THE
SNOW QUEEN
AND OTHER
WINTER TALES

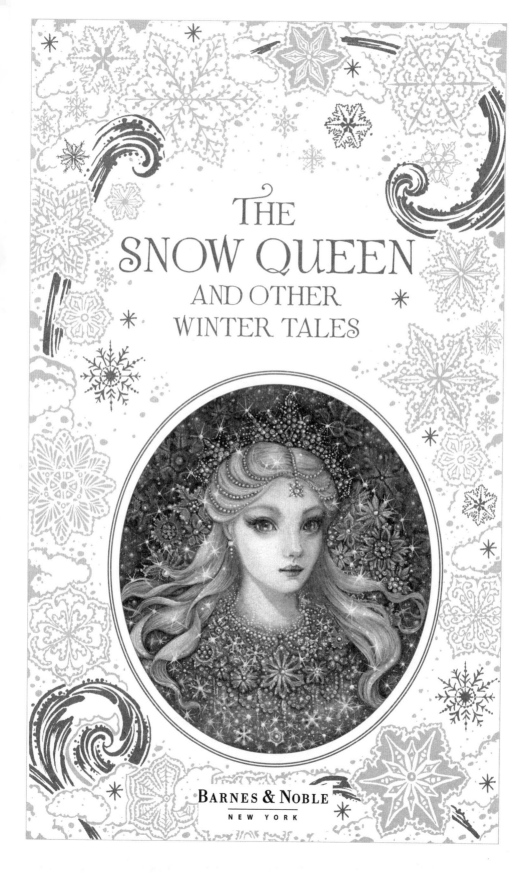

THE
SNOW QUEEN
AND OTHER
WINTER TALES

BARNES & NOBLE
NEW YORK

Cover art: Laurel Long
Cover design: Patrice Kaplan
Endpapers: Shutterstock

Barnes & Noble, Inc.
122 Fifth Avenue
New York, NY 10011

ISBN 978-1-4351-6069-9

Manufactured in China

2 4 6 8 10 9 7 5 3 1

Contents

Introduction

IN HIS CLASSIC FAIRY TALE "THE SNOW QUEEN," HANS CHRISTIAN Andersen tells of a magic mirror, fashioned by the devil, that distorts the image of everything reflected in it, making the world and its people appear ugly and repulsive. When the mirror falls to earth, it splinters into billions of pieces, some so tiny that they pierce the hearts of people without killing them, although "the heart at once became like a lump of ice." When a piece of the mirror lodges in the heart of Kay, a young boy in the story, he immediately becomes disdainful of the world around him, seeing only its most negative qualities. This numbing of Kay's soul sets the stage for his poetically just abduction by the Snow Queen to her wintry world of snow and ice.

Andersen's story is one of the more dramatic presentations of a winter theme in a fairy and folk tale, but it calls attention to the popularity of winter as a theme for such works. In the 100 tales collected for *The Snow Queen and Other Winter Tales*, chosen from the folk legacies of many different cultures, winter appears as a time, a setting, a backdrop—even as a variety of personifications including a snow-daughter, a frost-king, an ice maiden, and incarnations of the months of December, January, and February.

It's easy to understand why winter themes are so prevalent in these stories. Many were recorded by writers who lived in northern countries—Andersen was a native of Denmark, and Peter Christen Asbjørnsen a native of Norway—where winter climates and landscapes of snow and ice were a familiar part of their daily reality. But fairy and folk tales, by their nature, are distilled from the collective experiences of a culture, and every culture has traditions pertinent to the wintertime, as well as to other seasons and intervals. In many of these stories winter is presented as a bleak or harsh time, the end of a declining year soon to give way to the spring and a season of warmth and renewal. Personifications of winter are often depicted as characters who are emotionally cold and reserved or, like the Snow Queen, as indifferent in personality as they are coolly beautiful in appearance. But not all fairy tale treatments of winter are so negative and several feature friendly characters whom we associate with the wintertime, among them animated snowmen, lonely Christmas trees, and helpful reindeer.

Readers will find that a number of these stories echo one another, and that different cultures and countries work variations on common story treatments. A classic winter tale—several variants of which appear in these pages—tells the story of a young girl, usually a stepdaughter, who is dispatched to the wilds in the middle of a bleak winter's evening by a cruel stepmother to seek an impossible treat for a bratty, demanding stepsister: fresh strawberries, fresh apples, and the like. When the girl shows kindness to people she meets in the wilds, she is not only directed to a magical location where she can find the treat, but often endowed with a legacy appropriate for her generous spirit: great beauty, riches, marriage to a prince or king, and so on. When the stepmother sends her daughter on a similar mission in the hope of reaping the same rewards for her, the stepsister acts arrogantly towards the people in the wilds and is cursed with a dismal fate suitable for the selfish.

Goblins appear in various guises in a number of these stories and in the folklore of some countries—notably Greece, Turkey, and other southern European nations—their appearance is associated with Christmastime. The *kallikantzaroi* of Greece, for example, are malevolent goblins who spend most of the year underground sawing away at the world tree, trying to cause the collapse of the world. On the dawn of Christmas day, however, they are allowed to escape from their task and ascend to the earth's surface to wreak mischief on mortals. On January 6, the feast of the Epiphany and the end of the Christmas season, the *kallikantzaroi* return underground only to find that the world tree has healed in their absence and that they must begin their year's labor anew. Whether or not these goblins bear any relation to those who appear in tales by Andersen, Angelo M. Lewis, and others collected here, yuletide appears to be a season when goblins mingle with mortals, and not always with devious intent. One of the most famous goblin stories is the tale presented here as "The Story of the Goblins Who Stole a Sexton" by Charles Dickens. Originally published as a tale told within the tale of Dickens's series of sketches, *The Pickwick Papers* (1837), its account of curmudgeonly Gabriel Grub, who is accosted and chastised by a horde of goblins for forsaking the pleasures of home and hearth to dig graves on Christmas Eve, is clearly an anticipation of Ebenezer Scrooge's experiences in that most famous of all Christmas tales, *A Christmas Carol*, which Dickens would write six years later.

Christmas stories form an important subgenre of winter fairy and folktales, and among the best known and most loved is "The History of a Nutcracker" by Alexandre Dumas. One of the bestselling writers of the nineteenth century, Dumas modeled his tale on "The Nutcracker and the Mouse King," a story published a quarter of a century earlier by Prussian writer E.T.A. Hoffmann (whom Dumas acknowledges in his rendition). Dumas's version was translated from the French into English in 1847 as part of London book publisher Chapman and Hall's Picture Story Books series for young readers. It was Dumas's more precious treatment of Hoffmann's dramatic fairy tale that caught the eye of Ivan Vsevolozhsky, director of Russia's Imperial Theatres, in the early 1890s. Vsevolozhsky recommended the tale to Imperial Ballet Master Marius Petipa for adaptation to the ballet stage by Pyotr Ilyich Tchaikovsky, and Petipa wrote the libretto to pair with Tchaikovsky's score. *The Nutcracker* debuted at the St. Petersburg Imperial Theatre in 1892. It was only a modestly popular ballet until 1954, when New York City Ballet choreographer George Balanchine presented the version that has become a standard for the Christmas season ever since.

Their winter theme notwithstanding, the selections in *The Snow Queen and Other Winter Tales* are classic fairy and folk tales in their own right. They offer reading pleasures that can be enjoyed the whole year round.

The Snow Queen

(A Tale in Seven Stories)

HANS CHRISTIAN ANDERSEN

Story the First

Which Describes the Looking-glass and the Fragments

Well! We will begin. When we get to the end of the story we shall know more than we do now about a certain wicked goblin. He was one of the very worst, for he was Old Nick himself. One day he was in a very good temper, for he had made a mirror that possessed the power of making everything good and beautiful that was reflected in it shrink to almost nothing, whilst all that was worthless and bad looked still larger and worse. The most beautiful landscapes appeared like boiled spinach, and the best people looked repulsive, or stood on their heads and had no bodies. Their faces were so distorted that no one could recognize them, and if there was one freckle on any one's face, he might be sure that it would spread all over his nose and mouth. Old Nick thought this extremely amusing. When a good pious thought passed through any one's mind, it was reflected in the mirror as a grin, and the devil could not help laughing at his cunning invention. Those who went to the goblin's school—for he kept a school of his own—related everywhere that a miracle had taken place, and declared that now people could see for the first time how the world and mankind really looked. They carried the mirror about everywhere, till at last there was not a country nor any person who had not been distorted in it. Then they even wanted to fly up to Heaven with it to see the angels, but the higher they flew with the mirror the more hideously did it grin. They could hardly hold it, but still flying upwards, they came near the angels; then the grins of the mirror shook it so terribly, that it slipped from their hands and fell to the earth, where it was shattered into millions and billions of pieces. And now it caused far more unhappiness than before, for some pieces were no larger than a grain of sand. These flew about in the world, and when they got into any one's eyes, they would stay there, and then the people saw everything distorted, or could only see the bad side of a thing; for every fragment of the mirror retained the same power that the whole mirror had possessed. Some people even got a fragment into their heart, and that was a horrible thing; the heart at once became like a lump of ice. Some fragments were so large that they were used for window-panes; but it was a bad thing to look at one's friends through such windows. Other pieces were made into spectacles, and when people put these on, it was difficult for them to see straight or to be just; the evil one laughed till his sides shook—it tickled him so. But there were still some of these small fragments floating about in the air. Well, we shall hear about them.

Story the Second

A Little Boy and a Little Girl

In a large town, which contained so many people and houses that there was not room enough for everybody to possess a little garden of his own, and where therefore most of them had to content themselves with flowers in pots, there dwelled two poor children who had a somewhat larger garden than a flower-pot. They were not brother and sister, but they loved each other as much as if they had been. Their parents lived in two attics exactly opposite each other. Just where the roof of one house joined the other, and where a gutter ran between the two, there was a little window in each house; one had only to step across the gutter to get from one window to the other.

The parents of both children had a large wooden box standing outside, in which grew herbs they used in cooking, and a small rose-bush; there was one in each box, and they grew splendidly. The parents hit upon the idea of placing the boxes across the gutter, so that they almost reached from one window to the other, and looked just like two walls of flowers. Scarlet-runners hung down over the boxes, and the rose-bushes put forth long shoots which climbed up round the windows, and becoming entwined with those opposite, formed almost a triumphal arch of foliage and flowers. As the boxes were very high, and the children knew that they might not climb upon them, they often got permission to go out on the roof, and to sit on their little stools

2

under the roses, and there they played prettily.

Winter put an end to this pleasure. The windows were often quite frozen over; but then they would warm a penny on the stove and hold it against the frozen pane; in this way they made a little round peep-hole, behind which there sparkled a kind gentle eye, one at each window. These were the little boy and the little girl; he was called Kay, and her name was Gerda. In summer they could get to each other in one bound, but in winter they had to go up and down ever so many stairs and through the snow.

"Those are swarms of white bees," said the old grandmother.

"Have they a queen bee too? asked the little boy, for he knew that the real bees had one

"Certainly they have," said the grandmother. "She flies where they are thickest. She is the largest of all, and she never remains quiet on the ground; she flies up again into the black clouds. Many a time at midnight does she fly through the streets of the town looking in at the windows, and then they freeze in a wonderful way and look like flowers."

"Oh yes! we have seen that," said both children, and now they knew it was true.

"Can the Snow Queen come in here?" asked the little girl.

"Only let her come," said the boy; "I'll put her on the warm stove, and then she'll melt."

But grandmother smoothed her hair and told other tales. In the evening, when little Kay was at home and half undressed, he climbed up on a chair to the window, and peeped through the little hole; a few snow-flakes were falling outside, and one of them, the largest, remained lying on the edge of one of the flowerboxes. The snow-flake got larger and larger, and at last grew into a maiden, dressed in the finest white gauze, which was composed of millions of starry flakes. She was very beautiful and dainty, but made of ice—of dazzling, glittering ice. But still she was alive; her eyes sparkled like two stars, but there was no rest nor peace in them. She nodded at the window and beckoned with her hand. The little boy got frightened and jumped down from the chair; then it was just as if a larger bird was flying past the window.

There was a clear frost next day, and then spring came. The sun shone, the trees and bushes budded, the swallows built their nests, the windows were opened, and the little children sat once more in their little garden high up in the gutter on the top of the roof.

How splendidly the roses bloomed that summer! The little girl had learnt a psalm in which there was something about roses, and when she came to that part she thought of her own. She sang it to the little boy, and he sang it with her:

> The roses fade and die, but we
> Our Infant Lord shall surely see.

The little ones held each other by the hand, kissed the roses and, looking at God's fair sunshine, spoke to it as if the Child Jesus were there. What glorious summer days those were! How beautiful it was out there by those fragrant rose-trees, which seemed to wish that they might never stop blooming!

One day Kay and Gerda were looking at their picture-book full of animals and birds, when just as the clock in the great church-steeple struck five, Kay said:

"Oh! what a shooting pain I felt in my heart, and something has flown into my eye."

The little girl put her arms round his neck; he blinked his eyes—no, there was nothing to be seen.

"I believe it is gone," he said; but gone it was not. It happened to be one of those splinters of glass from the magic mirror which we have not forgotten—that hateful glass that made everything great and good that was reflected in it small and ugly, and in which all that was wicked and bad was made still more so, and every fault magnified.

Poor Kay had got a splinter right into his heart which would now soon become like a lump of ice. He no longer felt any pain, but the splinter was there.

"What are you crying for?" he said. "You look ugly when you cry. There's nothing the matter with me. Good gracious!" he suddenly cried out, "that rose there has a worm in it. And look, this one hangs quite crooked. They are ugly roses, after all. They look like the box in which they grow." And then he kicked the box and tore off the roses.

"Kay, what are you doing?" cried the little girl; and when he saw how frightened she was, he tore another rose off, and then sprang into his window away from dear little Gerda.

When she came to him afterwards with the picture-book, he said that it was only fit for babies in long clothes, and when his grandmother told them tales he always put in a "but." When he could, he would get behind, put on her spectacles, and speak just like her; he could do that wonderfully well, and people laughed at him. Soon he was able to mimic the speech and walk of everybody in the street. Everything that was peculiar or not nice about them, Kay could imitate, and people would say: "What a remarkable head that boy has!" But it was the glass that was in his heart. It was that too that made him tease even little Gerda, who was very fond indeed of him. His games were now different from what they had been before; they became quite sensible ones. One winter's day, when it was snowing, he came in with a large magnifying glass, and holding out one of the tails of his blue coat, let the snow fall upon it.

"Now look through the glass, Gerda," he said; each snowflake was much larger and looked like a splendid flower or a ten-cornered star. It was a beautiful sight. "Do you see how curiously they are made?" said Kay. "They are much more interesting than real flowers. And there is not a single fault in them; their points are absolutely regular. If only they would not melt!"

Soon after this Kay came in wearing thick gloves and with his sledge on his back; he called out to Gerda, "I have obtained permission to go sleighing in the large square where the other boys play," and away he went.

In the square the most daring boys often tied their sledges to the carts of the country people, and then they rode a good way with them. That was very fine. Whilst they were in the midst of their play, a large sledge came along. It was painted white all over, and in it sat some one wrapped in a rough white fur and wearing a rough white cap. The sledge rode round the square twice, and Kay, quickly binding his little sledge to it, rode away with it, faster and faster, through the neighboring streets. The person who was driving turned round and nodded to Kay in a friendly manner, just as if they knew each other, and every time that Kay wanted to unfasten his little sledge, the driver nodded again, and so Kay stayed on and rode out through the city-gates. Then the snow began to fall so thickly that the little boy could not see an inch before him, but still he rode on. At last he tried to undo the rope to get away from the great sledge, but it was of no use; his little carriage hung fast and flew along like the wind. Then he called out quite loudly, but no one heard him; the snow fell, and the sledge flew along, now and then giving a jump as if it were driving over hedges and ditches. The boy was quite frightened; he tried to say his prayers, but he could only remember his multiplication table.

The snow-flakes became larger and larger; at last they looked like large white chickens. All at once they fell aside, the large sledge stopped, and the person who had been driving got up from the seat; the cloak and the cap were made entirely of snow, and they were worn by a lady, tall and slender and dazzlingly white—it was the Snow Queen. "We have driven fast," she said; "but no one likes to be frozen. Creep under my fur." And placing Kay next to her in the sledge, she wrapped her cloak around him, and he seemed to be sinking in a snow-drift.

"Are you still cold?" she asked, and kissed him on the forehead. Oh! that kiss was colder than ice, it went right through his heart, which was already fast becoming a lump of ice. He felt as if he were going to die, but it was only for a moment, then he was all right again, and no longer felt the cold all around him.

"My sledge! Don't forget my sledge!" That was the first thing he thought of, and it was bound fast to one of the white chickens which flew on behind with the sledge on its back. The Snow Queen kissed Kay again, and then he forgot all about little Gerda, his grandmother, and all the folks at home.

"I will not give you any more kisses now," she said; "else I should kiss you to death."

Kay looked at her, she was so beautiful; he could not imagine a wiser and kinder face. She no longer appeared to him to be of ice as when she sat outside the window beckoning to him; in his eyes she was perfect, and he felt no fear at all. He told her he could do mental arithmetic, and in fractions, too; that he knew how many square miles there were in the country, and the number of its inhabitants. She smiled, and then it occurred to him that it was not enough after all that he knew, and he looked up into the great space above him. She flew on high with him up to the black clouds where the storm was raging and moaning, and it seemed to Kay as if it were singing old songs. They flew across forests and lakes, across sea and land. Under them the cold winds whistled, the wolves howled and the snow crackled, while above them flew the black cawing crows. The moon, large and bright, shone down upon all, and there Kay sat and gazed through the long winter's night; during the day he slept at the feet of the Snow Queen.

Story the Third

The Flower-Garden of the Sorceress

But how fared it with little Gerda when Kay did not return? Where could he be? No one knew, no one could tell. The boys said that they had seen him tying his sledge to another larger one which had driven into the streets and out through the gates of the town. No one knew where he was; many tears were shed, especially by little Gerda, who wept much and long. Then they said that he was dead: that he was drowned in the river that flowed not far from the school. Oh! what long dark winter days those were!

Now came spring with its warm sunshine.

"Kay is dead and gone!" said little Gerda.

"I don't believe it!" answered the sunshine.

"He is dead and gone," she said to the swallows.

"We don't believe it," they replied, and at last little Gerda did not believe it either.

"I will put on my new red shoes," she said, one morning, "those that Kay has never seen, and then I will go down to the river and ask after him."

It was still very early; she kissed her old grandmother, who was still asleep, put on her red shoes, and went quite alone through the gates of the town, down to the river.

"Is it true that you have taken away my little playmate from me? I will give you my red shoes, if you give him back to me."

It seemed to her as if the waves nodded in a strange way; so she took off her red shoes, which she liked more than anything she had, and threw them both into the river. But they fell close to the bank, and the little waves carried them back to her; it was just as if the river not having little Kay, would not take from her what she liked best. She, however, thought she had not thrown them in far enough, and so she crept into a boat that lay among the reeds; going to the farthest end of it she threw the shoes in from thence, and the boat, not being fastened, her movement caused it to glide away from the bank. Seeing this, she hastened to get out, but before she reached the other end the boat was more than a yard from the land, and was quickly gliding away.

Little Gerda was quite frightened and began to cry; but no one besides the sparrows heard her, and they could not carry her back to land. However, they flew along the banks, and sang as if to comfort her: "Here we are, here we are!"

The boat drifted along with the stream, and in it sat little Gerda, quite still, with only stockings on her feet; her small red shoes floated behind her, but they could not reach the boat, for it went along too quickly.

The banks on both sides were very pretty; beautiful flowers, old trees, and hills dotted with sheep and cows were there, but not a single human being was to be seen.

"Perhaps the river is carrying me to little Kay," thought Gerda, and then she became more cheerful, stood up and gazed for hours at the beautiful green banks. At last she came to a large cherry-orchard, in which there was a little house with curious red and blue windows; it also had a thatched roof, and outside stood two wooden soldiers who presented arms as she sailed by.

Gerda called out to them, thinking that they were alive, but of course they did not answer. She came quite close to them, for the stream was drifting the boat straight to the land.

Gerda called still louder, and then an old woman came out of the house, supporting herself on a crutch; she wore a large sun-hat, with the most beautiful flowers painted on it.

"Poor little thing!" said the old woman; "how ever did you come upon the great rushing stream, and get carried out so far into the world?" Then the old woman got into the water, and seizing the boat with her crutch, drew it to the shore, and took little Gerda out.

Gerda was pleased to reach dry land again, although she was somewhat afraid of the strange old woman.

"Come and tell me who you are, and where you come from," she said. And Gerda told her all, and the old woman shook her head and said "Hem, hem!" And when Gerda had told her all, and asked her whether she had not seen little Kay, she answered that he had not come by, but that he would probably do so yet. She told Gerda not to be sad, but to eat some cherries, and look at her flowers, which were finer than any in the picture-book, and each of which could tell a story. Then she took Gerda by the hand, led her into the little house, and closed the door.

The windows were very high, and the panes were red, blue and yellow, so that the daylight shone through them strangely in all kinds of colors. Upon the table stood the finest cherries, and Gerda was allowed to eat as many of them as she liked. While she ate, the old woman combed her hair with a golden comb, and the bright flaxen locks fell in beautiful ringlets round the small smiling face which looked as round and as blooming as a rose.

"I have long wished for such a dear little girl," said the old woman. "Now you will see how happily we shall live together." And as she combed little Gerda's hair, the child gradually forgot her foster-brother Kay, for the old woman was a sorceress. But she was not a wicked sorceress; she only practiced her charms for amusement, and wished very much to keep little Gerda. She therefore went into the garden, and stretched out her crutch towards all the rose-trees, and although they were blooming beautifully, they all sank into the black ground, and it was impossible to see where they had stood. The old woman was afraid that if Gerda saw the roses, she would think of her own, and then remember little Kay, and run away.

Then she took Gerda out into the flower-garden. How fragrant and lovely it was! Every imaginable flower, and those of every season, too, stood here in perfect bloom; no picture-book could be more richly or finely colored.

Gerda jumped for joy, and played till the sun went down behind the tall cherry-trees; then she was laid in a beautiful bed with red silk pillows embroidered with violets. She slept and dreamed as gloriously as only a queen can do on her wedding-day.

The next day she could again play with the flowers in the warm sunshine, and in this way many days passed. Gerda knew every flower; but although there were so many of them, it seemed as if one were missing, yet which she did not know. One day she was sitting gazing at the old woman's sun-hat with the painted flowers, and it happened that the finest one was a rose. The old woman had forgotten to make it disappear from her hat when she had charmed the others into the earth. But so it is, if one has not perfect command over one's thoughts.

"What! are there no roses here?" cried Gerda, and she ran among the beds searching and searching; but alas! there were none to be found. Then she sat down and wept, and her warm tears falling just on the spot where a rose-tree had sunk down, they moistened the earth, and the tree suddenly shot up as blooming as when it had sunk; Gerda embraced it, kissed the roses, and thought of the beautiful roses at home, and with them of little Kay, too.

"Oh! how I have been detained!" said the little girl. "I wanted to go and find little Kay. Don't you know where he is?" she asked the roses. "Do you think he is dead?"

"No, he is not dead," answered the roses. "We have been in the ground where all the dead are, but Kay was not there."

"Thank you," said little Gerda, and going to the flowers, she looked into their cups and asked: "Do you know where little Kay is?"

But every flower was standing in the sun dreaming its own fairy tale or story, and of these Gerda heard ever so many; none, however, knew anything about Kay.

What says the tiger-lily?

"Do you hear the drum? 'boom, boom!' There are only two notes, always, 'boom, boom!' Listen to the wailing chant of the women, listen to the cry of the priests. The Hindoo widow clad in her long red mantle stands upon the funeral pile; the flames leap up around her and her dead husband. But she thinks of the living one in that circle—of him, her son whose eyes burn more than fire, of him whose looks are greater torture to her heart than the flames which will soon reduce her body to ashes. Can the flame of the heart perish in the flames of the stake?"

"I don't understand that at all," said little Gerda.

"That is my tale," said the tiger-lily.

What says the convolvulus?

"Overhanging the narrow pathway stands an old knight's castle; the thick evergreen climbs up the ruined red walls, leaf upon leaf, right up to the balcony where a beautiful maiden stands. She bends over the balustrade and looks along the path. No rose on the bough is fresher than she; no apple-blossom, when swept from the tree by the breeze, floats lighter than she. How her rich silken garments rustle as she exclaims, "Does he not come yet?"

"Is it Kay you mean?" said little Gerda.

"I am only speaking of my tale, my dream," answered the convolvulus.

What says the little snowdrop?

"Between the trees a board is hanging by some ropes; it is a swing. Two pretty little girls in snow-white dresses and with long green silk ribbons fluttering from their hats are sitting on it swinging. Their brother, who is bigger than they, stands in the swing; he has his arm round the rope to hold himself, for in one hand he has a little dish and in the other a clay pipe. He is blowing soap bubbles; the swing flies on and the bubbles rise in beautiful varying colors. The last is still hanging to the bowl of the pipe and sways in the wind. The swing goes on; a little black dog, as light as the bubbles, stands on his hind legs and wants to get in too. But the swing flies up and the dog falls, barking and angry; they tease him, and the bubbles burst. A swinging plank, and a dissolving airy picture is my song."

"What you relate may be pretty, but you tell it so mournfully, and you don't mention little Kay at all."

What do the hyacinths say?

"There were three beautiful sisters, dainty and transparent One was dressed in red, another in blue, and the third in white; hand in hand they danced by the silent lake in the bright moonlight. They were not elves but human beings. Attracted by the sweet fragrance, they disappeared into the wood; here the fragrance became stronger. Three coffins, in which lay the beautiful maidens, glided from the thicket of the wood out across the lake; the fire-flies flew all around to light their way, like little floating torches. Do the dancing maidens sleep, or are they dead? The fragrance from the flowers says they are dead, and the evening bell tolls their knell."

"You make me feel quite sad," said little Gerda. "Your scent is so strong that it makes me think of the dead. Is little Kay then really dead? The roses have been down in the ground and they say 'No.'"

"Ding, dong!" tolled the hyacinth bells. "We are not tolling for little Kay, we don't know him; we do but sing our song, the only one we know."

Then Gerda went to the buttercups that were shining out from amongst the bright green leaves.

"You are bright little suns," said Gerda. "Tell me, do you know where I can find my playmate?"

The buttercups shone so brightly and again looked at Gerda. What song could they sing? It was not about Kay.

"On the first spring day the fair sun shone down so warm on a little courtyard, its rays falling on the white walls of the neighboring house. Close by bloomed the first yellow flower, glittering like gold in the warm sunbeams. The old grandmother sat outside in her chair; her grandchild, a poor but pretty servant-girl, was just going home again after a short visit. She kissed her grandmother, and there was gold, pure gold, in that blessed kiss. Gold,

gold everywhere, on the maiden's lips and in the early morning air! You see, that is my little story," said the buttercup.

"My poor old grandmother," sighed Gerda. "Yes, I have no doubt she longs and grieves for me just as she did for little Kay. But I shall soon be home again, and then I will bring Kay with me. It is no use asking the flowers; they only know their own song, and cannot give me any information." And then she tucked up her little dress, so that she might run faster; but the narcissus caught hold of her leg as she was jumping over it. So she stopped to look at the long yellow flower and said, "Perhaps you know something." And she bent down quite close to the flower, and what did it say?

"I can see myself! I can see myself!" said the narcissus. "Oh! how I smell! Up in the little corner room stands a little ballet-girl, half undressed; first she stands on one leg, then on the other, sometimes on both. She treads the whole world under her feet, yet she is nothing but a delusion. She pours some water out of a teapot upon a piece of stuff that she holds in her hand; it is her bodice. Cleanliness is a fine thing. Her white dress hangs on a peg; it has also been washed in the teapot and dried on the roof. She puts it on and ties a saffron-colored kerchief round her neck which makes the dress look whiter. Look how she struts on one stem! I can see myself! I can see myself!"

"I don't care for that at all," said Gerda. "You need not have told me that." And then she ran to the end of the garden.

The door was fastened, but she pressed against the rusty latch so that it gave way; the door opened, and little Gerda sprang out with bare feet into the wide world. She looked back three times, but there was no one following her; at last she could walk no more and sat down on a large stone. When she looked round, the summer was gone and it was late in autumn. It was impossible to see that in the beautiful garden, where there was always sunshine, and where the flowers of every season grew.

"Oh, how I have tarried!" said little Gerda. "Autumn has come already. I must not rest any longer." And she rose to go.

Oh! how tired and sore her little feet were! All around it looked cold and raw. The long willow-leaves were quite yellow, and the dew trickled down like water. One leaf fell after another, and only the sloe-thorn still bore fruit, but it was sour and set one's teeth on edge. Oh! how dark and miserable the whole world looked.

Story the Fourth

The Prince and the Princess

Gerda was obliged to rest again; just opposite the spot where she sat a great crow was hopping on the snow. It had sat looking at her and wagging its head for a long time; at last it said, "Caw, caw! Good-day, good-day!" It could not speak plainer than that, but it meant to be kind to the little girl, and asked where she was going all alone like that in the wide world. Gerda understood the word "alone" very well, and felt how much it expressed; so she related to the crow her whole life and adventures, and asked whether it had seen Kay.

The crow nodded very thoughtfully and said, "It may be, it may be."

"What! Do you think so?" cried the little girl, and almost hugged the crow to death as she kissed it.

"Gently, gently!" said the crow. "I believe—I know. I believe—it may be— little Kay—but he has doubtless forgotten you by this time for the princess."

"Does he live with a princess?" asked Gerda.

"Yes, listen!" said the crow. "But it is so difficult for me to speak your language. If you understand the crow's language[1] I could tell it you better."

"No, I have never learned it," said Gerda, "but my grandmother understood it and could speak it too. I wish I had learned it."

"It doesn't matter," said the crow. "I will speak as well as I can, but it will be very badly." Then he related what he knew.

"In the kingdom where we now are, there lives a princess who is excessively clever; she has read all the newspapers there are in the world, and forgotten them too, so clever is she. A little while ago she was sitting on the throne, and they say that it is not such a comfortable seat after all. Well, she began to sing a song and it was this: 'Why should I not marry?' Now listen, for there's something in this. She wished to marry, but she wanted a husband who could answer when he was spoken to—one who would not merely stand there and look grand, for that would be too tedious. So she assembled all her court ladies by the beat of the drum, and when they heard what she wished they were very pleased. 'I like that,' said each one; 'I was just thinking about it myself.' You may believe every word I say," added the crow. "I have a tame sweetheart, who goes about freely in the castle, and she told me all about it."

---

1. This is a kind of gibberish used by children, and is formed by adding syllables or letters to each word.

Of course his sweetheart was a crow too. For one crow seeks another, and a crow always remains a crow.

"The newspapers immediately appeared with a border of hearts and the initials of the princess. They said that every good-looking young man was free to go to the castle and talk to the princess; and he who spoke so that it could be heard that he felt at home, and who spoke best, would be chosen for the princess's husband. Yes, yes," said the crow, "you may believe me; it is all as true as I sit here. Young men came in streams. There was a deal of crowding and rushing; but no one succeeded either on the first or on the second day. They could all talk well when they were in the street, but when they entered the castle-gates, and saw the guards in silver and the footmen in gold on the staircases, and the great halls lighted up, they became confused. And when they stood before the throne where the princess sat, they could only repeat the last word she had uttered, and she had no wish to hear that over again. It was just as if the people had swallowed snuff and went to sleep while they were inside till they came back into the street, for it was only then that they found their tongues again. A whole row of them reached from the city-gates to the palace. I went there myself to see them," said the crow.

"They were hungry and thirsty, but at the castle not even a glass of water was given to them. A few of the wisest had taken some bread and butter with them, but they did not share it with their neighbors, for they thought, "let him look hungry, then the princess will not take him."

"But Kay, little Kay," said Gerda. "When did he come? Was he amongst the crowd?"

"Wait a bit! We're coming to him now. It was on the third day there came, gaily marching along to the palace, a little personage without horses or carriage; his eyes sparkled just like yours. He had beautiful long hair, but was very poorly dressed."

"That was Kay!" exclaimed Gerda, joyfully. "Oh, then I have found him," and she clapped her hands.

"He had a little knapsack on his back," said the crow.

"No, that must have been his sledge," said Gerda; "for he went away with that."

"It may have been," said the crow; "I did not look at it so closely. But this I know from my tame sweetheart, that when he passed through the castle-gates and saw the body-guards in silver and the footmen in gold on the staircases, he was not in the least embarrassed. He nodded to them and said: "How tedious it must be to stand on the stairs; I prefer to go in." The halls were brilliant with lights; privy councilors and ambassadors went about barefooted carrying golden vessels. It was enough to make any one feel serious. His boots creaked terribly, but he was not at all afraid."

"That was most certainly Kay," said Gerda. "I know he has new boots on; I heard them creaking in grandmother's room."

"Indeed they did creak," said the crow. "Yet he boldly went straight up to the princess, who was sitting on a pearl as large as a spinning-wheel; and standing all round in a great circle were all the court ladies, with their maids and their maids' maids, and all the courtiers, with their servants and their servants' servants, and the latter each had a man too. The nearer they stood to the door the prouder they were. One hardly dared to look at the men of the servants' servants, who always wear slippers, so proudly did they stand in the doorway."

"That must have been dreadful," said little Gerda. "But did Kay get the princess after all?"

"If I had not been a crow, I would have taken her myself, even though I am engaged. They say he spoke as well as I do when I speak crows' language: so my tame sweetheart told me. He was gay and good-looking. He said he had not come to woo, but only to hear the princess's wisdom. This he thought excellent, and she thought him very nice."

"Certainly that was Kay," said Gerda. "He was so clever; he could do fractions in his head. Oh, will you not take me to the palace?"

"Yes, that's easily said," replied the crow. "But how can we manage it? I'll talk it over with my sweetheart; she'll be able to advise us, for I must tell you that a little girl like you never obtains permission to enter the castle."

"Oh, but I shall," said Gerda. "When Kay hears that I am there, he'll come out at once and fetch me."

"Wait for me by those railings," said the crow, and wagging his head flew away.

It was late in the evening before the crow came back. "Caw, caw," he said. "She sends you her compliments, and here is a little roll for you which she took from the kitchen; there's bread enough there, and you must be hungry. It is impossible for you to enter the castle; you are barefooted. The guards in silver and the footmen in gold would not allow it. But don't cry; you shall get in. My sweetheart tells me there is a narrow back staircase that leads to the sleeping apartments, and she knows how to get the key."

They went into the garden and along the great avenue where the leaves were falling one after another; and when the lights in the castle had been extinguished in the same manner, the crow led little Gerda to a back door which stood ajar.

Oh, how Gerda's heart beat with fear and longing! She felt as if she were about to do something wrong, and after all she only wanted to know whether little Kay was there. Yes, it must be he; she had such a vivid recollection of his bright eyes and his long hair; she could see him smiling as he used to do when they sat under the roses at home.

He would no doubt be glad to see her: to hear what a long way she had come for his sake, and to know how grieved they had all been at home when he had not returned. Oh, what fear and joy she felt!

Now they were on the stairs; a little lamp was burning in a recess, and in the middle of the floor stood the tame crow, turning her head from side to side and looking at Gerda, who curtsied as her grandmother had taught her to do.

"My betrothed has spoken so highly of you, my little lady," said the tame crow; "your career, as people say, is very touching. If you will take the lamp, I will go before you. We will go straight along this way, then we shall meet no one."

"It seems to me as if some one were coming behind us," said Gerda, and something rushed past her like shadows on the wall: horses with flying manes and thin legs, huntsmen, and ladies and gentlemen on horseback.

"They are only dreams," said the crow; "they are come to fetch the thoughts of the lords and ladies out hunting. That's a good thing, for then you can look at them in their beds more safely. But I hope that when you rise to honors and dignities, you will show a grateful heart."

"Of course she will," said the crow from the forest. They now came into the first hall, the walls of which were covered with rose-colored satin, embroidered with flowers. Here the dreams again rushed by them, but so quickly that Gerda was unable to catch a glimpse of the great lords and ladies. Each hall was more splendid than the other; indeed, it was quite bewildering. At last they reached the sleeping apartments. The ceiling here was like a great palm-tree with leaves of costly crystal, and over the middle of the floor, two beds, each of which looked like a lily, hung suspended from a thick golden stem. The one in which the princess lay was white; the other was red, and in this Gerda had to seek for little Kay. She pushed one of the red leaves aside and saw a brown neck. Oh, that must be Kay! She called him loudly by his name, and held the lamp towards him; the dreams on horseback again rushed into the room—he awoke, turned his head, and—it was not little Kay.

The prince resembled him only in the neck; but he was young and handsome. And the princess peeped out of the white lily-leaf and asked who was there. Then little Gerda wept and told her whole story, and all that the crows had done for her.

"Poor child!" said the prince and princess; and then praised the crows, and said that they were not angry with them, but they were not to do so again. They would, moreover, be rewarded.

"Would you like to be free?" said the princess. "Or would you like a permanent appointment as court crows, with permission to have all the leavings in the kitchen?"

Both the crows bowed, and begged for a permanent appointment, for they thought of their old age, and said:

"It would be nice to have some provision for one's old age," as they called it.

And the prince got up from his bed and let Gerda sleep in it; he could not do more than that. She folded her little hands and thought, "How good both men and animals are!" Then she closed her eyes and slept sweetly. All the dreams came flying in again, looking like angels, and drawing a little sledge, on which sat Kay nodding to her; but it was all only a dream, and was therefore gone again as soon as she awoke.

The following day she was dressed from head to foot in silks and velvets, and was asked to remain in the castle and enjoy herself. But she only begged for a little carriage and one horse, and for a pair of boots, so that she might again go out into the wide world to look for Kay.

She obtained not only the boots but a muff also, and she was neatly dressed. When she was about to go, a new carriage made of pure gold drove up to the door, with the arms of the prince and princess shining upon it like a star, and the coachman, footmen, and outriders—for there were outriders too—all wearing golden crowns on their heads. The prince and princess themselves helped her into the carriage, and wished her every happiness. The crow from the wood, who was now married, accompanied her for the first three miles; he sat at her side, for he could not bear riding backwards. The other crow stood in the doorway flapping her wings: she did not go with them, for she suffered from headache since she had received her permanent appointment and got too much to eat. The carriage was lined inside with sugar-cakes, and under the seat were fruit and ginger-nuts.

"Farewell, farewell!" cried the prince and the princess; and little Gerda wept, and the crow wept. At the end of the first three miles the crow also bade her farewell, and this was the saddest parting of all; he flew into a tree, and flapped his black wings as long as he could see the carriage, which shone like bright sunshine.

Story the Fifth

The Little Robber-Girl

They drove through a dark wood, but the coach was as brilliant as a lighted torch; it dazzled the eyes of some robbers, who could not bear to see it.

"It's gold! It's gold!" they cried, and rushing forward, they seized the horses, killed the little jockeys, the coachmen and the footmen, and pulled little Gerda out of the carriage.

"She is plump and pretty, and has been fed on nuts," said the old robber-woman, who had a long stubbly beard and eyebrows that hung down over her eyes.

"She is as good as a fat little lamb; how nice she will taste!" And then she drew forth her shining knife that glittered horribly.

"Oh!" cried the woman at the same moment; she had been bitten by her own daughter—who was hanging on her back—in such a ferocious way that it would have pleased us to see it. "You ugly brat!" cried her mother, and had no time to kill Gerda.

"She shall play with me!" said the little robber-girl. "She shall give me her muff and her pretty dress, and sleep with me in my bed." And then she bit her mother again, making the robber-woman jump in the air and dance about. All the robbers laughed and said: "Look how she dances with her calf."

"I want to get into the carriage," said the little robber-girl. She would have her own way, too, for she was quite spoiled and very obstinate; so she and Gerda sat in it and drove over stumps and stones farther into the forest. The little robber-girl was as tall as Gerda, but stronger, and had broader shoulders and darker skin; her eyes were black and looked almost sad. She caught little Gerda round the waist and said: "They shall not kill you as long as I am not vexed with you. I suppose you are a princess?"

"No," said Gerda, and told her all that she had gone through, and how she loved little Kay.

The robber-girl looked at her very earnestly, shook her head a little and said, "They shall not kill you, even if I do get vexed with you; I'll do it myself then." And then she dried Gerda's eyes and put both her hands into the beautiful muff, which was soft and warm.

At last the coach stopped in the courtyard of a robber's castle. The walls were cracked from top to bottom; ravens and crows flew out of the open holes, and great mastiffs, each of which looked as if he could swallow a man, jumped up; but they did not bark, for that was forbidden.

In the large old smoky hall a bright fire was burning in the middle of the stone floor; the smoke curled up to the ceiling and had to find a way out for itself. A large cauldron of soup was boiling, and hares and rabbits were roasting on the spit.

"You shall sleep with me and all my little animals to-night," said the robber-girl. They had something to eat and drink, and then went to a corner where there lay some straw and carpets. Above them on laths and sticks were perched more than a hundred pigeons, who all appeared to be asleep, though they moved a little when the two little girls came up.

"All these belong to me," said the little robber-girl, and quickly seizing one of the nearest held it by its feet and shook it till it flapped its wings.

"Kiss it," she cried, beating it into Gerda's face. "Those are the wretches from the wood, those two; they would fly away at once, if they were not kept well locked up. And here is my old sweetheart, 'Ba,'" she said, as she dragged out a reindeer by the horns; it had a bright copper ring round its neck, and was tied up. "We have to hold him tight too, else he would spring away. Every evening I tickle his neck with my sharp knife; that makes him very frightened." And the little girl took a long knife out of a crack in the wall and passed it over the reindeer's neck; the poor animal kicked out, while the little robber-girl laughed and then pulled Gerda into bed with her.

"Are you going to keep the knife with you while you sleep?" asked Gerda, looking at it somewhat timidly.

"I always sleep with my knife," said the little robber-girl. "One never knows what may happen. But tell me again what you told me before about little Kay, and why you went out into the wide world."

And Gerda related it all over again while the wood-pigeons cooed up in their cage, and the other pigeons slept. The little robber-girl put her arm round Gerda's neck, held the knife in the other hand and was soon asleep and snoring. But Gerda could not close her eyes at all; she did not know whether she was to live or die. The robbers sat round the fire, singing and drinking, and the robber-woman turned somersaults. Oh, it was quite a horrible thing for the little girl to see all this!

Then the wood-pigeons said "Coo, coo! We have seen little Kay. A white hen was carrying his sledge, and he sat in the Snowqueen's carriage as it drove through the wood quite close to our nest. She blew upon us, and all the other young ones died except us two. Coo, coo!"

"What do you say up there?" cried Gerda, "Whither was the Snow Queen going? Can you tell me that?"

"She was probably going to Lapland, for there is always snow and ice there. Ask the reindeer, that is fastened up with a rope."

"There is ice and snow, there it is glorious and fine," said the reindeer. "There one can spring about freely in the great shining valleys. There the Snow Queen has her summer tent; but her finest castle is farther north, nearer the Pole, on the island they call Spitzbergen."

"Oh Kay, little Kay!" sighed Gerda.

"You must lie still," said the robber-girl, "or I shall stick my knife into you."

In the morning Gerda told her all that the wood-pigeons had said, and the little robber-girl looked grave, shook her head and said: "It doesn't matter! It doesn't matter! Do you know where Lapland is?" she asked the reindeer.

"Who should know better than I?" said the animal, and his eyes sparkled. "I was born and bred in Lapland; I have jumped about upon the snow-fields there."

"Listen," said the robber-girl to Gerda; "you see that all our men are away. Only mother is still here, and she will stay. But about mid-day she

20

drinks out of a big bottle and then she sleeps for a little while—then I will do something for you."

Then she jumped out of bed, clasped her mother round the neck, and pulled her beard, saying: "Good morning, my own dear nanny-goat!" Then her mother pulled her nose till it was black and blue; and that was all done out of pure love.

So when the mother had drunk out of her bottle and fallen asleep, the robber-girl went up to the reindeer and said: "It would give me great pleasure to tickle your neck a few times more with my sharp knife, for then you are really too funny; but it doesn't matter. I will loosen your rope and help you out so that you may run to Lapland; but you must put your best leg forward, and take this little girl to the Snow Queen's castle where her playmate is. You must have heard what she told me, for she spoke loud enough, and you were listening."

The reindeer jumped for joy. The robber-maiden lifted little Gerda on his back and took the precaution to tie her on, and even to give her a little cushion for a seat. "Here are your fur boots, too," she said, "for it will be cold; but the muff I will keep, it is so very pretty. But you shall not freeze on that account. Here you have my mother's large mittens; they will reach right up to your elbows. Get into them! Now you look just like my ugly mother about the hands."

But Gerda wept for joy.

"I can't bear to see you make such grimaces," said the little robber-girl. "You ought to look quite happy now. Here are two loaves and a ham, so you will not starve." These were tied on behind on the reindeer's back; the little robber-girl then opened the door, coaxed in all the big dogs, and cutting the rope with her sharp knife, said to the reindeer: "Now run! But mind you take good care of the little girl!"

And Gerda stretched out her hands with the great mittens to the robber-girl and said "Farewell!"

Then the reindeer galloped away across stumps and stones, through the great wood and across marshes and plains, as quickly as he could. The wolves howled and the ravens croaked, while the sky seemed to be spitting fire.

"Those are my old northern lights," said the reindeer; "see how they flash." And now he galloped along faster still, day and night. The loaves were eaten, and the ham too, and then they came to Lapland.

Story the Sixth

The Lapland Woman and the Finland Woman

They stopped at a little hut; it was a very humble one. The roof sloped down almost to the ground, and the door was so low that the family had to go on hands and knees when they went in and out. There was no one at home but an old woman who was cooking fish over an oil lamp. The reindeer told her Gerda's whole story, but his own first, for that seemed to him of much more importance; and Gerda was so numbed with the cold that she could not speak.

"Poor creatures!" said the woman; "you have still a long way to go. You must travel more than a hundred miles farther, to Finland, for that is where the Snow Queen lives and where she burns Bengal lights every evening. I will write a few words on a dried stock-fish, for I nave no paper. This you can take for me to a Finland woman there; she can give you more information than I."

And when Gerda was warmed and had had something to eat and drink, the woman wrote a few words on a dried stock-fish, and telling Gerda to take care of it, tied her again on the reindeer which galloped away. "Fut! Fut!" was heard up in the sky, and all night long the most beautiful blue northern lights were burning. At last they reached Finland and knocked at the chimney of the woman for whom they had a message; for she had not even a door.

It was so hot inside that the woman, who was small and dirty, wore scarcely anything. She immediately loosened little Gerda's dress and took off her mittens and boots—for else the heat would have been too great for her; she also laid a piece of ice on the reindeer's head, and then read what was written on the stock-fish. She read it three times, and then knew it by heart; so she put the fish into the soup-kettle, for it could be eaten, and she never wasted anything.

Then the reindeer told first his story and then that of little Gerda. The woman blinked her cunning eyes, but said nothing.

"You are very clever," said the reindeer; "I know you can tie all the winds of the world together with a piece of twine. If the sailor unties one knot, he has a fair wind; if he unties another, it blows hard; and if he unties the third and fourth, the storm will tear up a forest. Will you not give the little girl a potion that will make her as strong as twelve men and enable her to conquer the Snow Queen?"

"As strong as twelve men!" said the woman. "That would not be of much use." Then she went to a bed, took out a large skin and unrolled it; there were strange letters written on it, and the woman read till the sweat ran down from her forehead.

But the reindeer begged again so hard for little Gerda, and Gerda looked at the woman with such pleading and tearful eyes, that her own again began to twinkle, and drawing the reindeer into a corner, she whispered to him, whilst she placed some fresh ice on his head:

"Little Kay is, it is true, with the Snow Queen, but finds everything there to his taste and liking, and thinks it the best place in the world. That is, however, because he has a splinter of glass in his heart and a small grain of it in his eye; these will have to come out first, or he will never be a human being again, and the Snow Queen will retain her power over him."

"But can't you give little Gerda something to enable her to do all this?"

"I can give her no greater power than she already possesses; don't you see how great that is? Don't you see how both men and animals are obliged to serve her, and how well she has got on in the world barefooted? She cannot receive any power from us; she possesses it in her heart; it consists in her being a sweet innocent child. If she cannot herself get to the Snow Queen and remove the glass from little Kay, we cannot help her. Two miles from here the Snow Queen's garden begins; thither you can carry the little girl. Put her down by the great bush with the red berries that stands in the snow; don't stand chattering, but hasten to get back here." Then the woman lifted little Gerda upon the reindeer, who ran off as quickly as he could.

"Oh, I have left my boots and my mittens behind!" cried little Gerda.

The piercing cold reminded her of this; but the reindeer did not venture to stop. He ran on till he reached the bush with the red berries; there he put Gerda down and kissed her on her mouth. Large bright tears ran down the animal's cheeks, and then he galloped back as fast as he could. There stood poor Gerda, without shoes or gloves, in the middle of terrible icy Finland.

She ran on as quickly as she could till she met a whole regiment of snow-flakes coming along. They did not fall from the sky, for that was bright and shining with the northern lights; the snow-flakes ran along the ground, and the nearer they came, the larger they grew. Gerda remembered how large and curious the snow-flakes had looked when she saw them through the magnifying glass. But here they were larger still, and more terrible; they were alive; they were the Snow Queen's outposts, and had the strangest shapes. Some looked like great ugly porcupines; others like knots of serpents with outstretched heads; others, again, like small fat bears with bristling hair. All were dazzlingly white, and all were live snow-flakes. Then little Gerda said the Lord's Prayer; the cold was so intense that she could see her own breath; it came out of her mouth like smoke. Her breath became thicker and thicker, and took the form of little angels who grew larger and larger as soon as they touched the ground. All had helmets on their heads, and lances and shields in their hands; their numbers increased, and when Gerda had finished her prayer a whole legion stood around her. They thrust their lances against the horrible snowflakes, so that the latter flew into a hundred pieces; and little Gerda went forward safely and cheerfully. The angels stroked her hands and feet, so that she felt the cold less, and she hastened on to the Snow Queen's castle.

But now we must first see what Kay is doing. He was by no means thinking of little Gerda, and least of all that she was standing outside the castle.

Story the Seventh

Of the Snow Queen's Castle,
and What Happened There in the End

The walls of the castle were formed of driven snow, and the doors and windows of the cutting winds. There were more than a hundred halls in it, all just as the snowstorm had blown them together. The largest of them extended for several miles; they were all lit up by the strong northern light, and how large and empty, how icy cold and glittering they were! There were never any festivities here, not even a little bear's ball, for which the storm might have been the music, and at which the polar bears could have walked on their hind legs and shown off their grand manners. There were never any little games of snapdragon or touch, nor any tea-parties at which the young lady foxes might gossip. Empty, spacious, and cold were the halls of the Snow Queen. The northern lights burned so steadily that they could be counted when they stood highest and lowest. In the middle of this empty, endless hall of snow, there was a frozen lake broken into a thousand pieces; but each piece was so like the other that it was a perfect work of art. In the middle of the lake sat the Snow Queen when she was at home; then she used to say that she sat in the mirror of Understanding, and that it was the only and the best one in the world.

Little Kay was blue with cold, in fact almost black; but he did not notice it, for she had kissed away the icy chills and his heart was like a lump of ice. He dragged some sharp, flat pieces of ice to and fro, putting them together in every possible position, for he wanted to make something out of them. It was just as when we have little wooden tablets, and make figures out of them, calling it a Chinese puzzle. Kay was making figures too, and very artistic ones. It was the ice game of reason. In his eyes the figures were very extraordinary and of the greatest importance: the grain of glass in his eye was the cause of that. He made several complete figures which formed a written word; but he could never manage to make the word he wanted—the word "Eternity."

The Snow Queen had said, "If you can make that figure, you shall be your own master, and I will give you the whole world and a pair of new skates."

But he could not do it.

"Now I must rush off to warm countries," said the Snow Queen. "I will go and look into the black-pots." She meant the fire-spitting mountains Etna and Vesuvius, as they are called. "I'll whiten them a bit. That will be good for them and for the lemons and grapes too." And away flew the Snow Queen, leaving Kay alone in the great empty ice-halls so many miles in length. He sat there stiff, and still gazing at the pieces of ice, and thinking till his head was bursting; one would have thought he was frozen.

Just at that moment little Gerda entered the castle by the great gate. Cutting winds kept guard here, but they all seemed asleep; so she entered the great empty cold halls—and there she saw Kay.

She recognized him, flew to him, and clasped him round the neck, and held him tightly while she exclaimed, "Kay, dear little Kay! At last I have found you."

But he sat still, stiff and cold; then little Gerda wept hot tears, which fell upon his breast. They penetrated into his heart, thawed the lump of ice and consumed the little splinter of glass in it. He looked at her, and she sang:

> The roses fade and die, but we
> Our Infant Lord shall surely see.

Then Kay burst into tears; he cried so that the grain of glass was washed out of his eye. Now he recognized her and cried joyfully: "Gerda! dear little Gerda! Where have you been all this time? And where have I been?" And he looked all around him. "How cold it is here, and how vast and empty!" he said, as he clung to Gerda, who was laughing and crying for joy. There was such joy that even the ice-blocks danced about; and when they were tired and lay down, they formed themselves into the letters of which the Snow Queen had said that if he found them out he should be his own master, and she would give him the whole world and a pair of new skates.

And Gerda kissed his cheeks and they became blooming. She kissed his eyes and they shone like hers; she kissed his hands and feet, and he was happy. The Snow Queen might come home now; there stood his discharge written in glittering ice-blocks.

And they took each other by the hand and went forth from the great castle. They spoke of the grandmother and of the roses upon the roof, and wherever they walked the winds sank to rest and the sun came out. When they reached the bush with the red berries, the reindeer stood waiting there; he had brought another young one with him whose udder was full, and this one gave the children its warm milk and kissed them on the mouth. Then they carried Kay and Gerda first to the Finland woman, where they warmed themselves in the hot room and obtained information about the journey home; and then to the Lapland woman who had made new clothes for them and repaired their sledge.

The reindeer and the young one ran by their side and followed them as far as the boundaries of the country, where the first green leaves were budding; there they parted from the reindeer and the Lapland woman. "Farewell," they all said. And now they once more heard the little birds twittering and saw the green buds of the forest. Out of the latter came riding on a splendid horse which Gerda knew—for it had drawn the golden coach—a young girl, with a bright red cap on her head and pistols in her belt. It was the little robber-girl who had got tired of staying at home, and was now going north, and if that did not suit her, to another part of the world. She recognized Gerda at once, and Gerda recognized her too; it was a joyful meeting.

"You are a fine fellow to go gadding about like that," she said to little Kay. "I should like to know whether you deserve that people should run to the end of the world for your sake."

But Gerda patted her cheeks and asked after the prince and princess.

"They have gone to foreign countries," said the robber-girl.

"And the crow?" asked Gerda.

"Oh, the crow is dead," she replied. "The tame sweetheart is a widow now and wears a piece of black wool round her leg; she mourns very much, but it's all talk! But tell me now how you got on and how you managed to catch him."

And Gerda and Kay told their story.

"Snip, snap, snorum, porum, basilorum!" said the robber-girl, and taking both their hands she promised that if ever she should pass through their city, she would come and visit them. And with that she rode out into the wide world. Gerda and Kay went hand in hand, and wherever they went it was glorious spring with flowers and verdure. The church bells were ringing, and they recognized the high steeples and the great city in which they lived. They entered it, and went to their grandmother's door up the stairs and into the room, where everything stood in exactly the same spot as before. The clock went "tick, tick!" and the hands went round, but as they passed through the door they noticed that they had become grown-up people. The roses on the roof bloomed in at the open window, and there stood the little children's chairs; Kay and Gerda sat down each on their own, and held each other by the hand. They had forgotten the cold empty grandeur of the Snow Queen's castle like a bad dream. The grandmother sat in God's bright sunshine and read aloud from the Bible: "Except ye become as little children, ye shall in no wise enter into the kingdom of God."

And Kay and Gerda looked into each other's eyes, and all at once understood the old song:

> The roses fade and die, but we
> Our Infant Lord shall surely see.

There they both sat, grown up and yet children—children in heart; and it was summer—warm, pleasant summer.

Snow-White and Rose-Red

(FROM *THE BLUE FAIRY BOOK*)

A poor widow once lived in a little cottage with a garden in front of it, in which grew two rose trees, one bearing white roses and the other red. She had two children, who were just like the two rose trees; one was called Snow-White and the other Rose-Red, and they were the sweetest and best children in the world, always diligent and always cheerful; but Snow-White was quieter and more gentle than Rose-Red. Rose-Red loved to run about the fields and meadows, and to pick flowers and catch butterflies; but Snow-White sat at home with her mother and helped her in the household, or read aloud to her when there was no work to do. The two children loved each other so dearly that they always walked about hand in hand whenever they went out together, and when Snow-White said, "We will never desert each other," Rose-Red answered: "No, not as long as we live"; and the mother added: "Whatever one gets she shall share with the other." They often roamed about in the woods gathering berries and no beast offered to hurt them; on the contrary, they came up to them in the most confiding manner; the little hare would eat a cabbage leaf from their hands, the deer grazed beside them, the stag would bound past them merrily, and the birds remained on the branches and sang to them with all their might. No evil ever befell them; if they tarried late in the wood and night overtook them, they lay down together on the moss and slept till morning, and their mother knew they were quite safe, and never felt anxious about them. Once, when they had slept all night in the wood and had been wakened by the morning sun, they perceived a beautiful child in a shining white robe sitting close to their resting-place. The figure got up, looked at them kindly, but said nothing, and vanished into the wood. And when they looked round about them they became aware that they had slept quite close to a precipice, over which they would certainly have fallen had they gone on a few steps further in the darkness. And when they told their mother of their adventure, she said what they had seen must have been the angel that guards good children.

Snow-White and Rose-Red kept their mother's cottage so beautifully clean and neat that it was a pleasure to go into it. In summer Rose-Red looked after the house, and every morning before her mother awoke she placed a bunch of flowers before the bed, from each tree a rose. In winter Snow-White lit the fire and put on the kettle, which was made of brass, but so beautifully polished that it shone like gold. In the evening when the snowflakes fell their mother said: "Snow-White, go and close the shutters," and they drew round the fire, while the mother put on her spectacles and read aloud from a big book and the two girls listened and sat and span. Beside them on the ground lay a little lamb, and behind them perched a little white dove with its head tucked under its wings.

One evening as they sat thus cosily together someone knocked at the door as though he desired admittance. The mother said: "Rose-Red, open the door quickly; it must be some traveler seeking shelter." Rose-Red hastened to unbar the door, and thought she saw a poor man standing in the darkness outside; but it was no such thing, only a bear, who poked his thick black head through the door. Rose-Red screamed aloud and sprang back in terror, the lamb began to bleat, the dove flapped its wings, and Snow-White ran and hid behind her mother's bed. But the bear began to speak, and said: "Don't be afraid: I won't hurt you. I am half frozen, and only wish to warm myself a little." "My poor bear," said the mother, "lie down by the fire, only take care you don't burn your fur." Then she called out: "Snow-White and Rose-Red, come out; the bear will do you no harm; he is a good, honest creature." So they both came out of their hiding-places, and gradually the lamb and dove drew near too, and they all forgot their fear. The bear asked the children to beat the snow a little out of his fur, and they fetched a brush and scrubbed him till he was dry. Then the beast stretched himself in front of the fire, and growled quite happily and comfortably. The children soon grew quite at their ease with him, and led their helpless guest a fearful life. They tugged his fur with their hands, put their small feet on his back, and rolled him about here and there, or took a hazel wand and beat him with it; and if he growled they only laughed. The bear submitted to everything with the best possible good-nature, only when they went too far he cried: "Oh! children, spare my life!

Snow-White and Rose-Red,
Don't beat your lover dead."

When it was time to retire for the night, and the others went to bed, the mother said to the bear: "You can lie there on the hearth, in Heaven's name; it will be shelter for you from the cold and wet." As soon as day dawned the children led him out, and he trotted over the snow into the wood. From this time on the bear came every evening at the same hour, and lay down by the hearth and let the children play what pranks they liked with him; and they got so accustomed to him that the door was never shut till their black friend had made his appearance.

When spring came, and all outside was green, the bear said one morning to Snow-White: "Now I must go away, and not return again the whole summer." "Where are you going to, dear bear?" asked Snow-White. "I must go to the wood and protect my treasure from the wicked dwarfs. In winter, when the earth is frozen hard, they are obliged to remain underground, for they can't work their way through; but now, when the sun has thawed and warmed the ground, they break through and come up above to spy the land and steal what they can; what once falls into their hands and into their caves is not easily brought back to light." Snow-White was quite sad over their friend's departure, and when she unbarred the door for him, the bear, stepping out, caught a piece of his fur in the door-knocker, and Snow-White thought she caught sight of glittering gold beneath it, but she couldn't be certain of it; and the bear ran hastily away, and soon disappeared behind the trees.

A short time after this the mother sent the children into the wood to collect fagots. They came in their wanderings upon a big tree which lay felled on the ground, and on the trunk among the long grass they noticed something jumping up and down, but what it was they couldn't distinguish. When they approached nearer they perceived a dwarf with a wizened face and a beard a yard long. The end of the beard was jammed into a cleft of the tree, and the little man sprang about like a dog on a chain, and didn't seem to know what he was to do. He glared at the girls with his fiery red eyes, and screamed out: "What are you standing there for? Can't you come and help me?" "What were you doing, little man?" asked Rose-Red. "You stupid, inquisitive goose!" replied the dwarf; "I wanted to split the tree, in order to get little chips of wood for our kitchen fire; those thick logs that serve to make fires for coarse, greedy people like yourselves quite burn up all the little food we need. I had successfully driven in the wedge, and all was going well, but the cursed wood was so slippery that it suddenly sprang out, and the tree closed up so rapidly that I had no time to take my beautiful white beard out, so here I am stuck fast, and I can't get away; and you silly, smooth-faced, milk-and-water girls just stand and laugh! Ugh! what wretches you are!"

The children did all in their power, but they couldn't get the beard out; it was wedged in far too firmly. "I will run and fetch somebody," said Rose-Red. "Crazy blockheads!" snapped the dwarf; "what's the good of calling anyone else? You're already two too many for me. Does nothing better occur to you than that?" "Don't be so impatient," said Snow-White, "I'll see you get help," and taking her scissors out of her pocket she cut off the end of his beard. As soon as the dwarf felt himself free he seized a bag full of gold which was hidden among the roots of the tree, lifted it up, and muttered aloud: "Curse these rude wretches, cutting off a piece of my splendid beard!" With these words he swung the bag over his back, and disappeared without as much as looking at the children again.

Shortly after this Snow-White and Rose-Red went out to get a dish of fish. As they approached the stream they saw something which looked like an enormous grasshopper springing toward the water as if it were going to jump in. They ran forward and recognized their old friend the dwarf. "Where are you going to?" asked Rose-Red; "you're surely not going to jump into the water?" "I'm not such a fool," screamed the dwarf. "Don't you see that cursed fish is trying to drag me in?" The little man had been sitting on the bank fishing, when unfortunately the wind had entangled his beard in the line; and when immediately afterward a big fish bit, the feeble little creature had no strength to pull it out; the fish had the upper fin, and dragged the dwarf towards him. He clung on with all his might to every rush and blade of grass, but it didn't help him much; he had to follow every movement of the fish, and was in great danger of being drawn into the water. The girls came up just at the right moment, held him firm, and did all they could to disentangle his beard from the line; but in vain, beard and line were in a hopeless muddle. Nothing remained but to produce the scissors and cut the beard, by which a small part of it was sacrificed.

When the dwarf perceived what they were about he yelled to them: "Do you call that manners, you toadstools! to disfigure a fellow's face? It wasn't enough that you shortened my beard before, but you must now needs cut off the best bit of it. I can't appear like this before my own people. I wish you'd been at Jericho first." Then he fetched a sack of pearls that lay among the rushes, and without saying another word he dragged it away and disappeared behind a stone.

It happened that soon after this the mother sent the two girls to the town to buy needles, thread, laces, and ribbons. Their road led over a heath where huge boulders of rock lay scattered here and there. While trudging along they saw a big bird hovering in the air, circling slowly above them, but always descending lower, till at last it settled on a rock not far from them. Immediately afterward they heard a sharp, piercing cry. They ran forward, and saw with horror that the eagle had pounced on their old friend the dwarf, and was about to carry him off. The tender-hearted children seized ahold of the little man, and struggled so long with the bird that at last he let go his prey. When the dwarf had recovered from the first shock he screamed in his screeching voice: "Couldn't you have treated me more carefully? You have torn my thin little coat all to shreds, useless, awkward hussies that you are!" Then he took a bag of precious stones and vanished under the rocks into his cave. The girls were accustomed to his ingratitude, and went on their way and did their business in town. On their way home, as they were again passing the heath, they surprised the dwarf pouring out his precious stones on an open space, for he had thought no one would pass by at so late an hour. The evening sun shone on the glittering stones, and they glanced and gleamed so beautifully that the children stood still and gazed on them. "What are you standing there gaping for?" screamed the dwarf, and his ashen-gray face became scarlet with rage. He was about to go off with these angry words when a sudden growl was heard, and a black bear trotted out of the wood. The dwarf jumped up in great fright, but he hadn't time to reach his place of retreat, for the bear was already close to him. Then he cried in terror: "Dear Mr. Bear, spare me! I'll give you all my treasure. Look at those beautiful precious stones lying there. Spare my life! what pleasure would you get from a poor feeble little fellow like me? You won't feel me between your teeth. There, lay hold of these two wicked girls, they will be a tender morsel for you, as fat as young quails; eat them up, for heaven's sake." But the bear, paying no attention to his words, gave the evil little creature one blow with his paw, and he never moved again.

The girls had run away, but the bear called after them: "Snow-White and Rose-Red, don't be afraid; wait, and I'll come with you." Then they recognized his voice and stood still, and when the bear was quite close to them his skin suddenly fell off, and a beautiful man stood beside them, all dressed in gold. "I am a king's son," he said, "and have been doomed by that unholy little dwarf, who had stolen my treasure, to roam about the woods as a wild bear till his death should set me free. Now he has got his well-merited punishment."

Snow-White married him, and Rose-Red his brother, and they divided the great treasure the dwarf had collected in his cave between them. The old mother lived for many years peacefully with her children; and she carried the two rose trees with her, and they stood in front of her window, and every year they bore the finest red and white roses.

The King of the Swans

(TRADITIONAL GERMAN TALE)

There was once a little girl, who was named Delphine, so good and cheerful, that she was a favorite with everybody. This girl had a friend called Hilda, who was likewise a very good child, and they loved each other dearly.

It was in winter, and the snow was lying deep upon hill and field, when Hilda fell sick, and her parents were very anxious about her. She was quite unable to eat, and she was alternately burning hot, and shivering with cold; and, though she had several doctors and much physic, she did not become any better.

If any of her young friends visited her, she would often say, "Give me strawberries. Which of you will go, and find me some strawberries, that I may get well again?"

If her father and mother said, "Dear Hilda, it is winter, and there are no strawberries to be found at this season, Hilda would raise herself up in bed, and say, "Far away over the high hill there is a green slope; there I can see plenty of strawberries. Who will go, and fetch them for me?—only one of the nice red berries—only one!" The children left the room, and chatted together, and said, "What foolish things Hilda spoke in her dreams!" But Delphine was much troubled that she could not help her dear friend. All at once she said—"Who will go with me over the mountains to seek for strawberries? It will be some little comfort to poor Hilda, if she sees us going over the hill, and seeking for them." None of them would agree to go, but went straight home.

Delphine set out alone upon her way, and went through a forest. A small trodden footpath led up the hill, and down again on the other side, through another wood of tall oaks and beeches. She came to a place where three paths met: she stood still a moment, not knowing which to take, when, quite unexpectedly, she saw a little man approaching through the trees. He had a green hat upon his head, with a feather as white as snow. His dress was made of the softest swansdown; he carried an ivory bow at his shoulder, and a small silver hunting horn hung at his side. "What do you want here, my little damsel?" he said, with friendly voice.

"Ah!" said Delphine, "I have a sick friend who longs for strawberries, and says they will make her well again. I know very well that it is winter; but I think I shall be able to find something here that she will like, and I hope I shall not return quite empty-handed."

"Come with me," said the little hunter: "I will show you a place where you will find what you are come in search of."

He went on before her, and led her through many winding paths in the thicket, till at length the forest appeared lighter, and a warm spring-like air met them; and they at last stood at a grated iron door. The little man unlocked it, saying—"Now, if you go straight forward, you will find what you seek."

Delphine would have thanked the good-natured little man; but he had vanished instantly. She went on a few steps farther, and came to a green slope.

Here winter had disappeared. The sun shone warm in the cloudless blue heavens; the birds sang merrily; yet, a few steps farther, and she beheld the ground covered with the finest strawberries. How the good little maiden rejoiced! She quickly gathered a large bunch, and hastened back to take them to her dear sick friend.

But somehow it happened, that in her haste she could not find her way back. She came to the iron palisades which surrounded the wood; but all her attempts to find the gate were fruitless. She ran in great anxiety this way and that; but no gate was to be seen. Then she heard the sound of a whistle at a distance. "Thank God!" she said, "I hear a living sound: some one is probably there, who will show me the way." She hastened through the thicket, and was much astonished at what she beheld. At the end of a beautiful green meadow, there was a lake, in which many beautiful swans, both black and white, were swimming gracefully. In the middle of the lake there was a small island, upon which was a fine castle, surrounded by flower gardens and pleasure grounds. As she approached the shore of the lake, she perceived a little man sitting, but with a less friendly aspect than the little hunter in the forest. He had a large head, with rough hair; and a gray beard, so long that it reached his knees. In one hand he held a whistle, and in the other a switch.

Delphine felt rather afraid of speaking to him, and stood still at a little distance. She soon observed, that his office was to take care of the swans, and prevent them from going out of the water. When any did so, he whistled to them; and, if they did not obey him, then he employed his long switch, which had the property of stretching out, or becoming shorter, just as he pleased. Except this swan-herd, she saw no one; and there was no bridge over to the castle. So she took courage, and said to the gray-beard, "Good friend, cannot you show me the gate, which will lead me into the forest?"

The gray-beard looked at her in surprise, but did not speak: he merely made her understand by signs, that she should sit down; which she did. Then he whistled, and presently came a large swan from the lake, which laid itself down before him. The little old man seated himself on the swan's back, threw one of his arms round its neck; and away the trusty bird swam with him across the lake: there he alighted, and went into the castle.

Delphine waited some time, curious to see what would happen; but she did not feel afraid. At length she saw four black swans swim from a creek of the lake, harnessed to a beautiful little green boat, adorned with silver. The covering of the boat was formed like a pair of wings, and shaded two small seats, of which the foremost ended in the shape of a long swan's neck.

There sat the gray-beard, who looked much more agreeable than before. He gave Delphine a sign to step in, which she complied with, and they sailed gently across the lake; and, when they reached the shore, they left the boat, and the old man led her into the palace.

In a light-blue marble hall, the King of the Swans sat upon his throne, a bright golden crown upon his head, and many richly dressed attendants surrounded him. "What dost thou seek in my kingdom?" inquired the King.—"I have found what I sought," answered Delphine; "but I pray you to let some one direct me in the way home; for I find that I have wandered in the wrong direction."—"Very well," said the King," it shall be done; but it is the custom for all who enter this kingdom to give a present to the King of the Swans. What hast thou to offer?"

"Alas!" replied Delphine, "I have nothing at all. If I had known, I would have brought something with me from home."—"Thou hast strawberries," rejoined the King; "and I like strawberries above all things. Give me thy strawberries, and then one of my servants shall show thee the way home."

"Alas! I cannot give you all,"continued Delphine; "the strawberries are for my sick friend, who must die if she has no strawberries. But I will readily give you some of them." With these words, she took several fine strawberries, with the stems and leaves; tied them in a bunch with the ribbon which confined her hair; and handed them to the King. "Thanks, my little daughter," said the King; "now go: this man will attend thee; but do exactly what he bids thee." The old swan-herd waited ready for her. When she had taken leave of the King, Delphine was led into the garden, upon an open lawn; a fine white handkerchief was tied over her eyes; the old man whistled, and took her by the arm. She heard a rustling of wings; she felt the wind blow in her face, and felt colder and colder; but she could not see any thing.

At last the sound of wings ceased, and the old man set her upon the ground. "Now, my child, count twenty; then take off the bandage, but not before. Preserve it carefully: it will be required of thee at its proper time." She counted twenty; and, when she had taken off the bandage, she found herself standing on the hill, opposite the house of her friend Hilda, with frost and snow all around. She looked up to the sky, and there beheld a great bird, and the old man sitting upon it with his arm round its neck. Then she hastened to her friend Hilda, who was in bed, repeating the words, "Who will bring me strawberries to make me well?"—"There they are," said Delphine, and handed the bunch to Hilda. Every one was astonished, and wanted to know whence Delphine had brought them. But she had hardly begun to relate her wonderful adventures, before Hilda had eaten all the strawberries. Then the color returned to her face, and strength to her limbs; and Hilda said, "Thank God, and dear Delphine, now I am quite well!" She rose up, and was really quite restored.

Who can say how the parents thanked and blessed Delphine? She was a truly good and brave girl; and, when she grew up, everybody desired their children to be like her.

One day, as Delphine was walking in the meadows with her mother (she was now so tall, that those who had only seen her when a child could not have known her again to be the same), she looked up, and saw a black speck in the sky, which became larger, as it descended; and at last she saw that it was a prodigious black swan, far larger than our swans, and that it was flying down towards her. There was a tent, with golden gauze curtains upon the swan's back; and, when the swan had gently alighted on the ground, there came out of the tent a little man with friendly eyes—it was the King of the Swans. "I have heard," said he, "that in a short time thou wilt celebrate a joyful festival; and, as thou gavest me a present when a child, and hast grown up so good, and brave, and pure a maiden, I will make thee a present in return." Saying these words, he placed a costly crown upon her head. It was formed of gold, wrought in the form of strawberry leaves; and, between the leaves, there sparkled red rubies, diamonds, and purple amethysts; and the edge was a beautiful golden band.

Delphine and her mother could hardly thank the King for astonishment. But he did not give them time. The swan rose majestically in the air, and flew towards his home; and, at last, disappeared as a little spot in the clouds.

Many boys and girls have gone over the hill since that time to seek the land of the swans, and to find strawberries in winter, but have not found them.

Perhaps they were *more selfish*, and not so good as Delphine.

Heart of Ice

(From *The Green Fairy Book*)

Once upon a time there lived a King and Queen who were foolish beyond all telling, but nevertheless they were vastly fond of one another. It is true that certain spiteful people were heard to say that this was only one proof the more of their exceeding foolishness, but of course you will understand that these were not their own courtiers, since, after all, they *were* a King and Queen, and up to this time all things had prospered with them. For in those days the one thing to be thought of in governing a kingdom was to keep well with all the Fairies and Enchanters, and on no account to stint them of the cakes, the ells of ribbon, and similar trifles which were their due, and, above all things, when there was a christening, to remember to invite every single one, good, bad, or indifferent, to the ceremony. Now, the foolish Queen had one little son who was just going to be christened, and for several months she had been hard at work preparing an enormous list of the names of those who were to be invited, but she quite forgot that it would take nearly as long to read it over as it had taken to write it out. So, when the moment of the christening arrived the King—to whom the task had been entrusted—had barely reached the end of the second page and his tongue was tripping with fatigue and haste as he repeated the usual formula: "I conjure and pray you, Fairy so-and-so"— or "Enchanter such-a-one"—"to honor me with a visit, and graciously bestow your gifts upon my son."

To make matters worse, word was brought to him that the Fairies asked on the first page had already arrived and were waiting impatiently in the Great Hall, and grumbling that nobody was there to receive them. Thereupon he gave up the list in despair and hurried to greet those whom he had succeeded in asking, imploring their goodwill so humbly that most of them were touched, and promised that they would do his son no harm. But there happened to be among them a Fairy from a far country about whom they knew nothing, though her name had been written on the first page of the list. This Fairy was annoyed that after having taken the trouble to come so quickly, there had been no one to receive her, or help her to alight from the great ostrich on which she had traveled from her distant home, and now she began to mutter to herself in the most alarming way.

"Oh! prate away," said she, "your son will never be anything to boast of. Say what you will, he will be nothing but a Mannikin—"

No doubt she would have gone on longer in this strain, and given the unhappy little Prince half-a-dozen undesirable gifts, if it had not been for the good Fairy Genesta, who held the kingdom under her special protection, and who luckily hurried in just in time to prevent further mischief. When she had by compliments and entreaties pacified the unknown Fairy, and persuaded her to say no more, she gave the King a hint that now was the time to distribute the presents, after which ceremony they all took their departure, excepting the Fairy Genesta, who then went to see the Queen, and said to her:

"A nice mess you seem to have made of this business, madam. Why did you not condescend to consult me? But foolish people like you always think they can do without help or advice, and I observe that, in spite of all my goodness to you, you had not even the civility to invite me!"

"Ah! dear madam," cried the King, throwing himself at her feet; "did I ever have time to get as far as your name? See where I put in this mark when I abandoned the hopeless undertaking which I had but just begun!"

"There! there!" said the Fairy, "I am not offended. I don't allow myself to be put out by trifles like that with people I really am fond of. But now about your son: I have saved him from a great many disagreeable things, but you must let me take him away and take care of him, and you will not see him again until he is all covered with fur!"

At these mysterious words the King and Queen burst into tears, for they lived in such a hot climate themselves that how or why the Prince should come to be covered with fur they could not imagine, and thought it must portend some great misfortune to him.

However, Genesta told them not to disquiet themselves.

"If I left him to you to bring up," said she, "you would be certain to make him as foolish as yourselves. I do not even intend to let him know that he is your son. As for you, you had better give your minds to governing your kingdom properly." So saying, she opened the window, and catching up the little Prince, cradle and all, she glided away in the air as if she were skating upon ice, leaving the King and Queen in the greatest affliction. They consulted everyone who came near them as to what the Fairy could possibly have meant by saying that when they saw their son again he would be covered with fur. But nobody could offer any solution of the mystery, only they all seemed to agree that it must be something frightful, and the King and Queen made themselves more miserable than ever, and wandered about their palace in a way to make anyone pity them. Meantime the Fairy had carried off the little Prince to her own castle, and placed him under the care of a young peasant woman, whom she bewitched so as to make her think that this new baby was one of her own children. So the Prince grew up healthy and strong, leading the simple life of a young peasant, for the Fairy thought that he could have no better training; only as he grew older she kept him more and more with herself, that his mind might be cultivated and exercised as well as his body. But her care did not cease there: she resolved that he should be tried by hardships and disappointments and the knowledge of his fellowmen; for indeed she knew the Prince would need every advantage that she could give him, since, though he increased in years, he did not increase in height, but remained the tiniest of Princes. However, in spite of this he was exceedingly active and well formed, and altogether so handsome and agreeable that the smallness of his stature was of no real consequence. The Prince was perfectly aware that he was called by the ridiculous name of "Mannikin," but he consoled himself by vowing that, happen what might, he would make it illustrious.

In order to carry out her plans for his welfare the Fairy now began to send Prince Mannikin the most wonderful dreams of adventure by sea and land, and of these adventures he himself was always the hero. Sometimes he rescued a lovely Princess from some terrible danger, again he earned a kingdom by some brave deed, until at last he longed to go away and seek his fortune in a far country where his humble birth would not prevent his gaining honor and riches by his courage, and it was with a heart full of ambitious projects that he rode one day into a great city not far from the Fairy's castle. As he had set out intending to hunt in the surrounding forest he was quite simply dressed, and carried only a bow and arrows and a light spear; but even thus arrayed he looked graceful and distinguished. As he entered the city he saw that the inhabitants were all racing with one accord towards the market-place, and he also turned his horse in the same direction, curious to know what was going forward. When he reached the spot he found that certain foreigners of strange and outlandish appearance were about to make a proclamation to the assembled citizens, and he hastily pushed his way into the crowd until he was near enough to hear the words of the venerable old man who was their spokesman:

"Let the whole world know that he who can reach the summit of the Ice Mountain shall receive as his reward, not only the incomparable Sabella, fairest of the fair, but also all the realms of which she is Queen!" "Here," continued the old man after he had made this proclamation—"here is the list of all those Princes who, struck by the beauty of the Princess, have perished in the attempt to win her; and here is the list of these who have just entered upon the high emprise."

Prince Mannikin was seized with a violent desire to inscribe his name among the others, but the remembrance of his dependent position and his lack of wealth held him back. But while he hesitated the old man, with many respectful ceremonies, unveiled a portrait of the lovely Sabella, which was carried by some of the attendants, and after one glance at it the Prince delayed no longer, but, rushing forward, demanded permission to add his name to the list. When they saw his tiny stature and simple attire the strangers looked at each other doubtfully, not knowing whether to accept or refuse him. But the Prince said haughtily:

"Give me the paper that I may sign it," and they obeyed. What between admiration for the Princess and annoyance at the hesitation shown by her ambassadors the Prince was too much agitated to choose any other name than the one by which he was always known. But when, after all the grand titles of the other Princes, he simply wrote "Mannikin," the ambassadors broke into shouts of laughter.

"Miserable wretches!" cried the Prince; "but for the presence of that lovely portrait I would cut off your heads."

But he suddenly remembered that, after all, it *was* a funny name, and that he had not yet had time to make it famous; so he was calm, and enquired the way to the Princess Sabella's country.

Though his heart did not fail him in the least, still he felt there were many difficulties before him, and he resolved to set out at once, without even taking leave of the Fairy, for fear she might try to stop him. Everybody in the town who knew him made great fun of the idea of Mannikin's undertaking such an expedition, and it even came to the ears of the foolish King and Queen, who laughed over it more than any of the others, without having an idea that the presumptuous Mannikin was their only son!

Meantime the Prince was traveling on, though the direction he had received for his journey were none of the clearest.

"Four hundred leagues north of Mount Caucasus you will receive your orders and instructions for the conquest of the Ice Mountain."

Fine marching orders, those, for a man starting from a country near where Japan is nowadays!

However, he fared eastward, avoiding all towns, lest the people should laugh at his name, for, you see, he was not a very experienced traveler, and had not yet learned to enjoy a joke even if it were against himself. At night he slept in the woods, and at first he lived upon wild fruits; but the Fairy, who was keeping a benevolent eye upon him, thought that it would never do to let him be half-starved in that way, so she took to feeding him with all sorts of good things while he was asleep, and the Prince wondered very much that when he was awake he never felt hungry! True to her plan the Fairy sent him various adventures to prove his courage, and he came successfully through them all, only in his last fight with a furious monster rather like a tiger he had the ill luck to lose his horse. However, nothing daunted, he struggled on on foot, and at last reached a seaport. Here he found a boat sailing for the coast which he desired to reach, and, having just enough money to pay his passage, he went on board and they started. But after some days a fearful storm came on, which completely wrecked the little ship, and the Prince only saved his life by swimming a long, long way to the only land that was in sight, and which proved to be a desert island. Here he lived by fishing and hunting, always hoping that the good Fairy would presently rescue him. One day, as he was looking sadly out to sea, he became aware of a curious looking boat which was drifting slowly towards the shore, and which presently ran into a little creek and there stuck fast in the sand. Prince Mannikin rushed down eagerly to examine it, and saw with amazement that the masts and spars were all branched, and covered thickly with leaves until it looked like a little wood. Thinking from the stillness that there could be no one on board, the Prince pushed aside the branches and sprang over the side, and found himself surrounded by the crew, who lay motionless as dead men and in a most deplorable condition. They, too, had become almost like trees, and were growing to the deck, or to the masts, or to the sides of the vessel, or to whatever they had happened to be touching when the enchantment fell upon them. Mannikin was struck with pity for their miserable plight, and set to work with might and main to release them. With the sharp point of one of his arrows he gently detached their hands and feet from the wood which held them fast, and carried them on shore, one after another, where he rubbed their rigid limbs, and bathed them with infusions of various herbs with such success, that, after a few days, they recovered perfectly and were as fit to manage a boat as ever. You may be sure that the good Fairy Genesta had something to do with this marvelous cure, and she also put it into the Prince's head to rub the boat itself with the same magic herbs, which cleared it entirely, and not before it was time, for, at the rate at which it was growing before, it would very soon have become a forest! The gratitude of the sailors was extreme, and they willingly promised to land the Prince upon any coast he pleased; but, when he questioned them about the extraordinary thing that had happened to them and to their ship, they could in no way explain it, except that they said that, as they were passing along a thickly wooded coast, a sudden gust of wind had reached them from the land and enveloped them in a dense cloud of dust, after which everything in the boat that was not metal had sprouted and blossomed, as the Prince had seen, and that they themselves had grown gradually numb and heavy, and had finally lost all consciousness. Prince Mannikin was deeply interested in this curious story, and collected a quantity of the dust from the bottom of the boat, which he carefully preserved, thinking that its strange property might one day stand him in good stead.

Then they joyfully left the desert island, and after a long and prosperous voyage over calm seas they at length came in sight of land, and resolved to go on shore, not only to take in a fresh stock of water and provisions, but also to find out, if possible, where they were and in what direction to proceed.

As they neared the coast they wondered if this could be another uninhabited land, for no human beings could be distinguished, and yet that something was stirring became evident, for in the dust-clouds that moved near the ground small dark forms were dimly visible. These appeared to be assembling at the exact spot where they were preparing to run ashore, and what was their surprise to find they were nothing more nor less than large and beautiful spaniels, some mounted as sentries, others grouped in companies and regiments, all eagerly watching their disembarkation. When they found that Prince Mannikin, instead of saying, "Shoot them," as they had feared, said "Hi, good dog!" in a thoroughly friendly and ingratiating way, they crowded round him with a great wagging of tails and giving of paws, and very soon made him understand that they wanted him to leave his men with the boat and follow them. The Prince was so curious to know more about them that he agreed willingly; so, after arranging with the sailors to wait for him fifteen days, and then, if he had not come back, to go on their way without him, he set out with his new friends. Their way lay inland, and Mannikin noticed with great surprise that the fields were well cultivated and that the carts and ploughs were drawn by horses or oxen, just as they might have been in any other country, and when they passed any village the cottages were trim and pretty, and an air of prosperity was everywhere. At one of the villages a dainty little repast was set before the Prince, and while he was eating, a chariot was brought, drawn by two splendid horses, which were driven with great skill by a large spaniel. In this carriage he continued his journey very comfortably, passing many similar equipages upon the road, and being always most courteously saluted by the spaniels who occupied them. At last they drove rapidly into a large town, which Prince Mannikin had no doubt was the capital of the kingdom. News of his approach had evidently been received, for all the inhabitants were at their doors and windows, and all the little spaniels had climbed upon the wall and gates to see him arrive. The Prince was delighted with the hearty welcome they gave him, and looked round him with the deepest interest. After passing through a few wide streets, well paved, and adorned with avenues of fine trees, they drove into the courtyard of a grand palace, which was full of spaniels who were evidently soldiers. "The King's body-guard," thought the Prince to himself as he returned their salutations, and then the carriage stopped, and he was shown into the presence of the King, who lay upon a rich Persian carpet surrounded by several little spaniels, who were occupied in chasing away the flies lest they should disturb his Majesty. He was the most beautiful of all spaniels, with a look of sadness in his large eyes, which, however, quite disappeared as he sprang up to welcome Prince Mannikin with every demonstration of delight; after which he made a sign to his courtiers, who came one by one to pay their respects to the visitor. The Prince thought that he would find himself puzzled as to how he should carry on a conversation, but as soon as he and the King were once more left alone, a Secretary of State was sent for, who wrote from his Majesty's dictation a most polite speech, in which he regretted much that they were unable to converse, except in writing, the language of dogs being difficult to understand. As for the writing, it had remained the same as the Prince's own.

Mannikin thereupon wrote a suitable reply, and then begged the King to satisfy his curiosity about all the strange things he had seen and heard since his landing. This appeared to awaken sad recollections in the King's mind, but he informed the Prince that he was called King Bayard, and that a Fairy, whose kingdom was next his own, had fallen violently in love with him, and had done all she could to persuade him to marry her; but that he could not do so as he himself was the devoted lover of the Queen of the Spice Islands. Finally, the Fairy, furious at the indifference with which her love was treated, had reduced him to the state in which the Prince found him, leaving him unchanged in mind, but deprived of the power of speech; and, not content with wreaking her vengeance upon the King alone, she had condemned all his subjects to a similar fate, saying:

"Bark, and run upon four feet, until the time comes when virtue shall be rewarded by love and fortune."

Which, as the poor King remarked, was very much the same thing as if she had said, "Remain a spaniel for ever and ever."

Prince Mannikin was quite of the same opinion; nevertheless he said what we should all have said in the same circumstances:

"Your Majesty must have patience."

He was indeed deeply sorry for poor King Bayard, and said all the consoling things he could think of, promising to aid him with all his might if there was anything to be done. In short they became firm friends, and the King proudly displayed to Mannikin the portrait of the Queen of the Spice Islands, and he quite agreed that it was worth while to go through anything for the sake of a creature so lovely. Prince Mannikin in his turn told his own history, and the great undertaking upon which he had set out, and King Bayard was able to give him some valuable instructions as to which would be the best way for him to proceed, and then they went together to the place where the boat had been left. The sailors were delighted to see the Prince again, though they had known that he was safe, and when they had taken on board all the supplies which the King had sent for them, they started once more. The King and Prince parted with much regret, and the former insisted that Mannikin should take with him one of his own pages, named Mousta, who was charged to attend to him everywhere, and serve him faithfully, which he promised to do.

The wind being favorable they were soon out of hearing of the general howl of regret from the whole army, which had been given by order of the King, as a great compliment, and it was not long before the land was entirely lost to view. They met with no further adventures worth speaking of, and presently found themselves within two leagues of the harbor for which they were making. The Prince, however, thought it would suit him better to land where he was, so as to avoid the town, since he had no money left and was very doubtful as to what he should do next. So the sailors set him and Mousta on shore, and then went back sorrowfully to their ship, while the Prince and his attendant walked off in what looked to them the most promising direction. They soon reached a lovely green meadow on the border of a wood, which seemed to them so pleasant after their long voyage that they sat down to rest in the shade and amused themselves by watching the gambols

45

and antics of a pretty tiny monkey in the trees close by. The Prince pres-ently became so fascinated by it that he sprang up and tried to catch it, but it eluded his grasp and kept just out of arm's reach, until it had made him promise to follow wherever it led him, and then it sprang upon his shoulder and whispered in his ear:

"We have no money, my poor Mannikin, and we are altogether badly off, and at a loss to know what to do next."

"Yes, indeed," answered the Prince ruefully, "and I have nothing to give you, no sugar or biscuits, or anything that you like, my pretty one."

"Since you are so thoughtful for me, and so patient about your own affairs," said the little monkey, "I will show you the way to the Golden Rock, only you must leave Mousta to wait for you here."

Prince Mannikin agreed willingly, and then the little monkey sprang from his shoulder to the nearest tree, and began to run through the wood from branch to branch, crying, "Follow me."

This the Prince did not find quite so easy, but the little monkey waited for him and showed him the easiest places, until presently the wood grew thin-ner and they came out into a little clear grassy space at the foot of a moun-tain, in the midst of which stood a single rock, about ten feet high. When they were quite close to it the little monkey said:

"This stone looks pretty hard, but give it a blow with your spear and let us see what will happen."

So the Prince took his spear and gave the rock a vigorous dig, which split off several pieces, and showed that, though the surface was thinly coated with stone, inside it was one solid mass of pure gold.

Thereupon the little monkey said, laughing at his astonishment:

"I make you a present of what you have broken off; take as much of it as you think proper."

The Prince thanked her gratefully, and picked up one of the smallest of the lumps of gold; as he did so the little monkey was suddenly transformed into a tall and gracious lady, who said to him:

"If you are always as kind and persevering and easily contented as you are now you may hope to accomplish the most difficult tasks; go on your way and have no fear that you will be troubled any more for lack of gold, for that little piece which you modestly chose shall never grow less, use it as much as you will. But that you may see the danger you have escaped by your moderation, come with me." So saying she led him back into the wood by a different path, and he saw that it was full of men and women; their faces were pale and haggard, and they ran hither and thither seeking madly upon the ground, or in the air, starting at every sound, pushing and trampling upon one another in their frantic eagerness to find the way to the Golden Rock.

"You see how they toil," said the Fairy; "but it is all of no avail: they will end by dying of despair, as hundreds have done before them."

As soon as they had got back to the place where they had left Mousta the Fairy disappeared, and the Prince and his faithful Squire, who had greeted him with every demonstration of joy, took the nearest way to the city. Here they stayed several days, while the Prince provided himself with horses and attendants, and made many enquiries about the Princess Sabella, and the way to her kingdom, which was still so far away that he could hear but little, and that of the vaguest description, but when he presently reached Mount Caucasus it was quite a different matter. Here they seemed to talk of nothing but the Princess Sabella, and strangers from all parts of the world were traveling towards her father's Court.

The Prince heard plenty of assurances as to her beauty and her riches, but he also heard of the immense number of his rivals and their power. One brought an army at his back, another had vast treasures, a third was as handsome and accomplished as it was possible to be; while, as to poor Mannikin, he had nothing but his determination to succeed, his faithful spaniel, and his ridiculous name—which last was hardly likely to help him, but as he could not alter it he wisely determined not to think of it any more. After journeying for two whole months they came at last to Trelintin, the capital of the Princess Sabella's kingdom, and here he heard dismal stories about the Ice Mountain, and how none of those who had attempted to climb it had ever come back. He heard also the story of King Farda-Kinbras, Sabella's father. It appeared that he, being a rich and powerful monarch, had married a lovely Princess named Birbantine, and they were as happy as the day was long—so happy that as they were out sledging one day they were foolish enough to defy fate to spoil their happiness.

"We shall see about that," grumbled an old hag who sat by the wayside blowing her fingers to keep them warm. The King thereupon was very angry, and wanted to punish the woman; but the Queen prevented him, saying:

"Alas! sire, do not let us make bad worse; no doubt this is a Fairy!"

47

"You are right there," said the old woman, and immediately she stood up, and as they gazed at her in horror she grew gigantic and terrible, her staff turned to a fiery dragon with outstretched wings, her ragged cloak to a golden mantle, and her wooden shoes to two bundles of rockets. "You are right there, and you will see what will come of your fine goings on, and remember the Fairy Gorgonzola!" So saying she mounted the dragon and flew off, the rockets shooting in all directions and leaving long trails of sparks.

In vain did Farda-Kinbras and Birbantine beg her to return, and endeavor by their humble apologies to pacify her; she never so much as looked at them, and was very soon out of sight, leaving them a prey to all kinds of dismal forebodings. Very soon after this the Queen had a little daughter, who was the most beautiful creature ever seen; all the Fairies of the North were invited to her christening, and warned against the malicious Gorgonzola. She also was invited, but she neither came to the banquet nor received her present; but as soon as all the others were seated at table, after bestowing their gifts upon the little Princess, she stole into the Palace, disguised as a black cat, and hid herself under the cradle until the nurses and the cradle-rockers had all turned their backs, and then she sprang out, and in an instant had stolen the little Princess's heart and made her escape, only being chased by a few dogs and scullions on her way across the courtyard. Once outside she mounted her chariot and flew straight away to the North Pole, where she shut up her stolen treasure on the summit of the Ice Mountain, and surrounded it with so many difficulties that she felt quite easy about its remaining there as long as the Princess lived, and then she went home, chuckling at her success. As to the other Fairies, they went home after the banquet without discovering that anything was amiss, and so the King and Queen were quite happy. Sabella grew prettier day by day. She learnt everything a Princess ought to know without the slightest trouble, and yet something always seemed lacking to make her perfectly charming. She had an exquisite voice, but whether her songs were grave or gay it did not matter, she did not seem to know what they meant; and everyone who heard her said:

"She certainly sings perfectly; but there is no tenderness, no heart in her voice." Poor Sabella! how could there be when her heart was far away on the Ice Mountains? And it was just the same with all the other things that she did. As time went on, in spite of the admiration of the whole Court and the blind fondness of the King and Queen, it became more and more evident that something was fatally wrong: for those who love no one cannot long be loved; and at last the King called a general assembly, and invited the Fairies to attend, that they might, if possible, find out what was the matter. After explaining their grief as well as he could, he ended by begging them to see the Princess for themselves. "It is certain," said he, "that something is wrong—*what* it is I don't know how to tell you, but in some way your work is imperfect."

They all assured him that, so far as they knew, everything had been done for the Princess, and they had forgotten nothing that they could bestow on so good a neighbor as the King had been to them. After this they went to see Sabella; but they had no sooner entered her presence than they cried out with one accord:

"Oh! horror!—she has no heart!"

On hearing this frightful announcement, the King and Queen gave a cry of despair, and entreated the Fairies to find some remedy for such an unheard-of misfortune. Thereupon the eldest Fairy consulted her Book of Magic, which she always carried about with her, hung to her girdle by a thick silver chain, and there she found out at once that it was Gorgonzola who had stolen the Princess's heart, and also discovered what the wicked old Fairy had done with it.

"What shall we do? What shall we do?" cried the King and Queen in one breath.

"You must certainly suffer much annoyance from seeing and loving Sabella, who is nothing but a beautiful image," replied the Fairy, "and this must go on for a long time; but I think I see that, in the end, she will once more regain her heart. My advice is that you shall at once cause her portrait to be sent all over the world, and promise her hand and all her possessions to the Prince who is successful in reaching her heart. Her beauty alone is sufficient to engage all the Princes of the world in the quest."

This was accordingly done, and Prince Mannikin heard that already five hundred Princes had perished in the snow and ice, not to mention their squires and pages, and that more continued to arrive daily, eager to try their fortune. After some consideration he determined to present himself at Court; but his arrival made no stir, as his retinue was as inconsiderable as his stature, and the splendor of his rivals was great enough to throw even Farda-Kinbras himself into the shade. However, he paid his respects to the

King very gracefully, and asked permission to kiss the hand of the Princess in the usual manner; but when he said he was called "Mannikin," the King could hardly repress a smile, and the Princes who stood by openly shouted with laughter.

Turning to the King, Prince Mannikin said with great dignity:

"Pray laugh if it pleases your Majesty, I am glad that it is in my power to afford you any amusement; but I am not a plaything for these gentlemen, and I must beg them to dismiss any ideas of that kind from their minds at once," and with that he turned upon the one who had laughed the loudest and proudly challenged him to a single combat. This Prince, who was called Fadasse, accepted the challenge very scornfully, mocking at Mannikin, whom he felt sure had no chance against himself; but the meeting was arranged for the next day. When Prince Mannikin quitted the King's presence he was conducted to the audience hall of the Princess Sabella. The sight of so much beauty and magnificence almost took his breath away for an instant, but, recovering himself with an effort, he said:

"Lovely Princess, irresistibly drawn by the beauty of your portrait, I come from the other end of the world to offer my services to you. My devotion knows no bounds, but my absurd name has already involved me in a quarrel with one of your courtiers. Tomorrow I am to fight this ugly, overgrown Prince, and I beg you to honor the combat with your presence, and prove to the world that there is nothing in a name, and that you deign to accept Mannikin as your knight."

When it came to this the Princess could not help being amused, for, though she had no heart, she was not without humor. However, she answered graciously that she accepted with pleasure, which encouraged the Prince to entreat further that she would not show any favor to his adversary.

"Alas!" said she, "I favor none of these foolish people, who weary me with their sentiment and their folly. I do very well as I am, and yet from one year's end to another they talk of nothing but delivering me from some imaginary affliction. Not a word do I understand of all their pratings about love, and who knows what dull things besides, which, I declare to you, I cannot even remember."

Mannikin was quick enough to gather from this speech that to amuse and interest the Princess would be a far surer way of gaining her favor than to add himself to the list of those who continually teased her about that mysterious thing called "love" which she was so incapable of comprehending. So he began to talk of his rivals, and found in each of them something to make merry over, in which diversion the Princess joined him heartily, and so well did he succeed in his attempt to amuse her that before very long she declared that of all the people at Court he was the one to whom she preferred to talk.

The following day, at the time appointed for the combat, when the King, the Queen, and the Princess had taken their places, and the whole Court and the whole town were assembled to see the show, Prince Fadasse rode into the lists magnificently armed and accoutered, followed by twenty-four squires and a hundred men-at-arms, each one leading a splendid horse, while Prince Mannikin entered from the other side armed only with his spear and followed by the faithful Mousta. The contrast between the two champions was so great that there was a shout of laughter from the whole assembly; but when at the sounding of a trumpet the combatants rushed upon each other, and Mannikin, eluding the blow aimed at him, succeeded in thrusting Prince Fadasse from his horse and pinning him to the sand with his spear, it changed to a murmur of admiration.

So soon as he had him at his mercy, however, Mannikin, turning to the Princess, assured her that he had no desire to kill anyone who called himself her courtier, and then he bade the furious and humiliated Fadasse rise and thank the Princess to whom he owed his life. Then, amid the sounding of the trumpets and the shoutings of the people, he and Mousta retired gravely from the lists.

The King soon sent for him to congratulate him upon his success, and to offer him a lodging in the Palace, which he joyfully accepted. While the Princess expressed a wish to have Mousta brought to her, and, when the Prince sent for him, she was so delighted with his courtly manners and his marvelous intelligence that she entreated Mannikin to give him to her for her own. The Prince consented with alacrity, not only out of politeness, but because he foresaw that to have a faithful friend always near the Princess might some day be of great service to him. All these events made Prince Mannikin a person of much more consequence at the Court. Very soon after, there arrived upon the frontier the Ambassador of a very powerful King, who sent to Farda-Kinbras the following letter, at the same time demanding permission to enter the capital in state to receive the answer:

"I, Brandatimor, to Farda-Kinbras send greeting. If I had before this time seen the portrait of your beautiful daughter Sabella I should not have permitted all these adventurers and petty Princes to be dancing attendance and getting themselves frozen with the absurd idea of meriting her hand. For myself I am not afraid of any rivals, and, now I have declared my intention of marrying your daughter, no doubt they will at once withdraw their pretensions. My Ambassador has orders, therefore, to make arrangements for the Princess to come and be married to me without delay—for I attach no importance at all to the farrago of nonsense which you have caused to be published all over the world about this Ice Mountain. If the Princess really has no heart, be assured that I shall not concern myself about it, since, if anybody can help her to discover one, it is myself. My worthy father-in-law, farewell!"

The reading of this letter embarrassed and displeased Farda-Kinbras and Birbantine immensely, while the Princess was furious at the insolence of the demand. They all three resolved that its contents must be kept a profound secret until they could decide what reply should be sent, but Mousta contrived to send word of all that had passed to Prince Mannikin. He was naturally alarmed and indignant, and, after thinking it over a little, he begged an audience of the Princess, and led the conversation so cunningly up to the subject that was uppermost in her thoughts, as well as his own, that she presently told him all about the matter and asked his advice as to what it would be best to do. This was exactly what he had not been able to decide for himself; however, he replied that he should advise her to gain a little time by promising her answer after the grand entry of the Ambassador, and this was accordingly done.

The Ambassador did not at all like being put off after that fashion, but he was obliged to be content, and only said very arrogantly that so soon as his equipages arrived, as he expected they would do very shortly, he would give all the people of the city, and the stranger Princes with whom it was inundated, an idea of the power and the magnificence of his master. Mannikin, in despair, resolved that he would for once beg the assistance of the kind Fairy Genesta. He often thought of her and always with gratitude, but from the moment of his setting out he had determined to seek her aid only on the greatest occasions. That very night, when he had fallen asleep quite worn out with thinking over all the difficulties of the situation, he dreamed that the Fairy stood beside him, and said:

"Mannikin, you have done very well so far; continue to please me and you shall always find good friends when you need them most. As for this affair with the Ambassador, you can assure Sabella that she may look forward tranquilly to his triumphal entry, since it will all turn out well for her in the end."

The Prince tried to throw himself at her feet to thank her, but woke to find it was all a dream; nevertheless he took fresh courage, and went next day to see the Princess, to whom he gave many mysterious assurances that all would yet be well. He even went so far as to ask her if she would not be very grateful to anyone who would rid her of the insolent Brandatimor. To which she replied that her gratitude would know no bounds. Then he wanted to know what would be her best wish for the person who was lucky enough to accomplish it. To which she said that she would wish them to be as insensible to the folly called "love" as she was herself!

This was indeed a crushing speech to make to such a devoted lover as Prince Mannikin, but he concealed the pain it caused him with great courage.

And now the Ambassador sent to say that on the very next day he would come in state to receive his answer, and from the earliest dawn the inhabitants were astir, to secure the best places for the grand sight; but the good Fairy Genesta was providing them an amount of amusement they were far from expecting, for she so enchanted the eyes of all the spectators that when the Ambassador's gorgeous procession appeared, the splendid uniforms seemed to them miserable rags that a beggar would have been ashamed to wear, the prancing horses appeared as wretched skeletons hardly able to drag one leg after the other, while their trappings, which really sparkled with gold and jewels, looked like old sheepskins that would not have been good enough for a plough horse. The pages resembled the ugliest sweeps. The trumpets gave no more sound than whistles made of onion-stalks, or combs wrapped in paper; while the train of fifty carriages looked no better than fifty donkey carts. In the last of these sat the Ambassador with the haughty and scornful air which he considered becoming in the representative of so powerful a monarch: for this was the crowning point of the absurdity of the whole procession, that all who took part in it wore the expression of vanity and self-satisfaction and pride in their own appearance and all their surroundings which they believed their splendor amply justified.

The laughter and howls of derision from the whole crowd rose ever louder and louder as the extraordinary cortège advanced, and at last reached the ears of the King as he waited in the audience hall, and before the procession reached the palace he had been informed of its nature, and, supposing that it must be intended as an insult, he ordered the gates to be closed. You may imagine the fury of the Ambassador when, after all his pomp and pride, the King absolutely and unaccountably refused to receive him. He raved wildly both against King and people, and the cortège retired in great confusion, jeered at and pelted with stones and mud by the enraged crowd. It is needless to say that he left the country as fast as horses could carry him, but not before he had declared war, with the most terrible menaces, threatening to devastate the country with fire and sword.

Some days after this disastrous embassy King Bayard sent couriers to Prince Mannikin with a most friendly letter, offering his services in any difficulty, and enquiring with the deepest interest how he fared.

Mannikin at once replied, relating all that had happened since they parted, not forgetting to mention the event which had just involved Farda-Kinbras and Brandatimor in this deadly quarrel, and he ended by entreating his faithful friend to despatch a few thousands of his veteran spaniels to his assistance.

Neither the King, the Queen, nor the Princess could in the least understand the amazing conduct of Brandatimor's Ambassador; nevertheless the preparations for the war went forward briskly and all the Princes who had not gone on towards the Ice Mountain offered their services, at the same time demanding all the best appointments in the King's army. Mannikin was one of the first to volunteer, but he only asked to go as aide-de-camp to the Commander-in chief, who was a gallant soldier and celebrated for his victories. As soon as the army could be got together it was marched to the frontier, where it met the opposing force headed by Brandatimor himself, who was full of fury, determined to avenge the insult to his Ambassador and to possess himself of the Princess Sabella. All the army of Farda-Kinbras could do, being so heavily outnumbered, was to act upon the defensive, and before long Mannikin won the esteem of the officers for his ability, and of the soldiers for his courage, and care for their welfare, and in all the skirmishes which he conducted he had the good fortune to vanquish the enemy.

At last Brandatimor engaged the whole army in a terrific conflict, and though the troops of Farda-Kinbras fought with desperate courage, their general was killed, and they were defeated and forced to retreat with immense loss. Mannikin did wonders, and half-a-dozen times turned the retreating forces and beat back the enemy; and he afterwards collected troops enough to keep them in check until, the severe winter setting in, put an end to hostilities for a while.

He then returned to the Court, where consternation reigned. The King was in despair at the death of his trusty general, and ended by imploring Mannikin to take the command of the army, and his counsel was followed in all the affairs of the Court. He followed up his former plan of amusing the Princess, and on no account reminding her of that tedious thing called "love," so that she was always glad to see him, and the winter slipped by gaily for both of them.

The Prince was all the while secretly making plans for the next campaign; he received private intelligence of the arrival of a strong reinforcement of Spaniels, to whom he sent orders to post themselves along the frontier without attracting attention, and as soon as he possibly could he held a consultation with their Commander, who was an old and experienced warrior. Following his advice, he decided to have a pitched battle as soon as the enemy advanced, and this Brandatimor lost not a moment in doing, as he was perfectly persuaded that he was now going to make an end of the war and utterly vanquish Farda-Kinbras. But no sooner had he given the order to charge than the Spaniels, who had mingled with his troops unperceived, leaped each upon the horse nearest to him, and not only threw the whole squadron into confusion by the terror they caused, but, springing at the throats of the riders, unhorsed many of them by the suddenness of their attack; then turning the horses to the rear, they spread consternation everywhere, and made it easy for Prince Mannikin to gain a complete victory. He met Brandatimor in single combat, and succeeded in taking him prisoner; but he did not live to reach the Court, to which Mannikin had sent him: his pride killed him at the thought of appearing before Sabella under these altered circumstances. In the meantime Prince Fadasse and all the others who had remained behind were setting out with all speed for the conquest of the Ice Mountain, being afraid that Prince Mannikin might prove as successful in that as he seemed to be in everything else, and when Mannikin returned he heard of it with great annoyance. True he had been serving the Princess, but she only admired and praised him for his gallant deeds, and seemed no whit nearer bestowing on him the love he so ardently desired, and all the comfort Mousta could give him on the subject was that at least she loved no one else, and with that he had to content himself. But he determined that, come what might, he would delay no longer, but attempt the great undertaking for which he had come so far. When he went to take leave of the King and Queen they entreated him not to go, as they had just heard that Prince Fadasse, and all who accompanied him, had perished in the snow; but he persisted in his resolve. As for Sabella, she gave him her hand to kiss with precisely the same gracious indifference as she had given it to him the first time they met. It happened that this farewell took place before the whole Court, and so great a favorite had Prince Mannikin become that they were all indignant at the coldness with which the Princess treated him.

Finally the King said to him:

"Prince, you have constantly refused all the gifts which, in my gratitude for your invaluable services, I have offered to you, but I wish the Princess to present you with her cloak of marten's fur, and *that* I hope you will not reject!" Now this was a splendid fur mantle which the Princess was very fond of wearing, not so much because she felt cold, as that its richness set off to perfection the delicate tints of her complexion and the brilliant gold of her hair. However, she took it off, and with graceful politeness begged Prince Mannikin to accept it, which you may be sure he was charmed to do, and, taking only this and a little bundle of all kinds of wood, and accompanied only by two spaniels out of the fifty who had stayed with him when the war was ended, he set forth, receiving many tokens of love and favor from the people in every town he passed through. At the last little village he left his horse behind him, to begin his toilful march through the snow, which extended, blank and terrible, in every direction as far as the eye could see. Here he had appointed to meet the other forty-eight spaniels, who received him joyfully, and assured him that, happen what might, they would follow and serve him faithfully. And so they started, full of heart and hope. At first there was a slight track, difficult, but not impossible to follow; but this was soon lost, and the Pole Star was their only guide. When the time came to call a halt, the Prince, who had after much consideration decided on his plan of action, caused a few twigs from the faggot he had brought with him to be planted in the snow, and then he sprinkled over them a pinch of the magic powder he had collected from the enchanted boat. To his great joy they instantly began to sprout and grow, and in a marvelously short time the camp was surrounded by a perfect grove of trees of all sorts, which blossomed and bore ripe fruit, so that all their wants were easily

56

supplied, and they were able to make huge fires to warm themselves. The Prince then sent out several spaniels to reconnoitre, and they had the good luck to discover a horse laden with provisions stuck fast in the snow. They at once fetched their comrades, and brought the spoil triumphantly into the camp, and, as it consisted principally of biscuits, not a spaniel among them went supperless to sleep. In this way they journeyed by day and encamped safely at night, always remembering to take on a few branches to provide them with food and shelter. They passed by the way armies of those who had set out upon the perilous enterprise, who stood frozen stiffly, without sense or motion; but Prince Mannikin strictly forbade that any attempt should be made to thaw them. So they went on and on for more than three months, and day by day the Ice Mountain, which they had seen for a long time, grew clearer, until at last they stood close to it, and shuddered at its height and steepness. But by patience and perseverance they crept up foot by foot, aided by their fires of magic wood, without which they must have perished in the intense cold, until presently they stood at the gates of the magnificent Ice Palace which crowned the mountain, where, in deadly silence and icy sleep, lay the heart of Sabella. Now the difficulty became immense, for if they maintained enough heat to keep themselves alive they were in danger every moment of melting the blocks of solid ice of which the palace was entirely built, and bringing the whole structure down upon their heads; but cautiously and quickly they traversed courtyards and halls, until they found themselves at the foot of a vast throne, where, upon a cushion of snow, lay an enormous and brilliantly sparkling diamond, which contained the heart of the lovely Princess Sabella. Upon the lowest step of the throne was inscribed in icy letters, "Whosoever thou art who by courage and virtue canst win the heart of Sabella enjoy peacefully the good fortune which thou hast richly deserved."

Prince Mannikin bounded forward, and had just strength left to grasp the precious diamond which contained all he coveted in the world before he fell insensible upon the snowy cushion. But his good spaniels lost no time in rushing to the rescue, and between them they bore him hastily from the hall, and not a moment too soon, for all around them they heard the clang of the falling blocks of ice as the Fairy Palace slowly collapsed under the unwonted heat. Not until they reached the foot of the mountain did they pause to restore the Prince to consciousness, and then his joy to find himself the possessor of Sabella's heart knew no bounds.

With all speed they began to retrace their steps, but this time the happy Prince could not bear the sight of his defeated and disappointed rivals, whose frozen forms lined his triumphant way. He gave orders to his spaniels to spare no pains to restore them to life, and so successful were they that day by day his train increased, so that by the time he got back to the little village where he had left his horse he was escorted by five hundred sovereign Princes, and knights and squires without number, and he was so courteous and unassuming that they all followed him willingly, anxious to do him honor. But then he was so happy and blissful himself that he found it easy to be at peace with all the world. It was not long before he met the faithful Mousta, who was coming at the top of his speed hoping to meet the Prince, that he might tell him of the sudden and wonderful change that had come over the Princess, who had become gentle and thoughtful and had talked to him of nothing but Prince Mannikin, of the hardships she feared he might be suffering, and of her anxiety for him, and all this with a hundred tender expressions which put the finishing stroke to the Prince's delight. Then came a courier bearing the congratulations of the King and Queen, who had just heard of his successful return, and there was even a graceful compliment from Sabella herself. The Prince sent Mousta back to her, and he was welcomed with joy, for was he not her lover's present?

At last the travelers reached the capital, and were received with regal magnificence. Farda-Kinbras and Birbantine embraced Prince Mannikin, declaring that they regarded him as their heir and the future husband of the Princess, to which he replied that they did him too much honor. And then he was admitted into the presence of the Princess, who for the first time in her life blushed as he kissed her hand, and could not find a word to say. But the Prince, throwing himself on his knees beside her, held out the splendid diamond, saying:

"Madam, this treasure is yours, since none of the dangers and difficulties I have gone through have been sufficient to make me deserve it."

"Ah! Prince," said she, "if I take it, it is only that I may give it back to you, since truly it belongs to you already."

At this moment in came the King and Queen, and interrupted them by asking all the questions imaginable, and not infrequently the same over and over again. It seems that there is always one thing that is sure to be said about an event by everybody, and Prince Mannikin found that the question which he was asked by more than a thousand people on this particular occasion was:

"And didn't you find it very cold?"

The King had come to request Prince Mannikin and the Princess to follow him to the Council Chamber, which they did, not knowing that he meant to present the Prince to all the nobles assembled there as his son-in-law and successor. But when Mannikin perceived his intention, he begged permission to speak first, and told his whole story, even to the fact that he believed himself to be a peasant's son. Scarcely had he finished speaking when the sky grew black, the thunder growled, and the lightning flashed, and in the blaze of light the good Fairy Genesta suddenly appeared. Turning to Prince Mannikin, she said:

"I am satisfied with you, since you have shown not only courage but a good heart." Then she addressed King Farda-Kinbras, and informed him of the real history of the Prince, and how she had determined to give him the education she knew would be best for a man who was to command others. "You have already found the advantage of having a faithful friend," she added to the Prince, "and now you will have the pleasure of seeing King Bayard and his subjects regain their natural forms as a reward for his kindness to you."

Just then arrived a chariot drawn by eagles, which proved to contain the foolish King and Queen, who embraced their long-lost son with great joy, and were greatly struck with the fact that they did indeed find him covered with fur! While they were caressing Sabella and wringing her hands (which is a favorite form of endearment with foolish people) chariots were seen approaching from all points of the compass, containing numbers of Fairies.

"Sire," said Genesta to Farda-Kinbras, "I have taken the liberty of appointing your Court as a meeting-place for all the Fairies who could spare the time to come; and I hope you can arrange to hold the great ball, which we have once in a hundred years, on this occasion."

The King having suitably acknowledged the honor done him, was next reconciled to Gorgonzola, and they two presently opened the ball together. The Fairy Marsontine restored their natural forms to King Bayard and all his subjects, and he appeared once more as handsome a king as you could wish to see. One of the Fairies immediately despatched her chariot for the Queen of the Spice Islands, and their wedding took place at the same time as that of Prince Mannikin and the lovely and gracious Sabella. They lived happily ever afterwards, and their vast kingdoms were presently divided between their children.

The Prince, out of grateful remembrance of the Princess Sabella's first gift to him, bestowed the right of bearing her name upon the most beautiful of the martens, and that is why they are called *sables* to this day.

My Lady Legend

(TRADITIONAL SWEDISH TALE)

Hyu-u-u, hy-u-y-y," sang the Wind, and chased the Snowflakes till they flew down terrified, like a flock of white doves when the hawk pursues them. But outside of the window, right by the' corner, the flakes were captured; they could not fly any further, they were so tired.

"Here we will sink down," said they. "We, too, we, too," cried they who came after. So they rested against one another, row after row, till the snowdrift grew and became ever higher and higher.

"What are you doing here? Up with you!" cried the Wind. He likes a commotion and will not allow anything to remain still. He was angry. If he but caught a little flake, he would whirl about with her, away over land and sea, till the poor little thing became so dizzy that she did not know where she was, and she never saw father, mother or sisters again.

This is why the flakes in the drift were so frightened that they huddled close up to one another.

"Hold me in, hold me in," cried the little ones to each other, and turned perfectly white with fear.

Higher and higher the drift grew, because the flakes stood by each other faithfully; and when this is so, even the weak grow strong.

Inside in the warm room stood the children and looked out through the window.

"Oh! see how high the drift gets," said they, and pointed at it with their fingers. They stood on tiptoe so they could see it better, for they did not dare to go out and look at it. If they should do that, the north wind would come instantly and pinch their little cheeks with his cold, sharp fingers. He was angry with order, Old North Wind, and lashed without exception, all whom he came across, and the darker it grew at night, the angrier he grew also.

"Piff-paff, piff-paff!" sounded from the chimney place; it was the fire that snapped and crackled, and immediately the little ones who stood at the window, gathered around this cheerful companion. The small flames leaped from twig to twig and got both red and warm. Then there was a knock at the door.

"Come in, come in," shouted the rosy lips.

"Thank you, most kindly. Whew! it is dreadfully cold out," said she who came in through the door.

The stranger was a girl with gleaming eyes that sparkled in a wonderful manner. When she took off her hood, rich, waving curls fell about her forehead and cheeks, and reached far down on the full garments she wore.

"Oh! what a wonderful dress you have on," said little Elin; "it is not a bit like ours; it has neither waist nor sleeves, but it fits so nicely!"

"Do you think so?" replied the stranger, and smilingly shook her head. She took each one of the little ones by the hand, and smiled so tenderly that she immediately won their hearts, and little Mia laid her head upon the stranger's knee, and gazed into the sparkling eyes.

"Oh, listen to Boreas!" said one, "now he is tearing his beard! Think how good it was that you found our house, else perhaps you might have frozen. But your hands are not cold one bit," went on the child who was talking, taking the stranger girl's soft hands. "Why, you are real warm, and you have been out in such weather."

"I get warm at once when I am received as I was here," said the stranger, and smiled." And if I find it cold in one place, I go immediately to another."

"Oh! do you do that?" cried the children. "But is your horse never tired?" added they.

"Oh, no, oh, no! he never gets tired; he can travel from heaven to earth, and from the earth to the stars, and from the cold North Pole to the palm groves of the south in an instant."

"What a lot of lovely things you must see!"

She nodded, and then told them about many things she had seen and heard. She told about the wonders away in southern lands, where the air is laden with the perfume of a thousand flowers; she told about the icebergs at the Poles, about the Northern Lights, about winds and snowflakes. She knew what the waves say, what the trees whisper and the birds sing; yes, she could even understand what the straws, the matches and the tattered shoes on the brush heap think. About great and small, about what is on the earth and under the earth—yes, about everything she had something to tell.

And so the time flew fast, the fire went out, and the glowing coals began to fall apart, but none of the children had noticed it.

"Oh, stay, stay!" cried they, when she rose at last to go.

"Not longer now; not longer this time," she replied, and kissed them all.

"But you will surely come again, sweet one, come again!" said one of the children.

"You will be sure to come again, you look so kind," said another.

Then the stranger standing in the doorway nodded a farewell to them.

"But what is your name?" cried the children, for they had forgotten to ask it before.

"My name is Legend," answered the stranger, and was gone.

But when the world grows dark without, when old Jack Frost knocks at the window, and the cheerful fire crackles on the hearth, then Legend comes to tarry with those who receive her in a friendly spirit.

The Fir-Tree

HANS CHRISTIAN ANDERSEN

Far out in the forest grew a pretty little fir-tree. It had a favorable place; the sun shone brightly on it, and there was plenty of fresh air, while many taller comrades, both pines and firs, were thriving around it. The little fir-tree longingly desired to grow taller! It was indifferent to the warm sun and the fresh air, it took no notice of the peasant children, who ran about and chattered, when they had come out to gather strawberries and raspberries. Often they came with a basket full, and had threaded strawberries on a straw like beads; then they used to sit down near the little fir-tree and say: "What a pretty little tree this one is!" But this the tree did not like to hear at all.

In the following year it grew taller by a considerable shoot, and the year after by another one, for by the number of shoots which fir-trees have, we may discover how many years they have grown.

"Oh, that I were as tall a tree as the others!" sighed the little tree; "then I might spread out my branches far around, and look with my crown out into the wide world! The birds would build their nests in my boughs, and when the wind blew I could proudly nod, just like the others yonder!"

It took no delight in the sunshine, in the birds, nor in the red clouds which in the morning and evening passed over it. When the winter had come and the snow was lying white and sparkling on the ground, often a hare came running and jumped right over the little tree—oh, that annoyed it so much! But two winters passed, and in the third the little tree was already so high that the hare had to run round it. "To grow, to grow, to become tall and old, this is the most desirable thing in the world," thought the tree.

Every year in autumn woodcutters came and felled several of the biggest trees; the young tree, now well grown, shuddered, for the tall magnificent trees fell to the ground with a crash; and when their branches were hewn off, the trees looked so naked, long and slender, they were hardly to be recognized. Then they were placed upon carts, and horses drew them out of the wood. Whither were they going? What was to become of them? In spring, when the swallows and storks returned, the tree asked them: "Can you not tell me whither they have taken them? Have you not met them?"

The swallows knew nothing about them; but the stork looked pensive, nodded his head and said: "Yes. I think I know. When I left Egypt I passed by many new ships, and on the ships were splendid masts; I suppose these were the trees, for they smelt like fir-trees, and they looked very stately indeed!"

"I wish I were tall enough to go over the sea! I should like to know what the sea is. What does it look like?"

"To explain that," replied the stork, "would take me too long," and thus saying he flew away.

"Enjoy thy youth!" said the sunbeams; "take pleasure in thy vigorous growth, in the fresh life that is within thee."

The wind kissed the tree, and the dew shed tears over it; but the fir-tree did not understand them.

About Christmas-time people cut down many trees which were quite young and smaller than the fir-tree, which had no rest and always wished to be off. These young trees, the very best that could be found, kept all their branches; they were placed upon carts and drawn out of the wood by horses.

"What are they doing with them?" asked the fir-tree. "They are not taller than I am—nay, there was one much smaller! Why did they retain all their branches? Where are they conveying them to?"

"We can tell you; we know!" chirped the sparrows. "Down below in the town we have looked through the windows! We know where they are taken to! They come to the greatest splendor you can imagine! We have looked in at the windows and have seen them standing in the middle of a warm room covered with the most beautiful things: gilded apples, gingerbread, toys, and many, many wax candles."

"And then," asked the fir-tree, trembling all over, "what happens after that?"

"Why, that is all we have seen! But that was very beautiful."

"I wonder whether I am destined to receive such great splendor," exclaimed the fir-tree merrily. "That is far better than crossing the sea! How much I am longing for the time! I wish Christmas had arrived! Now I am tall and have grown to a good length like the others which they took away last year! I wish I were already placed on the cart or in the warm room adorned with all the bright and beautiful things! And then there is something much better and brighter to come, or why would they decorate the trees so beautifully? Yes, indeed, there is something more splendid and grand to follow! But what can it be? Oh, how I suffer with longing; I hardly know how I feel."

"Enjoy our presence," said the air and the sunshine; "delight in thy young life here in the forest."

But the tree did not enjoy anything, it grew and grew; winter and summer it was green, and people who saw it said that it was a beautiful tree.

Christmas came at last, and the tree was the first to be cut down. The axe entered deeply into its stem; the tree fell groaning to the ground; a pain and a faintness overcame it; it was unable to think of the happiness to come, it was sad that it had to leave its home, the spot where it had grown up; it knew well enough that it would never see again the dear old comrades, the little bushes and the flowers, and perhaps not even the birds. Parting was not at all pleasant. The tree did not recover until it was taken from the cart in a court-yard with other trees and heard a man say: "This one is very fine, we only want this one."

Two servants in livery soon came and carried the tree into a large, beautiful room. The walls were all covered with pictures, and by the side of the tile-stove stood big Chinese vases with lions on the lids; there were rocking-chairs, couches covered with silk, on a large table were displayed picture-books and toys of very great value—at least, so the children said. The fir-tree was put into a large vessel filled with sand; but nobody could see that it was a vessel, for it was covered all over with green cloth and placed on a handsome carpet of many colors. How the fir-tree trembled! What was to happen now? The young ladies of the house, aided by the servants, adorned the tree. They hung on its branches little nets cut out of colored paper and filled with sweets; gilded apples and walnuts were fastened to the tree, as if they grew on it, and more than a hundred small candles, red, blue, and white, were fixed to the branches. Dolls looking exactly like human beings—the tree had never seen anything of the like before—were hanging in the green foliage, and on the very top of the tree they fixed a glittering star of tinsel. It was very beautiful.

"To-night," they all said—"to-night it will shine!"

"Oh, that the evening had come!" thought the tree. "I wish the candles were lighted! And what will happen then? I wonder if the trees will come from the wood to look at me, or if the sparrows will look in at the windows. Am I to grow fast here and remain winter and summer adorned as I am now?"

Indeed, that was not a bad guess! Its longing made its bark ache; barkache for a tree is just as bad as a headache for us.

At last the candles were lighted. What a blaze of light! What a splendor! The tree trembled so much with joy in all its branches that one of the lights set fire to one of its boughs and scorched it.

"Heaven preserve us!" exclaimed the young ladies, and quickly extinguished the flame.

Now the tree was no longer allowed to tremble! That was dreadful. It was so afraid lest it might lose some of its ornaments; it was quite dazzled by all the splendor Then the folding-doors were thrown open, and the children rushed into the room as if they wished to upset the tree; the elders followed. For a moment the children stood silent with surprise, but only for a moment; then they shouted for joy till the room rang; they danced joyfully round the tree, and present after present was taken down from it.

"What are they doing?" thought the tree. "What is to happen?" The candles burnt gradually down to the boughs on which they were fastened and were put out, and then the children were allowed to plunder the tree. Oh, how they rushed at it; all its branches cracked, and had it not been fastened with the glittering star to the ceiling, they would have upset it. The children were dancing about with their beautiful toys. Nobody took any notice of the tree, except the old nurse, who came and looked at the branches, but only to see if there was not a fig or an apple left on them.

"A story! a story!" cried the children, while they pulled a small stout man towards the tree. He seated himself just underneath the tree, "for there we are in its green shade" he said, "and it will be an advantage to the tree to listen! But I shall only tell one story. Would you like to hear Ivede-Avede or Humpty Dumpty, who fell downstairs, but came to honors after all and married the princess?"

"Ivede-Avede!" cried some, "Humpty Dumpty!" cried others; there was a good deal of crying and shouting. Only the fir-tree was quite silent and thought to itself: "Am I not to take part in this?" but it had already done what it was expected to do.

And the man told the story of Humpty Dumpty who fell downstairs, and after all came to honors and married the princess. And the children clapped their hands and cried: "Go on, tell us another!" They wished also to hear the story of Ivede-Avede, but he only told that of Humpty Dumpty. The fir-tree was standing quite silent and thoughtful; the birds of the wood had never told such stories. "Humpty Dumpty fell downstairs, and yet married the princess. Thus it happens in the world," thought the fir-tree, and believed that it was all true, because such a nice man had told the story. "Well, well! Who knows? Perhaps I shall also fall downstairs and marry a princess!" And it looked forward with joy to being adorned again on the following day with toys, glitter, and fruit.

"To-morrow I shall not tremble!" it thought; "I shall enjoy all my splendor thoroughly. To-morrow I shall hear the story of Humpty Dumpty again, and perhaps also that of Ivede-Avede."

All night the tree was standing silent and thoughtful. In the morning the man-servants and housemaids entered the room. "Now," thought the tree, "they will adorn me again!" But they dragged it out of the room, upstairs into the garret, and placed it there in a dark corner, where no daylight reached it. "What does this mean?" thought the tree. "What am I to do here? What can I hear in such a place?" and it leaned against the wall, and thought and thought. And, indeed, it had time enough to think; for days and nights passed, but nobody came upstairs, and when at last somebody did come, it was only to store away some big chests. Thus the tree was quite hidden; one might have thought that they had entirely forgotten it.

"Now it is winter," thought the tree. "The ground is so hard and covered with snow that people cannot plant me again! Therefore, I think, they shelter me here until spring comes. How thoughtful! How kind people are to me! I only wish it was not quite so dark and so dreadfully lonely here! Not even a small hare is to be seen! How nice it was in the wood, when the snow covered the ground and the hare was running by; I should not even mind his jumping right over me, although then I could not bear the thought of it. It is awfully lonely here, indeed!"

"Squeak, squeak," a little mouse said just then, creeping timidly forward; another one soon followed. They sniffed at the fir-tree and slipped into its branches.

"Oh, that it were not so bitter cold," said the mice, "then we should feel quite comfortable here. Don't you think so, old fir-tree?"

"I am not old at all!" replied the fir-tree; "there are many much older than myself."

"Where do you come from?" asked the mice; "what do you know?" for they were very inquisitive. "Tell us about the most beautiful place on earth! Have you been there? Have you been in the pantry where cheeses lie on the shelves, and hams hang from the ceiling, where one can dance on tallow candles, and go in thin and come out fat?"

"I have not been there," said the tree; "but I know the wood where the sun shines and the birds sing." And then the tree told the mice all about its youth. The little mice, who had never heard anything like it before, listened attentively and exclaimed:

"You have seen a great deal, indeed; how happy you must have felt!"

"Do you think so?" said the tree, and reflected on its own story. "After all, those days were not unhappy." Then it told them all about Christmas Eve, when it was so beautifully adorned with cake and lights.

"You must have been very happy, you old fir-tree," replied the mice.

"I am not old at all," repeated the tree, "I only left the wood this winter; I am somewhat forward in my growth."

"How well you can tell stories," said the little mice. Next night they returned with four more little mice, whom they wished to hear what the tree had to relate; the more the tree told them, the more it remembered distinctly all that had happened, and it thought, "Those days were happy indeed, but they may come again. Humpty Dumpty fell downstairs, and married the princess after all; perhaps I may also marry a princess!" And then the fir-tree thought of a pretty little birch in the wood, which appeared to it a beautiful princess.

"Who is Humpty Dumpty?" asked the little mice. And then the tree had to relate the whole tale. It remembered every word of it, and the little mice were so delighted that they nearly jumped to the top of the tree for joy. The next night many more mice came to listen to the tree; and on Sunday two rats came; they, however, said the story was not pretty. The little mice were very sorry, for they began to think less of it.

"Do you know only that one story?" asked the rats.

"Only that one," said the tree, "and that I heard on the happiest night of my life; but then I did not know how happy I was."

"That is a very poor tale," said the rats. "Do you not know one about bacon and tallow candles—a sort of store-room story?"

"No," said the tree.

"We do not care for this one"; thus saying, the rats went off.

In the end also the little mice stayed away, and the tree sighed and said: "How pleasant it was to see all the lively little mice sitting round me when I talked! Now all this is passed. I should be very pleased if they came to fetch me away from here."

But whenever would that happen? One morning people came to tidy the garret; the chests were put aside, the tree was dragged out of its corner and thrown roughly to the ground; a man-servant carried it at once towards the staircase, where the sun was shining.

"Now life is beginning again," thought the tree; it felt the fresh air and the first sunbeams, and soon it was carried into the courtyard. All happened so quickly that the tree forgot to look at itself; there was so much about it to look at. The courtyard bordered on a garden, where all plants were in flower; the roses hung fresh and fragrant over the small fence; the lime-trees were blooming, and the swallows flew about, saying, "Twit, twit, twit, my husband has come!" but they did not mean the fir-tree.

"Now I shall live," exclaimed the fir tree joyfully, spreading out its branches; but alas! they were all withered and yellow; and it lay between weeds and nettles. The star of gilt paper was still fixed to its top and glittered in the sunshine. Some of the bright children who had been dancing round the tree so merrily on Christmas Eve were playing in the courtyard. One of the smallest came and tore the gilt star off.

"Look, what is still sticking to the ugly fir-tree!" said the child, treading on the branches, which cracked under its boots. And the tree looked at all the fresh and beautiful flowers in the garden; it looked at itself and wished that it had remained in the dark corner of the garret; it remembered its bright youth in the forest, the delightful Christmas Eve, the little mice, which had so quietly listened to the story of Humpty Dumpty.

"All is over," said the old tree. "Oh, that I had enjoyed myself while I could do so! All is passed away."

A man-servant came and chopped the tree into small pieces, until a large bundle was lying on the ground; then he placed them in the fire, under a large copper, where they blazed up brightly; the tree sighed deeply, and each sigh was as loud as a little pistol-shot; the children, who were playing near, came and sat down before the fire, and looking into it cried, "Pop, pop." But at each little shot, which was a deep sigh, the tree thought of a summer day in the wood, or a winter night there, when the stars sparkled; it remembered the Christmas Eve and Humpty Dumpty, the only fairy tale which it had heard and knew to tell, and then it was all burned up.

The boys played in the garden, and the smallest had fixed the gilt star which had adorned the tree on its happiest night on his breast. Now all had come to an end, the tree had come to an end, and also the story, for all stories come to an end!

The Three Dwarfs

(FROM *THE RED FAIRY BOOK*)

There was once upon a time a man who lost his wife, and a woman who lost her husband; and the man had a daughter and so had the woman. The two girls were great friends and used often to play together. One day the woman turned to the man's daughter and said:

"Go and tell your father that I will marry him, and then you shall wash in milk and drink wine, but my own daughter shall wash in water and drink it too."

The girl went straight home and told her father what the woman had said.

"What am I to do?" he answered. "Marriage is either a success or it is a failure."

At last, being of an undecided character and not being able to make up his mind, he took off his boot, and handing it to his daughter, said:

"Take this boot which has a hole in the sole, hang it up on a nail in the hayloft, and pour water into it. If it holds water I will marry again, but if it doesn't I won't." The girl did as she was bid, but the water drew the hole together and the boot filled up to the very top. So she went and told her father the result. He got up and went to see for himself, and when he saw that it was true and no mistake, he accepted his fate, proposed to the widow, and they were married at once.

On the morning after the wedding, when the two girls awoke, milk was standing for the man's daughter to wash in and wine for her to drink; but for the woman's daughter, only water to wash in and only water to drink. On the second morning, water to wash in and water to drink was standing for the man's daughter as well. And on the third morning, water to wash in and water to drink was standing for the man's daughter, and milk to wash in and wine to drink for the woman's daughter; and so it continued ever after. The woman hated her stepdaughter from the bottom of her heart, and did all she could to make her life miserable. She was as jealous as she could possibly be, because the girl was so beautiful and charming, while her own daughter was both ugly and repulsive.

One winter's day when there was a hard frost, and mountain and valley were covered with snow, the woman made a dress of paper, and calling the girl to her said:

"There, put on this dress and go out into the wood and fetch me a basket of strawberries!"

"Now Heaven help us," replied her stepdaughter; "strawberries don't grow in winter; the earth is all frozen and the snow has covered up everything; and why send me in a paper dress? it is so cold outside that one's very breath freezes; the wind will whistle through my dress, and the brambles tear it from my body."

"How dare you contradict me!" said her stepmother; "be off with you at once, and don't show your face again till you have filled the basket with strawberries."

Then she gave her a hard crust of bread, saying:

"That will be enough for you to-day," and she thought to herself: "The girl will certainly perish of hunger and cold outside, and I shan't be bothered with her any more."

The girl was so obedient that she put on the paper dress and set out with her little basket. There was nothing but snow far and near, and not a green blade of grass to be seen anywhere. When she came to the wood she saw a little house, and out of it peeped three little dwarfs. She wished them good-day, and knocked modestly at the door. They called out to her to enter, so she stepped in and sat down on a seat by the fire, wishing to warm herself and eat her breakfast. The Dwarfs said at once: "Give us some of your food!"

"Gladly," she said, and breaking her crust in two, she gave them the half.

Then they asked her what she was doing in the depths of winter in her thin dress.

"Oh," she answered, "I have been sent to get a basketful of strawberries, and I daren't show my face again at home till I bring them with me."

When she had finished her bread they gave her a broom and told her to sweep away the snow from the back door. As soon as she left the room to do so, the three little men consulted what they should give her as a reward for being so sweet and good, and for sharing her last crust with them.

The first said: "Every day she shall grow prettier."

The second: "Every time she opens her mouth a piece of gold shall fall out."

And the third: "A King shall come and marry her."

The girl in the meantime was doing as the Dwarfs had bidden her, and was sweeping the snow away from the back door, and what do you think she found there?—heaps of fine ripe strawberries that showed out dark red against the white snow. She joyfully picked enough to fill her basket, thanked the little men for their kindness, shook hands with them, and ran home to bring her stepmother what she had asked for. When she walked in and said; Good evening," a piece of gold fell out of her mouth. Then she told what had happened to her in the wood, and at every word pieces of gold dropped from her mouth, so that the room was soon covered with them.

"She's surely more money than wit to throw gold about like that," said her stepsister, but in her secret heart she was very jealous, and determined that she too would go to the wood and look for strawberries. But her mother refused to let her go, saying:

"My dear child, it is far too cold; you might freeze to death."

The girl however left her no peace, so she was forced at last to give in, but she insisted on her putting on a beautiful fur cloak, and she gave her bread and butter and cakes to eat on the way.

The girl went straight to the little house in the wood, and as before the three little men were looking out of the window. She took no notice of them, and without as much as "By your leave," or "With your leave," she flounced into the room, sat herself down at the fire, and began to eat her bread and butter and cakes.

"Give us some," cried the Dwarfs.

But she answered: "No, I won't, it's hardly enough for myself; so catch me giving you any."

When she had finished eating they said:

"There's a broom for you, go and clear up our back door."

"I'll see myself further," she answered rudely. "Do it yourselves; I'm not your servant."

When she saw that they did not mean to give her anything, she left the house in no amiable frame of mind. Then the three little men consulted what they should do to her, because she was so bad and had such an evil, covetous heart, that she grudged everybody their good fortune.

The first said: "She shall grow uglier every day."

The second: "Every time she speaks a toad shall jump out of her mouth."

And the third: "She shall die a most miserable death."

The girl searched for strawberries, but she found none, and returned home in a very bad temper. When she opened her mouth to tell her mother what had befallen her in the wood, a toad jumped out, so that everyone was quite disgusted with her.

Then the stepmother was more furious than ever, and did nothing but plot mischief against the man's daughter, who was daily growing more and more beautiful. At last, one day the wicked woman took a large pot, put it on the fire and boiled some yarn in it. When it was well scalded she hung it round the poor girl's shoulder, and giving her an axe, she bade her break a hole in the frozen river, and rinse the yarn in it. Her stepdaughter obeyed as usual, and went and broke a hole in the ice. When she was in the act of wringing out the yarn a magnificent carriage passed, and the King sat inside. The carriage stood still, and the King asked her:

"My child, who are you, and what in the wide world are you doing here?"

"I am only a poor girl," she answered, "and am rinsing out my yarn in the river." Then the King was sorry for her, and when he saw how beautiful she was he said:

"Will you come away with me?"

"Most gladly," she replied, for she knew how willingly she would leave her stepmother and sister, and how glad they would be to be rid of her.

So she stepped into the carriage and drove away with the King, and when they reached his palace the wedding was celebrated with much splendor. So all turned out just as the three little Dwarfs had said. After a year the Queen gave birth to a little son. When her stepmother heard of her good fortune she came to the palace with her daughter by way of paying a call, and took up her abode there. Now one day, when the King was out and nobody else near, the bad woman took the Queen by her head, and the daughter took her by her heels, and they dragged her from her bed, and flung her out of the window into the stream which flowed beneath it. Then the stepmother laid her ugly daughter in the Queen's place, and covered her up with the clothes, so that nothing of her was seen. When the King came home and wished to speak to his wife the woman called out:

"Quietly, quietly I this will never do; your wife is very ill, you must let her rest all to-day." The King suspected no evil, and didn't come again till next morning. When he spoke to his wife and she answered him, instead of the usual piece of gold a toad jumped out of her mouth. Then he asked what it meant, and the old woman told him it was nothing but weakness, and that she would soon be all right again.

But that same evening the scullion noticed a duck swimming up the gutter, saying as it passed:

> What does the King, I pray you tell,
> Is he awake or sleeps he well?

and receiving no reply, it continued:

> And all my guests, are they asleep?

and the Scullion answered:

> Yes, one and all they slumber deep.

Then the Duck went on:

> And what about my baby dear?

and he answered:

> Oh, it sleeps soundly, never fear.

Then the Duck assumed the Queen's shape, went up to the child's room, tucked him up comfortably in his cradle, and then swam back down the gutter again, in the likeness of a Duck. This was repeated for two nights, and on the third the Duck said to the Scullion:

"Go and tell the King to swing his sword three times over me on the threshold."

The Scullion did as the creature bade him, and the King came with his sword and swung it three times over the bird, and lo and behold! his wife stood before him once more, alive, and as blooming as ever.

The King rejoiced greatly, but he kept the Queen in hiding till the Sunday on which the child was to be christened. After the christening he said:

"What punishment does that person deserve who drags another out of bed, and throws him or her, as the case may be, into the water?"

Then the wicked old stepmother answered:

"No better fate than to be put into a barrel lined with sharp nails, and to be rolled in it down the hill into the water."

"You have pronounced your own doom," said the King; and he ordered a barrel to be made lined with sharp nails, and in it he put the bad old woman and her daughter. Then it was fastened down securely, and the barrel was rolled down the hill till it fell into the river.

The Selfish Giant

OSCAR WILDE

Every afternoon, as they were coming from school, the children used to go and play in the Giant's garden.

It was a large lovely garden, with soft green grass. Here and there over the grass stood beautiful flowers like stars, and there were twelve peach-trees that in the spring-time broke out into delicate blossoms of pink and pearl, and in the autumn bore rich fruit. The birds sat on the trees and sang so sweetly that the children used to stop their games in order to listen to them. "How happy we are here!" they cried to each other.

One day the Giant came back. He had been to visit his friend the Cornish ogre, and had stayed with him for seven years. After the seven years were over he had said all that he had to say, for his conversation was limited, and he determined to return to his own castle. When he arrived he saw the children playing in the garden.

"What are you doing there?" he cried in a very gruff voice, and the children ran away.

"My own garden is my own garden," said the Giant; "any one can understand that, and I will allow nobody to play in it but myself." So he built a high wall all round it, and put up a notice-board.

> *TRESPASSERS*
> *WILL BE*
> *PROSECUTED*

He was a very selfish Giant.

The poor children had now nowhere to play. They tried to play on the road, but the road was very dusty and full of hard stones, and they did not like it. They used to wander round the high wall when their lessons were over, and talk about the beautiful garden inside. "How happy we were there," they said to each other.

Then the Spring came, and all over the country there were little blossoms and little birds. Only in the garden of the Selfish Giant it was still winter. The birds did not care to sing in it as there were no children, and the trees forgot to blossom. Once a beautiful flower put its head out from the grass, but when it saw the notice-board it was so sorry for the children that it slipped back into the ground again, and went off to sleep. The only people who were pleased were the Snow and the Frost. "Spring has forgotten this garden," they cried, "so we will live here all the year round." The Snow covered up the grass with her great white cloak, and the Frost painted all the trees silver. Then they invited the North Wind to stay with them, and he came. He was wrapped in furs, and he roared all day about the garden, and blew the chimney-pots down. "This is a delightful spot," he said, "we must ask the Hail on a visit." So the Hail came. Every day for three hours he rattled on the roof of the castle till he broke most of the slates, and then he ran round and round the garden as fast as he could go. He was dressed in gray, and his breath was like ice.

"I cannot understand why the Spring is so late in coming," said the Selfish Giant, as he sat at the window and looked out at his cold white garden; "I hope there will be a change in the weather."

But the Spring never came, nor the Summer. The Autumn gave golden fruit to every garden, but to the Giant's garden she gave none. "He is too selfish," she said. So it was always Winter there, and the North Wind, and the Hail, and the Frost, and the Snow danced about through the trees.

One morning the Giant was lying awake in bed when he heard some lovely music. It sounded so sweet to his ears that he thought it must be the King's musicians passing by. It was really only a little linnet singing outside his window, but it was so long since he had heard a bird sing in his garden that it seemed to him to be the most beautiful music in the world. Then the Hail stopped dancing over his head, and the North Wind ceased roaring, and a delicious perfume came to him through the open casement. "I believe the Spring has come at last," said the Giant; and he jumped out of bed and looked out.

What did he see?

He saw a most wonderful sight. Through a little hole in the wall the children had crept in, and they were sitting in the branches of the trees. In every tree that he could see there was a little child. And the trees were so glad to have the children back again that they had covered themselves with blossoms, and were waving their arms gently above the children's heads. The birds were flying about and twittering with delight, and the flowers were looking up through the green grass and laughing. It was a lovely scene, only in one corner it was still winter. It was the farthest corner of the garden, and in it was standing a little boy. He was so small that he could not reach up to the branches of the tree, and he was wandering all round it, crying bitterly. The poor tree was still quite covered with frost and snow, and the North Wind was blowing and roaring above it. "Climb up! little boy," said the Tree, and it bent its branches down as low as it could; but the boy was too tiny.

And the Giant's heart melted as he looked out. "How selfish I have been!" he said; "now I know why the Spring would not come here. I will put that poor little boy on the top of the tree, and then I will knock down the wall, and my garden shall be the children's playground for ever and ever." He was really very sorry for what he had done.

So he crept downstairs and opened the front door quite softly, and went out into the garden. But when the children saw him they were so frightened that they all ran away, and the garden became winter again. Only the little boy did not run, for his eyes were so full of tears that he did not see the Giant coming. And the Giant stole up behind him and took him gently in his hand, and put him up into the tree. And the tree broke at once into blossom, and the birds came and sang on it, and the little boy stretched out his two arms and flung them round the Giant's neck, and kissed him. And the other children, when they saw that the Giant was not wicked any longer, came running back, and with them came the Spring. "It is your garden now, little children," said the Giant, and he took a great axe and knocked down the wall. And when the people were going to market at twelve o'clock they found the Giant playing with the children in the most beautiful garden they had ever seen.

All day long they played, and in the evening they came to the Giant to bid him good-bye.

"But where is your little companion?" he said: "the boy I put into the tree." The Giant loved him the best because he had kissed him.

"We don't know," answered the children; "he has gone away."

"You must tell him to be sure and come here to-morrow," said the Giant. But the children said that they did not know where he lived, and had never seen him before; and the Giant felt very sad.

Every afternoon, when school was over, the children came and played with the Giant. But the little boy whom the Giant loved was never seen again. The Giant was very kind to all the children, yet he longed for his first little friend, and often spoke of him. "How I would like to see him !" he used to say.

Years went over, and the Giant grew very old and feeble. He could not play about any more, so he sat in a huge armchair, and watched the children at their games, and admired his garden. "I have many beautiful flowers," he said; "but the children are the most beautiful flowers of all."

One winter morning he looked out of his window as he was dressing. He did not hate the Winter now, for he knew that it was merely the Spring asleep, and that the flowers were resting.

Suddenly he rubbed his eyes in wonder, and looked and looked. It certainly was a marvelous sight. In the farthest corner of the garden was a tree quite covered with lovely white blossoms. Its branches were all golden, and silver fruit hung down from them, and underneath it stood the little boy he had loved.

Downstairs ran the Giant in great joy, and out into the garden. He hastened across the grass, and came near to the child. And when he came quite close his face grew red with anger, and he said, "Who hath dared to wound thee?" For on the palms of the child's hands were the prints of two nails, and the prints of two nails were on the little feet.

"Who hath dared to wound thee?" cried the Giant; "tell me, that I may take my big sword and slay him."

"Nay!" answered the child; "but these are the wounds of Love."

"Who art thou?" said the Giant, and a strange awe fell on him, and he knelt before the little child.

And the child smiled on the Giant, and said to him, "You let me play once in your garden, to-day you shall come with me to my garden, which is Paradise."

And when the children ran in that afternoon, they found the Giant lying dead under the tree, all covered with white blossoms.

Lasse's Fur Overcoat

(Traditional Swedish Tale)

Lasse was a good boy, no one could deny that, but he sometimes behaved in rather a stupid manner. Still one could forgive him for that, so much the more, as other people sometimes do the same.

Just listen: It once happened that Lasse was to have a fur overcoat—for that is a necessary thing when it is very cold—and every man who could afford it had such an article of dress. So Lasse went to the city to buy fur, because there was none to be found in the village where he lived. He went to a dealer in furs.

"Good-day, Mr. Furdealer; I want to buy some pelts," said Lasse, and the man showed him some very fine skins. They were all white but one, which was black; but that made no difference, because the fur was to be turned inside. Yes, the black one ought to make a very fine coat, they both thought, so Lasse went home delighted with his purchase.

But Lasse intended to make the coat himself, because he was not unhandy with his needle; the worst part was the cutting out, for he did not know how to do that.

"But I will go to the other village folks and borrow patterns, then it will go all right," thought Lasse, and he started out. He went into the nearest neighbor's first.

"I am going to make a fur coat," said Lasse, "and I would be much obliged if I could borrow a pattern to cut it out by."

"That is a good thing to do," said the peasant, "but see here, do not make it too long, for that would be the worst thing that could happen."

The peasant was a short man, so short coats fitted him; Lasse, on the contrary, was tall, but the peasant never thought of that.

"Thank you for your advice," said Lasse, "I shall not forget it." And he went out.

After he was outside he thought like this:

"It would be a good thing to get several patterns and have more to go by; the coat would be so much the better." So he went into the sheriff's and made known his errand.

"By all means make the coat roomy and wide, or it will be good for nothing," said he, because he was thick about the waist. He did not remember that Lasse was thin, as young striplings usually are.

And Lasse thanked him for his advice, and promised to follow it, of course.

Then Lasse went from one to another through the whole village; one advised him to make long sleeves, another to put the fur on the outside, still another to turn it inside. An old soldier who was active and warm-blooded, as old warriors sometimes are, advised Lasse to leave holes for ventilation on the back, "else you will melt with the heat," said he.

After Lasse had been to every house, he went home and began to cut out the coat, and it was a queer one, for he followed the advice of each person. One sleeve was so short that it only reached to the elbow, while the other was so long that only the tips of his fingers could be seen. The lower part of the coat was so full that it would have reached around the sheriff's thick body, while the upper part was so narrow that Lasse could scarcely breathe. He turned the fur outside on the back, and as it was black and the skin light, it looked ridiculous. And on this piece he had cut a big hole, so he should not melt with the heat.

Well, he looked queer when he got the coat on. But he thought it was very fine, because he had followed the advice of so many wise folks. Then he went out to show himself to the village.

The big pigs in the garden were the first to see him, and they rushed up and down hill and tore up the ground. The animals had never seen anything so remarkable before as Lasse's fur coat, so they sprang out through the gate in terror, and squealed so loud that all the people who sat in the little cottages looked out of the windows.

"Oh, goodness gracious!" they cried when they saw Lasse, and old women, children and youths rushed out on the village street to examine the funny coat.

"Where are you going?" "What have you dressed yourself up so fine for?" they called after him, screaming and laughing.

Oh, look! he has a chimney on his back, and it is black with soot; hurrah! hurrah!" yelled a whole crowd of boys who ran after Lasse. And the dogs, children and pigs followed, till Lasse grew so ashamed of his coat that he ran home as fast as he could, the crowd at his heels.

A bull that was grazing on a hill, became angry at the noise, and when he caught sight of the great black patch of fur on Lasse's back, he started after him, roaring "Buuh!" caught him on his horns and tossed him right up in the air. Luckily for Lasse, he fell on the other side of the fence, or he might have been gored to death; but at last he reached his father's cot.

When he went in his mother was just going to settle the coffee, and in fright let the pot drop on the floor, so the hot coffee came on the cat's paws; she cried, "Yam, yam!" sprang upon the table and spit at Lasse, who stood shamefacedly in the door.

"What in the wide world has happened to you?" shrieked his father; "you have completely ruined the fur and made yourself the laughing stock of the whole village beside."

Yes, and then you frightened me so as to make me spoil the coffee and scald the cat's paws," Said his mother; but Lasse only cried.

"I have taken the advice of everybody in the whole town," said Lasse, "and still it is not right!"

Have you been to the tailor with it?" asked his father.

"No," said Lasse, "I never thought of that."

"Remember, that when a man wants to make a fur coat, he needs to ask the tailor, if he does not understand how to do it himself, but he should not ask anybody and everybody, because if he does, he is sure to make a fool of himself as you have done now."

So Lasse went to the tailor, but he has not been able to afford a new coat yet, because he was without one when I saw him yesterday, for the one he made was just good for nothing.

The Treasure

(TRADITIONAL RUSSIAN TALE)

In a certain kingdom there lived an old couple in great poverty. Sooner or later the old woman died. It was in winter, in severe and frosty weather. The old man went round to his friends and neighbors, begging them to help him to dig a grave for the old woman; but his friends and neighbors, knowing his great poverty, all flatly refused. The old man went to the priest, (but in that village they had an awfully grasping priest, one without any conscience), and says he:—

"Lend a hand, reverend father, to get my old woman buried."

"But have you got any money to pay for the funeral? if so, friend, pay up beforehand!"

"It's no use hiding anything from you. Not a single copeck have I at home. But if you'll wait a little, I'll earn some, and then I'll pay you with interest— on my word I'll pay you!"

The priest wouldn't so much as listen to the old man.

"If you haven't any money, don't you dare to come here," says he.

"What's to be done?" thinks the old man. "I'll go to the graveyard, dig a grave as I best can, and bury the old woman myself." So he took an axe and a shovel, and went to the graveyard. When he got there he began to prepare a grave. He chopped away the frozen ground on the top with the axe, and then he took to the shovel. He dug and dug, and at last he dug out a metal pot. Looking into it he saw that it was stuffed full of ducats that shone like fire. The old man was immensely delighted, and cried, "Glory be to Thee, O Lord! I shall have wherewithal both to bury my old woman, and to perform the rites of remembrance."

He did not go on digging the grave any longer, but took the pot of gold and carried it home. Well, we all know what money will do—everything went as smooth as oil! In a trice there were found good folks to dig the grave and fashion the coffin. The old man sent his daughter-in-law to purchase meat and drink and different kind of relishes—everything there ought to be at memorial feasts—and he himself took a ducat in his hand and hobbled back again to the pope's. The moment he reached the door, out flew the priest at him.

"You were distinctly told, you old lout, that you were not to come here without money; and now you've slunk back again."

"Don't be angry, reverence father," said the old man imploringly. "Here's gold for you. If you'll only bury my old woman, I'll never forget your kindness."

The priest took the money, and didn't know how best to receive the old man, where to seat him, with what words to smooth him down. "Well now, old friend! Be of good cheer; everything shall be done," said he.

The old man made his bow, and went home, and the priest and his wife began talking about him.

82

"There now, the old hunks!" they say. "So poor, forsooth, so poor! And yet he's paid a gold piece. Many a defunct person of quality have I buried in my time, but I never got so from anyone before."

The priest got under weigh with all his retinue, and buried the old crone in proper style. After the funeral the old man invited him to his house, to take part in the feast in memory of the dead. Well, they entered the cottage, and sat down to table—and there appeared from somewhere or other meat and drink and all sorts of snacks, everything in profusion. The reverend guest sat down, ate for three people, looked greedily at what was not his. The other guests finished their meal, and separated to go to their homes; then the priest also rose from the table. The old man went to speed him on his way. As soon as they got into the farmyard, and the priest saw they were alone at last, he began questioning the old man: "Listen, friend! confess to me, don't leave so much as a single sin on your soul—it's just the same before me as before God! How have you managed to get on at such a pace? You used to be a poor moujik, and now—marry! where did it come from? Confess, friend, whose breath have you stopped? whom have you pillaged?"

"What are you talking about, reverend father? I will tell you the exact truth. I have not robbed, nor plundered, nor killed anyone. A treasure tumbled into my hands of its own accord."

And he told him how it all happened. When the priest heard these words he actually shook all over with greediness. Going home, he did nothing by night and by day but think, "That such a wretched lout of a moujik should have come in for such a lump of money! Is there any way of tricking him now, and getting this pot of money out of him?" He told his wife about it, and he and she discussed the matter together, and held counsel over it.

"Listen, mother," says he; "we've a goat, haven't we?"

"Yes."

"All right, then; we'll wait until it's night, and then we'll do the job properly."

Late in the evening the priest dragged the goat indoors, killed it, and took off its skin—horns, beard, and all complete. Then he pulled the goat's skin over himself and said to his wife:

"Bring a needle and thread, mother, and fasten up the skin all round, so that it mayn't slip off."

So she took a strong needle, and some tough thread, and sewed him up in the goatskin. Well, at the dead of night, the priest went straight to the old man's cottage, got under the window, and began knocking and scratching. The old man hearing the noise, jumped up and asked:

"Who's there?"

"The Devil!"

"Ours is a holy spot!" shrieked the moujik, and began crossing himself and uttering prayers.

"Listen, old man," says the priest, "From me thou will not escape, although thou may'st pray, although thou may'st cross thyself; much better give me back my pot of money, otherwise I will make thee pay for it. See now, I pitied thee in thy misfortune, and I showed thee the treasure, thinking thou wouldst take a little of it to pay for the funeral, but thou hast pillaged it utterly."

The old man looked out of window—the goat's horns and beard caught his eye—it was the Devil himself, no doubt of it.

"Let's get rid of him, money and all," thinks the old man; "I've lived before now without money, and now I'll go on living without it."

So he took the pot of gold, carried it outside, flung it on the ground, and bolted indoors again as quickly as possible.

The priest seized the pot of money, and hastened home. When he got back, "Come," says he, "the money is in our hands now. Here, mother, put it well out of sight, and take a sharp knife, cut the thread, and pull the goatskin off me before anyone sees it."

She took a knife, and was beginning to cut the thread at the seam, when forth flowed blood, and the priest began to howl:

"Oh! it hurts, mother, it hurts! don't cut mother, don't cut!"

She began ripping the skin open in another place, but with just the same result. The goatskin had united with his body all round. And all that they tried, and all that they did, even to taking the money back to the old man, was of no avail. The goatskin remained clinging tight to the priest all the same. God evidently did it to punish him for his great greediness.

The Story of the Year

Hans Christian Andersen

It was in the latter part of the month of January. A violent snowstorm was raging; the snow whirled along the streets and lanes and covered the outside of the window-panes all over, whilst it fell down in larger masses from the roofs of the houses.

All the people in the street were seized with a sudden haste; they hurried along, often jostling against one another or falling into one another's arms, holding on tightly, so as to be safe for a moment at least. Carriages and horses looked as if they were powdered all over with sugar; the footmen were standing with their backs to the carriages, in order to shelter their faces from the cutting wind; foot-passengers eagerly sought the protection of the vehicles which moved slowly forward through the deep snow. When at last the storm had abated, and narrow paths were cleared along the fronts of the houses, people nevertheless often came to a dead stop when they met, neither wishing to step aside into the deep snow to make room for the other to pass.

Still and silently they were standing face to face, till at last they mutually arrived at the tacit compromise of exposing each one foot to the snow-heaps.

Towards the evening the wind ceased to blow; the sky looked as if it had been swept, and became higher and more transparent; the stars seemed to be quite new, and some of them were shining marvelously bright and clear; it was freezing so much that the snow creaked, and soon it was covered with a crust strong enough to carry the sparrows at daybreak, when they hopped up and down, where the snow had been shovelled away; but there was very little food to be found, and it was bitterly cold.

"Twit," said one to another, "this is what they call a new year; it is much worse than the last, and we might just as well have kept the old one. I am very dissatisfied, and I think I have good cause to be so."

"Yes; people were running about and firing salutes in honor of the new year," said a little sparrow, shivering with cold. "They were throwing pots and dishes against the doors, and were nearly out of their minds for joy, because the old year was gone. I was glad of it too, for I hoped we should soon have warmer days again; but nothing of the sort has happened yet; on the contrary, it freezes much harder than before. I think they must have made a mistake in their calculation of the time."

"There is no doubt about it," said a third, an old gray-headed bird. "They have a thing they call a calendar, which is entirely their own invention, and that is why they wish to regulate everything according to it; but that can't be so easily done. When Spring comes the new year begins; that is the course of nature—I go by that."

"But when will Spring come?" asked the others.

"It will come when the stork comes back; but he is very uncertain. Nobody here in town knows anything about him; they are better informed in the country. Shall we fly thither and wait? There we are certainly much nearer to Spring."

"That is all very well," said one of the sparrows, who had hopped about and chirped for a long time, without really saying anything. "I have found here in town comforts which I fear I should have to go without in the country. Near here, in a courtyard, live some people who had the happy thought of attaching two or three flower-pots to their house, so that their open ends are close to the wall, while the bottoms of the pots stand out; a hole is cut into each of them large enough for me to fly in and out; there my husband and I have built our nest, and there we have reared all our young ones. These people have of course done all this to have the pleasure of seeing us, otherwise I am sure they would not have done it. For their own pleasure, also, they strew out bread-crumbs, and thus we have food: we are, as it were, provided for. Therefore I think my husband and I will stay, although we are very discontented—yes, I think we shall stay."

"And we shall fly into the country to see if Spring is not yet coming." And off they went.

In the country the winter was harder still, and the glass showed a few degrees more cold than in town. The piercing wind swept over the snow-covered fields. The peasant sat in his sledge, with his hands wrapped in warm mittens, beating his arms across his chest to get warm, while his whip was lying on his knees; the lean horses ran so fast that they steamed; the snow creaked, and the sparrows hopped about in the ruts and froze. "Twit! When will Spring come? It takes a very long time."

"A very long time," resounded from the nearest snow-covered hill far over the field; it might have been an echo which one heard, or perhaps the language of the wonderful old man who sat in wind and weather on the top of snow-heaps; he was quite white, dressed like a peasant in a coarse white coat of frieze; he had long white hair, was very pale, and had large clear eyes.

"Who is the old man yonder?" asked the sparrows.

"I know," said an old raven sitting on the post of a railing, who was condescending enough to acknowledge that we are all small birds in the sight of the Lord, and who was therefore ready to talk to the sparrows and to give them information. "I know who the old man is. It is Winter, the old man of last year: he is not dead, as the calendar says, but is guardian to the young prince Spring, who is coming. Yes, winter is still swaying his scepter. Ugh! the cold makes you shiver, you little ones, does it not?"

"Yes; but is it not as I said?" asked the sparrow. "The calendar is only the invention of men, it is not arranged according to nature. They ought to leave such things to us, who are more sensitive."

Week after week passed by; the frozen lake was motionless, and looked like molten lead; damp, icy mists were hanging heavily over the country; the large black crows flew about in long rows without making a noise; it was as if everything in nature was asleep. Then a sunbeam glided over the icy surface of the lake, and made it shine like polished tin. The snow covering the fields and the hill no longer glittered as before; but the white man, Winter himself, was still sitting there and looking unswervingly southward; he did not notice that the snowy carpet sunk, as it were, into the ground, and that here and there little green spots came forth, and on these spots the sparrows flocked together.

"Twit, twit! is Spring coming now?"

"Spring!" It sounded over field and meadow, and through the dark woods, where bright green moss was shining on the trunks of the trees; and the two first storks arrived from the south, carrying on their backs two lovely little children, a boy and a girl; they kissed the earth in greeting, and wherever they set their feet, white flowers sprang forth out of the snow; hand in hand they went to the old ice-man, Winter, and tenderly clung to his breast. In a moment they had all three disappeared, while the whole country round them was enveloped in a thick damp mist, dense and heavy, which covered everything like a veil. Gradually the wind began to blow, and rushed with a roar against the mist and drove it away with violent blows; the sun shone brightly.

Winter had disappeared, but Spring's lovely children had seated themselves on the throne of the year.

"This is the new year!" cried the sparrows. "Now we shall get our due, and damages in addition, for the severe winter."

Wherever the two children directed their steps, green buds burst forth on the bushes and trees; the grass was shooting up; the cornfields became day by day greener and more lovely to look at. The little girl strewed flowers all around—there were no end of them in her frock, which she held up; however jealously she strewed them, they seemed to grow there. In her great zeal she poured forth a snow of blossoms over apple and pear trees, so that they stood there in all their splendor, before the green leaves had time to grow forth.

And she clapped her hands, and the boy followed her example; flocks of birds came flying, nobody knew where they came from, and chirped and sang: "Spring has come!"

That was wonderful to see. Many an old woman came out of her doorway into the sunshine, and basked in it, looking at the yellow flowers, blooming everywhere in the fields, and thinking that it was just like that in her young days; the world grew young again to her. "It is a blessing to be out here to-day," she said.

The wood still wore its dark green garments, made of buds, but the thyme had already come out, filling the air with sweet fragrance, and there were plenty of violets, anemones and primroses: every blade of grass was full of sap and strength. Truly that was a marvelous carpet, on which one could not help wishing to rest. There the two Spring children sat down hand in hand, singing and smiling, and continually growing. A mild rain fell down from Heaven; they did not notice it, the rain-drops mingled with their own tears of joy.

The two lovers kissed each other, and in a moment the green of the wood became alive. When the sun rose again all the woods were green.

Hand in hand the betrothed wandered under the fresh hanging roof of leaves, wherever the sunbeams and shadows produced a change of color in the green.

What delicate tints, what a sweet fragrance the new leaves had! The clear stream and brooks rippled merrily between the velvet-like rushes and over the colored pebbles. "So it was for ever and shall ever remain so," said all Nature. The cuckoo sang, the lark flew up—it was a beautiful Spring; but the willow trees wore woollen mittens over their blossoms; they were exceedingly careful, and that is tiresome.

Days and weeks passed by, and the heat came, as it were, rolling down; hot waves of air passed through the corn and made it yellower from day to day. The white water-lily of the north spread its large green leaves over the surface of the streams and lakes, and the fishes sought shade beneath them. In a spot where the trees of the wood sheltered it stood a farmer's cottage; the sun shone on its walls and warmed the unfolded roses, and the black juicy berries with which the cherry-trees were loaded. There sat the lovely wife of Summer, the same that we have seen as child and bride; her glances were fixed on the rising dark clouds, which, like mountains, in wave-like outlines, dark blue and heavy, were rising higher and higher. From three sides they came, continually growing, and seemed very much like a petrified reversed ocean gradually settling down on the forest, where everything, as if by magic, had become quiet. Not a breath of air was stirring; every bird was silent, there was an earnest expectation in the whole of Nature, but on the paths and roadways people in carriages, on horseback, and on foot, hastened to reach a shelter.

Suddenly there came a flash of light, as if the sun broke through the clouds again, flaming, dazzling, all-devouring; and then again it became dark, and the thunder rolled. Rain came pouring down in torrents; darkness and light, absolute silence and terrible noise, followed each other in quick succession. The wind moved the long, feather-like reeds on the moor like the waves of the sea; the branches of the trees were concealed in watery mist. Grass and corn lay beaten down and swamped, looking as if they could never rise again. Then the rain gradually ceased, the sun burst forth, drops of water glittered on the stalks and leaves like pearls, the birds began to sing, the fishes darted out of the water, the gnats played in the sunshine and out on a stone in the foaming water stood Summer himself, the strong man, with vigorous limbs, and wet, dripping hair, refreshed by the bath, basking in the sunshine.

All Nature seemed born anew, and stood forth in rich, strong, beautiful splendor; it was Summer, warm, sweet Summer.

Sweet and agreeable was the fragrance streaming forth from the rich clover field; the bees were humming yonder round the ruins of the old meeting-place; a bramble-bush wound itself round the stone altar, which, washed by the rain, was glittering in the sunshine, thither flew the queen with the whole swarm to prepare wax and honey. Only Summer saw it, and his vigorous spouse; for them the altar-table was covered with Nature's offerings.

The evening sky looked like gold; no church dome was ever so bright, and the moon was shining between the evening red and the dawn. It was Summer!

And days and weeks passed by. The shining scythes of the reapers glittered in the cornfields, the branches of the apple-trees were bending under the weight of the red and yellow fruit; the hops smelled sweetly and hung in large clusters, and under the hazel bushes, where the nuts grew in big bunches, sat Summer, with his serious wife.

"What a wealth!" she said; "blessings are spread everywhere. Wherever one turns it is pleasant to abide; and yet—I do not know why—I am longing for peace, rest; I cannot express what I feel. They are already plowing again. Men are insatiable; they always wish to gain more and more. See, the storks come in flocks and follow at a little distance behind the ploughs; it is the bird of Egypt which carried us through the air. Do you still remember when we two came hither to this northern land? We brought with us flowers, lovely sunshine, and green woods. The wind has dealt very roughly with them; they are becoming brown and dark like the trees of the south, but they do not carry golden fruit like those."

"You would like to see the golden fruit?" asked Summer. "Look up, then." He lifted his arm, and the leaves of the trees became red and golden. A splendor of color was spread over all the woods; the dog-rose hedge glittered with scarlet hips, the elder-trees were full of large bunches of dark-brown berries, the horse-chestnuts fell down out of their dark-green husks, and on the ground below violets were blooming for the second time.

But the queen of the year grew quieter and paler. "It is blowing very cold," she said; "the night brings damp mists. I am longing for the country where I passed my childhood."

And she saw the storks fly away. Not a single one remained; and she stretched out her hands after them, as if she wished to retain them. She looked up at the empty nests—in one a long-stalked cornflower, in another the yellow rape-seed were thriving, as if the nest was only intended to protect them and serve as a fence for them; and the sparrows flew up into the storks' nest.

"Twit! What has become of the master and his wife? They cannot bear it if the wind blows a little, and therefore they have left the country. I wish them a happy journey."

The leaves in the wood became more yellow day by day, and fell down one after another. The violent autumn winds were blowing; the year was far advanced, and on a couch of dry leaves rested the queen of the year, and looked with mild eyes at the sparkling stars, while her husband stood by her side. A gust of wind made the leaves rustle; a great many of them fell down, and suddenly she was gone; but a butterfly—the last of the year—flew through the cold air.

Damp fogs came, icy winds were blowing, and the dark long nights set in. The ruler of the year stood there, with white locks, but he was not aware of it; he thought snow-flakes were falling from the clouds.

A thin layer of snow was spread over the green fields, and the church bells were pealing forth the Christmas chimes.

"The bells are telling of Christ's birth," said the ruler of the year. "Soon the new rulers will be born, and I shall go to rest, like my wife: to rest in the shining star."

And out in the green pinewood the Christmas angel consecrated the young trees which he selected to serve at his festival.

"May there be joy in the homes under the green branches," said the old ruler of the year: in a few weeks his hair had become as white as snow. "The time for my rest draws near, and the young couple of the year will receive my crown and scepter."

"You are still in power," said the Christmas angel; "you must not yet go to rest. Let the snow still cover and warm the young seed. Learn to bear the thought that honor is done to another while you are still the ruler. Learn to be forgotten and yet to live. The hour of your deliverance approaches with Spring." "When is Spring coming?" said Winter. "He will come when the stork returns."

And Winter, ice-cold and broken down, with white locks and still whiter beard, was sitting on the top of the hill, where his predecessor had sat, and looked towards the south. The ice cracked, the snow creaked, the skaters enjoyed themselves on the smooth surface of the lake and the black of the ravens and crows stood in strong contrast to the white ground. Not a breath of air was stirring. Old Winter clenched his fists in the cold air, and the ice on the rivers and lakes was several feet thick.

Then the sparrows came out of town again and asked: "Who is the old man yonder?" And the raven was there again, or perhaps his son, which comes to the same thing, and replied to them: "It is Winter, the old man from last year. He is not dead, as the calendar says, but is the guardian of Spring, who is approaching."

"When will Spring come?" asked the sparrows; "then we shall have a better time and milder *regime*; the old one was good for nothing."

And Winter nodded pensively towards the dark leafless woods, where every tree showed the graceful outline of its branches, and during the long winter night icy fogs descended—the ruler dreamt of his young days, of his manhood, and at daybreak the whole forest was glittering with hoar-frost; that was Winter's summer dream, but the sunshine soon made the frost melt and drop down from the branches.

"When will Spring come?" asked the sparrows.

"Spring!" echoed the snow-covered hills: the sun shone more warmly, the snow melted, the birds chirped, "Spring is coming."

And the first stork came flying through the air, a second soon followed: each had a lovely child on his back. They descended in an open field, kissed the ground and kissed the silent old man; and as Moses disappeared on the mount, so he disappeared, carried away by the clouds.

The story of the year was ended.

"This is all very fine," said the sparrows; "it is beautiful too; but it is not according to the calendar, and therefore it must be wrong."

Little Lasse

(FROM *THE LILAC FAIRY BOOK*)

There was once a little boy whose name was Lars, and because he was so little he was called Little Lasse; he was a brave little man, for he sailed round the world in a pea-shell boat.

It was summer time, when the pea shells grew long and green in the garden. Little Lasse crept into the pea bed where the pea stalks rose high above his cap, and he picked seventeen large shells, the longest and straightest he could find.

Little Lasse thought, perhaps, that no one saw him; but that was foolish, for God sees everywhere.

Then the gardener came with his gun over his shoulder, and he heard something rustling in the pea bed.

"I think that must be a sparrow," he said. "Ras! Ras!" But no sparrows flew out, for Little Lasse had no wings, only two small legs. "Wait! I will load my gun and shoot the sparrows," said the gardener.

Then Little Lasse was frightened, and crept out on to the path.

"Forgive me, dear gardener!" he said. "I wanted to get some fine boats."

"Well, I will this time," said the gardener. "But another time Little Lasse must ask leave to go and look for boats in the pea bed."

"I will," answered Lasse; and he went off to the shore. Then he opened the shells with a pin, split them carefully in two, and broke small little bits of sticks for the rowers' seats. Then he took the peas which were in the shells and put them in the boats for cargo. Some of the shells got broken, some remained whole, and when all were ready Lasse had twelve boats. But they should not be boats, they should be large warships. He had three liners, three frigates, three brigs and three schooners. The largest liner was called *Hercules*, and the smallest schooner *The Flea*. Little Lasse put all the twelve into the water, and they floated as splendidly and as proudly as any great ships over the waves of the ocean.

And now the ships must sail round the world. The great island over there was Asia; that large stone Africa; the little island America; the small stones were Polynesia; and the shore from which the ships sailed out was Europe. The whole fleet set off and sailed far away to other parts of the world. The ships of the line steered a straight course to Asia, the frigates sailed to Africa, the brigs to America, and the schooners to Polynesia. But Little Lasse remained in Europe, and threw small stones out into the great sea.

Now, there was on the shore of Europe a real boat, father's own, a beautiful white-painted boat, and Little Lasse got into it. Father and mother had forbidden this, but Little Lasse forgot. He thought he should very much like to travel to some other part of the world.

"I shall row out a little way—only a very little way," he thought. The pea-shell boats had traveled so far that they only looked like little specks on the ocean. "I shall seize *Hercules* on the coast of Asia," said Lasse, "and then row home again to Europe."

He shook the rope that held the boat, and, strange to say, the rope became loose. Ditsch, ratsch, a man is a man, and so Little Lasse manned the boat.

Now he would row—and he could row, for he had rowed so often on the steps at home, when the steps pretended to be a boat and father's big stick an oar. But when Little Lasse wanted to row there were no oars to be found in the boat. The oars were locked up in the boat-house, and Little Lasse had not noticed that the boat was empty. It is not so easy as one thinks to row to Asia without oars.

What could Little Lasse do now? The boat was already some distance out on the sea, and the wind, which blew from land, was driving it still further out. Lasse was frightened and began to cry. But there was no one on the shore to hear him. Only a big crow perched alone in the birch tree; and the gardener's black cat sat under the birch tree, waiting to catch the crow. Neither of them troubled themselves in the least about Little Lasse, who was drifting out to sea.

Ah! how sorry Little Lasse was now that he had been disobedient and got into the boat, when father and mother had so often forbidden him to do so! Now it was too late, he could not get back to land. Perhaps he would be lost out on the great sea. What should he do?

When he had shouted until he was tired and no one heard him, he put his two little hands together and said, "Good God, do not be angry with Little Lasse." And then he went to sleep. For although it was daylight, old Nukku Matti was sitting on the shores of the "Land of Nod," and was fishing for little children with his long fishing rod. He heard the low words which Little Lasse said to God, and he immediately drew the boat to himself and laid Little Lasse to sleep on a bed of rose leaves.

Then Nukku Matti said to one of the Dreams, "Play with Little Lasse, so that he does not feel lonesome."

It was a little dream-boy, so little, so little, that he was less than Lasse himself; he had blue eyes and fair hair, a red cap with a silver band, and white coat with pearls on the collar. He came to Little Lasse and said, "Would you like to sail round the world?"

"Yes," said Lasse in his sleep, "I should like to."

"Come, then," said the dream-boy, "and let us sail in your pea-shell boats. You shall sail in *Hercules* and I shall sail in *The Flea*."

So they sailed away from the "Land of Nod," and in a little while *Hercules* and *The Flea* were on the shores of Asia away at the other end of the world, where the Ice Sea flows through Behring Straits into the Pacific Ocean. A long way off in the winter mist they could see the explorer Nordenskiöld with his ship *Vega* trying to find an opening between the ice. It was so cold, so cold; the great icebergs glittered strangely, and the huge whales now lived under the ice, for they could not make a hole through with their awkward heads. All around on the dreary shore there was snow and snow as far as the eye could see; little gray men in shaggy skins moved about, and drove in small sledges through the snow drifts, but the sledges were drawn by dogs.

"Shall we land here?" asked the dream-boy.

"No," said Little Lasse. "I am so afraid that the whales would swallow us up, and the big dogs bite us. Let us sail instead to another part of the world."

"Very well," said the dream-boy with the red cap and the silver band; "it is not far to America"—and at the same moment they were there.

The sun was shining and it was very warm. Tall palm trees grew in long rows on the shore and bore coconuts in their top branches. Men red as copper galloped over the immense green prairies and shot their arrows at the buffaloes, who turned against them with their sharp horns. An enormous cobra which had crept up the stem of a tall palm tree threw itself on to a little llama that was grazing at the foot. Knaps! it was all over the little llama.

"Shall we land here?" asked the dream-boy.

"No," said Little Lasse. "I am so afraid that the buffaloes will butt us, and the great serpent eat us up. Let us travel to another part of the world."

"Very well," said the dream-boy with the white coat, "it is only a little way to Polynesia"—and then they were there.

It was very warm there, as warm as in a hot bath in Finland. Costly spices grew on the shores: the pepper plant, the cinnamon tree, ginger, saffron; the coffee plant and the tea plant. Brown people with long ears and thick lips, and hideously painted faces, hunted a yellow-spotted tiger among the high bamboos on the shore, and the tiger turned on them and stuck its claws into one of the brown men. Then all the others took to flight.

"Shall we land here?" asked the dream-boy.

"No," said Little Lasse. "Don't you see the tiger away there by the pepper plant? Let us travel to another part of the world."

"We can do so," said the dream-boy with the blue eyes. "We are not far from Africa"—and as he said that they were there.

They anchored at the mouth of a great river where the shores were as green as the greenest velvet. A little distance from the river an immense desert stretched away. The air was yellow; the sun shone so hot, so hot as if it would burn the earth to ashes, and the people were as black as the blackest jet. They rode across the desert on tall camels; the lions roared with thirst, and the great crocodiles with their gray lizard heads and sharp white teeth gaped up out of the river.

"Shall we land here?" asked the dream-boy.

"No," said Little Lasse. "The sun would burn us, and the lions and the crocodiles would eat us up. Let us travel to another part of the world."

"We can travel back to Europe," said the dream-boy with the fair hair. And with that they were there.

They came to a shore where it was all so cool and familiar and friendly. There stood the tall birch tree with its drooping leaves; at the top sat the old crow, and at its foot crept the gardener's black cat. Not far away was a house which Little Lasse had seen before; near the house there was a garden, and in the garden a pea bed with long pea shells. An old gardener with a green coat walked about and wondered if the cucumbers were ripe. Fylax was barking on the steps, and when he saw Little Lasse he wagged his tail. Old Stina was milking the cows in the farmyard, and there was a very familiar lady in a check woollen shawl on her way to the bleaching green to see if the clothes were bleached. There was, too, a well-known gentleman in a yellow summer coat, with a long pipe in his mouth; he was going to see if the reapers had cut the rye. A boy and a girl were running on the shore and calling out, "Little Lasse! Come home for bread-and-butter!"

"Shall we land here?" asked the dream-boy, and he blinked his blue eyes roguishly.

"Come with me, and I shall ask mother to give you some bread-and-butter and a glass of milk," said Little Lasse.

"Wait a little," said the dream-boy. And now Little Lasse saw that the kitchen door was open, and from within there was heard a low, pleasant frizzling, like that which is heard when one whisks yellow batter with a wooden ladle into a hot frying-pan.

"Perhaps we should sail back to Polynesia now?" said the happy dream-boy.

"No; they are frying pancakes in Europe just now," said Little Lasse; and he wanted to jump ashore, but he could not. The dream-boy had tied him with a chain of flowers, so that he could not move. And now all the little dreams came about him, thousands and thousands of little children, and they made a ring around him and sang a little song:

> The world is very, very wide,
>> Little Lasse, Lasse,
> And though you've sailed beyond the tide,
> You can never tell how wide
> It is on the other side,
>> Lasse, Little Lasse.
> You have found it cold and hot,
> Little Lasse, Lasse;
> But in no land is God not,
>> Lasse, Little Lasse.
> Many men live there as here,
> But they all to God are dear,
>> Little Lasse, Lasse.
> When His angel is your guide,
>> Little Lasse, Lasse,
> Then no harm can e'er betide,
> Even on the other side
>> Where the wild beasts wander.
> But tell us now,
>> Whene'er you roam,
>> Do you not find the best is home
> Of all the lands you've looked upon,
>> Lasse, Little Lasse?

When the dreams had sung their song they skipped away, and Nukku Matti carried Lasse back to the boat. He lay there for a long time quite still, and he still heard the frying-pan frizzling at home of the fire, the frizzling was very plain, Little Lasse heard it quite near him; and so he woke up.

There he lay in the boat, where he had fallen asleep. The wind had turned, and the boat had drifted out with one wind and drifted in with another while Little Lasse slept, and what Lasse thought was frizzling in a frying-pan was the low murmur of the waves as they washed against the stones on the shore. But he was not altogether wrong, for the clear blue sea is like a great pan in which God's sun all day makes cakes for good children.

Little Lasse rubbed the sleep out of his eyes and looked around him. Everything was the same as before; the crow in the birch tree, the cat on the grass, and the pea-shell fleet on the shore. Some of the ships had foundered, and some had drifted back to land. *Hercules* had come back with its cargo from Asia, *The Flea* had arrived from Polynesia, and the other parts of the world were just where they were before.

Little Lasse did not know what to think. He had so often been in that grotto in the "Land of Nod" and did not know what tricks dreams can play. But Little Lasse did not trouble his head with such things; he gathered together his boats and walked up the shore back to the house.

His brother and sister ran to meet him, and called out from the distance, "Where have you been so long, Lasse? Come home and get some bread-and-butter." The kitchen door stood open, and inside was heard a strange frizzling.

The gardener was near the gate, watering the dill and parsley, the carrots and parsnips.

"Well," he said, "where has Little Lasse been so long?"

Little Lasse straightened himself up stiff, and answered: "I have sailed round the world in a pea-shell boat."

"Oh!" said the gardener.

He has forgotten Dreamland. But you have not forgotten it; you know that it exists. You know the beautiful grotto and the bright silver walls whose luster never fades, the sparkling diamonds which never grow dim, the music which never ceases its low, soft murmur through the sweet evening twilight. The airy fairy fancies of happy Dreamland never grow old; they, like the glorious stars above us, are always young. Perhaps you have caught a glimpse of their ethereal wings as they flew around your pillow. Perhaps you have met the same dream-boy with the blue eyes and the fair hair, the one who wore the red cap with the silver band and the white coat with pearls on the collar. Perhaps he has taken you to see all the countries of the world and the peoples, the cold waste lands and the burning deserts, the many colored men and the wild creatures in the sea and in the woods, so that you may earn many things, but come gladly home again. Yes, who knows? Perhaps you also have sailed round the wide world once in a pea-shell boat.

The Christmas Spruce-Tree

(Traditional Swedish Tale)

Among the high and stately trees in the forest, there grew a spruce-tree that was no taller than a man, and when a spruce-tree is no taller than that, it looks very small indeed.

But the other trees round about were so large and spread their branches out so far on all sides that the little spruce could not have grown taller even if she had chosen.

Although she was little, she both heard and saw and listened gladly to the conversation of the other trees, which was very learned and also depressing for the little bush, which could never become great.

"I am the glory of the forest," said the haughty oak; "look at my mighty trunk and my powerful branches, how they reach up towards heaven! The little worms bite off my buds and think thereby to hinder my growth, but what impression can the insects make on my strength and hardiness! I will upward, and upward I go, because it is my destiny to do so. I furnish planks for men, from which they build their ships, and then I defy the storms on the ocean as I did the thunder in the forest before."

"And I follow you on the foaming waves," said the tall, graceful pine, and waved her proud crown. "When the ships fly over the billows, I uphold the flapping sails; without masts the fleets would be helplessly lost among the foaming breakers. Yes, my calling is a high one," she ended.

"And we warm the dwellings of mankind when Winter comes hither from his summer palace at the North Pole," said the white-stemmed birch, and smilingly shook her fine, delicate branches; "and in summer men throw themselves gladly at my feet and enjoy the shade and fragrance which my luxurious branches spread around them."

"I flatter myself that I perform the same service to man that you do," said a tall fir-tree, and gracefully drooped her lovely branches towards the ground on which she had cast down many smooth, shining cones, which looked so beautiful on the new-fallen, white snow carpet, which Winter had spread there.

And so the Wind sighed through the forest, which nodded to him, for he was a friend of their childhood, and gladly seen by the trees, although he sometimes caught them so quickly in his arms that he threw them down.

"That boy, that boy!" said those that would remain standing, "he is always so wild; but one can afford to excuse him on account of his youth," and so they continued to nod to him.

But the little spruce had heard how the other trees talked about their high destination, and so she thought: "What destination have I, then?" But however much she thought about the thing, she never arrived at a clear understanding of it, and so she decided to ask the great trees about it.

So she questioned the oak, the pine and the fir, but they all bore their heads so high that they did not hear what the little one said. Only the birch took up her question.

"You have no vocation," said the birch, "because you can never grow large enough; you can only be a Christmas-tree," added she.

"And what is a Christmas-tree?" continued the little bush.

"That I cannot exactly say," replied the birch, "but sometimes when the days are the shortest, people come out here into the forest and when they see a spruce that is not of any use, they say, 'That will do for a Christmas spruce.' Then they chop down the bush and carry it away from the forest. What they afterwards do with it, I cannot tell; very likely throw it away, because it could not be used for anything." And the little spruce bush asked the hares that hopped past, and the owls that sat in the pines, and the squirrels that came to carry away the fir cones, but no one could say more than the birch; no one knew what vocation a Christmas spruce-tree had.

Then the little spruce bush wept because it had no calling, and could not be of any use in the world. And the tears hardened into clear, translucent drops, but we call them gum.

Then there came a boy into the forest with an axe in his hands, and when he saw the spruce-tree, he said:

"Perhaps that will do for a Christmas-tree." He chopped it down, laid it on a sled and dragged it home.

The boy, however, put a wooden foot under the spruce-tree and sold it and it was taken into a large handsome room and dressed up with fine paper and small colored candles; candies and packages were tied on the branches, so the little tree became perfectly confused with the many new things she saw.

But along towards evening the spruce was put into a large room, all by itself. Here everything was silent and still, and the little tree, who stood there in the darkness, began again to think gloomy thoughts.

But presently the door opened, and a lady came in and lighted the candles. How light and glowing it was within then! The little tree had never been able to think of anything so beautiful. From an adjoining room came the sound of clear, childish voices, singing a beautiful Christmas song. They sang:

> Upon this day is born a child,
> So was God's plan and pleasure:
> Its mother was a Virgin mild;—
> Christ, Son of God, our Treasure.

So ran the Christmas psalm, and the little spruce-tree stood spell-bound and listened. But the doors flew open, and a crowd of merry children rushed in.

"Oh! how pretty, how fine!" cried the troop of young creatures, and danced in a ring around the tree, while the father played on a violin and the tiniest child sat nodding and cooing in its mother's arms.

"Ah! now I know what I was made for," thought the little tree. "I was intended to give joy to the little ones, because I myself am so small and humble."

How the Beggar Boy Turned into Count Piro

(FROM *THE CRIMSON FAIRY BOOK*)

Once upon a time there lived a man who had only one son, a lazy, stupid boy, who would never do anything he was told. When the father was dying, he sent for his son and told him that he would soon be left alone in the world, with no possessions but the small cottage they lived in and a pear tree which grew behind it, and that, whether he liked it or not, he would have to work, or else he would starve. Then the old man died.

But the boy did not work; instead, he idled about as before, contenting himself with eating the pears off his tree, which, unlike other pear trees before or since, bore fruit the whole year round. Indeed, the pears were so much finer than any you could get even in the autumn, that one day, in the middle of the winter, they attracted the notice of a fox who was creeping by.

"Dear me; what lovely pears!" he said to the youth. "Do give me a basket of them. It will bring you luck!"

"Ah, little fox, but if I give you a basketful, what am I to eat?" asked the boy.

"Oh, trust me, and do what I tell you," said the fox; "I know it will bring you luck." So the boy got up and picked some of the ripest pears and put them into a rush basket. The fox thanked him, and, taking the basket in his mouth, trotted off to the king's palace and made his way straight to the king.

"Your Majesty, my master sends you a few of his best pears, and begs you will graciously accept them," he said, laying the basket at the feet of the king.

"Pears! at this season?" cried the king, peering down to look at them; "and, pray, who is your master?"

"The Count Piro," answered the fox.

"But how does he manage to get pears in midwinter?" asked the king.

"Oh, he has everything he wants," replied the fox; "he is richer even than you are, your Majesty."

"Then what can I send him in return for his pears?" said the king.

"Nothing, your Majesty, or you would hurt his feelings," answered the fox.

"Well, tell him how heartily I thank him, and how much I shall enjoy them." And the fox went away.

He trotted back to the cottage with his empty basket and told his tale, but the youth did not seem as pleased to hear as the fox was to tell.

"But, my dear little fox," said he, "you have brought me nothing in return, and I am so hungry!"

"Let me alone," replied the fox; "I know what I am doing. You will see, it will bring you luck."

A few days after this the fox came back again.

"I must have another basket of pears," said he.

"Ah, little fox, what shall I eat if you take away all my pears?" answered the youth.

"Be quiet, it will be all right," said the fox; and taking a bigger basket than before, he filled it quite full of pears. Then he picked it up in his mouth, and trotted off to the palace.

"Your Majesty, as you seemed to like the first basket of pears, I have brought you some more," said he, "with my master, the Count Piro's humble respects."

"Now, surely it is not possible to grow such pears with deep snow on the ground?" cried the king.

"Oh, that never affects them," answered the fox lightly; "he is rich enough to do anything. But to-day he sends me to ask if you will give him your daughter in marriage?"

"If he is so much richer than I am," said the king, "I shall be obliged to refuse. My honor would not permit me to accept his offer."

"Oh, your Majesty, you must not think that," replied the fox; "and do not let the question of a dowry trouble you. The Count Piro would not dream of asking anything but the hand of the princess."

"Is he really so rich that he can do without a dowry?" asked the king.

"Did I not tell your Majesty that he was richer than you?" answered the fox reproachfully.

"Well, beg him to come here, that we may talk together," said the king.

So the fox went back to the young man and said: "I have told the king that you are Count Piro, and have asked his daughter in marriage."

"Oh, little fox, what have you done?" cried the youth in dismay; "when the king sees me he will order my head to be cut off."

"Oh, no, he won't!" replied the fox; "just do as I tell you." And he went off to the town, and stopped at the house of the best tailor.

"My master, the Count Piro, begs that you will send him at once the finest coat that you have in your shop," said the fox, putting on his grandest air, "and if it fits him I will call and pay for it to-morrow! Indeed, as he is in a great hurry, perhaps it might be as well if I took it round myself." The tailor was not accustomed to serve counts, and he at once got out all the coats he had ready. The fox chose out a beautiful one of white and silver, bade the tailor tie it up in a parcel, and carrying the string in his teeth, he left the shop, and went to a horse-dealer's, whom he persuaded to send his finest horse round to the cottage, saying that the king had bidden his master to the palace.

Very unwillingly the young man put on the coat and mounted the horse, and rode up to meet the king, with the fox running before him.

"What am I to say to his Majesty, little fox?" he asked anxiously; "you know that I have never spoken to a king before."

"Say nothing," answered the fox, "but leave the talking to me. "Good morning, your Majesty," will be all that is necessary for you."

By this time they had reached the palace, and the king came to the door to receive Count Piro, and led him to the great hall, where a feast was spread. The princess was already seated at the table, but was as dumb as Count Piro himself.

"The Count speaks very little," the king said at last to the fox, and the fox answered: "He has so much to think about in the management of his property that he cannot afford to talk like ordinary people." The king was quite satisfied, and they finished dinner, after which Count Piro and the fox took leave.

The next morning the fox came round again.

"Give me another basket of pears," he said.

"Very well, little fox; but remember it may cost me my life," answered the youth.

"Oh, leave it to me, and do as I tell you, and you will see that in the end it will bring you luck," answered the fox; and plucking the pears he took them up to the king.

"My master, Count Piro, sends you these pears," he said, "and asks for an answer to his proposal."

"Tell the count that the wedding can take place whenever he pleases," answered the king, and, filled with pride, the fox trotted back to deliver his message.

"But I can't bring the princess here, little fox?" cried the young man in dismay.

"You leave everything to me," answered the fox; "have I not managed well so far?"

And up at the palace preparations were made for a grand wedding, and the youth was married to the princess.

After a week of feasting, the fox said to the king: "My master wishes to take his young bride home to his own castle."

"Very well, I will accompany them," replied the king; and he ordered his courtiers and attendants to get ready, and the best horses in his stable to be brought out for himself, Count Piro and the princess. So they all set out, and rode across the plain, the little fox running before them.

He stopped at the sight of a great flock of sheep, which was feeding peacefully on the rich grass. "To whom do these sheep belong?" asked he of the shepherd. "To an ogre," replied the shepherd.

"Hush," said the fox in a mysterious manner. "Do you see that crowd of armed men riding along? If you were to tell them that those sheep belonged to an ogre, they would kill them, and then the ogre would kill *you*! If they ask, just say the sheep belong to Count Piro; it will be better for everybody." And the fox ran hastily on, as he did not wish to be seen talking to the shepherd.

Very soon the king came up.

"What beautiful sheep!" he said, drawing up his horse. "I have none so fine in my pastures. Whose are they?"

"Count Piro's," answered the shepherd, who did not know the king.

"Well, he must be a very rich man," thought the king to himself, and rejoiced that he had such a wealthy son-in-law.

Meanwhile the fox had met with a huge herd of pigs, snuffling about the roots of some trees.

"To whom do these pigs belong?" he asked of the swineherd.

"To an ogre," replied he.

"Hush!" whispered the fox, though nobody could hear him; "do you see that troop of armed men riding towards us? If you tell them that the pigs belong to the ogre they will kill them, and then the ogre will kill you! If they ask, just say that the pigs belong to Count Piro; it will be better for everybody." And he ran hastily on.

Soon after the king rode up.

"What fine pigs!" he said, reining in his horse. "They are fatter than any I have got on my farms. Whose are they?"

"Count Piro's," answered the swineherd, who did not know the king; and again the king felt he was lucky to have such a rich son-in-law.

This time the fox ran faster than before, and in a flowery meadow he found a troop of horses feeding. "Whose horses are these?" he asked of the man who was watching them.

"An ogre's," replied he.

"Hush!" whispered the fox, "do you see that crowd of armed men coming towards us? If you tell them the horses belong to an ogre they will drive them off, and then the ogre will kill you! If they ask, just say they are Count Piro's; it will be better for everybody." And he ran on again.

In a few minutes the king rode up.

"Oh, what lovely creatures! how I wish they were mine!" he exclaimed. "Whose are they?"

"Count Piro's," answered the man, who did not know the king; and the king's heart leapt as he thought that if they belonged to his rich son-in-law they were as good as his.

At last the fox came to the castle of the ogre himself. He ran up the steps, with tears falling from his eyes, and crying:

"Oh, you poor, poor people, what a sad fate is yours!"

"What has happened?" asked the ogre, trembling with fright.

"Do you see that troop of horsemen who are riding along the road? They are sent by the king to kill you!"

"Oh, dear little fox, help us, we implore you!" cried the ogre and his wife.

"Well, I will do what I can," answered the fox. "The best place is for you both to hide in the big oven, and when the soldiers have gone by I will let you out."

The ogre and ogress scrambled into the oven as quick as thought, and the fox banged the door on them; just as he did so the king came up.

"Do us the honor to dismount, your Majesty," said the fox, bowing low. "This is the palace of Count Piro!"

"Why it is more splendid than my own!" exclaimed the king, looking round on all the beautiful things that filled the hall. But why are there no servants?"

"His Excellency the Count Piro wished the princess to choose them for herself," answered the fox, and the king nodded his approval. He then rode on, leaving the bridal pair in the castle. But when it was dark and all was still, the fox crept downstairs and lit the kitchen fire, and the ogre and his wife were burned to death. The next morning the fox said to Count Piro:

"Now that you are rich and happy, you have no more need of me; but, before I go, there is one thing I must ask of you in return: when I die, promise me that you will give me a magnificent coffin, and bury me with due honors."

"Oh, little, little fox, don't talk of dying," cried the princess, nearly weeping, for she had taken a great liking to the fox.

After some time the fox thought he would see if the Count Piro was really grateful to him for all he had done, and went back to the castle, where he lay down on the door-step, and pretended to be dead. The princess was just going out for a walk, and directly she saw him lying there, she burst into tears and fell on her knees beside him.

"My dear little fox, you are not dead," she wailed; "you poor, poor little creature, you shall have the finest coffin in the world!"

"A coffin for an animal?" said Count Piro. "What nonsense! just take him by the leg and throw him into the ditch."

Then the fox sprang up and cried: "You wretched, thankless beggar; have you forgotten that you owe all your riches to me?"

Count Piro was frightened when he heard these words, as he thought that perhaps the fox might have power to take away the castle, and leave him as poor as when he had nothing to eat but the pears off his tree. So he tried to soften the fox's anger, saying that he had only spoken in joke, as he had known quite well that he was not really dead. For the sake of the princess, the fox let himself be softened, and he lived in the castle for many years, and played with Count Piro's children. And when he actually did die, his coffin was made of silver, and Count Piro and his wife followed him to the grave.

How the Mice Are Whistling

(Traditional German Tale)

"Where are the mice whistling?" Do you know why when one wants to make fun of anybody's not thriving well, one says, "Where are the mice whistling?" In Reddebas there lived once upon a time a farmer called Martin Drews, who was rather wild and fierce, and would bear no restraint. The village folks called him "Mad Drews." At work he was capable, could thresh and mow as much as two or three others; but of God and His word he would not hear anything, and every Sunday and holiday, and many a week-day night, he would sit in the public-house at cards and gin, and would behave dreadfully. For he could drink more than any man, and stand more fatigue than a horse. If he had sat up through the night, he was yet quick and fresh at work during the day, and whoever sat down to drink with him was lost, and at cards he was still more dangerous. He made all his card-party stupid, or tired them out, and thus got their money. In short, he was a fellow against whom everybody ought to have been cautioned, and nobody could do anything against his fists. Thus Martin went on for many a day, like a regular heathen, and yet until now he had always fared well. Now it happened one Christmas Eve that he sat in the inn at Karnin playing at cards, and having plenty of trumps. As midnight drew near, the gamekeeper from Karnin, who was of the party, rose and said, "Throw the cards down, Drews, and let us say a Paternoster, so that the Evil One may not have any power over us this coming year."

Drews laughed at him and said, "Go along with your Evil One; that is nothing but parsons' talk, and spook for children and old women. The Devil has long been killed, and as far as he is concerned I will safely go through the world by day and night. What, you, a fellow that carries powder and shot, can still believe in these old tales!"

"Yes," said the keeper, "through the world with God and His word." And he stood up, folded his hands, and prayed; and all the others prayed with him, also the card-players, who had laid down their cards. But Martin snapped his fingers, shuffled the cards, and laughed. The game was broken up, for nobody would go on playing with him, and everybody went home. At last Drews left also.

As he was halfway between Karnin and Reddebas, on the big high-road to Hamburg, where the road turns off to Satel, he saw all of a sudden a red flame running through the bushes, and however bold he was, his skin was creepy all over his body, and his hair stood on end inside his cap. His fear actually got the better of him, and he could not help it; he took to his heels. When he had run along for some time he stood still to take breath, and said to himself, "Fie, Martin! Is that how you run away from the Devil? And yet it is nothing but children's tales—for who has ever seen the Devil? Go along, be a man and go at him, if he can be found."

Thus he made himself brave and turned back, and walked slowly to the place where half-an-hour ago his legs had become so nimble. Yet his heart beat under his ribs so loudly that you could have heard it at the distance of a gunshot. Still he pulled himself together, set his teeth firmly, and wanted to be a man. And when he came to the Satel road, where he had seen the funny flame running over the white snow, he stood still and called out with such a loud voice that the trees trembled, "Come out, Devil! come out, if you have any courage!"

And what happened? Upon his word the flame leapt like lightning over the snow just towards him, and he saw that it was like a glowing mouse, which jumped as if in high glee, and whistled quite finely, and was no bigger than an ordinary mouse; but it flickered and flared like hellish fire, and had a beautifully gilt comb on its head, and gnashed its fiery teeth as if it meant to bite him. And whether Martin liked it or not, he could not stand the flickering and snapping, and in a trice he took again to his heels. But he had so outrun his strength in the deep snow, and the fright had so upset him, that he was laid up miserably ill for a week or longer. Yet he was silent about his Christmas adventure, and his run in the snow, and did not tell a soul how he had got from Karnin to Reddebas.

And that was not the end of it, for evil things take their time, just as good things. He had called out the old black fiend, and now he would not give him up. Martin was so frightened of the place near the Satel road, that even in bright daylight nobody could have taken him there alive. When he had any journey to make towards Flemendorp or the sea, he always made a long detour. Yet Old Nick is very cunning, and knows how to find the way to where he wants to go. It was very peculiar in this mouse affair, that in spite of all the fear with which he remembered the flaming mouse on the snow, yet he felt a burning desire and impulse in his heart to see the fiery mouse once more. For thus it is that fear and desire draw a poor sinner to the Devil. His desire grew stronger day by day, and tormented him so much that he had no rest nor peace from it. And the greatest torment was near the time when God leaves the road open to the Devil, when he and all that wear witches' and evil spirits' caps may carry on their game. When all good Christians lie in their best sleep at midnight, Martin could hardly contain himself, however fearful he felt; it pulled him out of his warm bed, and out of the house into the sullen, dark, and dreary night, on to the high-road where it goes uphill from the village towards Karnin, and only greater fear and trembling drove him home again.

Thus the craving desire for and fear of the Devil, plagued him for three months, from Christmas to Easter, and the formerly merry and wild fellow became thoughtful and melancholy, so that his friends and neighbors wondered what might be the matter with him. Martin bravely resisted for some time, yet in the end the Devil got the better of him, and notwithstanding his fear he was driven towards the road to Satel. And as he came to it, surely there all was ready for him, and his fate was sealed. The very instant the fiery mouse was there, and jumped about him and behaved so nicely, and looked so pleasantly at him with its bright shining eyes, as if it would make friends; and then it ran in front of him towards the coppice, and stood still again and looked back at him, so as to say, "Come with me, come with me!" And however much his heart beat and thumped he could not help it, he must follow. And as the mouse came into the coppice, it crept under a round stone and disappeared, and instantly the stone looked as if it were on fire. When Martin saw that, his fear was gone, he bethought himself of old tales which his father used in old days to tell him of burning gold, and how one might conjure the Devil so that he could not pull the gold down with him.

Martin lost no time; he spread his hands in the form of a cross over the stone, nourished his hat over it, and cried, "Avaunt, Satan, thou hast no right over me!" And he stood boldly and daringly there until the cock crowed and the larks rose up in the air, and the bright day broke. Then he set to work, rolled the stone aside, and there lay a dead mouse and a big heap of red ducats. And he gathered his hat-crown full, and filled his pockets and boots, and then sneaked home without making a noise, and put the gold in his money-box. And having thus taken the first earnest-money from Satan, he was doomed. Many a night when all good people lie in a sweet slumber which covers all care, poor Martin had to turn out and stagger to the fatal stone, and stand shivering by it in fear and trembling.

This went on for a few years, and he had boxes and chests heaped full of gold, and stalked about like a lord in a splendid coat, silver spurs, and a hat with gold galloon. But every Christian could see that there was something wrong. And at last there started a rumour of fiery mice, and one farm-servant, who could no longer remain in his service for fear and awe, related that he had often seen the burning mice run over the farmyard, and that in the barns and stables nobody could save and hide himself from their whistling and nibbling.

And so it happened that when the evil fiend had so ensnared him that he no longer could burst his bonds, one Christmas Eve, between midnight and one o'clock, so many flaming mice came running across the farmyard that it shone like a big fire, and these jumping Devil's brats set fire to his house and barns and stables; and Martin Drews, with wife and children, with his cattle and horses, was burnt to ashes, and all the Devil's money with him—unless the mice have secretly carried it off. Only two or three miserable ducats were scratched up among the ashes. And ever since that time folks say, "Listen, how Martin's mice are whistling!" And where formerly Martin's house used to stand, that is behind the publican's orchard, there is ghostly whistling every night; and on each tree there sits an owl and screams, and I would not advise any one to go over that place in the dead, dark night-time.

Under the Willow Tree

HANS CHRISTIAN ANDERSEN

The country round the little town of Kjöge, in Zealand, is very bare. It is true that the town lies by the sea-shore, which is always beautiful, but still it might be more beautiful there than it really is: all around are flat fields, and it is a very long way to the forest. Still, when one is quite at home in a place, one can always find some attraction in it, for which one afterwards longs, even when in the most charming spot in the world. And we must freely confess that it looked very pretty in summer at the extreme edge of the little town, where a few humble gardens skirt the rivulet which flows into the sea there; this was also the opinion of two children who lived next to each other and played here, making their way through the gooseberry bushes to get to each other.

In one garden stood an elder-tree, in the other an old willow, and it was especially under the latter that the children were very fond of playing; this they were allowed to do, although the willow stood near the rivulet and they might easily have fallen into the water. But the eye of God watches over the little ones—otherwise it would be a bad look-out for them. They were, however, very careful with regard to the water; in fact, the boy was so afraid of it that it was impossible in summer-time to get him to go into the sea, in which the other children were very fond of splashing about. Accordingly, he was constantly being teased and laughed at, and had to bear it patiently. Once Johanna, the little girl who lived next door, dreamed that she was sailing in a boat and that Kanut waded out to her, so that the water first came up to his neck, then closed over his head, and that at last he disappeared altogether. From the moment when little Kanut heard of this dream, he would no longer bear the jeers of the other boys; for he was not afraid of going into the water now. Had not Johanna dreamed it? It is true that he never did it, but from that time the dream was his pride.

Their parents, who were poor people, often came together, and Kanut and Johanna played in the gardens and on the high road, where, beside the ditch stood a row of willow-trees, looking, it is true, far from beautiful with their polled tops, but then they were not there for ornament, but for use. The old willow in the garden was much finer, and under that the two children usually sat. In the little town itself there is a large market-place, and at the time of the annual fair this was covered with whole streets of tents and booths full of silk ribbons, boots, and all that one could wish for. There was a terrible crowd; and as it generally rained too, one could easily distinguish the odor of the peasants' frieze jackets, mingled, however, with the more agreeable fragrance of honey-cakes and gingerbread, of which there was a booth full. The best of it all was that the man who sold the cakes always lived during fair-time with little Kanut's parents, and there was generally a present of a piece of gingerbread now and then, of which Johanna, of course, got her share. But it was still more charming that the gingerbread dealer could tell tales about every possible thing, even about his gingerbread; indeed, one evening he told a story about it which made such a deep impression upon the children that they never forgot it, and therefore it is perhaps best that we should hear it too, especially as it is only a short one.

"On the counter," he said, "lay two cakes of gingerbread, one in the shape of a man with a hat, the other in the shape of a young woman without a hat; both their faces were on the side that was turned uppermost, and they were to be looked at only on that side, and not on the other, for people should never be looked at from the wrong side. The man carried on his left side a bitter almond—that was his heart; the maiden, on the other hand, was all honey-cake. They both lay as samples on the counter, and lay there so long, that at last they fell in love with each other; but neither told the other, as they ought to have done, if they had wanted anything to come of it.

"'He is a man—he ought to speak first,' she thought, but would have been quite satisfied, if she had only known that her love was returned. His ideas were far more extravagant, as is always the case with men. He dreamed that he was a real street boy, that he possessed four pennies, and that he bought the young woman and ate her up.

"And so they lay for days and weeks upon the counter and got dry, the thoughts of the young woman growing more and more tender and womanly.

"'It is enough for me that I have lain on the same counter with him,' she thought, and—crack!—she broke right in two.

"'If she had only known of my love, she would have held together a little longer,' thought he.

"That is the story, and here they are both," said the cake-seller. "They are remarkable for their history and for their silent love, which never led to anything. You may have them!" Saying which he gave Johanna the man, who was whole, and Kanut received the broken maiden; but the children were so affected by the story that they did not have the heart to eat the pair of lovers.

On the following day they took them into the churchyard, and sat down by the church wall, which is covered, summer and winter, with the most luxuriant ivy, as with a rich carpet. Here they stood the two gingerbread cakes between the green creepers in the sunshine, while they told a group of other children the story of the silent love which was so silly; that is to say, the love was silly, for of course the story was beautiful—on that they were all agreed. But when they looked at the gingerbread pair again, a big boy, purely out of mischief, had eaten up the broken maiden. The children wept about it, and afterwards—probably in order that the poor lover should not remain in the world alone—they ate him up too; but they never forgot the story.

The two children were always together by the elder-tree and under the willow, and the little girl sang the most beautiful songs with a voice as clear as a bell; Kanut, on the contrary, had not a note in him, but he knew the words, and that is at least something. The people of Kjöge, even to the wife of the fancy goods dealer, stood still and listened when Johanna sang. "What a very sweet voice the little girl has!" they would say.

Those were glorious days, but they did not last for ever. The neighbors became separated. The little girl's mother was dead, and her father intended to marry again—in the capital, too, where he had been promised a living somewhere as messenger, which post was said to be a very lucrative one. The neighbors parted in tears; that is to say, the children wept, but their parents promised to write to one another at least once a year.

Kanut was apprenticed to a shoemaker, for such a big boy could not be allowed to walk about idle any longer; and he was also confirmed.

Oh! how he would have liked to have been in Copenhagen with little Johanna on that joyous day, but he remained in Kjöge, and had never been to Copenhagen, although the capital is only five miles distant from the little town; but when the sky was clear Kanut had seen the towers of the city far away across the sea, and on his confirmation day he distinctly saw the golden cross on the church of the Virgin glittering in the sun.

How often his thoughts were with Johanna! Did she ever think of him? he wondered. Yes. Towards Christmas a letter came from her father to Kanut's parents, saying that they were getting on very well in Copenhagen, and that Johanna might look forward to great fortune on account of her fine voice; she had been engaged to sing at the theater, and was already earning a little money by that, out of which she sent her dear neighbors in Kjöge a whole dollar for a merry Christmas Eve; she had herself added in a postscript that they were to drink to her health, and in the same postscript was also written: "Kind regards to Kanut."

The whole family wept, and yet all this was so pleasant; but they wept for joy. Johanna had occupied Kanut's thoughts every day, and now he was convinced that she also thought of him, and the nearer the time came when he should have finished his apprenticeship, the more clearly did it appear to him that he loved Johanna dearly and that she must be his wife. At these thoughts a smile would come over his face and he would draw the thread twice as fast and press his foot against the knee-strap; he ran the awl deep into his finger, but that was nothing. He certainly did not intend to play the dumb lover, as the two gingerbread cakes had done; that story should be a good lesson for him.

Now he was a journeyman and his knapsack was packed; at length, for the first time in his life, he was to go to Copenhagen, where he already had a master. How surprised and pleased Johanna would be! She was now seventeen years old—he nineteen.

He wanted to buy a gold ring for her before leaving Kjöge, but it occurred to him that much finer things of that kind could be bought in Copenhagen. So he took leave of his parents, and on a rainy day late in autumn he set out on foot from his native town; the leaves were falling from the trees, and he arrived in the great city at his new master's, soaked through. He intended to pay his visit to Johanna's father on the following Sunday. The new journeyman's clothes were brought out and the new hat from Kjöge was put on; Kanut looked very well in it, having till that time always worn a cap. He found the house that he was looking for, and went up so many steps that it made him quite giddy to see how the people were piled on top of each other in the great city.

Everything in the room had a prosperous look, and Johanna's father received him in a very friendly manner; to the wife he was of course a stranger, but she shook hands with him, and gave him some coffee.

"Johanna will be pleased to see you," said the father; "you have indeed grown a very nice young man. Now you shall see her; she is a girl who causes me much pleasure, and with God's help will do so still more. She has her own room, and pays us for it." The father himself knocked politely at the door, as if he were a stranger, and then they went in.

And how pretty everything was in there! Such a little room was certainly not to be found in all Kjöge; the queen herself could not have a more charming one. There were carpets, there were window-curtains right down to the ground, and even a velvet chair, and all around flowers and pictures, and a mirror into which there was almost danger of stepping, for it was as large as a door. Kanut saw all this at a glance, and yet he saw only Johanna; she was a grown-up girl, and quite different from what Kanut had imagined her, but much more beautiful. In all Kjöge there was not a single maiden like her. How elegant she was, and how very strangely she looked at Kanut, but only for a moment, for the next she rushed towards him, as though she were about to kiss him! She certainly did not do so, but she was very near it. Yes, she certainly rejoiced at the sight of her old playmate. There were actually tears in her eyes, and then she had much to ask and much to talk about, from Kanut's parents down to the elder-tree and the willow, which she called elder-mother and willow-father, as if they had been people too; there was indeed no reason why they should not pass off as such, as well as the gingerbread cakes. Of these she also spoke, and of their silent love, as they lay upon the counter and broke in two, and at that she laughed quite heartily; but the blood mounted up into Kanut's cheeks and his heart beat quicker than ever. No, she was not proud at all. It was through her too—he saw that very well—that her parents invited him to spend the whole evening there; she poured out the tea and gave him a cup herself. Presently she took a book and read aloud, and it seemed to Kanut that the piece that she read was all about his love, so well did it fit in with his thoughts; then she sang a simple song, but it came from her lips like a story, and her own heart seemed to be overflowing with it. Yes, she was certainly fond of Kanut. The tears rolled down his cheeks—he could not help it, and he was unable to utter a single word; he appeared to himself as if he were struck dumb, and yet she pressed his hand and said: "You have a good heart, Kanut—always remain as you are."

That was an evening without its like; to sleep after it was impossible—neither did Kanut do so.

At parting, Johanna's father had said: "Now, I hope you will not forget us altogether. You will not allow the whole winter to pass before coming to see us?" So he could very well go again on the following Sunday, and he intended to do so. But every evening, after working hours—and they worked by candle-light too—Kanut went into the town; he walked through the street in which Johanna lived, and looked up at her windows, which were almost always lit up. Once he plainly saw the shadow of her face on the curtain—that was an eventful night. His master's wife did not like his roaming about every evening, as she called it, and she shook her head; but the master smiled, saying, "He is a young man."

"We shall see each other on Sunday, and I will tell her how she fills my heart and thoughts, and that she must be my little wife; it is true I am only a poor journeyman shoemaker, but I may become a master. I will work and strive—yes, I will tell her so. Nothing comes of silent love; that I learned from the gingerbread cakes." So thought Kanut.

Sunday came, and Kanut came, but how unfortunate it was! they were obliged to tell him that they were all invited out for that evening. Johanna pressed his hand and asked, "Have you been to the theater? You must go there. I sing on Wednesday, and if you can get out on that day, I will send you a ticket. My father knows where your master lives."

How kind it was of her! And on Wednesday afternoon he received a sealed envelope, without a word inside it, except the ticket; and in the evening Kanut went to the theater for the first time in his life. And what did he see? Johanna, so beautiful and charming, married, it is true, to a strange man, but that was all play-acting—something that they pretended; that Kanut knew, otherwise she would not have had the heart to send him a ticket so that he might see it; and all the people clapped their hands and shouted, and Kanut also shouted "Hurrah!"

Even the King smiled at Johanna, as if he were pleased with her. Heavens! how small Kanut felt; but he loved her very tenderly, and she was also fond of him—that he knew; but the man must say the first word—even the gingerbread maiden had been of that opinion. Indeed there was a great deal in that story.

As soon as Sunday came he went again, feeling as though he were going to take the sacrament; Johanna was alone, and received him. So it could not have chanced more luckily.

"I am glad that you have come," she said. "I was already thinking of sending my father to you, but I had an idea that you would come to-night; for I must tell you that I am going to France on Friday. I must, if I wish to do anything in the future."

But it seemed to Kanut as if the room were turning round and round; he felt as though his heart was going to burst. It is true no tears came into his eyes, but one could plainly see how grieved he was. "Dear honest, faithful soul!" she said; and with that Kanut's tongue was loosed, and he told her how dear she was to him, and that she must be his wife. While he uttered these words, he saw Johanna change color and turn pale; she let go his hand and replied earnestly and sadly: "Do not make yourself and me unhappy, Kanut. I will always be a kind sister to you, upon whom you can rely; but no more than that." And she passed her soft hand over his hot brow. "God gives us strength to bear much, if we but will it."

At that moment her step-mother entered the room.

"Kanut is quite beside himself at my going away," said Johanna. "Be a man"; and with that she laid her hand upon his shoulder. One would have thought that they had spoken only of the journey and of nothing else. "You are a child," she continued; "but now you must be good and reasonable, as under the willow-tree, when we were both children."

But it seemed to Kanut as though the world were out of joint; his thoughts were like a loose thread, fluttering to and fro in the wind. He stayed, not knowing whether they had asked him to stay; but they were kind and good, and Johanna poured him out some tea, and sang. The songs did not have the old ring, but were still so infinitely beautiful, almost heartbreaking. At last Kanut went; he did not offer her his hand, but she took it, saying, "I suppose you will give your sister your hand at parting, my old playmate." She smiled through the tears which were running down her cheeks, and repeated the word "Brother." Yes, that was indeed a beautiful consolation. Such was their parting.

She sailed to France; Kanut walked about in the dirty streets of Copenhagen. His shopmates asked him why he went about looking so miserable, and told him that he, a young fellow, ought to go out and enjoy himself with them.

They went together to a dancing saloon; there were many pretty girls, but none at all like Johanna, and here, where he had thought to forget her, she was most of all in his thoughts. "God gives us strength to bear much, if we but will it," she had said, and a kind of devotion came over him. He folded his hands; the violins struck up, and the girls danced around in a circle. Suddenly he started; it seemed to him as if he were in a place where he ought not to have taken Johanna, for after all she was with him there in his heart. So he went out, walked about the streets, and went past the house where she had lived; all was dark there—it was dark, empty, and lonesome everywhere. The world went its way, and Kanut went his.

Winter came and the waters froze over; it seemed as if everything were preparing itself for burial.

But when spring returned, and the first steamer went out, a longing seized Kanut to go far out into the world, but not to France.

He buckled on his knapsack and wandered far into Germany, from town to town, knowing no rest neither peace; only when he reached the beautiful old town of Nüremberg did he seem to become master again of his feet. He controlled himself sufficiently to stay there.

Nüremberg is a wonderful old town, looking as though it were cut out of an old picture-book. The streets run just as they themselves please, and the houses do not care about standing evenly in rows. Bow-windows and small turrets, scroll-work and statues project over the pavement, and high up from the roofs, gutters, in the form of dragons and long-legged dogs, run out into the middle of the street. Here on the market-place stood Kanut with his knapsack on his back; he was standing near one of the old fountains with the beautiful biblical and historical figures which are to be seen between the sparkling jets of water. A pretty servant-maid was just getting some water, and gave Kanut a draft; having a handful of roses, she also gave him one, and this seemed to him to be a good omen.

From the neighboring church the sound of the organ came out towards him; it sounded so homelike, that it seemed to come from the church at

Kjöge, and he went into the great cathedral. The sun shone in between the tall slender pillars through the stained-glass windows; Kanut's thoughts were filled with devotion, and a peaceful calm came over his soul.

He sought out a good master in Nüremberg, and stayed with him and learned the German language.

The old ditches round the town have been turned into small kitchen-gardens, but the high walls with their heavy towers are still standing. The ropemaker twists his rope on the wooden galleries along the inner side of the city wall, and here all around the elder grows up out of holes and crevices. It stretches its branches over the small lowly houses lying beneath, and in one of these lived the master with whom Kanut worked; the elder-tree hung its branches over the little attic window at which the young man sat.

Here he passed a summer and a winter; but when spring came it was no longer to be borne. The elder blossomed, and its fragrance reminded him so of home that it seemed as if he were again in the gardens of Kjöge: so Kanut left his master for another who lived farther in the town, where no elder-tree grew.

His workshop was near an old walled bridge, opposite an ever-splashing low water-mill; the rushing stream flowed past, hemmed in by houses which were all provided with old crumbling balconies. It looked as if the houses wanted to shake them all down into the water. Here no elder grew; here there was not even a flower-pot with a little green. But just opposite the workshop there stood a large old willow, clinging, as it were, to the house, so as not to be torn away by the stream, and stretching its boughs out over the water, like the willow-tree in the garden at Kjöge.

Yes, he had indeed removed from elder-tree mother to willow father; the tree here, especially on moonlight evenings, had something about it that went to his heart; it was, however, by no means the moonlight, but the old tree itself.

Anyhow, he could not bear it. Why not? Ask the willow-tree, ask the blossoming elder. And so he bade his Nüremberg master good-bye and went farther.

He never spoke to any one of Johanna, hiding his grief within him, and laying a deep significance upon the story of the two gingerbread cakes. Now he understood why the little man had had a bitter almond on his left side, for he himself had also a bitter taste there; and Johanna, who had always been so kind and friendly, she was honey-cake all over. It seemed as though the strap of his knapsack was so tight that he could hardly breathe; he loosened it, but it was no better than before. He saw only half the world around him; the other half he carried within him. That was how the matter stood.

It was only when he caught sight of the high mountains that his heart became lighter. Tears came into his eyes, and his thoughts turned towards the things about him.

The Alps seemed to him to be the folded wings of the earth; what if they should unfold themselves, these great pinions with their variegated pictures of dark forests, rushing torrents, clouds and masses of snow? On the last day the earth will lift up its great wings, soar up to Heaven, and burst like a soap-bubble in the light that streams from the Throne. "Oh! would that it were the last day!" sighed Kanut.

Silently he wandered through the land that seemed to him like a grass-grown orchard. Pretty young lacemakers nodded to him from the wooden balconies of the houses, the mountain-tops glowed in the red sunset, and when he saw the green lakes, overshadowed by the dark trees, he thought of the coast in the bay of Kjöge, and his heart was filled with sadness, but not with pain.

And farther on he saw the Rhine rolling along like a great wave, dashing itself into foam, and, with the rainbow fluttering overhead like a loose rib-bon, transforming itself into snow-white masses of clouds; it seemed to him as though this was the place where the clouds were made, and he thought of the water-mill at Kjöge, where the waters rush and foam.

He would gladly have remained here in the quiet town on the Rhine, but there were far too many elder and willow trees. He therefore proceeded farther, across the great lofty mountains, through the clefts in the preci-pices, and along paths which hung upon the sides of the rocks like swallows' nests. The waters rushed along far beneath him, and the clouds lay at his feet; he marched along in the warm summer sun, over thistles, alpine roses and snow, saying farewell to the lands of the North, and entering the region of blossoming chestnut-trees, vineyards, and fields of maize. The moun-tains formed a wall between him and all his recollections; and this was as it should be.

Before him lay a great magnificent city which they called Milan, and here he found a German master, who gave him employment; they were an old, pious couple in whose shop he worked, and they grew very fond of the quiet young journeyman, who spoke little, but worked the more, and who lived in such a pious and Christian way. It also seemed to him as though Heaven had taken the heavy burden from his heart.

His greatest pleasure was to occasionally ascend the mighty marble cathedral which seemed to him to be built of snow from his home, and shaped into images, tapering spires, and open halls adorned in many colors; from every corner, every spire and every niche the white statues smiled down upon him. Above him was the blue sky, beneath him lay the city and the far-stretching green plains of Lombardy, and towards the north were the high mountains with their eternal snows. At such moments he would think of the church at Kjöge, with its red ivy-clad walls, but he did not wish himself away; here, behind the mountains, he longed to be buried.

He had lived in Milan a year, and three years had passed since he had left home, when one day his master took him into the town, not to the circus to see the riding, but to the grand opera, and it was a building, too, worth seeing. The finest silken curtains hung down from seven balconies, and from the floor to the dizzy heights of the roof sat the grandest ladies with bouquets in their hands, as if they were going to a ball; the gentlemen were all in full dress, and many of them adorned with gold and silver. It was as light as in the brightest sunshine; the music was beautiful, and everything was much grander than in the theater at Copenhagen, although Johanna was there. But surely it was magic! The curtain went up, and here she was too! Here was Johanna, all dressed in gold and silk, with a golden crown on her head. She sang as only an angel can sing, coming down to the footlights as far as she could.

She smiled as only Johanna could smile, and looked straight at Kanut.

The poor fellow seized his master's hand and shouted "Johanna"; but no one else heard him, the music drowning everything. His master nodded, saying, "Yes, her name is Johanna"; and with that he took out a printed paper and showed Kanut her name, written out at length.

No, it was not a dream. Every one applauded and threw flowers and wreaths to her, and every time that she went off, she was called back; she was continually going off and coming on.

In the street the people crowded round her carriage and drew it along; Kanut was among the foremost and shouted the most lustily. When they had reached her house, which was all beautifully illuminated, he stood at the carriage-door, which sprang open, and Johanna got out. The light fell upon her sweet face, and she, though deeply moved, smilingly returned her thanks in a kind, friendly way. Kanut looked her straight in the face, and she looked full into his, but she did not know him. A man, on whose breast sparkled a star, gave her his arm—they were betrothed, people said.

Then Kanut went home and packed his knapsack; he felt that he must get back to his native place, to the elder and the willow-tree. Under that dear old willow-tree!—One can run over a whole lifetime in an hour.

The old couple begged him to stay, but no words could keep him back. It was all in vain that they reminded him of the coming winter, and told him that snow had already fallen on the mountains; he would be able, he said, to get along, with his knapsack on his back and supported by his staff, in the track of the slow rolling wagons, for which a way would have to be made.

He marched along towards the mountains, and crossing them descended into the valley; though wearied, he saw neither village nor house, and continued his march northwards. The stars gleamed overhead, his knees gave way, and his head became dizzy; down in the valley stars shone forth too, and it seemed as if the sky were also beneath him. He felt ill; the stars below became more numerous, and grew brighter and brighter, moving to and fro. It was a little town in which lights were flickering, and when he comprehended this he exerted his remaining strength and reached a miserable inn.

He remained there for the night and for the whole of the following day, for his body required rest and nourishment; it was thawing, and rain was falling in the valley. But early on the next morning a minstrel came into the village playing an air from Kanut's home, and then it was impossible for him to tarry any longer. He continued his journey towards the north, marching for days and days with such haste as if he were anxious to get home before all were dead there; but to no one did he speak of his longing; no one would have believed in the sorrow of his heart, the deepest sorrow that can exist. Such grief is not for the world, it is not entertaining—not even for friends; and he was a stranger in the strange lands through which he was passing to his home in the north.

It was evening; he was walking along the public high-road. The frost was beginning to make itself felt, and the country was becoming more and more flat, with more fields and meadows. By the road stood a large willow-tree;

everything looked so very home-like that he sat down under it. He felt very tired, his head began to nod, and his eyes closed in slumber, but still he knew that the willow-tree stretched its hanging branches out over him; the tree seemed to him to be an old mighty man. It seemed to be old willow-father himself, who took him up in his arms, and carried him, his tired son, back to the old homeland, to the open bleak shore of Kjöge, to the garden of his childhood's days. It was indeed the willow-tree itself, from Kjöge, which had wandered out in the world to seek him; now it had found him, and had led him back to the little garden by the brook, and here stood Johanna in her splendor, as he had last seen her, and crying out "Welcome" to him.

Before him stood two peculiar forms, although they seemed much more human than when he had seen them in his childhood, for they too had altered; they were the two gingerbread cakes, the man and the woman, turning their right side towards him and looking very well.

"Many thanks," said they to Kanut. "You have loosened our tongues to freely express our thoughts, otherwise nothing would come of them, and now something has come of them: we are engaged."

Then they went hand in hand through the streets of Kjöge and looked very respectable even on their wrong side—there was no fault to be found with them. They walked straight towards the church, Kanut and Johanna following; the latter also went hand in hand, and the church stood there just as ever, with its red walls, clad with green ivy. Both the great doors of the church flew open, the organ pealed forth, and they walked up the broad aisle.

"Our master first," said the gingerbread bridal pair, making way for Kanut and Johanna, who knelt down at the altar; she bent her head over his face and icy-cold tears fell from her eyes. It was the ice round her heart melting by his strong love; the tears fell upon his burning cheeks and—awoke him, and he found himself sitting under the old willow-tree, in a strange land, on a cold wintry evening. From the clouds fell icy hail and beat upon. his face.

"That was the most beautiful hour of my life," said he, "and it was—a dream. Oh God! let me dream again!" He closed his eyes once more; he slept and dreamed.

Towards morning snow fell. The wind blew it in drifts over him, but he slept on. The villagers going to church found a working lad sitting by the roadside; he was dead, frozen to death—under the willow-tree.

Jack Dreadnought

(Traditional Magyar Tale)

A poor widow had a son who was so courageous that not even the devil's mother would have frightened him, and therefore he was named in his childhood Jack Dreadnought. His mother was in continual terror lest something dreadful might happen to her son, as he was so plucky, nay foolhardy, and determined to use all possible means to teach him to fear. For this reason she sent him to the clergyman of the village as "mendicant," and requested the minister to use all his knowledge in trying to teach her son to fear. The clergyman left nothing untried to make the boy frightened; he told him all sorts of ghostly and horrible tales, but these, instead of frightening the lad, made him only more anxious to make the acquaintance of ghosts similar to those mentioned in the tales. The clergyman thereupon hit upon the idea of introducing some sham ghosts in order to break Jack Dreadnought's intrepidity.

He fixed upon the three nights before Christmas; on these nights the lad had to go to ring the bells at midnight in the tower that stood at the very end of the village, and the clergyman thought that he could find some opportunity of frightening Jack. He took an old cassock and stuffed it with straw and placed it before the tower door with one hand on the handle. Midnight came and Jack went to ring the bells and discovered the dummy in the cassock. "Who are you?" he called out, but received no reply. "Very well," said the boy, "if you won't answer I will tell you this, that if you don't clear off from that door I'll kick you in the stomach that you will turn twelve somersaults." As there was no reply, Jack in his rage took hold of the dummy's collar and threw him on the ground with such violence that it rolled away three fathoms, and then, as if nothing had happened, went up into the tower, rang the bells, and went home. The clergyman, as his first experiment did not succeed, made two dummies the next day, which were exactly alike; one he placed in the same position as before at the door of the tower, the other near the bell ropes.

At midnight Jack again went to ring the bells and, as before, made short work of the first dummy; as he did not receive any reply he took him by the collar and threw him on the ground. When he went up into the tower and saw that the rope was held by another, he thought it was the first one, and thus addressed him, "Well, my friend, you've come here, have you? You hadn't enough with the first fall? Answer me or I will dash you on the ground so that you will not be able to get up again," and as the dummy did not reply Jack took it by the throat and pitched it from the window of the tower, and it whizzed through the air. The clergyman had had two unsuccessful experiments but he had great confidence in the third. He made three dummies this time, two were placed as before and the third he stood on the bell so that it might prevent it ringing. Jack Dreadnought dealt with the two first dummies as on the previous night, but as he was about to ring, to his astonishment, he discovered the dummy on the bell; he was not frightened, but when he saw that it would not come down, after a polite request, took it angrily by one leg and pitched it through the window like a cat. The clergyman had now come to the conclusion that he was unable to teach Jack fear, and now commenced to plan how he might get rid of him. The next morning he called him, and thus spoke to him: "Jack, you are a fine courageous fellow; go, take my gray horse, and as much provisions as you think will last you three days, and go into the world and follow your nose; do not stop all day, but take up your night quarters wherever darkness finds you. Do this for three days, and settle down where you spend the third night, and you will be prosperous."

The clergyman thought that Jack would perish on the way; but we shall see whether he did. Jack started off the first day, and in the evening came to a narrow, round timber hut, which was rather high, and he decided to sleep there. As he found it empty he made a fire in its center and commenced to fry some bacon; all of a sudden he felt something dripping, he looked up and saw something like a human form dangling in the air. "Well, upon my word," shouted he, "the devil won't leave me alone even here: get down from there, will you, or do you expect me to take you down?" No reply came, and Jack, with a clever jump, caught hold of one of his legs, and brought it down, but the head was torn off and fell down. Only then he discovered that it was a hanged man, but he did not think much of it, and stayed there all night. He traveled the whole of the next day; in the evening he reached an inn and asked for a room, and received in reply that they had an empty room on the upper floor, the only one vacant; but that no one could sleep there, as the place was haunted. "What!" shouted Jack; "Oh! I know those ghosts; let me have a dish of good food, a mouthful of good wine, and a burning candle in the upper room, and I will sleep there. I swear by Beelzebub that the ghosts will come no more!" The innkeeper tried to dissuade Jack from his foolhardy attempt, but he would not give way.

He was shown into the room; it was a large apartment on the upper floor. Jack placed the lighted candle in the middle; a dishful of food and a jug of wine by the side of it; and settled own in a chair, waiting for the awful ghosts. No sooner had the clock struck midnight than, all of a sudden, a fearful chorus of animal noises was to he heard, like the howling of dogs, neighing of horses, bellowing of cattle, roaring of wild beasts, bleating of sheep and of goats, and also crying, laughing, and clanking of chains. Jack was quite delighted with the nocturnal concert; but, all of a sudden a big skull rolled in through the door and stopped by the side of the dish. Jack stared at it, and, instead of the skull, he saw an old monk standing before him with long heavy chains. "Good evening, brother friar!" shouted Jack, "pray have supper with me." "I'm going from here," said the friar, "and I want you to come too; I will show you something." "With pleasure," replied Jack, "will you lead the way, you devil, or you reverend gentleman?" Thereupon Jack followed the friar with the lighted candle. When they arrived at the stairs the friar insisted upon his going first, but Jack would not; and the friar was obliged to lead the way. Next they came to a narrow landing at the top of the cellar stairs. Here, again, the friar invited him to go first, but he would not; and so the apparition had to go first. But, as soon as he went down a few steps, Jack gave the friar such a push with such dexterity that he went head over heels down the steps and broke his neck. In the morning the innkeeper had the friar buried. He made Jack a handsome present, and the latter continued his journey.

Jack Dreadnought rode the whole next day, and in the evening again came to an inn, where he could not get any room except up stairs, where no one else would sleep, on account of ghostly visitors. Jack took the room and was again enjoying his supper in the center, when the old clock struck midnight. The same sort of music struck his ear as on the previous night, and, amid a great crash, a human hand dropped from the ceiling to near his dish. Jack, in cold blood, took up the hand and threw it behind the door. Another hand fell and went the same way. Now a leg came, and this, too, went behind the door. Then came its fellow, which was soon despatched to the rest. At last

126

a big skull dropped right into the middle of the dish and broke it. Jack got into a rage, and threw the skull violently behind the door; and, on looking back, he found, instead of the limbs, an immense ghost standing behind the door, whom Jack at once taxed with the damage done to the dish, demanding payment. The ghost replied, "Very well; I will pay for it, if you come with me." Jack consented, and they went off together; as before, he always insisted on the ghost going first. They came to a long winding staircase, and down into a huge cellar. Jack opened his eyes and mouth wide when he found in the cellar three vats full of gold, six vats of silver, and twelve vats of copper coins. Then the ghost said to him, "There, choose a vat full of coins for your dish, and take it whenever you like." But Jack, however, did not touch the money, but replied, "Not I; do you suppose that 1 will carry that money? Whoever brought it here, let him take it away." "Well done," replied the ghost; "I see I've found my man at last. Had you touched the treasure you would have died a sudden death; but now, since you are such a fine courageous fellow, the like of whom I have never seen before, settle down in this place and use the treasure in peace; nobody will ever disturb or haunt you any more." After these words the ghost disappeared.

Jack became the owner of the immense treasure, and married the innkeeper's only daughter, who was very pretty, and lives with her to this day, if he has not died since, enjoying life and spending the money he found in the vats in the cellar.

Tilly's Christmas

LOUISA MAY ALCOTT

I'm so glad to-morrow is Christmas, because I'm going to have lots of presents."

"So am I glad, though I don't expect any presents but a pair of mittens."

"And so am I; but I sha'n't have any presents at all."

As the three little girls trudged home from school they said these things, and as Tilly spoke, both the others looked at her with pity and some surprise, for she spoke cheerfully, and they wondered how she could be happy when she was so poor she could have no presents on Christmas.

"Don't you wish you could find a purse full of money right here in the path?" said Kate, the child who was going to have "lots of presents."

"Oh, don't I, if I could keep it honestly!" and Tilly's eyes shone at the very thought.

"What would you buy?" asked Bessy, rubbing her cold hands, and longing for her mittens.

"I'd buy a pair of large, warm blankets, a load of wood, a shawl for mother, and a pair of shoes for me; and if there was enough left, I'd give Bessie a new hat, and then she needn't wear Ben's old felt one," answered Tilly.

The girls laughed at that; but Bessy pulled the funny hat over her ears, and said she was much obliged, but she'd rather have candy.

"Let's look, and may be we can find a purse. People are always going about with money at Christmas-time, and some one may lose it here," said Kate.

So, as they went along the snowy road, they looked about them, half in earnest, half in fun. Suddenly, Tilly sprang forward, exclaiming,—

"I see it! I've found it!"

The others followed, but all stopped disappointed; for it wasn't a purse, it was only a little bird. It lay upon the snow with its wings spread and feebly fluttering, as if too weak to fly. Its little feet were benumbed with cold; its once bright eyes were dull with pain, and instead of a blithe song, it could only utter a faint chirp, now and then, as if crying for help.

"Nothing but a stupid old robin. How provoking!" cried Kate, sitting down to rest.

"I sha'n't touch it; I found one once, and took care of it, and the ungrateful thing flew away the minute it was well," said Bessy, creeping under Kate's shawl, and putting her hands under her chin to warm them.

"Poor little birdie! How pitiful he looks, and how glad he must be to see some one coming to help him. I'll take him up gently, and carry him home to mother. Don't be frightened, dear, I'm your friend;" and Tilly knelt down in the snow, stretching her hand to the bird with the tenderest pity in her face.

Kate and Bessy laughed.

"Don't stop for that thing; it's getting late and cold: let's go on and look for the purse," they said, moving away.

"You wouldn't leave it to die!" cried Tilly. "I'd rather have the bird than the money; so I sha'n't look any more. The purse wouldn't be mine, and I should only be tempted to keep it; but this poor thing will thank and love me, and I'm so glad I came in time."

Gently lifting the bird, Tilly felt its tiny cold claws cling to her hand, and saw its dim eyes brighten as it nestled down with a grateful chirp.

"Now I've got a Christmas present after all," she said, smiling, as they walked on. "I always wanted a bird, and this one will be such a pretty pet for me."

"He'll fly away the first chance he gets, and die anyhow; so you'd better not waste your time over him," said Bessy.

"He can't pay you for taking care of him, and my mother says it isn't worth while to help folks that can't help us," added Kate.

"My mother says, 'Do as you'd be done by'; and I'm sure I'd like any one to help me, if I was dying of cold and hunger. 'Love your neighbor as yourself,' is another of her sayings. This bird is my little neighbor, and I'll love him and care for him, as I often wish our rich neighbor would love and care for us," answered Tilly, breathing her warm breath over the benumbed bird, who looked up at her with confiding eyes, quick to feel and know a friend.

"What a funny girl you are," said Kate, "caring for that silly bird, and talking about loving your neighbor in that sober way. Mr. King don't care a bit for you, and never will, though he knows how poor you are; so I don't think your plan amounts to much."

"I believe it, though; and shall do my part anyway. Good-night. I hope you'll have a merry Christmas, and lots of pretty things," answered Tilly, as they parted.

Her eyes were full, and she felt so poor as she went on alone toward the little old house where she lived. It would have been so pleasant to know that she was going to have some of the pretty things all children love to find in their full stockings on Christmas morning. And pleasanter still to have been able to give her mother something nice. So many comforts were needed, and there was no hope of getting them; for they could barely get food and fire.

"Never mind, birdie, we'll make the best of what we have, and be merry in spite of everything. You shall have a happy Christmas, anyway; and I know God won't forget us, if every one else does."

She stopped a minute to wipe her eyes, and lean her cheek against the bird's soft breast, finding great comfort in the little creature, though it could only love her, nothing more.

"See, mother, what a nice present I've found," she cried, going in with a cheery face that was like sunshine in the dark room.

"I'm glad of that, deary; for I haven't been able to get my little girl anything but a rosy apple. Poor bird! Give it some of your warm bread and milk."

"Why, mother, what a big bowlful! I'm afraid you gave me all the milk," said Tilly, smiling over the nice steaming supper that stood ready for her.

"I've had plenty, dear. Sit down and dry your wet feet, and put the bird in my basket on this warm flannel."

Tilly peeped into the closet and saw nothing there but dry bread.

"Mother's given me all the milk, and is going without her tea, 'cause she knows I'm hungry. Now I'll surprise her, and she shall have a good supper too. She is going to split wood, and I'll fix it while she's gone."

So Tilly put down the old tea-pot, carefully poured out a part of the milk, and from her pocket produced a great plummy bun, that one of the schoolchildren had given her, and she had saved for her mother. A slice of the dry bread was nicely toasted, and the bit of butter set by for her put on it. When her mother came in there was the table drawn up in a warm place, a hot cup of tea ready, and Tilly and birdie waiting for her.

Such a poor little supper, and yet such a happy one; for love, charity, and contentment were guests there, and that Christmas Eve was a blither one than that up at the great house, where lights shone, fires blazed, a great tree glittered, and music sounded, as the children danced and played.

"We must go to bed early, for we've only wood enough to last over to-morrow. I shall be paid for my work the day after, and then we can get some," said Tilly's mother, as they sat by the fire.

"If my bird was only a fairy bird, and would give us three wishes, how nice it would be! Poor dear, he can't give me anything; but it's no matter," answered Tilly, looking at the robin, who lay in the basket with his head under his wing, a mere little feathery bunch.

"He can give you one thing, Tilly,—the pleasure of doing good. That is one of the sweetest things in life; and the poor can enjoy it as well as the rich."

As her mother spoke, with her tired hand softly stroking her little daughter's hair, Tilly suddenly started and pointed to the window, saying, in a frightened whisper,—

"I saw a face,—a man's face, looking in! It's gone now; but I truly saw it."

"Some traveler attracted by the light, perhaps; I'll go and see," And Tilly's mother went to the door.

No one was there. The wind blew cold, the stars shone, the snow lay white on field and wood, and the Christmas moon was glittering in the sky.

"What sort of a face was it?" asked Tilly's mother, coming back.

"A pleasant sort of face, I think; but I was so startled, I don't quite know what it was like. I wish we had a curtain there," said Tilly.

"I like to have our light shine out in the evening; for the road is dark and lonely just here, and the twinkle of our lamp is pleasant to people's eyes as they go by. We can do so little for our neighbors, I am glad to cheer the way for them. Now put these poor old shoes to dry, and go to bed, deary; I'll come soon."

Tilly went, taking her bird with her to sleep in his basket near by, lest he should be lonely in the night.

Soon the little house was dark and still, and no one saw the Christmas spirits at their work that night.

When Tilly opened the door next morning, she gave a loud cry, clapped her hands, and then stood still, quite speechless with wonder and delight. There, before the door, lay a great pile of wood, all ready to burn, a big bundle and a basket, with a lovely nosegay of winter roses, holly, and evergreen tied to the handle.

"Oh, mother, did the fairies do it?" cried Tilly, pale with her happiness, as she seized the basket while her mother took in the bundle.

"Yes, dear, the best and dearest fairy in the world, called 'Charity.' She walks abroad at Christmas time, does beautiful deeds like this, and does not stay to be thanked," answered her mother with full eyes, as she undid the parcel.

There they were,—the warm, thick blankets, the comfortable shawl, the new shoes, and, best of all, a pretty winter hat for Bessy. The basket was full of good things to eat, and on the flowers lay a paper saying, —

"For the little girl who loves her neighbor as herself."

"Mother, I really think my bird is a fairy bird, and all these splendid things come from him," said Tilly, laughing and crying with joy.

It really did seem so, for, as she spoke, the robin flew to the table, hopped to the nosegay, and perching among the roses, began to chirp with all his little might. The sun streamed in on flowers, bird, and happy child, and no one saw a shadow glide away from the window; no one ever knew that Mr. King had seen and heard the little girls the night before, or dreamed that the rich neighbor had learned a lesson from the poor neighbor.

And Tilly's bird was a fairy bird; for by her love and tenderness to the helpless thing, she brought good gifts to herself, happiness to the unknown giver of them, and a faithful little friend who did not fly away, but stayed with her till the snow was gone, making summer for her in the winter-time.

Adventures of an Indian Brave

(FROM THE ORANGE FAIRY BOOK)

A long, long way off, right away in the west of America, there once lived an old man who had one son. The country round was covered with forests, in which dwelt all kinds of wild beasts, and the young man and his companions used to spend whole days in hunting them, and he was the finest hunter of all the tribe.

One morning, when winter was coming on, the youth and his companions set off as usual to bring back some of the mountain goats and deer to be salted down, as he was afraid of a snow-storm; and if the wind blew and the snow drifted the forest might be impassable for some weeks. The old man and the wife, however, would not go out, but remained in the wigwam making bows and arrows.

It soon grew so cold in the forest that at last one of the men declared they could walk no more, unless they could manage to warm themselves.

"That is easily done," said the leader, giving a kick to a large tree. Flames broke out in the trunk, and before it had burnt up they were as hot as if it had been summer. Then they started off to the place where the goats and deer were to be found in the greatest numbers, and soon had killed as many as they wanted. But the leader killed most, as he was the best shot.

"Now we must cut up the game and divide it," said he; and so they did, each one taking his own share; and, walking one behind the other, set out for the village. But when they reached a great river the young man did not want the trouble of carrying his pack any further, and left it on the bank.

"I am going home another way," he told his companions. And taking another road he reached the village long before they did.

"Have you returned with empty hands?" asked the old man, as his son opened the door.

"Have I *ever* done that, that you put me such a question?" asked the youth. "No; I have slain enough to feast us for many moons, but it was heavy, and I left the pack on the bank of the great river. Give me the arrows, I will finish making them, and you can go to the river and bring home the pack!"

So the old man rose and went, and strapped the meat on his shoulder; but as he was crossing the ford the strap broke and the pack fell into the river. He stooped to catch it, but it swirled past him. He clutched again; but in doing so he over-balanced himself and was hurried into some rapids, where he was knocked against some rocks, and he sank and was drowned, and his body was carried down the stream into smoother water when it rose to the surface again. But by this time it had lost all likeness to a man, and was changed into a piece of wood.

The wood floated on, and the river got bigger and bigger and entered a new country. There it was borne by the current close to the shore, and a woman who was down there washing her clothes caught it as it passed, and drew it out, saying to herself: "What a nice smooth plank! I will use it as a table to put my food upon." And gathering up her clothes she took the plank with her into her hut.

When her supper time came she stretched the board across two strings which hung from the roof, and set upon it the pot containing a stew that smelled very good. The woman had been working hard all day and was very hungry, so she took her biggest spoon and plunged it into the pot. But what was her astonishment and disgust when both pot and food vanished instantly before her!

"Oh, you horrid plank, you have brought me ill-luck!" she cried. And taking it up she flung it away from her.

The woman had been surprised before at the disappearance of her food, but she was more astonished still when, instead of the plank, she beheld a baby. However, she was fond of children and had none of her own, so she made up her mind that she would keep it and take care of it. The baby grew and throve as no baby in that country had ever done, and in four days he was a man, and as tall and strong as any brave of the tribe.

"You have treated me well," he said, "and meat shall never fail to your house. But now I must go, for I have much work to do."

Then he set out for his home.

It took him many days to get there, and when he saw his son sitting in his place his anger was kindled, and his heart was stirred to take vengeance upon him. So he went out quickly into the forest and shed tears, and each tear became a bird. "Stay there till I want you," said he; and he returned to the hut.

"I saw some pretty new birds, high up in a tree yonder," he remarked. And the son answered: "Show me the way and I will get them for dinner."

The two went out together, and after walking for about half an hour the old man stopped. "That is the tree," he said. And the son began to climb it.

Now a strange thing happened. The higher the young man climbed the higher the birds seemed to be, and when he looked down the earth below appeared no bigger than a star. Sill he tried to go back, but he could not, and though he could not see the birds any longer he felt as if something were dragging him up and up.

He thought that he had been climbing that tree for days, and perhaps he had, for suddenly a beautiful country, yellow with fields of maize, stretched before him, and he gladly left the top of the tree and entered it. He walked through the maize without knowing where he was going, when he heard a sound of knocking, and saw two old blind women crushing their food between two stones. He crept up to them on tiptoe, and when one old woman passed her dinner to the other he held out his hand and took it and ate if for himself.

"How slow you are kneading that cake," cried the other old woman at last.

"Why, I have given you your dinner, and what more do you want?" replied the second.

"You didn't; at least I never got it," said the other.

"I certainly thought you took it from me; but here is some more." And again the young man stretched out his hand; and the two old women fell to quarreling afresh. But when it happened for the third time the old women suspected some trick, and one of them exclaimed:

"I am sure there is a man here; tell me, are you not my grandson?"

"Yes," answered the young man, who wished to please her, "and in return for your good dinner I will see if I cannot restore your sight; for I was taught in the art of healing by the best medicine man in the tribe." And with that he left them, and wandered about till he found the herb which he wanted. Then he hastened back to the old women, and begging them to boil him some water, he threw the herb in. As soon as the pot began to sing he took off the lid, and sprinkled the eyes of the women, and sight came back to them once more.

There was no night in that country, so, instead of going to bed very early, as he would have done in his own hut, the young man took another walk. A splashing noise near by drew him down to a valley through which ran a large river, and up a waterfall some salmon were leaping. How their silver sides glistened in the light, and how he longed to catch some of the great fellows! But how could he do it? He had beheld no one except the old women, and it was not very likely that they would be able to help him. So with a sigh he turned away and went back to them, but, as he walked, a thought struck him. He pulled out one of his hairs which hung nearly to his waist, and it instantly became a strong line, nearly a mile in length.

"Weave me a net that I may catch some salmon," said he. And they wove him the net he asked for, and for many weeks he watched by the river, only going back to the old women when he wanted a fish cooked.

At last, one day, when he was eating his dinner, the old woman who always spoke first, said to him:

"We have been very glad to see you, grandson, but now it is time that you went home." And pushing aside a rock, he saw a deep hole, *so* deep that he could not see to the bottom. Then they dragged a basket out of the house, and tied a rope to it. "Get in, and wrap this blanket round your head," said they; "and, whatever happens, don't uncover it till you get to the bottom." Then they bade him farewell, and he curled himself up in the basket.

Down, down, down he went; would he *ever* stop going? But when the basket *did* stop, the young man forgot what he had been told, and put his head out to see what was the matter. In an instant the basket moved, but, to his horror, instead of going down, he felt himself being drawn upwards, and shortly after he beheld the faces of the old women.

"You will never see your wife and son if you will not do as you are bid," said they. "Now get in, and do not stir till you hear a crow calling."

This time the young man was wiser, and though the basket often stopped, and strange creatures seemed to rest on him and to pluck at his blanket, he held it tight till he heard the crow calling. Then he flung off the blanket and sprang out, while the basket vanished in the sky.

He walked on quickly down the track that led to the hut, when, before him, he saw his wife with his little son on her back.

"Oh! there is father at last," cried the boy; but the mother bade him cease from idle talking.

"But, mother, it is true; father is coming!" repeated the child. And, to satisfy him, the woman turned round and perceived her husband.

Oh, how glad they all were to be together again! And when the wind whistled through the forest, and the snow stood in great banks round the door, the father used to take the little boy on his knee and tell him how he caught salmon in the Land of the Sun.

The Town Mouse and the Country Mouse

PETER CHRISTEN ASBJØRNSEN

Once upon a time a town mouse met a country mouse on the outskirts of a wood. The country mouse was sitting under a hazel thicket plucking nuts.

"Busy harvesting, I see," said the town mouse. "Who would think of our meeting in this out-of-the-way part of the world?"

"Just so," said the country mouse.

"You are gathering nuts for your winter store?" said the town mouse.

"I am obliged to do so if we intend having anything to live upon during the winter," said the country mouse.

"The husk is big and the nut full this year, enough to satisfy any hungry body," said the town mouse.

"Yes, you are right there," said the country mouse; and then she related how well she lived and how comfortable she was at home.

The town mouse maintained that she was the better off, but the country mouse said that nowhere could one be so well off as in the woods and hills. The town mouse, however, declared she was best off; and as they could not agree on this point they promised to visit one another at Christmas, then they could see for themselves which was really the most comfortable.

The first visit was to be paid by the town mouse.

Now, although the country mouse had moved down from the mountains for the winter, the road was long and tiring and one had to travel up hill and down dale; the snow lay thick and deep, so the town mouse found it hard work to get on and she became both tired and hungry before she reached the end of her journey.

How nice it will be to get some food, she thought.

The country mouse had scraped together the best she had. There were nut kernels, polypoly and other sorts of roots, and many other good things which grow in woods and fields. She kept it all in a hole far under the ground, so the frost could not reach it, and close by was a running spring, open all the winter, so she could drink as much water as she liked. There was an abundance of all she had, and they ate both well and heartily; but the town mouse thought it was very poor fare indeed.

"One can, of course, keep body and soul together on this," said she; "but I don't think much of it. Now you must be good enough to visit me and taste what we have."

Yes, that she would, and before long she set out. The town mouse had gathered together all the scraps from the Christmas fare which the woman of the house had dropped on the floor during the holidays—bits of cheese, butter and tallow ends, cake-crumbs, pastry and many other good things. In the dish under the ale-tap she had drink enough; in fact, the place was full of all kinds of dainties.

They ate and fared well; the country mouse seemed never to have had enough; she had never tasted such delicacies. But then she became thirsty, for she found the food both strong and rich, and now she wanted something to drink.

"We haven't far to go for the beer we shall drink," said the town mouse, and jumped upon the edge of the dish and drank till she was no longer thirsty; she did not drink too much, for she knew the Christmas beer was strong. The country mouse, however, thought the beer a splendid drink; she had never tasted anything but water, so she took one sip after another, but as she could not stand strong drink she became tipsy before she left the dish.

The drink got into her head and down into her toes and she began running and jumping about from one beer barrel to the other, and to dance and tumble about on the shelves amongst the cups and mugs; she squeaked and screeched as if she were both drunk and mad. About her being drunk there was very little doubt.

"You must not carry on as if you had just come from the backwoods and make such a row and noise," said the town mouse; "the master of the house is a bailiff and he is very strict indeed," she added.

The country mouse said she didn't care either for bailiffs or beggars. But the cat sat at the top of the cellar steps, lying in wait, and heard all the chatter and noise. When the woman of the house went down to draw some beer and lifted the trap door the cat slipped by into the cellar and struck its claws into the country mouse. Then there was quite another sort of dance.

The town mouse slid back into her hole and sat in safety looking on, while the country mouse suddenly became sober when she felt the claws of the cat in her back.

"Oh, my dear bailiff, oh, dearest bailiff, be merciful and spare my life and I will tell you a fairy tale," she said.

"Well, go on," said the cat.

"Once upon a time there were two little mice," said the country mouse, squeaking slowly and pitifully, for she wanted to make the story last as long as she could.

"Then they were not lonely," said the cat dryly and curtly.

"And they had a steak which they were going to fry."

"Then they could not starve," said the eat.

"And they put it out on the roof to cool," said the country mouse.

"Then they did not burn themselves," said the cat.

"But there came a fox and a crow and ate it all up," said the country mouse.

"Then I'll eat you," said the cat. But just at that moment the woman shut the trap door with a slam, which so startled the cat that she let go her hold of the mouse. One bound, and the country mouse found herself in the hole with the town mouse.

From there a passage led out into the snow, and you may be sure the country mouse did not wait long before she set out homewards.

138

"And this is what you call living well and being best off," she said to the town mouse. "Heaven preserve me from having such a fine place and such a master! Why, I only just got away with my life!"

Twelve by the Mail

Hans Christian Andersen

It was intensely cold, the sky was studded with stars, there was no breath of air stirring.

"Boom!" An old earthen pot was flung against the neighbor's door. "Bang, bang!" A gun was fired off. They were greeting the New Year. It was New Year's Eve! The church-clock was striking Midnight.

"Ta-ta-ra, ta-ta-ra!" The heavy mail-coach came lumbering up and stopped before the gate of the town. There were twelve passengers in it, for all seats were occupied.

"Hip, hip, hurrah!" cried the people in the houses of the town, where they were keeping New Year's Night, and rose when the clock struck twelve with their glasses in their hands, drinking the health of the New Year.

"A Happy New Year to you!" was the cry. "A pretty wife! plenty of money! no trouble and sorrow!"

Such were the good wishes expressed amid clinking of glasses. There was singing and ringing! Before the gate of the town stopped the mail-coach with twelve guests, the passengers.

And who were these strangers? Each of them had his passport and luggage with him; they even brought presents for you, for me, and for all the inhabitants of the little town. But who were they, what did they intend to do, and what did they bring with them?

"Good morning!" they called out to the sentry at the town-gate

"Good morning!" answered the sentry, for the clock had already struck twelve o'clock.

"Your names? your business?" the sentry asked the first who left the coach.

139

"Look for yourself in my passport," replied the man. "I am I!" And he was indeed a man, clad in a large bearskin and wearing fur boots. "I am the man on whom many people set their hopes. Come and see me to-morrow and I shall give you a New Year's gift. I throw coppers and silver among the people, and give balls—to wit, thirty-one; but more nights I cannot sacrifice. My ships are frozen in, but in my office it is warm and pleasant. My name is January; I am a merchant, and carry all my accounts with me."

Then the second alighted from the coach. He was a jovial fellow; he was theatrical manager, arranger of masquerades and all sorts of amusements that one could think of. His luggage consisted of a big cask.

"We shall drive the cat out of this cask at carnival time," he said. "I shall give you and myself pleasure. We shall be merry every day. I have not too long to live—in fact, of all the family my life is the shortest, for I shall only become twenty-eight days old. Sometimes they allow me one day more, but I don't trouble myself about that. Hurrah!"

"You must not shout so!" said the sentry.

"Why shouldn't I?" replied the man. "I am Prince Carnival, traveling under the name of Februarius."

Then the third left the coach. He looked the very picture of fasting; he carried his nose very high, for he was related to the "forty knights," and he was a weather-prophet. But this is not a remunerative trade, and therefore he was in favor of fasting. He had a bunch of violets in his button-hole, but it was very small.

"March, March!" cried the fourth after him, slapping his shoulders, "do you not smell something? Come quick into the guardroom; they are drinking punch there, which is your favorite beverage; I can smell it outside. March, Mr. Martius!" But it was not true, he only wished to tease him by making him an April fool; for with such merriment the fourth generally made his entrance into the town. He looked very smart, worked but very little, and kept more holidays than others. "I wish there was a little more steadiness in the world," he said, "but sometimes one is in good, sometimes in bad, humor, always according to circumstances; one has continually to change one's dress, for sometimes it rains and sometimes the sun shines. I am a sort of house-agent and undertaker; I can laugh and weep according to circumstances. I have my summer-clothes here in my portmanteau, but it would be foolish to put them on. Here I am! On Sundays I take a walk in shoes and white silk stockings, and with a muff."

After him a lady alighted from the coach. Her name was Miss May. She wore a summer dress and galoshes, her frock was of a light green, and anemones adorned her hair; she smelt so strongly of thyme that the sentry could not help sneezing. "Health and prosperity to you," she said, greeting him. How pretty she was! She was a singer, but not a theatrical vocalist, nor a ballad-singer; she was a songstress of the grove; she roamed about in the green forests and sang for her own pleasure and amusement.

"Now comes the young married woman," they cried from inside the coach, and a young, beautiful and distinguished-looking woman stepped out. One could see that Mrs. June was not accustomed to do much for herself, but rather to be waited upon. On the longest day in the year she gave a great dinner-party, that her guests might have time to eat the numerous courses which were served. Although she had her own carriage, she traveled like the others by the mail, in order to show people that she was not haughty. But she was not unaccompanied, for her younger brother Julius was with her. He looked very well fed, wore summer clothes and a straw hat. He had but little luggage, as it was burdensome to carry in the great heat; he had only a pair of bathing-drawers with him.

Then the mother alighted, Mrs. August, a wholesale fruiterer, the proprietress of many fish-ponds and a farmer, wearing a large crinoline; she was stout and hot, worked hard, and carried the beer out to her laborers in the field herself. "In the sweat of thy brow thou shalt eat thy bread," she used to say; "that is written in the Bible. When the work is done follow the excursions into the country, dance and play under the green trees, and the harvest festivals." She was an excellent housekeeper.

After her a man came out of the coach who was a painter; he was the famous colorist, September; he would repair to the woods and change the color of the leaves according to his ideas; and soon it gleamed with crimson, russet, and gold. The master could whistle like a starling; he was a quick worker, and decorated his beer-jug with a twining branch of hops, so that it looked beautiful; he had a strong sense of beauty. There he stood with his color-box, which made up his whole luggage.

He was followed by a landowner, who only thought of ploughing and preparing the field in the seed-month, and who was fond of field sports.

Mr. October had his dog and gun with him, and carried nuts in his game-bag. "Crack, crack!" He had a great deal of luggage, including even an English plow; he talked about agriculture, but on account of the coughing and groaning of his neighbor one could not hear much of it.

It was November who coughed so much when he got out. He suffered a great deal from colds, and blew his nose continually; and yet he declared that he must accompany the servant-girls to their new places and initiate them into their winter service; his cold, he thought, would soon be better when he began woodcutting, for he was a master woodcutter, and the president of the guild. He passed his evenings cutting wood for skates, for he knew well, he said, that in a few weeks these articles would be in great demand for the people's amusement.

Finally, the last passenger made her appearance—the old mother December, carrying a foot-warmer with her. The old woman was shivering with cold, but her eyes were as bright as two stars. She held a flower-pot in her arm, in which a little fir-tree was growing. "This tree," she said, "I will take care of and cherish, that it may thrive and grow very tall, till Christmas Eve; it must reach from the floor to the ceiling, and will be covered with glittering lights, gilded apples, and cut-out figures. The foot-warmer warms me like a stove; I shall take a story-book out of my pocket and read it aloud, until all the children in the room are quiet, and all the little figures on the tree become alive; and the little wax angel on the top of the tree opens his wings of tinsel, flies down from his green resting-place, and kisses all the children and grown-up people in the room. Nay, he also kisses the poor children who stand outside in the street and sing the Christmas song of the 'Star of Bethlehem.'"

"Well, the coach may drive off," said the sentry, "now we have all the twelve. And the luggage cart may come up."

"First let the twelve come in to me," said the captain of the guard, "one after the other. I shall keep their passports here; they are all available for one month; when it is gone I shall give them a character on the passports. Now, Mr. January, please walk in."

And Mr. January accepted the invitation.

When a year is gone, I shall tell you what the twelve passengers have brought you, myself, and all of us. At present I do not know it, and perhaps they do not know it themselves; for it is a strange time we live in.

The Elf Maiden

(FROM *THE BROWN FAIRY BOOK*)

Once upon a time two young men living in a small village fell in love with the same girl. During the winter, it was all night except for an hour or so about noon, when the darkness seemed a little less dark, and then they used to see which of them could tempt her out for a sleigh ride with the Northern Lights flashing above them, or which could persuade her to come to a dance in some neighboring barn. But when the spring began, and the light grew longer, the hearts of the villagers leapt at the sight of the sun, and a day was fixed for the boats to be brought out, and the great nets to be spread in the bays of some islands that lay a few miles to the north. Everybody went on this expedition, and the two young men and the girl went with them.

They all sailed merrily across the sea chattering like a flock of magpies, or singing their favorite songs. And when they reached the shore, what an unpacking there was! For this was a noted fishing ground, and here they would live, in little wooden huts, till autumn and bad weather came round again.

The maiden and the two young men happened to share the same hut with some friends, and fished daily from the same boat. And as time went on, one of the youths remarked that the girl took less notice of him than she did of his companion. At first he tried to think that he was dreaming, and for a long while he kept his eyes shut very tight to what he did not want to see, but in spite of his efforts, the truth managed to wriggle through, and then the young man gave up trying to deceive himself, and set about finding some way to get the better of his rival.

The plan that he hit upon could not be carried out for some months; but the longer the young man thought of it, the more pleased he was with it, so he made no sign of his feelings, and waited patiently till the moment came. This was the very day that they were all going to leave the islands, and sail back to the mainland for the winter. In the bustle and hurry of departure, the cunning fisherman contrived that their boat should be the

143

last to put off, and when everything was ready, and the sails about to be set, he suddenly called out:

"Oh, dear, what shall I do! I have left my best knife behind in the hut. Run, like a good fellow, and get it for me, while I raise the anchor and loosen the tiller."

Not thinking any harm, the youth jumped back on shore and made his way up the steep bank. At the door of the hut he stopped and looked back, then started and gazed in horror. The head of the boat stood out to sea, and he was left alone on the island.

Yes, there was no doubt of it—he was quite alone; and he had nothing to help him except the knife which his comrade had purposely dropped on the ledge of the window. For some minutes he was too stunned by the treachery of his friend to think about anything at all, but after a while he shook himself awake, and determined that he would manage to keep alive somehow, if it were only to revenge himself.

So he put the knife in his pocket and went off to a part of the island which was not so bare as the rest, and had a small grove of trees. From one of these he cut himself a bow, which he strung with a piece of cord that had been left lying about the huts.

When this was ready the young man ran down to the shore and shot one or two sea-birds, which he plucked and cooked for supper.

In this way the months slipped by, and Christmas came round again. The evening before, the youth went down to the rocks and into the copse, collecting all the drift wood the sea had washed up or the gale had blown down, and he piled it up in a great stack outside the door, so that he might not have to fetch any all the next day. As soon as his task was done, he paused and looked out towards the mainland, thinking of Christmas Eve last year, and the merry dance they had had. The night was still and cold, and by the help of the Northern Lights he could almost sea across to the opposite coast, when, suddenly, he noticed a boat, which seemed steering straight for the island. At first he could hardly stand for joy, the chance of speaking to another man was so delightful; but as the boat drew near there was something, he could not tell what, that was different from the boats which he had been used to all his life, and when it touched the shore he saw that the people that filled it were beings of another world than ours. Then he hastily stepped behind the wood stack, and waited for what might happen next.

The strange folk one by one jumped on to the rocks, each bearing a load of something that they wanted. Among the women he remarked two young girls, more beautiful and better dressed than any of the rest, carrying between them two great baskets full of provisions. The young man peeped out cautiously to see what all this crowd could be doing inside the tiny hut, but in a moment he drew back again, as the girls returned, and looked about as if they wanted to find out what sort of a place the island was.

Their sharp eyes soon discovered the form of a man crouching behind the bundles of sticks, and at first they felt a little frightened, and started as if they would run away. But the youth remained so still, that they took courage and laughed gaily to each other. "What a strange creature, let us try what he is made of," said one, and she stooped down and gave him a pinch.

Now the young man had a pin sticking in the sleeve of his jacket, and the moment the girl's hand touched him she pricked it so sharply that the blood came. The girl screamed so loudly that the people all ran out of their huts to see what was the matter. But directly they caught sight of the man they turned and fled in the other direction, and picking up the goods they had brought with them scampered as fast as they could down to the shore. In an instant, boat, people, and goods had vanished completely.

In their hurry they had, however, forgotten two things: a bundle of keys which lay on the table, and the girl whom the pin had pricked, and who now stood pale and helpless beside the wood stack.

"You will have to make me your wife," she said at last, "for you have drawn my blood, and I belong to you."

"Why not? I am quite willing," answered he. "But how do you suppose we can manage to live till summer comes round again?"

"Do not be anxious about that," said the girl; "if you will only marry me all will be well. I am very rich, and all my family are rich also."

Then the young man gave her his promise to make her his wife, and the girl fulfilled her part of the bargain, and food was plentiful on the island all through the long winter months, though he never knew how it got there. And by-and-by it was spring once more, and time for the fisher-folk to sail from the mainland.

"Where are we to go now?" asked the girl, one day, when the sun seemed brighter and the wind softer than usual.

"I do not care where I go," answered the young man; "what do you think?"

The girl replied that she would like to go somewhere right at the other end of the island, and build a house, far away from the huts of the fishing-folk. And he consented, and that very day they set off in search of a sheltered spot on the banks of a stream, so that it would be easy to get water.

In a tiny bay, on the opposite side of the island they found the very thing, which seemed to have been made on purpose for them; and as they were tired with their long walk, they laid themselves down on a bank of moss among some birches and prepared to have a good night's rest, so as to be fresh for work next day. But before she went to sleep the girl turned to her husband, and said: "If in your dreams you fancy that you hear strange noises, be sure you do not stir, or get up to see what it is."

"Oh, it is not likely we shall hear any noises in such a quiet place," answered he, and fell sound asleep.

Suddenly he was awakened by a great clatter about his ears, as if all the workmen in the world were sawing and hammering and building close to him. He was just going to spring up and go to see what it meant, when he luckily remembered his wife's words and lay still. But the time till morning seemed very long, and with the first ray of sun they both rose, and pushed aside the branches of the birch trees. There, in the very place they had chosen, stood a beautiful house—doors and windows, and everything all complete!

"Now you must fix on a spot for your cow-stalls," said the girl, when they had breakfasted off wild cherries; "and take care it is the proper size, neither too large nor too small." And the husband did as he was bid, though he wondered what use a cow-house could be, as they had no cows to put in it. But as he was a little afraid of his wife, who knew so much more than he, he asked no questions.

This night also he was awakened by the same sounds as before, and in the morning they found, near the stream, the most beautiful cow-house that ever was seen, with stalls and milk-pails and stools all complete, indeed, everything that a cow-house could possibly want, except the cows. Then the girl bade him measure out the ground for a storehouse, and this, she said, might be as large as he pleased; and when the storehouse was ready she proposed that they should set off to pay her parents a visit.

The old people welcomed them heartily, and summoned their neighbors, for many miles round, to a great feast in their honor. In fact, for several weeks there was no work done on the farm at all; and at length the young man and his wife grew tired of so much play, and declared that they must return to their own home. But, before they started on the journey, the wife whispered to her husband: "Take care to jump over the threshold as quick as you can, or it will be the worse for you."

The young man listened to her words, and sprang over the threshold like an arrow from a bow; and it was well he did, for, no sooner was he on the other side, than his father-in-law threw a great hammer at him, which would have broken both his legs, if it had only touched them.

When they had gone some distance on the road home, the girl turned to her husband and said: "Till you step inside the house, be sure you do not look back, whatever you may hear or see."

And the husband promised, and for a while all was still; and he thought no more about the matter till he noticed at last that the nearer he drew to the house the louder grew the noise of the trampling of feet behind him. As he laid his hand upon the door he thought he was safe, and turned to look. There, sure enough, was a vast herd of cattle, which had been sent after him by his father-in-law when he found that his daughter had been cleverer than he. Half of the herd were already through the fence and cropping the grass on the banks of the stream, but half still remained outside and faded into nothing, even as he watched them.

However, enough cattle were left to make the young man rich, and he and his wife lived happily together, except that every now and then the girl vanished from his sight, and never told him where she had been. For a long time he kept silence about it; but one day, when he had been complaining of her absence, she said to him: "Dear husband, I am bound to go, even against my will, and there is only one way to stop me. Drive a nail into the threshold, and then I can never pass in or out."

And so he did.

The Three Wishes

(TRADITIONAL SPANISH TALE)

Many years ago there was an old married man who, although poor, had worked very diligently all his life on his little piece of ground. One winter's night, as this old man was seated with his wife in front of their comfortable hearth in social chat, instead of giving thanks to God for the benefits they enjoyed, they spent the time in enumerating the good things possessed by their neighbors, and in wishing that they belonged to them.

"Instead of my little hut, which is on bad soil, and only fit to house a donkey in, I would like to have the farm of old Polainas!" exclaimed the old man.

"And I," added his wife, who was annoyed that he did not aspire higher, "instead of that, would like to have our neighbor's house, which is nearly new."

"And I," continued her husband, "instead of our old donkey, which can scarcely carry an empty sack, would like to have Polainas's mule!"

"And I," exclaimed the wife, "would like to have such a fat porker as our neighbor has to kill! Some people seem only to wish for a thing in order to get it. How I should like to see my wishes accomplished!"

Scarcely had she uttered these words than they beheld a most beautiful little woman standing in front of the fire. She was so small that her height could not have been more than eighteen inches, whilst she wore a crown like a queen's upon her head. Her tunic and veil were almost transparent, and seemed made of white smoke, whilst the sparks from the fire crackled and jumped like fireworks about her, and sparkled around her as glittering spangles. In her hand she bore a little golden scepter, the end of which was formed by a gleaming ruby.

"I am the Fairy Fortunata," she said to them. "I was passing by here, and I have heard your complaints. I have so much anxiety to accomplish your desires that I come to promise you the realization of three wishes: one to you," she said to the wife; "the other to you," to the husband, "and the third has to be mutual, and agreeable to the desire of you both. This last I will agree to in person tomorrow, when I will return at this time; and until then I leave you to think of what it shall be."

When she had said these words, the beautiful fairy sprang through the flames and disappeared in a cloud of smoke.

I leave to the imagination of our fair readers the delight of the worthy couple, and the number of wishes, numerous as suitors at the door of a Minister, which presented themselves to their minds. Their desires were so many that, not knowing which to select, they determined to defer the definite selection to the following day. After having had all the night to think the matter over, they began to discuss entirely different things. In a little while their conversation recurred to their wealthy neighbors.

"I was at their house to-day," said the husband; "they were making black puddings. Ah, such black puddings! It would have done you good to see them!"

"I would like to have one of them here." replied the wife, "to roast on the ashes for supper."

Scarcely had she uttered the words than there appeared upon the ashes the most delicious-looking black pudding that could possibly be imagined.

The woman remained staring at it with open mouth and eyes starting out of her head. But her husband jumped up in despair, and after striding up and down the room, tearing his hair in desperation, said:—"Through your gluttony, you greedy woman, we have lost one of the wishes! Good heavens, what a woman this is! More stupid than a goose! It makes me desperate; I detest you and the black pudding too, and I wish it were stuck on to your nose!"

No sooner had he spoken than there was the black pudding hanging from the place indicated!

Then was the old man struck with horror and his wife with desperation.

"You see what you have done, evil tongue!" exclaimed she, as she made useless exertions to tear the appendage from her nose; "if I employed my wish badly, at least it was to my own disadvantage and not to the disadvantage of any one else; but the sin carries its punishment with it, for I will not have any other wish, nor desire anything else than that the black pudding be taken off my nose."

"Wife, for heaven's sake! What of the new house?"

"Nothing!"

"Wife, for heaven's sake, think of the farm!"

"It does not matter."

"My dear, let us wish for a fortune, and then we will have a golden case for the black pudding."

"I will not hear of it."

"Then you would have us left just as we were before?"

"That is all that I wish for."

And for all that the man could say, nothing could alter his wife's determination, who grew more and more enraged with her double nose, and could scarcely keep off the dog and the cat, who both wished to make free with it.

When, on the following night, the fairy appeared and asked them what was their last wish, they said to her: "We see how blind and foolish it is of men to fancy that the realization of their wishes will make them happy."

Nor is happiness in the accomplishment of our wishes, but in the not having any. He is rich who possesses what he wants; but happy is he who wishes for nothing.

A Christmas Miracle

HARRISON S. MORRIS

You have never heard of Alcala? Well, it is a little village nestling between the Spanish hills, a league from great Madrid. There is a ring of stone houses, each with its white-walled patio and grated windows; each with its balcony, whence now and then a laughing face looks down upon the traveler. There is an ancient inn by the roadside, a time-worn church, and above, on the hill-top, against the still blue sky, the castle, dusky with age, but still keeping a feudal dignity, though half its yellow walls have crumbled away.

This is the Alcala into which I jogged one winter evening in search of rest and entertainment after a long day's journey on mule-back.

The inn was in a doze when my footsteps broke the silence of its stone court-yard; but presently a woman came through an inner door to answer my summons, and I was speedily cast under the quiet spell of the place by finding myself behind a screen of leaves, with a straw-covered bottle at my elbow and a cold fowl within comfortable reach.

The bower where I sat was unlighted save by the waning sun, and I could see but little of its long vista, without neglecting a very imperious appetite. The lattice was covered, I thought, with vine-leaves, and I felt sure, too, that some orange boughs, reaching across the patio wall, mingled with the foliage above my head. But all I was certain of was the relish of the fowl and the delicious refreshment of the cool wine. Having finished these, I lay back in my chair, luxuriating in the sense of healthy fatigue, and going over again, in fancy, the rolling roads of my journey.

I believe I, also, fell into the prevailing slumber of the place, lulled by the soft atmosphere and gentle wine, and might have slept there till morning had a furious sneeze not awakened me with a start. I looked confusedly about in the dusk, but could see nothing save, at last, the tip of a lighted cigarette in the remote depths of the bower. I called out,—

"Who's there?" and was answered, courteously, by a deep, gruff voice in Spanish,—

"It is I, señor, Jose Rosado."

"Are you a guest of 'La Fonda'?" said I, for I had learned that this was the name of the inn, and was a little doubtful whether I had fallen into the hands of friend or foe.

"Ha! ha! ha!" with a long explosion of guttural sounds, was my only answer. Then, after a brightening of the cigarette-fire, to denote that the smoker was puffing it into life, he said,—

"I, señor, am the host."

At this I drew my chair closer, and found, in the thin reflection of the cigarette, a round, bronzed face beaming with smiles and picturing easy good health.

It was winter in Spain, but the scent of flowers was abroad, and the soft, far-off stars twinkled through the moving leaves. What wonder, then, that we fell into talk,—I, the inquiring traveler, he, the arch-gossip of Alcala,— and talked till the moon rose high into the night?

"And who lives in the castle on the hill?" I asked, after hearing the private history of half the town.

"Ah," said mine host, as if preparing to swallow a savory morsel, "there's a bit of gossip; there's a story, indeed!" He puffed away for a minute in mute satisfaction, and then began.

"That is a noble family, the Aranjuez. None can remember in Alcala when there was not a noble Aranjuez living in its castle, and they have led our people bravely in all the wars of Spain. I remember as a boy—"

But, having become acquainted with mine host's loquacity, I broke in with a question more to the point,—

"Who, Señor Jose, lives in the castle now?"

He would have answered without a suspicion of my ruse, had not a bell just then rung solemnly forth, awakening the still night, and arousing Jose Rosado from his comfortable bench, promptly to his feet.

"Come," he said; "that is for the Christmas Mass. I will tell you as we go."

The little inn was lively enough as we emerged from the bower and crossed the court-yard towards the road. The woman who had prepared my supper came forth arrayed in a capulet of white and scarlet, and two younger girls who accompanied her wore veils and long, black robes which fell about their forms like Oriental garments. Two or three men, attendants and hostlers of the place, were also about to start, trigged out in queer little capes and high-crowned hats. All this fine apparel, mine host informed me, was peculiar to Christmas, and I soon found the highway full of peasants in similar garb.

As we got off, Jose Rosado resumed his story, which was brief enough to beguile us just to the church-door.

"You ask me, señor, who lives in the castle now? The Donna Isabella is alone there, now, the only survivor of the noble race, except—except señor" (he laid a peculiar emphasis on the word), "except a willful son, whom she has disowned and driven from her house. He is a handsome lad, and married, here in Alcala, the beauty of the town, in spite of his mother's wounded pride. It was a love-match of stolen wooing and secret wedding,—but, ha! ha! *we* saw it all, knew it all, before even they did themselves. Many an evening have I met them on these roads, billing and cooing like the doves on La Fonda's eaves. They were made by nature for each other, though, and even the rage of the proud Donna Isabella could never part them."

"And do they still live in the town?" I asked.

"Oh, yes," said Jose; "over there in the white house where the olive trees are, at the bottom of the long hill."

I looked in the direction whither he pointed, but I could see little in the dim moonlight save a white wall amid dense shadows.

"And is Donna Isabella a very old lady?" I asked, because very old ladies are often charged with peculiar severity to very young ones.

"No, no, no," said Jose Rosado, with a quick turn of the head to each no. "She's a widow lady of middle age; very proud and very handsome. You shall see her presently, for she has consented to take part in the Christmas play at the church."

152

As I had come a long journey to see this same Christmas play, my expectation was doubly aroused as we approached the old edifice, whose open belfry and rows of cloisters stood before us at the top of the hill we were ascending.

As we entered, the bells stopped ringing, for it was precisely midnight, and the priest at the altar began to say the Christmas Masses. When he had reached the Gospel, he was interrupted by the appearance of a matron, dressed all in white, who stood at the end of the nave. She was clad like the Madonna, and was accompanied by Joseph, who wore the garb of a mountaineer, with a hatchet in his hand. An officious little officer with a halberd opened the way through the crowd before these personages, and they came solemnly up the aisle towards the chancel, which had been arrayed to represent Bethlehem, the Madonna reciting, as she moved forward, a plaintive song about her homelessness. Joseph replied cheeringly, and led her under a roof of leaves in the sanctuary, formed in the manner of a stable, in which we could see the manger against the wall. Here she took rest from her journey, while a little crib, wherein lay the Bambino—or waxen image of the Babe—all adorned with ribbons and laces, was brought from the sacristy and placed in the straw at her feet.

As the Madonna passed us, Jose Rosado nudged me, and whispered audibly enough to make the crowd about us turn and stare,—

"Hist! here's the Donna Isabella, señor! She looks like a saint to-night!"

I watched her closely as she went by me, and marked, under the meek expression assumed by the Virgin, a more characteristic one of severe resolution. She was, however, a queenly woman, in the ripest stage of maturity, but she bore herself, in the part she had taken, with a matronly grace something too conscious for the lowly Mary.

As she seated herself on the heap of straw, a little boy in a surplice, representing an angel, with wings of crimped lawn at his shoulders, was raised in a chair, by a cord and pulley, to the very top of the sanctuary arch, where he sang a carol to the shepherds,—

> Shepherds, hasten all
> With flying feet from your retreat;
> On rustic pipes now play
> Your sweetest, sweetest lay;

for"—so ran the song—"Mary and the King of Heaven are in yonder cave."

At this, an orchestra, concealed behind the high altar, set up a tooting from bagpipes, and flute, and violin, which served as a prelude to the appearance of the shepherds, who were concealed in the gallery.

Up they got, with long cloaks and crooked staffs, murmuring their surprise and incredulity at what the angel had said; some pretending to grumble at being awakened from sleep, others anxious to prove the truth of the strange tidings.

Then the angel sang a more appealing ditty still, whereat they were all about ready to advance, when one of their number, of a skeptical turn, urged them to avoid such fanciful matters and give heed to their sheep, who would otherwise become the prey of the wolf.

Hereupon, an old shepherd appeared, who gave three loud knocks with his crook, and denounced those who should disobey the heavenly messenger. The practical man was thus silenced, and they expressed their willingness to go to the manger,—and at the same moment an angel appeared to guide them thither.

They descended from the gallery to the outer porch of the church and knocked loudly at the door, saying, as if to the innkeeper at Bethlehem:

> Pray, good master of the inn,
> Open the door and let us in.

But Joseph became alarmed at the approach of such a number of rustics, and inquired who they were. They held a songful colloquy with him; but he continued to refuse them admittance, until an angel again intervened, this time in the form of a tall acolyte from the sanctuary, accompanied by two little angelic choristers. He reassured Joseph, and invited the shepherds to enter and worship the Babe. They came up the aisle flourishing their be-ribboned crooks and singing in praise of the Child, but they were sorely vexed, when they saw the stable, that so humble a place had been found for His shelter. Joseph explained, in several couplets, that no other house would receive them, and the shepherds replied in several others, mingling sympathy and good advice, intended not for Joseph, but for the throng, who listened in religious awe.

After paying due homage to the child and Mary, the shepherds exchanged some more verses with Joseph, and then retired to the other end of the church, singing in chorus as they went.

All these ceremonies had so claimed my attention that I had given scarcely any heed to the Virgin. She was seated humbly in the straw beside the little crib, in which still nestled the Bambino, and, with eyes cast down in maternal thoughtfulness, she was a lovely object there beneath the roof of the leafy stable. She did not appear to notice the actors in the drama; and now, when three young girls, in gayest holiday attire, came forward with distaffs that streamed with bright ribbons, and knelt before her, she reached forth a hand as if to bless them, but kept her eyes turned meekly upon the ground.

As these three girls retired from the manger, another and larger band appeared beneath the gallery opposite the shepherds, singing in sweet voices a salutation to the three who had just left the chancel. These made answer that they had come from the stable where the Savior was born; and so, in alternate questions and answers, they described all that they had seen. The two groups, having advanced a step or two at each stanza, now met, and went back to the manger together, singing the same air the shepherds had previously sung.

When they arrived at the stable they made their offering, setting up a tent the while, ornamented with plenteous ribbons and flowers, among which blackbirds, thrushes, turtle-doves and partridges fluttered about at the ends of cords to which they were fastened. They brought with them, also, bunches of purple grapes and strings of yellow apples, chaplets of dried prunes and heaps of walnuts and chestnuts. After arranging these rustic offerings, the shepherdesses returned, singing in chorus as they went:

> In Bethlehem, at midnight,
> > The Virgin mother bore her child.
> This world contains no fairer sight
> > Than this fair Babe and Mary mild.
> Well may we sing at sight like this,
> > Gloria in Excelsis.

I now had another unobstructed view of Donna Isabella, and Jose Rosado's gossip, intensified by her romantic appearance as the Virgin, had given me a deep interest in her every movement.

She reached down into the little crib to lift out the Bambino, and I could plainly see a look of astonishment rise to her face as she started back, both hands held wide apart, as if having encountered something they were unprepared to touch. Then she turned hurriedly to Joseph and whispered a word in his ear, whereupon he too bent with surprise over the little crib. After gazing at it a moment, he reached down and lifted out, not the waxen Bambino, but a sweet young baby that smiled and reached its tiny arms from Joseph towards the white Virgin.

Donna Isabella was visibly affected at this, and took the tender infant into her arms, caressing and soothing it, while it fondled her face and white head-dress.

The audience had now become aware that, instead of the waxen image in the crib, there had been found a living baby, and the impetuous and susceptible minds of the Spanish peasants had jumped at the conclusion that they had witnessed a new miracle. They crowded up to the manger, telling their beads and murmuring prayers, while they pushed and jostled each other madly for a glimpse of the holy infant.

One of the acolytes reached his arms forth to take it from Donna Isabella and bring it to the chancel rail for the crowd to see, but she held it more closely to her bosom, and refused to let it go from her. As she stood there, a tall and stately figure, folded in the white gown of the Virgin and wearing the close head-dress which concealed all save her splendid face, she seemed the creation of some old painter, and the curious crowd of peasants was hushed into admiration by her beauty and her tenderness for the child. She, too, became a part of the strange miracle. The infant Christ had been born anew among them, and lay there in his very mother's arms, an object of mystery and worship. As the silence of wonder ensued, Donna Isabella seemed to collect her startled senses, and looked around her as if expecting the mother of the child to come and claim it. A woman of her resolution was not to be hurried into superstitious follies by some pretty trick or accident. But the little one lay so softly in her arms and reached with such tiny, appealing fingers at her throat, that she began to feel a motherly fondness for it. And, moreover, had it not been sent her, who was alone now in the great castle on the hill, as a mysterious gift of Providence? Ought she not to feel it a sacred charge, coming as it did, from the very manger, to her arms?

Thus thinking, the Donna Isabella came slowly to the chancel rail, and, holding forth the infant at arms' length, she said:

"Good people of Alcala, my part in the Christmas play is done. The good Lord has sent me this little one to take care of; and here, before you all, I accept the charge and promise to cherish and love it. If any of you know its mother, say that the Donna Isabella has carried it to the castle of Aranjuez, and tell her to follow it there, for where her child is, there the mother should be also." This broke the spell. The silent crowd fell into murmurs and gestures, and each one asked his neighbor where the child belonged. There was no longer any doubt. It was merely a human child; but the mystery of the manger surrounded it with a hallowed interest, and everybody was eager to discover its parents and bear them the good news of its adoption by the great lady.

Now, Jose Rosado was too old a hand, too jolly a host, to be long deceived. He whispered me his views as we stood near the leafy stable, and they were to the effect that the wayward son of the Aranjuez knew more about the child in the manger than any one else thereabouts.

And Jose was right; for, before the bustle of inquiry had quite died away, from out the sacristy door came a young girl wearing a veil and dressed in the long black gown of the Christmas ceremonies. She walked demurely through the crowd, which parted for her with inquiring looks, and, going straight up to the chancel, dropped on her knees before the Donna Isabella. She held down her head and made no motion; but all knew instinctively that she was the mother of the child.

The noble Virgin stooped and raised her head with a loving compassion. She put aside her veil and moved as if to kiss her, but one look at the mother's face turned her kindness into rage. She cried, "What, you?" and overwhelmed at the discovery sank down on the straw of the stable, clasping the child with a firmer hold, as if to shield it from a foe.

It was a sore conflict for an unyielding will like that of the Donna Isabella; but the part she had played in the sacred ceremonies and the surrounding emblems of peace and good-will were softening influences. More potent even than these was the persuasive contact of the little hands which opened and shut in playful touches at her throat. I could see from the varying expressions of her face that she questioned herself. Should she yield? The pride of birth, the disobedience of a youthful son to a mother of her indulgent nature, the stigma of a low connection upon a noble family name—all these things pleaded urgently, No. She looked up vindictively at the gaping congregation, which seemed spellbound in wanton curiosity, wherewith was mingled not a little religious dread. And then, again, she turned her eyes down upon the innocent face beside her bosom, so guileless, to be the cause of such varying passions in the throng about it. No, she could not give it up. All the old maternal instincts were aroused in her, and the firmness of her will was redoubled by the sentiment of love for her grandchild. Was it not her son's child, then, as well as this woman's? Surely, she had a right to keep it, and, glancing up with this last plea for possession on her lips, she saw beside the kneeling wife a new figure, whose presence made her pause and falter.

Only for an instant, however, for a kindlier light came into her clear eyes, and reaching forth the one arm which was free she threw it around her son's neck and kissed him fondly, while the little child which had wrought the change,—a latter-day miracle of broken affections made whole, of bitter wounds healed by the touch of innocence,—lay there between them, striving, with its playful hands, to catch at its mother's bowing head.

As Jose Rosado and I walked homeward through the pale-blue moonlight, we did not say much. I was deeply moved by the touching scene I had beheld; and he was exceedingly reflective.

At last, as we neared La Fonda's vine-run walls, he said:

"Señor, do you think the miracles are all over nowadays?"

"I know not, Señor Jose," I answered; "but there are certainly strange potencies lurking in the depths of a mother's love."

House Island

(TRADITIONAL NORWEGIAN TALE)

There lived in Norway, not far from the city of Drontheim, a rich and prosperous gentleman. He had an only daughter, called Aslog, the fame of whose beauty spread far and wide. The greatest men of the country sought her, but all were alike unsuccessful in their suit. Her father, who thought his daughter delayed her choice only that she might choose the better, forbore to interfere, and exulted in her prudence. But when, at length, the richest and noblest had tried their fortune with as little success as the rest, he grew angry, called his daughter, and said to her:—

"Hitherto I have left you to your free choice, but since I see that you reject all without any distinction, and the very best of your suitors seem not good enough for you, I will keep measures no longer with you. What! shall my family become extinct, and my inheritance pass away into the hands of strangers? I will break your stubborn spirit. I give you now till the festival of the great Winter-night; by that time you must make your decision, or prepare to accept the husband whom I myself shall select."

Now Aslog secretly loved a youth named Orm, handsome, noble and brave. She loved him with her whole soul, and would sooner die than bestow her hand on another. But Orm was poor, and poverty compelled him to keep his love as secret as her own.

When Aslog saw the darkness of her father's countenance, and heard his angry words, she turned pale as death, for she knew his temper, and doubted not but that he would put his threats into execution. Without uttering a word in reply, she retired to her chamber, and pondered vainly how to escape the storm that hung over her. The great festival approached nearer and nearer, and her anguish increased every day.

At last the lovers resolved on flight. Orm knew a secure place, where they could hide until they found an opportunity of quitting the country. So at night, when all were asleep, he led the trembling Aslog over the snow and ice-fields away to the mountains. The moon and the stars lighted them on their way. They had under their arms a few articles of dress and some skins of animals, which were all they could carry. They ascended the mountains the whole night long, till they reached a lonely spot inclosed with lofty rocks. Here Orm conducted the weary Aslog into a cave, the low and narrow entrance to which was hardly perceptible, but it soon enlarged to a great hall, reaching deep into the mountain. He kindled a fire, and they now, reposing on their skins, sat in the deepest solitude far away from all the world.

Orm was the first who had discovered this cave, which is shown to this very day. But as no one then knew anything of it, they were safe from the pursuit of Aslog's father. They passed the whole winter in this retirement, contented and even happy; for they knew they were married, and belonged to one another, and no cruel father could separate them more. Orm used to go a-hunting, and Aslog stayed at home in the cave, minded the fire, and prepared the necessary food. Frequently did she mount the points of the rocks, but her eyes, did they wander ever so far, saw only glittering snow-fields.

The spring now came on—the woods were green—the meadows put on their various colors, people began to wander out for summer pleasuring, and Aslog could but rarely and with circumspection venture to leave the cave. One evening Orm came in with the intelligence that he had recognized her father's servants in the distance, and that he could hardly have been unobserved by them. "They will surround this place," continued he, "and never rest till they have found us; we must quit our retreat, then, without a moment's delay."

They accordingly descended on the other side of the mountain, and reached the strand, where they fortunately found a boat. Orm pushed off, and the boat drove into the open sea. They had escaped their pursuers, but they were now exposed to dangers of another kind: whither should they turn? They could not venture to land, for Aslog's father was lord of the whole coast, and they would infallibly fall into his hands. Nothing then remained for them but to commit their bark to the wind and waves. They were driven along the entire night. At break of day the coast had disappeared, and they saw nothing but the sky, the sea, and the waves. They had not brought one morsel of food with them, and thirst and hunger began now to torment them. Three days did they toss about in this state of misery, and Aslog, faint and exhausted, saw nothing but certain death before her.

At length, on the evening of the third day, they discovered an island of tolerable magnitude, and surrounded by a number of smaller ones. Orm immediately steered for it, but, just as he came near it, there suddenly rose a violent wind, and the sea rolled every moment higher and higher. He turned about with a view of approaching it on another side, but with no better success; his vessel, as often as it neared the island, was driven back as if by an invisible power. "God help us!" he cried, and crossed himself, and looked on poor Aslog, who seemed to be dying of weakness before his eyes. But scarcely had the exclamation passed his lips when the storm ceased, the waves subsided, and the vessel came to the shore without encountering any hindrance. Orm jumped out on the beach; some mussels that he found on the strand strengthened and revived the exhausted Aslog, so that she was soon able to leave the boat.

The island was overgrown with low dwarf shrubs, and seemed to be uninhabited; but when they had reached the middle of it, they discovered a house, which appeared to be half under the surface of the earth. In the hope of meeting with human help, the wanderers approached it. They listened, but the most perfect silence reigned there. Orm at length opened the door, and they both walked in: but what was their surprise, to find everything regulated and arranged as if for inhabitants, yet not a single living creature visible. The fire was burning on the hearth, in the middle of the room, and a kettle with fish hung on it, apparently only waiting for some one to take it up and eat it. The beds were made, and ready to receive their wearied tenants. Orm and Aslog stood for some time dubious, and looked on with a certain degree of awe, but at last, overcome by hunger, they took up the food and ate. When they had satisfied their appetites, and still discovered no human being, they gave way to weariness, and laid themselves in the beds, which looked so peaceful and inviting to their wearied limbs.

They had expected to be awakened in the night by the owners of the house on their return home, but their expectation was not fulfilled; they slept undisturbed till the morning sun shone in upon them. No one appeared on any of the following days, and it seemed as if some invisible power had made ready the house for their reception. They spent the whole summer in perfect happiness: they were, to be sure, solitary, yet they did not miss mankind. The wild birds' eggs, and the fish they caught, yielded them provisions in abundance.

When autumn came, Aslog brought forth a son. In the midst of their joy at this, they were surprised by a wonderful apparition. The door opened on a sudden, and an old woman stepped in. She wore a handsome blue dress; there was something proud, but at the same time something strange, in her appearance.

"Do not be afraid," said she, "at my unexpected appearance. I am the owner of this house, and I thank you for the clean and neat state in which you have kept it, and for the good order in which I find everything with you. I would willingly have come sooner, but I had no power to do so till this little heathen (pointing to the new-born babe) was come to the light. Now I have free access. Only fetch no priest from the mainland to christen it, or I must depart again. If you will in this matter comply with my wishes, you may not only continue to live here, but all the good that ever you can wish for I will do you. Whatever you take in hand shall prosper; good luck shall follow you wherever you go. But break this condition, and depend upon it that misfortune after misfortune will come on you, and even on this child will I avenge myself. If you want anything, or are in danger, you have only to pronounce my name three times, and I will appear and lend you assistance. I am of the race of the old giants, and my name is Guru. But beware of uttering in my presence the name of Him whom no giant may hear of, and never venture to make the sign of the cross, or to cut it on beam or board in the house. You may dwell in this house the whole year long, only be so good as to give it up to me on Yule evening, when the sun is at the lowest, as then we celebrate our great festival, and then only are we permitted to be merry. At least, if you should not be willing to go out of the house, keep yourselves up in the loft as quiet as possible the whole day long, and as you value your lives do not look down into the room below until midnight is past. After that you may take possession of everything again."

When the old woman had thus spoken she vanished, and Aslog and Orm lived without any disturbance, contented and happy. Orm never made a cast of his net without getting a plentiful draught; he never shot an arrow from his bow that it was not sure to hit; in short, whatever they took in hand, were it ever so trifling, evidently prospered.

When Christmas came, they cleaned up the house in the best manner, set everything in order, kindled a fire on the hearth, and as the twilight approached they went up to the loft, where they remained quite still and quiet. At length it grew dark; they thought they heard a sound of whizzing and snorting in the air, such as the swans used to make in the winter time. There was a hole in the roof over the fireplace, which might be opened and shut either to let in the light from above, or to afford a free passage for the smoke. Orm lifted up the lid, which was covered with a skin, and put out his head. But what a wonderful sight then presented itself to his eyes! The little islands around were all lit up with countless blue lights, which moved about without ceasing, jumped up and down, then skipped to the shore, assembled together, and came nearer and nearer to the large island where Orm and Aslog lived. At last they reached it, and arranged themselves in a circle around a large stone not far from the shore, and which Orm well knew. But what was his surprise when he saw that the stone had now completely assumed the form of a man, though a monstrous and gigantic one! He could clearly perceive that the little blue lights were borne by Dwarfs whose pale clay-colored faces, with their huge noses and red eyes, disfigured too by birds' bills and owls' eyes, were supported by misshapen bodies, and they tottered and wabbled about here and there, so that they seemed to be at the same time merry and in pain.

Suddenly, the circle opened; the little ones retired on each side, and Guru—who was the woman Guru, whom Orm recognized immediately, though she had risen in stature and size so as to be almost as gigantic as the stone man—advanced towards it. She threw both her arms round the image, which immediately seemed to receive life and motion. Then the Dwarfs, with wonderful capers and grimaces, began a song, or, to speak more properly, a howl, with which the whole island resounded and almost trembled at the noise. Orm, quite terrified, drew in his head, and he and Aslog remained in the dark, so still that they hardly ventured to draw their breath.

The procession moved on towards the house, as might be clearly perceived by the nearer approach of the shouting and crying. They were now all come in, light and active; the Dwarfs were heard jumping about on the benches, and heavy and loud sounded at intervals the steps of the giants. Orm and his wife listened to the clattering of the plates, and the shouts of joy with which they celebrated their banquet. When it was over and midnight drew near, they began to dance to that ravishing fairy-tune, which some have heard in the rocky glens, and learned by listening to the underground musicians. As soon as Aslog caught the sound of this air, she felt an irresistible longing to see the dance. Nor was Orm able to keep her back. "Let me look," said she, "or my heart will burst." She took her child and placed herself at the extreme end of the loft, whence, without being observed, she could see all that passed. Long did she gaze, without taking off her eyes for an instant, on the dance—on the bold and wonderful springs of the little creatures, who seemed to float in the air, and not so much as to touch the ground, while the ravishing melody of the Elves filled her whole soul. The child, meanwhile, which lay in her arms grew sleepy and drew its breath heavily, and, without ever thinking on the promise she had given the old woman, she made, as is usual, the sign of the cross over the mouth of the child, and said, "Christ bless you, my babe!"

The instant she had spoken the word there was raised a horrible, piercing cry. The Dwarfs tumbled head over heels out at the door with terrible crushing and crowding, their lights went out, and in a few minutes the whole house was clear of them and left desolate. Orm and Aslog, frightened to death, hid themselves in the most retired nook they could find. They did not venture to stir till daybreak, and not till the sun shone through the hole in the roof down on the fireplace did they feel courage enough to descend from the loft.

The table remained still covered as the underground people had left it; all their vessels, which were of silver, and manufactured in the most beautiful manner, lay upon it. In the middle of the room, there stood upon the ground a huge copper kettle half full of sweet mead, and by the side of it a drinking-horn of pure gold. In the corner rested, against the wall, a stringed instrument, not unlike a dulcimer, which, as people believe, the Giantesses used to play on. They gazed on what was before them, full of admiration, but without venturing to lay their hands on anything; how great and fearful was their amazement, when, on turning about, they saw sitting at the table an immense figure, which Orm instantly recognized as the Giant whom Guru had animated by her embrace. He was now a cold and hard stone. While they were standing gazing on it, Guru herself entered the room in her giant form. She wept so bitterly, that her tears trickled down on the ground. It was long ere her sobbing permitted her to utter a single word; at last she spoke:—

"Great affliction have you brought on me, and henceforth I must weep while I live; yet as I know that you have not done this with evil intentions, I forgive you, though it were a trifle for me to crush the whole house like an egg-shell over your heads."

"What have we done?" cried Orm and Aslog, penetrated with the deepest sorrow.

"Alas!" answered she, "my husband, whom I love more than myself, there he sits, petrified for ever; never again will he open his eyes! Three hundred years lived I with my father on the island of Kunnan, happy in the innocence of youth, as the fairest among the Giant-maidens. Mighty heroes sued for my hand; the sea around that island is still filled with the rocky fragments which they hurled against each other in their combats. Andfind won the victory, and I plighted myself to him. But ere I was married came the detestable Odin into the country, who overcame my father, and drove us all from the island. My father and sisters fled to the mountains, and since that time my eyes have beheld them no more. Andfind and I saved ourselves on this island, where we for a long time lived in peace and quiet, and thought it would never be interrupted. But destiny, which no one escapes, had determined it otherwise. Oluf came from Britain. They called him the Holy, and Andfind instantly found that his voyage would be inauspicious to the Giants. When he heard how Oluf's ship rushed through the waves, he went down to the strand and blew the sea against him with all his strength. The waves swelled up like mountains. But Oluf was still more mighty than he; his ship flew unchecked through the billows like an arrow from a bow. He steered direct for our island. When the ship was so near that Andfind thought he could reach it with his hands, he grasped at the forepart with his right hand, and was about to drag it down to the bottom, as he had often done with other ships. But Oluf, the terrible Oluf, stepped forward, and crossing his hands over each other, he cried with a loud voice, "Stand there as a stone till the last day," and in the same instant my unhappy husband became a mass of rock. The ship sailed on unimpeded, and ran direct against the mountain, which it cut through, and separated from it the little island which lies out yonder.

"Ever have I passed my life alone and forlorn. On Yule-eve alone can petrified Giants receive back their life for the space of seven hours, if one of their race embraces them, and is at the same time willing to sacrifice a hundred years. I loved my husband too well not to bring him back to life every time that I could do it, even at this price, and I have not even counted how often I have done it, that I might not know the hour when I myself should share his fate, and at the moment when I threw my arms around him become stone like him. But, alas! even this comfort is taken from me; I can never more by any embrace awake him. He has heard the Name which I dare not utter, and never again will he see the light until the dawn of the last day shall bring it.

"I now go hence, and you will behold me no more. All that is here in the house I give you; my dulcimer alone will I keep. But let no one venture to fix his habitation on the small islands that lie around here. There dwell the little underground people whom you saw at the festival, and I will protect them as long as I live!"

With these words Guru vanished. The next spring Orm took the golden horn and the silverware to Drontheim, where no one knew him. The value of these precious metals was so great that he was able to purchase everything requisite for a wealthy man. He laded his ship with his purchases, and returned back to the island, where he spent many years in unalloyed happiness, and Aslog's father was soon reconciled to his wealthy son-in-law.

The huge image remained sitting in the house; no human power was able to move it. So hard was the stone, that hammer and axe flew in pieces without making the slightest impression upon it. The giant sat there till a holy man came to the island, who with one single word removed him back to his former station, where he stands to this hour. The copper kettle, which the underground people left behind them, was preserved as a memorial upon the island, which bears the name of House Island to the present day.

The Little Match Girl

HANS CHRISTIAN ANDERSEN

It was terribly cold; it snowed and was almost dark on this, the last evening of the year. In the cold and darkness, a poor little girl, with bare head and naked feet, went along the streets. When she left home, it is true, she had had slippers on, but what was the use of that? They were very large slippers; her mother had worn them till then, so big were they. So the little girl lost them as she sped across the street, to get out of the way of two carts driving furiously along. One slipper was not to be found again, and a boy had caught up the other and run away with it. So the little girl had to walk with naked feet, which were red and blue with cold. She carried a lot of matches in a red apron, and a box of them in her hand. No one had bought anything of her the live-long day; no one had given her a penny.

Shivering with cold and hunger, she crept along, poor little thing, a picture of misery.

The snow-flakes covered her beautiful fair hair, which fell in long tresses about her neck: but she did not think of that now. Lights were shining in all the windows, and there was a tempting smell of roast goose, for it was New Year's Eve. Yes, she was thinking of that.

In a corner formed by two houses, one of which projected beyond the other, she crouched down in a little heap. Although she had drawn her feet up under her, she became colder and colder; she dared not go home, for she had not sold any matches nor earned a single penny.

She would certainly be beaten by her father, and it was cold at home, too; they had only the roof above them, through which the wind whistled, although the largest cracks had been stopped up with straw and rags.

Her hands were almost numb with cold. One little match might do her good, if she dared take only one out of the box, strike it on the wall and warm her fingers. She took one out and lit it. How it sputtered and burned!

It was a warm, bright flame, like a little candle, when she held her hands over it; it was a wonderful little light, and it really seemed to the child as though she was sitting in front of a great iron stove with polished brass feet and brass ornaments. How the fire burned up, and how nicely it warmed one! The little girl was already stretching out her feet to warm these too, when— out went the little flame, the stove vanished, and she had only the remains of the burned match in her hand.

She struck a second one on the wall; it threw a light, and where this fell upon the wall, the latter became transparent, like a veil; she could see right into the room. A white table-cloth was spread upon the table, which was decked with shining china dishes, and there was a glorious smell of roast goose stuffed with apples and dried plums. And what pleased the poor little girl more than all was that the goose hopped down from the dish, and with a knife and fork sticking in its breast, came waddling across the floor straight up to her. Just at that moment out went the match, and only the thick, damp, cold wall remained. So she lighted another match, and at once she sat under the beautiful Christmas tree; it was much larger and better dressed than the one she had seen through the glass doors at the rich merchant's. The green boughs were lit up with thousands of candles, and gaily-painted figures, like those in the shop-windows, looked down upon her. The little girl stretched her hands out towards them and—out went the match. The Christmas can-dles rose higher and higher till they were only the stars in the sky; one of them fell, leaving a long fiery trail behind it.

"Now, some one is dying," thought the little girl, for she had been told by her old grandmother, the only person she had ever loved, and who was now dead, that when a star falls a soul goes up to heaven.

She struck another match on the wall; it was alight once more, and before her stood her old grandmother, all dazzling and bright, and looking very kind and loving.

"Grandmother!" cried the little girl. "Oh! take me with you. I know that you will go away when the match is burned out; you will vanish like the warm stove, like the beautiful roast goose, and the large and splendid Christmas-tree." And she quickly lighted the whole box of matches, for she did not wish to let her grandmother go. The matches burned with such a blaze that it was lighter than day, and the old grandmother had never appeared so beautiful nor so tall before. Taking the little girl in her arms, she flew up with her, high, endlessly high, above the earth; and there they knew neither cold, nor hunger, nor sorrow—for they were with God.

But in the cold dawn, the poor little girl was still sitting—with red cheeks and a smile upon her lips—in the corner, leaning against the wall: frozen to death on the last evening of the Old Year. The New Year's sun shone on the little body. The child sat up stiffly, holding her matches, of which a box had been burnt. "She must have tried to warm herself," some one said. No one knew what beautiful things she had seen, nor into what glory she had entered with her grandmother on the joyous New Year.

The Story of the Goblins Who Stole a Sexton

Charles Dickens

In an old abbey town, down in this part of the country, a long, long while ago—so long, that the story must be a true one, because our great-grandfathers implicitly believed it—there officiated as sexton and grave-digger in the churchyard, one Gabriel Grub. It by no means follows that because a man is a sexton, and constantly surrounded by the emblems of mortality, therefore he should be a morose and melancholy man; your undertakers are the merriest fellows in the world, and I once had the honor of being on intimate terms with a mute, who in private life, and off duty, was as comical and jocose a little fellow as ever chirped out a devil-may-care song, without a hitch in his memory, or drained off the contents of a good stiff glass without stopping for breath. But, notwithstanding these precedents to the contrary, Gabriel Grub was an ill-conditioned, cross-grained, surly fellow—a morose and lonely man, who consorted with nobody but himself, and an old wicker bottle which fitted into his large deep waistcoat pocket—and who eyed each merry face, as it passed him by, with such a deep scowl of malice and ill-humor, as it was difficult to meet, without feeling something the worse for.

A little before twilight one Christmas Eve, Gabriel shouldered his spade, lighted his lantern, and betook himself towards the old churchyard; for he had got a grave to finish by next morning, and feeling very low, he thought it might raise his spirits, perhaps, if he went on with his work at once. As he wended his way, up the ancient street, he saw the cheerful light of the blazing fires gleam through the old casements, and heard the loud laugh and the cheerful shouts of those who were assembled around them; he marked the bustling preparations for next day's cheer, and smelled the numerous savory odors consequent thereupon, as they steamed up from the kitchen windows in clouds. All this was gall and wormwood to the heart of Gabriel Grub; and when groups of children, bounded out of the houses, tripped across the road, and were met, before they could knock at the opposite door, by half a dozen curly-headed little rascals who crowded round them as they flocked up-stairs to spend the evening in their Christmas games, Gabriel smiled grimly, and clutched the handle of his spade with a firmer grasp, as he thought of measles, scarlet-fever, thrush, whooping-cough, and a good many other sources of consolation besides.

In this happy frame of mind, Gabriel strode along: returning a short, sullen growl to the good-humored greetings of such of his neighbors as now and then passed him: until he turned into the dark lane which led to the churchyard. Now, Gabriel had been looking forward to reaching the dark lane, because it was, generally speaking, a nice, gloomy, mournful place, into which the townspeople did not much care to go, except in broad daylight, and when the sun was shining; consequently, he was not a little indignant to hear a young urchin roaring out some jolly song about a merry Christmas, in this very sanctuary, which had been called Coffin Lane ever since the days of the old abbey, and the time of the shaven-headed monks. As Gabriel walked on, and the voice drew nearer, he found it proceeded from a small boy, who was hurrying along, to join one of the little parties in the old street, and who, partly to keep himself company, and partly to prepare himself for the occasion, was shouting out the song at the highest pitch of his lungs. So Gabriel waited until the boy came up, and then dodged him into a corner, and rapped him over the head with his lantern five or six times, to teach him to modulate his voice. And as the boy hurried away with his hand to his head, singing quite a different sort of tune, Gabriel Grub chuckled very heartily to himself, and entered the churchyard: locking the gate behind him.

He took off his coat, put down his lantern, and getting into the unfinished grave, worked at it for an hour or so, with right good will. But the earth was hardened with the frost, and it was no very easy matter to break it up, and shovel it out; and although there was a moon, it was a very young one, and shed little light upon the grave, which was in the shadow of the church. At any other time, these obstacles would have made Gabriel Grub very moody and miserable, but he was so well pleased with having stopped the small boy's singing, that he took little heed of the scanty progress he had made, and looked down into the grave, when he had finished work for the night, with grim satisfaction: murmuring as he gathered up his things:

> Brave lodgings for one, brave lodgings for one,
> A few feet of cold earth, when life is done;
> A stone at the head, a stone at the feet,
> A rich, juicy meal for the worms to eat;
> Rank grass overhead, and damp clay around,
> Brave lodgings for one, these, in holy ground!

"Ho! ho!" laughed Gabriel Grub, as he sat himself down on a flat tombstone which was a favorite resting-place of his; and drew forth his wicker bottle. "A coffin at Christmas! A Christmas Box. Ho! ho! ho!"

"Ho! ho! ho!" repeated a voice which sounded close behind him.

Gabriel paused in some alarm, in the act of raising the wicker bottle to his lips: and looked round. The bottom of the oldest grave about him, was not more still and quiet, than the churchyard in the pale moonlight. The cold hoar-frost glistened on the tombstones, and sparkled like rows of gems, among the stone carvings of the old church. The snow lay hard and crisp upon the ground, and spread over the thickly-strewn mounds of earth so white and smooth a cover, that it seemed as if corpses lay there, hidden only by their winding sheets. Not the faintest rustle broke the profound tranquillity of the solemn scene. Sound itself appeared to be frozen up, all was so cold and still.

"It was the echoes," said Gabriel Grub, raising the bottle to his lips again.

"It was *not*," said a deep voice.

Gabriel started up, and stood rooted to the spot with astonishment and terror; for his eyes rested on a form that made his blood run cold.

Seated on an upright tombstone, close to him, was a strange unearthly figure, whom Gabriel felt at once was no being of this world. His long fantastic legs which might have reached the ground, were cocked up, and crossed after a quaint, fantastic fashion; his sinewy arms were bare, and his hands rested on his knees. On his short round body, he wore a close covering, ornamented with small slashes; a short cloak dangled at his back; the collar was cut into curious peaks, which served the goblin in lieu of ruff or neckerchief; and his shoes curled up at his toes into long points. On his head, he wore a broad-brimmed sugar-loaf hat, garnished with a single feather. The hat was covered with the white frost; and the goblin looked as if he had sat on the same tombstone very comfortably, for two or three hundred years. He was sitting perfectly still; his tongue was put out, as if in derision; and he was grinning at Gabriel Grub with such a grin as only a goblin could call up.

"It was *not* the echoes," said the goblin.

Gabriel Grub was paralysed, and could make no reply.

"What do you do here on Christmas Eve?" said the goblin sternly.

"I came to dig a grave, sir," stammered Gabriel Grub.

"What man wanders among graves and churchyards on such a night as this?" cried the goblin.

"Gabriel Grub! Gabriel Grub!" screamed a wild chorus of voices that seemed to fill the churchyard. Gabriel looked fearfully round—nothing was to be seen.

"What have you got in that bottle?" said the goblin.

"Hollands, sir," replied the sexton, trembling more than ever; for he had bought it of the smugglers, and he thought that perhaps his questioner might be in the excise department of the goblins.

"Who drinks Hollands alone, and in a churchyard, on such a night as this?" said the goblin.

"Gabriel Grub! Gabriel Grub!" exclaimed the wild voices again.

The goblin leered maliciously at the terrified sexton, and then raising his voice, exclaimed:

"And, who, then, is our fair and lawful prize?"

To this inquiry the invisible chorus replied, in a strain that sounded like the voices of many choristers singing to the mighty swell of the old church organ—a strain that seemed borne to the sexton's ears upon a gentle wind, and to die away as it passed on ward; but the burden of the reply was still the same, "Gabriel Grub! Gabriel Grub!"

The goblin grinned a broader grin than before, as he said, "Well, Gabriel, what do you say to this?"

The sexton gasped for breath.

"What do you think of this, Gabriel?" said the goblin, kicking up his feet in the air on either side the tombstone, and looking at the turned-up points with as much complacency as if he had been contemplating the most fashionable pair of Wellingtons in all Bond Street.

"It's—it's—very curious, sir," replied the sexton, half dead with fright; "very curious, and very pretty, but I think I'll go back and finish my work, sir, if you please."

"Work!" said the goblin, "what work?"

"The grave, sir; making the grave," stammered the sexton.

"Oh, the grave, eh?" said the goblin; "who makes graves at a time when all other men are merry, and takes a pleasure in it?"

Again the mysterious voices replied, "Gabriel Grub! Gabriel Grub!"

"I'm afraid my friends want you, Gabriel," said the goblin, thrusting his tongue further into his cheek than ever—and a most astonishing tongue it was—"I'm afraid my friends want you, Gabriel," said the goblin.

"Under favor, sir," replied the horror-stricken sexton, "I don't think they can, Sir; they don't know me, sir; I don't think the gentlemen have ever seen me, Sir."

"Oh yes they have," replied the goblin; "we know the man with the sulky face and grim scowl, that came down the street to-night, throwing his evil looks at the children, and grasping his burying spade the tighter. We know the man who struck the boy in the envious malice of his heart, because the boy could be merry, and he could not. We know him, we know him."

Here, the goblin gave a loud shrill laugh, which the echoes returned twenty-fold: and throwing his legs up in the air, stood upon his head, or rather upon the very point of his sugar-loaf hat, on the narrow edge of the tombstone: whence he threw a somerset with extraordinary agility, right to the sexton's feet, at which he planted himself in the attitude in which tailors generally sit upon the shopboard.

"I—I—am afraid I must leave you, sir," said the sexton, making an effort to move.

"Leave us!" said the goblin, "Gabriel Grub going to leave us. Ho! ho! ho!"

As the goblin laughed, the sexton observed, for one instant, a brilliant illumination within the windows of the church, as if the whole building were lighted up; it disappeared, the organ pealed forth a lively air, and whole troops of goblins, the very counterpart of the first one, poured into the churchyard, and began playing at leap-frog with the tombstones: never stopping for an instant to take breath, but "overing" the highest among them, one after the other, with the utmost marvelous dexterity. The first goblin was a most astonishing leaper, and none of the others could come near him; even in the extremity of his terror the sexton could not help observing, that while his friends were content to leap over the common-sized gravestones, the first one took the family vaults, iron railings and all, with as much ease as if they had been so many street posts.

At last the game reached to a most exciting pitch; the organ played quicker and quicker; and the goblins leaped faster and faster: coiling themselves up, rolling head over heels upon the ground, and bounding over the tombstones like foot-balls. The sexton's brain whirled round with the rapidity of the motion he beheld, and his legs reeled beneath him, as the spirits flew before his eyes: when the goblin king, suddenly darting towards him, laid his hand upon his collar, and sank with him through the earth.

When Gabriel Grub had had time to fetch his breath, which the rapidity of his descent had for the moment taken away, he found himself in what appeared to be a large cavern, surrounded on all sides by crowds of goblins, ugly and grim; in the center of the room, on an elevated seat, was stationed his friend of the churchyard; and close beside him stood Gabriel Grub himself, without power of motion.

"Cold to-night," said the king of the goblins, "very cold. A glass of something warm, here!"

At this command, half a dozen officious goblins, with a perpetual smile upon their faces, whom Gabriel Grub imagined to be courtiers, on that account, hastily disappeared, and presently returned with a goblet of liquid fire, which they presented to the king.

"Ah!" cried the goblin, whose cheeks and throat were transparent, as he tossed down the flame, "this warms one, indeed! Bring a bumper of the same, for Mr. Grub."

It was in vain for the unfortunate sexton to protest that he was not in the habit of taking anything warm at night; one of the goblins held him while another poured the blazing liquid down his throat; the whole assembly screeched with laughter as he coughed and choked, and wiped away the tears which gushed plentifully from his eyes, after swallowing the burning draught.

"And now," said the king, fantastically poking the taper corner of his sugar-loaf hat into the sexton's eye, and thereby occasioning him the most exquisite pain: "and now, show the man of misery and gloom a few of the pictures from our own great storehouse!"

As the goblin said this, a thick cloud which obscured the remoter end of the cavern rolled gradually away, and disclosed, apparently at a great distance, a small and scantily furnished, but neat and clean apartment. A crowd of little children were gathered round a bright fire, clinging to their mother's gown, and gambolling round her chair. The mother occasionally rose, and drew aside the window-curtain, as if to look for some expected object; a frugal meal was ready spread upon the table, and an elbow chair was placed near the fire. A knock was heard at the door: the mother opened it, and the children crowded round her, and clapped their hands for joy, as their father entered. He was wet and weary, and shook the snow from his garments, as the children crowded round him, and seizing his cloak, hat, stick, and gloves, with busy zeal, ran with them from the room. Then, as he sat down to his meal before the fire, the children climbed about his knee, and the mother sat by his side, and all seemed happiness and comfort.

But a change came upon the view, almost imperceptibly. The scene was altered to a small bedroom, where the fairest and youngest child lay dying; the roses had fled from his cheek, and the light from his eye; and even as the sexton looked upon him, with an interest he had never felt or known before, he died. His young brothers and sisters crowded round his little bed, and seized his tiny hand, so cold and heavy; but they shrank back from its touch, and looked with awe on his infant face; for calm and tranquil as it was, and sleeping in rest and peace as the beautiful child seemed to be, they saw that he was dead, and they knew that he was an Angel looking down upon, and blessing them, from a bright and happy Heaven.

Again the light cloud passed across the picture, and again the subject changed. The father and mother were old and helpless now, and the number of those about them was diminished more than half; but content and cheerfulness sat on every face, and beamed in every eye, as they crowded round the fireside, and told and listened to old stories of earlier and bygone days. Slowly and peacefully the father sank into the grave, and, soon after, the sharer of all his cares and troubles followed him to a place of rest. The few, who yet survived them, knelt by their tomb, and watered the green turf which covered it with their tears; then rose, and turned away: sadly and mournfully, but not with bitter cries, or despairing lamentations, for they knew that they should one day meet again; and once more they mixed with the busy world, and their content and cheerfulness were restored. The cloud settled upon the picture, and concealed it from the sexton's view.

"What do you think of *that*?" said the goblin, turning his large face towards Gabriel Grub.

Gabriel murmured out something about its being very pretty, and looked somewhat ashamed, as the goblin bent his fiery eyes upon him.

"*You* a miserable man!" said the goblin, in a tone of excessive contempt. "You!" He appeared disposed to add more, but indignation choked his utterance, so he lifted up one of his very pliable legs, and flourishing it above his head a little, to insure his aim, administered a good sound kick to Gabriel Grub; immediately after which, all the goblins in waiting crowded round the wretched sexton, and kicked him without mercy: according to the established and invariable custom of courtiers upon earth, who kick whom royalty kicks, and hug whom royalty hugs.

"Show him some more!" said the king of the goblins.

At these words the cloud was dispelled, and a rich and beautiful landscape was disclosed to view—there is just such another, to this day, within half a mile of the old abbey town. The sun shone from out the clear blue sky, the water sparkled beneath his rays, and the trees looked greener, and the flowers more gay, beneath his cheering influence. The water rippled on, with a pleasant sound; the trees rustled in the light wind that murmured among their leaves; the birds sang upon the boughs; and the lark carolled on high her welcome to the morning. Yes, it was morning: the bright, balmy morning of summer; the minutest leaf, the smallest blade of grass, was instinct with life. The ant crept forth to her daily toil, the butterfly fluttered and basked in the warm rays of the sun; myriads of insects spread their transparent wings, and revelled in their brief but happy existence. Man walked forth, elated with the scene; and all was brightness and splendor.

"*You* a miserable man!" said the king of the goblins, in a more contemptuous tone than before. And again the king of the goblins gave his leg a flourish; again it descended on the shoulders of the sexton; and again the attendant goblins imitated the example of their chief.

Many a time the cloud went and came, and many a lesson it taught to Gabriel Grub, who, although his shoulder smarted with pain from the frequent application of the goblin's feet, looked on with an interest that nothing could diminish. He saw that men who worked hard, and earned their scanty bread with lives of labor, were cheerful and happy; and that to the most ignorant, the sweet face of nature was a never-failing source of cheerfulness and joy. He saw those who had been delicately nurtured, and tenderly brought up, cheerful under privations, and superior to suffering, that would have crushed many of a rougher grain, because they bore within their own bosoms the materials of happiness, and contentment, and peace. He saw that women, the tenderest and most fragile of all God's creatures, were the oftenest superior to sorrow, adversity, and distress; and he saw that it was because they bore, in their own hearts, an inexhaustible well-spring of affection and devotion. Above all, he saw that men like himself, who snarled at the mirth and cheerfulness of others, were the foulest weeds on the fair surface of the earth; and setting all the good of the world against the evil, he came to the conclusion that it was a very decent and respectable sort of world after all. No sooner had he formed it, than the cloud which closed over the last picture seemed to settle on his senses, and lull him to repose. One by one, the goblins faded from his sight; and as the last one disappeared, he sunk to sleep.

The day had broken when Gabriel Grub awoke, and found himself lying, at full length on the flat gravestone in the churchyard, with the wicker bottle lying empty by his side, and his coat, spade, and lantern, all well whitened by the last night's frost, scattered on the ground. The stone on which he had first seen the goblin seated stood bolt upright before him, and the grave at which he had worked, the night before, was not far off. At first he began to doubt the reality of his adventures, but the acute pain in his shoulders when he attempted to rise assured him that the kicking of the goblins was certainly not ideal. He was staggered again, by observing no traces of footsteps in the snow on which the goblins had played at leap-frog with the gravestones, but he speedily accounted for this circumstance when he remembered that, being spirits, they would leave no visible impression behind them. So, Gabriel Grub got on his feet as well as he could, for the pain in his back; and brushing the frost off his coat, put it on, and turned his face towards the town.

But he was an altered man, and he could not bear the thought of return-ing to a place where his repentance would be scoffed at, and his reformation disbelieved. He hesitated for a few moments; and then turned away to wan-der where he might, and seek his bread elsewhere.

The lantern, the spade, and the wicker bottle were found, that day, in the churchyard. There were a great many speculations about the sexton's fate, at first, but it was speedily determined that he had been carried away by the goblins; and there were not wanting some very credible witnesses who had distinctly seen him whisked through the air on the back of a chestnut horse blind of one eye, with the hind-quarters of a lion and the tail of a bear. At length all this was devoutly believed; and the new sexton used to exhibit to the curious, for a trifling emolument, a good-sized piece of the church weathercock which had been accidentally kicked off by the aforesaid horse in his aerial flight, and picked up by himself in the churchyard, a year or two afterwards.

Unfortunately these stories were somewhat disturbed by the unlooked-for reappearance of Gabriel Grub himself, some ten years afterwards, a ragged, contented, rheumatic old man. He told his story to the clergyman, and also to the mayor; and in course of time it began to be received, as a matter of history, in which form it has continued down to this very day. The believers in the weathercock tale, having misplaced their confidence once, were not easily prevailed upon to part with it again, so they looked as wise as they could, shrugged their shoulders, touched their foreheads, and mur-mured something about Gabriel Grub having drunk all the Hollands, and then fallen asleep on the flat tombstone; and they affected to explain what he supposed he had witnessed in the goblin's cavern, by saying that he had seen the world, and grown wiser. But this opinion, which was by no means a popular one at any time, gradually died off; and be the matter how it may, as Gabriel Grub was afflicted with rheumatism to the end of his days, this story has at least one moral, if it teach no better one—and that is, that if a man turns sulky and drinks by himself at Christmas time, he may make up his mind to be not a bit the better for it: let the spirits be never so good, or let them be even as many degrees beyond proof, as those which Gabriel Grub saw in the goblin's cavern.

The Rich Brother and the Poor Brother

(FROM *THE LILAC FAIRY BOOK*)

There was once a rich old man who had two sons, and as his wife was dead, the elder lived with him, and helped him to look after his property. For a long time all went well; the young man got up very early in the morning, and worked hard all day, and at the end of every week his father counted up the money they had made, and rubbed his hands with delight, as he saw how big the pile of gold in the strong iron chest was becoming. "It will soon be full now, and I shall have to buy a larger one," he said to himself, and so busy was he with the thought of his money, that he did not notice how bright his son's face had grown, nor how he sometimes started when he was spoken to, as if his mind was far away.

One day, however, the old man went to the city on business, which he had not done for three years at least. It was market day, and he met with many people he knew, and it was getting quite late when he turned into the inn yard, and bade an ostler saddle his horse, and bring it round directly. While he was waiting in the hall, the landlady came up for a gossip, and after a few remarks about the weather and the vineyards she asked him how he liked his new daughter-in-law, and whether he had been surprised at the marriage.

The old man stared as he listened to her. "Daughter-in-law? Marriage?" said he. "I don't know what you are talking about! I've got no daughter-in-law, and nobody has been married lately, that I ever heard of."

Now this was exactly what the landlady, who was very curious, wanted to find out; but she put on a look of great alarm, and exclaimed:

"Oh, dear! I hope I have not made mischief. I had no idea—or, of course, I would not have spoken—but"—and here she stopped and fumbled with her apron, as if she was greatly embarrassed.

"As you have said so much you will have to say a little more," retorted the old man, a suspicion of what she meant darting across him; and the woman, nothing loth, answered as before.

"Ah, it was not all for buying or selling that your handsome son has been coming to town every week these many months past. And not by the shortest way, either! No, it was over the river he rode, and across the hill and past the cottage of Miguel the vine-keeper, whose daughter, they say, is the prettiest girl in the whole country side, though she is too white for *my* taste," and then the landlady paused again, and glanced up at the farmer, to see how he was taking it. She did not learn much. He was looking straight before him, his teeth set. But as she ceased to talk, he said quietly, "Go on."

"There is not much more to tell," replied the landlady, for she suddenly remembered that she must prepare supper for the hungry men who always stopped at the inn on market days, before starting for home, "but one fine morning they both went to the little church on top of the hill, and were married. My cousin is servant to the priest, and she found out about it and told me. But good-day to you, sir; here is your horse, and I must hurry off to the kitchen."

It was lucky that the horse was sure-footed and knew the road, for his bridle hung loose on his neck, and his master took no heed of the way he was going. When the farm-house was reached, the man led the animal to the stable, and then went to look for his son.

"I know everything—you have deceived me. Get out of my sight at once—I have done with you," he stammered, choking with passion as he came up to the young man, who was cutting a stick in front of the door, whistling gaily the while.

"But, father—"

"You are no son of mine; I have only one now. Begone, or it will be the worse for you," and as he spoke he lifted up his whip.

The young man shrank back. He feared lest his father should fall down in a fit, his face was so red and his eyes seemed bursting from his head. But it was no use staying: perhaps next morning the old man might listen to reason, though in his heart the son felt that he would never take back his words. So he turned slowly away, and walked heavily along a path which ended in a cave on the side of his hill, and there he sat through the night, thinking of what had happened.

Yes, he had been wrong, there was no doubt of that, and he did not quite know how it had come about. He had *meant* to have told his father all about it, and he was sure, *quite* sure, that if once the old man had seen his wife, he would have forgiven her poverty on account of her great beauty and goodness. But he had put it off from day to day, hoping always for a better opportunity, and now this was the end!

If the son had no sleep that night, no more had the father, and as soon as the sun rose, he sent a messenger into the great city with orders to bring back the younger brother. When he arrived the farmer did not waste words, but informed him that he was now his only heir, and would inherit all his lands and money, and that he was to come and live at home, and to help manage the property.

Though very pleased at the thought of becoming such a rich man—for the brothers had never cared much for each other—the younger would rather have stayed where he was, for he soon got tired of the country, and longed for a town life. However, this he kept to himself, and made the best of things, working hard like his brother before him.

In this way the years went on, but the crops were not so good as they had been, and the old man gave orders that some fine houses he was building in the city should be left unfinished, for it would take all the savings to complete them. As to the elder son, he would never even hear his name mentioned, and died at last without ever seeing his face, leaving to the younger, as he had promised, all his lands, as well as his money.

Meanwhile, the son whom he had disinherited had grown poorer and poorer. He and his wife were always looking out for something to do, and never spent a penny that they could help, but luck was against them, and at the time of his father's death they had hardly bread to eat or clothes to cover them. If there had been only himself, he would have managed to get on somehow, but he could not bear to watch his children becoming weaker day by day, and swallowing his pride, at length he crossed the mountains to his old home where his brother was living.

It was the first time for long that the two men had come face to face, and they looked at each other in silence. Then tears rose in the eyes of the elder, but winking them hastily away, he said:

"Brother, it is not needful that I should tell you how poor I am; you can see that for yourself. I have not come to beg for money, but only to ask if you will give me those unfinished houses of yours in the city, and I will make them watertight, so that my wife and children can live in them, and that will save our rent. For as they are, they profit you nothing."

And the younger brother listened and pitied him, and gave him the houses that he asked for, and the elder went away happy.

For some years things went on as they were, and then the rich brother began to feel lonely, and thought to himself that he was getting older, and it was time for him to be married. The wife he chose was very wealthy, but she was also very greedy, and however much she had, she always wanted more. She was, besides, one of those unfortunate people who invariably fancy that the possessions of other people must be better than their own. Many a time her poor husband regretted the day that he had first seen her, and often her meanness and shabby ways put him to shame. But he had not the courage to rule her, and she only got worse and worse.

After she had been married a few months the bride wanted to go into the city and buy herself some new dresses. She had never been there before, and when she had finished her shopping, she thought she would pay a visit to her unknown sister-in-law, and rest for a bit. The house she was seeking was in a broad street, and *ought* to have been very magnificent, but the carved stone portico enclosed a mean little door of rough wood, while a row of beautiful pillars led to nothing. The dwelling on each side were in the same unfinished condition, and water trickled down the walls. Most people would have considered it a wretched place, and turned their backs on it as soon as they could, but this lady saw that by spending some money the houses could be made as splendid as they were originally intended to be, and she instantly resolved to get them for herself.

Full of this idea she walked up the marble staircase, and entered the little room where her sister-in-law sat, making clothes for her children. The bride seemed full of interest in the houses, and asked a great many questions about them, so that her new relations liked her much better than they expected, and hoped they might be good friends. However, as soon as she reached home, she went straight to her husband, and told him that he must get back those houses from his brother, as they would exactly suit her, and she could easily make them into a palace as fine as the king's. But her husband only told her that she might buy houses in some other part of the town, for she could not have those, as he had long since made a gift of them to his brother, who had lived there for many years past.

At this answer the wife grew very angry. She began to cry, and made such a noise that all the neighbors heard her and put their heads out of the windows, to see what was the matter. "It was absurd," she sobbed out, "quite unjust. Indeed, if you came to think of it, the gift was worth nothing, as when her husband made it he was a bachelor, and since then he had been married, and she had never given her consent to any such thing." And so she lamented all day and all night, till the poor man was nearly worried to death; and at last he did what she wished, and summoned his brother in a court of law to give up the houses which, he said, had only been lent to him. But when the evidence on both sides had been heard, the judge decided in favor of the poor man, which made the rich lady more furious than ever, and she determined not to rest until she had gained the day. If one judge would not give her the houses another should, and so time after time the case was tried over again, till at last it came before the highest judge of all, in the city of Evora. Her husband was heartily tired and ashamed of the whole affair, but his weakness in not putting a stop to it in the beginning had got him into this difficulty, and now he was forced to go on.

On the same day the two brothers set out on their journey to the city, the rich one on horseback, with plenty of food in his knapsack, the poor one on foot with nothing but a piece of bread and four onions to eat on the way. The road was hilly and neither could go very fast, and when night fell, they were both glad to see some lights in a window a little distance in front of them.

The lights turned out to have been placed there by a farmer, who had planned to have a particularly good supper as it was his wife's birthday, and bade the rich man enter and sit down, while he himself took the horse to the stable. The poor man asked timidly if he might spend the night in a corner, adding that he had brought his own supper with him. Another time permission might have been refused him, for the farmer was no lover of humble folk, but now he gave the elder brother leave to come in, pointing out a wooden chair where he could sit.

Supper was soon served, and very glad the younger brother was to eat it, for his long ride had made him very hungry. The farmer's wife, however, would touch nothing, and at last declared that the only supper she wanted

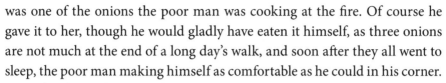

was one of the onions the poor man was cooking at the fire. Of course he gave it to her, though he would gladly have eaten it himself, as three onions are not much at the end of a long day's walk, and soon after they all went to sleep, the poor man making himself as comfortable as he could in his corner.

A few hours later the farmer was aroused by the cries and groans of his wife.

"Oh, I feel so ill, I'm sure I'm going to die," wept she. "It was that onion, I know it was. I wish I had never eaten it. It must have been poisoned."

"If the man has poisoned you he shall pay for it," said her husband, and seizing a thick stick he ran downstairs and began to beat the poor man, who had been sound asleep, and had nothing to defend himself with. Luckily, the noise aroused the younger brother, who jumped up and snatched the stick from the farmer's hand, saying:

"We are both going to Evora to try a law-suit. Come too, and accuse him there if he has attempted to rob you or murder you, but don't kill him now, or you will get yourself into trouble."

"Well, perhaps you are right," answered the farmer, "but the sooner that fellow has his deserts, the better I shall be pleased," and without more words he went to the stables and brought out a horse for himself and also the black Andalusian mare ridden by the rich man, while the poor brother, fearing more ill-treatment, started at once on foot.

Now all that night it had rained heavily, and did not seem likely to stop, and in some places the road was so thick with mud that it was almost impossible to get across it. In one spot it was so very bad that a mule laden with baggage had got stuck in it, and tug as he might, his master was quite unable to pull him out. The muleteer in despair appealed to the two horseman, who were carefully skirting the swamp at some distance off, but they paid no heed to his cries, and he began to talk cheerfully to his mule, hoping to keep up his spirits, declaring that if the poor beast would only have a little patience help was sure to come.

And so it did, for very soon the poor brother reached the place, bespattered with mud from head to foot, but ready to do all he could to help with the mule and his master. First they set about finding some stout logs of wood to lay down on the marsh so that they could reach the mule, for by this time his frantic struggles had broken his bridle, and he was deeper in than ever. Stepping cautiously along the wood, the poor man contrived to lay hold of the animal's tail, and with a desperate effort the mule managed to regain his footing on dry ground, but at the cost of leaving his tail in the poor man's hand. When he saw this the muleteer's anger knew no bounds, and forgetting that without the help given him he would have lost his mule altogether, he began to abuse the poor man, declaring that he had ruined his beast, and the law would make him pay for it. Then, jumping on the back of the mule, which was so glad to be out of the choking mud that he did not seem to mind the loss of his tail, the ungrateful wretch rode on, and that evening reached the inn at Evora, where the rich man and the farmer had already arrived for the night.

Meanwhile the poor brother walked wearily along, wondering what other dreadful adventures were in store for him.

"I shall certainly be condemned for one or other of them," thought he sadly; "and after all, if I *have* to die, I would rather choose my own death than leave it to my enemies," and as soon as he entered Evora he looked about for a place suitable for carrying out the plan he had made. At length he found what he sought, but as it was too late and too dark for him to make sure of success, he curled himself up under a doorway, and slept till morning.

Although it was winter, the sun rose in a clear sky, and its rays felt almost warm when the poor man got up and shook himself. He intended it to be the day of his death, but in spite of that, and of the fact that he was leaving his wife and children behind him, he felt almost cheerful. He had struggled so long, and was so very, very tired; but he would not have minded that if he could have proved his innocence, and triumphed over his enemies. However, they had all been too clever for him, and he had no strength to fight any more. So he mounted the stone steps that led to the battlements of the city, and stopped for a moment to gaze about him.

It happened that an old sick man who lived near by had begged to be carried out and to be laid at the foot of the wall so that the beams of the rising sun might fall upon him, and he would be able to talk with his friends as they passed by to their work. Little did he guess that on top of the battlements, exactly over his head, stood a man who was taking his last look at the same sun, before going to his death that awaited him. But so it was; and as the steeple opposite was touched by the golden light, the poor man shut his eyes and sprang forward. The wall was high, and he flew rapidly through the air, but it was not the ground he touched, only the body of the sick man, who rolled

184

over and died without a groan. As for the other, he was quite unhurt, and was slowly rising to his feet when his arms were suddenly seized and held.

"You have killed our father, do you see? do you see?" cried two young men, "and you will come with us this instant before the judge, and answer for it."

"Your father? but I don't know him. What do you mean?" asked the poor man, who was quite bewildered with his sudden rush through the air, and could not think why he should be accused of this fresh crime. But he got no reply, and was only hurried through the streets to the court-house, where his brother, the muleteer, and the farmer had just arrived, all as angry as ever, all talking at once, till the judge entered and ordered them to be silent.

"I will hear you one by one," he said, and motioned the younger brother to begin.

He did not take long to state his case. The unfinished houses were his, left him with the rest of the property by his father, and his brother refused to give them up. In answer, the poor man told, in a few words, how he had begged the houses from his brother, and produced the deed of gift which made him their owner.

The judge listened quietly and asked a few questions; then he gave his verdict.

"The houses shall remain the property of the man to whom they were given, and to whom they belong. And as you," he added, turning to the younger brother, "brought this accusation knowing full well it was wicked and unjust, I order you, besides losing the houses, to pay a thousand pounds damages to your brother."

The rich man heard the judge with rage in his heart, the poor man with surprise and gratitude. But he was not safe yet, for now it was the turn of the farmer. The judge could hardly conceal a smile at the story, and inquired if the wife was dead before the farmer left the house, and received for answer that he was in such a hurry for justice to be done that he had not waited to see. Then the poor man told his tale, and once more judgment was given in his favor, while twelve hundred pounds was ordered to be paid him. As for the muleteer, he was informed very plainly that he had proved himself mean and ungrateful for the help that had been given him, and as a punishment he must pay to the poor man a fine of fifty pounds, and hand him over the mule till his tail had grown again.

Lastly, there came the two sons of the sick man.

"This is the wretch who killed our father," they said, "and we demand that he should die also."

"How did you kill him?" asked the judge, turning to the accused, and the poor man told how he had leaped from the wall, not knowing that anyone was beneath.

"Well, this is my judgment," replied the judge, when they had all spoken: "Let the accused sit under the wall, and let the sons of the dead man jump from the top and fall on him and kill him, and if they will not do this, then they are condemned to pay eight hundred pounds for their false accusation."

The young men looked at each other, and slowly shook their heads.

"We will pay the fine," said they, and the judge nodded.

So the poor man rode the mule home, and brought back to his family enough money to keep them in comfort to the end of their days.

What the Christmas Star Sees

(Traditional Danish Tale)

Under the Angel's Wings

In the dim twilight a young mother sits by the window. Her little son, her only one, is on her lap. It is so charming to sit quietly in a corner near the window, while darkness gently settles about you, and watch the stars rise from the deep shadows in the sky, glittering forth, one by one.

She clasps her arms fondly around her little boy, and says, softly: "Look, how all the small stars smile and twinkle at us. They have something to tell."

"What is it, mama?" asks her little boy. His mother continues:

"'We are but very small spots,' say the stars to you and to me, 'of all the splendor within the sky. But soon Christmas comes with the child Jesus, and to him it all belongs. He sends an angel through the darkness, with gifts for all his children below. The angel keeps them under his wings. He will give you all that you wish for, that you may know how well Jesus loves you.'"

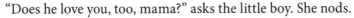

"Does he love you, too, mama?" asks the little boy. She nods.

"And papa?"

"Yes." she says, drawing a long breath, "he loves him so well that neither papa nor I really know *how* well."

"That was my testimonial!" exclaims a merry voice behind them—papa's voice. They had not seen him enter the room. "Well, what do you wish, little one? Wish, wish, while it is time!"

The little boy meditates and seems irresolute. On a sudden he looks smilingly into their faces, and says: "First, I must find my place under the angel's wings."

"He knows how to wish for plenty, the little fellow!" exclaims his father. "He wants all at once."

"Look!" ejaculates the boy, pointing to the sky. A light is kindled there. Slowly, in a wide, gleaming circle, it shoots across the firmament, and disappears within it.

"A shooting-star! Your wish will be fulfilled, my own boy," says his mother, clasping the child more tightly in her arms, while he claps his hands delightedly.

"Have it; have it all!" merrily resumes his father. "But you must be sure and return home. Do not let the angel fly away with you! I would not lose you for all the wealth of heaven, my little boy."

"Oh, do not say it in such a manner," exclaims his wife, pressing her hand against her heart in sudden alarm; "you make me so afraid."

"My pious little wife!" answers he; "how can these foolish shooting-stars frighten you? Now I leave you for my work, and in the mean time you may cherish your hopes about divine things. A mother does this all the better when she is alone."

With moistened eyes she turns towards him, whispering: "I wish both of us could do it."

"I am more easily contented than both of you," he returns, smiling upon her; "I shall not ask for heaven, but am contented with the earth, where I have you and the boy."

Kissing his two dear ones, he leaves them. A young man, with all the joy in life yet before him, he is so wise and self-reliant, so strong and good, too.

But mother sits alone with her little son. One shooting-star falls after another, and for every one of them she takes him more firmly in her arms.

Another evening: Christmas night.

The young mother again sits alone with her little boy, her only one, on her lap. It is sad to sit with such a treasure in your arms, while the darkness settles about you—it is sad to watch the glowing cheeks and the eyes which sparkle, not from a yearning or glee, but because the violent coughing takes his breath away and shakes the little body. Mother folds her quivering hands around the glowing forehead. Father is sitting immovable, watching his child.

Healthy and fresh, with rosy cheeks, did he fall asleep the previous evening; hot and feverish did he awake in the morning. The Christmas joy vanished, giving room for the shadows of anxiety which fell upon the home. The physician came and went during the day; now he is expected back.

Suddenly the coughing stops, a gleam of relief spreading upon the child's countenance. He recovers his breath and turns to his mother, whispering:

"Mama! Will I find my place under the angel's wings to-night?" This was his thought and longing for many days and weeks. But mother can only nod; she dares not venture to answer the question.

"Mama, kiss me! Papa, come here!"

His mother bends over him, and his father kisses the little face. There is a happy smile, a faint struggle, and a deep silence at last.

In the room, where stood a Christmas-tree which will not be lighted, sits the young mother, alone. The door is opened, and her husband walks softly in. Bending over her, he looks into her tearless eyes.

"The shooting-star," he says, at length, "spoke the truth. Your boy and mine is now under the angel's wings. We both believe it, you and I."

She feels that she is alone no more.

A feeble ray from the Christmas star reaches the sorrow as well as the joy. Its blessed light comes from the little figure under the angel's wings.

A Christmas Gift

We are in the large city. The clocks show that it is late in the afternoon. The streets are crowded with people who all know that the following night is Christmas Eve, and are anxious not to be late on any account.

Straight through the crowds a little boy and girl, brother and sister, are rushing along, closely followed by a big dog and a small puppy. The latter is really rolling along rather than trudging with the rest of the company. When there seems to be danger ahead, the big dog snatches her offspring from the ground, carrying the little ball-like creature in her mouth, until the number of rapidly moving feet diminishes, and the passage becomes less dangerous. This little company of four is as busy as if some one's life depended upon its movements, and such is, indeed, the case.

The big dog's name is Ada, and she is doomed to be hanged. The puppy has no name; but he will be drowned.

Ada had developed of late two rather disagreeable habits. One of these is that she is always abundantly well supplied with puppies. Although she does not mean to give any one trouble with her large family, the latter surely gives her considerable cause for worry. Mama says that the puppies are dirty little fellows, and papa declares that there is no end of bother on their account. At length he becomes impatient, and in his extreme annoyance declares that in the afternoon Ada must be hanged, and the puppy drowned. No pleading or coaxing helped this time, as had been the case before; papa would not listen; he was too seriously annoyed.

What a great sorrow had descended upon the children to darken the bright Christmas Day! For over an hour they were crying over the poor puppy and his dear mother, upon whose soft pelt their little heads had often rested. But, suddenly, John is struck by an idea. Lifting his head from the soft pillow he dries his eyes, and says: "I know, sister, what we must do. We will make somebody a Christmas present of Ada and the dear puppy. I never heard that anybody was allowed to hang or drown their Christmas gifts."

Emma assented at once, whereupon all four started on their expedition. They determined to go first to Aunt Lizzie, who was so tender and good.

"Here we are, Aunt Lizzie!" they cried, when at length they were confronted by this lady; "here is Ada and the puppy. We are going to make you a Christmas present of them, Aunt Lizzie!"

"God forbid!" exclaimed Aunt Lizzie, "I will never keep them in my house. What are you thinking of?"

"Oh, *do* take them, auntie!" prayed Emma. "If nobody will have them, they must be killed."

"Tut, tut, children," said the dear old lady, by way of comforting. "They are only a couple of animals, after all."

"Animals?" ejaculated Emma. "It's Ada and her pup, Aunt Lizzie, please remember."

Upon this the four comrades went away in a rather disconsolate state of mind. After all, Aunt Lizzie was not as nice as they had thought her. Now she should not get the two sweet animals, even if she went down on her knees and prayed for them.

They went from one house to another. At every place they presented their Christmas gift, but without success. It was continually declined, and the situation grew more and more painful.

Now they were, as above described, rushing onward in high speed.

Suddenly Emma stopped, flushed and breathless. "I cannot walk farther," declared she; "I am getting too tired. But let us go and make Uncle Peter a Christmas present of Ada and the pup!"

"No, I am afraid of that," answered John; "Uncle Peter is *so* queer, says mama; he can't bear to see any one around."

"Yes, but mama says that he has humane feelings, anyway. I don't know what *that* is. I heard mama say that he had once had great sorrows. Now, I don't know what that is, either; but some days ago I gave him the first stocking I had made for my big doll, and he smiled at it, and kissed me. Let us go and bring him our Christmas presents! I wonder what mama means by great sorrows, but it must be something dreadful." Emma turned around and led the procession, until all were standing in a row before Uncle Peter's rocking-chair.

"Here, Uncle Peter," say the children—"here we bring you Ada and her pup; they are a Christmas gift for you."

"How is that?" asks Uncle Peter, in wonder. But Emma's arms are already around his neck, and she sobs into his ear: "Ada and her pup were to be killed, and that would be so—so dreadful to us, such a great sorrow, Uncle Peter. You know what that means, for you have had some yourself, haven't you!"

What is the matter with Uncle Peter? He starts, suddenly pushing Emma away from him, presses both hands against his forehead, but suddenly jumps from his chair and walks up to Ada, addressing her in his deep, strong voice: "Do you wish to stay by such an old fellow as I, old lady?"

Ada proceeds to make an appropriate remark in her own tongue. Uncle Peter seems to understand her answer; he turns to the children, exclaiming: "I never heard the like! Ada says she intends to keep Christmas here for her pup, and we are invited, all three!"

How *could* Ada think of such a thing! Well, there is no moment to be lost; it is already late in the afternoon. A number of hurried visits are made to many different stores, and at length the preparations are finished.

A beautiful Christmas-tree is lighted in Uncle Peter's study. His furniture looks quite amazed at the strange spectacle.

But the door is opened, admitting the surprised faces of mama and papa. Uncle Peter nods and beams upon them with his large, benevolent face.

"Children, children!" exclaims mama. "Why did you run away in such a manner? Papa and I were very uneasy about you."

"We could not come home yet, mama," objects John. "Ada keeps Christmas for her puppy, and we are all invited, you know!"

A ray from the Christmas star kisses his eager, upturned face, and his mother follows its example.

Number 101

"Follow me," whispers the twinkling star, "to narrow dwellings, where hearts grow faint and weary; to dreary places, where the name which a mother gave her child is changed into a number."

There is a large and quiet-looking building, lonely, situated in the outskirts of the city, with high and firm walls, the monotony of which is broken by no ornament except the regular lines of small, curious windows. These look, in fact, rather like the small, deep-set eyes of an old, irascible bachelor than spaces through which the sunlight, which God gave to mankind before anything else was created, can penetrate the darkness within and conjure away the shadows.

Twilight settles upon the large building, and one window after another is lighted. They look like long rows of tired, sleepy eyes, as they shine forth, in a thoughtless, passive manner, through the misty evening air. Do they tell us of the many deadened hopes and stifled aspirations of those who dwell under the roof of this building?

They do. Behind every one of them a spoiled life is slowly dragged along under the benumbing influence of the somber place, under a code of rules and regulations as rigidly enforced as observed, under a system which induces forgetfulness on one important point above all—namely, that man's acts are not always man's nature.

Prisoner Number 101—name forgotten—is proud of having behaved well. Soon his time will be out, so he will again become an honest member of society. The crime was bought by the sacrifice of so-and-so many years of freedom, bought and honestly paid for. An honest deal, and nothing else, says Number 101.

I see him behind the little window at the right end of the second row, as he sits on a narrow bench, leaning forward, with his elbows upon his knees and with folded hands, glancing through the iron bars into the darkness outside, towards one little twinkling star high above the black earth and its codes of rules and regulations.

Number 101 is thinking, although there is—officially—no personality behind the thoughts. "Halloo!" cry the thoughts, undaunted by the heavy doors and iron bars; but the well-known places and figures do not return the greeting as confidentially as of old. There is one sweet, girlish face at the remembrance of which the prisoner's heart waxes warm, although it is not known—officially—that Number 101 possesses a heart; but it turns away from him like all the other acquaintances, whereat he clinches both hands against the small speck of the dark sky visible through the little window in the wall.

"That is not the right way to treat a prisoner who served his time," say the thoughts. "Beware! Any one who scoffs at me, exonerated as I am now, will be duly punished, like all other offenders. There is justice even for an offender when he has paid his debts to justice."

The thoughts pursue their course from one place to another, and Number 101 holds his head high, for he has paid his debts.

But in the center of the whirling mass of thoughts there is one dark point which seems to frighten the thinker, like a vacuum horrifies nature. It seems possessed of a singular influence, both attractive and repulsive. The thoughts are afraid of this dark point, and yet they must approach it. Prisoner Number 101 buries his head in his two strong hands, but "visions come again" of things departed.

A woman in a ragged dress is standing on the market-place. She has sold her last lamb; baby's lambkin must change owner, that money might be procured. Even baby cannot live on her love for her sweet lambkin; even sweet baby—healthy and fresh in her rags—needs a crumb of bread now and then.

The poor woman sells her lamb, and her five thin fingers are eagerly seizing an equally thin roll of paper money. Tears rise in her eyes, as they came into a pair of blossom-blue ones at home when lambkin departed.

There is a rush of feet. Five strong fingers grasp the tiny roll of money with which lambkin was bought, and Prisoner Number 101 darts away into the crowd.

"Stop thief!"

Number 101—name already forgotten—stands before the bar and tells frankly of his guilt.

"How could you do it?'" asked the judge, looking from his strong, well-built figure to the poor woman in her ragged dress.

The strong man bends his head before the stern gaze of the man of law. He wishes to fall on his knees and pray forgiveness; but to produce a scene in the court-room where inquisitive eyes are watching from every corner, trying to catch every bit of sensational news—that would never do. So the guilty man hides his feelings, and no sensation occurs, and as there are no extenuating circumstances, he must pay his debt in full.

Number 101 lifts his head and waves his hand at the dark thoughts, repeating: "I have paid it all."

"You have not," say the thoughts.

"I have," firmly asserts the prisoner.

"You could not," repeat the thoughts. "Do you not know that you could pay none of your debts, even by sacrificing your whole life?"

"When I leave this room a free man, I am exonerated, and no one will dare say a word about the debt," continues the lonely man.

But the thoughts are persistent, and resume: "People will scowl at you, and close their doors on you; nay, even be afraid to touch you. No man or woman can ever blot out the brand for theft which you carry."

"They dare not do it. There is justice in the land, and I am exonerated. No one shall scowl at me."

Steps sound and resound in the spacious halls outside; at length a rap at the door starts Number 101 from his revery. At nine o'clock the light is made out; it is time to go to bed, and the prisoner knows it.

At nine sharp Number 101 is in bed, like all other prisoners. The light goes out, and darkness rolls its mask down over the lonely man. But thoughts will roam about, so far and wide, until one little figure after another finds its way in under the mask, and carry the sleeper's spirit away into dreamland.

No man or woman can ever blot out—

The little twinkling star lifts the dark veil, and sheds its silver rays upon the figure in the narrow bed, in the narrow room, behind the high walls.

Prisoner Number 101 has gone to sleep with a smile upon his face, dreaming that he has returned to baby, for whom he brings a new lambkin with beautiful, white wool, and a golden collar.

The Strange Adventures of Little Maia

(FROM *THE OLIVE FAIRY BOOK*)

Once upon a time there lived a woman who had a pretty cottage and garden right in the middle of a forest. All through the summer she was quite happy tending her flowers and listening to the birds singing in the trees, but in the winter, when snow lay on the ground and wolves came howling about the door, she felt very lonely and frightened. "If I only had a child to speak to, however small, what a comfort it would be!" she said to herself. And the heavier the snow fell the oftener she repeated the words. And at last a day arrived when she could bear the silence and solitude no longer, and set off to walk to the nearest village to beg someone to sell her or lend her a child.

The snow was very deep, and reached above her ankles, and it took her almost an hour to go a few hundred yards.

"It will be dark at this rate before I get to the first house," thought she, and stopped to look about her. Suddenly a little woman in a high-crowned hat stepped from behind a tree in front of her.

"This is a bad day for walking! Are you going far?" inquired the little woman.

"Well, I want to go to the village; but I don't see how I am ever to get there," answered the other.

"And may I ask what important business takes you there?" asked the little woman, who was really a witch.

"My house is so dreary, with no one to speak to; I cannot stay in it alone, and I am seeking for a child—I don't mind how small she is—who will keep me company."

"Oh, if that is all, you need go no further," replied the witch, putting her hand in her pocket. "Look, here is a barley corn, as a favor you shall have it for twelve shillings, and if you plant it in a flower-pot, and give it plenty of water, in a few days you will see something wonderful."

This promise raised the woman's spirits. She gladly paid down the price, and as soon as she returned home she dug a hole in a flower-pot and put in the seed.

For three days she waited, hardly taking her eyes from the flower-pot in its warm corner, and on the third morning she saw that, while she was asleep, a tall red tulip had shot up, sheathed in green leaves.

"What a beautiful blossom," cried the woman, stooping to kiss it, when, as she did so, the red petals burst asunder, and in the midst of them was a lovely little girl only an inch high. This tiny little creature was seated on a mattress of violets, and covered with a quilt of rose leaves, and she opened her eyes and smiled at the woman as if she had known her all her life.

"Oh! you darling; I shall never be lonely any more!" she exclaimed in rapture; and the baby nodded her head as much as to say:

"No, of course you won't!"

The woman lost no time in seeking for a roomy walnut-shell, which she lined thickly with white satin, and on it she placed the mattress, with the child, whom she called Maia, upon it. This was her bed, and stood on a chair close to where her foster-mother was sleeping; but in the morning she was lifted out, and placed on a leaf in the middle of a large bowl of water, and given two white horse-hairs to row herself about with. She was the happiest baby that ever was seen, and passed the whole day singing to herself, in a language of her own, that nobody else could understand.

For some weeks the two lived together and never grew tired of each other's society, and then a terrible misfortune happened. One night, when the foster-mother lay sound asleep after a hard day's work, a big, ugly, wet frog hopped in through the open window and stood staring at Maia under her quilt of rose leaves.

"Dear me! that is quite a pretty little girl," thought the frog to herself; "she would make a nice wife for my son." And picking up the walnut cradle in her mouth, she hopped with it to the edge of a stream which ran through the garden.

"Come and see what I have brought you," called the old frog, when she reached her home in the mud.

"Croak! croak! croak!" uttered the son, gazing with pleasure at the sleeping child.

"Hush; don't make such a noise or you will wake her!" whispered the mother. "I mean her to be a wife for you, and while we are preparing for the wedding we will set her on that water-lily leaf in the middle of the brook, so that she may not be able to run away from us."

It was on this green floating prison that Maia awoke, frightened and puzzled, with the first rays of the sun. She stood up straight on the leaf, looking about her for a way of escape, and, finding none, she sat down again and began to weep bitterly. At length her sobs were heard by the old frog, who was busy in her house at the bottom of the marsh, twisting rushes into a soft carpet for Maia's feet, and twining reeds and grapes over the doorway, to make it look pretty for the bride.

"Ah! the poor child feels lost and unhappy," she thought pitifully, for her heart was kind. "Well, I have just done, and then my son and I will go to fetch her. When she sees how handsome he is she will be all smiles again." And in a few minutes they both appeared beside the leaf.

"This is your future husband. Did you ever see anyone like him?" asked the proud mother, pushing him forward. But, after one glance, Maia only cried the more; and the little fishes who lived in the stream came swimming round to see what was the matter.

"It is absurd that such a pretty creature should be forced to take a husband whom she does not want," said they to each other. "And such an ugly one too! However, we can easily prevent it." And by turns they gnawed the stem of the lily-leaf close to the root, till at length it was free, and taking it in their mouths they bore Maia far away, till the little stream grew into a great river.

Oh, how Maia enjoyed that voyage, when once she became quite certain that the frogs could no longer reach her. Past many towns she went, and the people on the banks all turned to look at her, and exclaimed:

"What a lovely little girl! Where can she have come from?"

"What a lovely little girl!" twittered the birds in the bushes. And a blue butterfly fell in love with her, and would not leave her; so she took off her sash, which just matched him, and tied it round his body, so that with this new kind of horse she traveled much faster than before.

Unluckily, a great cockchafer, who was buzzing over the river, happened to catch sight of her, and caught her up in his claws. The poor butterfly was terribly frightened at the sight of him, and he struggled hard to free himself, so that the sash bow gave way, and he flew off into the sunshine. But Maia wasn't so fortunate, and though the cockchafer collected honey from the flowers for her dinner, and told her several times how pretty she was, she could not feel at ease with him. The cockchafer noticed this, and summoned his sisters to play with her; but they only stared rudely, and said:

"Where did you pick up that strange object? She is very ugly to be sure, but one ought to pity her for she has only two legs."

"Yes, and no feelers," added another; "and she is so thin! Well, our brother has certainly very odd taste!"

"Indeed he has!" echoed the others. And they repeated it so loud and so often that, in the end, he believed it too, and snatching her up from the tree where he had placed her, set her down upon a daisy which grew near the ground.

Here Maia stayed for the whole summer, and really was not at all unhappy. She ventured to walk about by herself, and wove herself a bed of some blades of grass, and placed it under a clover leaf for shelter. The red cups that grew in the moss held as much dew as she wanted, and the cockchafer had taught her how to get honey. But summer does not last for ever, and by-and-by the flowers withered, and instead of dew there was snow and ice. Maia did not know what to do, for her clothes were worn to rags, and though she tried to roll herself up in a dry leaf it broke under her fingers. It soon was plain to her that if she did not get some other shelter she would die of hunger and cold.

So, gathering up all her courage, she left the forest and crossed the road into what had been, in the summer, a beautiful field of waving corn, but was now only a mass of hard stalks. She wandered on, seeing nothing but the sky above her head, till she suddenly found herself close to an opening which seemed to lead underground.

"It will be warm, at any rate," thought Maia, "and perhaps the person who lives there will give me something to eat. At any rate, I can't be worse off than I am now." And she walked boldly down the passage. By-and-by she came to a door which stood ajar, and, peeping in, discovered a whole room full of corn. This gave her heart, and she went on more swiftly, till she reached a kitchen where an old field mouse was baking a cake.

"You poor little animal," cried the mouse, who had never seen anything like her before, "you look starved to death! Come and sit here and get warm, and share my dinner with me."

Maia almost wept with joy at the old mouse's kind words. She needed no second bidding, but ate more than she had ever done in her life, though it was not a breakfast for a humming-bird! When she had quite finished she put out her hand and smiled, and the old mouse said to her:

"Can you tell stories? If so you may stay with me till the sun gets hot again, and you shall help me with my house. But it is dull here in the winter unless you have somebody clever enough to amuse you."

Yes, Maia had learned a great many stories from her foster-mother, and, besides, there were all her own adventures, and her escapes from death. She knew also how a room should be swept, and never failed to get up early in the morning and have everything clean and tidy for the old mouse.

So the winter passed away pleasantly, and Maia began to talk of the spring, and of the time when she would have to go out into the world again and seek her fortune.

"Oh, you need not begin to think of *that* for a while yet," answered the field-mouse. "Up on the earth they have a proverb:

> When the day lengthens
> Then the cold strengthens;

it has been quite warm up to now, and the snow may fall any time. Never a winter goes by without it, and *then* you will be very thankful you are *here*, and not outside! But I dare say it is quiet for a young thing like you," she added, "and I have invited my neighbor the mole to come and pay us a visit. He has been asleep all these months, but I hear he is waking up again. You would be a lucky girl if he took into his head to marry you, only, unfortunately, he is blind, and cannot see how pretty you are." And for this blindness Maia felt truly glad, as she did not want a mole for a husband.

198

However, by-and-by he paid his promised visit, and Maia did not like him at all. He might be as rich and learned as possible, but he hated the sun, and the trees, and the flowers, and all that Maia loved best. To be sure, being blind, he had never seen them, and, like many other people, he thought that anything *he* did not know was not worth knowing. But Maia's tales amused him, though he would not for the world have let her see it, and he admired her voice when she sang:

> Mary, Mary, quite contrary,
> How does your garden grow?
> Hush-a-bye, baby, on the tree-top;

though he told her that it was all nonsense, and that trees and gardens were mere foolishness. When she was *his* wife he would teach her things better worth learning.

"Meanwhile," he said, with a grand air, "I have burrowed a passage from this house to my own, in which you can walk; but I warn you not to be frightened at a great dead creature that has fallen through a hole in the roof, and is lying on one side."

"What sort of creature is it?" asked Maia eagerly.

"Oh, I really can't tell you," answered the mole, indifferently; "it is covered with something soft, and it has two thin legs, and a long sharp thing sticking out of its head."

"It is a bird," cried Maia joyfully, "and I love birds! It must have died of cold," she added, dropping her voice. "Oh! good Mr. Mole, do take me to see it!"

"Come then, as I am going home," replied the mole. And calling to the old field-mouse to accompany them, they all set out.

"Here it is," said the mole at last; "dear me, how thankful I am Fate did not make me a bird. They can't say anything but "twit, twit," and die with the first breath of cold."

"Ah, yes, poor useless creature," answered the field-mouse. But while they were talking, Maia crept round to the other side and stroked the feathers of the little swallow, and kissed his eyes.

All that night she lay awake, thinking of the swallow lying dead in the passage. At length she could bear it no longer, and stole away to the place where the hay was kept, and wove a thick carpet. Next she went to the field-mouse's store of cotton which she picked in the summer from some of the marsh flowers, and carrying them both down the passage, she tucked the cotton underneath the bird and spread the hay quilt over him.

"Perhaps you were one of the swallows who sang to me in the summer," said she. "I wish I could have brought you to life again; but now, good-bye!" And she laid her face, wet with tears, on the breast of the bird. Surely she felt a faint movement against her cheek? Yes, there it was again! Suppose the bird was not dead after all, but only senseless with cold and hunger! And at this thought Maia hastened back to the house, and brought some grains of corn, and a drop of water in a leaf. This she held close to the swallow's beak, which he opened unconsciously, and when he had sipped the water she gave him the grains one by one.

"Make no noise, so that no one may guess you are not dead," she said. "To-night I will bring you some more food, and I will tell the mole that he must stuff up the hole again, as it makes the passage too cold for me to walk in. And now farewell." And off she went, back to the field-mouse, who was sound asleep.

After some days of Maia's careful nursing, the swallow felt strong enough to talk, and he told Maia how he came to be in the place where she found him. Before he was big enough to fly very high he had torn his wing in a rosebush, so that he could not keep up with his family and friends when they took their departure to warmer lands. In their swift course they never noticed that their little brother was not with them, and at last he dropped on the ground from sheer fatigue, and must have rolled down the hole into the passage.

It was very lucky for the swallow that both the mole and the field-mouse thought he was dead, and did not trouble about him, so that when the spring *really* came, and the sun was hot, and blue hyacinths grew in the woods and primroses in the hedges, he was as tall and strong as any of his companions.

"You have saved my life, dear little Maia," said he; "but now the time has come for me to leave you—unless," he added, "you will let me carry you on my back far away from this gloomy prison."

Maia's eyes sparkled at the thought, but she shook her head bravely.

"Yes, you must go; but I must stay behind," she answered. "The field-mouse has been good to me, and I cannot desert her like that. Do you think you can open the hole for yourself?" she asked anxiously. "If so, you had better begin now, for this evening we are to have supper with the mole, and it would never do for my foster-mother to find you working at it."

"That is true," answered the swallow. And flying up to the roof,—which, after all, was not very high above them—he set to work with his bill, and soon let a flood of sunshine into the dark place.

"*Won't* you come with me, Maia?" said he. And though her heart longed for the trees and the flowers, she answered as before:

"No, I cannot."

That one glimpse of the sun was all Maia had for some time, for the corn sprung up so thickly over the hole and about the house, that there might almost as well have been no sun at all. However, though she missed her bird friend every moment, she had no leisure to be idle, for the field-mouse had told her that very soon she was to be married to the mole, and kept her spinning wool and cotton for her outfit. And as she had never in her life made a dress, four clever spiders were persuaded to spend the days underground, turning the wool and cotton into tiny garments. Maia liked the clothes, but hated the thought of the blind mole, only she did not know how to escape him. In the evenings, when the spiders were going to their homes for the night, she would walk with them to the door and wait till a puff of wind blew the corn ears apart, and she could see the sky.

"If the swallow would only come now," she said to herself, "I would go with him to the end of the world." But he never came!

"Your outfit is all finished," said the field-mouse one day when the berries were red and the leaves yellow, "and the mole and I have decided that your wedding shall be in four weeks' time."

"Oh, not so soon! not so soon!" cried Maia, bursting into tears; which made the field-mouse very angry, and declare that Maia had no more sense than other girls, and did not know what was good for her. Then the mole arrived, and carried her on his back to see the new house he had dug for her, which was so very far under ground that Maia's tiny legs could never bring her up even as high as the field-mouse's dwelling, from which she might see the sunlight. Her heart grew heavier and heavier as the days went by, and in the last evening of all she crept out into the field among the stubble, to watch the sun set before she bade it good-bye for ever.

"Farewell, farewell," she said "and farewell to my little swallow. Ah! if he only knew, he would come to help me."

"Twit! twit," cried a voice just above her; and the swallow fluttered to the ground beside her. "You look sad; are you *really* going to let that ugly mole marry you?"

"I shall soon die, that is one comfort," she answered weeping. But the swallow only said:

"Tut! tut! get on my back, as I told you before, and I will take you to a land where the sun always shines, and you will soon forget that such a creature as a mole ever existed."

"Yes, I will come," said Maia.

Then the swallow tore off one of the corn stalks with his strong beak, and bade her tie it safely to his wing. And they started off, flying, flying south for many a day.

Oh! how happy Maia was to see the beautiful earth again! A hundred times she longed for the swallow to stop, but he always told her that the best was yet to be; and they flew on and on, only halting for short rests, till they reached a place covered with tall white marble pillars, some standing high, wreathed in vines, out of which endless swallows' heads were peeping; others lying stretched among the flowers, white, yellow, and blue.

"I live up there," said the swallow, pointing to the tallest of the pillars. "But such a house would never do for you, as you would only fall out of it and kill yourself. So choose one of those flowers below, and you shall have it for your own, and sleep all night curled up in its leaves."

"I will have that one," answered Maia, pointing to a white flower shaped like a star, with a tiny crinkled wreath of red and yellow in its center, and a long stem that swayed in the wind; "that one is the prettiest of all, and it smells so sweet." Then the swallow flew down towards it; but as they drew near they saw a tiny little manikin with a crown on his head, and wings on his shoulders, balancing himself on one of the leaves. "Ah, that is the king of the flower-spirits," whispered the swallow. And the king stretched out his hands to Maia, and helped her to jump from the swallow's back.

"I have waited for you for a long while," said he, "and now you have come at last to be my queen."

And Maia smiled, and stood beside him as all the fairies that dwelt in the flowers ran to fetch presents for her; and the best of them all was a pair of lovely gauzy blue wings to help fly about like one of themselves.

So instead of marrying the mole, Little Maia was crowned a queen, and the fairies danced round her in a ring, while the swallow sang the wedding song.

The Snowman

Hans Christian Andersen

I t is so bitterly cold that my whole body creaks," said the snowman. "The wind is wonderfully invigorating. How that glowing thing up there is staring at me!" He meant the sun, who was just setting. "He shall not make me wink; I will hold the pieces tightly." For you must know that he had two large triangular pieces of red tile in the place of eyes in his head; an old rake represented his mouth, and therefore he had also teeth.

He was born amidst the cheering of the boys, and greeted by the tinkling of sleigh-bells and the cracking of whips.

The sun set, the full moon rose large, round and clear on the blue sky. "There he is again on the other side!" said the snowman. Of course he fancied the sun was showing himself again. "I thought I had cured him of staring. Now let him hang there, and give me a light, that I may see myself. I wish I knew how to move, I should so much like to walk about. If I could, I should like to go down and slide on yonder ice, as I have seen the boys do; but I don't know how—I can't even walk."

"Away, away!" barked the old dog in the yard; he was somewhat hoarse, and could no longer well pronounce the proper "Wow, wow." He had become hoarse when he used to live indoors and lie all day long under the warm stove. "The sun will soon teach you how to run; I have seen him teach your predecessor last year, and his predecessors before him. Away, away, they are all gone."

"I do not understand you, friend," said the snowman. "Do you mean to say that she up there is to teach me walking?" He meant the moon. "I have certainly seen her walk a little while ago when I looked her straight in the face, but now she comes creeping from the other side."

"You are dreadfully ignorant," replied the dog, "but that is no wonder, for you have only just been put up. She whom you see up there is the moon; he whom you have seen going off a little while ago was the sun; he is returning to-morrow, and is sure to teach you how to run down into the ditch. We shall soon have a change in the weather, I feel it by the pain I have in my left hind leg; the weather is going to change."

"I do not understand him," said the snowman, "but it strikes me that he speaks of something disagreeable. He who was so staring at me and afterwards went off—the sun, as he calls him—is not my friend; so much I know for certain."

"Away, away," barked the dog; turned three times round himself, and crept back into his kennel to sleep.

The weather really changed. On the next morning the whole country was enveloped in a dense fog; later on an icy wind began to blow, it was bitter cold; but when the sun rose, what a splendor! Trees and bushes were covered with a hoar-frost, they looked like a wood of white coral; all the branches seemed to be strewed over with shiny white blossoms. The many delicate boughs and twigs, which are in the summer completely hidden by the rich foliage, were all visible now. It looked very much like a snowy white cobweb; every twig seemed to send forth rays of white light. The birch-tree moved its branches in the wind, as the trees do in the summer; it was marvelously beautiful to look at.

And when the sun rose the whole glittered and sparkled as if small diamonds had been strewed over them, while on the snowy carpet below large diamonds or innumerable lights seemed to shine even more white than the snow.

"How charming!" said a young girl who stepped out into the garden with a young man. Both stopped near the snowman, and then looked admiringly at the glittering trees. "There is no more beautiful scene in the summer," she said, and her eyes were beaming. "And we can't possibly have such a fellow there in the summer," replied the young man, pointing at the snowman.

The girl laughed, nodded at the snowman, and then both walked over the snow, so that it creaked under their feet like starch.

"Who were these two?" asked the snowman of the dog. "You are longer in the yard than I; do you know them?"

"Certainly I do," replied the dog. "She has stroked me, and he has given me a meat-bone. I shall never bite those two."

"But what are they?" asked the snowman again.

"Lovers," was the dog's answer. "They are going to live together in one kennel, and gnaw on the same bone. Away, away!"

"Are they beings like ourselves?" asked the snowman.

"They are members of the master's family," replied the dog. "Of course one knows very little if one has only been born yesterday. I can see that from you! I have the age and the knowledge too. I know all in the house. I also knew a time when I was not obliged to be chained up here in the cold. Away, away!"

"The cold is splendid," said the snowman. "Go on, tell me more; but you must not rattle so with the chain, for you make me shudder if you do."

"Away, away!" barked the dog. "They say I was once a dear little boy. Then I used to lie on a chair covered with velvet, up in the mansion, or sit on the mistress's lap; they kissed me upon the mouth and wiped my paws with an embroidered handkerchief. They called me Ami, dear sweet Ami. But later on I became too big for them, and they gave me to the housekeeper; thus I came down into the basement. You can look in at the window from the place where you are standing. You can look down into the room where I was one day master, for master I was at the housekeeper's. The rooms were not so grand as above in the mansion, but they were more homely; I was not continually touched and pulled about by the children, and the food was just as good, if not better, than at the mansion. I had my own cushion, and there was a stove in the room, which is at this time of the year the best thing in the world. I used to creep under the stove; there was enough room for me. I am still dreaming of this stove. Away, away!"

"Does a stove look nice?" asked the snowman. "Does it resemble me?"

"The very contrary of you! It is as black as a raven and has a long neck with a broad brass band round it. It eats so much fuel that the fire comes out of its mouth. One must keep at its side, close by or underneath it; there one is very comfortable. Perhaps you can see it from your place."

The snowman looked and noticed something, brightly polished with a broad brass band round it; in its lower parts the fire was visible. A strange feeling overcame the snowman; he had no idea what it was, nor could he explain the cause of it; but all beings, even those who are not snowmen, know it.

"Why did you leave her?" asked the snowman, for he had a notion that the stove was a woman. "How could you leave such a place?"

"I was compelled to," replied the dog; "they threw me out of the house and fastened me up here with the chain. I had bitten the youngest son of the squire in the leg, because he pushed away the bone which I was gnawing with his foot. Bone for bone, I think. But this they took very ill of me, and from this time forward I was chained up. And I have lost my voice, too—do you not hear how hoarse I am? Away, away! I can no longer bark like other dogs. Away, away! That was how it ended."

The snowman was no longer listening to him; he looked unswervingly at the basement into the housekeeper's room, where the stove was standing on its four iron legs, as high as the snowman.

"What a strange noise I hear within me," he said. "Shall I never get in there? It is such an innocent wish of mine, and they say innocent wishes are sure to be fulfilled. I must go in there, and lean against her, even if I must break the window."

"You will never get in there," said the dog, "and if you come close to the stove you are gone. Away, away!"

"I am already now as good as gone," replied the snowman, "I believe I am fainting."

The snowman was all day long looking in at the window. In the dawn the room appeared still more inviting; a gentle light shined out of the stove, not like that of the moon or the sun, but such light as only a stove can produce after being filled with fuel. When the door of the room was opened, the flame burst out at the mouth of the stove—that was its custom. And the flame was reflected on the white face and breast of the snowman, and made him appear quite ruddy.

"I can no longer stand it," he said; "how well it suits her to put out her tongue!"

The night was long, but it did not appear so to the snowman, for he was standing there deeply lost in his pleasant thoughts, which were so freezing that it creaked.

In the morning the window-panes of the basement were covered with ice; the most beautiful ice-flowers that one could wish for were upon them; but they concealed the stove.

The ice on the window-panes would not thaw; the snowman could not see the stove which he imagined to be such a lovely woman. It groaned and creaked within him; it was the very weather to please a snowman; but he did not rejoice—how could he have been happy with this great longing for the stove?

"That is a dreadful disease for a snowman," said the dog; "I suffered myself from it one day, but I have got over it. Away, away!" he barked. "We shall soon have a change in the weather," he added.

The weather changed; it was beginning to thaw. The warmer it became, the more the snowman vanished away. He said nothing, he did not complain; that is the surest sign.

One morning he broke down; and lo! in the place where he had stood, something like a broomstick was sticking in the ground, round which the boys had built him up.

"Well, now I understand why he had such a great longing," said the dog; "I see there is an iron hook attached to the stick, which people use to clean stoves with; the snowman had a stove-scraper in his body, that has moved him so. Now all is over. Away, away!"

And soon the winter was gone. "Away, away," barked the hoarse dog, but the girls in the house were singing:

> Thyme, green thyme, come out, we sing.
> Soon will come the gentle spring;
> Ye willow trees, your catkins don:
> The sun shines bright and days roll on.
> Cuckoo and lark sing merrily too,
> We also will sing Cuckoo! cuckoo!

And nobody thought of the snowman.

The Underground Workers

(FROM *THE VIOLET FAIRY BOOK*)

On a bitter night somewhere between Christmas and the New Year, a man set out to walk to the neighboring village. It was not many miles off, but the snow was so thick that there were no roads, or walls, or hedges left to guide him, and very soon he lost his way altogether, and was glad to get shelter from the wind behind a thick juniper tree. Here he resolved to spend the night, thinking that when the sun rose he would be able to see his path again.

So he tucked his legs snugly under him like a hedgehog, rolled himself up in his sheepskin, and went to sleep. How long he slept, I cannot tell you, but after awhile he became aware that some one was gently shaking him, while a stranger whispered, "My good man, get up! If you lie there any more, you will be buried in the snow, and no one will ever know what became of you."

The sleeper slowly raised his head from his furs, and opened his heavy eyes. Near him stood a long thin man, holding in his hand a young fir tree taller than himself. "Come with me," said the man, "a little way off we have made a large fire, and you will rest far better there than out upon this moor." The sleeper did not wait to be asked twice, but rose at once and followed the stranger. The snow was falling so fast that he could not see three steps in front of him, till the stranger waved his staff, when the drifts parted before them. Very soon they reached a wood, and saw the friendly glow of a fire.

"What is your name?" asked the stranger, suddenly turning round.

"I am called Hans, the son of Long Hans," said the peasant.

In front of the fire three men were sitting clothed in white, just as if it was summer, and for about thirty feet all round winter had been banished. The moss was dry and the plants green, while the grass seemed all alive with the hum of bees and cockchafers. But above the noise the son of Long Hans could hear the whistling of the wind and the crackling of the branches as they fell beneath the weight of the snow.

"Well! you son of Long Hans, isn't this more comfortable than your juniper bush?" laughed the stranger, and for answer Hans replied he could not thank his friend enough for having brought him here, and, throwing off his sheepskin, rolled it up as a pillow. Then, after a hot drink which warmed both their hearts, they lay down on the ground. The stranger talked for a little to the other men in a language Hans did not understand, and after listening for a short time he once more fell asleep.

When he awoke, neither wood nor fire was to be seen, and he did not know where he was. He rubbed his eyes, and began to recall the events of the night, thinking he must have been dreaming; but for all that, he could not make out how he came to be in this place.

Suddenly a loud noise struck on his ear, and he felt the earth tremble beneath his feet. Hans listened for a moment, then resolved to go towards the place where the sound came from, hoping he might come across some human being. He found himself at length at the mouth of a rocky cave in which a fire seemed burning. He entered, and saw a huge forge, and a crowd of men in front of it, blowing bellows and wielding hammers, and to each anvil were seven men, and a set of more comical smiths could not be found if you searched all the world through! Their heads were bigger than their little bodies, and their hammers twice the size of themselves, but the strongest men on earth could not have handled their iron clubs more stoutly or given lustier blows.

The little blacksmiths were clad in leather aprons, which covered them from their necks to their feet in front, and left their backs naked. On a high stool against the wall sat the man with the pinewood staff, watching sharply the way the little fellows did their work, and near him stood a large can, from which every now and then the workers would come and take a drink. The master no longer wore the white garments of the day before, but a black jerkin, held in its place by a leathern girdle with huge clasps.

From time to time he would give his workmen a sign with his staff, for it was useless to speak amid such a noise.

If any of them had noticed that there was a stranger present they took no heed of him, but went on with what they were doing. After some hours' hard labor came the time for rest, and they all flung their hammers to the ground and trooped out of the cave.

Then the master got down from his seat and said to Hans:

"I saw you come in, but the work was pressing, and I could not stop to speak to you. To-day you must be my guest, and I will show you something of the way in which I live. Wait here for a moment, while I lay aside these dirty clothes." With these words he unlocked a door in the cave, and bade Hans pass in before him.

Oh, what riches and treasures met Hans' astonished eyes! Gold and silver bars lay piled on the floor, and glittered so that you could not look at them! Hans thought he would count them for fun, and had already reached the five hundred and seventieth when his host returned and cried, laughing:

"Do not try to count them, it would take too long; choose some of the bars from the heap, as I should like to make you a present of them."

Hans did not wait to be asked twice, and stooped to pick up a bar of gold, but though he put forth all his strength he could not even move it with both hands, still less lift it off the ground.

"Why, you have no more power than a flea," laughed the host; "you will have to content yourself with feasting your eyes upon them!"

So he bade Hans follow him through other rooms, till they entered one bigger than a church, filled, like the rest, with gold and silver. Hans wondered to see these vast riches, which might have bought all the kingdoms of the world, and lay buried, useless, he thought, to anyone.

"What is the reason," he asked of his guide, "that you gather up these treasures here, where they can do good to nobody? If they fell into the hands of men, everyone would be rich, and none need work or suffer hunger."

"And it is exactly for that reason," answered he, "that I must keep these riches out of their way. The whole world would sink to idleness if men were not forced to earn their daily bread. It is only through work and care that man can ever hope to be good for anything."

Hans stared at these words, and at last he begged that his host would tell him what use it was to anybody that this gold and silver should lie mouldering there, and the owner of it be continually trying to increase his treasure, which already overflowed his store rooms.

"I am not really a man," replied his guide, "though I have the outward form of one, but one of those beings to whom is given the care of the world. It is my task and that of my workmen to prepare under the earth the gold and silver, a small portion of which finds its way every year to the upper world, but only just enough to help them carry on their business. To none comes wealth without trouble: we must first dig out the gold and mix the grains with earth, clay, and sand. Then, after long and hard seeking, it will be found in this state, by those who have good luck or much patience. But, my friend, the hour of dinner is at hand. If you wish to remain in this place, and feast your eyes on this gold, then stay till I call you."

In his absence Hans wandered from one treasure chamber to another, sometimes trying to break off a little lump of gold, but never able to do it. After awhile his host came back, but so changed that Hans could not believe it was really he. His silken clothes were of the brightest flame color, richly trimmed with gold fringes and lace; a golden girdle was round his waist, while his head was encircled with a crown of gold, and precious stones twinkled about him like stars in a winter's night, and in place of his wooden stick he held a finely worked golden staff.

The lord of all this treasure locked the doors and put the keys in his pocket, then led Hans into another room, where dinner was laid for them. Table and seats were all of silver, while the dishes and plates were of solid gold. Directly they sat down, a dozen little servants appeared to wait on them, which they did so cleverly and so quickly that Hans could hardly believe they had no wings. As they did not reach as high as the table, they were often obliged to jump and hop right on to the top to get at the dishes. Everything was new to Hans, and though he was rather bewildered he enjoyed himself very much, especially when the man with the golden crown began to tell him many things he had never heard of before.

"Between Christmas and the New Year," said he, "I often amuse myself by wandering about the earth watching the doings of men and learning something about them. But as far as I have seen and heard I cannot speak well of them. The greater part of them are always quarreling and complaining of each other's faults, while nobody thinks of his own."

Hans tried to deny the truth of these words, but he could not do it, and sat silent, hardly listening to what his friend was saying. Then he went to sleep in his chair, and knew nothing of what was happening.

Wonderful dreams came to him during his sleep, where the bars of gold continually hovered before his eyes. He felt stronger than he had ever felt during his waking moments, and lifted two bars quite easily on to his back. He did this so often that at length his strength seemed exhausted, and he sank almost breathless on the ground. Then he heard the sound of cheerful voices, and the song of the blacksmiths as they blew their bellows—he even felt as if he saw the sparks flashing before his eyes. Stretching himself, he awoke slowly, and here he was in the green forest, and instead of the glow of the fire in the underworld the sun was streaming on him, and he sat up wondering why he felt so strange.

At length his memory came back to him, and as he called to mind all the wonderful things he had seen he tried in vain to make them agree with those that happen every day. After thinking it over till he was nearly mad, he tried at last to believe that one night between Christmas and the New Year he had met a stranger in the forest, and had slept all night in his company before a big fire; the next day they had dined together, and had drunk a great deal more than was good for them—in short, he had spent two whole days revelling with another man. But here, with the full tide of summer around him, he could hardly accept his own explanation, and felt that he must have been the plaything or sport of some magician.

Near him, in the full sunlight, were the traces of a dead fire, and when he drew close to it he saw that what he had taken for ashes was really fine silver dust, and that the half burnt firewood was made of gold.

Oh, how lucky Hans thought himself; but where should he get a sack to carry his treasure home before anyone else found it? But necessity is the mother of invention: Hans threw off his fur coat, gathered up the silver ashes so carefully in it that none remained behind, laid the gold sticks on top, and tied up the bag thus made with his girdle, so that nothing should fall out. The load was not, in point of fact, very heavy, although it seemed so to his imagination, and he moved slowly along till he found a safe hiding-place for it.

In this way Hans suddenly became rich—rich enough to buy a property of his own. But being a prudent man, he finally decided that it would be best for him to leave his old neighborhood and look for a home in a distant part of the country, where nobody knew anything about him. It did not take him long to find what he wanted, and after he had paid for it there was plenty of money left over. When he was settled, he married a pretty girl who lived near by, and had some children, to whom on his death-bed he told the story of the lord of the underworld, and how he had made Hans rich.

Christmas with the Baron

ANGELO J. LEWIS

I

Once upon a time—fairy tales always begin with once upon a time—once upon a time there lived in a fine old castle on the Rhine a certain Baron von Schrochslofsleschshoffinger. You will not find it an easy name to pronounce; in fact, the baron never tried it himself but once, and then he was laid up for two days afterwards; so in future we will merely call him "the baron," for shortness, particularly as he was rather a dumpy man.

After having heard his name, you will not be surprised when I tell you that he was an exceedingly bad character. For a baron, he was considered enormously rich; a hundred and fifty pounds a year would not be thought much in this country; but still it will buy a good deal of sausage, which, with wine grown on the estate, formed the chief sustenance of the baron and his family.

Now, you will hardly believe that, notwithstanding he was the possessor of this princely revenue, the baron was not satisfied, but oppressed and ground down his unfortunate tenants to the very last penny he could possibly squeeze out of them. In all his exactions he was seconded and encouraged by his steward, Klootz, an old rascal who took a malicious pleasure in his master's cruelty, and who chuckled and rubbed his hands with the greatest apparent enjoyment when any of the poor landholders could not pay their rent, or afforded him any opportunity for oppression.

Not content with making the poor tenants pay double value for the land they rented, the baron was in the habit of going round every now and then to their houses and ordering anything he took a fancy to, from a fat pig to a pretty daughter, to be sent up to the castle. The pretty daughter was made parlor-maid, but as she had nothing a year, and to find herself, it wasn't what would be considered by careful mothers an eligible situation. The fat pig became sausage, of course.

Things went on from bad to worse, till, at the time of our story, between the alternate squeezings of the baron and his steward, the poor tenants had very little left to squeeze out of them. The fat pigs and pretty daughters had nearly all found their way up to the castle, and there was little left to take.

The only help the poor fellows had was the baron's only daughter, Lady Bertha, who always had a kind word, and frequently something more substantial, for them when her father was not in the way.

Now, I'm not going to describe Bertha, for the simple reason that if I did you would imagine that she was the fairy I'm going to tell you about, and she isn't. However, I don't mind giving you a few outlines.

In the first place, she was exceedingly tiny,—the nicest girls, the real lovable little pets, always are tiny,—and she had long silken black hair, and a dear, dimpled little face full of love and mischief. Now, then, fill up the outline with the details of the nicest and prettiest girl you know, and you will have a slight idea of her. On second thoughts, I don't believe you will, for your portrait wouldn't be half good enough; however, it will be near enough for you.

Well, the baron's daughter, being all your fancy painted her and a trifle more, was naturally much distressed at the goings-on of her unamiable parent, and tried her best to make amends for her father's harshness. She generally managed that a good many pounds of the sausage should find their way back to the owners of the original pig; and when the baron tried to squeeze the hand of the pretty parlor-maid, which he occasionally did after dinner, Bertha had only to say, in a tone of mild remonstrance, "Pa!" and he dropped the hand instantly and stared very hard the other way.

Bad as this disreputable old baron was, he had a respect for the goodness and purity of his child. Like the lion tamed by the charm of Una's innocence, the rough old rascal seemed to lose in her presence half his rudeness, and, though he used awful language to her sometimes (I dare say even Una's lion roared occasionally), he was more tractable with her than with any other living being. Her presence operated as a moral restraint upon him, which, possibly, was the reason that he never stayed down-stairs after dinner, but always retired to a favorite turret, which, I regret to say, he had got so in the way of doing every afternoon that I believe he would have felt unwell without it.

The hour of the baron's afternoon symposium was the time selected by Bertha for her errands of charity. Once he was fairly settled down to his second bottle, off went Bertha, with her maid beside her carrying a basket, to bestow a meal on some of the poor tenants, among whom she was always received with blessings.

At first these excursions had been undertaken principally from charitable motives, and Bertha thought herself plentifully repaid in the love and thanks of her grateful pensioners.

Of late, however, another cause had led her to take even stronger interest in her walks, and occasionally to come in with brighter eyes and a rosier cheek than the gratitude of the poor tenants had been wont to produce.

The fact is, some months before the time of our story, Bertha had noticed in her walks a young artist, who seemed to be fated to be invariably sketching points of interest in the road she had to take. There was one particular tree, exactly in the path which led from the castle-gate, which he had sketched from at least four points of view, and Bertha began to wonder what there could be so very particular about it.

At last, just as Carl von Sempach had begun to consider where on earth he could sketch the tree from next, and to ponder seriously upon the feasibility of climbing up into it and taking it from *that* point of view, a trifling accident occurred which gave him the opportunity of making Bertha's acquaintance,—which, I don't mind stating confidentially, was the very thing he had been waiting for.

It so chanced that, on one particular afternoon, the maid, either through awkwardness, or possibly through looking more at the handsome painter than the ground she was walking on, stumbled and fell.

Of course, the basket fell, too, and equally of course, Carl, as a gentleman, could not do less than offer his assistance in picking up the damsel and the dinner.

The acquaintance thus commenced was not suffered to drop; and handsome Carl and our good little Bertha were fairly over head and ears in love, and had begun to have serious thoughts of a cottage in a wood, *et cœtera*, when their felicity was disturbed by their being accidentally met, in one of their walks, by the baron.

Of course the baron, being himself so thorough an aristocrat, had higher views for his daughter than marrying her to a "beggarly artist," and accordingly he stamped, and swore, and threatened Carl with summary punishment with all sorts of weapons, from heavy boots to blunderbusses, if ever he ventured near the premises again.

This was unpleasant; but I fear it did not *quite* put a stop to the young people's interviews, though it made them less frequent and more secret than before.

Now, I am quite aware this was not at all proper, and that no properly regulated young lady would ever have had meetings with a young man her papa didn't approve of.

But then it is just possible Bertha might not have been a properly regulated young lady. I only know she was a dear little pet, worth twenty model young ladies, and that she loved Carl very dearly.

And then consider what a dreadful old tyrant of a papa she had! My dear girl, it's not the slightest use your looking so provokingly correct; it's my deliberate belief that if you had been in her shoes (they'd have been at least three sizes too small for you, but that doesn't matter) you would have done precisely the same.

Such was the state of things on Christmas Eve in the year— Stay! fairy tales never have a year to them, so, on second thoughts, I wouldn't tell the date if I knew,—but I don't.

Such was the state of things, however, on the particular 24th of December to which our story refers—only, if anything, rather more so.

The baron had got up in the morning in an exceedingly bad temper; and those about him had felt its effects all through the day.

His two favorite wolf-hounds, Lutzow and Teufel, had received so many kicks from the baron's heavy boots that they hardly knew at which end their tails were; and even Klootz himself scarcely dared to approach his master.

In the middle of the day two of the principal tenants came to say that they were unprepared with their rent, and to beg for a little delay.

The poor fellows represented that their families were starving, and entreated for mercy; but the baron was only too glad that he had at last found so fair an excuse for venting his ill-humor.

He loaded the unhappy defaulters with every abusive epithet he could devise (and being called names in German is no joke, I can tell you); and, lastly, he swore by everything he could think of that, if their rent was not paid on the morrow, themselves and their families should be turned out of doors to sleep on the snow, which was then many inches deep on the ground. They still continued to beg for mercy, till the baron became so exasperated that he determined to put them out of the castle himself. He pursued them for that purpose as far as the outer door, when fresh fuel was added to his anger.

Carl, who, as I have hinted, still managed, notwithstanding the paternal prohibition, to see Bertha occasionally, and had come to wish her a merry Christmas, chanced at this identical moment to be saying good-by at the door, above which, in accordance with immemorial usage, a huge bush of mistletoe was suspended. What they were doing under it at the moment of the baron's appearance, I never knew exactly; but his wrath was tremendous!

I regret to say that his language was unparliamentary in the extreme. He swore until he was mauve in the face; and if he had not providentially been seized with a fit of coughing, and sat down in the coal-scuttle,—mistaking it for a three-legged stool,—it is impossible to say to what lengths his feelings might have carried him.

Carl and Bertha picked him up, rather black behind, but otherwise not much the worse for his accident.

In fact, the diversion of his thoughts seemed to have done him good; for, having sworn a little more, and Carl having left the castle, he appeared rather better.

II

After enduring so many and various emotions, it is hardly to be wondered at that the baron required some consolation; so, after having changed his trousers, he took himself off to his favorite turret to allay, by copious potations, the irritations of his mind.

Bottle after bottle was emptied, and pipe after pipe was filled and smoked. The fine old Burgundy was gradually getting into the baron's head; and, altogether, he was beginning to feel more comfortable.

The shades of the winter afternoon had deepened into the evening twilight, made dimmer still by the aromatic clouds that came, with dignified deliberation, from the baron's lips, and curled and floated up to the carved ceiling of the turret, where they spread themselves into a dim canopy, which every successive cloud brought lower and lower.

The fire, which had been piled up mountain-high earlier in the afternoon, and had flamed and roared to its heart's content ever since, had now got to that state—the perfection of a fire to a lazy man—when it requires no poking or attention of any kind, but just burns itself hollow, and then tumbles in, and blazes jovially for a little time, and then settles down to a genial glow, and gets hollow, and tumbles in again.

The baron's fire was just in this delightful *da capo* condition, most favorable of all to the enjoyment of the *dolce far niente*.

For a little while it would glow and kindle quietly, making strange faces to itself, and building fantastic castles in the depths of its red recesses, and then the castles would come down with a crash, and the faces disappear, and a bright flame spring up and lick lovingly the sides of the old chimney; and the carved heads of improbable men and impossible women, hewn so deftly round the panels of the old oak wardrobe opposite, in which the baron's choicest vintages were deposited, were lit up by the flickering light, and seemed to nod and wink at the fire in return, with the familiarity of old acquaintances.

Some such fancy as this was disporting itself in the baron's brain; and he was gazing at the old oak carving accordingly, and emitting huge volumes of smoke with reflective slowness, when a clatter among the bottles on the table caused him to turn his head to ascertain the cause.

The baron was by no means a nervous man; however, the sight that met his eyes when he turned round did take away his presence of mind a little; and he was obliged to take four distinct puffs before he had sufficiently regained his equilibrium to inquire, "Who the—Pickwick—are you?" (The baron said "Dickens," but, as that is a naughty word, we will substitute "Pickwick," which is equally expressive, and not so wrong.) Let me see; where was I? Oh, yes!" Who the Pickwick are you?"

Now, before I allow the baron's visitor to answer the question, perhaps I had better give a slight description of his personal appearance.

If this was not a true story, I should have liked to have made him a model of manly beauty; but a regard for veracity compels me to confess that he was not what would be generally considered handsome; that is, not in figure, for his face was by no means unpleasing.

His body was, in size and shape, not very unlike a huge plum-pudding, and was clothed in a bright-green, tightly-fitting doublet, with red holly-berries for buttons.

His limbs were long and slender in proportion to his stature, which was not more than three feet or so.

His head was encircled by a crown of holly and mistletoe.

The round red berries sparkled amid his hair, which was silver-white, and shone out in cheerful harmony with his rosy, jovial face. And that face! it would have done one good to look at it.

In spite of the silver hair, and an occasional wrinkle beneath the merry, laughing eyes, it seemed brimming over with perpetual youth. The mouth, well garnished with teeth, white and sound, which seemed as if they could do ample justice to holiday cheer, was ever open with a beaming, genial smile, expanding now and then into hearty laughter. Fun and good-fellowship were in every feature.

The owner of the face was, at the moment when the baron first perceived him, comfortably seated upon the top of the large tobacco-jar on the table, nursing his left leg.

The baron's somewhat abrupt inquiry did not appear to irritate him; on the contrary, he seemed rather amused than otherwise.

"You don't ask prettily, old gentleman," he replied; "but I don't mind telling you, for all that. I'm King Christmas."

"Eh?" said the baron.

"Ah!" said the goblin. Of course, you have guessed he was a goblin?

"And pray what's your business here?" said the baron.

"Don't be crusty with a fellow," replied the goblin. "I merely looked in to wish you the compliments of the season. Talking of crust, by the way, what sort of a tap is it you're drinking?" So saying, he took up a flask of the baron's very best and poured out about half a glass. Having held the glass first on one side and then on the other, winked at it twice, sniffed it, and gone through the remainder of the pantomime in which connoisseurs indulge, he drank it with great deliberation, and smacked his lips scientifically. "Hum! Johannisberg! and not so *very* bad—for you. But I tell you what it is, baron, you'll have to bring out better stuff than this when I put my legs on your mahogany."

"Well, you are a cool fish," said the baron. "However, you're rather a joke, so, now you're here, we may as well enjoy ourselves. Smoke?"

"Not anything you're likely to offer me!"

"Confound your impudence!" roared the baron, with a horribly complicated oath. "That tobacco is as good as any in all Rhineland."

"That's a nasty cough you've got, baron. Don't excite yourself, my dear boy; I dare say you speak according to your lights. I don't mean Vesuvians, you know, but your opportunities for knowing anything about it. Try a weed out of my case, and I expect you'll alter your opinion."

The baron took the proffered case and selected a cigar. Not a word was spoken till it was half consumed, when the baron took it, for the first time, from his lips, and said, gently, with the air of a man communicating an important discovery in the strictest confidence, "Das ist gut!"

"Thought you'd say so," said the visitor. "And now, as you like the cigar, I should like you to try a thimbleful of what I call wine. I must warn you, though, that it is rather potent, and may produce effects you are not accustomed to."

"Bother that, if it is as good as the weed," said the baron; "I haven't taken my usual quantity by four bottles yet."

"Well, don't say I didn't warn you, that's all. I don't think you'll find it unpleasant, though it is rather strong when you're not accustomed to it." So saying, the goblin produced from some mysterious pocket a black, big-bellied bottle, crusted, apparently, with the dust of ages.

It did strike the baron as peculiar, that the bottle, when once produced, appeared nearly as big round as the goblin himself; but he was not the sort of man to stick at trifles, and he pushed forward his glass to be filled just as composedly as if the potion had been shipped and paid duty, in the most commonplace way.

The glass was filled and emptied, but the baron uttered not his opinion. Not in words, at least, but he pushed forward his glass to be filled again in a manner that sufficiently bespoke his approval.

"Aha! you smile!" said the goblin. And it was a positive fact; the baron was smiling; a thing he had not been known to do in the memory of the oldest inhabitant. "That's the stuff to make your hair curl, isn't it?"

"I believe you, my b-o-o-oy!" The baron brought out this earnest expression of implicit confidence with true unction. "It warms one *here!*"

Knowing the character of the man, one would have expected him to put his hand upon his stomach. But he didn't; he laid it upon his *heart.*

"The spell begins to operate, I see," said the goblin. "Have another glass?"

The baron had another glass, and another after that.

The smile on his face expanded into an expression of such geniality that the whole character of his countenance was changed, and his own mother wouldn't have known him. I doubt myself—inasmuch as she died when he was exactly a year and three months old—whether she would have recognized him under any circumstances; but I merely wish to express that he was changed almost beyond recognition.

"Upon my word," said the baron, at length, "I feel so light I almost think I could dance a hornpipe. I used to, once, I know. Shall I try?"

"Well, if you ask my advice," replied the goblin, "I should say, decidedly, don't. 'Barkis is willing,' I dare say, but trousers are weak, and you might split 'em."

"Hang it all," said the baron, "so I might. I didn't think of that. But still I feel as if I must do something juvenile!"

"Ah! that's the effect of your change of nature," said the goblin. "Never mind, I'll give you plenty to do presently."

"Change of nature! What do you mean, you old conundrum?" said the baron.

"You're another," said the goblin. "But never mind. What I mean is just this. What you are now feeling is the natural consequence of my magic wine, which has changed you into a fairy. That's what's the matter, sir."

"A fairy! me!" exclaimed the baron. "Get out. I'm too fat."

"Fat! Oh! that's nothing. We shall put you in regular training, and you'll soon be slim enough to creep into a lady's stocking. Not that you'll be called upon to do anything of the sort; but I'm merely giving you an idea of your future figure."

"No, no," said the baron; "me thin! that's too ridiculous. Why, that's worse than being a fairy. You don't mean it, though, do you? I do feel rather peculiar."

"I do, indeed," said the visitor. "You don't dislike it, do you?"

"Well, no, I can't say I do, entirely. It's queer, though, I feel so uncommon friendly. I feel as if I should like to shake hands or pat somebody on the back."

"Ah!" said the goblin, "I know how it is. Rum feeling, when you're not accustomed to it. But come; finish that glass, for we must be off. We've got a precious deal to do before morning, I can tell you. Are you ready?"

"All right," said the baron. "I'm just in the humor to make a night of it."

"Come along, then," said the goblin.

They proceeded for a short time in silence along the corridors of the old castle. They carried no candle, but the baron noticed that everything seemed perfectly light wherever they stood, but relapsed into darkness as soon as they had passed by. The goblin spoke first.

"I say, baron, you've been an uncommon old brute in your time, now, haven't you?"

"H'm," said the baron, reflectively; "I don't know. Well, yes, I rather think I have."

"How jolly miserable you've been making those two young people, you old sinner! You know who I mean."

"Eh, what? You know that, too?" said the baron.

"Know it; of course I do. Why, bless your heart, I know everything, my dear boy. But you *have* made yourself an old tyrant in that quarter, considerably. Ar'n't you blushing, you hard-hearted old monster?"

"Don't know, I'm sure," said the baron, scratching his nose, as if that was where he expected to feel it. "I believe I have treated them badly, though, now I come to think of it."

At this moment they reached the door of Bertha's chamber The door opened of itself at their approach.

"Come along," said the goblin; "you won't wake her. Now, old flinty-heart, look there."

The sight that met the baron's view was one that few fathers could have beheld without affectionate emotion. Under ordinary circumstances, however, the baron would not have felt at all sentimental on the subject, but to-night something made him view things in quite a different light.

I shouldn't like to make affidavit of the fact, but it's my positive impression that he sighed.

Now, my dear reader, don't imagine I'm going to indulge your impertinent curiosity with an elaborate description of the sacred details of a lady's sleeping apartment. *You're* not a fairy, you know, and I don't see that it can possibly matter to you whether fair Bertha's dainty little bottines were tidily placed on a chair by her bedside, or thrown carelessly, as they had been taken off, upon the hearth-rug, where her favorite spaniel reposed, warming his nose in his sleep before the last smouldering embers of the decaying fire; or whether her crinoline—but if she did wear a crinoline, what can that possibly matter to you?

All I shall tell you is, that everything looked snug and comfortable; but, somehow, any place got that look when Bertha was in it.

And now a word about the jewel in the casket—pet Bertha herself. Really, I'm at a loss to describe her. How do you look when you're asleep?—Well, it wasn't like *that*; not a bit! Fancy a sweet girl's face, the cheek faintly flushed with a soft, warm tint, like the blush in the heart of the opening rose, and made brighter by the contrast of the snowy pillow on which it rested; dark silken hair, curling and clustering lovingly over the tiniest of tiny ears, and the softest, whitest neck that ever mortal maiden was blessed with; long silken eyelashes, fringing lids only less beautiful than the dear earnest eyes they cover. Fancy all this, and fancy, too, if you can, the expression of perfect goodness and purity that lit up the sweet features of the slumbering maiden with a beauty almost angelic, and you will see what the baron saw that night. Not quite all, however, for the baron's vision paused not at the bedside before him, but had passed on from the face of the sleeping maiden to another face as lovely, that of the young wife, Bertha's mother, who had, years before, taken her angel beauty to the angels.

The goblin spoke to the baron's thought. "Wonderfully like her, is she not, baron?" The baron slowly inclined his head.

"You made her very happy, didn't you?" The tone in which the goblin spoke was harsh and mocking.

"A faithful husband, tender and true! She must have been a happy wife, eh, baron?"

The baron's head had sunk upon his bosom. Old recollections were thronging into his awakened memory. Solemn vows to love and cherish somewhat strangely kept. Memories of bitter words and savage oaths showered at a quiet and uncomplaining figure, without one word in reply. And, last, the memory of a fit of drunken passion, and a hasty blow struck with a heavy hand. And then of three months of fading away; and last, of her last prayer—for her baby and him.

"A good husband makes a good father, baron. No wonder you are somewhat chary of rashly intrusting to a suitor the happiness of a sweet flower like this. Poor child! it is hard, though, that she must think no more of him she loves so dearly. See! she is weeping even in her dreams. But you have good reasons, no doubt. Young Carl is wild, perhaps, or drinks, or gambles, eh? What! none of these? Perhaps he is wayward and uncertain; and you fear that the honeyed words of courtship might turn to bitter sayings in matrimony. They do, sometimes, eh, baron? By all means guard her from such a fate as that. Poor, tender flower! Or who knows, worse than that, baron! Hard words break no bones, they say, but angry men arc quick, and a blow is soon struck, eh?"

The goblin had drawn nearer and nearer, and laid his hand upon the baron's arm, and the last words were literally hissed into his ears.

The baron's frame swayed to and fro under the violence of his emotion. At last, with a cry of agony, he dashed his hands upon his forehead. The veins were swollen up like thick cords, and his voice was almost inarticulate in its unnatural hoarseness.

"Tortures! release me! Let me go, let me go and do something to forget the past, or I shall go mad and die!"

He rushed out of the room and paced wildly down the corridor, the goblin following him. At last, as they came near the outer door of the castle, which opened of itself as they reached it, the spirit spoke:

223

"This way, baron, this way. I told you there was work for us to do before morning, you know."

"Work!" exclaimed the baron, absently, passing his fingers through his tangled hair; "oh! yes, work! the harder the better; anything to make me forget."

The two stepped out into the courtyard, and the baron shivered, though, as it seemed, unconsciously, at the breath of the frosty midnight air. The snow lay deep on the ground, and the baron's heavy boots sank into it with a crisp, crushing sound at every tread.

He was bareheaded, but seemed unconscious of the fact, and tramped on, as if utterly indifferent to anything but his own thoughts. At last, as a blast of the night wind, keener than ordinary, swept over him, he seemed for the first time to feel the chill. His teeth chattered, and he muttered, "Cold, very cold."

"Ay, baron," said the goblin, "it is cold even to us, who are healthy and strong, and warmed with wine. Colder still, though, to those who are hungry and half-naked, and have to sleep on the snow."

"Sleep? snow?" said the baron. "Who sleeps on the snow? Why, I wouldn't let my dogs be out on such a night as this."

"Your dogs, no!" said the goblin; "I spoke of meaner animals—your wretched tenants. Did you not order, yesterday, that Wilhelm and Friedrich, if they did not pay their rent tomorrow, should be turned out to sleep on the snow? A snug bed for the little ones, and a nice white coverlet, eh? Ha! ha! twenty florins or so is no great matter, is it? I'm afraid their chance is small; nevertheless, come and sec."

The baron hung his head. A few minutes brought him to the first of the poor dwellings, which they entered noiselessly. The fireless grate, the carpet-less floor, the broken windowpanes, all gave sufficient testimony to the want and misery of the occupants. In one corner lay sleeping a man, a woman, and three children, and nestling to each other for the warmth which their ragged coverlet could afford. In the man, the baron recognized his tenant Wilhelm, one of those who had been with him to beg for indulgence on the previous day.

The keen features, and bones almost starting through the pallid skin, showed how heavily the hand of hunger had been laid upon all.

The cold night wind moaned and whistled through the many flaws in the ill-glazed, ill-thatched tenement, and rustled over the sleepers, who shivered even in their sleep.

"Ha, baron!" said the goblin, "death is breathing in their faces even now, you see; it is hardly worth while to lay them to sleep in the snow, is it? They would sleep a little sounder, that's all."

The baron shuddered, and then, hastily pulling the warm coat from his own shoulders, he spread it over the sleepers.

"Oho!" said the goblin; "bravely done, baron! By all means keep them warm to-night; they'll enjoy the snow more to-morrow, you know."

Strange to say, the baron, instead of feeling chilled when he had removed his coat, felt a strange glow of warmth spread from the region of the heart over his entire frame. The goblin's continual allusions to his former intention, which he had by this time totally relinquished, hurt him, and he said, rather pathetically,—

"Don't talk of that again, good goblin. I'd rather sleep on the snow myself."

"Eh! what?" said the goblin; "you don't mean to say you're sorry? Then what do you say to making these poor people comfortable?"

"With all my heart," said the baron, "if we had only anything to do it with."

"You leave that to me," said the goblin. "Your brother fairies are not far off, you may be sure."

As he spoke he clapped his hands thrice, and before the third clap had died away the poor cottage was swarming with tiny figures, whom the baron rightly conjectured to be the fairies themselves.

Now, you may not be aware (the baron was not, until that night) that there are among the fairies trades and professions, just as with ordinary mortals.

However, there they were, each with the accompaniments of his or her particular business, and to it they went manfully. A fairy glazier put in new panes to the shattered windows, fairy carpenters replaced the doors upon their hinges, and fairy painters, with inconceivable celerity, made cupboards and closets as fresh as paint could make them; one fairy housemaid laid and lit a roaring fire, while another dusted and rubbed chairs and tables to a miraculous degree of brightness; a fairy butler uncorked bottles of fairy wine, and a fairy cook laid out a repast of most tempting appearance.

The baron, hearing a tapping above him, cast his eyes upward, and beheld a fairy slater rapidly repairing a hole in the roof; and when he bent them down again they fell on a fairy doctor mixing a cordial for the sleepers. Nay, there was even a fairy parson, who, not having any present employment, contented himself with rubbing his hands and looking pleasant, probably waiting till somebody might want to be christened or married.

Every trade, every profession or occupation appeared, without exception, to be represented; nay, we beg pardon, with one exception only, for the baron used to say, when afterwards relating his experiences to bachelor friends,—

"You may believe me or not, sir, there was every mortal business under the sun, *but deil a bit of a lawyer.*"

The baron could not long remain inactive. He was rapidly seized with a violent desire to do something to help, which manifested itself in insane attempts to assist everybody at once. At last, after having taken all the skin off his knuckles in attempting to hammer in nails in aid of the carpenter, and then nearly tumbling over a fairy housemaid, whose broom he was offering to carry, he gave it up as a bad job, and stood aside with his friend the goblin.

He was just about to inquire how it was that the poor occupants of the house were not awakened by so much din, when a fairy Sam Slick, who had been examining the cottager's old clock with a view to a thorough repair, touched some spring within it, and it made the usual purr preparatory to striking. When, lo! and behold, at the very first stroke, cottage, goblin, fairies, and all disappeared into utter darkness, and the baron found himself in his turret-chamber, rubbing his toe, which he had just hit with considerable force against the fender. As he was only in his slippers, the concussion was unpleasant, and the baron rubbed his toe for a good while.

After he had finished with his toe he rubbed his nose, and, finally, with a countenance of deep reflection, scratched the bump of something or other at the top of his head.

The old clock on the stairs was striking three, and the fire had gone out.

The baron reflected for a short time longer, and finally decided that he had better go to bed, which he did accordingly.

III

The morning dawned upon the very ideal, as far as weather was concerned, of a Christmas-day. A bright winter sun shone out just vividly enough to make everything look genial and pleasant, and yet not with sufficient warmth to mar the pure, unbroken surface of the crisp, white snow, which lay like a never-ending white lawn upon the ground, and glittered in myriad silver flakes upon the leaves of the sturdy evergreens.

I am afraid the baron had not had a very good night; at any rate, I know that he was wide-awake at an hour long before his usual time of rising.

He lay first on one side, and then on the other, and then, by way of variety, turned on his back, with his magenta nose pointing perpendicularly towards the ceiling; but it was all of no use. Do what he would, he couldn't get to sleep, and at last, not long after daybreak, he tumbled out of bed and proceeded to dress.

Even after he was out of bed his fidgetiness continued. It did not strike him, until after he had got one boot on, that it would be a more natural proceeding to put his stockings on first; after which he caught himself in the act of trying to put his trousers on over his head.

In a word, the baron's mind was evidently preoccupied; his whole air was that of a man who felt a strong impulse to do something or other, but could not quite make up his mind to it.

At last, however, the good impulse conquered, and this wicked old baron, in the stillness of the calm, bright Christmas morning, went down upon his knees and prayed.

Stiff were his knees and slow his tongue, for neither had done such work for many a long day past; but I have read in the Book of the joy of angels over a repenting sinner.

There needs not much eloquence to pray the publican's prayer, and who shall say but there was gladness in heaven that Christmas morn.

The baron's appearance down-stairs at such an early hour occasioned quite a commotion. Nor were the domestics reassured when the baron ordered a bullock to be killed and jointed instantly, and all the available provisions in the larder, including sausage, to be packed up in baskets, with a good store of his own peculiar wine.

One ancient retainer was heard to declare, with much pathos, that he feared master had gone insane.

However, insane or not, they knew the baron must be obeyed, and in an exceedingly short space of time he sallied forth, accompanied by three servants carrying the baskets, and wondering what in the name of fortune their master would do next.

He stopped at the cottage of Wilhelm, which he had visited with the goblin on the previous night. The labors of the fairies did not seem to have produced much lasting benefit, for the appearance of everything around was as wretched as could be.

The poor family thought that the baron had come himself to turn them out of house and home; and the children huddled up timidly to their mother for protection, while the father attempted some words of entreaty for mercy.

The pale, pinched features of the group, and their looks of dread and wretchedness, were too much for the baron.

"Eh! what! what do you mean, confound you? Turn you out? Of course not: I've brought you some breakfast. Here! Fritz—Carl; where are the knaves? Now, then, unpack, and don't be a week about it. Can't you see the people are hungry, ye villains? Here, lend me the corkscrew."

This last being a tool the baron was tolerably accustomed to, he had better success than with those of the fairy carpenters; and it was not long before the poor tenants were seated before a roaring fire, and doing justice, with the appetite of starvation, to a substantial breakfast.

The baron felt a queer sensation in his throat at the sight of the poor people's enjoyment, and had passed the back of his hand twice across his eyes when he thought no one was looking; but his emotion fairly rose to boiling when the poor father, Wilhelm, with tears in his eyes, and about a quarter of a pound of beef in his mouth, sprang up from the table and flung himself at the baron's knees, invoking blessings on him for his goodness.

"Get up, you audacious scoundrel!" roared the baron. "What the deuce do you mean by such conduct, eh? confound you!"

At this moment the door opened, and in walked Mynheer Klootz, who had heard nothing of the baron's change of intentions, and who, seeing Wilhelm at the baron's feet, and hearing the latter speaking, as he thought, in an angry tone, at once jumped to the conclusion that Wilhelm was entreating for longer indulgence. He rushed at the unfortunate man and collared him. "Not if we know it," exclaimed he; "you'll have the wolves for bedfellows tonight, I reckon. Come along, my fine fellow." As he spoke he turned his back towards the baron, with the intention of dragging his victim to the door.

The baron's little gray eyes twinkled, and his whole frame quivered with suppressed emotion, which, after the lapse of a moment, vented itself in a kick, and such a kick! Not one of your *Varsovianna* flourishes, but a kick that employed every muscle from hip to toe, and drove the worthy steward up against the door like a ball from a catapult.

Misfortunes never come singly, and so Mynheer Klootz found with regard to the kick, for it was followed, without loss of time, by several dozen others, as like it as possible, from the baron's heavy boots.

Wounded lions proverbially come badly off, and Fritz and Carl, who had suffered from many an act of petty tyranny on the part of the steward, thought they could not do better than follow their master's example, which they did to such good purpose, that when the unfortunate Klootz did escape from the cottage at last, I don't believe he could have had any *os sacrum* left.

After having executed this little act of poetical justice, the baron and his servants visited the other cottages, in all of which they were received with dread and dismissed with blessings.

Having completed his tour of charity, the baron returned home to breakfast, feeling more really contented than he had done for many a long year. He found Bertha, who had not risen when he started, in a considerable state of anxiety as to what he could possibly have been doing. In answer to her inquiries, he told her, with a roughness he was far from feeling, to "mind her own affairs."

The gentle eyes filled with tears at the harshness of the reply; perceiving which, the baron was beyond measure distressed, and chucked her under the chin in what was meant to be a very conciliatory manner.

"Eh! what, my pretty, tears? No, surely. Bertha must forgive her old father. I didn't mean it, you know, my pet; and yet, on second thoughts, yes, I did, too." Bertha's face was overcast again. "My little girl thinks she has no business anywhere, eh! Is that it? Well, then, my pet, suppose you make it your business to write a note to young Carl von Sempach, and say I'm afraid I was rather rude to him yesterday, but if he'll overlook it, and come take a snug family dinner and a slice of the pudding with us to-day—"

"Why, pa, you don't mean—yes, I do really believe you do—"

The baron's eyes were winking nineteen to the dozen.

"Why, you dear, dear, dear old pa!" and at the imminent risk of upsetting the breakfast table, Bertha rushed at the baron, and flinging two soft white arms about his neck, kissed him—oh! how she *did* kiss him! I shouldn't have thought, myself, she could possibly have had any left for Carl; but I dare say Bertha attended to his interests in that respect somehow.

IV

Well, Carl came to dinner, and the baron was, not very many years after, promoted to the dignity of a grandpapa, and a very jolly old grandpapa he made.

Is that all you wanted to know? About Klootz? Well, Klootz got over the kicking, but he was dismissed from the baron's service; and on examination of his accounts it was discovered that he had been in the habit of robbing the baron of nearly a third of his yearly income, which he had to refund; and with the money he was thus compelled to disgorge, the baron built new cottages for his tenants, and new-stocked their farms. Nor was he poorer in the end, for his tenants worked with the energy of gratitude, and he was soon many times richer than when the goblin visited him on that Christmas Eve.

And was the goblin ever explained? Certainly not. How dare you have the impertinence to suppose such a thing?

An empty bottle, covered with cobwebs, was found the next morning in the turret-chamber, which the baron at first imagined must be the bottle from which the goblin produced his magic wine; but as it was found, on examination, to be labeled "Old Jamaica Rum," of course that could not have had anything to do with it. However it was, the baron never thoroughly enjoyed any other wine after it, and as he did not thenceforth get intoxicated, on an average, more than two nights a week, or swear more than eight oaths a day, I think King Christmas may be considered to have thoroughly reformed him.

And he always maintained, to the day of his death, that he was changed into a fairy, and became exceedingly angry if contradicted.

Who doesn't believe in fairies after this? I only hope King Christmas may make a few more good fairies this year, to brighten the homes of the poor with the light of Christmas charity.

Truly, we need not look far for alms-men. Cold and hunger, disease and death, are around us at all times; but at no time do they press more heavily on the poor than at this jovial Christmas season.

Shall we shut out, in our mirth and jollity, the cry of the hungry poor? or shall we not rather remember, in the midst of our happy family circles, round our well-filled tables and before our blazing fires, that our brothers are starving out in the cold, and that the Christmas song of the angels was "Good-will to men"?

Rübezahl

(FROM *THE BROWN FAIRY BOOK*)

Over all the vast under-world the mountain Gnome Rübezahl was lord; and busy enough the care of his dominions kept him. There were the endless treasure chambers to be gone through, and the hosts of gnomes to be kept to their tasks. Some built strong barriers to hold back the fiery rivers in the earth's heart, and some had scalding vapors to change dull stones to precious metal, or were hard at work filling every cranny of the rocks with diamonds and rubies; for Rübezahl loved all pretty things. Sometimes the fancy would take him to leave those gloomy regions, and come out upon the green earth for a while, and bask in the sunshine and hear the birds sing. And as gnomes live many hundreds of years he saw strange things. For, the first time he came up, the great hills were covered with thick forests, in which wild animals roamed, and Rübezahl watched the fierce fights between bear and bison, or chased the gray wolves, or amused himself by rolling great rocks down into the desolate valleys, to hear the thunder of their fall echoing among the hills. But the next time he ventured above ground, what was his surprise to find everything changed! The dark woods were hewn down, and in their place appeared blossoming orchards surrounding cosy-looking thatched cottages; for every chimney the blue smoke curled peacefully into the air, sheep and oxen fed in the flowery meadows, while from the shade of the hedges came the music of the shepherd's pipe. The strangeness and pleasantness of the sight so delighted the gnome that he never thought of resenting the intrusion of these unexpected guests, who, without saying "by your leave" or "with your leave," had made themselves so very much at home upon is hills; nor did he wish to interfere with their doings, but left them in quiet possession of their homes, as a good householder leaves in peace the swallows who have built their nests under his eaves. He was indeed greatly minded to make friends with this being called "man," so, taking the form of an old field laborer, he entered the service of a farmer. Under his care all the crops flourished exceedingly, but the master proved to be wasteful and ungrateful, and Rübezahl soon left him, and went to be shepherd to his next neighbor. He tended the flock so diligently, and knew so well where to lead the sheep to the sweetest pastures, and where among the hills to look for any who strayed away, that they too prospered under his care, and not one was lost or torn by wolves; but this new master was a hard man, and begrudged him his well-earned wages. So he ran away and went to serve the judge. Here he upheld the law with might and main, and was a terror to thieves and evildoers; but the judge was a bad man, who took bribes, and despised the law. Rübezahl would not be the tool of an unjust man, and so he told his master, who thereupon ordered him to be thrown in prison. Of course that did not trouble the gnome at all, he simply got out through the keyhole, and went away down to his underground palace, very much disappointed by his first experience of mankind. But, as time went on, he forgot the disagreeable things that had happened to him, and thought he would take another look at the upper world.

So he stole into the valley, keeping himself carefully hidden in copse or hedgerow, and very soon met with an adventure; for, peeping through a screen of leaves, he saw before him a green lawn where stood a charming maiden, fresh as the spring, and beautiful to look upon. Around her upon the grass lay her young companions, as if they had thrown themselves down to rest after some merry game. Beyond them flowed a little brook, into which a waterfall leapt from a high rock, filling the air with its pleasant sound, and making a coolness even in the sultry noontide. The sight of the maiden so pleased the gnome that, for the first time, he wished himself a mortal; and, longing for a better view of the gay company, he changed himself into a raven and perched upon an oak-tree which overhung the brook. But he soon found that this was not at all a good plan. He could only see with a raven's eyes, and feel as a raven feels; and a nest of field-mice at the foot of the tree interested him far more than the sport of the maidens. When he understood this he flew down again in a great hurry into the thicket, and took the form of a handsome young man—that was the best way—and he fell in love with the girl then and there. The fair maiden was the daughter of the king of the country, and she often wandered in the forest with her play fellows gathering the wild flowers and fruits, till the midday heat drove the merry band to the shady lawn by the brook to rest, or to bathe in the cool waters. On this particular morning the fancy took them to wander off again into the wood.

This was Master Rübezahl's opportunity. Stepping out of his hiding-place he stood in the midst of the little lawn, weaving his magic spells, till slowly all about him changed, and when the maidens returned at noon to their favorite resting-place they stood lost in amazement, and almost fancied that they must be dreaming. The red rocks had become white marble and alabaster; the stream that murmured and struggled before in its rocky bed, flowed in silence now in its smooth channel, from which a clear fountain leapt, to fall again in showers of diamond drops, now on this side now on that, as the wandering breeze scattered it.

Daisies and forget-me-nots fringed its brink, while tall hedges of roses and jasmine ringed it round, making the sweetest and daintiest bower imaginable. To the right and left of the waterfall opened out a wonderful grotto, its walls and arches glittering with many-colored rock-crystals, while in every niche were spread out strange fruits and sweetmeats, the very sight of which made the princess long to taste them. She hesitated a while, however, scarcely able to believe her eyes, and not knowing if she should enter the enchanted spot or fly from it. But at length curiosity prevailed, and she and her companions explored to their heart's content, and tasted and examined everything, running hither and thither in high glee, and calling merrily to each other.

At last, when they were quite weary, the princess cried out suddenly that nothing would content her but to bathe in the marble pool, which certainly did look very inviting; and they all went gaily to this new amusement. The princess was ready first, but scarcely had she slipped over the rim of the pool when down—down—down she sank, and vanished in its depths before her frightened playmates could seize her by so much as a lock of her floating golden hair!

Loudly did they weep and wail, running about the brink of the pool, which looked so shallow and so clear, but which had swallowed up their princess before their eyes. They even sprang into the water and tried to dive after her, but in vain; they only floated like corks in the enchanted pool, and could not keep under water for a second.

They saw at last that there was nothing for it but to carry to the king the sad tidings of his beloved daughter's disappearance. And what great weeping and lamentation there was in the palace when the dreadful news was told! The king tore his robes, dashed his golden crown from his head, and hid his face in his purple mantle for grief and anguish at the loss of the princess.

After the first outburst of wailing, however, he took heart and hurried off to see for himself the scene of this strange adventure, thinking, as people will in sorrow, that there might be some mistake after all. But when he reached the spot, behold, all was changed again! The glittering grotto described to him by the maidens had completely vanished, and so had the marble bath, the bower of jasmine; instead, all was a tangle of flowers, as it had been of old. The king was so much perplexed that he threatened the princess's playfellows with all sorts of punishments if they would not confess something about her disappearance; but as they only repeated the same story he presently put down the whole affair to the work of some sprite or goblin, and tried to console himself for his loss by ordering a grand hunt; for kings cannot bear to be troubled about anything long.

Meanwhile the princess was not at all unhappy in the palace of her elfish lover.

When the water-nymphs, who were hiding in readiness, had caught her and dragged her out of the sight of her terrified maidens, she herself had not had time to be frightened. They swam with her quickly by strange underground ways to a palace so splendid that her father's seemed but a poor cottage in comparison with it, and when she recovered from her astonishment she found herself seated upon a couch, wrapped in a wonderful robe of satin fastened with a silken girdle, while beside her knelt a young man who whispered the sweetest speeches imaginable in her ear. The gnome, for he it was, told her all about himself and his great underground kingdom, and presently led her through the many rooms and halls of the palace, and showed her the rare and wonderful things displayed in them till she was fairly dazzled at the sight of so much splendor. On three sides of the castle lay a lovely garden with masses of gay, sweet flowers, and velvet lawns all cool and shady, which pleased the eye of the princess. The fruit trees were hung with golden and rosy apples, and nightingales sang in every bush, as the gnome and the princess wandered in the leafy alleys, sometimes gazing at the moon, sometimes pausing to gather the rarest flowers for her adornment. And all the time he was thinking to himself that never, during the hundreds of years he had lived, had he seen so charming a maiden. But the princess felt no such happiness; in spite of all the magic delights around her she was sad, though she tried to seem content for fear of displeasing the gnome. However, he soon perceived her melancholy, and in a thousand ways strove to dispel the cloud, but in vain. At last he said to himself: "Men are sociable creatures, like bees or ants. Doubtless this lovely mortal is pining for company. Who is there I can find for her to talk to?"

Thereupon he hastened into the nearest filed and dug up a dozen or so of different roots—carrots, turnips, and radishes—and laying them carefully in an elegant basket brought them to the princess, who sat pensive in the shade of the rose-bower.

"Loveliest daughter of earth," said the gnome, "banish all sorrow; no more shall you be lonely in my dwelling. In this basket is all you need to make this spot delightful to you. Take this little many-colored wand, and with a touch give to each root the form you desire to see."

With this he left her, and the princess, without an instant's delay, opened the basket, and touching a turnip, cried eagerly: "Brunhilda, my dear Brunhilda! come to me quickly!" And sure enough there was Brunhilda, joyfully hugging and kissing her beloved princess, and chattering as gaily as in the old days.

This sudden appearance was so delightful that the princess could hardly believe her own eyes, and was quite beside herself with the joy of having her dear playfellow with her once more. Hand in hand they wandered about the enchanted garden, and gathered the golden apples from the trees, and when they were tired of this amusement the princess led her friend through all the wonderful rooms of the palace, until at last they came to the one in which were kept all the marvelous dresses and ornaments the gnome had given to his hoped-for bride. There they found so much to amuse them that the hours passed like minutes. Veils, girdles, and necklaces were tried on and admired, the imitation Brunhilda knew so well how to behave herself, and showed so much taste that nobody would ever have suspected that she was nothing but a turnip after all. The gnome, who had secretly been keeping an eye upon them, was very pleased with himself for having so well understood the heart of a woman; and the princess seemed to him even more charming than before. She did not forget to touch the rest of the roots with her magic wand, and soon had all her maidens about her, and even, as she had two tiny radishes to spare, her favorite cat, and her little dog whose name was Beni.

And now all went cheerfully in the castle. The princess gave to each of the maidens her task, and never was mistress better served. For a whole week she enjoyed the delight of her pleasant company undisturbed. They all sang, they danced, they played from morning to night; only the princess noticed that day by day the fresh young faces of her maidens grew pale and wan, and the mirror in the great marble hall showed her that she alone still kept her rosy bloom, while Brunhilda and the rest faded visibly. They assured her that all was well with them; but, nevertheless, they continued to waste away, and day by day it became harder to them to take part in the games of the princess, till at last, one fine morning, when the princess started from bed and hastened out to join her gay playfellows, she shuddered and started back at the sight of a group of shrivelled crones, with bent backs and trembling limbs, who supported their tottering steps with staves and crutches, and coughed dismally. A little nearer to the hearth lay the once frolicsome Beni, with all four feet stretched stiffly out, while the sleek cat seemed too weak to raise his head from his velvet cushion.

The horrified princess fled to the door to escape from the sight of this mournful company, and called loudly for the gnome, who appeared at once, humbly anxious to do her bidding.

"Malicious Sprite," she cried, "why do you begrudge me my playmates—the greatest delight of my lonely hours? Isn't this solitary life in such a desert bad enough without your turning the castle into a hospital for the aged? Give my maidens back their youth and health this very minute, or I will never love you!"

"Sweetest and fairest of damsels," cried the gnome, "do not be angry; everything that is in my power I will do—but do not ask the impossible. So long as the sap was fresh in the roots the magic staff could keep them in the forms you desired, but as the sap dried up they withered away. But never trouble yourself about that, dearest one, a basket of fresh turnips will soon set matters right, and you can speedily call up again every form you wish to see. The great green patch in the garden will prove you with a more lively company."

So saying the gnome took himself off. And the princess with her magic wand touched the wrinkled old women, and left them the withered roots they really were, to be thrown upon the rubbish heap; and with light feet skipped off across to the meadow to take possession of the freshly filled basket. But to her surprise she could not find it anywhere. Up and down the garden she searched, spying into every corner, but not a sign of it was to be found. By the trellis of grape vines she met the gnome, who was so much embarrassed at the sight of her that she became aware of his confusion while he was still quite a long way off.

"You are trying to tease me," she cried, as soon as she saw him. "Where have you hidden the basket? I have been looking for it at least an hour."

"Dear queen of my heart," answered he, "I pray you to forgive my carelessness. I promised more than I could perform. I have sought all over the land for the roots you desire; but they are gathered in, and lie drying in musty cellars, and the fields are bare and desolate, for below in the valley winter reigns, only here in your presence spring is held fast, and wherever your foot is set the gay flowers bloom. Have patience for a little, and then without fail you shall have your puppets to play with."

Almost before the gnome had finished, the disappointed princess turned away, and marched off to her own apartments, without deigning to answer him.

The gnome, however, set off above ground as speedily as possible, and disguising himself as a farmer, bought an ass in the nearest market-town, and brought it back loaded with sacks of turnip, carrot, and radish seed. With this he sowed a great field, and sent a vast army of his goblins to watch and tend it, and to bring up the fiery rivers from the heart of the earth near enough to warm and encourage the sprouting seeds. Thus fostered they grew and flourished marvelously, and promised a goodly crop.

The princess wandered about the field day by day, no other plants or fruits in all her wonderful garden pleased her as much as these roots; but still her eyes were full of discontent. And, best of all, she loved to while away the hours in a shady fir-wood, seated upon the bank of a little stream, into which she would cast the flowers she had gathered and watch them float away.

The gnome tried hard by every means in his power to please the princess and win her love, but little did he guess the real reason of his lack of success. He imagined that she was too young and inexperienced to care for him; but that was a mistake, for the truth was that another image already filled her heart. The young Prince Ratibor, whose lands joined her father's, had won the heart of the princess; and the lovers had been looking forward to the coming of their wedding-day when the bride's mysterious disappearance took place. The sad news drove Ratibor distracted, and as the days went on, and nothing could be heard of the princess, he forsook his castle and the society of men, and spent his days in the wild forests, roaming about and crying her name aloud to the trees and rocks. Meanwhile, the maiden, in her gorgeous prison, sighed in secret over her grief, not wishing to arouse the gnome's suspicions. In her own mind she was wondering if by any means she might escape from her captivity, and at last she hit upon a plan.

By this time spring once more reigned in the valley, and the gnome sent the fires back to their places in the deeps of the earth, for the roots which they had kept warm through all the cruel winter hand now come to their full size. Day by day the princess pulled up some of them, and made experiments with them, conjuring up now this longed-for person, and now that, just for the pleasure of seeing them as they appeared; but she really had another purpose in view.

One day she changed a tiny turnip into a bee, and sent him off to bring her some news of her lover.

"Fly, dear little bee, towards the east," said she, "to my beloved Ratibor, and softly hum into his ear that I love him only, but that I am a captive in the gnome's palace under the mountains. Do not forget a single word of my greeting, and bring me back a message from my beloved."

So the bee spread his shining wings and flew away to do as he was bidden; but before he was out of sight a greedy swallow made a snatch at him, and to the great grief of the princess her messenger was eaten up then and there.

After that, by the power of the wonderful wand she summoned a cricket, and taught him this greeting:

"Hop, little cricket, to Ratibor, and chirp in his ear that I love him only, but that I am held captive by the gnome in his palace under the mountains."

So the cricket hopped off gaily, determined to do his best to deliver his message; but, alas! a long-legged stork who was prancing along the same road caught him in her cruel beak, and before he could say a word he had disappeared down her throat.

These two unlucky ventures did not prevent the princess from trying once more.

This time she changed the turnip into a magpie.

"Flutter from tree to tree, chattering bird," said she, "till you come to Ratibor, my love. Tell him that I am a captive, and bid him come with horses and men, the third day from this, to the hill that rises from the Thorny Valley."

The magpie listened, hopped awhile from branch to branch, and then darted away, the princess watching him anxiously as far as she could see.

Now Prince Ratibor was still spending his life in wandering about the woods, and not even the beauty of the spring could soothe his grief.

One day, as he sat in the shade of an oak tree, dreaming of his lost princess, and sometimes crying her name aloud, he seemed to hear another voice reply to his, and, starting up, he gazed around him, but he could see no one, and he had just made up his mind that he must be mistaken, when the same voice called again, and, looking up sharply, he saw a magpie which hopped to and fro among the twigs. Then Ratibor heard with surprise that the bird was indeed calling him by name.

"Poor chatterpie," said he; "who taught you to say that name, which belongs to an unlucky mortal who wishes the earth would open and swallow up him and his memory for ever?"

Thereupon he caught up a great stone, and would have hurled it at the magpie, if it had not at that moment uttered the name of the princess.

This was so unexpected that the prince's arm fell helplessly to his side at the sound, and he stood motionless.

But the magpie in the tree, who, like all the rest of his family, was not happy unless he could be for ever chattering, began to repeat the message the princess had taught him; and as soon as he understood it, Prince Ratibor's heart was filed with joy. All his gloom and misery vanished in a moment, and he anxiously questioned the welcome messenger as to the fate of the princess.

But the magpie knew no more than the lesson he had learnt, so he soon fluttered away; while the prince hurried back to his castle to gather together a troop of horsemen, full of courage for whatever might befall.

The princess meanwhile was craftily pursuing her plan of escape. She left off treating the gnome with coldness and indifference; indeed, there was a look in her eyes which encouraged him to hope that she might some day return his love, and the idea pleased him mightily. The next day, as soon as the sun rose, she made her appearance decked as a bride, in the wonderful robes and jewels which the fond gnome had prepared for her. Her golden hair was braided and crowned with myrtle blossoms, and her flowing veil sparkled with gems. In these magnificent garments she went to meet the gnome upon the great terrace.

"Loveliest of maidens," he stammered, bowing low before her, "let me gaze into your dear eyes, and read in them that you will no longer refuse my love, but will make me the happiest being the sun shines upon."

So saying he would have drawn aside her veil; but the princess only held it more closely about her.

"Your constancy has overcome me," she said; "I can no longer oppose your wishes. But believe my words, and suffer this veil still to hide my blushes and tears."

"Why tears, beloved one?" cried the gnome anxiously; "every tear of yours falls upon my heart like a drop of molten gold. Greatly as I desire your love, I do not ask a sacrifice."

"Ah!" cried the false princess, "why do you misunderstand my tears? My heart answers to your tenderness, and yet I am fearful. A wife cannot always charm, and though *you* will never alter, the beauty of mortals is as a flower that fades. How can I be sure that you will always be as loving and charming as you are now?"

"Ask some proof, sweetheart," said he. "Put my obedience and my patience to some test by which you can judge of my unalterable love."

"Be it so," answered the crafty maiden. "Then give me just one proof of your goodness. Go! count the turnips in yonder meadow. My wedding feast must not lack guests. They shall provide me with bride-maidens too. But beware lest you deceive me, and do not miss a single one. That shall be the test of your truth towards me."

Unwilling as the gnome was to lose sight of his beautiful bride for a moment, he obeyed her commands without delay, and hurried off to begin his task. He skipped along among the turnips as nimble as a grasshopper, and had soon counted them all; but, to be quite certain that he had made no mistake, he thought he would just run over them again. This time, to his great annoyance, the number was different; so he reckoned them for the third time, but now the number was not the same as either of the previous ones! And this was hardly to be wondered at, as his mind was full of the princess's pretty looks and words.

As for the maiden, no sooner was her deluded lover fairly out of sight than she began to prepare for flight. She had a fine fresh turnip hidden close at hand, which she changed into a spirited horse, all saddled and bridled, and, springing upon its back, she galloped away over hill and dale till she reached the Thorny Valley, and flung herself into the arms of her beloved Prince Ratibor.

Meanwhile the toiling gnome went through his task over and over again till his back ached and his head swam, and he could no longer put two and two together; but as he felt tolerably certain of the exact number of turnips in the field, big and little together, he hurried back eager to prove to his beloved one what a delightful and submissive husband he would be. He felt very well satisfied with himself as he crossed the mossy lawn to the place where he had left her; but, alas! she was no longer there.

He searched every thicket and path, he looked behind every tree, and gazed into every pond, but without success; then he hastened into the palace and rushed from room to room, peering into every hole and corner and calling her by name; but only echo answered in the marble halls—there was neither voice nor footstep.

Then he began to perceive that something was amiss, and, throwing off the mortal form that encumbered him, he flew out of the palace, and soared high into the air, and saw the fugitive princess in the far distance just as the swift horse carried her across the boundary of his dominions.

Furiously did the enraged gnome fling two great clouds together, and hurl a thunderbolt after the flying maiden, splintering the rocky barriers which had stood a thousand years. But his fury was vain, the thunderclouds melted away into a soft mist, and the gnome, after flying about for a while in despair, bewailing to the four winds his unhappy fate, went sorrowfully back to the palace, and stole once more through every room, with many sighs and lamentations. He passed through the gardens which for him had lost their charm, and the sight of the princess's footprints on the golden sand of the pathway renewed his grief. All was lonely, empty, sorrowful; and the forsaken gnome resolved that he would have no more dealings with such false creatures as he had found men to be.

Thereupon he stamped three times upon the earth, and the magic palace, with all its treasures, vanished away into the nothingness out of which he had called it; and the gnome fled once more to the depths of his underground kingdom.

While all this was happening, Prince Ratibor was hurrying away with his prize to a place of safety. With great pomp and triumph he restored the lovely princess to her father, and was then and there married to her, and took her back with him to his own castle.

But long after she was dead, and her children too, the villagers would tell the tale of her imprisonment underground, as they sat carving wood in the winter nights.

The King o' the Cats

One winter's evening the sexton's wife was sitting by the fireside with her big black cat, Old Tom, on the other side, both half-asleep and waiting for the master to come home. They waited and they waited, but still he didn't come, till at last he came rushing in, calling out, "Who's Tommy Tildrum?" in such a wild way that both his wife and his cat stared at him to know what was the matter.

"Why, what's the matter?" said his wife, "and why do you want to know who Tommy Tildrum is?"

"Oh, I've had such an adventure. I was digging away at old Mr. Fordyce's grave when I suppose I must have dropped asleep, and only woke up by hearing a cat's *Miaou*."

"*Miaou!*" said Old Tom in answer.

"Yes, just like that! So I looked over the edge of the grave, and what do you think I saw?"

"Now, how can I tell?" said the sexton's wife.

"Why, nine black cats all like our friend Tom here, all with a white spot on their chestesses. And what do you think they were carrying? Why, a small coffin covered with a black velvet pall, and on the pall was a small coronet all of gold, and at every third step they took they cried all together, *Miaou—*"

"*Miaou!*" said Old Tom again.

"Yes, just like that!" said the Sexton; "and as they came nearer and nearer to me I could see them more distinctly, because their eyes shone out with a sort of green light. Well, they all came towards me, eight of them carrying the coffin, and the biggest cat of all walking in front for all the world like—but look at our Tom, how he's looking at me. You'd think he knew all I was saying."

"Go on, go on," said his wife; "never mind Old Tom."

"Well, as I was a-saying, they came towards me slowly and solemnly, and at every third step crying all together, *Miaou—*"

"*Miaou!*" said Old Tom again.

"Yes, just like that, till they came and stood right opposite Mr. Fordyce's grave, where I was, when they all stood still and looked straight at me. I did feel queer, that I did! But look at Old Tom; he's looking at me just like they did."

"Go on, go on," said his wife; "never mind Old Tom."

"Where was I? Oh, they all stood still looking at me, when the one that wasn't carrying the coffin came forward and, staring straight at me, said to me—yes, I tell 'ee, *said* to me—with a squeaky voice, 'Tell Tom Tildrum that Tim Toldrum's dead,' and that's why I asked you if you knew who Tom Tildrum was, for how can I tell Tom Tildrum Tim Toldrum's dead if I don't know who Tom Tildrum is?"

"Look at Old Tom, look at Old Tom!" screamed his wife.

And well he might look, for Tom was swelling and Tom was staring, and at last Tom shrieked out, "What—old Tim dead! then I'm the King o' the Cats!" and rushed up the chimney and was never more seen.

The Goblin and the Huckster

HANS CHRISTIAN ANDERSEN

Once upon a time there was a real student; he lived in an attic and possessed nothing at all. But once upon a time there was also a real huckster; he lived on the ground-floor, and the whole house belonged to him. The goblin remained friends with him, for at the huckster's they always had a big plum-pudding every Christmas Eve, with a fine large piece of butter in it. That the huckster could afford, and therefore the goblin stayed in the huckster's shop, and that was very interesting. One evening the student came in through the back door to buy some candles and cheese. He had no one to send, so he came himself. He got what he wanted, and the huckster and his wife both nodded him a good evening. Madam was a woman who could do more than merely nod; she had an extraordinary power of speech. The student nodded too, but suddenly stood still reading the sheet of paper in which the cheese was wrapped up. It was a leaf that had been torn out of an old book—a leaf out of a book that ought not to have been torn up, a book that was full of poetry.

"Here's some more of the same kind," said the huckster; "I gave an old woman a little coffee for the book. If you give me twopence you shall have the rest."

"Very well," said the student, "give me the book instead of the cheese; I can eat my bread and butter without cheese. It would be a sin to tear the book up entirely. You are a fine fellow and a practical man, but you know as much about poetry as that cask there."

Now this was very rude, especially towards the cask, but the huckster laughed and the student laughed, for it was only said in fun. But the goblin was angry that people should dare to say such things to a huckster who was a landlord—and who sold the best butter.

When night came and the shop was closed, and all were in bed with the exception of the student, the goblin came out, went into the bedroom, and took madam's tongue away. She did not want it while she was asleep; and on whatever object in the room he placed it that object acquired speech and voice, and told its thoughts and feelings just like madam. But only one object at a time could use it, which was a blessing, otherwise they would all have spoken at once.

The goblin placed the mouthpiece on the cask in which lay the old newspapers. "Is it really true," he asked, "that you don't know anything about poetry?"

"Certainly I do," replied the cask. "Poetry is something they always put at the bottom of newspapers, and which is sometimes cut out. I daresay I have a great deal more of it in me than the student, and yet I am only a poor cask compared to the huckster."

Then the goblin placed the tongue on the coffee-mill. Mercy on us! how it rattled away! And he put it on the butter-cask, and on the till—all were of the same opinion as the waste-paper cask, and the opinion of the majority must be respected.

"Now I'll tell the student." And with these words the goblin stole quietly up the backstairs to the attic where the student lived. The student had still a candle burning, and the goblin peeped through the keyhole and saw him reading in the torn book that he had got from the shop downstairs.

But how light it was up there! Out of the book shone a bright beam, which grew up into a thick stem and into a mighty tree, that rose and spread its branches far over the student. Every leaf was fresh, and every blossom was a beautiful maiden's head, some with dark sparkling eyes, others with wonderfully clear blue ones; every fruit was a shining star, and there was a sound of glorious singing in the student's room.

No, such splendor the little goblin had never dreamed of, let alone seen or heard. He remained standing there on tiptoe, peeping and peeping till the light in the garret went out. Probably the student had blown it out and gone to bed, but the goblin remained standing there all the same, for he could still hear the sweet glorious singing—a beautiful lullaby for the student, who had lain down to rest.

"What an incomparable place this is!" said the goblin; "I never expected such a thing. I should like to live with the student." Then the little man thought it over—he was a sensible little man too—but he sighed: "The student has no plum-pudding," and then he went down again to the huckster's. And it was a good thing too that he did come back, for the cask had almost worn out madam's tongue: it had already spoken out at one side all that was contained in it, and was just about to turn round to give it out from the other side too, when the goblin entered and put madam's tongue back into its right place. But from that time forth the whole shop, from the till down to the firewood, took its views from the cask; and all paid it so much respect, and reposed so much confidence in it, that when the huckster afterwards read the art and dramatic criticism in the newspaper she was foolish enough to believe it came from the cask.

But the goblin no longer sat quietly listening to the wisdom and understanding to be heard down in the shop; no, as soon as the light glimmered down from the garret in the evening, he felt as if the rays were strong cables, drawing him up, and he was obliged to go and peep through the keyhole. There a feeling of greatness came rushing over him, such as we feel beside the ever-rolling sea when the storm sweeps over it, and he burst into tears; he did not know himself why he wept, but a peculiar and very pleasant feeling was mingled with his tears. How wonderfully glorious it must be to sit with the student under that tree! but that could not be—he must content himself with the keyhole, and be glad of that. There he stood in the cold passage with the autumn wind blowing down from the trap-door in the loft; it was cold, very cold, but that the little fellow only felt when the light in the attic was put out and the sounds in the wonderful tree died away. Ugh! then he felt frozen, and he crept down to his warm corner again—it was cozy and comfortable there!

When Christmas came, and with it the plum-pudding and the great lump of butter, why, then the huckster was Number One.

But in the middle of the night the goblin was awakened by a terrible noise and a banging at the shutters, against which the people outside were knocking as hard as they could. The night watchman blew his horn, for a great fire had broken out. Was it in the house itself, or at the neighbor's? Where was it? A panic ensued. The huckster's wife was so bewildered that she took her gold earrings from her ears and put them into her pocket so that she might save at least something; the huckster made a dash for his bank-notes, and the maid for her black silk mantle—for her means allowed her that luxury. Every one wanted to save the best thing they had; the goblin wanted to do that too, and in a few leaps he was up the stairs and in the room of the student who was calmly standing at the open window gazing at the fire that raged in the house of the neighbor opposite. The goblin seized the book lying on the table, put it into his red cap, and clasped it with both hands; the greatest treasure in the house was saved, and now he ran up and away, out upon the roof of the house, on to the chimney. There he sat in the light of the flames from the burning house opposite, both hands pressed over his red cap in which the treasure lay, and now he knew the real inclinations of his heart and knew to whom it really belonged. But when the fire was extinguished, and the goblin again began to reflect calmly, well—

"I will divide myself between the two," he said, "I cannot give the huckster up altogether on account of the pudding!"

And that was only human after all. Most of us stick to the huckster for the sake of the pudding.

The Headless Dwarfs

(FROM *THE VIOLET FAIRY BOOK*)

There was once a minister who spent his whole time in trying to find a servant who would undertake to ring the church bells at midnight, in addition to all his other duties.

Of course it was not everyone who cared to get up in the middle of the night, when he had been working hard all day; still, a good many had agreed to do it. But the strange thing was that no sooner had the servant set forth to perform his task than he disappeared, as if the earth had swallowed him up. No bells were rung, and no ringer ever came back. The minister did his best to keep the matter secret, but it leaked out for all that, and the end of it was that no one would enter his service. Indeed, there were even those who whispered that the minister himself had murdered the missing men!

It was to no purpose that Sunday after Sunday the minister gave out from his pulpit that double wages would be paid to anyone that would fulfil the sacred duty of ringing the bells of the church. No one took the slightest notice of any offer he might make, and the poor man was in despair, when one day, as he was standing at his house door, a youth known in the village as Clever Hans came up to him. "I am tired of living with a miser who will not give me enough to eat and drink," said he, "and I am ready to do all you want." "Very good, my son," replied the minister, "you shall have the chance of proving your courage this very night. To-morrow we will settle what your wages are to be."

Hans was quite content with this proposal, and went straight into the kitchen to begin his work, not knowing that his new master was quite as stingy as his old one. In the hope that his presence might be a restraint upon them, the minister used to sit at the table during his servants' meals, and would exhort them to drink much and often, thinking that they would not be able to eat as well, and beef was dearer than beer. But in Hans he had met his match, and the minister soon found to his cost that in his case at any rate a full cup did not mean an empty plate.

About an hour before midnight, Hans entered the church and locked the door behind him, but what was his surprise when, in place of the darkness and silence he expected, he found the church brilliantly lighted, and a crowd of people sitting round a table playing cards. Hans felt no fear at this strange sight, or was prudent enough to hide it if he did, and, going up to the table, sat down amongst the players. One of them looked up and asked, "My friend, what are you doing here?" and Hans gazed at him for a moment, then laughed and answered, "Well, if anybody has a right to put that question, it is I! And if *I* do not put it, it will certainly be wiser for you not to do so!"

Then he picked up some cards, and played with the unknown men as if he had known them all his life. The luck was on his side, and soon the money of the other gamblers found its way from their pockets into his. On the stroke of midnight the cock crew, and in an instant lights, table, cards, and people all had vanished, and Hans was left alone.

He groped about for some time, till he found the staircase in the tower, and then began to feel his way up the steps.

On the first landing a glimmer of light came through a slit in the wall, and he saw a tiny man sitting there, without a head. "Ho! ho! my little fellow, what are you doing there?" asked Hans, and, without waiting for an answer, gave him a kick which sent him flying down the stairs. Then he climbed higher still, and finding as he went dumb watchers sitting on every landing, treated them as he had done the first.

At last he reached the top, and as he paused for a moment to look round him he saw another headless man cowering in the very bell itself, waiting till Hans should seize the bell-pull in order to strike him a blow with the clapper, which would soon have made an end of him.

"Stop, my little friend!" cried Hans. "That is not part of the bargain! Perhaps you saw how your comrades walked down stairs, and you are going after them. But as you are in the highest place you shall make a more digni-fied exit, and follow them through the window!"

With these words he began to climb the ladder, in order to take the little man from the bell and carry out his threat.

At this the dwarf cried out imploringly, "Oh, brother! spare my life, and I promise that neither I nor my comrades will ever trouble you any more. I am small and weak, but who knows whether some day I shall not be able to reward you."

"You wretched little shrimp," replied Hans, "a great deal of good your gratitude is likely to do me! But as I happen to be feeling in a cheerful mood to-night I will let you have your life. But take care how you come across me again, or you may not escape so easily!"

The headless man thanked him humbly, slid hastily down the bell rope, and ran down the steps of the tower as if he had left a fire behind him. Then Hans began to ring lustily.

When the minister heard the sound of the midnight bells he wondered greatly, but rejoiced that he had at last found some one to whom he could trust this duty. Hans rang the bells for some time, then went to the hay-loft, and fell fast asleep.

Now it was the custom of the minister to get up very early, and to go round to make sure that the men were all at their work. This morning everyone was in his place except Hans, and no one knew anything about him. Nine o'clock came, and no Hans, but when eleven struck the minister began to fear that he had vanished like the ringers who had gone before him. When, however, the servants all gathered round the table for dinner, Hans at last made his appearance stretching himself and yawning.

"Where have you been all this time?" asked the minister.

"Asleep," said Hans.

"Asleep!" exclaimed the minister in astonishment. "You don't mean to tell me that you can go on sleeping till mid-day?"

"That is exactly what I do mean," replied Hans. "If one works in the night one must sleep in the day, just as if one works in the day one sleeps in the night. If you can find somebody else to ring the bells at midnight I am ready to begin work at dawn; but if you want me to ring them I must go on sleeping till noon at the very earliest."

The minister tried to argue the point with him, but at length the following agreement was come to. Hans was to give up the ringing, and was to work like the rest from sunrise to sunset, with the exception of an hour after breakfast and an hour after dinner, when he might go to sleep. "But, of course," added the minister carelessly, "it may happen now and then, especially in winter, when the days are short, that you will have to work a little longer, to get something finished."

"Not at all!" answered Hans. "Unless I were to leave off work earlier in summer, I will not do a stroke more than I have promised, and that is from dawn to dark; so you know what you have to expect."

A few weeks later the minister was asked to attend a christening in the neighboring town. He bade Hans come with him, but, as the town was only a few hours' ride from where he lived, the minister was much surprised to see Hans come forth laden with a bag containing food.

"What are you taking that for?" asked the minister. "We shall be there before dark."

"Who knows?" replied Hans. "Many things may happen to delay our journey, and I need not remind you of our contract that the moment the sun sets I cease to be your servant. If we don't reach the town while it is still daylight I shall leave you to shift for yourself."

The minister thought he was joking, and made no further remark. But when they had left the village behind them, and had ridden a few miles, they found that snow had fallen during the night, and had been blown by the wind into drifts. This hindered their progress, and by the time they had entered the thick wood which lay between them and their destination the sun was already touching the tops of the trees. The horses ploughed their way slowly through the deep soft snow and as they went Hans kept turning to look at the sun, which lay at their backs.

"Is there anything behind you?" asked the minister. "Or what is it you are always turning round for?"

"I turn round because I have no eyes in the back of my neck," said Hans.

"Cease talking nonsense," replied the minister, "and give all your mind to getting us to the town before nightfall."

Hans did not answer, but rode on steadily, though every now and then he cast a glance over his shoulder.

When they arrived in the middle of the wood the sun sank altogether. Then Hans reined up his horse, took his knapsack, and jumped out of the sledge.

"What are you doing? Are you mad?" asked the minister, but Hans answered quietly, "The sun is set and my work is over, and I am going to camp here for the night."

In vain the master prayed and threatened, and promised Hans a large reward if he would only drive him on. The young man was not to be moved.

"Are you not ashamed to urge me to break my word?" said he. "If you want to reach the town to-night you must go alone. The hour of my freedom has struck, and I cannot go with you."

"My good Hans," entreated the minister, "I really ought not to leave you here. Consider what danger you would be in! Yonder, as you see, a gallows is set up, and two evil-doers are hanging on it. You could not possibly sleep with such ghastly neighbors."

"Why not?" asked Hans. "Those gallows birds hang high in the air, and my camp will be on the ground; we shall have nothing to do with each other." As he spoke, he turned his back on the minister, and went his way.

There was no help for it, and the minister had to push on by himself, if he expected to arrive in time for the christening. His friends were much surprised to see him drive up without a coachman, and thought some accident had happened. But when he told them of his conversation with Hans they did not know which was the most foolish, master or man.

It would have mattered little to Hans had he known what they were saying or thinking of him. He satisfied his hunger with the food he had in his knapsack, lit his pipe, pitched his tent under the boughs of a tree, wrapped himself in his furs, and went sound asleep. After some hours, he was awakened by a sudden noise, and sat up and looked about him. The moon was shining brightly above his head, and close by stood two headless dwarfs, talking angrily. At the sight of Hans the little dwarfs cried out:

"It is he! It is he!" and one of them stepping nearer exclaimed, "Ah, my old friend! it is a lucky chance that has brought us here. My bones still ache from my fall down the steps of the tower. I dare say you have not forgotten that night! Now it is the turn of your bones. Hi! comrades, make haste! make haste!"

Like a swarm of midges, a host of tiny headless creatures seemed to spring straight out of the ground, and every one was armed with a club. Although they were so small, yet there were such numbers of them and they struck so hard that even a strong man could do nothing against them. Hans thought his last hour was come, when just as the fight was at the hottest another little dwarf arrived on the scene.

"Hold, comrades!" he shouted, turning to the attacking party. "This man once did me a service, and I am his debtor. When I was in his power he granted me my life. And even if he did throw you downstairs, well, a warm bath soon cured your bruises, so you must just forgive him and go quietly home."

The headless dwarfs listened to his words and disappeared as suddenly as they had come. As soon as Hans recovered himself a little he looked at his rescuer, and saw he was the dwarf he had found seated in the church bell.

"Ah!" said the dwarf, seating himself quietly under the tree. "You laughed at me when I told you that some day I might do you a good turn. Now you see I was right, and perhaps you will learn for the future not to despise any creature, however small."

"I thank you from my heart," answered Hans. "My bones are still sore from their blows, and had it not been for you I should indeed have fared badly."

"I have almost paid my debt," went on the little man, "but as you have suffered already, I will do more, and give you a piece of information. You need not remain any longer in the service of that stingy minister, but when you

251

get home to-morrow go at once to the north corner of the church, and there you will find a large stone built into the wall, but not cemented like the rest. The day after to-morrow the moon is full, and at midnight you must go to the spot and get the stone out of the wall with a pickaxe. Under the stone lies a great treasure, which has been hidden there in time of war. Besides church plate, you will find bags of money, which have been lying in this place for over a hundred years, and no one knows to whom it all belongs. A third of this money you must give to the poor, but the rest you may keep for yourself." As he finished, the cocks in the village crowed, and the little man was nowhere to be seen. Hans found that his limbs no longer pained him, and lay for some time thinking of the hidden treasure. Towards morning he fell asleep.

The sun was high in the heavens when his master returned from the town.

"Hans," said he, "what a fool you were not to come with me yesterday! I was well feasted and entertained, and I have money in my pocket into the bargain," he went on, rattling some coins while he spoke, to make Hans understand how much he had lost.

"Ah, sir," replied Hans calmly, "in order to have gained so much money you must have lain awake all night, but I have earned a hundred times that amount while I was sleeping soundly."

"How did you manage that?" asked the minister eagerly, but Hans answered, "It is only fools who boast of their farthings; wise men take care to hide their crowns."

They drove home, and Hans neglected none of his duties, but put up the horses and gave them their food before going to the church corner, where he found the loose stone, exactly in the place described by the dwarf. Then he returned to his work.

The first night of the full moon, when the whole village was asleep, he stole out, armed with a pickaxe, and with much difficulty succeeded in dislodging the stone from its place. Sure enough, there was the hole, and in the hole lay the treasure, exactly as the little man had said.

The following Sunday he handed over the third part to the village poor, and informed the minister that he wished to break his bond of service. As, however, he did not claim any wages, the minister made no objections, but allowed him to do as he wished. So Hans went his way, bought himself a large house, and married a young wife, and lived happily and prosperously to the end of his days.

The Quern at the Bottom of the Sea

PETER CHRISTEN ASBJØRNSEN

O nce upon a time in the old, old days there were two brothers, one of whom was rich and the other poor. When Christmas Eve came the poor brother had not a morsel in the house, neither of meat nor bread; and so he went to his rich brother, and asked for a trifle for Christmas, in heaven's name. It was not the first time the brother had helped him, but he was always very close-fisted, and was not particularly glad to see him this time.

"If you'll do what I tell you, you shall have a whole ham," he said. The poor brother promised he would, and was very grateful into the bargain.

"There it is, and now go to the devil! "said the rich brother, and threw the ham across to him.

"Well, what I have promised I must keep," said the other one. He took the ham, and set out. He walked and walked the whole day, and as it was getting dark he came to a place where the lights were shining brightly. "This is most likely the place," thought the man with the ham.

In the wood-shed stood an old man with a long white beard, cutting firewood for Christmas.

"Good evening," said he with the ham.

"Good evening to you," said the man. "Where are you going so late?"

"I am going to the devil—that is to say, if I am on the right way," answered the poor man.

"Yes, you are quite right; this is his place," said the old man. "When you get in they will all want to buy your ham, for ham is scarce food here; but you must not sell it unless you get the hand-quern, which stands just behind the door. When you come out again I'll teach you how to use it. You will find it useful in many ways."

The man with the ham thanked him for all the information and knocked at the door.

When he got in it happened just as the old man had said. All the imps, both big and small, flocked around him like ants in a field, and the one out-bid the other for the ham.

'Well," said the man, "my good woman and I were to have it for Christmas Eve, but since you want it so badly I will let you have it. But if I am going to part with it, I want that hand-quern which stands behind the door."

The devil did not like to part with it, and higgled and haggled with the man, but he stuck to what he had said, and in the end the devil had to part with the quern.

When the man came out he asked the old wood-cutter how he was to use the quern, and when he had learned this, he thanked the old man and set out homeward, as quickly as he could; but after all he did not get home till the clock struck twelve on Christmas Eve.

"Where in all the world have you been? "said his wife. "Here have I been sitting, hour after hour, waiting and watching for you, and have not had as much as two chips to lay under the porridge pot."

"Well, I couldn't get back before," said the man. "I have had a good many things to look after, and I've had a long way to walk as well; but now I'll show you something," said he and put the quern on the table. He asked it first to grind candles, then a cloth, and then food and beer, and everything else that was good for Christmas cheer; and as he spoke the quern brought them forth. The woman crossed herself time after time and wanted to know where her husband had got the quern from; but this he would not tell her.

"It does not matter where I got it from; you see the quern is good and the mill stream is not likely to freeze," said the man. So he ground food and drink and all good things during Christmas; and the third day he invited his friends, as he wanted to give them a feast. When the rich brother saw all that was in the house, he became both angry and furious, for he begrudged his brother everything.

"On Christmas Eve he was so needy that he came to me and asked for a trifle in heaven's name; and now he gives a feast, as if he were both a count and a king," said the brother. "Where did you get all your riches from?" he said to his brother.

"From just behind the door," he answered, for he did not care to tell his brother much about it. But later in the evening, when he had drunk a little freely, he could no longer resist, but brought out the quern.

"There you see that which has brought me all my riches," he said, and so he let the quern grind first one thing and then another.

When the brother saw this he was determined to have the quern at all cost, and at last it was settled he should have it, but three hundred dollars was to be the price of it. The brother was, however, to keep it till the harvest began; "for if I keep it so long I can grind out food for many years to come," he thought.

During that time you may be sure the quern did not rust, and when the harvest began the rich brother got it; but the other had taken great care not to show him how to use it.

It was evening when the rich brother got the quern home, and in the morning he asked his wife to go out and help the haymakers; he would get the breakfast ready for himself to-day, he said.

When it was near breakfast time he put the quern on the breakfast table.

"Grind herrings and broth, and do it quickly and well," said the man, and the quern began to bring forth herrings and broth, and first filled all the dishes and tubs, and afterward began flooding the whole kitchen.

The man fiddled and fumbled and tried to stop the quern, but however much he twisted and fingered it, the quern went on grinding, and in a little while the broth reached so high that the man was very near drowning. He then pulled open the parlor door, but it was not very long before the quern had filled the parlor also, and it was just in the very nick of time that the man put his hand down into the broth and got hold of the latch, and when he had got the door open, he was soon out of the parlor, you may be sure. He rushed out, and the herrings and the broth came pouring out after him, like a stream, down the fields and meadows.

The wife, who was out haymaking, now thought it took too long a time to get the breakfast ready.

"If my husband doesn't call us soon we must go home whether or no: I don't suppose he knows much about making broth, so I must go and help him," said the wife to the haymakers.

They began walking homewards, but when they had got a bit up the hill they met the stream of broth with the herrings tossing about in it and the man himself running in front of it all.

"I wish all of you had a hundred stomachs each!" shouted the man; "but take care you don't get drowned." And he rushed past them as if the Evil One was at his heels, down to where his brother lived. He asked him for heaven's sake to take back the quern, and that at once; "If it goes on grinding another hour the whole parish will perish in broth and herrings," he said. But the brother would not take it back on any account before his brother had paid him three hundred dollars more, and this he had to do. The poor brother now had plenty of money, and before long he bought a farm much grander than the one on which his rich brother lived, and with the quern he ground so much gold that he covered the farmstead with gold plates and, as it lay close to the shore, it glittered and shone far out at sea. All those who sailed past wanted to call and visit the rich man in the golden house, and everybody wanted to see the wonderful quern, for its fame had spread far and wide, and there was no one who had not heard it spoken of.

After a long while there came a skipper who wanted to see the quern; he asked if it could grind salt. Yes, that it could, said he who owned it; and when the skipper heard this he wanted the quern by hook or crook, cost what it might, for if he had it he thought he need not sail far away across dangerous seas for cargoes of salt.

At first the man did not want to part with it, but the skipper both begged and prayed, and at last he sold it and got many, many thousand dollars for it.

As soon as the skipper had got the quern on his back, he did not stop long, for he was afraid the man would change his mind, and as for asking how to use it he had no time to do that; he made for his ship as quickly as he could, and when he had got out to sea a bit he had the quern brought up on deck.

"Grind salt, and that both quickly and well," said the skipper, and the quern began to grind out salt so that it spurted to all sides.

When the skipper had got the ship filled he wanted to stop the quern, but however much he tried and whatever he did the quern went on grinding, and the mound of salt grew higher and higher, and at last the ship sank.

There at the bottom of the sea stands the quern grinding till this very day, and that is the reason why the sea is salt.

How Little Brother Set Free His Big Brothers

(FROM *THE BROWN FAIRY BOOK*)

In a small hut, right in the middle of the forest, lived a man, his wife, three sons and a daughter. For some reason, all the animals seemed to have left that part of the country, and food grew very scarce; so, one morning, after a night of snow, when the tracks of beasts might be easily seen, the three boys started off to hunt.

They kept together for some time, till they reached a place where the path they had been following split into two, and one of the brothers called his dog and went to the left, while the others took the trail to the right. These had not gone far when their dogs scented a bear, and drove him out from the thicket. The bear ran across a clearing, and the elder brother managed to place an arrow right in his head.

They both took up the bear, and carried it towards home, meeting the third at the spot where they had parted from him. When they reached home they threw the bear down on the floor of the hut saying,

"Father, here is a bear which we killed; now we can have some dinner."

But the father, who was in a bad temper, only said:

"When I was a young man we used to get two bears in one day."

The sons were rather disappointed at hearing this, and though there was plenty of meat to last for two or three days, they started off early in the morning down the same trail that they had followed before. As they drew near the fork a bear suddenly ran out from behind a tree, and took the path on the right. The two elder boys and their dogs pursued him, and soon the second son, who was also a good shot, killed him instantly with an arrow. At the fork of the trail, on their way home, they met the youngest, who had taken the left-hand road, and had shot a bear for himself. But when they threw the two bears triumphantly on the floor of the hut their father hardly looked at them, and only said:

"When *I* was a young man I used to get three bears in one day."

The next day they were luckier than before, and brought back three bears, on which their father told them that *he* had always killed four. However, that did not prevent him from skinning the bears and cooking them in a way of his own, which he thought very good, and they all ate an excellent supper.

Now these bears were the servants of the great bear chief who lived in a high mountain a long way off. And every time a bear was killed his shadow returned to the house of the bear chief, with the marks of his wounds plainly to bee seen by the rest.

The chief was furious at the number of bears the hunters had killed, and determined that he would find some way of destroying them. So he called another of his servants, and said to him:

"Go to the thicket near the fork, where the boys killed your brothers, and directly they or the dogs see you return here as fast as ever you can. The mountain will open to let you in, and the hunters will follow you. Then I shall have them in my power, and be able to revenge myself."

The servant bowed low, and started at once for the fork, where he hid himself in the bushes.

By-and-by the boys came in sight, but this time there were only two of them, as the youngest had stayed at home. The air was warm and damp, and the snow soft and slushy, and the elder brother's bowstring hung loose, while the bow of the younger caught in a tree and snapped in half. At that moment the dogs began to bark loudly, and the bear rushed out of the thicket and set off in the direction of the mountain. Without thinking that they had nothing to defend themselves with, should the bear turn and attack them, the boys gave chase. The bear, who knew quite well that he could not be shot, sometimes slackened his pace and let the dogs get quite close; and in this way the elder son reached the mountain without observing it, while his brother, who had hurt his foot, was still far behind.

As he ran up, the mountain opened to admit the bear, and the boy, who was close on his heels, rushed in after him, and did not know where he was till he saw bears sitting on every side of him, holding a council. The animal he had been chasing sank panting in their midst, and the boy, very much frightened, stood still, letting his bow fall to the ground.

"Why are you trying to kill all my servants?" asked the chief. "Look round and see their shades, with arrows sticking in them. It was I who told the bear to-day how he was to lure you into my power. I shall take care that

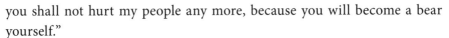

you shall not hurt my people any more, because you will become a bear yourself."

At this moment the second brother came up—for the mountain had been left open on purpose to tempt him also—and cried out breathlessly: "Don't you see that the bear is lying close to you? Why don't you shoot him?" And, without waiting for a reply, pressed forward to drive his arrow into the heart of the bear. But the elder one caught his raised arm, and whispered: "Be quiet! can't you tell where you are?" Then the boy looked up and saw the angry bears about him. On the one side were the servants of the chief, and on the other the servants of the chief's sister, who was sorry for the two youths, and begged that their lives might be spared. The chief answered that he would not kill them, but only cast a spell over them, by which their heads and bodies should remain as they were, but their arms and legs should change into those of a bear, so that they would go on all fours for the rest of their lives. And, stooping over a spring of water, he dipped a handful of moss in it and rubbed it over the arms and legs of the boys. In an instant the transformation took place, and two creatures, neither beast nor human, stood before the chief.

Now the bear chief of course knew that the boys' father would seek for his sons when they did not return home, so he sent another of his servants to the hiding-place at the fork of the trail to see what would happen. He had not waited long, when the father came in sight, stooping as he went to look for his sons' tracks in the snow. When he saw the marks of snow-shoes along the path on the right he was filled with joy, not knowing that the servant had made some fresh tracks on purpose to mislead him; and he hastened forward so fast that he fell headlong into a pit, where the bear was sitting. Before he could pick himself up the bear had quietly broken his neck, and, hiding the body under the snow, sat down to see if anyone else would pass that way.

Meanwhile the mother at home was wondering what had become of her two sons, and as the hours went on, and their father never returned, she made up her mind to go and look for him. The youngest boy begged her to let him undertake the search, but she would not hear of it, and told him he must stay at home and take care of his sister. So, slipping on her snow-shoes, she started on her way.

As no fresh snow had fallen, the trail was quite easy to find, and she walked straight on, till it led her up to the pit where the bear was waiting for her. He grasped her as she fell and broke her neck, after which he laid her in the snow beside her husband, and went back to tell the bear chief.

Hour after hour dragged heavily by in the forest hut, and at last the brother and sister felt quite sure that in some way or other all the rest of the family had perished. Day after day the boy climbed to the top of a tall tree near the house, and sat there till he was almost frozen, looking on all sides through the forest openings, hoping that he might see someone coming along. Very soon all the food in the house was eaten, and he knew he would have to go out and hunt for more. Besides, he wished to seek for his parents.

The little girl did not like being left alone in the hut, and cried bitterly; but her brother told her that there was no use sitting down quietly to starve, and that whether he found any game or not he would certainly be back before the following night. Then he cut himself some arrows, each from a different tree, and winged with the feathers of four different birds. He then made himself a bow, very light and strong, and got down his snow-shoes. All this took some time, and he could not start that day, but early next morning he called his little dog Redmouth, whom he kept in a box, and set out.

After he had followed the trail for a great distance he grew very tired, and sat upon the branch of a tree to rest. But Redmouth barked so furiously that the boy thought that perhaps his parents might have been killed under its branches, and stepping back, shot one of his arrows at the root of the tree. Whereupon a noise like thunder shook it from top to bottom, fire broke out, and in a few minutes a little heap of ashes lay in the place where it had stood.

Not knowing quite what to make of it all, the boy continued on the trail, and went down the right-hand fork till he came to the clump of bushes where the bears used to hide.

Now, as was plain by his being able to change the shape of the two brothers, the bear chief knew a good deal of magic, and he was quite aware that the little boy was following the trail, and he sent a very small but clever bear servant to wait for him in the bushes and to try to tempt him into the mountain. But somehow his spells could not have worked properly that day, as the bear chief did not know that Redmouth had gone with his master, or he would have been more careful. For the moment the dog ran round the bushes barking loudly, the little bear servant rushed out in a fright, and set out for the mountains as fast as he could.

The dog followed the bear, and the boy followed the dog, until the mountain, the house of the great bear chief, came in sight. But along the road the snow was so wet and heavy that the boy could hardly get along, and then the thong of his snow-shoes broke, and he had to stop and mend it, so that the bear and the dog got so far ahead that he could scarcely hear the barking. When the strap was firm again the boy spoke to his snow-shoes and said:

"Now you must go as fast as you can, or, if not, I shall lose the dog as well as the bear." And the snow-shoes sang in answer that they would run like the wind.

As he came along, the bear chief's sister was looking out of the window, and took pity on this little brother, as she had on the two elder ones, and waited to see what the boy would do, when he found that the bear servant and the dog had already entered the mountain.

The little brother was certainly very much puzzled at not seeing anything of either of the animals, which had vanished suddenly out of his sight. He paused for an instant to think what he should do next, and while he did so he fancied he heard Redmouth's voice on the opposite side of the mountain. With great difficulty he scrambled over steep rocks, and forced a path through tangled thickets; but when he reached the other side the sound appeared to start from the place from which he had come. Then he had to go all the way back again, and at the very top, where he stopped to rest, the barking was directly beneath him, and he knew in an instant where he was and what had happened.

"Let my dog out at once, bear chief!" cried he. "If you do not, I shall destroy your palace." But the bear chief only laughed, and said nothing. The boy was very angry at his silence, and aiming one of his arrows at the bottom of the mountain, shot straight through it.

As the arrow touched the ground a rumbling was heard, and with a roar a fire broke out which seemed to split the whole mountain into pieces. The bear chief and all his servants were burnt up in the flames, but his sister and all that belonged to her were spared because she had tried to save the two elder boys from punishment.

As soon as the fire had burnt itself out the little hunter entered what was left of the mountain, and the first thing he saw was his two brothers—half bear, half boy.

"Oh, help us! help us!" cried they, standing on their hind legs as they spoke, and stretching out their fore-paws to him.

"But how am I to help you?" asked the little brother, almost weeping. "I can kill people, and destroy trees and mountains, but I have no power over men." And the two elder brothers came up and put their paws on his shoulders, and they all three wept together.

The heart of the bear chief's sister was moved when she saw their misery, and she came gently up behind, and whispered:

"Little boy, gather some moss from the spring over there, and let your brothers smell it."

With a bound all three were at the spring, and as the youngest plucked a handful of wet moss, the two others sniffed at it with all their might. Then the bearskin fell away from them, and they stood upright once more.

"How can we thank you? how can we thank you?" they stammered, hardly able to speak; and fell at her feet in gratitude. But the bear's sister only smiled, and bade them go home and look after the little girl, who had no one else to protect her.

And this the boys did, and took such good care of their sister that, as she was very small, she soon forgot that she had ever had a father and mother.

The Cat and the Mouse in Partnership

(FROM *THE YELLOW FAIRY BOOK*)

A cat had made acquaintance with a mouse, and had spoken so much of the great love and friendship she felt for her, that at last the Mouse consented to live in the same house with her, and to go shares in the house-keeping. "But we must provide for the winter or else we shall suffer hunger," said the Cat. "You, little Mouse, cannot venture everywhere in case you run at last into a trap." This good counsel was followed, and a little pot of fat was bought. But they did not know where to put it. At length, after long consultation, the Cat said, "I know of no place where it could be better put than in the church. No one will trouble to take it away from there. We will hide it in a corner, and we won't touch it till we are in want." So the little pot was placed in safety; but it was not long before the Cat had a great longing for it, and said to the Mouse, "I wanted to tell you, little Mouse, that my cousin has a little son, white with brown spots, and she wants me to be godmother to it. Let me go out to-day, and do you take care of the house alone."

"Yes, go certainly," replied the Mouse, "and when you eat anything good, think of me; I should very much like a drop of the red christening wine."

But it was all untrue. The Cat had no cousin, and had not been asked to be godmother. She went straight to the church, slunk to the little pot of fat, began to lick it, and licked the top off. Then she took a walk on the roofs of the town, looked at the view, stretched herself out in the sun, and licked her lips whenever she thought of the little pot of fat. As soon as it was evening she went home again.

"Ah, here you are again!" said the Mouse; "you must certainly have had an enjoyable day."

"It went off very well," answered the Cat.

"What was the child's name?" asked the Mouse.

"Top Off," said the Cat drily.

"Topoff!" echoed the Mouse, "it is indeed a wonderful and curious name. Is it in your family?"

"What is there odd about it?" said the Cat. "It is not worse than Breadthief, as your godchild is called."

Not long after this another great longing came over the Cat. She said to the Mouse, "You must again be kind enough to look after the house alone, for I have been asked a second time to stand godmother, and as this child has a white ring round its neck, I cannot refuse."

The kind Mouse agreed, but the Cat slunk under the town wall to the church, and ate up half of the pot of fat. "Nothing tastes better," said she, "than what one eats by oneself," and she was very much pleased with her day's work. When she came home the Mouse asked, "What was this child called?"

"Half Gone," answered the Cat.

"Halfgone! what a name! I have never heard it in my life. I don't believe it is in the calendar."

Soon the Cat's mouth began to water once more after her licking business. "All good things in threes," she said to the Mouse; "I have again to stand godmother. The child is quite black, and has very white paws, but not a single white hair on its body. This only happens once in two years, so you will let me go out?"

"Topoff! Halfgone!" repeated the Mouse, "they are such curious names; they make me very thoughtful."

"Oh, you sit at home in your dark gray coat and your long tail," said the Cat, "and you get fanciful. That comes of not going out in the day."

The Mouse had a good cleaning out while the Cat was gone, and made the house tidy; but the greedy Cat ate the fat every bit up.

"When it is all gone one can be at rest," she said to herself, and at night she came home sleek and satisfied. The Mouse asked at once after the third child's name.

"It won't please you any better," said the Cat, "he was called Clean Gone."

"Cleangone!" repeated the Mouse. "I do not believe that name has been printed any more than the others. Cleangone! What can it mean?" She shook her head, curled herself up, and went to sleep.

From this time on no one asked the Cat to stand godmother; but when the winter came and there was nothing to be got outside, the Mouse remembered their provision and said, "Come, Cat, we will go to our pot of fat which we have stored away; it will taste very good."

"Yes, indeed," answered the Cat; "it will taste as good to you as if you stretched your thin tongue out of the window."

They started off, and when they reached it they found the pot in its place, but quite empty!

"Ah," said the Mouse," "now I know what has happened! It has all come out! You are a true friend to me! You have eaten it all when you stood godmother; first the top off, then half of it gone, then——"

"Will you be quiet!" screamed the Cat. "Another word and I will eat you up."

"Clean-gone" was already on the poor Mouse's tongue, and scarcely was it out than the Cat made a spring at her, seized and swallowed her.

You see that is the way of the world.

The Girl Who Trod on a Loaf

Hans Christian Andersen

The story of the girl who trod on a loaf of bread in order to avoid soiling her shoes, and how she was punished for it, is well known; it is written down—nay, even printed. Ingé was the girl's name; she was a poor child, but proud and haughty; there was a bad foundation in her, as the saying is. Already, when quite a small child, it amused her greatly to catch flies, pull their wings off, and to transform them into creeping things. Later on she took cockchafers and beetles, stuck them on a needle, and held a green leaf or a little piece of paper close to their feet. Then the poor animal seized it, and turned it over and over in its struggles to get free from the needle. "Now the cockchafer is reading," said Ingé", "look how it turns the leaf over." As years passed by she became rather worse than better, but she was beautiful, and that was her misfortune; otherwise something else might have happened to her than what really happened.

"Your bad disposition ought to be thoroughly rooted out," her own mother said to her. "As a child you have often trampled upon my apron, but I am afraid you will one day trample on my heart."

And that she really did.

She went into the country, and entered the service of some rich people who treated her like their own child, and dressed her accordingly; she looked very well, but her haughtiness increased.

When she had been there about a year, her mistress said to her: "Ingé, you ought to go for once to see your parents."

And Ingé went off, but only in order to show herself in her native place; she wished people to see how grand she had become. But when she came to the entrance of the village and saw the young men and girls chatting there, and her own mother near them, resting on a stone, and having a bundle of sticks in front of her which she had picked up in the wood, Ingé turned back; she was ashamed to think that she, who was so well clad, had a poor ragged woman for a mother, who picked up sticks in the wood. And she was not sorry that she returned; she was only angry.

Again six months passed by, and her mistress said: "You ought to go home again and visit your parents, Ingé. I will give you a large loaf of bread for them. I am sure they will be pleased to see you."

Ingé put her best dress and her new shoes on, raised her skirt, and walked very carefully that she might be clean and neat about the feet and for that no one could find fault with her. But when she came to the point where the path runs over the moor, where it was muddy, and where many puddles had formed, she threw the loaf down and trod on it, in order to keep her shoes clean; but while she was thus standing with one foot on the loaf and the other raised up in order to go on, the loaf sank down with her deeper and deeper, and she entirely disappeared. A large puddle with bubbles on it was all that was left to show where she had sunk. That is the story.

But what became of Ingé? She sank down into the ground, and came to the Marsh Woman below, where she was brewing. The Marsh Woman is a sister of the Elfin Girls, who are known well enough, for there are songs and pictures of them; but of the Marsh Woman people only know that when in the summer mists rise in the meadows, she is brewing below. Ingé sank down to the Marsh Woman's brewery, but there nobody can bear to stay long. The dung hole is a splendid drawing-room compared to the Marsh Woman's brewery. Every vessel smells so disagreeably that one almost faints, and in addition the barrels are so closely packed that if there were a small opening between them through which one might creep, it would be impossible because of the wet toads and fat serpents which abide there. In this place Ingé arrived; all the horrible creeping things were so icy cold, that she shuddered all over, and then she became more and more rigid. She stuck fast to the loaf, which dragged her down as an amber button attracts a straw.

The Marsh Woman was at home. There were visitors at the brewery, for Old Bogey and his grandmother inspected it. And Old Bogey's grandmother is a wicked old woman, who is never idle; she never rode out on visits without having her needlework with her, and also here she had not forgotten it. She sewed little bits of leather to be attached to men's shoes, so that they continually wander about without being able to settle anywhere; she embroidered cobwebs of lies, and made crochet-work of foolish words which had fallen to the ground: all this was for men's disadvantage and destruction. Yes, indeed! She knew how to sew, to embroider, and to crochet—this old grandmother.

She saw Ingé, put her spectacles on, and looked at her again.

"That's a girl who possesses talents," she said; "and I request you to let me have the little one as a memento of my visit here. She will make a suitable statue in my grandson's ante-room."

And she was given to her, and thus Ingé came into still lower regions. People do not go there directly, but they can get there by a circuitous road, when they have the necessary talents. That was an endless ante-room; one felt quite dizzy if one looked forward or backward. A crowd of people, exhausted to death, were standing here and waiting for the gate of mercy to be opened to them. They had to wait a long time. Large, fat, waddling spiders spun cobwebs, which lasted thousands of years, over their feet, and cut like iron foot-traps and copper chains; besides this, every soul was filled with everlasting restlessness—a restlessness of misery. The miser was standing there, and had forgotten the key of his money-box; the key was in the keyhole, he knew that. It would lead us too far to enumerate all the tortures and misery which were seen there. Ingel felt inexpressible pain when she had to stand there as a statue; it was as if she had been tied to the loaf.

"That is the consequence of trying to keep one's feet clean and tidy," she said to herself. "Look how they stare at me!"

And indeed the eyes of all were fixed upon her; their wicked desires were looking out of their eyes and speaking out of their mouths, without a sound being heard. They were dreadful to look at.

"It must be a pleasure to look at me!" thought Ingé. "I have a pretty face and fine clothes." And then she turned her eyes, for she could not move her neck—it was too stiff. She had forgotten that she had been much soiled in the Marsh Woman's brewery. Her dress was covered with slime; a snake had fixed itself in her hair, and hung down her back; out of every fold of her dress a toad looked forth, croaking like a short-winded pug-dog. That was very disagreeable. "But the others down here look just as dreadful," she thought, and thus consoled herself.

The worst of all, however, was the terrible hunger she felt. Could she not stoop down and break off a piece from the loaf on which she was standing? No, her back was stiff, her arms and hands were rigid, her whole body was like a pillar of stone; she could only turn her eyes in her head, but right round, so she could also see behind her. It was an awful aspect. And then flies came and ran to and fro over her eyes. She blinked, but they did not fly away, for they could not, as their wings were torn off, and they were transformed into creeping things. It was a horrible pain, which was increased by hunger, and at last it seemed to her as if there was nothing left in her body. "If this is to last much longer," she said, "I shall not be able to bear it." But she had to bear it. Then a hot tear fell upon her head, and rolled over her face and her breast, down to the loaf upon which she stood; and another tear fell, and many others more. Who do you think was weeping for Ingé? Her mother was still alive! The tears of grief which a mother sheds over her child always reach it, but they do not redeem; they burn and augment the torture—this unbearable hunger, and not to be able to reach the loaf upon which she was standing with her feet! She had a feeling as if her whole interior had consumed itself. She was like a thin hollow reed which takes in every sound; she heard everything distinctly that was spoken about her on earth, but what she heard was hard and evil. Although her mother shed a great many tears over her, and was sad, she could not help saying, "Pride goes before a fall. That was your misfortune, Ingé You have much grieved your mother."

Her mother and all on earth knew of the sin which she had committed; they knew that she had trod on the loaf, and that she had sunk and disappeared, for the cowherd had seen it from the slope near the marsh land.

"How you have grieved your mother, Ingé!" said the mother. "I had a sort of presentiment."

"I wish I had never been born!" thought Ingé; "it would have been much better. Of what use are my mother's tears now?" She heard how her master and mistress, the good people who had taken care of her like parents, said that she was a sinful child who had despised God's gifts, and trod upon them with her feet. The gates of mercy would be very slowly opened to her!

"They ought to have chastised me, and driven out the whims, if I had any," thought Ingé.

She heard that a song was composed about her—the haughty girl who had trod on a loaf to keep her shoes clean—and that it was sung all over the country.

"That one must bear so much evil, and have to suffer so much!" thought Ingé. "Others ought to be punished too for their sins! But, of course, then there would be much to be punished. Alas! how I am tortured!"

Her mind now became harder than her exterior. "In such company," she said, "it is impossible to become better, and I don't wish to become better. Look how they stare at me!" Her mind was full of wrath and malice against all men. "At last those up there have something to talk about! Alas! how I am tortured!"

She also heard how her story was told to children, and how the little ones called her wicked Ingé. They said she was so ugly and wicked she ought to be severely punished. Again and again hard words were uttered about her by children. Yet, one day, while grief and hunger were gnawing her hollow body, she heard her name pronounced and her story told to an innocent child—a little girl—and she also heard that the little one burst into tears at the story of the haughty, vain Ingé and did not add anything about her faults. A young innocent child cried and asked mercy for her. She felt very strange; she would have much liked to cry herself, but she could not do it: she was unable to cry, and that was another torture.

"But will Ingé never come up again?" asked the little girl.

"No, never," was the answer.

"But if she says 'please,' and asks pardon, and promises never to do it again?"

"Then, yes; but she will not ask to be pardoned," they told the child.

"I should like her so much to do it," said the little girl, and was quite inconsolable. "I will give my doll and all my toys if she may only come up. It is too terrible—poor Ingé."

These words touched Ingé to the depth of her heart; they did her good. It was the first time any one had said, "Poor Ingé," and did not add anything about her faults. A young innocent child cried and asked mercy for her. She felt very strange; she would have much liked to cry herself, but she could not do it: she was unable to cry, and that was another torture.

While years passed on above, no change took place below. She more rarely heard words from above; she was less spoken of. Then suddenly one day a sigh reached her ear: "Ingé! Ingé! how sad you have made me. I have said it would be so!" It was the last sigh of her dying mother. Sometimes she heard her name mentioned by her former master and mistress, and these were pleasant words when the lady said: "Shall I ever, see you again, Ingé? One does not know where one comes to!"

But Ingé was convinced that her kind mistress would never come to the place where she was.

Again a long while passed—a long bitter time. Then Ingé heard her name pronounced once more, and saw two stars sparkling above her. These were two kind eyes which had closed on earth. So many years had passed since the little girl had been inconsolable and had wept over "poor Ingé," that the child had become an old woman, whom God was calling back again, and in the hour when thoughts of various periods of her life came back to her mind she remembered how she had once as a little child cried bitterly when she heard the story of Ingé. And the old lady had such a lively recollection, in the hour of death, of the impression the story had made upon her that she exclaimed: "My God and Lord, have I not sometimes, like Ingé!, trampled Thy blessings under my feet, without thinking it wrong? Have I not walked about with haughtiness? But in Thy mercy Thou hast not let me sink, but supported me. Oh, do not forsake me in my last hour!" The eyes of the old lady closed, and the eyes of her soul opened to see hidden things. She, whose last thoughts Ingé had so much occupied, saw now how deep she had sunk, and at this sight the pious woman burst into tears; in Heaven she was standing like a child and crying for poor Ingé! And these tears and prayers resounded like an echo in the hollow outside shell that enclosed the fettered tortured soul; the never-dreamed-of love from above overwhelmed her; an angel of God was shedding tears over her. Why was this granted her?

The tortured soul collected as it were in thought every action she had done on earth, and Ingé trembled in tears such as she had never wept. Grief at herself filled her, she felt as if the gates of mercy could never be thrown open to her; and while in contrition she recognized this, a beam of light rushed down to her in the precipice with a force much stronger than that of the sunbeam which melts the snowman that boys have put up, and much quicker than the snowflake melts that falls on the warm lips of a child, and becomes a drop of water; the petrified shape of Ingé dissolved into mist—a little bird flew up with the quickness of lightning into the upper world.

But the bird was timid and shy towards all that surrounded it; it was ashamed of itself, ashamed to face the living creatures, and quickly concealed itself in a dark hole in an old weather-beaten wall. There it sat and cowered, trembling all over and unable to utter a single sound: it had no voice. It sat there a long time before it could see all the splendor around it; indeed it was very beautiful! The air was fresh and mild, the moon threw her silvery light over the earth; trees and bushes breathed forth fragrance, and the place where it sat was pleasant; its feathers were pure and fine. How love and brightness pervaded all creation! The bird wanted to burst into song, and to sing forth all that filled its breast, but was unable to do it; it would gladly have sung like the cuckoo and nightingale in spring. But God, who hears the soundless hymn of praise of the worm, also heard the notes of praise which filled its breast, as the psalms of David were heard before they were expressed in word and tune.

For weeks these soundless songs stirred in the bird's breast; a good deed had to be performed to make them burst forth!

Holy Christmastime approached. A peasant set up a pole near the wall and tied a bunch of oats to it, that the birds of the air might also have a pleasant Christmas and a good feed in this blissful time. When the sun rose on Christmas morn and shined upon the oats, the twittering birds flew in flocks round the pole. Then also a "tweet, tweet" sounded from a hole in the wall—the swelling thought became a sound, the weak "tweet, tweet," a whole song of joy, the thought of a good deed was called to life, the bird left its hiding-place; in Heaven it was known what sort of bird this was!

The winter was hard, the water frozen over, and the birds and the animals in the wood had little food. Our little bird flew over the highroad, and found a grain of corn here and there in the ruts the sleighs made, and a few crumbs at the halting-places; it ate but few, but called all the other starving sparrows that they might have some food. It flew into the towns, looked all round, and where a loving hand had strewn bread-crumbs on a window-sill for the birds, it only ate a single crumb, leaving all to the other birds.

In the course of the winter the bird had gathered so many crumbs and given them to other birds, that altogether they equalled the weight of the whole loaf on which Ingé had trodden to keep her shoes clean. And when the last bread-crumb was found and given away, the gray wings of the bird turned white and expanded.

"There flies a sea-swallow over the water," said the children who saw the white bird; it dived down into the sea and then rose up again into the bright sunshine; it glittered, and it was impossible to see what became of it—they said it flew into the sun.

Niels and the Giants

(FROM *THE CRIMSON FAIRY BOOK*)

On one of the great moors over in Jutland, where trees won't grow because the soil is so sandy and the wind so strong, there once lived a man and his wife, who had a little house and some sheep, and two sons who helped them to herd them. The elder of the two was called Rasmus, and the younger Niels. Rasmus was quite content to look after sheep, as his father had done before him, but Niels had a fancy to be a hunter, and was not happy till he got hold of a gun and learned to shoot. It was only an old muzzle-loading flint-lock after all, but Niels thought it a great prize, and went about shooting at everything he could see. So much did he practice that in the long run he became a wonderful shot, and was heard of even where he had never been seen. Some people said there was very little in him beyond this, but that was an idea they found reason to change in the course of time.

The parents of Rasmus and Niels were good Catholics, and when they were getting old the mother took it into her head that she would like to go to Rome and see the Pope. The others didn't see much use in this, but she had her way in the end: they sold all the sheep, shut up the house, and set out for Rome on foot. Niels took his gun with him.

"What do you want with that?" said Rasmus; "we have plenty to carry without it." But Niels could not be happy without his gun, and took it all the same.

It was in the hottest part of summer that they began their journey, so hot that they could not travel at all in the middle of the day, and they were afraid to do it by night lest they might lose their way or fall into the hands of robbers. One day, a little before sunset, they came to an inn which lay at the edge of a forest.

"We had better stay here for the night," said Rasmus.

"What an idea!" said Niels, who was growing impatient at the slow progress they were making. "We can't travel by day for the heat, and we remain where we are all night. It will be long enough before we get to Rome if we go on at this rate."

Rasmus was unwilling to go on, but the two old people sided with Niels, who said, "The nights aren't dark, and the moon will soon be up. We can ask at the inn here, and find out which way we ought to take."

So they held on for some time, but at last they came to a small opening in the forest, and here they found that the road split in two. There was no sign-post to direct them, and the people in the inn had not told them which of the two roads to take.

"What's to be done now?" said Rasmus. "I think we had better have stayed at the inn."

"There's no harm done," said Niels. "The night is warm, and we can wait here till morning. One of us will keep watch till midnight, and then waken the other."

Rasmus chose to take the first watch, and the others lay down to sleep. It was very quiet in the forest, and Rasmus could hear the deer and foxes and other animals moving about among the rustling leaves. After the moon rose he could see them occasionally, and when a big stag came quite close to him he got hold of Niels' gun and shot it.

Niels was wakened by the report. "What's that?" he said.

"I've just shot a stag," said Rasmus, highly pleased with himself.

"That's nothing," said Niels. "I've often shot a sparrow, which is a much more difficult thing to do."

It was now close on midnight, so Niels began his watch, and Rasmus went to sleep. It began to get colder, and Niels began to walk about a little to keep himself warm. He soon found that they were not far from the edge of the forest, and when he climbed up one of the trees there he could see out over the open country beyond. At a little distance he saw a fire, and beside it there sat three giants, busy with broth and beef. They were so huge that the spoons they used were as large as spades, and their forks as big as hay-forks: with these they lifted whole bucketfuls of broth and great joints of meat out of an enormous pot which was set on the ground between them. Niels was startled and rather scared at first, but he comforted himself with the thought that the giants were a good way off, and that if they came nearer he could easily hide among the bushes. After watching them for a little, however, he began to get over his alarm, and finally slid down the tree again, resolved to get his gun and play some tricks with them.

When he had climbed back to his former position, he took good aim, and waited till one of the giants was just in the act of putting a large piece of meat

273

into his mouth. *Bang!* went Niels' gun, and the bullet struck the handle of the fork so hard that the point went into the giant's chin, instead of his mouth.

"None of your tricks," growled the giant to the one who sat next him. "What do you mean by hitting my fork like that, and making me prick myself?"

"I never touched your fork," said the other. "Don't try to get up a quarrel with me."

"Look at it, then," said the first. "Do you suppose I stuck it into my own chin for fun?"

The two got so angry over the matter that each offered to fight the other there and then, but the third giant acted as peace-maker, and they again fell to their eating. While the quarrel was going on, Niels had loaded the gun again, and just as the second giant was about to put a nice tit-bit into his mouth, *bang!* went the gun again, and the fork flew into a dozen pieces.

This giant was even more furious than the first had been, and words were just coming to blows, when the third giant again interposed.

"Don't be fools," he said to them; "what's the good of beginning to fight among ourselves, when it is so necessary for the three of us to work together and get the upper hand over the king of this country. It will be a hard enough task as it is, but it will be altogether hopeless if we don't stick together. Sit down again, and let us finish our meal; I shall sit between you, and then neither of you can blame the other."

Niels was too far away to hear their talk, but from their gestures he could guess what was happening, and thought it good fun.

"Thrice is lucky," said he to himself; "I'll have another shot yet."

This time it was the third giant's fork that caught the bullet, and snapped in two.

"Well," said he, "if I were as foolish as you two, I would also fly into a rage, but I begin to see what time of day it is, and I'm going off this minute to see who it is that's playing these tricks with us."

So well had the giant made his observations, that though Niels climbed down the tree as fast as he could, so as to hide among the bushes, he had just got to the ground when the enemy was upon him.

"Stay where you are," said the giant, "or I'll put my foot on you, and there won't be much of you left after that."

Niels gave in, and the giant carried him back to his comrades.

"You don't deserve any mercy at our hands," said his captor "but as you are such a good shot you may be of great use to us, so we shall spare your life, if you will do us a service. Not far from here there stands a castle, in which the king's daughter lives; we are at war with the king, and want to get the upper hand of him by carrying off the princess, but the castle is so well guarded that there is no getting into it. By our skill in magic we have cast sleep on every living thing in the castle, except a little black dog, and, as long as he is awake, we are no better off than before; for, as soon as we begin to climb over the wall, the little dog will hear us, and its barking will waken all the others again. Having got you, we can place you where you will be able to shoot the dog before it begins to bark, and then no one can hinder us from getting the princess into our hands. If you do that, we shall not only let you off, but reward you handsomely."

Niels had to consent, and the giants set out for the castle at once. It was surrounded by a very high rampart, so high that even the giants could not touch the top of it. "How am I to get over that?" said Niels.

"Quite easily," said the third giant; "I'll throw you up on it."

"No, thanks," said Niels. "I might fall down on the other side, or break my leg or neck, and then the little dog wouldn't get shot after all."

"No fear of that," said the giant; "the rampart is quite wide on the top, and covered with long grass, so that you will come down as softly as though you fell on a feather-bed."

Niels had to believe him, and allowed the giant to throw him up. He came down on his feet quite unhurt, but the little black dog heard the dump, and rushed out of its kennel at once. It was just opening its mouth to bark, when Niels fired, and it fell dead on the spot.

"Go down on the inside now," said the giant, "and see if you can open the gate to us."

Niels made his way down into the courtyard, but on his way to the outer gate he found himself at the entrance to the large hall of the castle. The door was open, and the hall was brilliantly lighted, though there was no one to be seen. Niels went in here and looked round him: on the wall there hung a huge sword without a sheath, and beneath it was a large drinking-horn, mounted with silver. Niels went closer to look at these, and saw that the horn had letters engraved on the silver rim: when he took it down and turned it round, he found that the inscription was:—

Whoever drinks the wine I hold
Can wield the sword that hangs above;
Then let him use it for the right,
And win a royal maiden's love.

Niels took out the silver stopper of the horn, and drank some of the wine, but when he tried to take down the sword he found himself unable to move it. So he hung up the horn again, and went further in to the castle. "The giants can wait a little," he said.

Before long he came to an apartment in which a beautiful princess lay asleep in a bed, and on a table by her side there lay a gold-hemmed handkerchief. Niels tore this in two, and put one half in his pocket, leaving the other half on the table. On the floor he saw a pair of gold-embroidered slippers, and one of these he also put in his pocket. After that he went back to the hall, and took down the horn again. "Perhaps I have to drink all that is in it before I can move the sword," he thought; so he put it to his lips again and drank till it was quite empty. When he had done this, he could wield the sword with the greatest of ease, and felt himself strong enough to do anything, even to fight the giants he had left outside, who were no doubt wondering why he had not opened the gate to them before this time. To kill the giants, he thought, would be using the sword for the right; but as to winning the love of the princess, that was a thing which the son of a poor sheep-farmer need not hope for.

When Niels came to the gate of the castle, he found that there was a large door and a small one, so he opened the latter.

"Can't you open the big door?" said the giants; "we shall hardly be able to get in at this one."

"The bars are too heavy for me to draw," said Niels; "if you stoop a little you can quite well come in here." The first giant accordingly bent down and entered in a stooping posture, but before he had time to straighten his back again Niels made a sweep with the sword, and off went the giant's head. To push the body aside as it fell was quite easy for Niels, so strong had the wine made him, and the second giant as he entered met the same reception. The third was slower in coming, so Niels called out to him: "Be quick," he said, "you are surely the oldest of the three, since you are so slow in your movements, but I can't wait here long; I must get back to my own people as

276

soon as possible." So the third also came in, and was served in the same way. It appears from the story that giants were not given fair play!

By this time day was beginning to break, and Niels thought that his folks might already be searching for him, so, instead of waiting to see what took place at the castle, he ran off to the forest as fast as he could, taking the sword with him. He found the others still asleep, so he woke them up, and they again set out on their journey. Of the night's adventures he said not a word, and when they asked where he got the sword, he only pointed in the direction of the castle, and said, "Over that way." They thought he had found it, and asked no more questions.

When Niels left the castle, he shut the door behind him, and it closed with such a bang that the porter woke up. He could scarcely believe his eyes when he saw the three headless giants lying in a heap in the courtyard, and could not imagine what had taken place. The whole castle was soon aroused, and then everybody wondered at the affair: it was soon seen that the bodies were those of the king's great enemies, but how they came to be there and in that condition was a perfect mystery. Then it was noticed that the drinking-horn was empty and the sword gone, while the princess reported that half of her handkerchief and one of her slippers had been taken away. *How* the giants had been killed seemed a little clearer now, but *who* had done it was as great a puzzle as before. The old knight who had charge of the castle said that in his opinion it must have been some young knight, who had immediately set off to the king to claim the hand of the princess. This sounded likely, but the messenger who was sent to the Court returned with the news that no one there knew anything about the matter.

"We must find him, however," said the princess; "for if he is willing to marry me I cannot in honor refuse him, after what my father put on the horn." She took council with her father's wisest men as to what ought to be done, and among other things they advised her to build a house beside the highway, and put over the door this inscription:—"Whoever will tell the story of his life, may stay here three nights for nothing." This was done, and many strange tales were told to the princess, but none of the travelers said a word about the three giants.

In the meantime Niels and the others tramped on towards Rome. Autumn passed, and winter was just beginning when they came to the foot of a great range of mountains, towering up to the sky. "Must we go over these?" said they. "We shall be frozen to death or buried in the snow."

"Here comes a man," said Niels; "let us ask him the way to Rome." They did so, and were told that there was no other way.

"And is it far yet?" said the old people, who were beginning to be worn out by the long journey. The man held up his foot so that they could see the sole of his shoe; it was worn as thin as paper, and there was a hole in the middle of it.

"These shoes were quite new when I left Rome," he said, "and look at them now; that will tell you whether you are far from it or not."

This discouraged the old people so much that they gave up all thought of finishing the journey, and only wished to get back to Denmark as quickly as they could. What with the winter and bad roads they took longer to return than they had taken to go, but in the end they found themselves in sight of the forest where they had slept before.

"What's this?" said Rasmus. "Here's a big house built since we passed this way before."

"So it is," said Peter; "let's stay all night in it."

"No, we can't afford that," said the old people; "it will be too dear for the like of us."

However, when they saw what was written above the door, they were all well pleased to get a night's lodging for nothing. They were well received, and had so much attention given to them, that the old people were quite put out by it. After they had got time to rest themselves, the princess's steward came to hear their story.

"You saw what was written above the door," he said to the father. "Tell me who you are and what your history has been."

"Dear me, I have nothing of any importance to tell you," said the old man, "and I am sure we should never have made so bold as to trouble you at all if it hadn't been for the youngest of our two sons here."

"Never mind that," said the steward; "you are very welcome if you will only tell me the story of your life."

"Well, well, I will," said he, "but there is nothing to tell about it. I and my wife have lived all our days on a moor in North Jutland, until this last year, when she took a fancy to go to Rome. We set out with our two sons but turned back long before we got there, and are now on our way home again.

That's all my own story, and our two sons have lived with us all their days, so there is nothing more to be told about them either."

"Yes there is," said Rasmus; "when we were on our way south, we slept in the wood near here one night, and I shot a stag."

The steward was so much accustomed to hearing stories of no importance that he thought there was no use going further with this, but reported to the princess that the newcomers had nothing to tell.

"Did you question them all?" she said.

"Well, no; not directly," said he; "but the father said that none of them could tell me any more than he had done."

"You are getting careless," said the princess; "I shall go and talk to them myself."

Niels knew the princess again as soon as she entered the room, and was greatly alarmed, for he immediately supposed that all this was a device to discover the person who had run away with the sword, the slipper and the half of the handkerchief, and that it would fare badly with him if he were discovered. So he told his story much the same as the others did (Niels was not very particular), and thought he had escaped all further trouble, when Rasmus put in his word. "You've forgotten something, Niels," he said; "you remember you found a sword near here that night I shot the stag."

"Where is the sword?" said the princess.

"I know," said the steward, "I saw where he laid it down when they came in;" and off he went to fetch it, while Niels wondered whether he could make his escape in the meantime. Before he had made up his mind, however, the steward was back with the sword, which the princess recognized at once.

"Where did you get this?" she said to Niels.

Niels was silent, and wondered what the usual penalty was for a poor sheep-farmer's son who was so unfortunate as to deliver a princess and carry off things from her bed-room.

"See what else he has about him," said the princess to the steward, and Niels had to submit to be searched: out of one pocket came a gold-embroidered slipper, and out of another the half of a gold-hemmed handkerchief.

"That is enough," said the princess; "*now* we needn't ask any more questions. Send for my father the king at once."

"Please let me go," said Niels; "I did you as much good as harm, at any rate."

"Why, who said anything about doing harm?" said the princess. "You must stay here till my father comes."

The way in which the princess smiled when she said this gave Niels some hope that things might not be bad for him after all, and he was yet more encouraged when he thought of the words engraven on the horn, though the last line still seemed too good to be true. However, the arrival of the king soon settled the matter: the princess was willing and so was Niels, and in a few days the wedding bells were ringing. Niels was made an earl by that time, and looked as handsome as any of them when dressed in all his robes. Before long the old king died, and Niels reigned after him; but whether his father and mother stayed with him, or went back to the moor in Jutland, or were sent to Rome in a carriage and four, is something that all the historians of his reign have forgotten to mention.

The Lime-Tree

(TRADITIONAL RUSSIAN TALE)

One evening Vanyusha (Johnny) was sitting with his grandfather, and asked his grandfather: "Whence comes it that bears' paws are like our hands and feet?" His grandfather replied: "Listen, Johnny. I will tell you what I have myself heard from ancient people. Ancient people said bears were like human beings, like us orthodox Christians. In a certain village there lived a poor cottager. His cottage was wretched; he had no pony; a cow he never even thought of; he had no firewood. Winter came, and it was cold in his unwarmed room. The cottager took his axe, and went with it into the wood. An enchanted tree—a lime-tree—presented itself to his sight. He struck it with his axe, and now to cut it down; but the lime-tree addressed him in human speech: 'I will give you all that you want. If you have no riches, if you have no wife, I will give you all.' The peasant said: 'Very good, mother, if you make me richer than any of the peasants. But I have no pony, no cow, and my cottage is wretched.' The lime-tree said: 'Go home; all shall be yours.' The peasant went. A new house was his: fences of stout boards, horses that were ready to fly, and store-rooms full of corn. The cottager was not satisfied, because his wife was not handsomer. What was to be done? ' I'll go off quick to Mother Lime-tree.' He took his axe, and went off into the wood.

"He went into the wood to the lime-tree, and struck it with his axe. 'What do you want?' 'Mother Lime-tree, among mankind there are wives and wives, but mine is such a disagreeable one. Do me a service: give me a handsome wife.' The lime-tree said: 'Go home.' The peasant went. His wife came to meet him—such a beauty—blood and milk, and store-rooms full of everything good. Well, the cottager began to live comfortably with his young wife, and thought: 'It is a fine thing for us to live possessed of riches, but we're under a superior authority. Is it impossible for me to be the superior authority myself?' He thought it over with his wife. He went again to the enchanted lime-tree.

"He went into the wood, he struck it with his axe. 'What do you want, peasant?' 'What, indeed, Mother Lime-tree! It's a fine thing for us to live in possession of riches; but we're under a superior authority. Is it impossible for me to be head-borough myself?' 'Very well: go home; all shall be yours.' No sooner had the cottager got home, when a letter came for him—the cottager was to be head-borough. The cottager got used to living as head-borough, and thought to himself: 'It's a fine thing to be head-borough, but all is under the control of the lord of the manor. Is it impossible for me to be the lord myself?' He considered the matter with his wife, they consulted together, and he went off again to the lime-tree.

"He went up to it, and struck it with his axe. The tree asked him: 'What do you want?' 'Thanks to you, mother, for all; but how not to doff my cap before the lord, to become the lord myself?' 'What is to be done with you? Go home; it shall all be yours.' Scarcely had he got home, when up drove the lord-lieutenant, and brought him a letter from the king, that 'he was to be a gentleman.' It was advantageous to be a gentleman. He began to give entertainments and banquets. 'It's a fine thing to be a gentleman, but without an official position! Was it impossible for him to become an official?' They thought and talked it over. He went off to the lime-tree and struck it with his axe. 'What do you want, peasant?' 'I thank you, mother, for all; but is it impossible for me to be an official?' 'Well, then, go home!' No sooner had he got home, when a royal letter arrived—he was invested with orders. 'It's a fine thing to be decorated, but all is under the control of the lord-lieutenant.

Is it impossible for me to be lord-lieutenant myself?' He thought it over with his wife, went off into the wood to the enchanted tree, the lime-tree.

"He came to the lime-tree and struck it with his axe. It said: 'What do you want, peasant? With what are you discontented?' 'I thank you, mother, for everything; but is it impossible for me to be lord-lieutenant myself, and to have a rich patrimony?' 'It is difficult to effect this. But what is to be done with you? Go home!' The cottager had scarcely got home, when a letter arrived—the cottager was to be lord-lieutenant, and was presented with an estate of inheritance. The cottager became used to living as lord-lieutenant—indeed, by descent, he was not a peasant. 'It's a fine thing for me to live as lord-lieutenant, but all is under the control of the king.' He considered; he went off into the wood to the enchanted tree, the lime-tree.

"He came to it, and struck it with his axe. The tree inquired: 'What do you want?' 'All is excellent; I thank you for all; but is it impossible for me to be king myself?' The lime-tree began to try to persuade him. 'Foolish man, for what are you asking? Consider what you were, and what you have become. From a cottager you have become a man of high rank and everything; but an emperor is chosen by God.' The lime-tree endeavored to persuade him with all manner of arguments that he had better not make the request, but all in vain. The cottager would not budge, but insisted that it should make him emperor. The lime-tree said to him: 'It is impossible to effect this, and it will not be done; you will lose, too, what you have already obtained!' But the cottager still insisted. The lime-tree said: 'Become a bear, and your wife a she-bear!' And he became a bear, and she a she-bear. They went off bears."

The grandson inquired: "Grandfather, can this be a true story?" "In reality 'tis a fable. Do not desire what is impossible; be content with a little. If you desire much, you will lose what you have obtained."

The Story of a Mother

Hans Christian Andersen

Amother sat by her little child; she was very sad, for she feared it would die. It was quite pale, and its little eyes were closed, and sometimes it drew a heavy deep breath, almost like a sigh; and then the mother gazed more sadly than ever on the poor little creature. Some one knocked at the door, and a poor old man walked in. He was wrapped in something that looked like a great horse-cloth; and he required it truly to keep him warm, for it was cold winter; the country everywhere lay covered with snow and ice, and the wind blew so sharply that it cut one's face.

The little child had dozed off to sleep for a moment, and the mother, seeing that the old man shivered with the cold, rose and placed a small mug of beer on the stove to warm for him. The old man sat and rocked the cradle; and the mother seated herself on a chair near him, and looked at her sick child who still breathed heavily, and took hold of its little hand.

"You think I shall keep him, do you not?" she said. "Our all-merciful God will surely not take him away from me."

The old man, who was indeed Death himself, nodded his head in a peculiar manner, which might have signified either Yes, or No; and the mother cast down her eyes, while the tears rolled down her cheeks. Then her head became heavy, for she had not closed her eyes for three days and nights, and she slept, but only for a moment. Shivering with cold, she started up and looked round the room. The old man was gone, and her child—it was gone too!—the old man had taken it with him. In the corner of the room the old clock began to strike; "whirr" went the chains, the heavy weight sank to the ground, and the clock stopped; and the poor mother rushed out of the house calling for her child. Out in the snow sat a woman in long black garments, and she said to the mother, "Death has been with you in your room. I saw him hastening away with your little child; he strides faster than the wind, and never brings back what he has taken away."

"Only tell me which way he has gone," said the mother; "tell me the way, I will find him."

283

"I know the way," said the woman in the black garments; "but before I tell you, you must sing to me all the songs that you have sung to your child; I love these songs, I have heard them before. I am Night, and I saw your tears flow as you sang."

"I will sing them all to you," said the mother; "but do not detain me now. I must overtake him, and find my child."

But Night sat silent and still. Then the mother wept and sang, and wrung her hands. And there were many songs, and yet even more tears; till at length Night said, "Go to the right, into the dark forest of fir-trees; for I saw Death take that road with your little child."

Within the wood the mother came to cross roads, and she knew not which to take. Just by stood a thorn-bush; it had neither leaf nor flower, for it was the cold winter time, and icicles hung on the branches. "Have you not seen Death go by, with my little child?" she asked.

"Yes," replied the thorn-bush; "but I will not tell you which way he has taken until you have warmed me in your bosom. I am freezing to death here, and turning to ice."

Then she pressed the bramble to her bosom quite close, so that it might be thawed, and the thorns pierced her flesh, and great drops of blood flowed; but the bramble shot forth fresh green leaves, and they became flowers on the cold winter's night, so warm is the heart of a sorrowing mother. Then the bramble-bush told her the path she must take. She came at length to a great lake, on which there was neither ship nor boat to be seen. The lake was not frozen sufficiently for her to pass over on the ice, nor was it open enough for her to wade through; and yet she must cross it, if she wished to find her child. Then she laid herself down to drink up the water of the lake, which was of course impossible for any human being to do; but the bereaved mother thought that perhaps a miracle might take place to help her. "You will never succeed in this," said the lake; "let us make an agreement together which will be better. I love to collect pearls, and your eyes are the purest I have ever seen. If you will weep those eyes away in tears into my waters, then I will take you to the large hothouse where Death dwells and rears flowers and trees, every one of which is a human life."

"Oh, what would I not give to reach my child!" said the weeping mother; and as she still continued to weep, her eyes fell into the depths of the lake, and became two costly pearls.

Then the lake lifted her up, and wafted her across to the opposite shore as if she were on a swing, where stood a wonderful building many miles in length. No one could tell whether it was a mountain covered with forests and full of caves, or whether it had been built. But the poor mother could not see, for she had wept her eyes into the lake. "Where shall I find Death, who went away with my little child?" she asked.

"He has not arrived here yet," said an old gray-haired woman, who was walking about, and watering Death's hothouse. "How have you found your way here? and who helped you?"

"God has helped me," she replied. "He is merciful; will you not be merciful too? Where shall I find my little child?"

"I did not know the child," said the old woman; "and you are blind. Many flowers and trees have faded to-night, and Death will soon come to transplant them. You know already that every human being has a life-tree or a life-flower, just as may be ordained for him. They look like other plants; but they have hearts that beat. Children's hearts also beat: from that you may perhaps be able to recognize your child. But what will you give me, if I tell you what more you will have to do?"

"I have nothing to give," said the afflicted mother; "but I would go to the ends of the earth for you."

"I can give you nothing to do for me there," said the old woman; "but you can give me your long black hair. You know yourself that it is beautiful, and it pleases me. You can take my white hair in exchange, which will be something in return."

"Do you ask nothing more than that?" said she. "I will give it to you with pleasure."

And she gave up her beautiful hair, and received in return the white locks of the old woman. Then they went into Death's vast hothouse, where flowers and trees grew together in wonderful profusion. Blooming hyacinths, under glass bells, and peonies, like strong trees. There grew water-plants, some quite fresh, and others looking sickly, which had water-snakes twining round them, and black crabs clinging to their stems. There stood noble palm-trees, oaks, and plantains, and beneath them bloomed thyme and parsley. Each tree and flower had a name; each represented a human life, and belonged to men still living, some in China, others in Greenland, and in all parts of the world. Some large trees had been planted in little pots, so that they were cramped for room, and seemed about to burst the pot to pieces; while many weak little flowers were growing in rich soil, with moss all around them, carefully tended and cared for. The sorrowing mother bent over the little plants, and heard the human heart beating in each, and recognized the beatings of her child's heart among millions of others.

"That is it," she cried, stretching out her hand towards a little crocus-flower which hung down its sickly head.

"Do not touch the flower," exclaimed the old woman; "but place yourself here; and when Death comes—I expect him every minute—do not let him pull up that plant, but threaten him that if he does you will serve the other flowers in the same manner. This will make him afraid; for he must account to God for each of them. None can be uprooted, unless he receives permission to do so."

There rushed through the hothouse a chill of icy coldness, and the blind mother felt that Death had arrived.

"How did you find your way hither?" asked he; "how could you come here faster than I have?"

"I am a mother," she answered.

And Death stretched out his hand towards the delicate little flower; but she held her hands tightly round it, and held it fast at same time, with the most anxious care, lest she should touch one of the leaves. Then Death breathed upon her hands, and she felt his breath colder than the icy wind, and her hands sank down powerless.

"You cannot prevail against me," said Death.

"But a God of mercy can," said she.

"I only do His will," replied Death. "I am his gardener. I take all His flowers and trees, and transplant them into the gardens of Paradise in an unknown land. How they flourish there, and what that garden resembles, I may not tell you."

"Give me back my child," said the mother, weeping and imploring; and she seized two beautiful flowers in her hands, and cried to Death, "I will tear up all your flowers, for I am in despair."

"Do not touch them," said Death. "You say you are unhappy; and would you make another mother as unhappy as yourself?"

"Another mother!" cried the poor woman, setting the flowers free from her hands.

"There are your eyes," said Death. "I fished them up out of the lake for you. They were shining brightly; but I knew not they were yours. Take them back—they are clearer now than before—and then look into the deep well which is close by here. I will tell you the names of the two flowers which you wished to pull up; and you will see the whole future of the human beings they represent, and what you were about to frustrate and destroy."

Then she looked into the well; and it was a glorious sight to behold how one of them became a blessing to the world, and how much happiness and joy it spread around. But she saw that the life of the other was full of care and poverty, misery and woe.

"Both are the will of God," said Death.

"Which is the unhappy flower, and which is the blessed one?" she said.

"That I may not tell you," said Death; "but thus far you may learn, that one of the two flowers represents your own child. It was the fate of your child that you saw,—the future of your own child."

Then the mother screamed aloud with terror, "Which of them belongs to my child? Tell me that. Deliver the unhappy child. Release it from so much misery. Rather take it away. Take it to the kingdom of God. Forget my tears and my entreaties; forget all that I have said or done."

"I do not understand you," said Death. "Will you have your child back? or shall I carry him away to a place that you do not know?"

Then the mother wrung her hands, fell on her knees, and prayed to God, "Grant not my prayers, when they are contrary to Thy will, which at all times must be the best. Oh, hear them not;" and her head sank on her bosom.

Then Death carried away her child to the unknown land.

Andras Baive

(FROM *THE ORANGE FAIRY BOOK*)

Once upon a time there lived in Lapland a man who was so very strong and swift of foot that nobody in his native town of Vadsö could come near him if they were running races in the summer evenings. The people of

Vadsö were very proud of their champion, and thought that there was no one like him in the world, till, by-and-by, it came to their ears that there dwelt among the mountains a Lapp, Andras Baive by name, who was said by his friends to be even stronger and swifter than the bailiff. Of course not a creature in Vadsö believed *that*, and declared that if it made the mountaineers happier to talk such nonsense, why, let them!

The winter was long and cold, and the thoughts of the villagers were much busier with wolves than with Andras Baive, when suddenly, on a frosty day, he made his appearance in the little town of Vadsö. The bailiff was delighted at this chance of trying his strength, and at once went out to seek Andras and to coax him into giving proof of his vigor. As he walked along his eyes fell upon a big eight-oared boat that lay upon the shore, and his face shone with pleasure. "That is the very thing," laughed he, "I will make him jump over that boat." Andras was quite ready to accept the challenge, and they soon settled the terms of the wager. He who could jump over the boat without so much as touching it with his heel was to be the winner, and would get a large sum of money as the prize. So, followed by many of the villagers, the two men walked down to the sea.

An old fisherman was chosen to stand near the boat to watch fair play, and to hold the stakes, and Andras, as the stranger was told to jump first. Going back to the flag which had been stuck into the sand to mark the starting place, he ran forward, with his head well thrown back, and cleared the boat with a mighty bound. The lookers-on cheered him, and indeed he well deserved it; but they waited anxiously all the same to see what the bailiff would do. On he came, taller than Andras by several inches, but heavier of build. He too sprang high and well, but as he came down his heel just grazed the edge of the boat. Dead silence reigned amidst the townsfolk, but Andras only laughed and said carelessly:

"Just a little too short, bailiff; next time you must do better than that."

The bailiff turned red with anger at his rival's scornful words, and answered quickly: "Next time you will have something harder to do." And turning his back on his friends, he went sulkily home. Andras, putting the money he had earned in his pocket, went home also.

The following spring Andras happened to be driving his reindeer along a great fiord to the west of Vadsö. A boy who had met him hastened to tell the bailiff that his enemy was only a few miles off; and the bailiff, disguising himself as a Stalo, or ogre, called his son and his dog and rowed away across the fiord to the place where the boy had met Andras.

Now the mountaineer was lazily walking along the sands, thinking of the new hut that he was building with the money that he had won on the day of his lucky jump. He wandered on, his eyes fixed on the sands, so that he did not see the bailiff drive his boat behind a rock, while he changed himself into a heap of wreckage which floated in on the waves. A stumble over a stone recalled Andras to himself, and looking up he beheld the mass of wreckage. "Dear me! I may find some use for that," he said; and hastened down to the sea, waiting till he could lay hold of some stray rope which might float towards him. Suddenly—he could not have told why—a nameless fear seized upon him, and he fled away from the shore as if for his life. As he ran he heard the sound of a pipe, such as only ogres of the Stalo kind were wont to use; and there flashed into his mind what the bailiff had said when they jumped the boat: "Next time you will have something harder to do." So it was no wreckage after all that he had seen, but the bailiff himself.

It happened that in the long summer nights up in the mountain, where the sun never set, and it was very difficult to get to sleep, Andras had spent many hours in the study of magic, and this stood him in good stead now. The instant he heard the Stalo music he wished himself to become the feet of a reindeer, and in this guise he galloped like the wind for several miles. Then he stopped to take breath and find out what his enemy was doing. Nothing he could see, but to his ears the notes of a pipe floated over the plain, and ever, as he listened, it drew nearer.

A cold shiver shook Andras, and this time he wished himself the feet of a reindeer calf. For when a reindeer calf has reached the age at which he begins first to lose his hair he is so swift that neither beast nor bird can come near him. A reindeer calf is the swiftest of all things living. Yes; but not so swift as a Stalo, as Andras found out when he stopped to rest, and heard the pipe playing!

For a moment his heart sank, and he gave himself up for dead, till he remembered that, not far off, were two little lakes joined together by a short though very broad river. In the middle of the river lay a stone that was always covered by water, except in very dry seasons, and as the winter rains had been very heavy, he felt quite sure that not even the top of it could be seen. The next minute, if anyone had been looking that way, he would have beheld a small reindeer calf speeding northwards, and by-and-by giving a great spring, which landed him in the midst of the stream. But, instead of sinking to the bottom, he paused a second to steady himself, then gave a second spring which landed him on the further shore. He next ran on to a little hill where he saw down and began to neigh loudly, so that the Stalo might know exactly where he was.

"Ah! *there* you are," cried the Stalo, appearing on the opposite bank; "for a moment I really thought I had lost you."

"No such luck," answered Andras, shaking his head sorrowfully. By this time he had taken his own shape again.

"Well, but I don't see how I am to get to you," said the Stalo, looking up and down.

"Jump over, as I did," answered Andras; "it is quite easy."

"But I could not jump this river; and I don't know how you did," replied the Stalo.

"I should be ashamed to say such things," exclaimed Andras. "Do you mean to tell me that a jump, which the weakest Lapp boy would make nothing of, is beyond your strength?"

The Stalo grew red and angry when he heard these words, just as Andras meant him to do. He bounded into the air and fell straight into the river. Not that *that* would have mattered, for he was a good swimmer; but Andras drew out the bow and arrows which every Lapp carries, and took aim at him. His aim was good, but the Stalo sprang so high into the air that the arrow flew between his feet. A second shot, directed at his forehead, fared no better, for this time the Stalo jumped so high to the other side that the arrow passed between his finger and thumb. Then Andras aimed his third arrow a little over the Stalo's head, and when he sprang up, just an instant too soon, it hit him between the ribs.

Mortally wounded as he was, the Stalo was not yet dead, and managed to swim to the shore. Stretching himself on the sand, he said slowly to Andras:

"Promise that you will give me an honorable burial, and when my body is laid in the grave go in my boat across the fiord, and take whatever you find in my house which belongs to me. My dog you must kill, but spare my son, Andras."

Then he died; and Andras sailed in his boat away across the fiord and found the dog and boy. The dog, a fierce, wicked-looking creature, he slew with one blow from his fist, for it is well known that if a Stalo's dog licks the blood that flows from his dead master's wounds the Stalo comes to life again. That is why no *real* Stalo is ever seen without his dog; but the bailiff, being only half a Stalo, had forgotten him, when he went to the little lakes in search of Andras. Next, Andras put all the gold and jewels which he found in the boat into his pockets, and bidding the boy get in, pushed it off from the shore, leaving the little craft to drift as it would, while he himself ran home. With the treasure he possessed he was able to buy a great herd of reindeer; and he soon married a rich wife, whose parents would not have him as a son-in-law when he was poor, and the two lived happy for ever after.

How Geirald the Coward Was Punished

(FROM *THE BROWN FAIRY BOOK*)

Once upon a time there lived a poor knight who had a great many children, and found it very hard to get enough for them to eat. One day he sent his eldest son, Rosald, a brave and honest youth, to the neighboring town to do some business, and here Rosald met a young man named Geirald, with whom he made friends.

Now Geirald was the son of a rich man, who was proud of the boy, and had all his life allowed him to do whatever he fancied, and, luckily for the father, he was prudent and sensible, and did not waste money, as many other rich young men might have done. For some time he had set his heart on traveling into foreign countries, and after he had been talking for a little while to Rosald, he asked if his new friend would be his companion on his journey.

"There is nothing I should like better," answered Rosald, shaking his head sorrowfully; "but my father is very poor, and he could never give me the money."

"Oh, if that is your only difficulty, it is all right," cried Geirald. "My father has more money than he knows what to do with, and he will give me as much as I want for both of us; only, there is one thing you must promise me, Rosald, that, supposing we have any adventures, you will let the honor and glory of them fall to me."

"Yes, of course, that is only fair," answered Rosald, who never cared about putting himself forward. "But I cannot go without telling my parents. I am sure they will think me lucky to get such a chance."

As soon as the business was finished, Rosald hastened home. His parents were delighted to hear of his good fortune, and his father gave him his own sword, which was growing rusty for want of use, while his mother saw that his leather jerkin was in order.

"Be sure you keep the promise you made to Geirald," said she, as she bade him good-bye, "and, come what may, see that you never betray him."

Full of joy Rosald rode off, and the next day he and Geirald started off to seek adventures. To their disappointment their own land was so well governed that nothing out of the common was very likely to happen, but directly they crossed the border into another kingdom all seemed lawlessness and confusion.

They had not gone very far, when, riding across a mountain, they caught a glimpse of several armed men hiding amongst some trees in their path, and remembered suddenly some talk they had heard of a band of twelve robbers who lay in wait for rich travelers. The robbers were more like savage beasts than men, and lived somewhere at the top of the mountain in caves and holes in the ground. They were all called "Hankur," and were distinguished one from another by the name of a color—blue, gray, red, and so on, except their chief, who was known as Hankur the Tall. All this and more rushed into the minds of the two young men as they saw the flash of their swords in the moonlight.

"It is impossible to fight them—they are twelve to two," whispered Geirald, stopping his horse in the path. "We had much better ride back and take the lower road. It would be stupid to throw away our lives like this."

"Oh, we can't turn back," answered Rosald, "we should be ashamed to look anyone in the face again! And, besides, it is a grand opportunity to show what we are made of. Let us tie up our horses here, and climb up the rocks so that we can roll stones down on them."

"Well, we might try that, and then we shall always have our horses," said Geirald. So they went up the rocks silently and carefully.

The robbers were lying all ready, expecting every moment to see their victims coming round the corner a few yards away, when a shower of huge stones fell on their heads, killing half the band. The others sprang up the rock, but as they reached the top the sword of Rosald swung round, and one man after another rolled down into the valley. At last the chief managed to spring up, and, grasping Rosald by the waist, flung away his sword, and the two fought desperately, their bodies swaying always nearer the edge. It seemed as if Rosald, being the smaller of the two, *must* fall over, when, with his left hand, he drew the robber's sword out of its sheath and plunged it into his heart. Then he took from the dead man a beautiful ring set with a large stone, and put it on his own finger.

The fame of this wonderful deed soon spread through the country, and people would often stop Geirald's horse, and ask leave to see the robber's ring, which was said to have been stolen from the father of the reigning king. And Geirald showed them the ring with pride, and listened to their words of praise, and no one would ever have guessed anyone else had destroyed the robbers.

In a few days they left the kingdom and rode on to another, where they thought they would stop through the remainder of the winter, for Geirald liked to be comfortable, and did not care about traveling through ice and snow. But the king would only grant them leave to stop on condition that, before the winter was ended, they should give him some fresh proof of the courage of which he had heard so much. Rosald's heart was glad at the king's message, and as for Geirald, he felt that as long as Rosald was there all would go well. So they both bowed low and replied that it was the king's place to command and theirs to obey.

"Well, then," said his Majesty, "this is what I want you to do: In the north-east part of my kingdom there dwells a giant, who has an iron staff twenty yards long, and he is so quick in using it, that even fifty knights have no chance against him. The bravest and strongest young men of my court have fallen under the blows of that staff; but, as you overcame the twelve robbers so easily, I feel that I have reason to hope that you may be able to conquer the giant. In three days from this you will set out."

"We will be ready, your Majesty," answered Rosald; but Geirald remained silent.

"How can we possibly fight against a giant that has killed fifty knights?" cried Geirald, when they were outside the castle. "The king only wants to get rid of us! He won't think about us for the next three days—that is one comfort—so we shall have plenty of time to cross the borders of the kingdom and be out of reach."

"We mayn't be able to kill the giant, but we certainly can't run away till we have tried," answered Rosald. "Besides, think how glorious it will be if we *do* manage to kill him! I know what sort of weapon I shall use. Come with me now, and I will see about it." And, taking his friend by the arm, he led him into a shop where he bought a huge lump of solid iron, so big that they could hardly lift it between them. However, they just managed to carry it to a blacksmith's where Rosald directed that it should be beaten into a thick club, with a sharp spike at one end. When this was done to his liking he took it home under his arm.

Very early on the third morning the two young men started on their journey, and on the fourth day they reached the giant's cave before he was out of bed. Hearing the sound of footsteps, the giant got up and went to the entrance to see who was coming, and Rosald, expecting something of the sort, struck him such a blow on the forehead that he fell to the ground. Then, before he could rise to his feet again, Rosald drew out his sword and cut off his head.

"It was not so difficult after all, you see," he said, turning to Geirald. And placing the giant's head in a leathern wallet which was slung over his back, they began their journey to the castle.

As they drew near the gates, Rosald took the head from the wallet and handed it to Geirald, whom he followed into the king's presence.

"The giant will trouble you no more," said Geirald, holding out the head. And the king fell on his neck and kissed him, and cried joyfully that he was the "bravest knight in all the world, and that a feast should be made for him and Rosald, and that the great deed should be proclaimed throughout the kingdom." And Geirald's heart swelled with pride, and he almost forgot that it was Rosald and not he, who had slain the giant.

By-and-by a whisper went round that a beautiful lady who lived in the castle would be present at the feast, with twenty-four lovely maidens, her attendants. The lady was the queen of her own country, but as her father and mother had died when she was a little girl, she had been left in the care of this king who was her uncle.

She was now old enough to govern her own kingdom, but her subjects did not like being ruled by a woman, and said that she must find a husband to help her in managing her affairs. Prince after prince had offered himself, but the young queen would have nothing to say to any of them, and at last told her ministers that if she was to have a husband at all she must choose him for herself, as she would certainly not marry any of those whom they had selected for her. The ministers replied that in that case she had better manage her kingdom alone, and the queen, who knew nothing about business, got things into such a confusion that at last she threw them up altogether, and went off to her uncle.

Now when she heard how the two young men had slain the giant, her heart was filled with admiration of their courage, and she declared that if a feast was held she would certainly be present at it.

And so she was; and when the feast was over she asked the king, her guardian, if he would allow the two heroes who had killed the robbers and slain the giant to fight a tourney the next day with one of her pages. The king gladly gave his consent, and ordered the lists to be made ready, never doubting that two great champions would be eager for such a chance of adding to their fame. Little did he guess that Geirald had done all he could to persuade Rosald to steal secretly out of the castle during the night, "for," said he, "I don't believe they are pages at all, but well-proved knights, and how can we, so young and untried, stand up against them?"

"The honor will be all the higher if we gain the day," answered Rosald; but Geirald would listen to nothing, and only declared that he did not care about honor, and would rather be alive than have every honor in the world heaped upon him. Go he would, and as Rosald had sworn to give him his company, he must come with him.

Rosald was much grieved when he heard these words, but he knew that it was useless attempting to persuade Geirald, and turned his thoughts to forming some plan to prevent this disgraceful flight. Suddenly his face brightened. "Let us change clothes," he said, "and *I* will do the fighting, while you shall get the glory. Nobody will ever know." And to this Geirald readily consented.

Whether Geirald was right or not in thinking that the so-called page was really a well-proved knight, it is certain that Rosald's task was a very hard one. Three times they came together with a crash which made their horses reel; once Rosald knocked the helmet off his foe, and received in return such a blow that he staggered in his saddle. Shouts went up from the lookers-on, as first one and then the other seemed gaining the victory; but at length Rosald planted his spear in the armor which covered his adversary's breast and bore him steadily backward. "Unhorsed! unhorsed!" cried the people; and Rosald then himself dismounted and helped his adversary to rise.

In the confusion that followed it was easy for Rosald to slip away and return Geirald his proper clothes. And in these, torn and dusty with the fight, Geirald answered the king's summons to come before him.

"You have done what I expected you to do," said he, "and now, choose your reward."

"Grant me, sire, the hand of the queen, your niece," replied the young man, bowing low, "and I will defend her kingdom against all her enemies."

"She could choose no better husband," said the king, "and if she consents I do." And he turned towards the queen, who had not been present during the fight, but had just slipped into a seat by his right hand. Now the queen's eyes were very sharp, and it seemed to her that the man who stood before her, tall and handsome though he might be, was different in many slight ways, and in one in particular, from the man who had fought the tourney. How there could be any trickery she could not understand, and why the real victor should be willing to give up his prize to another was still stranger; but something in her heart warned her to be careful. She answered: "You may be satisfied, uncle, but *I* am not. One more proof I must have; let the two young men now fight against each other. The man *I* marry must be the man who killed the robbers and the giant, and overcame my page." Geirald's face grew pale as he heard these words. He knew there was no escape from him now, though he did not doubt for one moment that Rosald would keep his compact loyally to the last. But how would it be possible that even Rosald should deceive the watchful eyes of the king and his court, and still more those of the young queen whom he felt uneasily had suspected him from the first?

The tourney was fought, and in spite of Geirald's fears Rosald managed to hang back to make attacks which were never meant to succeed, and to allow strokes which he could easily have parried to attain their end. At length, after a great show of resistance, he fell heavily to the ground. And as he fell he knew that it was not alone the glory that was his rightfully which he gave up, but the hand of the queen that was more precious still.

But Geirald did not even wait to see if he was wounded; he went straight to the wall where the royal banner waved and claimed the reward which was now his.

The crowd of watchers turned towards the queen, expecting to see her stoop and give some token to the victor. Instead, to the surprise of everyone, she merely smiled gracefully, and said that before she bestowed her hand one more test must be imposed, but this should be the last. The final tourney should be fought; Geirald and Rosald should meet singly two knights of the king's court, and he who could unhorse his foe should be master of herself and of her kingdom. The combat was fixed to take place at ten o'clock the following day.

All night long Geirald walked about his room, not daring to face the fight that lay in front of him, and trying with all his might to discover some means of escaping it. All night long he moved restlessly from door to window; and when the trumpets sounded, and the combatants rode into the field, he alone was missing. The king sent messengers to see what had become of him, and he was found, trembling with fear, hiding under his bed. After that there was no need of any further proof. The combat was declared unnecessary, and the queen pronounced herself quite satisfied, and ready to accept Rosald as her husband.

"You forgot one thing," she said, when they were alone. "I recognized my father's ring which Hankur the Tall had stolen, on the finger of your right hand, and I knew that it was you and not Geirald who had slain the robber band. *I* was the page who fought you, and again I saw the ring on your finger, though it was absent from his when he stood before me to claim the prize. That was why I ordered the combat between you, though your faith to your word prevented my plan being successful, and I had to try another. The man who keeps his promise at all costs to himself is the man I can trust, both for myself and for my people."

So they were married, and returned to their own kingdom, which they ruled well and happily. And many years after a poor beggar knocked at the palace gates and asked for money, for the sake of days gone by—and this was Geirald.

At the Uttermost Parts of the Sea

HANS CHRISTIAN ANDERSEN

Large ships were sent high up to the North Pole, in order to find out the uttermost limits, the last sea-shores, and to try how far it was possible for men to advance up there.

They were already sailing for a long, long time, through fogs and ice, and their crews had to bear many hardships; at last the winter had come and the sun had disappeared from those regions; they knew there would now be a night many, many weeks long. As far as the eye could reach it was one single ice block; the ships were anchored to it, the snow was piled up in large heaps, and huts were made of it in the shape of beehives—some as large as the old barrows, some, on the other hand, only big enough to accommodate two or four men. It was, however, not quite dark; the northern lights were shining red and blue, it was a lasting, magnificent firework. The snow glittered and sparkled, so that the night was one single long twilight. When it was brightest the natives came in troops, wonderful to look at in their hairy, rough fur clothing; they came in sleighs, consisting of ice-blocks, and brought hides and skins in large bundles with them; thus the snow huts received warm foot-rugs, for the skins were either used as such or as counterpanes. The sailors made up their beds under the snow roof; while it froze outside till it creaked, very much harder than it freezes with us in the winter. We were still in the latter part of autumn, and they thought of this up there; they remembered the yellow leaves on the trees in their native country. The clock pointed out that it was evening and time for going to bed, and in one of the snow huts two were already stretching themselves out to rest. The youngest of them had with him his best and dearest treasure from home, the Bible which his grandmother had given him on parting. Every night the Holy Scriptures were resting under his head, and he knew from his childhood what was written in it; he read it daily when he was lying on his couch, and often those holy words came into his mind which run: "If I take the wings of the morning, and fly to the uttermost parts of the sea, even there Thou art with me, and Thy right hand shall uphold me!"

Under the influence of the eternal Word and of true belief he closed his eyes, and sleep overcame him, and a dream which was a revelation of the Holy Ghost in God. His soul was alive and active while the body was resting; he felt this life, and it seemed to him as if dear, well-known airs were sounding and gentle summer breezes floating over him, and from his resting-place he saw it shine over him as if it was penetrating from outside through the snow-crust. He raised his head, but the beaming brightness was, however, not the reflection of the snow-crust, but the great wings of an angel, into whose gentle sweet face he gazed up. As if from the cup of a lily the angel rose from the leaves of the Bible, spreading his arms wide, and the walls of the snow-hut sank into the ground as if they were a light, airy veil of fog; the green meadows and hills of home lay around him, with the red-brown woods, in the still sunshine of a beautiful autumn day; the stork's nest was empty, but some apples still hung on the wild crab-tree, although it was already leafless; the red hips glittered, and a starling was whistling in the green cage over the window of a peasant's cottage, his home. The starling was whistling tunes that it had learned, and the grandmother was hanging green leaves on its cage, just as her grandson had always done. The daughter of the village blacksmith, young and beautiful, was standing at the well, drawing water, and nodded to the grandmother, who nodded to her and showed her a letter which had come from far, far away. The letter had come this very morning from the cold region near the North Pole, where the grandson was in the hand of God. They smiled and cried; and he, up there, in the ice and snow, under the wings of the angel, he too smiled and cried in his spirit with them, for he saw and heard them.

The letter was read aloud, and the words from the Holy Scripture: "At the uttermost parts of the sea Thy right hand shall uphold me." Round him sounded a beautiful psalm, and the angel let his wings sink down like a veil over the sleeping man. The vision had disappeared, it was dark in the snow-hut, but the Bible rested under his head, faith and hope dwelled in his heart. God was with him, and he carried his home in his heart—"at the uttermost parts of the sea."

The Snow-Daughter and the Fire-Son

(FROM *THE YELLOW FAIRY BOOK*)

There was once upon a time a man and his wife, and they had no children, which was a great grief to them. One winter's day, when the sun was shining brightly, the couple were standing outside their cottage, and the woman was looking at all the little icicles which hung from the roof. She sighed, and turning to her husband said, "I wish I had as many children as there are icicles hanging there." "Nothing would please me more either," replied her husband. Then a tiny icicle detached itself from the roof, and dropped into the woman's mouth, who swallowed it with a smile, and said, "Perhaps I shall give birth to a snow child now!" Her husband laughed at his wife's strange idea, and they went back into the house.

But after a short time the woman gave birth to a little girl, who was as white as snow and as cold as ice. If they brought the child anywhere near the fire, it screamed loudly till they put it back into some cool place. The little maid throve wonderfully, and in a few months she could run about and speak. But she was not altogether easy to bring up, and gave her parents much trouble and anxiety, for all summer she insisted on spending in the cellar, and in the winter she would sleep outside in the snow, and the colder it was the happier she seemed to be. Her father and mother called her simply "Our Snow-daughter," and this name stuck to her all her life.

One day her parents sat by the fire, talking over the extraordinary behavior of their daughter, who was disporting herself in the snowstorm that raged outside. The woman sighed deeply and said, "I wish I had given birth to a Fire-son!" As she said these words, a spark from the big wood fire flew into the woman's lap, and she said with a laugh, "Now perhaps I shall give birth to a Fire-son!" The man laughed at his wife's words, and thought it was a good joke. But he ceased to think it a joke when his wife shortly afterwards gave birth to a boy, who screamed lustily till he was put quite close to the fire, and who nearly yelled himself into a fit if the Snow-daughter came anywhere near him. The Snow-daughter herself avoided him as much as she could, and always crept into a corner as far away from him as possible. The parents called the boy simply "Our Fire-son," a name which stuck to him all his life. They had a great deal of trouble and worry with him too; but he throve and grew very quickly, and before he was a year old he could run about and talk. He was as red as fire, and as hot to touch, and he always sat on the hearth quite close to the fire, and complained of the cold; if his sister were in the room he almost crept into the flames, while the girl on her part always complained of the great heat if her brother were anywhere near. In summer the boy always lay out in the sun, while the girl hid herself in the cellar: so it happened that the brother and sister came very little into contact with each other—in fact, they carefully avoided it.

Just as the girl grew up into a beautiful woman, her father and mother both died one after the other. Then the Fire-son, who had grown up in the meantime into a fine, strong young man, said to his sister, "I am going out into the world, for what is the use of remaining on here?"

"I shall go with you," she answered, "for, except you, I have no one in the world, and I have a feeling that if we set out together we shall be lucky."

The Fire-son said, "I love you with all my heart, but at the same time I always freeze if you are near me, and you nearly die of heat if I approach you! How shall we travel about together without being odious the one to the other?"

"Don't worry about that," replied the girl, "for I've thought it all over, and have settled on a plan which will make us each able to bear with the other! See, I have had a fur cloak made for each of us, and if we put them on I shall not feel the heat so much nor you the cold." So they put on the fur cloaks, and set out cheerfully on their way, and for the first time in their lives quite happy in each other's company.

For a long time the Fire-son and the Snow-daughter wandered through the world, and when at the beginning of winter they came to a big wood they determined to stay there till spring. The Fire-son built himself a hut where he always kept up a huge fire, while his sister with very few clothes on stayed outside night and day. Now it happened one day that the King of the land held a hunt in this wood, and saw the Snow-daughter wandering about in the open air. He wondered very much who the beautiful girl clad in such garments could be, and he stopped and spoke to her. He soon learned that she could not stand heat, and that her brother could not endure cold. The

King was so charmed by the Snow-daughter, that he asked her to be his wife. The girl consented, and the wedding was held with much state. The King had a huge house of ice made for his wife underground, so that even in summer it did not melt. But for his brother-in-law he had a house built with huge ovens all round it, that were kept heated all day and night. The Fire-son was delighted, but the perpetual heat in which he lived made his body so hot, that it was dangerous to go too close to him.

One day the King gave a great feast, and asked his brother-in-law among the other guests. The Fire-son did not appear till everyone had assembled, and when he did, everyone fled outside to the open air, so intense was the heat he gave forth. Then the King was very angry and said, "If I had known what a lot of trouble you would have been, I would never have taken you into my house." Then the Fire-son replied with a laugh, "Don't be angry, dear brother! I love heat and my sister loves cold—come here and let me embrace you, and then I'll go home at once." And before the King had time to reply, the Fire-son seized him in a tight embrace. The King screamed aloud in agony, and when his wife, the Snow-daughter, who had taken refuge from her brother in the next room, hurried to him, the King lay dead on the ground burnt to a cinder. When the Snow-daughter saw this she turned on her brother and flew at him. Then a fight began, the like of which had never been seen on earth. When the people, attracted by the noise, hurried to the spot, they saw the Snow-daughter melting into water and the Fire-son burn to a cinder. And so ended the unhappy brother and sister.

The Happy Prince

OSCAR WILDE

High above the city, on a tall column, stood the statue of the Happy Prince. He was gilded all over with thin leaves of fine gold, for eyes he had two bright sapphires, and a large red ruby glowed on his sword-hilt.

He was very much admired indeed. "He is as beautiful as a weathercock," remarked one of the Town Councilors who wished to gain a reputation for having artistic tastes; "only not quite so useful," he added, fearing lest people should think him unpractical, which he really was not.

"Why can't you be like the Happy Prince?" asked a sensible mother of her little boy who was crying for the moon. "The Happy Prince never dreams of crying for anything."

"I am glad there is some one in the world who is quite happy," muttered a disappointed man as he gazed at the wonderful statue.

"He looks just like an angel," said the Charity Children as they came out of the cathedral in their bright scarlet cloaks, and their clean white pinafores.

"How do you know?" said the Mathematical Master, "you have never seen one."

"Ah! but we have, in our dreams," answered the children; and the Mathematical Master frowned and looked very severe, for he did not approve of children dreaming.

One night there flew over the city a little Swallow. His friends had gone away to Egypt six weeks before, but he had stayed behind, for he was in love with the most beautiful Reed. He had met her early in the spring as he was flying down the river after a big yellow moth, and had been so attracted by her slender waist that he had stopped to talk to her.

"Shall I love you?" said the Swallow, who liked to come to the point at once, and the Reed made him a low bow. So he flew round and round her, touching the water with his wings, and making silver ripples. This was his courtship, and it lasted all through the summer.

"It is a ridiculous attachment," twittered the other Swallows, "she has no money, and far too many relations;" and indeed the river was quite full of Reeds. Then, when the autumn came, they all flew away.

After they had gone he felt lonely, and began to tire of his lady-love. "She has no conversation," he said, "and I am afraid that she is a coquette, for she is always flirting with the wind." And certainly, whenever the wind blew, the Reed made the most graceful curtsies. "I admit that she is domestic," he continued, "but I love traveling, and my wife, consequently, should love traveling also."

"Will you come away with me?" he said finally to her; but the Reed shook her head, she was so attached to her home.

"You have been trifling with me," he cried, "I am off to the Pyramids. Good-bye!" and he flew away.

All day long he flew, and at night-time he arrived at the city. "Where shall I put up?" he said; "I hope the town has made preparations."

Then he saw the statue on the tall column." I will put up there," he cried; "it is a fine position with plenty of fresh air." So he alighted just between the feet of the Happy Prince.

"I have a golden bedroom," he said softly to himself as he looked round, and he prepared to go to sleep; but just as he was putting his head under his wing a large drop of water fell on him. "What a curious thing!" he cried, "there is not a single cloud in the sky, the stars are quite clear and bright, and yet it is raining."

Then another drop fell.

But before he had opened his wings, a third drop fell, and he looked up, and saw—Ah! what did he see?

The eyes of the Happy Prince were filled with tears, and tears were running down his golden cheeks. His face was so beautiful in the moonlight that the little Swallow was filled with pity.

"Who are you?" he said.

"I am the Happy Prince."

"Why are you weeping then?" asked the Swallow; "you have quite drenched me."

"When I was alive and had a human heart," answered the statue, "I did not know what tears were, for I lived in the Palace of Sans-Souci, where sorrow is not allowed to enter. In the daytime I played with my companions in the garden, and in the evening I led the dance in the Great Hall. Round the garden ran a very lofty wall, but I never cared to ask what lay beyond it, everything about me was so beautiful. My courtiers called me the Happy Prince, and happy indeed I was, if pleasure be happiness. So I lived, and so I died. And now that I am dead they have set me up here so high that I can see all the ugliness and all the misery of my city, and though my heart is made of lead yet I cannot choose but weep."

"What, is he not solid gold?" said the Swallow to himself. He was too polite to make any personal remarks out loud.

"Far away," continued the statue in a low musical voice, "far away in a little street there is a poor house. One of the windows is open and through it I can see a woman seated at a table. Her face is thin and worn, and she has coarse, red hands all pricked by the needle, for she is a seamstress. She is embroidering passion-flowers on a satin gown for the loveliest of the Queen's maids-of-honor to wear the next Court-ball. In a bed in the corner of the room her little boy is lying ill. He has a fever, and is asking for oranges. His mother has nothing to giv him but river water, so he is crying. Swallow, Swallow, little Swallow, will you not bring her the ruby out of my sword-hilt? My feet are fastened to this pedestal and I cannot move.

"I am waited for in Egypt," said the Swallow. "My frinds are flying up and down the Nile, and talking to the large lotus-flowers. Soon they will go to sleep in the tomb of the great King. The King is there himself in his painted coffin. He is wrapped in yellow linen, and embalmed with spices. Round his neck is a chain of pale green jade, and his hands are like withered leaves."

"Swallow, Swallow, little Swallow," said the Prince, "will you not stay with me for one night, and be my messenger? The boy is so thirsty, and the mother so sad."

"I don't think I like boys," answered the Swallow. "Last summer, when I was staying on the river, there were two rude boys, the miller's sons, who were always throwing stones at me. They never hit me, of course; we swallows fly far too well for that, and besides, I come of a family famous for its agility; but still, it was a mark of disrespect."

But the Happy Prince looked so sad that the little Swallow was sorry. "It is very cold here," he said; "but I will stay with you for one night, and be your messenger."

"Thank you, little Swallow," said the Prince.

So the Swallow picked out the great ruby from the Prince's sword, and flew away with it in his beak over the roofs of the town.

He passed by the cathedral tower, where the white marble angels were sculptured. He passed by the palace and heard the sound of dancing. A beautiful girl came out on the balcony with her lover. "How wonderful the stars are," he said to her, "and how wonderful is the power of love!" "I hope my dress will be ready in time for the State-ball," she answered; "I have ordered passion-flowers to be embroidered on it; but the seamstresses are so lazy."

He passed over the river, and saw the lanterns hanging to the masts of the ships. He passed over the Ghetto, and saw the old Jews bargaining with each other, and weighing out money in copper scales. At last he came to the poor house and looked in. The boy was tossing feverishly on his bed, and the mother had fallen asleep, she was so tired. In he hopped, and laid the great ruby on the table beside the woman's thimble. Then he flew gently round the bed, fanning the boy's forehead with his wings. "How cool I feel," said the boy, "I must be getting better;" and he sank into a delicious slumber.

Then the Swallow flew back to the Happy Prince, and told him what he had done. "It is curious," he remarked, "but I feel quite warm now, although it is so cold."

"That is because you have done a good action," said the Prince. And the little Swallow began to think, and then he fell asleep. Thinking always made him sleepy.

When day broke he flew down to the river and had a bath. "What a remarkable phenomenon," said the Professor of Ornithology as he was passing over the bridge. "A swallow in winter!" And he wrote a long letter about it to the local newspaper. Every one quoted it, it was full of so many words that they could not understand.

"To-night I go to Egypt," said the Swallow, and he was in high spirits at the prospect. He visited all the public monuments, and sat a long time on top of the church steeple. Wherever he went the Sparrows chirruped, and said to each other, "What a distinguished stranger!" so he enjoyed himself very much.

When the moon rose he flew back to the Happy Prince. "Have you any commissions for Egypt?" he cried; "I am just starting."

"Swallow, Swallow, little Swallow," said the Prince, "will you not stay with me one night longer?"

"I am waited for in Egypt," answered the Swallow. "To-morrow my friends will fly up to the Second Cataract. The river-horse couches there among the bulrushes, and on a great granite throne sits the God Memnon. All night long he watches the stars, and when the morning star shines he utters one cry of joy, and then he is silent. At noon the yellow lions come down to the water's edge to drink. They have eyes like green beryls, and their roar is louder than the roar of the cataract."

"Swallow, Swallow, little Swallow," said the Prince, "far away across the city I see a young man in a garret. He is leaning over a desk covered with papers, and in a tumbler by his side there is a bunch of withered violets. His hair is brown and crisp, and his lips are red as a pomegranate, and he has large and dreamy eyes. He is trying to finish a play for the Director of the Theater, but he is too cold to write any more. There is no fire in the grate, and hunger has made him faint."

"I will wait with you one night longer," said the Swallow, who really had a good heart. "Shall I take him another ruby?"

"Alas! I have no ruby now," said the Prince; "my eyes are all that I have left. They are made of rare sapphires, which were brought out of India a thousand years ago. Pluck out one of them and take it to him. He will sell it to the jeweller, and buy food and firewood, and finish his play."

"Dear Prince," said the Swallow, "I cannot do that;" and he began to weep.

"Swallow, Swallow, little Swallow," said the Prince, "do as I command you."

So the Swallow plucked out the Prince's eye, and flew away to the student's garret. It was easy enough to get in, as there was a hole in the roof. Through this he darted, and came into the room. The young man had his head buried in his hands, so he did not hear the flutter of the bird's wings, and when he looked up he found the beautiful sapphire lying on the withered violets.

"I am beginning to be appreciated," he cried; "this is from some great admirer. Now I can finish my play," and he looked quite happy.

The next day the Swallow flew down to the harbor. He sat on the mast of a large vessel and watched the sailors hauling big chests out of the hold with ropes. "Heave a-hoy!" they shouted as each chest came up. "I am going to Egypt!" cried the Swallow, but nobody minded, and when the moon rose he flew back to the Happy Prince.

"I am come to bid you good-bye," he cried.

"Swallow, Swallow, little Swallow," said the Prince, "will you not stay with me one night longer?"

"It is winter," answered the Swallow, "and the chill snow will soon be here. In Egypt the sun is warm on the green palm-trees, and the crocodiles lie in the mud and look lazily about them. My companions are building a nest in the Temple of Baalbec, and the pink and white doves are watching them, and cooing to each other. Dear Prince, I must leave you, but I will never forget you, and next spring I will bring you back two beautiful jewels in place of those you have given away. The ruby shall be redder than a red rose, and the sapphire shall be as blue as the great sea."

"In the square below," said the Happy Prince, "there stands a little match-girl. She has let her matches fall in the gutter, and they are all spoiled. Her father will beat her if she does not bring home some money, and she is crying. She has no shoes or stockings, and her little head is bare. Pluck out my other eye, and give it to her, and her father will not beat her."

"I will stay with you one night longer," said the Swallow, "but I cannot pluck out your eye. You would be quite blind then."

"Swallow, Swallow, little Swallow," said the Prince, "do as I command you."

So he plucked out the Prince's other eye, and darted down with it. He swooped past the match-girl, and slipped the jewel into the palm of her hand. "What a lovely bit of glass," cried the little girl; and she ran home, laughing.

Then the Swallow came back to the Prince. "You are blind now," he said, "so I will stay with you always."

"No, little Swallow," said the poor Prince, "you must go away to Egypt."

"I will stay with you always," said the Swallow, and he slept at the Prince's feet.

All the next day he sat on the Prince's shoulder, and told him stories of what he had seen in strange lands. He told him of the red ibises, who stand in long rows on the banks of the Nile, and catch gold fish in their beaks; of the Sphinx, who is as old as the world itself, and lives in the desert, and knows everything; of the merchants, who walk slowly by the side of their camels, and carry amber beads in their hands; of the King of the Mountains of the Moon, who is as black as ebony, and worships a large crystal; of the great green snake that sleeps in a palm-tree, and has twenty priests to feed it with honey-cakes; and of the pygmies who sail over a big lake on large flat leaves, and are always at war with the butterflies.

"Dear little Swallow," said the Prince, "you tell me of marvelous things, but more marvelous than anything is the suffering of men and of women. There is no Mystery so great as Misery. Fly over my city, little Swallow, and tell me what you see there."

So the Swallow flew over the great city, and saw the rich making merry in their beautiful houses, while the beggars were sitting at the gates. He flew into dark lanes, and saw the white faces of starving children looking out listlessly at the black streets. Under the archway of a bridge two little boys were lying in one another's arms to try and keep themselves warm. "How hungry we are!" they said. "You must not lie here," shouted the Watchman, and they wandered out into the rain.

Then he flew back and told the Prince what he had seen.

"I am covered with fine gold," said the Prince, "you must take it off, leaf by leaf, and give it to my poor; the living always think that gold can make them happy."

Leaf after leaf of the fine gold the Swallow picked off, till the Happy Prince looked quite dull and gray. Leaf after leaf of the fine gold he brought to the poor, and the children's faces grew rosier, and they laughed and played games in the street. "We have bread now!" they cried.

Then the snow came, and after the snow came the frost. The streets looked as if they were made of silver, they were so bright and glistening; long icicles like crystal daggers hung down from the eaves of the houses, everybody went about in furs, and the little boys wore scarlet caps and skated on the ice.

The poor little Swallow grew colder and colder, but he would not leave the Prince, he loved him too well. He picked up crumbs outside the baker's door when the baker was not looking, and tried to keep himself warm by flapping his wings.

But at last he knew that he was going to die. He had just strength to fly up to the Prince's shoulder once more. "Good-bye, dear Prince!" he murmured, "will you let me kiss your hand?"

"I am glad that you are going to Egypt at last, little Swallow," said the Prince, "you have stayed too long here; but you must kiss me on the lips, for I love you."

"It is not to Egypt that I am going," said the Swallow. "I am going to the House of Death. Death is the brother of Sleep, is he not?"

And he kissed the Happy Prince on the lips, and fell down dead at his feet.

At that moment a curious crack sounded inside the statue, as if something had broken. The fact is that the leaden heart had snapped right in two. It certainly was a dreadfully hard frost.

Early the next morning the Mayor was walking in the square below in company with the Town Councilors. As they passed the column he looked up at the statue: "Dear me! how shabby the Happy Prince looks!" he said.

"How shabby indeed!" cried the Town Councilors, who always agreed with the Mayor, and they went up to look at it

"The ruby has fallen out of his sword, his eyes are gone, and he is golden no longer," said the Mayor; "in fact, he is little better than a beggar!"

"Little better than a beggar," said the Town Councilors.

"And here is actually a dead bird at his feet!" continued the Mayor. "We must really issue a proclamation that birds are not to be allowed to die here." And the Town Clerk made a note of the suggestion.

So they pulled down the statue of the Happy Prince. "As he is no longer beautiful he is no longer useful," said the Art Professor at the University.

Then they melted the statue in a furnace, and the Mayor held a meeting of the Corporation to decide what was to be done with the metal. "We must have another statue, of course," he said, "and it shall be a statue of myself."

"Of myself," said each of the Town Councilors, and they quarreled. When I last heard of them they were quarreling still.

"What a strange thing!" said the overseer of the workmen at the foundry. "This broken lead heart will not melt in the furnace. We must throw it away." So they threw it on a dust-heap where the dead Swallow was also lying.

"Bring me the two most precious things in the city," said God to one of His Angels; and the Angel brought Him the leaden heart and the dead bird.

"You have rightly chosen," said God, "for in my garden of Paradise this little bird shall sing for evermore, and in my city of gold the Happy Prince shall praise me."

The Stones of Plouhinec

(FROM *THE LILAC FAIRY BOOK*)

Perhaps some of you may have read a book called "Kenneth; or the Rear-Guard of the Grand Army" of Napoleon. If so, you will remember how the two Scotch children found in Russia were taken care of by the French soldiers and prevented as far as possible from suffering from the horrors of the terrible Retreat. One of the soldiers, a Breton, often tried to make them forget how cold and hungry they were by telling them tales of his native country, Brittany, which is full of wonderful things. The best and warmest place round the camp fire was always given to the children, but even so the bitter frost would cause them to shiver. It was then that the Breton would begin: "Plouhinec is a small town near Hennebonne by the sea," and would continue until Kenneth or Effie would interrupt him with an eager question. Then he forgot how his mother had told him the tale, and was obliged to begin all over again, so the story lasted a long while, and by the time it was ended the children were ready to be rolled up in whatever coverings could be found, and go to sleep. It is this story that I am going to tell to you.

Plouhinec is a small town near Hennebonne by the sea. Around it stretches a desolate moor, where no corn can be grown, and the grass is so coarse that no beast grows fat on it. Here and there are scattered groves of fir trees, and small pebbles are so thick on the ground that you might almost take it for a beach. On the further side, the fairies, or korigans, as the people called them, had set up long long ago two rows of huge stones; indeed, so tall and heavy were they, that it seemed as if all the fairies in the world could not have placed them upright.

Not far off them this great stone avenue, and on the banks of the little river Intel, there lived a man named Marzinne and his sister Rozennik. They always had enough black bread to eat, and wooden shoes or sabots to wear, and a pig to fatten, so the neighbors thought them quite rich; and what was still better, they thought themselves rich also.

Rozennik was a pretty girl, who knew how to make the best of everything, and she could, if she wished, have chosen a husband from the young men of Plouhinec, but she cared for none of them except Bernèz, whom she had played with all her life, and Bernez, though he worked hard, was so very very poor that Marzinne told him roughly he must look elsewhere for a wife. But whatever Marzinne might say Rozennik smiled and nodded to him as before, and would often turn her head as she passed, and sing snatches of old songs over her shoulder.

Christmas Eve had come, and all the men who worked under Marzinne or on the farms round about were gathered in the large kitchen to eat the soup flavored with honey followed by rich puddings, to which they were always invited on this particular night. In the middle of the table was a large wooden bowl, with wooden spoons placed in a circle round it, so that each might dip in his turn. The benches were filled, and Marzinne was about to give the signal, when the door was suddenly thrown open, and an old man came in, wishing the guests a good appetite for their supper. There was a pause, and some of the faces looked a little frightened; for the newcomer was well known to them as a beggar, who was also said to be a wizard who cast spells over the cattle, and caused the corn to grow black, and old people to die, of what, nobody knew. Still, it was Christmas Eve, and besides it was as well not to offend him, so the farmer invited him in, and gave him a seat at the table and a wooden spoon like the rest.

There was not much talk after the beggar's entrance, and everyone was glad when the meal came to an end, and the beggar asked if he might sleep in the stable, as he should die of cold if he were left outside. Rather unwillingly Marzinne gave him leave, and bade Bernez take the key and unlock the door. There was certainly plenty of room for a dozen beggars, for the only occupants of the stable were an old donkey and a thin ox; and as the night was bitter, the wizard lay down between them for warmth, with a sack of reeds for a pillow.

He had walked far that day, and even wizards get tired sometimes, so in spite of the hard floor he was just dropping off to sleep, when midnight struck from the church tower of Plouhinec. At this sound the donkey raised her head and shook her ears, and turned towards the ox.

"Well, my dear cousin," said she, "and how have you fared since last Christmas Eve, when we had a conversation together?"

Instead of answering at once, the ox eyed the beggar with a long look of disgust.

"What is the use of talking," he replied roughly, "when a good-for-nothing creature like that can hear all we say?"

"Oh, you mustn't lose time in grumbling," rejoined the donkey gaily, "and don't you see that the wizard is asleep?"

"His wicked pranks do not make him rich, certainly," said the ox, "and he isn't even clever enough to have found out what a piece of luck might befall him a week hence."

"What piece of luck?" asked the donkey.

"Why, don't you know," inquired the ox, "that once very hundred years the stones on Plouhinec heath go down to drink at the river, and that while they are away the treasures underneath them are uncovered?"

"Ah, I remember now," replied the donkey, "but the stones return so quickly to their places, that you certainly would be crushed to death unless you have in your hands a bunch of crowsfoot and of five-leaved trefoil."

"Yes, but that is not enough," said the ox; "even supposing you get safely by, the treasure you have brought with you will crumble into dust if you do not give in exchange a baptized soul. It is needful that a Christian should die before you can enjoy the wealth of Plouhinec."

The donkey was about to ask some further questions, when she suddenly found herself unable to speak: the time allowed them for conversation was over.

"Ah, my dear creatures," thought the beggar, who had of course heard everything, "you are going to make me richer than the richest men of Vannes or Lorient. But I have no time to lose; to-morrow I must begin to hunt for the precious plants."

He did not dare to seek too near Plouhinec, lest somebody who knew the story might guess what he was doing, so he went away further towards the south, where the air was softer and the plants are always green. From the instant it was light, till the last rays had faded out of the sky, he searched every inch of ground where the magic plants might grow; he scarcely gave himself a minute to eat and drink, but at length he found the crowsfoot in a little hollow! Well, that was certainly a great deal, but after all, the crowsfoot was of no use without the trefoil, and there was so little time left.

He had almost give up hope, when on the very last day before it was necessary that he should start for Plouhinec, he came upon a little clump of trefoil, half hidden under a rock. Hardly able to breathe from excitement, he sat down and hunted eagerly through the plant which he had torn up. Leaf after leaf he threw aside in disgust, and he had nearly reached the end when he gave a cry of joy—the five-leaved trefoil was in his hand.

The beggar scrambled to his feet, and without a pause walked quickly down the road that led northwards. The moon was bright, and for some hours he kept steadily on, not knowing how many miles he had gone, nor even feeling tired. By and bye the sun rose, and the world began to stir, and stopping at a farmhouse door, he asked for a cup of milk and slice of bread and permission to rest for a while in the porch. Then he continued his journey, and so, towards sunset on New Year's Eve, he came back to Plouhinec.

As he was passing the long line of stones, he saw Bernèz working with a chisel on the tallest of them all.

"What are you doing there?" called the wizard, "do you mean to hollow out for yourself a bed in that huge column?"

"No," replied Bernèz quietly, "but as I happened to have no work to do to-day, I thought I would just carve a cross on this stone. The holy sign can never come amiss."

"I believe you think it will help you to win Rozennik," laughed the old man.

Bernèz ceased his task for a moment to look at him.

"Ah, so you know about that," replied he; "unluckily Marzinne wants a brother-in-law who has more pounds than I have pence."

"And suppose I were to give you more pounds than Marzinne ever dreamed of?" whispered the sorcerer glancing round to make sure that no one overheard him.

"You?"

"Yes, I."

"And what am I to do to gain the money," inquired Bernèz, who knew quite well that the Breton peasant gives nothing for nothing.

"What I want of you only needs a little courage," answered the old man.

"If that is all, tell me what I have got to do, and I will do it," cried Bernèz, letting fall his chisel. "If I have to risk thirty deaths, I am ready."

When the beggar knew that Bernèz would give him no trouble, he told him how, during that very night, the treasures under the stones would be uncovered, and how in a very few minutes they could take enough to make them both rich for life. But he kept silence as to the fate that awaited the man who was without the crowsfoot and the trefoil, and Bernèz thought that nothing but boldness and quickness were necessary. So he said:

"Old man, I am grateful, indeed, for the chance you have given me, and there will always be a pint of my blood at your service. Just let me finish carving this cross. It is nearly done, and I will join you in the fir wood at whatever hour you please."

"You must be there without fail an hour before midnight," answered the wizard, and went on his way.

As the hour struck from the great church at Plouhinec, Bernèz entered the wood. He found the beggar already there with a bag in each hand, and a third slung round his neck.

"You are punctual," said the old man, "but we need not start just yet. You had better sit down and think what you will do when your pockets are filled with gold and silver and jewels."

"Oh, it won't take me long to plan out that," returned Bernèz with a laugh. "I shall give Rozennik everything she can desire, dresses of all sorts, from cotton to silk, and good things of all kinds to eat, from white bread to oranges."

"The silver you find will pay for all that, and what about the gold?"

"With the gold I shall make rich Rozennik's relations and every friend of hers in the parish," replied he.

"So much for the gold; and the jewels?"

"Then," cried Bernèz, "I will divide the jewels amongst everybody in the world, so that they may be wealthy and happy; and I will tell them that it is Rozennik who would have it so."

"Hush! it is close on midnight—we must go," whispered the wizard, and together they crept to the edge of the wood.

With the first stroke of twelve a great noise arose over the silent heath, and the earth seemed to rock under the feet of the two watchers. The next moment by the light of the moon they beheld the huge stones near them leave their places and go down the slope leading to the river, knocking against each other in their haste. Passing the spot where stood Bernèz and the beggar, they were lost in the darkness. It seemed as if a procession of giants had gone by.

"Quick," said the wizard, in a low voice, and he rushed towards the empty holes, which even in the night shone brightly from the treasures within them. Flinging himself on his knees, the old man began filling the wallets he had brought, listening intently all the time for the return of the stones up the hill, while Bernèz more slowly put handfuls of all he could see into his pockets.

The sorcerer had just closed his third wallet, and was beginning to wonder if he could carry away any more treasures when a low murmur as of a distant storm broke upon his ears.

The stones had finished drinking, and were hastening back to their places.

On they came, bent a little forward, the tallest of them all at their head, breaking everything that stood in their way. At the sight Bernèz stood transfixed with horror, and said,

"We are lost! They will crush us to death."

"Not me!" answered the sorcerer, holding up the crowsfoot and the five-leaved trefoil, "for these will preserve me. But in order to keep my riches, I was obliged to sacrifice a Christian to the stones, and an evil fate threw you in my way." And as he spoke he stretched out the magic herbs to the stones, which were advancing rapidly. As if acknowledging a power greater than theirs, the monstrous things instantly parted to the right and left of the wizard, but closed their ranks again as they approached Bernèz.

The young man did not try to escape, he knew it was useless, and sank on his knees and closed his eyes. But suddenly the tall stone that was leading stopped straight in front of Bernèz, so that no other could get past.

It was the stone on which Bernèz had carved the cross, and it was now a baptized stone, and had power to save him.

So the stone remained before the young man till the rest had taken their places, and then, darting like a bird to its own hole, came upon the beggar, who, thinking himself quite safe, was staggering along under the weight of his treasures.

Seeing the stone approaching, he held out the magic herbs which he carried, but the baptized stone was no longer subject to the spells that bound the rest, and passed straight on its way, leaving the wizard crushed into powder in the heather.

Then Bernèz went home, and showed his wealth to Marzinne, who this time did not refuse him as a brother-in-law, and he and Rozennik were married, and lived happy for ever after.

My Own Self

(TRADITIONAL ENGLISH TALE)

In a tiny house in the North Countrie, far away from any town or village, there lived not long ago, a poor widow all alone with her little son, a six-year-old boy.

The house-door opened straight on to the hill-side, and all round about were moorlands and huge stones, and swampy hollows; never a house nor a sign of life wherever you might look, for their nearest neighbors were the "ferlies" in the glen below, and the "will-o'-the-wisps" in the long grass along the path-side.

And many a tale she could tell of the "good folk" calling to each other in the oak-trees, and the twinkling lights hopping on to the very window sill, on dark nights; but in spite of the loneliness, she lived on from year to year in the little house, perhaps because she was never asked to pay any rent for it.

But she did not care to sit up late, when the fire burnt low, and no one knew what might be about; so, when they had had their supper she would make up a good fire and go off to bed, so that if anything terrible *did* happen, she could always hide her head under the bed-clothes. This, however, was far too early to please her little son; so when she called him to bed, he would go on playing beside the fire, as if he did not hear her.

He had always been bad to do with since the day he was born, and his mother did not often care to cross him; indeed, the more she tried to make him obey her, the less heed he paid to anything she said, so it usually ended by his taking his own way.

But one night, just at the fore-end of winter, the widow could not make up her mind to go off to bed, and leave him playing by the fireside; for the wind was tugging at the door, and rattling the window-panes, and well she knew that on such a night, fairies and such like were bound to be out and about, and bent on mischief. So she tried to coax the boy into going at once to bed:

"The safest bed to bide in, such a night as this!" she said: but no, he wouldn't.

Then she threatened to "give him the stick," but it was no use.

The more she begged and scolded, the more he shook his head; and when at last she lost patience and cried that the fairies would surely come and fetch him away, he only laughed and said he wished they *would*, for he would like one to play with.

At that his mother burst into tears, and went off to bed in despair, certain that after such words something dreadful would happen; while her naughty little son sat on his stool by the fire, not at all put out by her crying.

But he had not long been sitting there alone, when he heard a fluttering sound near him in the chimney, and presently down by his side dropped the tiniest wee girl you could think of; she was not a span high, and had hair like spun silver, eyes as green as grass, and cheeks red as June roses.

The little boy looked at her with surprise.

"Oh!" said he; "what do they call ye?"

"My own self," she said in a shrill but sweet little voice, and she looked at him too. "And what do they call ye?"

"Just my own self too?" he answered cautiously; and with that they began to play together.

She certainly showed him some fine games. She made animals out of the ashes that looked and moved like life; and trees with green leaves waving

317

over tiny houses, with men and women an inch high in them, who, when she breathed on them, fell to walking and talking quite properly.

But the fire was getting low, and the light dim, and presently the little boy stirred the coals with a stick, to make them blaze; when out jumped a red-hot cinder, and where should it fall, but on the fairy-child's tiny foot.

Thereupon she set up such a squeal, that the boy dropped the stick, and clapped his hands to his ears; but it grew to so shrill a screech, that it was like all the wind in the world, whistling through one tiny keyhole.

There was a sound in the chimney again, but this time the little boy did not wait to see what it was, but bolted off to bed, where he hid under the blankets and listened in fear and trembling to what went on.

A voice came from the chimney speaking sharply:

"Who's there, and what's wrong?" it said.

"It's my own self," sobbed the fairy child; "and my foot's burnt sore. O-o-h!"

"Who did it?" said the voice angrily; this time it sounded nearer, and the boy, peeping from under the clothes, could see a white face looking out from the chimney-opening.

"Just my own self too!" said the fairy-child again.

"Then if ye did it your own self," cried the elf-mother shrilly, "what's the use o' making all this fash about it?"—and with that she stretched out a long thin arm, and caught the creature by its ear, and, shaking it roughly, pulled it after her, out of sight up the chimney.

The little boy lay awake a long time, listening, in case the fairy mother should come back after all; and next evening after supper, his mother was surprised to find that he was willing to go to bed whenever she liked.

"He's taking a turn for the better at last!" she said to herself; but he was thinking just then that, when next a fairy came to play with him, he might not get off quite so easily as he had done this time.

The Last Dream of the Old Oak

(A Christmas Story)

Hans Christian Andersen

In a wood, high up on the steep shore, near the open sea, stood a very old oak tree. It was three hundred and sixty-five years old, but all this long time had not appeared any longer to the tree than the same number of days to us human beings. We are awake in the daytime, we sleep at night, and then we have our dreams. It is different with a tree; it is awake during three seasons, and only begins to sleep towards the winter. Winter is its resting-time, its night after a long day, consisting of spring, summer, and autumn.

On many a warm summer day the ephemera—the fly that lives but one day—danced round its crown, lived and felt happy in the sunshine, and then the little creature rested a moment in quiet contentment on one of the large fresh oak leaves, and the oak tree would say: "Poor little one! your whole life is but one day! How very short! It is sad indeed!"

"Sad? What do you mean by that?" the ephemera used to ask. "All around me it is so wonderfully light, warm, and beautiful, and that makes me glad."

"But only one day, and then it is all over!" "Over," repeated the ephemera; "What does *over* mean? Is it not over with you too?"

"No; I live perhaps thousands of your days, and my days consist of entire seasons! That is so long that you are unable to reckon it up!"

"No. I don't understand you! You have thousands of my days, but I have thousands of moments in which I can be merry and happy. Does all the splendor of this world cease to exist when you die?"

"No," said the tree; "that will probably last much longer—indefinitely longer than I am able to imagine."

"But then we have both the same time to live, only we reckon differently." And the ephemera danced and flew about in the air, rejoicing in the possession of its wonderful wings of gauze and velvet; it enjoyed the warm air, which was saturated with the spicy fragrance of the clover fields, the dog roses, the lilac and honeysuckle, the garden hedges, thyme, the primrose, and the mint. The fragrance was so strong that the ephemera was almost intoxicated with it. The day was long and beautiful, full of joy and sweet pleasures, and when the sun set the little fly always felt agreeably tired of all the delight. Its wings would no longer support it, and gently and slowly it glided down on the waving blades of grass, nodded as an ephemera can nod, and fell asleep, peacefully and joyfully. It was dead. "Poor little ephemera," said the oak, "that was really too short a life."

The same dance, the same questions and answers, the same falling asleep, occurred again on every summer day; all repeated itself through whole generations of ephemeras, which all felt equally merry and happy.

The oak stood awake in the spring, its morning; the summer, its midday; and the autumn, its evening; soon its resting-time, night, was approaching. The winter was at hand. Already the storms sang "Good night! good night!" Here dropped a leaf, there dropped a leaf. "We will stir you and shake you! Go to sleep, go to sleep! We shall sing you to sleep, we shall shake you to sleep, and surely it will do your old twigs good; they will crackle with delight and joy. Sleep sweetly! sleep sweetly! It is your three hundred and sixty-fifth night; properly speaking you are only a stripling! Sleep sweetly! The clouds will throw snow down and make you a covering to keep your feet warm! Sleep sweetly—and pleasant dreams!"

The oak stood there, deprived of its foliage, to go to rest for the whole long winter and to dream many a dream; all was of something that had happened to it, as in the dreams of human beings. The large tree was once small—nay, an acorn had been its cradle. According to human calculation, it was now living its fourth century; it was the largest and best tree in the wood, and over-towered by far all the other trees with its crown. It was seen from a great distance out at sea, and served as a landmark to the sailors. Of course, it had no idea that so many eyes looked for it. High up in its green crown the wood-pigeon built her nest, and the cuckoo made its voice heard; and in autumn, when its leaves looked like hammered copper, the birds of passage rested themselves there before they flew across the sea. Now, however, it was winter; the tree stood there without leaves, and one could see how crooked and knotty the branches were that grew out of the stem. Crows and jackdaws came and sat alternately on it while they talked about the hard times which were now beginning, and how difficult it was to find food in the winter.

Towards the holy Christmas time the tree dreamt a most beautiful dream. It had a distinct notion of the festive time, and it seemed to the tree as if all the church bells round about were merrily pealing, and as if all this took place on a bright, mild, and warm summer day. Fresh and green its mighty crown spread forth, the sunbeams were playing between the leaves and branches, the air was filled with the fragrance of herbs and blossoms; colored butterflies chased each other, the ephemeras danced about as if all was only there for them to enjoy. All the tree had seen happening round it during many years passed before it in a festive procession. It saw the knights and noble ladies of bygone days on horseback, with waving plumes on their heads, the falcons on their wrists, riding through the wood; the bugle sounded, the hounds barked; it saw hostile warriors in colored garments, with glittering arms, spears, and halberds, pitching tents and striking them again; the watch-fires were burning while they sang and slept under the branches of the oak tree; it saw lovers in quiet happiness meet at its trunk in the moonlight and cut their names, their initials, into the dark-green bark. Guitars and Æolian harps were once—many, many years ago—hung in the branches of the oak by merry travelers; now they were hanging there again, and their wonderful sounds rang forth. The wood-pigeons cooed as if they wished to tell what the tree was feeling, and the cuckoo called out to it how many days it had yet to live. Then the tree felt new life streaming into it, down to the smallest root and high up into the topmost branches and leaves. It felt how it spread and extended—nay, it felt, by means of its roots, that there was also warmth and life deep below in the earth; its force was increasing, it grew higher and higher, the trunk shot up, there was no resting; more and more it grew, the crown became fuller, spread out, and raised itself, and in measure as the tree grew, its happiness and its longing to reach higher and higher increased, right up to the bright warm sun. It had already grown up into the clouds, which sailed under it like flights of birds of passage, or large white swans. Every leaf of the tree had the gift of sight, as if they had eyes to see. The stars became visible to it in broad daylight; they were large and sparkling, each of them glittered as mildly and clearly as a pair of eyes; they recalled to its memory well-known kind eyes—children's eyes, lovers' eyes—who had met under the tree. It was a marvelous moment, so full of joy and delight! And yet amidst all this joy the tree felt a desire, a longing wish, that all the other trees down in the wood—all the bushes, all the herbs and flowers—might be able to rise with it, see all this splendor, and feel this joy. The great majestic oak, with all its grandeur, was not quite happy without having them all, great and small, around it, and these feelings of longing passed through all the leaves and branches as vigorously as they would pass through a human breast. The crown of the tree was rocking to and fro as if it were seeking something in its deep longing; it was looking back. Then it smelt the fragrance of the thyme, and soon the still stronger scent of the honeysuckle and violet; it seemed as if the cuckoo was answering it.

Yes, through the clouds the green tops of the wood became visible, and below the oak recognized the other trees—how they grew and rose. Bushes and herbs shot high up, several tearing themselves up by the roots and flying up the quicker. The birch tree was the quickest of all; like a white flash of lightning its slender stem shot up in a zigzag line, the branches surrounding it like green gauze and flags. The whole wood, even the brown feathery reed, grew up; the birds followed and sang, and on a long blade of grass which fluttered in the air like a green silk ribbon sat a grasshopper, cleaning his wings with his legs; the cockchafers and the bees were humming; every bird was singing as well as it could; sounds and songs of joy and gladness rose up to Heaven.

"But where is the little blue flower that grows near the water," cried the oak, "and the harebell and the little daisy?" Indeed, the old oak wished to have them all around it.

"Here we are! Here we are!" echoed from all sides.

"But where is the beautiful thyme of last summer?—and wasn't there a bed of snowdrops here last year?—and the crab-apple that bloomed so beautifully, and the splendor of the woods during the whole year! Oh! that it were only born now, that it were only here now; then it could be with us!"

"We are here! We are here!" sounded voices still higher, as if they had flown up in advance.

"No! that is too beautiful to be believed!" exclaimed the old oak. "I have them all, both great and small; not one is forgotten! How is all this happiness imaginable? How is it possible?"

"In God's eternal kingdom it is possible and imaginable," sounded through the air.

The old tree, which was incessantly growing, felt its roots tearing themselves away from the earth. "That is right so, that is the best of all," said the old tree. "No fetters are holding me any longer; I can rise to the highest light and splendor, and all my beloved ones are with me, both great and small. All! All!"

That was the dream of the old oak, and while it thus dreamed a terrible storm was raging over land and sea—on holy Christmas Eve. The sea was rolling heavy waves against the shore; the tree, which crackled and groaned, was torn out of the ground by the roots at the very moment when it was dreaming that its roots tore themselves out of the earth. It fell to the ground. Its three hundred and sixty-five years had now passed away like the one day of the ephemera.

On Christmas morn, when the sun rose, the storm had abated. All the church bells were merrily pealing; out of every chimney top, even from the smallest and humblest cottage, the smoke rose up in blue clouds, like the smoke which rose from the altars of the Druids when they offered thankofferings. The sea became gradually calm; and on board a large ship which had been struggling all night with the storm, and happily got through it, all the flags were hoisted as a sign of Christmas joy.

"The tree is gone! The old oak, our landmark on the coast," said the sailors, "it has fallen during last night's storm. Who can replace it? No one!"

Such a funeral oration, short and sincere, was pronounced on the tree, which lay stretched out on the snow near the shore; and over it passed the sound of the psalms from the ship—songs of Christmas joy, and of the redemption of the human soul through Christ, and of eternal life:

> Christians, awake! salute the happy morn.
>> Whereon the Savior of the world was born;
>> Rise to adore the mystery of love
>> Which hosts of angels chanted from above.
>> Hallelujah. Hallelujah.

Thus sounded the old hymn, and every one on board the ship felt himself edified by song and prayer, as the old tree had done in its last most beautiful dream, on Christmas morn.

The Six Hungry Beasts

(FROM *THE CRIMSON FAIRY BOOK*)

Once upon a time there lived a man who dwelt with his wife in a little hut, far away from any neighbors. But they did not mind being alone, and would have been quite happy, if it had not been for a marten, who came every night to their poultry yard, and carried off one of their fowls. The man laid all sorts of traps to catch the thief, but instead of capturing the foe, it happened that one day he got caught himself, and falling down, struck his head against a stone, and was killed.

Not long after the marten came by on the look out for his supper. Seeing the dead man lying there, he said to himself: "That is a prize, this time I have done well"; and dragging the body with great difficulty to the sledge which was waiting for him, drove off with his booty. He had not driven far when he met a squirrel, who bowed and said: "Good-morning, godfather! what have you got behind you?"

The marten laughed and answered: "Did you ever hear anything so strange? The old man that you see here set traps about his hen-house, thinking to catch me but he fell into his own trap, and broke his own neck. He is very heavy; I wish you would help me to draw the sledge." The squirrel did as he was asked, and the sledge moved slowly along.

By-and-by a hare came running across a field, but stopped to see what wonderful thing was coming. "What have you got there?" she asked, and the marten told his story and begged the hare to help them pull.

The hare pulled her hardest, and after a while they were joined by a fox, and then by a wolf, and at length a bear was added to the company, and *he* was of more use than all the other five beasts put together. Besides, when the whole six had supped off the man he was not so heavy to draw.

The worst of it was that they soon began to get hungry again, and the wolf, who was the hungriest of all, said to the rest:

"What shall we eat *now*, my friends, as there is no more man?"

"I suppose we shall have to eat the smallest of us," replied the bear, and the marten turned round to seize the squirrel who was much smaller than any of the rest. But the squirrel ran up a tree like lightning, and the marten remembering, just in time, that *he* was the next in size, slipped quick as thought into a hole in the rocks.

"What shall we eat *now*?" asked the wolf again, when he had recovered from his surprise.

"We must eat the smallest of us," repeated the bear, stretching out a paw towards the hare; but the hare was not a hare for nothing, and before the paw had touched her, she had darted deep into the wood.

Now that the squirrel, the marten, and the hare had all gone, the fox was the smallest of the three who were left, and the wolf and the bear explained that they were very sorry, but they would have to eat *him*. Michael, the fox, did not run away as the others had done, but smiled in a friendly manner, and remarked: "Things taste so stale in a valley; one's appetite is so much better up on a mountain." The wolf and the bear agreed, and they turned out of the hollow where they had been walking, and chose a path that led up the mountain side. The fox trotted cheerfully by his two big companions, but on the way he managed to whisper to the wolf: "Tell me, Peter, when I am eaten, what will you have for your next dinner?"

This simple question seemed to put out the wolf very much. What *would* they have for their next dinner, and, what was more important still, who would there be to eat it? They had made a rule always to dine off the smallest of the party, and when the fox was gone, why of course, *he* was smaller than the bear.

These thoughts flashed quickly through his head, and he said hastily:

"Dear brothers, would it not be better for us to live together as comrades, and everyone to hunt for the common dinner? Is not my plan a good one?"

"It is the best thing I have ever heard," answered the fox; and as they were two to one the bear had to be content, though in his heart he would much have preferred a good dinner at once to any friendship.

For a few days all went well; there was plenty of game in the forest, and even the wolf had as much to eat as he could wish. One morning the fox as usual was going his rounds when he noticed a tall, slender tree, with a magpie's nest in one of the top branches. Now the fox was particularly fond of young magpies, and he set about making a plan by which he could have one for dinner. At last he hit upon something which he thought would do, and accordingly he sat down near the tree and began to stare hard at it.

"What are you looking at, Michael?" asked the magpie, who was watching him from a bough.

"I'm looking at this tree. It has just struck me what a good tree it would be to cut my new snow-shoes out of." But at this answer the magpie screeched loudly, and exclaimed: "Oh, not this tree, dear brother, I implore you! I have built my nest on it, and my young ones are not yet old enough to fly."

"It will not be easy to find another tree that would make such good snow-shoes," answered the fox, cocking his head on one side, and gazing at the tree thoughtfully; "but I do not like to be ill-natured, so if you will give me one of your young ones I will seek my snow-shoes elsewhere."

Not knowing what to do the poor magpie had to agree, and flying back, with a heavy heart, he threw one of his young ones out of the nest. The fox seized it in his mouth and ran off in triumph, while the magpie, though deeply grieved for the loss of his little one, found some comfort in the thought that only a bird of extraordinary wisdom would have dreamed of saving the rest by the sacrifice of the one. But what do you think happened? Why, a few days later, Michael the fox might have been seen sitting under the very same tree, and a dreadful pang shot through the heart of the magpie as he peeped at him from a hole in the nest.

"What are you looking at?" he asked in a trembling voice.

"At this tree. I was just thinking what good snow-shoes it would make," answered the fox in an absent voice, as if he was not thinking of what he was saying.

"Oh, my brother, my dear little brother, don't do that," cried the magpie, hopping about in his anguish. "You know you promised only a few days ago that you would get your snow-shoes elsewhere."

"So I did; but though I have searched through the whole forest, there is not a single tree that is as good as this. I am very sorry to put you out, but really it is not my fault. The only thing I can do for you is to offer to give up my snow-shoes altogether if you will throw me down one of your young ones in exchange."

And the poor magpie, in spite of his wisdom, was obliged to throw another of his little ones out of the nest; and this time he was not able to console himself with the thought that he had been much cleverer than other people.

He sat on the edge of his nest, his head drooping and his feathers all ruffled, looking the picture of misery. Indeed he was so different from the gay, jaunty magpie whom every creature in the forest knew, that a crow who was flying past, stopped to inquire what was the matter. "Where are the two young ones who are not in the nest?" asked he.

"I had to give them to the fox," replied the magpie in a quivering voice; "he has been here twice in the last week, and wanted to cut down my tree for the purpose of making snow-shoes out of it, and the only way I could buy him off was by giving him two of my young ones."

"Oh, you fool," cried the crow, "the fox was only trying to frighten you. He could not have cut down the tree, for he has neither axe nor knife. Dear me, to think that you have sacrificed your young ones for nothing! Dear, dear! how could you be so very foolish!" And the crow flew away, leaving the magpie overcome with shame and sorrow.

The next morning the fox came to his usual place in front of the tree, for he was hungry, and a nice young magpie would have suited him very well for dinner. But this time there was no cowering, timid magpie to do his bidding, but a bird with his head erect and a determined voice.

"My good fox," said the magpie putting his head on one side and looking very wise—"my good fox, if you take my advice, you will go home as fast as you can. There is no use your talking about making snow-shoes out of this tree, when you have neither knife nor axe to cut it down with!"

"Who has been teaching you wisdom?" asked the fox, forgetting his manners in his surprise at this new turn of affairs.

"The crow, who paid me a visit yesterday," answered the magpie.

"The crow was it?" said the fox, "well, the crow had better not meet me for the future, or it may be the worse for him."

As Michael, the cunning beast, had no desire to continue the conversation, he left the forest; but when he came to the high road he laid himself at full length on the ground, stretching himself out, just as if he was dead. Very soon he noticed, out of the corner of his eye, that the crow was flying towards him, and he kept stiller and stiffer than ever, with his tongue hanging out of his mouth. The crow, who wanted her supper very badly, hopped quickly towards him, and was stooping forward to peck at his tongue when the fox gave a snap, and caught him by the wing. The crow knew that it was of no use struggling, so he said:

"Ah, brother, if you are really going to eat me, do it, I beg of you, in good style. Throw me first over this precipice, so that my feathers may be strewn here and there, and that all who see them may know that your cunning is greater than mine." This idea pleased the fox, for he had not yet forgiven the crow for depriving him of the young magpies, so he carried the crow to the edge of the precipice and threw him over, intending to go round by a path he knew and pick him up at the bottom. But no sooner had the fox let the crow go than he soared up into the air, and hovering just out of teach of his enemy's jaws, he cried with a laugh: "Ah, fox! you know well how to catch, but you cannot keep."

With his tail between his legs, the fox slunk into the forest. He did not know where to look for a dinner, as he guessed that the crow would have flown back before him, and put every one on their guard. The notion of going to bed supperless was very unpleasant to him, and he was wondering what in the world he should do, when he chanced to meet with his old friend the bear.

This poor animal had just lost his wife, and was going to get some one to mourn over her, for he felt her loss greatly. He had hardly left his comfortable cave when he had come across the wolf, who inquired where he was going. "I am going to find a mourner," answered the bear, and told his story.

"Oh, let me mourn for you," cried the wolf.

"Do you understand how to howl?" said the bear.

"Oh, certainly, godfather, certainly," replied the wolf; but the bear said he should like to have a specimen of his howling, to make sure that he knew his business. So the wolf broke forth in his song of lament: "Hu, hu, hu, hum, hoh," he shouted, and he made such a noise that the bear put up his paws to his ears, and begged him to stop.

"You have no idea how it is done. Be off with you," said he angrily.

A little further down the road the hare was resting in a ditch, but when she saw the bear, she came out and spoke to him, and inquired why he looked so sad. The bear told her of the loss of his wife, and of his search after a mourner that could lament over her in the proper style. The hare instantly offered her services, but the bear took care to ask her to give him a proof of her talents, before he accepted them. "Pu, pu, pu, pum, poh," piped the hare; but this time her voice was so small that the bear could hardly hear her. "That is not what I want," he said, "I will bid you good morning."

It was after this that the fox came up, and he also was struck with the bear's altered looks, and stopped. "What is the matter with you, godfather?" asked he, "and where are you going?"

328

"I am going to find a mourner for my wife," answered the bear.

"Oh, do choose me," cried the fox, and the bear looked at him thoughtfully.

"Can you howl well?" he said.

"Yes, beautifully, just listen," and the fox lifted up his voice and sang—weeping: "Lou, lou, lou! the famous spinner, the baker of good cakes, the prudent housekeeper is torn from her husband! Lou, lou, lou! she is gone! she is gone!"

"Now at last I have found some one who knows the art of lamentation," exclaimed the bear, quite delighted; and he led the fox back to his cave, and bade him begin his lament over the dead wife who was lying stretched out on her bed of gray moss. But this did not suit the fox at all.

"One cannot wail properly in this cave," he said, "it is much too damp. You had better take the body to the storehouse. It will sound much finer there." So the bear carried his wife's body to the storehouse, while he himself went back to the cave to cook some pap for the mourner. From time to time he paused and listened for the sound of wailing, but he heard nothing. At last he went to the door of the storehouse, and called to the fox:

"Why don't you howl, godfather? What are you about?"

And the fox, who, instead of weeping over the dead bear, had been quietly eating her, answered:

"There only remain now her legs and the soles of her feet. Give me five minutes more and they will be gone also!"

When the bear heard that he ran back for the kitchen ladle, to give the traitor the beating he deserved. But as he opened the door of the storehouse, Michael was ready for him, and slipping between his legs, dashed straight off into the forest. The bear, seeing that the traitor had escaped, flung the ladle after him, and it just caught the tip of his tail, and that is how there comes to be a spot of white on the tails of all foxes.

Pretty Maruschka

(Traditional Slovakian Tale)

Far away in the hazy purple of antiquity, when all stepmothers were wicked, and all younger sons were successful, there lived on the confines of a forest a woman who had two daughters: the one her own, the other only a stepchild. Naturally, the love of the mother was concentrated on her own Helena, and, as naturally, she disliked Maruschka, who was the fairest, the gentlest, and the most pious of the two girls.

Little did pretty Maruschka know of her own surpassing beauty—a fact proving to us how remote from the present age was that in which these damsels lived. Her hair was like the waving gold of the cornfield when the wind soughs over it, and her eyes were as the blue forget-me-not which smiles and glimmers in a quiet nook by the brookside. She was slim and graceful; her step was light, for her heart was free. Wherever she went she brought cheerfulness and smiles; like the little golden sunbeams which pierce among the tree-shadows of a forest, and light up unexpected beauties where all before was gloom; now painting a saffron butterfly, now kindling an emerald moss-tuft, now making a scarlet lily flame against the dusk of the forest glades behind.

Helena was dressed by her mother in gay colors for Sunday and Feast-day, but poor little Maruschka had only a dingy gray gown, cast off by her sister. Helena wore black shoes with silver buckles, but pretty Maruschka clattered up the churchyard path in wooden clogs. Helena wore a false gold chain of great links round her neck, but her half-sister had only a turquoise-colored ribbon and a little silver cross with a crystal in it—that was her only ornament—and that had been given her by a lady whom she had guided into the road, when she had lost her way in the forest.

As the mother and the two girls went to church on Sundays, the lads were all in the yard hanging about the tombstones; and the old woman heard them whisper, "There is pretty Maruschka"; but never once did they say, "See pretty Helena." So she was angry, and hated the golden-haired, blue-eyed maiden. At home she made her do all the hard work—scrub the floors, cook the victuals,

330

mend the clothes—whilst Helena stood all day before her glass, combing her hair and adorning herself with trinkets, and wishing it were Sunday that she might flare before the eyes of the young men in the churchyard.

Helena and her mother did all that lay in their power to make the little girl's life miserable. They scolded her, they beat her, they devised schemes of annoyance for her, but never could they ruffle the sweet temper of Maruschka. One day, in the depth of winter, Helena cried out, "Ah, me! would that I had a bunch of violets in my bosom to-morrow, when I go to church. Run, Maruschka, run into the forest and pluck them for me, that I may have them to smell at whilst the priest gives us his sermon."

"Oh, my sister!" answered Maruschka, "who ever heard of violets being gathered in midwinter, under the deep snow?"

"Idle hussey!" screamed Helena; "go at once and fetch them. Have them I will, and you shall not come back without them." Then the mother chimed in with, "Mind and bring a large bunch, or you shall not be taken in here for the night. Go!" and she caught her, thrust her from the house, and slammed the door behind her.

Bitterly weeping, the poor maiden wandered into the forest. The snow lay deep everywhere, undinted by human foot; white wreaths hung on the bushes, and the sombre pine-boughs were frosted over with snow. Here were the traces of a hare, there the prints of a badger. An owl called from the depths of the forest. The girl lost her way. Dusk came on, and a few stars looked through the interlacing boughs overhead, watching Maruschka. An icy wind moaned through the trees, shaking the pines as though they quaked with mortal fear, and then they bent their branches and shot their loads of snow in dust to the ground. Strange harp-like sounds reverberated through the gloom, and gratings of bough on bough, which seemed as though the wood demons were gnawing at fallen timbers. Now a great black crow, which had been brooding among dark firs and pines, startled by the footfall and sobs of the maiden, expanded his wings, and, with a harsh scream, rushed away, noisily, sending the life-blood with a leap to the girl's heart. Suddenly, before her—far up on a hill-top—a light appeared, ruddy and flickering. Maruschka, inspired with hope, made for it, scrambling up a rocky slope through deep snow-drifts. She reached the summit, and beheld a great fire. Around this fire were twelve rough stones, and on each stone sat a man. Three were gray-bearded, three were middle-aged, three were youths;

and the last three were the youngest and fairest. They spake not, but looked intently on the roaring flames. He who sat in the seat of honor had a long staff in his hand. His hair was white, and fluttering in the cold wind.

Maruschka was startled, and watched them with astonishment for a little while; then mustering courage, she stepped within the circle and said:—

"Dear, good friends, please suffer me to warm myself a little while at the fire, for, indeed, I am perishing with cold." He with the flowing white hair raised his head, and said—

"Yes, child, approach. But what brings you here?"

"I am seeking violets," she answered.

"Violets! It is not the time for violets, when the snow lies deep?"

"Ah, sir! I know that well; but sister Helena and mother have bidden me bring them violets, and if I do not I must perish in the cold. You, kind shepherds, tell me where I may find violets!" Then the white aged one arose from his seat, stepped to one of the blooming youths, put his staff into his hand, and said—

"Brother March, take thou the pre-eminence." Then the Month March sat himself on the chief stone, and waved his staff over the fire. Instantly the flames rushed up and blazed with greater brilliancy, the snow began to thaw, the hazel-bushes were covered with catkins, and glossy buds appeared on the beech. Green herbs thrust up through the moist soil, a primrose gleamed from a dusky bank, and a sweet fragrance of violets was wafted by on a gentle breeze. Under a bush, the ground was purple with their scented blossoms. "Quick, Maruschka, pluck!" ordered March. The girl hastily gathered a handful. Then she courtesied to the twelve Months, thanked them cordially, and hurried home.

Helena was amazed when her half-sister came with the bunch to the door. She opened it to her, and the house was filled with the delicious odor.

"Where did you find them?" she asked.

"High up on the mountain, under a hawthorn bush."

Helena took the flowers, and set them in her bosom. She let her mother smell at them, but she never gave one to Maruschka.

When they came home from church next day, Helena cast off her gay shawls, and sat down to supper. But she had no appetite for what was on the table. She was angry with her sister; for all the lads had fixed their eyes on Maruschka, and had not even been attracted to her by the fragrant bunch of violets. "How beautiful is Maruschka to-day!" had said some of the older people; and none had spoken a good word of her.

So she sat and sighed, and hated the pretty girl more and more.

"Oh that I had strawberries!" she said. "I can eat nothing this evening but strawberries. Run, Maruschka, into the forest and gather me a dishful."

"Dear sister, this is not the time of the year for strawberries. Who ever heard of strawberries ripening under the snow?"

But the stepmother angrily exclaimed: "Run, Maruschka, fetch them at once, as your sister has ordered, or I will strike you dead"; and she thrust her from the door.

The poor girl cried bitterly; she looked back at the firelight which glimmered through the casement, and thought how warm it was within, whilst without it was so piercingly cold. But she dared not return unless she had with her the desired fruit. So she plunged into the forest. The snow lay deep, and nowhere was a human footprint. Snow began to fall in fine powder, whitening her shoulders, clinging to the folds of her gray dress, and forming a cap of ice on her golden hair. In that dull rayless night there was no light to show the blue ribbon, which strayed among the tree boles, or to twinkle on the crystal of the silver cross.

Presently Maruschka saw, high up on the summit of a rugged hill, a blazing fire. She scrambled to it, and there she found the Twelve sitting solemn and silent around the flames, and the Ice Month, with his staff, sat still on the seat of honor.

"Dear, good friends, please suffer me to warm myself a little while at the fire," she asked in a beseeching voice; "for, indeed, I am perishing with cold."

Then the one with the drifting white locks raised his head and said—

"Yes, child, approach. But what brings you here?"

"I am seeking strawberries," she answered.

"Strawberries! It is not the time for strawberries when the snow lies deep?"

"Ah, sir! I know that well; but sister Helena and mother have bidden me bring them strawberries, or they will strike me dead. You, kind shepherds, tell me where I may find strawberries."

Then the white Ice Month arose from his seat, stepped across the area to one of the young men, put the staff into his hand, and said—

"Brother June, take thou the pre-eminence." Then the Month June sat himself on the chief stone, and waved his staff over the fire. Instantly it glowed like molten gold, beams of glory streamed from it through the forest, and it shone like a sun resting on the earth. Overhead, the clouds flamed and curled in wreaths of light-tinted rose, carnation, and purple, athwart a sky blue as the forget-me-not. Every trace of snow vanished, and the earth was buried in green. The trees were covered with rustling leaves. Blue-bells gleamed under their shadows, and then died away. Red-robin blushed in tufts, and then shed its ragged petals. Wild roses burst into glorious flower, and the soft air was charged with the scent of the sweet-briar. From among the forest-glades called, in cool notes, a wood-dove. The thrush began to warble, and the blackbird to pipe. A bright-eyed squirrel danced among the fresh green leaves on the tree-tops. Beside a brown stone was a patch of sloping green. It was dotted with little white stars with golden hearts. Now the leaves drop off, and the hearts swell, and flush, and glow, and become crimson.

"Quick, Maruschka, pluck!" said June.

Then the girl joyfully hurried to the slope, and gathered an apronful of the luscious strawberries.

She courtesied to the twelve Months, thanked them cordially, and hurried home.

Helena was astonished as she saw her come to the house, and she ran to open the door. The whole cottage was fragrant with the odor of the strawberries.

"Where did you gather them?' asked Helena.

"High up on the mountains, under a brown rock." Helena took the strawberries, and ate them with her mother. She never offered even one to pretty Maruschka.

Next day, Helena had again no appetite for her supper.

"Oh, if I had only ripe apples!" she said; and then, turning to her sister, she ordered, "Run, Maruschka, run into the wood and gather me some ripe apples."

"Dear sister, this is not the time of the year for apples. Who ever heard of apples ripening in an icy wind?"

But her stepmother cried out, "Run, Maruschka, fetch the apples as your sister has required, or I will strike you dead."

And she thrust her from the door into the cold winter night-air.

The maiden hastened, sobbing, into the wood; the snow lay deep, and nowhere was there a human footprint. The new moon glimmered in a clear sky, and sent its feeble beams into the forest deeps, forming little trembling, silvery pools of light, which appeared and vanished, and formed again. And a low wind whispered a great secret in the trees, but so faint was the tone that none could make out what it said. There was a little opening in the wood; in the midst stood a gray wolf looking up at the moon and howling; but when Maruschka came near, it fled, and was lost among the shadows. The poor maiden shivered with cold, and her teeth chattered. Her lips were purple and her cheeks white; and the tears, as they formed, froze on her long eyelashes. She would have sunk on a snowdrift and died, had she not seen, up high on a rugged hill-top, a blazing fire. Towards it she made her way, and found it to be the same she had seen before. Round about, solemn and silent, sat the Twelve, and the Ice Month was on the seat of honor, clasping the staff of power.

"Dear, good friends, please suffer me to warm myself a little while at the fire," she asked, in supplicating tones; "for, indeed, I am perishing with cold."

Then the one with the long white hair and frosty beard raised his head, and said: "Yes, child, approach; but what brings you here?"

"I am seeking ripe apples," she answered.

"Ripe apples! It is not the time for ripe apples, when the snow lies deep?"

"Ah, sir! I know that well; but sister Helena and mother have bidden me bring them ripe apples, or they will strike me dead. You, kind shepherds, tell me where I may find ripe apples."

Then the Ice Month arose from his seat, stepped to one of the elder men, put the staff into his hand, and said—

"Brother September, take thou the pre-eminence."

Then the Month September sat himself on the chief stone, and waved his staff over the fire. Whereat it glowed like a furnace, red and fierce; sparks flew about, and volumes of glaring hot smoke, like the vapor of molten metal, rolled up to heaven. In a moment the snow was gone. The trees were covered with sere leaves; the oak foliage was brown and crumpled, that of the ash yellow as sulphur; other trees seemed leafed with copper. Stray leaves floated past and were whirled by little wind-eddies into rustling heaps. A few yellow flowers shook in the hot air. Pinks hung over the rocks, covering their faces with wandering shadows. Ladyfern waved and wafted its pleasant odor. A constant hum of bees and beetles and flies sounded through the wood. Maruschka looked about her for apples, and beheld a tree on whose branches hung the ruddy fruit.

"Quick, Maruschka, shake!" commanded September. Then she shook, and there fell an apple; she shook again, and there fell another. "Quick, Maruschka, hasten home!" said the Month.

Then she courtesied to the Twelve, thanked them cordially, and returned to the house of her stepmother.

Helena marveled not a little when she saw the red apples.

"How many have you plucked?" she asked.

"Only two."

"Where did you find them?"

"High up, on the mountain-top, on a tree weighed down with them."

"Why did you not gather more? Did you not eat them on your way home?" asked Helena, fiercely.

"Oh, dear sister, I have not tasted one! I shook once, and down fell an apple; I shook twice, and there fell another. I might not bring away more."

Helena struck her, and drove her to the kitchen. Then she tasted one of the apples. Never before had she eaten one so sweet and juicy. The stepmother ate the second.

"Mother!" exclaimed Helena, "give me my fur dress. I will go to the hill and bring some apples. That hussey has eaten all she took except two."

Then she wrapped herself up, and hurried into the wood. The snow lay deep, and nowhere was a human footprint. Helena lost herself; but presently she was aware of a hill, and a fire burning at the summit. She hastened to the light. There she saw a great blaze, and round it sat the twelve Months, silent and solemn. He with the long snowy locks sat on the seat of honor, holding the rod of power. Helena stared at them, then, pushing through the circle, went to the fire, and began to warm herself.

"What seek you here?" asked the Ice Month, with a frown wrinkling his white brow.

"That is no business of yours," answered Helena, sharply, over her shoulder.

The Ice Month shook his head, and, raising his arm, waved the staff over the fire.

Instantly the flames sank, and the fire was reduced to a glowing spark. The clouds rolled over the sky, and, bursting, discharged snow in such quantities that nothing was visible in earth and heaven but drifting white particles. An icy wind rumbled in the forest and roared round the hill. Helena fled. Everywhere white fleeting spots—whirling, falling, rising, scudding!

She ran this way, then that; she stumbled over a fallen log, she gathered herself up and ran again; then she plunged into a deep drift; and the white cold down from the breast of heaven whirled and fell, and rose, and fleeted, and danced this side of her, and dropped here on her, and rested there on her, and lodged on this limb, and built up a white heap on that limb, then bridged over one fold and filled up another. She shook herself, and the particles fell off. But then they began their work again: they spangled her with white, they wove a white net, they filled up the interstices of her lace, they built a mound over her arm, they buried her foot, they raised a cairn above her bosom. Then they spun a dance around the white face which looked up at them, and began to whiten it still more; lastly, they smoothed the sheet over her, and the work was done.

The mother looked out of the window and wondered that Helena did not return. Hour after hour passed, and her daughter came not.

"Maybe the apples are so sweet that she cannot eat enough," thought the mother. "I will go seek them too."

So she wrapped herself up in a thick shawl and went forth.

The snow lay deep, and nowhere was a human footprint. She called Helena, but received no answer. Then she lost her way. The snow fell, and the wind howled.

Maruschka sat over the fire and cooked supper.

Mother and sister came back no more.

The Owl and the Eagle

(FROM *THE ORANGE FAIRY BOOK*)

Once upon a time, in a savage country where the snow lies deep for many months in the year, there lived an owl and an eagle. Though they were so different in many ways they became great friends, and at length set up house together, one passing the day in hunting and the other the night. In this manner they did not see very much of each other—and perhaps agreed all the better for that; but at any rate they were perfectly happy, and only wanted one thing, or, rather, two things, and that was a wife for each.

"I really am too tired when I come home in the evening to clean up the house," said the eagle.

"And I am much too sleepy at dawn after a long night's hunting to begin to sweep and dust," answered the owl. And they both made up their minds that wives they must have.

They flew about in their spare moments to the young ladies of their acquaintance, but the girls all declared they preferred one husband to two. The poor birds began to despair, when, one evening, after they had been for a wonder hunting together, they found two sisters fast asleep on their two beds. The eagle looked at the owl and the owl looked at the eagle.

"They will make capital wives if they will only stay with us," said they. And they flew off to give themselves a wash, and to make themselves smart before the girls awoke.

For many hours the sisters slept on, for they had come a long way, from a town where there was scarcely anything to eat, and felt weak and tired. But by-and-by they opened their eyes and saw the two birds watching them.

"I hope you are rested?" asked the owl politely.

"Oh, yes, thank you," answered the girls. "Only we are so very hungry. Do you think we could have something to eat?"

"Certainly!" replied the eagle. And he flew away to a farmhouse a mile or two off, and brought back a nest of eggs in his strong beak; while the owl, catching up a tin pot, went to a cottage where lived an old woman and her cow, and entering the shed by the window dipped the pot into the pail of new milk that stood there.

The girls were so much delighted with the kindness and cleverness of their hosts that, when the birds inquired if they would marry them and stay there for ever, they accepted without so much as giving it a second thought. So the eagle took the younger sister to wife, and the owl the elder, and never was a home more peaceful than theirs!

All went well for several months, and then the eagle's wife had a son, while, on the same day, the owl's wife gave birth to a frog, which she placed directly on the banks of a stream near by, as he did not seem to like the house. The children both grew quickly, and were never tired of playing together, or wanted any other companions.

One night in the spring, when the ice had melted, and the snow was gone, the sisters sat spinning in the house, awaiting their husbands' return. But long though they watched, neither the owl nor the eagle ever came; neither that day nor the next, nor the next, nor the next. At last the wives gave up all hope of their return; but, being sensible women, they did not sit down and cry, but called their children, and set out, determined to seek the whole world over till the missing husbands were found.

Now the women had no idea in which direction the lost birds had gone, but they knew that some distance off was a thick forest, where good hunting was to be found. It seemed a likely place to find them, or, at any rate, they might hear something of them, and they walked quickly on, cheered by the thought that they were doing something. Suddenly the younger sister, who was a little in front, gave a cry of surprise.

"Oh! look at that lake!" she said, "we shall never get across it."

"Yes we shall," answered the elder; "I know what to do." And taking a long piece of string from her pocket, fastened it into the frog's mouth, like a bit.

"You must swim across the lake," she said, stooping to put him in, "and we will walk across on the line behind you." And so they did, till they got to about the middle of the lake, when the frog boy stopped.

"I don't like it, and I won't go any further," cried he sulkily. And his mother had to promise him all sorts of nice things before he would go on again.

When at last they reached the other side, the owl's wife untied the line from the frog's mouth and told him he might rest and play by the lake till they got back from the forest. Then she and her sister and the boy walked on, with the great forest looming before them. But they had by this time come far and were very tired, and felt glad enough to see some smoke curling up from a little hut in front of them.

"Let us go in and ask for some water," said the eagle's wife; and in they went.

The inside of the hut was so dark that at first they could see nothing at all; but presently they heard a feeble croak from one corner. But sisters turned to look, and there, tied by wings and feet, and their eyes sunken, were the husbands that they sought. Quick as lightning the wives cut the deer-thongs which bound them; but the poor birds were too weak from pain and starvation to do more than utter soft sounds of joy. Hardly, however, were they set free, than a voice of thunder made the two sisters jump, while the little boy clung tightly round his mother's neck.

"What are you doing in my house?" cried she. And the wives answered boldly that now they had found their husbands they meant to save them from such a wicked witch.

"Well, I will give you your chance," answered the ogress, with a hideous grin; "we will see if you can slide down this mountain. If you can reach the bottom of the cavern, you shall have your husbands back again." And as she spoke she pushed them before her out of the door to the edge of a precipice, which went straight down several hundreds of feet. Unseen by the witch, the frog's mother fastened one end of the magic line about her, and whispered to the little boy to hold fast the other. She had scarcely done so when the witch turned round.

"You don't seem to like your bargain," said she; but the girl answered:

"Oh, yes, I am quite ready. I was only waiting for you!" And sitting down she began her slide. On, on, she went, down to such a depth that even the witch's eyes could not follow her; but she took for granted that the woman was dead, and told the sister to take her place. At that instant, however, the head of the elder appeared above the rock, brought upwards by the magic line. The witch gave a howl of disgust, and hid her face in her hands; thus giving the younger sister time to fasten the cord to her waist before the ogress looked up.

"You can't expect such luck twice," she said; and the girl sat down and slid over the edge. But in a few minutes she too was back again, and the witch saw that she had failed, and feared lest her power was going. Trembling with rage though she was, she dared not show it, and only laughed hideously.

"I sha'n't let my prisoners go as easily as all that!" she said. "Make my hair grow as thick and as black as yours, or else your husbands shall never see daylight again."

"That is quite simple," replied the elder sister; "only you must do as we did—and perhaps you won't like the treatment."

"If *you* can bear it, of course *I* can," answered the witch. And so the girls told her they had first smeared their heads with pitch and then laid hot stones upon them.

"It is very painful," said they, "but there is no other way that we know of. And in order to make sure that all will go right, one of us will hold you down while the other pours on the pitch."

And so they did; and the elder sister let down her hair till it hung over the witch's eyes, so that she might believe it was her own hair growing. Then the other brought a huge stone, and, in short, there was an end of the witch. The sisters were savages who had never seen a missionary.

So when the sisters saw that she was dead they went to the hut, and nursed their husbands till they grew strong. Then they picked up the frog, and all went to make another home on the other side of the great lake.

How Grannas-Nils Became Such a Hero

(Traditional Swedish Tale)

Before this Grannas-Nils had not had a reputation for being a stout man, either in courage or his arms.

When he had to go out in the dark to give the horses food, he would have at least a farm boy with him, and when it was to be proved who was the stronger, he kept out of the way, as you shall soon hear. But no one can tell what people will do before they are tested, and it was so with Grannas-Nils, too.

It was towards Christmas-time, and the master of the house had errands to the city after one thing and another; and as Nils took care of the horses, he had to go, of course.

Now he was a little cast down in spirits, for a rumor had spread that two thieves had broken loose and roamed in the neighborhood, so Nils would gladly have left the city by daylight, of course, but that could not be, for he wanted to take home a cask of "weak drink," and it would not be ready before evening. But when Nils had got the Christmas drink bound fast to his sleigh, he had everything in order, and drove out through the toll-gate.

There he sat on the load, and it grew darker and darker. When he came to the forest it was black as coal, but the snow was so white that he could find his way, however.

Now Nils thought gloomy things and grew so frightened that he thought he saw a robber in every bush, who longed for his life and load. He whipped up the horses, and they galloped along the road till he came to a place where high mountains rose on both sides. Here two beggars were walking along, but Nils did not see what kind of folks they were, but thought they were the thieves, and their canes looked exactly like guns or other fatal weapons.

But as the man was obliged to keep on, he gave the horses a cut, so they went ahead still faster; and then it happened that just as he was opposite the beggars, the bung flew out of the beer cask with a dreadful explosion, because the drink had begun to work.

But Nils thought they were shooting at him, and could not believe it was anything but blood that was running when he heard the Christmas drink splashing. He expected to die every minute, and so he drove as if his life depended on it. When he at last came home, and found he was alive, he began to recover himself. But he was sure he had been pursued by two robbers.

When he came into the kitchen he told how he had been out, and that robbers had attacked both his life and load, and shot at him so the balls whistled by his ears. But he had defended himself like a man, and had arrived safely home with everything.

It so happened that the sheriff arrested the two thieves the next day after Grannas-Nils was out, and then it was plain that Nils spoke the truth. Yes, one could see blood tracks on the road—it was the "weak drink" that had run out—and the tracks followed the sledge a long way, and one could see by them that the bandits had followed Nils a long distance, the sheriff said. The strangest thing was, the thieves had not a single scratch on them, from which the blood could have flowed, and they would not own that they had met the servant on the road, but that was nothing to go by, for such folks are so sly and will never tell the truth, said the sheriff.

But the talk about Nils and his bravery spread far and wide, and a little was added here, and a little there, so it became a perfect feat of war he had performed; and his bravery was not shown in vain.

One day the minister sent a special message to Grannas-Nils to come to church the next Sunday.

Of course Nils went, and after the service was over, the minister came forward in the church, and made a most unusually beautiful speech about courage and God's help in time of trouble, so the women wept and long before the minister told the name, everybody knew it was Nils to whom he referred.

After he had finished he took up a medal which hung on a fine ribbon; the whole thing had come from the king himself, and it was now hung around Nils's neck, so people should see what sort of a person Nils was, for it said on it that the brave servant honestly earned it.

But the poor beggars knew nothing of it, and the "weak drink" cask could not speak.

And that is the way Grannas-Nils became such a hero.

The Metal Pig

HANS CHRISTIAN ANDERSEN

In the city of Florence, not far from the *Piazza del Granduca*, runs a little cross-street, called, I think, *Porta Rosa*. In this street, in front of a kind of market-hall where vegetables are sold, there lies a pig artistically wrought out of metal. The fresh clean water pours from the mouth of the animal, which has become a blackish green from age; only the snout shines as if it were polished, and that it is too by many hundreds of children and beggars, who lay hold of it with their hands as they put their mouth to the animal's snout to drink. It is quite a picture to see the well-shaped animal clasped by a pretty and half-naked boy who lays his red lips against its snout.

Every one who comes to Florence can easily find the place; he need only ask the first beggar he comes across for the metal pig, and he will find it.

It was an evening late in winter. The mountains were covered with snow; but it was moonlight, and moonlight in Italy is as good as the light of a dark northern winter's day, and indeed better, for the air is bright and exhilarating, while in the north the cold gray leaden skies seem to press us to the earth, to the cold, damp earth, which will one day press upon our coffin.

In the garden of the grand duke's castle, where thousands of roses bloom, even in winter, a little ragged boy had been sitting under the pines all day long—a boy who might serve as a type of Italy, pretty and smiling, but yet suffering. He was hungry and thirsty, but no one gave him anything, and when it got dark and the garden had to be closed, the gatekeeper drove him out. For a long time he stood dreaming on the bridge that crosses the Arno, gazing at the stars that were reflected in the water between him and the splendid marble bridge *Delia Trinità*.

He made his way towards the metal pig, and, half kneeling down, wound his arms round it, then putting his mouth to the shining snout, drank the fresh water in deep drafts. Close by lay some salad leaves and a few chestnuts; these were his supper. There was no one in the street but himself; it belonged to him alone, and somewhat comforted he lay down upon the pig's back, bending forward so that his curly head rested on that of the animal, and before he knew it he was asleep.

It was midnight—the metal pig stirred, and he heard it say distinctly, "You little boy! hold on tight, for I am going to run," and away it ran with him; it was a wonderful ride. First they reached the *Piazza del Granduca*, and the metal horse that carries the duke's statue neighed aloud, while the painted coats-of-arms on the council-house looked like transparent pictures, and Michaelangelo's David swung his sling; there was a strange life stirring. The metal groups representing Perseus and the Rape of the Sabine women stood there as if they were alive; a cry of deadly anguish escaped them and re-echoed across the splendid square.

At the *Palazza degli Uffizi*, in the arcade, where the nobility assemble for the carnival festivities, the metal pig stopped. "Hold tight," said the animal, "hold tight, for we are going upstairs."

The little boy spoke not a word, for he was half trembling and half delighted. They passed through a long gallery in which the boy had been before. The walls were hung with pictures, and here stood statues and busts, all in the most excellent light, as if it were broad day; but the most beautiful of all was when the door of a side-room opened. The little boy remembered the beautiful things he had seen there, but that night everything was in its highest splendor. There stood a lovely woman, as beautiful as only Nature or the greatest master of sculpture could form her. She moved her glorious limbs, dolphins sprang about her feet, and immortality shone out of her eyes. The world calls her the Venus de Medici. At her side are marble statues in which the spirit of life has entered into the stone. There are handsome undraped figures of men—one is sharpening a sword, and is called the Grinder; the

Wrestling Gladiators form another group, the sword being sharpened and the struggle being for the Goddess of Beauty.

The boy was dazzled by so much splendor; the walls were radiant with colors, and everything had life and movement. The picture of Venus was there in duplicate, the earthly one as yielding and as amorous as when Titian had pressed her to his heart. It was wonderful to behold. They were two beautiful women; their graceful limbs reclined on soft pillows, their bosom heaved, and their heads moved so that their rich tresses fell upon their well-shaped shoulders, whilst the dark eyes expressed the feelings that were coursing through their veins; but none of the pictures ventured to leave their frames entirely. The Goddess of Beauty herself, the Gladiators, and the Grinder remained in their places, for the halo of glory that shone out from the Madonna, Jesus, and John restrained them. The sacred pictures were no longer pictures; they were the saints themselves.

What splendor and what beauty they passed in going from hall to hall! The boy saw it all, for the metal pig went step by step through all this glory and magnificence. Every fresh sight effaced the remembrance of the last, but one picture impressed itself deeply upon his soul, and particularly on account of the happy smiling children it represented—he had seen it once by daylight.

Many, no doubt, pass this picture with indifference, and yet it contains a treasure of poetry. It is Christ descending into Hell; but these are not the damned by whom he is surrounded—they are heathens. The picture was painted by Angiolo Bronzino, a native of Florence. The most beautiful thing about it is the expression on the children's faces—the full confidence that they will get to Heaven. Two little ones are already embracing; one stretches out his hand to another, who stands below him, and points to himself as if he were saying: "I am going to Heaven." The elder ones look uncertain, though hopeful, or humbly bow down in adoration before the Lord Jesus. Longer than upon any other did the boy's gaze rest upon this picture, and the metal pig stopped before it. A low sigh was heard; did it come from the picture or from the animal? The boy lifted up his hands towards the smiling children; then the pig ran away with him—away through the open vestibule.

"Thanks and blessings upon you, you beautiful creature," said the little boy, caressing the metal pig as it ran down the steps.

"Thanks and blessings upon yourself," said the pig. "I have helped you and you have helped me, for only when I have an innocent child on my back

I have the power to run. You see that I may even go under the rays of the lamp that hangs before the image of the Virgin, though I may not venture into the church. But if you are with me I can look in from without through the open doors. Don't get down from my back, for if you do I shall lie dead as you see me in the daytime at the *Porta Rosa*."

"I will stay with you, my dear creature," said the boy, and so they went on in hot haste through the streets of Florence, out into the square before the church of Santa Croce. The folding-doors flew open, and the light shone forth from the altar through the church into the deserted square.

A wonderful blaze of light streamed out from a monument in the left aisle, around which a thousand moving stars formed as it were a halo of glory. A coat of arms stands proudly on the grave—a red ladder on a blue ground—and seemed to glow like fire; it was the grave of Galileo. The monument is very simple, but the red ladder on the blue ground is full of meaning—an emblem as it were of art, the path of which always leads up a burning ladder, and to heaven. All the prophets of the mind soar up towards Heaven, like Elijah.

To the right, in the aisle, every figure on the magnificent tombs seemed endowed with life. Here stood Michaelangelo, there Dante with a laurel wreath upon his brow, Alfieri and Macchiavelli; these great men, the pride of Italy, lie side by side.[1] It is a grand church, far more beautiful than the marble cathedral at Florence, though not so large.

It seemed as if the marble draperies of the statues moved, as if these great figures held up their heads and regarded, amidst song and music, the bright altar blazing with light, where white-robed choristers swung the golden censers; the strong fragrance streamed out of the church into the open square.

The boy stretched out his hand towards the stream of light, and in a twinkling the metal pig hurried away with him; he had to cling tightly, and the wind whistled about his ears; he heard the church doors creaking

---

1. Opposite the grave of Galileo is that of Michaelangelo. On the monument is his bust and three figures representing Sculpture, Painting, and Architecture. Close by is Dante's monument (the body itself was interred at Ravenna), on which is seen Italy pointing to a colossal statue of the poet, while Poetry weeps over his loss. A few steps farther is Alfieri's monument, adorned with laurels, the lyre and masks, while a figure of Italy weeps over his bier. Macchiavelli closes the series of celebrated men.

on their hinges as they closed, and at the same time he seemed to lose consciousness—he felt an icy shudder pass through him, and he opened his eyes.

It was morning, and he was still sitting on the metal pig, which stood in the *Porta Rosa*, but he had slipped half off his back.

Fear and trembling seized the boy at the thought of her whom he called mother, and who had sent him out yesterday to get some money; he had nothing, and he was hungry and thirsty. Once more he put his arms round the pig's neck, kissed it on the snout, and, nodding to it, wandered away into one of the narrowest streets, hardly wide enough for a laden donkey. A great iron-clamped door stood ajar; passing through this, he went up some stone stairs with dirty walls and a rope for a balustrade, till he reached an open gallery hung with rags. From here a flight of steps led down into the yard, where there was a fountain with great iron wires running to all the stories of the house; by this means one pail after another was swung up, while the roller creaked and the pail danced about so that the water splashed down into the yard. Here again a tumble-down stone staircase led upwards; two Prussian sailors were descending quickly, and almost knocked the poor boy down. They were returning from their nocturnal carouse. A woman, plump but no longer young, with rich black hair, followed them.

"What do you bring home?" she asked the boy.

"Don't be angry," he pleaded; "I got nothing—nothing at all." And he seized his mother's dress, as if to kiss it. They went into the little room; I will not describe it, but only say that there stood in it a pot with handles—called a *marito*—filled with burning coals. This she took in her arms, warmed her fingers, and pushed the boy with her elbow.

"You must have got some money," she said.

The boy wept, and she kicked him so that he cried aloud.

"Will you be quiet, or I'll break your screaming head?" and she lifted up the fire-pot that she held in her hands.

The boy bent down to the ground with a cry of terror. At this a neighbor came in, also with a *marito* in her arms. "Felicita," she said, "what are you doing to the child?"

"The child is mine," answered Felicita. "I can murder him if I like, and you too, Giannina." And she again lifted up her fire-pot. The other woman raised hers to defend herself, and both pots crashed together so violently that

347

the fragments, fire and ashes, flew all over the room; at the same moment the boy rushed out at the door, across the yard and out of the house.

The poor child ran till he could scarcely breathe; he stopped at the church, whose great doors had opened before him last night, and went in. All was bright as the boy knelt down by the first grave on the right, that of Michaelangelo, and soon he was sobbing aloud.

People came and went, and Mass was performed, but no one noticed the boy; only one elderly citizen stood still, looked at him—and then went away like the rest.

Hunger and thirst tormented the child, and he was quite faint and ill; so he crept into a corner between the marble monuments and went to sleep. Towards evening he was awakened by some one pulling his sleeve, and jumping up, he found the old citizen before him.

"Are you ill? Where do you live? Have you been here all day?" were a few of the many questions that the old man put to him. They were answered, and the old man took him into his little house, which was close by in a side-street. They entered a glove-maker's workshop, in which the wife was busily sewing when they arrived. A little white poodle, so closely shaven that his pink skin could be seen, was capering about upon the table and gambolled before the boy.

"Innocent souls recognize each other," said the woman, caressing both the dog and the boy. The latter was given food and drink by the good people, and they said they would permit him to stay with them for the night, promising him that next day Father Giuseppe should go and speak to his mother. He was given a humble little cot; but for him, who had often been obliged to sleep on the hard stone ground, it seemed like a royal couch. How sweetly he slept, dreaming of the beautiful pictures and of the metal pig!

Next morning Father Giuseppe went out; the poor child was by no means glad, for he knew that the object of this errand was to send him back to his mother. He kissed the lively little dog, and the woman nodded at them both.

What news did Father Giuseppe bring? He spoke with his wife for a long time, and the latter nodded and stroked the boy. "He is a beautiful child," said she. "He may become a good glove-maker like you are, and he has such delicate and pliable fingers. The Madonna intended him for a glove-maker."

So the boy stayed in the house, and the woman herself taught him to sew; he ate well, slept well, became very cheerful, and began to tease Bellissima, as the little dog was called. The woman threatened him with her finger, scolded him and got angry. That went to the boy's heart, and he sat thoughtful in his little room. This looked out into the street where skins were being dried; thick iron bars were before the windows. He could not sleep; the metal pig was continually running in his mind, and suddenly he heard a pit-a-pat outside. That must be a pig, he thought. So he ran to the window, but there was nothing to be seen; it had passed already.

"Help the signor to carry his box of colors," said madam the following morning to the boy, when her young neighbor, the artist, passed, carrying the box and a large canvas rolled up. The boy shouldered the box and followed the painter, who took the way leading to the gallery, and went up the same steps which were so well known to the boy since the night he had ridden on the metal pig. He knew the statues and the pictures, the beautiful marble Venus and the one who lived on the canvas; he again saw the Madonna, Jesus and John. They stopped before the picture by Bronzino, in which Christ is descending into hell, and the children are all smiling around him in sweet expectation of Heaven. The poor boy smiled too, for here he was in his Heaven!

"You may go home now," said the artist when the boy had stood there till the other had set up his easel.

"May I look at your painting?" asked the boy. "May I see how you get the picture upon this white canvas?"

"I'm not going to paint yet," replied the man, taking up his black chalk. His hand moved quickly, his eye measuring the great picture, and although only a thin line was visible, the figure of Christ was already on the canvas, as in the painted picture.

"But why don't you go home?" said the painter; and silently the boy walked home, sat down at the table and learned to sew gloves.

But the whole day his thoughts were in the picture gallery, and therefore he pricked his fingers and was very awkward, though he did not tease Bellissima. When evening came, and the house-door stood open for a moment, he slipped out; it was still cold, but a very fine bright starlight night. Away he wandered through the already deserted streets, and was soon standing before the metal pig, over which he bent, kissed its polished snout, and seated himself on its back. "You blessed creature," he cried, "how I have longed for you! We must have a ride to-night."

The metal pig lay motionless, and the fresh stream gushed forth from his mouth. The boy was sitting on his back like a rider, when something pulled him by the clothes. He looked down, and there was Bellissima, the little clean-shaven Bellissima, barking as if it wanted to say, "Do you see, I'm here too; why are you sitting there?" No fiery dragon could have startled the boy so much as did the little dog in this place. Bellissima in the street, and undressed too, as the old dame called it! What would be the end of it? The dog only went out in winter enveloped in a little lambskin which had been cut out for him and sewn. The skin, which was adorned with bows and bells, was fastened with a red ribbon round his neck and under his body. In this costume the dog looked like a little kid when in winter he got permission to trip out with his mistress. Now Bellissima was out and undressed too: what would be the end of it? All the boy's fancies had vanished, but still he kissed the metal pig and then took Bellissima in his arms. The little creature was trembling with cold, so the boy ran as fast as he could.

"What are you running away with there?" cried two soldiers whom he met and at whom Bellissima barked. "Where did you steal that pretty dog?" they asked, taking it from him.

"Oh, give it me back," pleaded the boy.

"If you did not steal it, you may go home and say that the dog may be had at the guard-house." They gave him the name of the street and went away with Bellissima.

This was a great calamity. The boy did not know whether he should jump into the Arno, or go home and confess all; they would certainly kill him, he thought. "But I will gladly be killed; then I shall go to Jesus and the Madonna." So he went home, principally for the sake of getting killed. The door was closed, and he could not reach the knocker. There was no one in the street, but a stone lay there, and with this he banged at the door.

"Who's there?" cried somebody inside.

"It's I," he said "Bellissima is gone. Open the door and kill me."

Everybody was terror-stricken concerning poor Bellissima, but especially madam. She immediately looked at the wall, where the dog's coat generally hung, and there was the little lambskin.

"Bellissima at the guard-house," she cried aloud. "You wicked child! How did you entice it out? It will freeze. The delicate little thing among those rough soldiers!"

Her husband had to go after it at once—the woman lamented and the boy wept. All the inmates of the house came together, and among them the painter. He took the boy between his knees, cross-questioned him, and in fragments got to know the whole story of the metal pig and the picture gallery: it was pretty unintelligible. He comforted the little fellow, and tried to pacify the old woman; but she was not satisfied till her husband arrived with Bellissima, who had been amongst the soldiers. There was great rejoicing, and the painter caressed the boy and gave him a handful of pictures.

Oh! what beautiful bits and comical heads there were, and the metal pig was actually among them too! Oh, nothing could be more delightful! It had been put there on the paper by a few strokes, and even the house behind it was also given.

Whoever could draw and paint, could collect the whole world round him! The first spare moment he had on the following day the boy seized a pencil and tried to copy the drawing of the metal pig on the back of one of the pictures. He succeeded; it was rather crooked, it is true, rather up and down, one leg thick and another thin, but still it was recognizable, and he rejoiced at it himself. The pencil would not go just as it should—he saw that very well; the following day a second metal pig stood by the side of the first, and it looked a hundred times better. The third was already so good that every one could recognize it.

But the glove-sewing went on very badly, and the orders given in the town were but slowly got out; the metal pig had taught the boy that all pictures can be drawn on paper, and the city of Florence is a picture-book for any one who will turn over its pages. On the *Piazza del Trinità* stands a slender pillar, on the top of which is the Goddess of Justice, blindfolded, and holding the scales in her hand. She was soon on paper, and it was the glovemaker's young apprentice who had put her there.

His collection of pictures increased, but still it contained only drawings of things without life, when one day Bellissima came springing up to him. "Stand still," he said, "then you shall be made beautiful and get into my collection."

But Bellissima would not stand still, so it had to be bound fast. Its head and tail were tied, but as it still barked and jumped, the string had to be pulled tighter. Just then his mistress came in.

"You wicked boy! The poor creature!" was all that she could utter. She pushed the boy aside, kicked him, and turned him out of the house, calling him a most ungrateful good-for-nothing, and a very wicked child, and tearfully she kissed her little halfstrangled Bellissima.

Just at that moment the painter came down the stairs; and this is the turning-point of the story.

In the year 1834 there was an exhibition in the Academy of Arts at Florence. Two pictures placed side by side attracted a number of spectators. The smaller of the two represented a merry little boy, who sat drawing, with a small white, curiously shorn poodle for his model; but the animal would not stand still, and was therefore tied up with a string, both by its head and tail. There was a life and truth about the picture that appealed to every one. The painter, it was said, was a young Florentine, who had been picked up from the streets when a child, and brought up by an old glove-maker, and had taught himself to draw. A now celebrated painter had discovered this talent, as the boy was being sent away for tying up madam's pet, the little poodle, and taking it for his model.

The glove-maker's apprentice had become a great painter; that was evident from the picture, but especially from the larger one beside it. Here there was only a single figure, a ragged but handsome boy, who was lying asleep in the streets, leaning against the metal pig in the *Porta Rosa*. All the spectators knew the spot. The child's arms rested upon the pig's head; he was fast asleep, and the lamp which hung before the image of the Madonna threw a strong effective light upon his pale, handsome face. It was a wonderfully beautiful picture, and was set in a large gilt frame, on the corner of which was hung a laurel wreath; but a black band was wound among the green leaves and a long streamer of crape hung down from it.

A few days before, the young artist had—died!

How the Stalos Were Tricked

(FROM *THE ORANGE FAIRY BOOK*)

Mother, I have seen such a wonderful man," said a little boy one day, as he entered a hut in Lapland, bearing in his arms the bundle of sticks he had been sent out to gather.

"Have you, my son; and what was he like?" asked the mother, as she took off the child's sheepskin coat and shook it on the doorstep.

"Well, I was tired of stooping for the sticks, and was leaning against a tree to rest, when I heard a noise of 'sh-'sh, among the dead leaves. I thought perhaps it was a wolf, so I stood very still. But soon there came past a tall man—oh! twice as tall as father—with a long red beard and a red tunic fastened with a silver girdle, from which hung a silver-handled knife. Behind him followed a great dog, which looked stronger than any wolf, or even a bear. But why are you so pale, mother?"

"It was the Stalo," replied she, her voice trembling; "Stalo the man-eater! You did well to hide, or you might never had come back. But, remember that, though he is so tall and strong, he is very stupid, and many a Lapp has escaped from his clutches by playing him some clever trick."

Not long after the mother and son had held this talk, it began to be whispered in the forest that the children of an old man called Patto had vanished one by one, no one knew whither. The unhappy father searched the country for miles round without being able to find as much as a shoe or a handkerchief, to show him where they had passed, but at length a little boy came with news that he had seen the Stalo hiding behind a well, near which the children used to play. The boy had waited behind a clump of bushes to see what would happen, and by-and-by he noticed that the Stalo had laid a cunning trap in the path to the well, and that anybody who fell over it would roll into the water and drown there.

And, as he watched, Patto's youngest daughter ran gaily down the path, till her foot caught in the strings that were stretched across the steepest place. She slipped and fell, and in another instant had rolled into the water within reach of the Stalo.

As soon as Patto heard this tale his heart was filled with rage, and he vowed to have his revenge. So he straightway took an old fur coat from the hook where it hung, and putting it on went out into the forest. When he reached the path that led to the well he looked hastily round to be sure that no one was watching him, then laid himself down as if he had been caught in the snare and had rolled into the well, though he took care to keep his head out of the water.

Very soon he heard a 'sh-'sh of the leaves, and there was the Stalo pushing his way through the undergrowth to see what chance he had of a dinner. At the first glimpse of Patto's head in the well he laughed loudly, crying:

"Ha! ha! This time it is the old ass! I wonder how *he* will taste?" And drawing Patto out of the well, he flung him across his shoulders and carried him home. Then he tied a cord round him and hung him over the fire to roast, while he finished a box that he was making before the door of the hut, which he meant to hold Patto's flesh when it was cooked. In a very short time the box was so nearly done that it only wanted a little more chipping out with an axe; but this part of the work was easier accomplished indoors, and he called to one of his sons who were lounging inside to bring him the tool.

The young man looked everywhere, but he could not find the axe, for the very good reason that Patto had managed to pick it up and hide it in his clothes.

"Stupid fellow! what is the use of you?" grumbled his father angrily; and he bade first one and then another of his sons to fetch him the tool, but they had no better success than their brother.

"I must come myself, I suppose!" said Stalo, putting aside the box. But, meanwhile, Patto had slipped from the hook and concealed himself behind the door, so that, as Stalo stepped in, his prisoner raised the axe, and with one blow the ogre's head was rolling on the ground. His sons were so frightened at the sight that they all ran away.

And in this manner Patto avenged his dead children.

But though Stalo was dead, his three sons were still living, and not very far off either. They had gone to their mother, who was tending some reindeer on the pastures, and told her that by some magic, they knew not what, their father's head had rolled from his body, and they had been so afraid that something dreadful would happen to them that they had come to take refuge with her. The ogress said nothing. Long ago she had found out how stupid her sons were, so she just sent them out to milk the reindeer, while she returned to the other house to bury her husband's body.

Now, three days' journey from the hut on the pastures two brothers Sodno dwelt in a small cottage with their sister Lyma, who tended a large herd of reindeer while they were out hunting. Of late it had been whispered from one to another that the three young Stalos were to be seen on the pastures, but the Sodno brothers did not disturb themselves, the danger seemed too far away.

Unluckily, however, one day, when Lyma was left by herself in the hut, the three Stalos came down and carried her and the reindeer off to their own cottage. The country was very lonely, and perhaps no one would have known in which direction she had gone had not the girl managed to tie a ball of thread to the handle of a door at the back of the cottage and let it trail behind her. Of course the ball was not long enough to go all the way, but it lay on the edge of a snowy track which led straight to the Stalos' house.

When the brothers returned from their hunting they found both the hut and the sheds empty. Loudly they cried: "Lyma! Lyma!" But no voice answered them; and they fell to searching all about, lest perchance their sister might have dropped some clue to guide them. At length their eyes dropped on the thread which lay on the snow, and they set out to follow it.

On and on they went, and when at length the thread stopped the brothers knew that another day's journey would bring them to the Stalos' dwelling. Of course they did not dare to approach it openly, for the Stalos had the strength of giants, and besides, there were three of them; so the two Sodnos climbed into a big bushy tree which overhung a well.

"Perhaps our sister may be sent to draw water here," they said to each other.

But it was not till the moon had risen that the sister came, and as she let down her bucket into the well, the leaves seemed to whisper "Lyma! Lyma!"

The girl started and looked up, but could see nothing, and in a moment the voice came again.

"Be careful—take no notice, fill your buckets, but listen carefully all the while, and we will tell you what to do so that you may escape yourself and set free the reindeer also."

So Lyma bent over the well lower than before, and seemed busier than ever.

"You know," said her brother, "that when a Stalo finds that anything has been dropped into his food he will not eat a morsel, but throws it to his dogs. Now, after the pot has been hanging some time over the fire, and the broth is nearly cooked, just rake up the log of wood so that some of the ashes fly into the pot. The Stalo will soon notice this, and will call you to give all the food to the dogs; but, instead, you must bring it straight to us, as it is three days since we have eaten or drunk. That is all you need do for the present."

Then Lyma took up her buckets and carried them into the house, and did as her brothers had told her. They were so hungry that they ate the food up greedily without speaking, but when there was nothing left in the pot, the eldest one said:

"Listen carefully to what I have to tell you. After the eldest Stalo has cooked and eaten a fresh supper, he will go to bed and sleep so soundly that not even a witch could wake him. You can hear him snoring a mile off, and then you must go into his room and pull off the iron mantle that covers him, and put it on the fire till it is almost red hot. When that is done, come to us and we will give you further directions."

"I will obey you in everything, dear brothers," answered Lyma; and so she did.

It had happened that on this very evening the Stalos had driven in some of the reindeer from the pasture, and had tied them up to the wall of the house so that they might be handy to kill for next day's dinner. The two Sodnos had seen what they were doing, and where the beasts were secured; so, at midnight, when all was still, they crept down from their tree and seized the reindeer by the horns which were locked together. The animals were frightened, and began to neigh and kick, as if they were fighting together, and the noise became so great that even the eldest Stalo was awakened by it, and *that* was a thing which had never occurred before. Raising himself in his bed, he called to his youngest brother to go out and separate the reindeer or they would certainly kill themselves.

The young Stalo did as he was bid, and left the house; but no sooner was he out of the door than he was stabbed to the heart by one of the Sodnos, and fell without a groan. Then they went back to worry the reindeer, and the noise became as great as ever, and a second time the Stalo awoke.

"The boy does not seem to be able to part the beasts," he cried to his second brother; "go and help him, or I shall never get to sleep." So the brother went, and in an instant was struck dead as he left the house by the sword of the eldest Sodno. The Stalo waited in bed a little longer for things to get quiet, but as the clatter of the reindeer's horns was as bad as ever, he rose angrily from his bed muttering to himself:

"It is extraordinary that they cannot unlock themselves; but as no one else seems able to help them I suppose I must go and do it."

Rubbing his eyes, he stood up on the floor and stretched his great arms and gave a yawn which shook the walls. The Sodnos heard it below, and posted themselves, one at the big door and one at the little door at the back, for they did not know what their enemy would come out at.

The Stalo put out his hand to take his iron mantle from the bed, where it always lay, but the mantle was not there. He wondered where it could be, and who could have moved it, and after searching through all the rooms, he found it hanging over the kitchen fire. But the first touch burnt him so badly that he let it alone, and went with nothing, except a stick in his hand, through the back door.

The young Sodno was standing ready for him, and as the Stalo passed the threshold struck him such a blow on the head that he rolled over with a crash and never stirred again. The two Sodnos did not trouble about him, but quickly stripped the younger Stalos of their clothes, in which they dressed themselves. Then they sat still till the dawn should break and they could find out from the Stalos' mother where the treasure was hidden.

With the first rays of the sun the young Sodno went upstairs and entered the old woman's room. She was already up and dressed, and sitting by the window knitting, and the young man crept in softly and crouched down on the floor, laying his head on her lap. For a while he kept silence, then he whispered gently:

"Tell me, dear mother, where did my eldest brother conceal his riches?"

"What a strange question! Surely you must know," answered she.

"No, I have forgotten; my memory is so bad."

"He dug a hole under the doorstep and placed it there," said she. And there was another pause.

By-and-by the Sodno asked again:

"And where may my second brother's money be?"

"Don't you know that either?" cried the mother in surprise.

"Oh, yes; I did once. But since I fell upon my head I can remember nothing."

"It is behind the oven," answered she. And again was silence.

"Mother, dear mother," said the young man at last, "I am almost afraid to ask you; but I really have grown so stupid of late. Where did I hide my own money?"

But at this question the old woman flew into a passion, and vowed that if she could find a rod she would bring his memory back to him. Luckily, no rod was within her reach, and the Sodno managed, after a little, to coax her back into good humor, and at length she told him that the youngest Stalo had buried his treasure under the very place where she was sitting.

"Dear mother," said Lyma, who had come in unseen, and was kneeling in front of the fire. "Dear mother, do you know who it is you have been talking with?"

The old woman started, but answered quietly:

"It is a Sodno, I suppose?"

"You have guessed right," replied Lyma.

The mother of the Stalos looked round for her iron cane, which she always used to kill her victims, but it was not there, for Lyma had put it in the fire.

"Where is my iron cane?" asked the old woman.

"There!" answered Lyma, pointing to the flames.

The old woman sprang forwards and seized it, but her clothes caught fire, and in a few minutes she was burned to ashes.

So the Sodno brothers found the treasure, and they carried it, and their sister and the reindeer, to their own home, and were the richest men in all Lapland.

A Hoax

(Traditional Russian Tale)

A good many years ago there came to the hut of an old peasant a soldier, who asked for a night's lodging.

"Come in, soldier, and welcome! Only you must tell me some stories all through the night, for you have been all over the world, I suppose, and have seen a great number of things and know so much."

"What am I to tell you, fiction or fact?"

"Something that has happened to yourself."

So the soldier began telling the peasant where he had been, how he had lived, and what he had seen and, after talking away for a long time he came to a stop, saying that he had nothing more of interest to tell. But the peasant was not satisfied, and declared that he would not sleep unless the soldier told him more tales.

The soldier thought and thought, and then it suddenly struck him that it would be rather fun to try and deceive the peasant somehow or another as he was rather good at that.

"Master, master!" he cried, "do you know what it is that is lying in the loft by your side?"

"Why, a soldier to be sure. What else?"

"No, you have not guessed right; feel with your hand!"

The peasant did so, and it felt as if a wolf were lying by his side. He was greatly alarmed.

"Don't be afraid of me," said the soldier; "feel yourself, and you will find that you are very much the same sort of animal!"

The peasant obeyed, and felt the thick fur of a bear all round him.

"Now listen, master," said the soldier; "we have no business to lie in the loft now; besides, when the people see us they will take us for real animals, and that would never do, we should be in great danger and that is just what we must avoid. Let us be off now so that no one may see us."

So they got up and ran out of the hut into the fields and far away. Suddenly they came across an old horse which belonged to the peasant.

"Come, let us eat up that horse, for I am hungry!" said the wolf.

"No, please don't, it is my horse!"

"Well, and what of that? Better let us eat it than starve."

So they ate it and ran on farther. It was quite daylight when they came into another field, where they saw an old woman, the peasant's wife, coming along.

"Come, my friend!" said the wolf, "let us eat up this old woman!"

"But she is my wife!" replied the bear.

"Your wife, indeed! What next?"

And they finished off the old woman also.

In this way the wolf and bear passed the whole summer, eating people or animals, whichever came first. When the winter arrived, the wolf said to his companion,—

"Come, let us find a bear's den in the forest yonder; you can get into it first and hide, while I keep watch at the opening, so that should any hunters happen to see us, they would shoot me first. But mind, as soon as you see that they have killed me and begin stripping off my skin, you must at once run out of the den and jump over my skin. The moment you do that you will be changed into yourself—a man—again."

They found a very suitable den in the forest, into which the bear went, while the wolf lay at the mouth.

They lay there for some time without anything happening to them. At last some hunters came riding along. When they saw the wolf they at once shot him, and then commenced tearing off his skin. At that moment the bear rushed out of his den, and with one leap tumbled right over the wolf's skin and ran off as hard as ever he could, and—down came the peasant, head-over-heels, from his loft in his own hut.

"Oh dear! oh dear!" he cried; "I have broken my back!"

"What is the matter with you, old man ?" asked his wife from the top of the stove. "What made you fall off the loft just as if you had been drinking?"

"Oh, you don't understand anything!" began the peasant. "You see the soldier and I changed into wild beasts; he into a wolf, I into a bear, and so we ran about all through the summer and winter. We ate up our old horse, and we even ate you up also, old woman."

The woman was greatly astonished, and thought her husband was going mad, while the soldier burst out into a hearty laugh.

"What!" cried the peasant, stupefied with amazement; "what, soldier! do you mean to say that you are lying in the loft?"

"Of course, where else should I be? Do you really suppose that the hunters killed me? Oh, what a joke! Why, you old donkey, it was nothing but a hoax; I wanted to have a little fun out of you. While you were half-asleep I told the story, and you actually thought that it really was taking place. I have often done this sort of thing, and am always greatly amused at the result."

The Frost-King;
or, The Power of Love

Louisa May Alcott

Three little Fairies sat in the fields eating their breakfast; each among the leaves of her favorite flower, Daisy, Primrose, and Violet, were happy as Elves need be.

The morning wind gently rocked them to and fro, and the sun shone warmly down upon the dewy grass, where butterflies spread their gay wings, and bees with their deep voices sung among the flowers; while the little birds hopped merrily about to peep at them.

On a silvery mushroom was spread the breakfast; little cakes of flower-dust lay on a broad green leaf, beside a crimson strawberry, which, with sugar from the violet, and cream from the yellow milkweed, made a fairy meal, and their drink was the dew from the flowers' bright leaves.

"Ah me," sighed Primrose, throwing herself languidly back, "how warm the sun grows! give me another piece of strawberry, and then I must hasten away to the shadow of the ferns. But while I eat, tell me, dear Violet, why are you all so sad? I have scarce seen a happy face since my return from Rose Land; dear friend, what means it?"

"I will tell you," replied little Violet, the tears gathering in her soft eyes. "Our good Queen is ever striving to keep the dear flowers from the power of the cruel Frost-King; many ways she tried, but all have failed. She has sent messengers to his court with costly gifts; but all have returned sick for want of sunlight, weary and sad; we have watched over them, heedless of sun or shower, but still his dark spirits do their work, and we are left to weep over our blighted blossoms. Thus have we striven, and in vain; and this night our Queen holds council for the last time. Therefore are we sad, dear Primrose, for she has toiled and cared for us, and we can do nothing to help or advise her now."

"It is indeed a cruel thing," replied her friend; "but as we cannot help it, we must suffer patiently, and not let the sorrows of others disturb our happiness. But, dear sisters, see you not how high the sun is getting? I have my locks to curl, and my robe to prepare for the evening; therefore I must be gone, or I shall be brown as a withered leaf in this warm light." So, gathering a tiny mushroom for a parasol, she flew away; Daisy soon followed, and Violet was left alone.

Then she spread the table afresh, and to it came fearlessly the busy ant and bee, gay butterfly and bird; even the poor blind mole and humble worm were not forgotten; and with gentle words she gave to all, while each learned something of their kind little teacher; and the love that made her own heart bright shone alike on all.

The ant and bee learned generosity, the butterfly and bird contentment, the mole and worm confidence in the love of others; and each went to their home better for the little time they had been with Violet.

Evening came, and with it troops of Elves to counsel their good Queen, who, seated on her mossy throne, looked anxiously upon the throng below, whose glittering wings and rustling robes gleamed like many-colored flowers.

At length she rose, and amid the deep silence spoke thus:—

"Dear children, let us not tire of a good work, hard though it be and wearisome; think of the many little hearts that in their sorrow look to us for help. What would the green earth be without its lovely flowers, and what a lonely home for us! Their beauty fills our hearts with brightness, and their love with tender thoughts. Ought we then to leave them to die uncared for and alone? They give to us their all; ought we not to toil unceasingly, that they may bloom in peace within their quiet homes? We have tried to gain the love of the stern Frost-King, but in vain; his heart is hard as his own icy land; no love can melt, no kindness bring it back to sunlight and to joy. How then may we keep our frail blossoms from his cruel spirits? Who will give us counsel? Who will be our messenger for the last time? Speak, my subjects."

Then a great murmuring arose, and many spoke, some for costlier gifts, some for war; and the fearful counseled patience and submission.

Long and eagerly they spoke, and their soft voices rose high.

Then sweet music sounded on the air, and the loud tones were hushed, as in wondering silence the Fairies waited what should come.

Through the crowd there came a little form, a wreath of pure white violets lay among the bright locks that fell so softly round the gentle face, where a deep blush glowed, as, kneeling at the throne, little Violet said:—

"Dear Queen, we have bent to the Frost-King's power, we have borne gifts unto his pride, but have we gone trustingly to him and spoken fearlessly of his evil deeds? Have we shed the soft light of unwearied love around his cold heart, and with patient tenderness shown him how bright and beautiful love can make even the darkest lot?

"Our messengers have gone fearfully, and with cold looks and courtly words offered him rich gifts, things he cared not for, and with equal pride has he sent them back.

"Then let me, the weakest of your band, go to him, trusting in the love I know lies hidden in the coldest heart.

"I will bear only a garland of our fairest flowers; these will I wind about him, and their bright faces, looking lovingly in his, will bring sweet thoughts to his dark mind, and their soft breath steal in like gentle words. Then, when he sees them fading on his breast, will he not sigh that there is no warmth there to keep them fresh and lovely? This will I do, dear Queen, and never leave his dreary home, till the sunlight falls on flowers fair as those that bloom in our own dear land."

Silently the Queen had listened, but now, rising and placing her hand on little Violet's head, she said, turning to the throng below:—

"We in our pride and power have erred, while this, the weakest and lowliest of our subjects, has from the innocence of her own pure heart counseled us more wisely than the noblest of our train. All who will aid our brave little messenger, lift your wands, that we may know who will place their trust in the Power of Love."

Every fairy wand glistened in the air, as with silvery voices they cried, "Love and little Violet."

Then down from the throne, hand in hand, came the Queen and Violet, and till the moon sank did the Fairies toil, to weave a wreath of the fairest flowers. Tenderly they gathered them, with the night-dew fresh upon their leaves, and as they wove chanted sweet spells, and whispered fairy blessings on the bright messengers whom they sent forth to die in a dreary land, that their gentle kindred might bloom unharmed.

At length it was done; and the fair flowers lay glowing in the soft starlight, while beside them stood the Fairies, singing to the music of the wind-harps:—

> We are sending you, dear flowers,
> Forth alone to die,
> Where your gentle sisters may not weep
> O'er the cold graves where you lie;
> But you go to bring them fadeless life
> In the bright homes where they dwell,
> And you softly smile that 't is so,
> As we sadly sing farewell.
>   O plead with gentle words for us,
> And whisper tenderly
> Of generous love to that cold heart,
> And it will answer ye;
> And though you fade in a dreary home,
> Yet loving hearts will tell
> Of the joy and peace that you have given:
> Flowers, dear flowers, farewell!

The morning sun looked softly down upon the broad green earth, which like a mighty altar was sending up clouds of perfume from its breast, while flowers danced gayly in the summer wind, and birds sang their morning hymn among the cool green leaves. Then high above, on shining wings, soared a little form. The sunlight rested softly on the silken hair, and the winds fanned lovingly the bright face, and brought the sweetest odors to cheer her on.

Thus went Violet through the clear air, and the earth looked smiling up to her, as, with the bright wreath folded in her arms, she flew among the soft, white clouds.

On and on she went, over hill and valley, broad rivers and rustling woods, till the warm sunlight passed away, the winds grew cold, and the air thick with falling snow. Then far below she saw the Frost-King's home. Pillars of hard, gray ice supported the high, arched roof, hung with crystal icicles. Dreary gardens lay around, filled with withered flowers and bare, drooping trees; while heavy clouds hung low in the dark sky, and a cold wind murmured sadly through the wintry air.

With a beating heart Violet folded her fading wreath more closely to her breast, and with weary wings flew onward to the dreary palace.

Here, before the closed doors, stood many forms with dark faces and harsh, discordant voices, who sternly asked the shivering little Fairy why she came to them.

Gently she answered, telling them her errand, beseeching them to let her pass ere the cold wind blighted her frail blossoms. Then they flung wide the doors, and she passed in.

Walls of ice, carved with strange figures, were around her; glittering icicles hung from the high roof, and soft, white snow covered the hard floors. On a throne hung with clouds sat the Frost-King; a crown of crystals bound his white locks, and a dark mantle wrought with delicate frost-work was folded over his cold breast.

His stern face could not stay little Violet, and on through the long hall she went, heedless of the snow that gathered on her feet, and the bleak wind that blew around her; while the King with wondering eyes looked on the golden light that played upon the dark walls as she passed.

The flowers, as if they knew their part, unfolded their bright leaves, and poured forth their sweetest perfume, as, kneeling at the throne, the brave little Fairy said,—

"O King of blight and sorrow, send me not away till I have brought back the light and joy that will make your dark home bright and beautiful again. Let me call back to the desolate gardens the fair forms that are gone, and their soft voices blessing you will bring to your breast a never failing joy. Cast by your icy crown and scepter, and let the sunlight of love fall softly on your heart.

"Then will the earth bloom again in all its beauty, and your dim eyes will rest only on fair forms, while music shall sound through these dreary halls, and the love of grateful hearts be yours. Have pity on the gentle flower-spirits, and do not doom them to an early death, when they might bloom in fadeless beauty, making us wiser by their gentle teachings, and the earth brighter by their lovely forms. These fair flowers, with the prayers of all Fairy Land, I lay before you; O send me not away till they are answered."

And with tears falling thick and fast upon their tender leaves, Violet laid the wreath at his feet, while the golden light grew ever brighter as it fell upon the little form so humbly kneeling there.

The King's stern face grew milder as he gazed on the gentle Fairy, and the flowers seemed to look beseechingly upon him; while their fragrant voices sounded softly in his ear, telling of their dying sisters, and of the joy it gives to bring happiness to the weak and sorrowing. But he drew the dark mantle closer over his breast and answered coldly,—

"I cannot grant your prayer, little Fairy; it is my will the flowers should die. Go back to your Queen, and tell her that I cannot yield my power to please these foolish flowers."

Then Violet hung the wreath above the throne, and with weary feet went forth again, out into the cold, dark gardens, and still the golden shadows followed her, and wherever they fell, flowers bloomed and green leaves rustled.

Then came the Frost-Spirits, and beneath their cold wings the flowers died, while the Spirits bore Violet to a low, dark cell, saying as they left her, that their King was angry that she had dared to stay when he had bid her go.

So all alone she sat, and sad thoughts of her happy home came back to her, and she wept bitterly. But soon came visions of the gentle flowers dying in their forest homes, and their voices ringing in her ear, imploring her to save them. Then she wept no longer, but patiently awaited what might come.

Soon the golden light gleamed faintly through the cell, and she heard little voices calling for help, and high up among the heavy cobwebs hung poor little flies struggling to free themselves, while their cruel enemies sat in their nets, watching their pain.

With her wand the Fairy broke the bands that held them, tenderly bound up their broken wings, and healed their wounds; while they lay in the warm light, and feebly hummed their thanks to their kind deliverer.

Then she went to the ugly brown spiders, and in gentle words told them, how in Fairy Land their kindred spun all the elfin cloth, and in return the Fairies gave them food, and then how happily they lived among the cool green leaves, spinning garments for their neighbors. "And you too," said she, "shall spin for me, and I will give you better food than helpless insects. You shall live in peace, and spin your delicate threads into a mantle for the stern King; and I will weave golden threads amid the gray, that when folded over his cold heart gentle thoughts may enter in and make it their home."

And while she gayly sung, the little weavers spun their silken threads, the flies on glittering wings flew lovingly above her head, and over all the golden light shone softly down.

When the Frost-Spirits told their King, he greatly wondered, and often stole to look at the sunny little room where friends and enemies worked peacefully together. Still the light grew brighter, and floated out into the cold air, where it hung like bright clouds above the dreary gardens, whence all the Spirits' power could not drive it; and green leaves budded on the naked trees, and flowers bloomed; but the Spirits heaped snow upon them, and they bowed their heads and died.

At length the mantle was finished, and amid the gray threads shone golden ones, making it bright; and she sent it to the King, entreating him to wear it, for it would bring peace and love to dwell within his breast.

But he scornfully threw it aside, and bade his Spirits take her to a colder cell, deep in the earth; and there with harsh words they left her.

Still she sang gayly on, and the falling drops kept time so musically, that the King in his cold ice-halls wondered at the low, sweet sounds that came stealing up to him.

Thus Violet dwelt, and each day the golden light grew stronger; and from among the crevices of the rocky walls came troops of little velvet-coated moles, praying that they might listen to the sweet music, and lie in the warm light.

"We lead," said they, "a dreary life in the cold earth; the flower-roots are dead, and no soft dews descend for us to drink, no little seed or leaf can we find. Ah, good Fairy, let us be your servants: give us but a few crumbs of your daily bread, and we will do all in our power to serve you."

And Violet said, "Yes"; so day after day they labored to make a pathway through the frozen earth, that she might reach the roots of the withered flowers; and soon, wherever through the dark galleries she went, the soft light fell upon the roots of flowers, and they with new life spread forth in the warm ground, and forced fresh sap to the blossoms above. Brightly they bloomed and danced in the soft light, and the Frost-Spirits tried in vain to harm them, for when they came beneath the bright clouds their power to do evil left them.

From his dark castle the King looked out on the happy flowers, who nodded gayly to him, and in sweet odors strove to tell him of the good little Spirit, who toiled so faithfully below, that they might live. And when he turned from the brightness without, to his stately palace, it seemed so cold and dreary, that he folded Violet's mantle round him, and sat beneath the faded wreath upon his ice-carved throne, wondering at the strange warmth that came from it; till at length he bade his Spirits bring the little Fairy from her dismal prison.

Soon they came hastening back, and prayed him to come and see how lovely the dark cell had grown. The rough floor was spread with deep green moss, and over wall and roof grew flowery vines, filling the air with their sweet breath; while above played the clear, soft light, casting rosy shadows on the glittering drops that lay among the fragrant leaves; and beneath the vines stood Violet, casting crumbs to the downy little moles who ran fearlessly about and listened as she sang to them.

When the old King saw how much fairer she had made the dreary cell than his palace rooms, gentle thoughts within whispered him to grant her prayer, and let the little Fairy go back to her friends and home; but the Frost-Spirits breathed upon the flowers and bid him see how frail they were, and useless to a King. Then the stern, cold thoughts came back again, and he harshly bid her follow him.

With a sad farewell to her little friends she followed him, and before the throne awaited his command. When the King saw how pale and sad the gentle face had grown, how thin her robe, and weak her wings, and yet how lovingly the golden shadows fell around her and brightened as they lay upon the wand, which, guided by patient love, had made his once desolate home so bright, he could not be cruel to the one who had done so much for him, and in kindly tone he said,—

"Little Fairy, I offer you two things, and you may choose between them. If I will vow never more to harm the flowers you may love, will you go back to your own people and leave me and my Spirits to work our will on all the other flowers that bloom? The earth is broad, and we can find them in any land, then why should you care what happens to their kindred if your own are safe? Will you do this?"

"Ah!" answered Violet sadly, "do you not know that beneath the flowers' bright leaves there beats a little heart that loves and sorrows like our own? And can I, heedless of their beauty, doom them to pain and grief, that I might save my own dear blossoms from the cruel foes to which I leave them? Ah no! sooner would I dwell for ever in your darkest cell, than lose the love of those warm, trusting hearts."

"Then listen," said the King, "to the task I give you. You shall raise up for me a palace fairer than this, and if you can work that miracle I will grant your prayer or lose my kingly crown. And now go forth, and begin your task; my Spirits shall not harm you, and I will wait till it is done before I blight another flower."

Then out into the gardens went Violet with a heavy heart; for she had toiled so long, her strength was nearly gone. But the flowers whispered their gratitude, and folded their leaves as if they blessed her; and when she saw the garden filled with loving friends, who strove to cheer and thank her for her care, courage and strength returned; and raising up thick clouds of mist, that hid her from the wondering flowers, alone and trustingly she began her work.

As time went by, the Frost-King feared the task had been too hard for the Fairy; sounds were heard behind the walls of mist, bright shadows seen to pass within, but the little voice was never heard. Meanwhile the golden light had faded from the garden, the flowers bowed their heads, and all was dark and cold as when the gentle Fairy came.

And to the stern King his home seemed more desolate and sad; for he missed the warm light, the happy flowers, and, more than all, the gay voice and bright face of little Violet. So he wandered through his dreary palace, wondering how he had been content to live before without sunlight and love.

And little Violet was mourned as dead in Fairy-Land, and many tears were shed, for the gentle Fairy was beloved by all, from the Queen down to the humblest flower. Sadly they watched over every bird and blossom which she had loved, and strove to be like her in kindly words and deeds. They wore cypress wreaths, and spoke of her as one whom they should never see again.

Thus they dwelt in deepest sorrow, till one day there came to them an unknown messenger, wrapped in a dark mantle, who looked with wondering eyes on the bright palace, and flower-crowned Elves, who kindly welcomed him, and brought fresh dew and rosy fruit to refresh the weary stranger. Then he told them that he came from the Frost-King, who begged the Queen and all her subjects to come and see the palace little Violet had built; for the veil of mist would soon be withdrawn, and as she could not make a fairer home than the ice-castle, the King wished her kindred near to comfort and to bear her home. And while the Elves wept, he told them how patiently she had toiled, how her fadeless love had made the dark cell bright and beautiful.

These and many other things he told them; for little Violet had won the love of many of the Frost-Spirits, and even when they killed the flowers she had toiled so hard to bring to life and beauty, she spoke gentle words to them, and sought to teach them how beautiful is love. Long stayed the messenger, and deeper grew his wonder that the Fairy could have left so fair a home, to toil in the dreary palace of his cruel master, and suffer cold and weariness, to give life and joy to the weak and sorrowing. When the Elves had promised they would come, he bade farewell to happy Fairy-Land, and flew sadly home.

At last the time arrived, and out in his barren garden, under a canopy of dark clouds, sat the Frost-King before the misty wall, behind which were heard low, sweet sounds, as of rustling trees and warbling birds.

Soon through the air came many-colored troops of Elves. First the Queen, known by the silver lilies on her snowy robe and the bright crown in her hair, beside whom flew a band of Elves in crimson and gold, making sweet music on their flower-trumpets, while all around, with smiling faces and bright eyes, fluttered her loving subjects.

On they came, like a flock of brilliant butterflies, their shining wings and many-colored garments sparkling in the dim air; and soon the leafless trees were gay with living flowers, and their sweet voices filled the gardens with music. Like his subjects, the King looked on the lovely Elves, and no longer wondered that little Violet wept and longed for her home. Darker and more desolate seemed his stately home, and when the Fairies asked for flowers, he felt ashamed that he had none to give them.

369

At length a warm wind swept through the gardens, and the mist-clouds passed away, while in silent wonder looked the Frost-King and the Elves upon the scene before them.

Far as eye could reach were tall green trees, whose drooping boughs made graceful arches, through which the golden light shone softly, making bright shadows on the deep green moss below, where the fairest flowers waved in the cool wind, and sang, in their low, sweet voices, how beautiful is Love.

Flowering vines folded their soft leaves around the trees, making green pillars of their rough trunks. Fountains threw their bright waters to the roof, and flocks of silver-winged birds flew singing among the flowers, or brooded lovingly above their nests. Doves with gentle eyes cooed among the green leaves, snow-white clouds floated in the sunny sky, and the golden light, brighter than before, shone softly down.

Soon through the long aisles came Violet, flowers and green leaves rustling as she passed. On she went to the Frost-King's throne, bearing two crowns, one of sparkling icicles, the other of pure white lilies, and kneeling before him, said,—

"My task is done, and, thanks to the Spirits of earth and air, I have made as fair a home as Elfin hands can form. You must now decide. Will you be King of Flower-Land, and own my gentle kindred for your loving friends? Will you possess unfading peace and joy, and the grateful love of all the green earth's fragrant children? Then take this crown of flowers. But if you can find no pleasure here, go back to your own cold home, and dwell in solitude and darkness, where no ray of sunlight or of joy can enter.

"Send forth your Spirits to carry sorrow and desolation over the happy earth, and win for yourself the fear and hatred of those who would so gladly love and reverence you. Then take this glittering crown, hard and cold as your own heart will be, if you will shut out all that is bright and beautiful. Both are before you. Choose."

The old King looked at the little Fairy, and saw how lovingly the bright shadows gathered round her, as if to shield her from every harm; the timid birds nestled in her bosom, and the flowers grew fairer as she looked upon them; while her gentle friends, with tears in their bright eyes, folded their hands beseechingly, and smiled on her.

Kind thoughts came thronging to his mind, and he turned to look at the two palaces. Violet's, so fair and beautiful, with its rustling trees, calm, sunny skies, and happy birds and flowers, all created by her patient love and care. His own, so cold and dark and dreary, his empty gardens where no flowers could bloom, no green trees dwell, or gay birds sing, all desolate and dim;— and while he gazed, his own Spirits, casting off their dark mantles, knelt before him and besought him not to send them forth to blight the things the gentle Fairies loved so much. "We have served you long and faithfully," said they, "give us now our freedom, that we may learn to be beloved by the sweet flowers we have harmed so long. Grant the little Fairy's prayer; and let her go back to her own dear home. She has taught us that Love is mightier than Fear. Choose the Flower crown, and we will be the truest subjects you have ever had."

Then, amid a burst of wild, sweet music, the Frost-King placed the Flower crown on his head, and knelt to little Violet; while far and near, over the broad green earth, sounded the voices of flowers, singing their thanks to the gentle Fairy, and the summer wind was laden with perfumes, which they sent as tokens of their gratitude; and wherever she went, old trees bent down to fold their slender branches round her, flowers laid their soft faces against her own, and whispered blessings; even the humble moss bent over the little feet, and kissed them as they passed.

The old King, surrounded by the happy Fairies, sat in Violet's lovely home, and watched his icy castle melt away beneath the bright sunlight; while his Spirits, cold and gloomy no longer, danced with the Elves, and waited on their King with loving eagerness. Brighter grew the golden light, gayer sang the birds, and the harmonious voices of grateful flowers, sounding over the earth, carried new joy to all their gentle kindred.

> Brighter shone the golden shadows;
> On the cool wind softly came
> The low, sweet tones of happy flowers,
> Singing little Violet's name.
> 'Mong the green trees was it whispered,
> And the bright waves bore it on
> To the lonely forest flowers,
> Where the glad news had not gone.
>
> Thus the Frost-King lost his kingdom,
> And his power to harm and blight

Violet conquered, and his cold heart
    Warmed with music, love, and light;
And his fair home, once so dreary,
    Gay with lovely Elves and flowers,
Brought a joy that never faded
    Through the long bright summer hours.

Thus, by Violet's magic power,
    All dark shadows passed away,
And o'er the home of happy flowers
    The golden light for ever lay.
Thus the Fairy mission ended,
    And all Flower-Land was taught
The "Power of Love," by gentle deeds
    That little Violet wrought.

Ian, the Soldier's Son

(From *The Orange Fairy Book*)

There dwelt a knight in Grianaig of the land of the West, who had three daughters, and for goodness and beauty they had not their like in all the isles. All the people loved them, and loud was the weeping when one day, as the three maidens sat on the rocks on the edge of the sea, dipping their feet in the water, there arose a great beast from under the waves and swept them away beneath the ocean. And none knew whither they had gone, or how to seek them.

Now there lived in a town a few miles off a soldier who had three sons, fine youths and strong, and the best players at shinny in that country. At Christmastide that year, when families met together and great feasts were held, Ian, the youngest of the three brothers, said:

"Let us have a match at shinny on the lawn of the knight of Grianaig, for his lawn is wider and the grass smoother than ours."

372

But the others answered:

"Nay, for he is in sorrow, and he will think of the games that we have played there when his daughters looked on."

"Let him be pleased or angry as he will," said Ian; "we will drive our ball on his lawn to-day."

And so it was done, and Ian won three games from his brothers. But the knight looked out of his window, and was wroth; and bade his men bring the youths before him. When he stood in his hall and beheld them, his heart was softened somewhat; but his face was angry as he asked:

"Why did you choose to play shinny in front of my castle when you knew full well that the remembrance of my daughters would come back to me? The pain which you have made me suffer you shall suffer also."

"Since we have done you wrong," answered Ian, the youngest, "build us a ship, and we will go and seek your daughters. Let them be to windward, or to leeward, or under the four brown boundaries of the sea, we will find them before a year and a day goes by, and will carry them back to Grianaig."

In seven days the ship was built, and great store of food and wine placed in her. And the three brothers put her head to the sea and sailed away, and in seven days the ship ran herself on to a beach of white sand, and they all went ashore. They had none of them ever seen that land before, and looked about them. Then they saw that, a short way from them, a number of men were working on a rock, with one man standing over them.

"What place is this?" asked the eldest brother. And the man who was standing by made answer:

"This is the place where dwell the three daughters of the knight of Grianaig, who are to be wedded to-morrow to three giants."

"How can we find them?" asked the young man again. And the over-looker answered:

"To reach the daughters of the knight of Grianaig you must get into this basket, and be drawn by a rope up the face of this rock."

"Oh, that is easily done," said the eldest brother, jumping into the basket, which at once began to move—up, and up, and up—till he had gone about half-way, when a fat black raven flew at him and pecked him till he was nearly blind, so that he was forced to go back the way he had come.

After that the second brother got into the creel; but he fared no better, for the raven flew upon him, and he returned as his brother had done.

"Now it is my turn," said Ian. But when he was halfway up the raven set upon him also.

"Quick! quick!" cried Ian to the men who held the rope. "Quick! quick! or I shall be blinded!" And the men pulled with all their might, and in another moment Ian was on top, and the raven behind him.

"Will you give me a piece of tobacco?" asked the raven, who was now quite quiet.

"You rascal! Am I to give you tobacco for trying to peck my eyes out?" answered Ian.

"That was part of my duty," replied the raven; "but give it to me, and I will prove a good friend to you." So Ian broke off a piece of tobacco and gave it to him. The raven hid it under his wing, and then went on: "Now I will take you to the house of the big giant, where the knight's daughter sits sewing, sewing, till even her thimble is wet with tears." And the raven hopped before him till they reached a large house, the door of which stood open. They entered and passed through one hall after the other, until they found the knight's daughter, as the bird had said.

"What brought you here?" asked she. And Ian made answer:

"Why may I not go where you can go?"

"I was brought hither by a giant," replied she.

"I know that," said Ian; "but tell me where the giant is, that I may find him."

"He is on the hunting hill," answered she; "and nought will bring him home save a shake of the iron chain which hangs outside the gate. But, there, neither to leeward, nor to windward, nor in the four brown boundaries of the sea, is there any man that can hold battle against him, save only Ian, the soldier's son, and he is now but sixteen years old, and how shall he stand against the giant?"

"In the land whence I have come there are many men with the strength of Ian," answered he. And he went outside and pulled at the chain, but he could not move it, and fell on to his knees. At that he rose swiftly, and gathering up his strength, he seized the chain, and this time he shook it so that the link broke. And the giant heard it on the hunting hill, and lifted his head, thinking—

"It sounds like the noise of Ian, the soldier's son," said he; "but as yet he is only sixteen years old. Still, I had better look to it." And home he came.

"Are you Ian, the soldier's son?" he asked, as he entered the castle.

374

"No, of a surety," answered the youth, who had no wish that they should know him.

"Then who are you in the leeward, or in the windward, or in the four brown boundaries of the sea, who are able to move my battle-chain?"

"That will be plain to you after wrestling with me as I wrestle with my mother. And one time she got the better of me, and two times she did not."

So they wrestled, and twisted and strove with each other till the giant forced Ian to his knee.

"You are the stronger," said Ian; and the giant answered:

"All men know that!" And they took hold of each other once more, and at last Ian threw the giant, and wished that the raven were there to help him. No sooner had he wished his wish than the raven came.

"Put your hand under my right wing and you will find a knife sharp enough to take off his head," said the raven. And the knife was so sharp that it cut off the giant's head with a blow.

"Now go and tell the daughter of the knight of Grianaig; but take heed lest you listen to her words, and promise to go no further, for she will seek to help you. Instead, seek the middle daughter, and when you have found her, you shall give me a piece of tobacco for reward."

"Well have you earned the half of all I have," answered Ian. But the raven shook his head.

"You know only what has passed, and nothing of what lies before. If you would not fail, wash yourself in clean water, and take balsam from a vessel on top of the door, and rub it over your body, and to-morrow you will be as strong as many men, and I will lead you to the dwelling of the middle one."

Ian did as the raven bade him, and in spite of the eldest daughter's entreaties, he set out to seek her next sister. He found her where she was seated sewing, her very thimble wet from the tears which she had shed.

"What brought you here?" asked the second sister.

"Why may I not go where you can go?" answered he; "and why are you weeping?"

"Because in one day I shall be married to the giant who is on the hunting hill."

"How can I get him home?" asked Ian.

"Nought will bring him but a shake of that iron chain which hangs outside the gate. But there is neither to leeward, nor to westward, nor in the four brown boundaries of the sea, any man that can hold battle with him, save Ian, the soldier's son, and he is now but sixteen years of age."

"In the land whence I have come there are many men with the strength of Ian," said he. And he went outside and pulled at the chain, but he could not move it, and fell on his knees. At that he rose to his feet, and gathering up his strength mightily, he seized the chain, and this time he shook it so that three links broke. And the second giant heard it on the hunting hill, and lifted his head, thinking—

"It sounds like the noise of Ian, the soldier's son," said he; "but as yet he is only sixteen years old. Still, I had better look to it." And home he came.

"Are you Ian, the soldier's son?" he asked, as he entered the castle.

"No, of a surety," answered Ian, who had no wish that this giant should know him either; "but I will wrestle with you as if I were he."

Then they seized each other by the shoulder, and the giant threw him on his two knees. "You are the stronger," cried Ian; "but I am not beaten yet." And rising to his feet, he threw his arms round the giant.

Backwards and forwards they swayed, and first one was uppermost and then the other; but at length Ian worked his leg round the giant's and threw him to the ground. Then he called to the raven, and the raven came flapping towards him, and said: "Put your hand under my right wing, and you will find there a knife sharp enough to take off his head." And sharp indeed it was, for with a single blow, the giant's head rolled from his body.

"Now wash yourself with warm water, and rub yourself over with oil of balsam, and to-morrow you will be as strong as many men. But beware of the words of the knight's daughter, for she is cunning, and will try to keep you at her side. So farewell; but first give me a piece of tobacco."

"That I will gladly," answered Ian breaking off a large bit.

He washed and rubbed himself that night, as the raven had told him, and the next morning he entered the chamber where the knight's daughter was sitting.

"Abide here with me," she said, "and be my husband. There is silver and gold in plenty in the castle." But he took no heed, and went on his way till he reached the castle where the knight's youngest daughter was sewing in the hall. And tears dropped from her eyes on to her thimble.

"What brought you here?" asked she. And Ian made answer:

"Why may I not go where you can go?"

"I was brought hither by a giant."

"I know full well," said he.

"Are you Ian, the soldier's son?" asked she again. And again he answered:

"Yes, I am; but tell me, why are you weeping?"

"To-morrow the giant will return from the hunting hill, and I must marry him," she sobbed. And Ian took no heed, and only said: "How can I bring him home?"

"Shake the iron chain that hangs outside the gate."

And Ian went out, and gave such a pull to the chain that he fell down at full length from the force of the shake. But in a moment he was on his feet again, and seized the chain with so much strength that four links came off in his hand. And the giant heard him in the hunting hill, as he was putting the game he had killed into a bag.

"In the leeward, or the windward, or in the four brown boundaries of the sea, there is none who could give my chain a shake save only Ian, the soldier's son. And if he has reached me, then he has left my two brothers dead behind him." With that he strode back to the castle, the earth trembling under him as he went.

"Are you Ian, the soldier's son?" asked he. And the youth answered:

"No, of a surety."

"Then who are you in the leeward, or the windward, or in the four brown boundaries of the sea, who are able to shake my battle chain? There is only Ian, the soldier's son, who can do this, and he is but now sixteen years old.

"I will show you who I am when you have wrestled with me," said Ian. And they threw their arms round each other, and the giant forced Ian on to his knees; but in a moment he was up again, and crooking his leg round the shoulders of the giant, he threw him heavily to the ground. "Stumpy black raven, come quick!" cried he; and the raven came, and beat the giant about the head with his wings, so that he could not get up. Then he bade Ian take out a sharp knife from under his feathers, which he carried with him for cutting berries, and Ian smote off the giant's head with it. And so sharp was that knife that, with one blow, the giant's head rolled on the ground.

"Rest now this night also," said the raven, "and to-morrow you shall take the knight's three daughters to the edge of the rock that leads to the lower world. But take heed to go down first yourself, and let them follow after you. And before I go you shall give me a piece of tobacco."

"Take it all," answered Ian, "for well have you earned it."

"No; give me but a piece. You know what is behind you, but you have no knowledge of what is before you." And picking up the tobacco in his beak, the raven flew away.

So the next morning the knight's youngest daughter loaded asses with all the silver and gold to be found in the castle, and she set out with Ian the soldier's son for the house where her second sister was waiting to see what would befall. She also had asses laden with precious things to carry away, and so had the eldest sister, when they reached the castle where she had been kept a prisoner. Together they all rode to the edge of the rock, and then Ian lay down and shouted, and the basket was drawn up, and in it they got one by one, and were let down to the bottom. When the last one was gone, Ian should have gone also, and left the three sisters to come after him; but he had forgotten the raven's warning, and bade them go first, lest some accident should happen. Only, he begged the youngest sister to let him keep the little gold cap which, like the others, she wore on her head; and then he helped them, each in her turn, into the basket.

Long he waited, but wait as he might, the basket never came back, for in their joy at being free the knight's daughters had forgotten all about Ian, and had set sail in the ship that had brought him and his brothers to the land of Grianaig.

At last he began to understand what had happened to him, and while he was taking counsel with himself what had best be done, the raven came to him.

"You did not heed my words," he said gravely.

"No, I did not, and therefore am I here," answered Ian, bowing his head.

"The past cannot be undone," went on the raven. "He that will not take counsel will take combat. This night, you will sleep in the giant's castle. And now you shall give me a piece of tobacco."

"I will. But, I pray you, stay in the castle with me."

"That I may not do, but on the morrow I will come."

And on the morrow he did, and he bade Ian go to the giant's stable where stood a horse to whom it mattered nothing if she journeyed over land or sea.

"But be careful," he added, "how you enter the stable, for the door swings without ceasing to and fro, and if it touches you, it will cause you to cry out. I will go first and show you the way."

"Go," said Ian. And the raven gave a bob and a hop, and thought he was quite safe, but the door slammed on a feather of his tail, and he screamed loudly.

Then Ian took a run backwards, and a run forwards, and made a spring; but the door caught one of his feet, and he fell fainting on the stable floor. Quickly the raven pounced on him, and picked him up in his beak and claws, and carried him back to the castle, where he laid ointments on his foot till it was as well as ever it was.

"Now come out to walk," said the raven, "but take heed that you wonder not at aught you may behold; neither shall you touch anything. And, first, give me a piece of tobacco."

Many strange things did Ian behold in that island, more than he had thought for. In a glen lay three heroes stretched on their backs, done to death by three spears that still stuck in their breasts. But he kept his counsel and spake nothing, only he pulled out the spears, and the men sat up and said:

"You are Ian the soldier's son, and a spell is laid upon you to travel in our company, to the cave of the black fisherman."

So together they went till they reached the cave, and one of the men entered, to see what should be found there. And he beheld a hag, horrible to look upon, seated on a rock, and before he could speak, she struck him with her club, and changed him into a stone; and in like manner she dealt with the other three. At the last Ian entered.

"These men are under spells," said the witch, "and alive they can never be till you have anointed them with the water which you must fetch from the island of Big Women. See that you do not tarry." And Ian turned away with a sinking heart, for he would fain have followed the youngest daughter of the knight of Grianaig.

"You did not obey my counsel," said the raven, hopping towards him, "and so trouble has come upon you. But sleep now, and to-morrow you shall mount the horse which is in the giant's stable, that can gallop over sea and land. When you reach the island of Big Women, sixteen boys will come to meet you, and will offer the horse food, and wish to take her saddle and bridle from her. But see that they touch her not, and give her food yourself, and yourself lead her into the stable, and shut the door. And be sure that for every turn of the lock given by the sixteen stable lads you give one. And now you shall break me off a piece of tobacco."

The next morning Ian arose, and led the horse from the stable, without the door hurting him, and he rode across the sea to the island of the Big Women, where the sixteen stable lads met him, and each one offered to take his horse, and to feed her, and to put her into the stable. But Ian only answered:

"I myself will put her in and will see to her." And thus he did. And while he was rubbing her sides the horse said to him:

"Every kind of drink will they offer you, but see you take none, save whey and water only." And so it fell out; and when the sixteen stable-boys saw that he would drink nothing, they drank it all themselves, and one by one lay stretched around the board.

Then Ian felt pleased in his heart that he had withstood their fair words, and he forgot the counsel that the horse had likewise given him saying:

"Beware lest you fall asleep, and let slip the chance of getting home again"; for while the lads were sleeping sweet music reached his ears, and he slept also.

When this came to pass the steed broke through the stable door, and kicked him and woke him roughly.

"You did not heed my counsel," said she; "and who knows if it is not too late to win over the sea? But first take that sword which hangs on the wall, and cut off the heads of the sixteen grooms."

Filled with shame at being once more proved heedless, Ian arose and did as the horse bade him. Then he ran to the well and poured some of the water into a leather bottle, and jumping on the horse's back rode over the sea to the island where the raven was waiting for him.

"Lead the horse into the stable," said the raven, "and lie down yourself to sleep, for to-morrow you must make the heroes to live again, and must slay the hag. And have a care not to be so foolish to-morrow as you were to-day."

"Stay with me for company," begged Ian; but the raven shook his head, and flew away.

In the morning Ian awoke, and hastened to the cave where the old hag was sitting, and he struck her dead as she was, before she could cast spells on him. Next he sprinkled the water over the heroes, who came to life again, and together they all journeyed to the other side of the island, and there the raven met them.

"At last you have followed the counsel that was given you," said the raven; "and now, having learned wisdom, you may go home again to Grianaig.

There you will find that the knight's two eldest daughters are to be wedded this day to your two brothers, and the youngest to the chief of the men at the rock. But her gold cap you shall give to me and, if you want it, you have only to think of me and I will bring it to you. And one more warning I give you. If anyone asks you whence you came, answer that you have come from behind you; and if anyone asks you whither you are going, say that you are going before you."

So Ian mounted the horse and set her face to the sea and her back to the shore, and she was off, away and away till she reached the church of Grianaig, and there, in a field of grass, beside a well of water, he leaped down from his saddle.

"Now," the horse said to him, "draw your sword and cut off my head." But Ian answered:

"Poor thanks would that be for all the help I have had from you."

"It is the only way that I can free myself from the spells that were laid by the giants on me and the raven; for I was a girl and he was a youth wooing me! So have no fears, but do as I have said."

Then Ian drew his sword as she bade him, and cut off her head, and went on his way without looking backwards. As he walked he saw a woman standing at her house door. She asked him whence he had come, and he answered as the raven had told him, that he came from behind. Next she inquired whither he was going, and this time he made reply that he was going on before him, but that he was thirsty and would like a drink.

"You are an impudent fellow," said the woman; "but you shall have a drink." And she gave him some milk, which was all she had till her husband came home.

"Where is your husband?" asked Ian, and the woman answered him:

"He is at the knight's castle trying to fashion gold and silver into a cap for the youngest daughter, like unto the caps that her sisters wear, such as are not to be found in all this land. But, see, he is returning; and now we shall hear how he has sped."

At that the man entered the gate, and beholding a strange youth, he said to him: "What is your trade, boy?"

"I am a smith," replied Ian. And the man answered:

"Good luck has befallen me, then, for you can help me to make a cap for the knight's daughter."

"You cannot make that cap, and you know it," said Ian.

"Well, I must try," replied the man, "or I shall be hanged on a tree; so it were a good deed to help me."

"I will help you if I can," said Ian; "but keep the gold and silver for yourself, and lock me into the smithy to-night, and I will work my spells." So the man, wondering to himself, locked him in.

As soon as the key was turned in the lock Ian wished for the raven, and the raven came to him, carrying the cap in his mouth.

"Now take my head off," said the raven. But Ian answered:

"Poor thanks were that for all the help you have given me."

"It is the only thanks you can give me," said the raven, "for I was a youth like yourself before spells were laid on me."

Then Ian drew his sword and cut off the head of the raven, and shut his eyes so that he might see nothing. After that he lay down and slept till morning dawned, and the man came and unlocked the door and shook the sleeper.

"Here is the cap," said Ian drowsily, drawing it from under his pillow. And he fell asleep again directly.

The sun was high in the heavens when he woke again, and this time he beheld a tall, brown-haired youth standing by him.

"I am the raven," said the youth, "and the spells are broken. But now get up and come with me."

Then they two went together to the place where Ian had left the dead horse; but no horse was there now, only a beautiful maiden.

"I am the horse," she said, "and the spells are broken"; and she and the youth went away together.

In the meantime the smith had carried the cap to the castle, and bade a servant belonging to the knight's youngest daughter bear it to her mistress. But when the girl's eyes fell on it, she cried out:

"He speaks false; and if he does not bring me the man who really made the cap I will hang him on the tree beside my window."

The servant was filled with fear at her words, and hastened and told the smith, who ran as fast as he could to seek for Ian. And when he found him and brought him into the castle, the girl was first struck dumb with joy; then she declared that she would marry nobody else. At this some one fetched to her the knight of Grianaig, and when Ian had told his tale, he vowed that the maiden was right, and that his elder daughters should never wed with men who had not only taken glory to themselves which did not belong to them, but had left the real doer of the deeds to his fate.

And the wedding guests said that the knight had spoken well; and the two elder brothers were fain to leave the country, for no one would hold converse with them.

The Elves

THE BROTHERS GRIMM

A shoemaker, by no fault of his own, had become so poor that at last he had nothing left but leather for one pair of shoes. So in the evening, he cut out the shoes which he wished to begin to make the next morning, and as he had a good conscience, he lay down quietly in his bed, commended himself to God, and fell asleep.

In the morning, after he had said his prayers, and was just going to sit down to work, the two shoes stood quite finished on his table. He was astounded, and knew not what to say to it. He took the shoes in his hands to observe them closer, and they were so neatly made that there was not one bad stitch in them, just as if they were intended as a masterpiece.

Soon after, a buyer came in, and as the shoes pleased him so well, he paid more for them than was customary, and, with the money, the shoemaker was able to purchase leather for two pairs of shoes. He cut them out at night, and next morning was about to set to work with fresh courage; but he had no need to do so, for, when he got up, they were already made, and buyers also were not wanting, who gave him money enough to buy leather for four pairs of shoes. The following morning, too, he found the four pairs made; and so it went on constantly, what he cut out in the evening was finished by the morning, so that he soon had his honest independence again, and at last became a wealthy man.

Now it befell that one evening not long before Christmas, when the man had been cutting out, he said to his wife, before going to bed, "What think you if we were to stay up to-night to see who it is that lends us this helping hand?"

The woman liked the idea, and lighted a candle, and then they hid themselves in a corner of the room, behind some clothes which were hanging up there, and watched. When it was midnight, two pretty little naked men came, sat down by the shoemaker's table, took all the work which was cut out before them and began to stitch, and sew, and hammer so skillfully and so quickly with their little fingers that the shoemaker could not turn away his eyes for astonishment. They did not stop until all was done, and stood finished on the table, and they ran quickly away.

Next morning the woman said, "The little men have made us rich, and we really must show that we are grateful for it. They run about so, and have nothing on, and must be cold. I'll tell thee what I'll do: I will make them little shirts, and coats, and vests, and trousers, and knit both of them a pair of stockings, and do thou, too, make them two little pairs of shoes."

The man said, "I shall be very glad to do it"; and one night, when everything was ready, they laid their presents all together on the table instead of the cut-out work, and then concealed themselves to see how the little men would behave. At midnight they came bounding in, and wanted to get to work at once, but as they did not find any leather cut out, but only the pretty little articles of clothing, they were at first astonished, and then they showed intense delight. They dressed themselves with the greatest rapidity, putting the pretty clothes on, and singing,

> Now we are boys so fine to see,
> Why should we longer cobblers be?

Then they danced and skipped and leapt over chairs and benches. At last they danced out of doors.

From that time forth they came no more, but as long as the shoemaker lived all went well with him, and all his undertakings prospered.

Well Done, Ill Paid

Peter Christen Asbjørnsen

Once upon a time there was a man who was going to the forest for firewood. On his way he met a bear.

"Give me your horse, or I will kill all your sheep next summer!" said the bear.

"Oh dear! oh dear!" said the man, "there is not a chip of wood in the house. You must let me drive home a cartload of wood, or we shall be frozen to death; but I will come back with the horse to-morrow for you."

Well, that would do; but it was understood that if he did not return he would lose all his sheep during the summer. The man loaded his sledge with wood, and drove homewards; but he was not very pleased with the arrangement he had made, you can imagine. On the way he met a fox.

"Why do you look so sad?" asked the fox.

"Oh, I met a bear up yonder," said the man, "and I had to promise that at this time to-morrow he should have my horse. If he does not get it, he said he would tear all my sheep to pieces next summer."

"Oh, nothing worse than that?" said the fox. "If you will give me your fattest ram I will soon get you out of your difficulty."

The man promised this, and said he would be sure to keep his word.

"When you come to the bear to-morrow with the horse," said the fox, "I will be up in the mountain, and will shout out to you. When the bear asks who it is, you must say it is Peter, the huntsman, who is the finest shot in the world. Afterwards you must use your own wits."

The next day the man set out, and when he met the bear some one up in the mountain began shouting.

"Whst! what's that?" said the bear.

"Oh, that's Peter, the huntsman. He is the finest shot in the world," said the man. "I know him by his voice."

"Have you seen any bear about here, Erik?" came from the wood.

"Say no!" said the bear.

"No, I have not seen any bear," said Erik.

385

"What's that standing by your sledge then?" came from the wood.

"Say it is the root of an old tree," whispered the bear.

"Oh, it's only the root of an old tree," said Erik.

"Such roots we generally load our sledges with," came from the wood; "if you are not able to do so, I will come and help you."

"Say you can do it yourself, and put me on the sledge."

"No, thanks, I can manage by myself," said the man, and rolled the bear on to the sledge.

"Such roots we generally tie down," came from the wood; "do you want any help?"

"Say you can do it yourself, and tie me down," said the bear.

"No, thanks, I can do it," said Erik, and began tying down the bear with all the ropes he had, till the bear could not move a paw.

"Such roots we generally strike an axe into, when we have tied it down," came from the wood, "for then one can steer the sledge better down the big hills."

"Pretend to strike the axe into me," whispered the bear.

But the man took the axe and split the skull of the bear, who was killed on the spot. So Erik and the fox became good friends and got on well together, but when they came to the farm, the fox said:

"I should like to go in with you, but I don't like your dogs. I will wait here till you come with the ram. But remember to pick me out one that is very fat."

Yes, the man would do so, and thanked the fox besides for his help. When he had put the horse into the stable he went across to the sheep-pen.

"Where are you going?" asked his wife.

"Oh, I am only going over to the sheep-pen to fetch a fat ram for that good fox who saved our horse," said the man, "as I have promised him one."

"Why on earth give that thief of a fox any ram?" said the woman. "We have got the horse quite safe and the bear besides, and the fox has stolen more geese from us than the ram is worth; or, if he hasn't already taken them, he is sure to do so sometime. No, take the most savage pair of those dogs of yours and let loose on him, then perhaps we'll get rid of that thieving old rascal," said the woman.

The man thought this was sensible advice and took two of his savage red dogs, put them in a bag and set out with them.

"Have you got the ram?" said the fox.

"Yes, come and fetch it," said the man, undoing the string round the bag and setting the dogs at the fox.

"Ugh!" said the fox bounding away, "the old saying, 'Well done, ill paid' is only too true; and now I find it is also true that one's relations are one's worst enemies," said he, as he saw the red dogs at his heels.

The Ice Maiden

Hans Christian Andersen

Little Rudy

Let us visit Switzerland and wander through that glorious mountain-land where the forests climb up the steep rocky walls; let us ascend to the dazzling snow-fields above, and descend again to the green valleys beneath, through which streams and rivulets rush along as hastily as if they could not reach the sea and disappear fast enough. The sun sends its scorching rays into the deep valley, and also falls upon the heavy masses of snow up above, so that in the course of years the latter melt into glimmering blocks of ice, and are formed into rolling avalanches and piled-up glaciers. Two such glaciers lie in the broad ravines below the "Schreckhorn" and the "Wetterhorn," near the little mountain town of Grindelwald; they are wonderful to behold, and for that reason they attract every summer many strangers from all parts of the world. They come across the high snow-covered mountains, and also through the deep valleys, and then they have to ascend for several hours; as they ascend, the valley sinks deeper and deeper, until, upon looking down into it, it appears as if viewed from a balloon. Above them the thick clouds often hang like a heavy veil around the mountain peaks, whilst down in the valley where numerous brown wooden houses lie scattered about, there may still be a stray sunbeam, bringing into brilliant relief a patch of green, as if it were transparent. Down below the waters go roaring along, dashing themselves into foam, while up above they ripple and purl, looking like silver ribbons streaming down the rocks.

On both sides of the way which leads up to the mountain there are wooden houses. Every house has its potato-garden, and this is indispensable, for there are many mouths to feed in the cottages, children, who are always ready for their meals, being plentiful. They pop up in all directions and crowd round the traveler, whether he is on foot or driving; the whole troop of children carry on a trade, offering for sale pretty little carved houses, models of those that are built here in the mountains. Whether there be rain or sunshine, the children are there with their wares.

Some twenty years ago there often stood here, but always at a little distance from the other children, a little boy who was also desirous of doing some business. He used to stand there looking very grave and holding his box of carved goods tightly with both hands as if he really had no wish to give it up; but it was this very gravity and the fact of his being such a very little fellow that led people to notice him, call him up to them, and buy most from him—he himself did not know why. An hour's walk higher up the mountain lived his grandfather who cut out the pretty little houses, and there in the old man's room stood a great cupboard crowded with all kinds of carved things, nut-crackers, knives and forks, boxes with leaf-work and leaping chamois—in fact, a haven of delight for any child. But the boy— Rudy was his name—looked with greater pleasure and longing at the old gun which hung down from one of the beams in the roof, and which his grandfather had promised him he should one day have, when he was tall and strong enough to use it.

Small as he was, the boy had to mind the goats, and if ever there was a good goatherd who knew how to climb, it was Rudy; he even clambered a little higher than the goats, for he loved to take the birds' nests from the tree-tops. He was bold and daring, but he was only seen to smile when he stood near a roaring waterfall, or heard the thunder of a rolling avalanche. He never played with the other children; he only came near them when his grandfather sent him down the mountain to sell things. And Rudy did not care particularly about selling; he preferred climbing about alone among the mountains, or sitting with his grandfather and hearing him tell of the olden days, and of the people in the village of Meiringen near by, where he had been born. The old man said that the race who lived had not always been there; that they were wanderers, and had come from the far north, where their ancestors had lived and had been called Swedes. Rudy was very proud of knowing this, but he also learned a good deal from other sources, such as those members of the family who belonged to the animal world.

There was a large dog, called Ajola, who had belonged to Rudy's father, and there was also a tom-cat. The tom-cat especially Rudy held in high honor, for he had learnt climbing from him.

"Come out upon the roof with me!" the cat had said, very distinctly and intelligibly too; for young children, before they are able to speak, understand fowls and ducks very well. Cats and dogs then speak as intelligibly as our parents, but we have to be very young; at that age even grandfather's stick neighs and becomes a whole horse with head, legs, and tail. Some children keep this intelligence much longer than others, and of these it is said that they are very backward, and have remained children very long. That's what people say!

"Come out upon the roof with me, Rudy!" was about the first thing that the cat had said, and Rudy had understood. "All that people say about falling down is mere fancy; you will not fall unless you are afraid. Come on! Put one of your paws here, and the other there; then feel with your fore-paws. You must use your eyes and be active in your limbs. If you come to a hole, jump and hold tight; that's what I do!"

And so little Rudy did too; that is why he so often sat on the shelving roof with the tom-cat and up in the tree-tops, and even up on the high ledges of the rocks where the cat could not follow him.

"Higher up!" said trees and bushes. "Look how we climb, how high we reach, and how we hold fast even to the very narrowest ledges."

Rudy reached the mountain-tops even before the sun touched them, and there he drank his morning draft, the fresh invigorating mountain air—the draft that only the good God knows how to prepare, and of which mankind can only read the recipe, in which is included fresh fragrance from the mountain herbs, and from the mint and thyme of the valley. All that is heavy is absorbed by the lowering clouds, and these being diffused over the pine-tops by the wind, the spirit of the fragrance becomes air, light and ever fresh; this was Rudy's morning draft.

The sunbeams—those daughters of the sun who bring blessings with them—kissed his cheeks, while Giddiness stood on the watch without daring to approach him: the swallows from his-grandfather's house, upon which there were no less than seven nests, flew up to him and the goats, singing: "We and you! You and we!" They brought greetings from home, from his grandfather, and even from the two hens, the only birds in the house, with which, however, Rudy was never intimate.

Young as he was he had traveled, and no short journey either for such a little fellow. He was born in the Canton of Valais and had been carried across the mountains; he had recently walked as far as the "Staubbach," which flutters in the wind like a silver veil before the snow-clad dazzling white mountain of the Jungfrau. He had also been to the great glaciers at Grindelwald; but that was a sad story, for his mother had found her death there, and there, his grandfather used to say, little Rudy had lost all his childish merriment. "Before the boy was a year old, he laughed more than he cried," his mother had written, "but from the time that he fell into the crevasse in the ice, a great change had come over him." His grandfather seldom spoke about the matter, but it was known all over the mountain.

Rudy's father had been a postillion, and the great dog which was now in his grandfather's hut had always accompanied him in his journeys across the Simplon down to the Lake of Geneva. Some relatives of Rudy on his father's side still lived in the Rhone valley, in the Canton Valais; his uncle was a famous chamois-hunter and a well-known Alpine guide. Rudy was only a year old when he lost his father, and his mother now longed to return with her child to her relatives in the Bernese Oberland. Her father lived a few hours' journey from Grindelwald; he was a wood-carver, and his trade enabled him to live comfortably.

In the month of June she set out homewards with her child, in the company of two chamois hunters, across the Gemmi to reach Grindelwald. They had already accomplished the greater part of the journey and had crossed the high ridges and come into the snow-field; already they perceived their native valley with all its well-known raftered houses, and had now only to cross one great glacier. The snow had recently fallen and hid a crevasse; not one of those, it is true, which reach down to the abyss below where the water rushed along, but still far deeper than a man's height. The young woman, who was carrying her child, slipped, sank down and disappeared; not a cry, not a groan was heard—nothing but the weeping of the babe.

More than an hour passed before her two companions obtained some ropes and poles from the nearest hut to aid them in their efforts, and after much exertion two dead bodies, as they appeared to be, were brought up out of the crevasse. Every means was employed to bring them back to life; with the child they were successful, but not with the mother, and so the old grand-father received into his house only his daughter's son—an orphan, the boy who laughed more than he cried. It seemed, however, as if the laughing had gone out of him, and the change must have taken place in the crevasse, in the cold unearthly ice-world, where the souls of the condemned are imprisoned until the Day of Judgment, as the Swiss peasant believes.

A rushing torrent, turned to ice and pressed as it were into blocks of green crystal, lies the glacier there, one great block of ice overtopping the other; and in the depths beneath the stream of melted ice and snow tears along where deep hollows and immense crevasses yawn. It is a marvelous palace of crystal, and in it lives the Ice Maiden, the queen of the glaciers. She, who slays and crushes, is half a child of the air, half the mighty ruler of the stream: therefore is she able to speed, with the swiftness of the chamois, to the highest peaks of the snow-clad mountains, where the bold climber has first to cut footsteps for himself in the ice. She sails upon a thin pine twig down the rushing stream, bounding from one rock to the other, with her long snow-white hair fluttering about her, and her bluish-green robe shining like the water in the deep Swiss lakes.

"To crush and to hold fast is in my power!" she cries. "A beautiful boy they stole from me—a boy whom I had kissed, but not kissed to death. He is again among the living; he tends the goats upon the mountain, climbing upwards, ever higher, away from others, but not from me. He is mine—I will have him!"

She gave the Spirit of Giddiness orders to act for her, for it was summer-time and too hot for the Ice Maiden in the green valley where the mint grows; so the Spirit—or rather, Spirits, for there were three of them—went up hill and down dale. This Spirit has many brothers, a whole troop of them, and the Ice-maiden chose the strongest among the many who exercise their power both within and without. They sit on the railings of steps and towers, they run like squirrels along the brink of the precipice, and jumping over parapets and bridges they tread the air as the swimmer does the water, luring their victims onwards and down into the abyss. The Spirit of Giddiness and the Ice Maiden both grasp after mankind as the polypus grasps after all that comes near it. The Spirit was to seize Rudy.

"Seize him, indeed!" said the Spirit; "I can't do it. That monster of a cat has taught him to climb. This boy has a power of his own that keeps me at a distance, and I am unable to get at him when he hangs from a branch over an abyss; however much I should like to tickle the soles of his feet, or send him flying head over heels through the air, I cannot manage it."

"We'll manage it some day," said the Ice Maiden. "You or I! I! I!"

"No, no!" rang out all around her, like a mountain echo of the pealing of the church bells; but it was the chant of a harmonious choir of other spirits of Nature—kind, loving spirits, the daughters of the rays of the sun. These encamp every evening in a circle around the mountain peaks, and spread out their rose-colored wings which, becoming redder and redder with the sinking sun, cast a glow over the lofty peaks, which is called by men the Alpine glow. When the sun has sunk they retire into the mountain tops, right into the white snow, where they slumber till the sun rises, when they again come forth. They are particularly fond of flowers, butterflies, and people, and among the latter they had taken a great fancy to Rudy.

"You shall not catch him! You shall not have him!" they said.

"I have caught bigger and stronger ones than he," said the Ice Maiden.

Then the daughters of the sun sang a song of the wanderer whose cloak the storm had torn away; the wind had taken the covering but not the man. "You can seize him, but you cannot hold him, you children of strength; he is stronger, more ethereal than even we. He ascends higher than our mother the sun; he possesses the magic word that binds winds and waters, and that compels them to serve and to obey him. You loosen the heavy oppressive weight, and he soars higher."

Glorious were the tones of the bell-like choir.

Every morning the sun's rays came through the one little window in the grandfather's hut, and shone upon the sleeping child. The daughters of the sun's rays kissed him, for they wished to thaw, melt, and dispel the icy kisses that the queenly maiden of the glaciers had given him as he lay in his dead mother's lap in the deep crevasse, and from which he had been saved as by a miracle.

The Journey to the New Home

Rudy was now eight years old. His uncle, who lived on the other side of the mountains, in the Rhone valley, wished to have the boy with him, so that he might learn something and get on better. His grandfather also thought this was for the best, and let him go.

So Rudy took his departure. Besides his grandfather there were several others to whom he had to bid farewell. First there was Ajola, the old dog.

"Your father was the postillion and I was the post-dog," said Ajola. "We used to travel backwards and forwards across the mountains, and I know both the men and the dogs on the other side. Talking was never much in my line, but now that we shall probably not be able to exchange a word for a long time, I will say a little more than usual. I will tell you a story that has been running in my head a long time and that I have ruminated upon at some length; I don't understand it, and you will not understand it either, but that doesn't matter. But this much I have made out of it: things are not dealt out quite equally in this world, either to dogs or to mankind. We are not all born to lie in people's laps or to drink milk. I have not been used to it; but I have seen a little dog traveling in a post-chaise and occupying the place of a human being. The lady who was his mistress, or whose master he was, carried a feeding-bottle full of milk with her, from which she fed the dog; she also gave him some sweets, but as he only sniffed at them and would not eat them, she gobbled them up herself. I was running along in the mud at the side of the carriage as hungry as a dog can be, and chewing the cud of my own thoughts, which seemed to tell me that things were not quite as they should be—but there is much that is not. Would you like to lie in laps and drive in carriages? I wish it you from the bottom of my heart. But you can't bring it about yourself; I have not been able to do so either by barking or whining."

These were Ajola's words, and Rudy threw his arms round his neck and kissed him heartily on his wet nose; then he took the cat in his arms, but he struggled to be free.

"You are getting too strong for me, and I don't want to use my claws against you. Climb away over the mountains, for I have taught you how! But never imagine that it is possible to fall; in this way you will always have a sure footing."

With that the cat sprang away, for he did not want Rudy to read in his eyes how sorry he was.

The hens were strutting about in the hut; one of them had lost its tail, a traveler who pretended to be a sportsman, having shot it off, mistaking the poor fowl for a bird of prey.

"Rudy is going over the hills!" said one of them.

"He is in a great hurry, too," said the other, "and I'm not fond of saying good-bye"; and with that they both hopped away.

He also bade farewell to the goats, who bleated and wanted to follow him; it was very touching.

Two able guides of the district, who were going across the mountains near the Gemmi, took Rudy with them on foot. It was a stiff journey for such a little fellow, but he was very strong, and his courage did not sink.

The swallows flew a little way with them. "We and you! You and we!" they sang. The road led across the rushing Lütschine, which falls from the dark clefts of the Grindelwald glacier in numerous small streams. The trunks of fallen trees and blocks of stone serve here as bridges. Having reached the alderwood on the other side, they began to ascend the mountain where the glacier had loosened itself from the side of the rock, and now they marched along the glacier over blocks of ice and round them. Sometimes Rudy went on hands and knees, sometimes upright; his eyes sparkled with joy, and he trod so firmly in his iron-tipped mountain shoes that it seemed as if he wished to leave behind him the impression of each footstep. The black earth which the mountain stream had cast upon the glacier gave it the appearance of being somewhat thawed, but still the bluish-green glassy ice shone through. They had to go round the little pools which had formed themselves, dammed up by blocks of ice, and in making one of these circuits they came near a great boulder which lay rocking on the edge of a crevasse in the ice; the stone lost its balance and, rolling down, the echo of its fall thundered up out of the deep abyss of the glacier.

The way continued to lead uphill; the glacier itself extended upwards like a stream covered with blocks of ice heaped up one on the other, and wedged in between two steep walls of rock. Rudy thought for a moment how he had lain with his mother deep down in one of these heart-chilling crevasses, as he had been told; but such thoughts were soon banished, and the story left no more impression upon him than the many others he had been told. Now and then, when the men thought the way was somewhat too difficult for the lad, they lent him a hand, but he did not tire, and on the slippery ice he stood as firmly as a chamois. They now came to rocky ground, sometimes striding between bare cliffs, sometimes passing between fir trees and out again into the green meadows, always through ever-changing scenery. All around them towered the snow-clad mountains, whose names—the "Jungfrau," the "Monk," and the "Eiger"—were known not only to Rudy but to every child in the country. Rudy had never been up so high before, and had never trodden the wide-spreading sea of snow which now lay before him with its motionless billows, from which the wind occasionally carried away a snow-flake as it blows along the foam from the waves of the sea. The glaciers stand here hand-in-hand, as it were; each of them is a palace of crystal for the Ice Maiden, whose power and will it is to seize and to bury. The sun shone warm and the snow glittered as if it had been strewn with sparkling bluish-white diamonds. Innumerable insects, especially butterflies and bees, lay dead in heaps upon the snow; they had ventured too high, or the wind had carried them up till they expired in the cold. Around the Wetterhorn there hung a threatening cloud, looking like a bundle of fleecy black wool, and sinking with the weight of what it contained within it—a "Föhn," one of the most violent storms when it breaks loose.

The impression of the whole journey, the night passed on the mountain, the remainder of the road, the deep crevasses where the water had worn away the rock during a period of time at the computation of which the brain reels—all this impressed itself indelibly upon Rudy's memory.

A deserted stone building on the other side of the sea of snow afforded shelter for the night. Here they found some charcoal and branches of pine-trees. A fire was soon kindled and a shakedown of some kind arranged; the men sat near the fire smoking their pipes and drinking the warm spiced beverage which they had themselves prepared, and of which Rudy also got his share. Tales were told of the mysterious state of the Alpine land, of the strange gigantic snakes in the deep lakes, of the spectral host that carry off sleepers at night through the air to the wonderful floating city of Venice, and of the wild shepherd who drives his black sheep over the pastures; if these had not been seen, the tinkling of their bells and the uncanny bleating of the flocks had undoubtedly been heard. Rudy listened with intense curiosity, but without any fear, for that he did not know; and while he listened he fancied he heard the weird bellowing of the spectral herd. It became more and more distinct, and the men hearing it too, sat listening to it in silence, telling Rudy not to go to sleep.

It was a "Föhn"—that violent hurricane that hurls itself from the mountains down into the valley, which snaps trees in its fury as if they were mere reeds, and which carries the wooden huts from one bank of a river to the other as we move men on a chess-board.

After the lapse of an hour they told Rudy that it was now all over, and that he might go to sleep; wearied by his long march, he slept as if it had been his bound duty to do so.

The next morning they again started on their way. The sun that day shone upon mountains, glaciers, and snow-fields that were all new to Rudy. They had entered the Canton Valais, and were upon that side of the range which is seen from Grindelwald, but still far distant from his new home. Other ravines, other pastures, woods, and rocky paths unfolded themselves, and other houses and other people were seen. But what kind of beings were these?

They were misshapen, uncanny wretches and podgy yellowish faces, their necks hanging down like bags with great ugly lumps of flesh. They were the cretins—dragging their miserable bodies along, and looking with stupid eyes at the strangers; the women were even more hideous than the men. Were these the people in his new home?

The Uncle

In his uncle's house, where Rudy now lived, the people were, thank God, such as he had been accustomed to see. There was only one cretin, a poor imbecile lad, one of those unfortunate creatures who in their destitute state are always traveling about in the Canton Valais from house to house, and who stay a few months in each family. Poor Saperli happened to be there when Rudy arrived.

Rudy's uncle was still a brave hunter, and could also earn his living as a cooper; his wife was a lively little woman with a face like a bird, eyes like an eagle, and a long neck covered all over with down.

Everything here was new to Rudy—dress, manners and customs, and even the language; but this his young ear would soon learn to understand. Things here looked quite prosperous compared to his former home with his grandfather. The room was larger; the walls were adorned with chamois horns and brightly polished guns; over the door hung a picture of the Virgin Mary, in front of which stood some fresh Alpine roses and a burning lamp.

His uncle was, as we have already mentioned, one of the ablest chamois-hunters of the whole district, and also one of the best guides. Rudy was now to become the pet of this household; it is true there was one already—an old dog who had formerly been used for hunting, but was now too blind and deaf to be of any use. But his good qualities of earlier days had not been forgotten, and he was therefore considered as one of the family and well taken care of. Rudy stroked the dog, who, however, did not take up easily with strangers, and such Rudy was at first. But he did not long remain so, and soon won his way to everybody's heart.

"It's not so bad in Canton Valais," said his uncle. "We have chamois here, which do not die off so fast as the wild goats, and things are much better than they used to be. Whatever they may say about the good old days, I think ours are better, and a hole having been made in the bag, we get a current of air now through our confined valley. Something better always turns up when worn-out things are done away with."

When his uncle became very communicative, he would relate stories of his youthful days, and even go back to the stirring times of his father, when Valais was still, as he expressed it, a closed bag, full of sick people, miserable cretins. "But the French soldiers came, and they were capital doctors, killing both the disease and the sufferers. The French were good at conquering in more ways than one, and even their girls were not behindhand at it." In saying this the uncle would nod at his wife, who was French by birth, and laugh. "The French had even tried their hand at conquering stones, and had succeeded well too. They had cut a road through the solid rock across the Simplon—such a road that I can say to a child of three years old, "Just go down to Italy; only mind you keep to the high road," and if it only keeps to the high road the child will come to Italy safe enough." Then the uncle would sing a French song, shout "Hurrah!" and "Long live Napoleon Buonaparte!"

Here Rudy for the first time heard of France and of Lyons, the great city on the Rhone, where his uncle had been. His uncle said that before many years had passed Rudy would become an able chamois-hunter, and that he had the right stuff in him for it; he taught him how to hold a gun, how to aim and fire. During the hunting season he took him to the mountains and made him drink the warm blood of the chamois, which prevents the hunter from becoming giddy; he also taught him to know the time when the avalanches are likely to roll down the different mountains—at noontide or in the evening, according as the sun's rays took effect. He taught him to observe the movements of the chamois when leaping, so that he might always come down firmly on his feet; he showed him how to hold himself up by his elbows, loins, and legs if there was no other support in the crevice of the rock, and how it was even possible, if necessary, to hang on by one's neck. He told him that the chamois were cunning and had outposts, but that the hunters must be more cunning than they, and put them off the scent.

One day, when Rudy was out hunting with his uncle, the latter hung his coat and hat upon his Alpine staff, and the chamois mistook the coat for the man. The mountain path was very narrow, indeed; it was scarcely a path at all, but only a narrow shelf along the yawning abyss. The snow that lay here was half thawed; and as the earth crumbled away beneath one's tread, Rudy's uncle lay down and crept forward. Every fragment that detached itself from the rock fell bounding from one side of the chasm to the other till it found a resting-place at the bottom. Rudy stood about a hundred paces behind his uncle on a firm projecting point of rock; from this post he could see a great vulture circling in the air and remain hovering above his uncle, whom the bird wished to hurl into the abyss with a blow from its wing, in order to make him its prey. The hunter had only eyes for the chamois, which with its young was to be seen on the other side of the chasm; Rudy kept his gaze fixed on the bird, for he understood what it wanted, and therefore stood ready to discharge his gun. Suddenly the chamois made a spring and his uncle fired and struck the animal with the deadly bullet, but the young kid sprang away, as if for a long life it had been exercised in danger and flight. The great bird, frightened by the report of the gun, winged its way in another direction, and Rudy's uncle knew nothing of the danger through which he had passed till he was told of it by the lad.

As they were now wending their way homewards in the best of humors, the uncle whistling a song of his youthful days, they suddenly heard a peculiar noise very near them; they looked around them, and there, high up on the slope of the mountain, the covering of snow rose and fell in billows like the motion of a large sheet of linen when the wind plays under it. The crust of snow, only a little while before as smooth and firm as a marble slab, suddenly burst, resolving itself into a foaming cataract which rushed down with a roar like that of distant thunder. It was an avalanche rolling, not indeed over Rudy and his uncle, but near them—all too near!

"Hold fast, Rudy!" cried his uncle; "hold fast with all your might!"

Rudy threw his arms round the trunk of the nearest tree, his uncle climbing up above him and holding fast to the branches, while the avalanche rolled along a few feet distant from them. But the rush of air that swept along with it like the wings of the storm, snapped the trees and bushes all around as if they had been only dry reeds, hurling them far and wide. Rudy lay crouched upon the ground. The tree to which he held fast looked as though it had been sawn in two, and the upper part had been flung far off; there amidst the shattered branches lay his uncle with his head dashed to pieces. His hand was still warm, but his face was not recognizable. Rudy stood pale and trembling; it was the first shock of his life, the first terror he had ever experienced.

Late in the evening he reached home with the fatal tidings—that home which was now turned into a house of mourning. The wife could find no words nor tears: it was only when they brought the body home that her grief found utterance. The poor cretin crept into his bed, and was seen no more the whole of the next day; it was only towards evening that he came up to Rudy.

"Will you write a letter for me?" he asked. "Saperli can't write, but Saperli can take the letter to the post-office."

"A letter from you?" asked Rudy. "And to whom?"

"To our Lord Christ!"

"To whom do you say?"

And the idiot, as the cretin was called, looked with a touching expression at Rudy, folded his hands, and said solemnly and piously:

"Jesus Christ! Saperli wants to send Him letter; ask Him let Saperli lie dead and not the master of the house here."

Rudy pressed his hand and said:

"The letter would not go, and cannot bring him back to us."

It was no easy task for Rudy to make Saperli understand how impossible it was.

"Now you are the support of the house," said his aunt and foster-mother, and such Rudy became.

Babette

Who is the best shot in the Canton Valais? That the chamois well knew.

"Beware of Rudy!" they might have said.

"Who is the handsomest hunter?"

"Why, Rudy!" said the girls; but they did not add:

"Beware of Rudy!"

Not even the sober mothers said that, for he nodded in quite as friendly a way to them as to the young girls. He was so brave and merry, his cheeks so brown, his teeth so white, and his black eyes so sparkling; he was altogether a handsome fellow, and twenty years old. He did not mind the coldest ice-water when he went swimming, and he would turn and twist about in it like a fish. He could climb better than any one else, sticking to the cliffs like a snail, and what kind of muscles and sinews he had was evident when he jumped, an art which he had first learned from the cat and afterwards from the chamois. Rudy was the best guide to whom one could trust oneself, and he could have made a good income by that calling. For the cooper's trade, which his uncle had also taught him, he had no inclination, his greatest pleasure being chamois-hunting, which brought in money too. Rudy would be a good match, it was said, if he only did not aspire beyond his station. He was such a dancer that the girls dreamt about him, and more than one carried him about in her waking thoughts too.

"He kissed me while we were dancing," said Annette, the schoolmaster's daughter, to her dearest friend; but she ought not to have told this even to her dearest friend. Such secrets are not easily kept; they are like sand in a sieve, they run through. It was soon known that Rudy, brave and good as he was, kissed when he danced, and yet it was not her he had kissed whom he would have liked to kiss most of all.

"O-ho!" said an old hunter; "he has kissed Annette. He has begun with A, and he'll kiss right through the alphabet."

A kiss while dancing was all that the busy tongues could find to say about him up to the present; he certainly had kissed Annette, and yet she was by no means the flower of his heart.

Down in the valley near Bex, amidst the great walnut-trees, by a small rushing mountain stream, lived the rich miller. The dwelling-house was a large three-storied building with small turrets; its roof was of thin wood covered with tin plates, which shone both in sunshine and moonshine. On the highest turret was a weather-cock—a glittering arrow piercing an apple—an allusion to Tell's feat. The mill looked very neat and prosperous, and would have looked pretty in a picture, or well in a description, but the miller's daughter would not have been so easy to paint or to describe—so at least Rudy would have said. And yet her image was engraved on his heart, and the eyes in this image blazed so that they kindled a fire there. It had burst out suddenly, like other fires; and the strangest part of it was that the miller's daughter, the pretty Babette, had no suspicion of it, for she and Rudy had never spoken a word to each other.

The miller was rich, and these riches placed Babette very high and made her a difficult catch. "But," thought Rudy, "nothing is so high that one may not reach it. All one has to do is to climb on, and one cannot fall if one doesn't think of it." This had been one of his earliest lessons.

It happened once that Rudy had some business to transact at Bex; it was a long journey, for in those days there was not yet any railway. From the Rhone glacier, along the foot of the Simplon, amidst the varying landscape presented by the numerous mountain heights, stretches the broad valley of Valais with its noble stream, the Rhone, which often overflows its banks, covering fields and roads and destroying everything in its course. Between the towns of Sion and St. Moritz the valley takes a turn, making a bend like an elbow, and becomes so narrow behind St. Moritz that there is only room for the bed of the river and the narrow carriage road. An old tower stands like a sentinel before the Canton Valais which ends here, and from it can be seen, across the stone bridge, the toll-house on the other side; it is the boundary of the Canton Vaud and the next town, not very distant in Bex. At every step can be seen an increasing luxuriance in the vegetation; it is as if we were in a garden of chestnut and walnut trees. Here and there cypress and pomegranate blossoms peep forth, and it is as sunny and warm here as if one were in Italy. Rudy arrived in Bex, and after having finished his business took a walk about the town, but not even a miller's boy, let alone Babette, could he see. This was not as it should be.

Evening came on, and the air was laden with the fragrance of wild thyme and the blossoming limes, while the wooded mountain slopes seemed to be covered with a shimmering sky-blue veil. Far and wide reigned a stillness, not as of sleep or death, but as if the whole of Nature were holding its breath, as if she were posing for her image to be photographed on the blue vault of Heaven. Here and there amidst the trees in the green fields stood the posts supporting the telegraph wires that ran through the silent valley. Against one of these leaned an object so motionless that it might have been mistaken for the trunk of a tree; it was Rudy, standing there as still as everything at that moment around him. He was not asleep, neither was he dead; but just as great events in the world, and matters of vital importance to individuals, often fly along the telegraph lines without the wires indicating it by the slightest quiver or sound, so were thoughts of mighty importance passing through Rudy's mind: the happiness of his life, the one thought that now constantly occupied him. His eyes were fixed on one point—a light that glimmered through the foliage from the parlor of the miller's house, where Babette lived. Rudy stood there so still that one would have thought he was taking aim at a chamois, but he himself was at that moment like the chamois, which will often stand as if hewn out of the rock, for minutes together, and then, when a stone rolls down, suddenly bound forward and rush away. And so it was with Rudy; an idea had just flashed through his mind.

"Never despair!" he cried. "A visit to the mill to say good evening to the miller and good evening to Babette. One can't fail as long as one has confidence. Babette must see me some time or other if I am to be her husband!"

Rudy laughed, for he was in a merry mood, and strode towards the mill; he knew what he wanted—he wanted Babette.

The stream flowed along over the yellow pebbles, and willows and lime-trees hung over the rolling waters, as Rudy went up the path leading to the miller's house. But as the children sing:

There was no one at home but the cat!

The cat standing on the steps put up its back and said "Mew." But Rudy had no mind for this kind of talk; he knocked, but no one heard him, no one opened the door for him. "Mew," said the cat again; and if Rudy had still been a child, he would have understood that language and known that the cat wanted to say, "There is no one at home here." But, as it was, he had to go across to the mill, and there he was told that the miller had gone to Interlaken, and taken Babette with him, to the great shooting festival which was to commence the following day, and which lasted a whole week. People from all the German cantons would be there. Poor Rudy! we may well say. He had not chosen a lucky day for his visit to Bex, and he might go back now. He did so, too, marching back through St. Moritz and Sion to his home in the valley; but he did not despair. When the sun rose the next morning, it found him in the best of spirits, for those, unlike the sun, had never sunk.

"Babette is in Interlaken," said Rudy to himself; "many days' journey from here. It is a long way if one follows the high road, but it is not so far if one cuts across the mountains, and that road just suits a chamois-hunter. I have been that way before, it leads to my home where I lived with my grandfather when I was a boy. And there is a shooting match at Interlaken! I'll go and try to get the first prize, and I'll be with Babette, when I've made her acquaintance."

With his light knapsack, containing his Sunday best, upon his back, and his gun and game-bag slung across his shoulder, Rudy started to take the shortest way across the mountains, which was no mean distance after all. But the festival was only to commence that day and lasted the whole week and more; and he had been told that during that time the miller and Babette would stay with their relatives in Interlaken. So Rudy crossed the Gemmi, intending to descend near Grindelwald. He strode merrily onwards in the fresh, light, invigorating mountain air. The valley sank lower and lower and the horizon extended; one after another the snowy peaks rose, and soon the whole Alpine range lay there in its dazzling purity. Rudy knew every mountain; he was now approaching the Schreckhorn, which stretches its white-powdered stone finger high up into the blue sky.

At last he had crossed the highest ridge, and now the pastures sloped down to the valley which had been his home. Both the air and his mind were light. Hill and dale were luxuriant in flowers and foliage, and his heart was full of those youthful feelings in which old age and death are out of the question: in which all is life, power, and enjoyment! He felt as free and as light as a bird. The swallows flew past him, and sang as they had sung in his childhood: "We and you! You and we!" All sang of flight and joy.

Beneath him lay the velvety green meadows, dotted with brown wooden cottages, while the murmuring Lutschine rolled along. He beheld the glacier with the green crystal edges and the soiled snow, and looking down into the deep crevasses saw both the upper and the lower glacier. The sound of the church bells came up to him as if they wished to ring him a welcome to his home; his heart beat faster, and became so filled with old memories that Babette was quite crowded out for a moment.

He once more strode along the road where, when a little boy, he had stood with the other children and sold carved toy-houses.

Yonder, behind the fir-trees, still stood his grandfather's house, but strangers lived in it now. Children came running up towards him and wanted him to buy; one offered him a mountain rose, which Rudy took as a good omen and thought of Babette. Soon he had crossed the bridge where the two streams unite; here the foliage was thicker, and the walnut trees afforded a pleasant shade. Soon he saw the waving flags bearing a white cross on a red ground, the standard both of the Swiss and the Danes; and before him lay Interlaken.

"It is indeed a splendid town and has no equal," thought Rudy. It was a little Swiss town in its Sunday dress. It was not like other towns, a somber heap of heavy stone houses, looking cold and stiff. No, here it looked as if the wooden houses had come down from the mountains into the green valley, and had ranged themselves side by side along the dear river which flows along swift as an arrow; they were a little irregular, but still formed a handsome street. The grandest of all the streets had certainly grown very much since Rudy had been here as a boy. It seemed to him as if it had been made up of all the pretty little houses which his grandfather had carved, and with which the cupboard at home had been filled, and that these had increased very much in size, like the old chestnut trees. Every house was called an hotel, and had a deal of carved wood work around the windows and balconies; the projecting roofs were gaily painted, and before each house was a flower garden leading on to the broad paved high road. This was lined by houses on one side only; otherwise the fresh green meadow in which the cows grazed, with the tinkling Alpine bells on their necks, would have been hidden. This meadow was encircled by high mountains which receded a little as if it were in the center, so that the snow-clad glittering peak of the Jungfrau, the most beautifully shaped of all Swiss mountains, could be distinctly seen.

What a number of finely dressed ladies and gentlemen from foreign parts, what a crowd of country-people from the different cantons there was! Every marksman wore his number in a band round his hat. There was music and singing of all kinds: hand-organs, trumpets, shouting and noise. The houses and bridges were adorned with emblems and verses. Flags and banners were waving, and shot upon shot was being fired. That was the sweetest music to Rudy's ears, and amidst all this turmoil he quite forgot Babette, on whose account only he had come.

The marksmen were crowding round the targets, and Rudy was soon among them. He proved himself the best shot, and was more fortunate than any of them; for he always hit the bull's eye.

"Who can the stranger be?" people asked. "He speaks the French of Canton Valais, and he also makes himself understood very well in our German," said some.

"He is said to have lived in the neighborhood of Grindelwald when he was a boy," said one of the sportsmen.

The young stranger was full of life, too; his eyes sparkled, and his aim and his arm were steady, therefore he always hit the mark. Good fortune brings courage, and courage Rudy always had. He soon had a circle of friends gathered round him; every one honored him and paid him homage. Babette had quite vanished from his thoughts. Suddenly a heavy hand was laid upon his shoulder, and a deep voice said to him in French: "Aren't you from the Canton Valais?"

Rudy turned round and saw a stout man with a ruddy, pleased face; it was the wealthy miller of Bex. His great body hid dainty little Babette, who, however, soon came to the fore with her bright dark eyes.

It had flattered the wealthy miller that it was a marksman from his own canton who had proved to be the best shot, and was honored by every one. Rudy was certainly born under a lucky star; those whom he had come all this way to see, but had forgotten when on the spot, now sought him out.

When people meet others from their part of the country far from home they always speak and make each other's acquaintance Rudy, by his shooting, was the first man in the festival, just as the miller at home in Bex was first by reason of his money and his fine mill. So the two men shook hands, which they had never done before; Babette too held out her hand to Rudy frankly, and he pressed it, and looked at her so hard that she blushed deeply.

The miller spoke of the long way they had come, and of the many large towns they had seen; in his opinion they had performed quite a journey, having traveled by steamer, rail, and coach.

"I came the shorter way," said Rudy. "I came over the mountains. There is no road too high for a man to pass along."

"But he may break his neck!" said the miller; "and you look just the kind of man to break your neck some day, you are so daring."

"Oh! one does not fall as long as one does not think of it," said Rudy.

The miller's relations in Interlaken, with whom the miller and Babette were staying, invited Rudy to come and see them—for was he not of the same canton as the miller? This invitation was very acceptable to Rudy; good fortune favored him, as it always does those who depend upon their own efforts and remember that "Providence gives us the nuts, but does not crack them for us." Rudy was treated by the miller's relations as if he belonged to the family, and they drank to the health of the best shot; Babette clinked glasses with Rudy too, and he returned thanks for the toast.

In the evening they all went for a walk along the beautiful road past the stately hotels and under the old walnut-trees, and there were so many people and such crowding that Rudy was obliged to offer Babette his arm. He told her how happy he was to have met people from the Canton Vaud, for Vaud and Valais were good neighborly cantons. He expressed his pleasure so heartily that Babette could not resist squeezing his hand. They walked on side by side as if they had been old acquaintances, she chatting on, and Rudy thinking how admirably she commented upon the dress and walk of the foreign ladies. She said that she really did not want to make fun of them, for she knew that they might be good, upright people; she herself had a god-mother who was a grand English lady. Eighteen years before, when Babette was christened, the lady was staying at Bex, and having acted as godmother to her had given her the costly brooch which she was now wearing. Her god-mother had twice written to her, and this year they were to have met her and her daughter here in Interlaken; "the daughters were old maids—nearly thirty," said Babette, who was only eighteen.

The sweet little mouth was not still a moment, and everything that Babette said sounded in Rudy's ears as matters of the greatest importance, while he in his turn told her all he had to tell—how often he had been in Bex, how well he knew the mill, and how often he had seen Babette, while she had most probably never noticed him, and lastly how he had gone to the mill filled with thoughts he could not express, and found her and her father gone to a place far away—not so far, however, but that one could clamber over the wall to it by a short cut.

All this he said, and much more; he told her how fond he was of her, and that he had come here for her sake and not on account of the shooting.

Babette became silent when she heard all this; it seemed as if he were asking her to bear too much.

Whilst they wandered on, the sun sank behind the great mountain wall.

The "Jungfrau" stood out in all her glory, encircled by the dark green wreath formed by the neighboring heights. Every one stood still to gaze at the beautiful sight; even Rudy and Babette enjoyed it too.

"Nowhere is it more beautiful than here!" said Babette.

"Nowhere!" said Rudy, looking at Babette.

"To-morrow I must return home!" he said, a few moments later.

"Come and see us at Bex!" whispered Babette, "my father will be very pleased."

On the Way Back

What a number of things Rudy had to carry when the following day he set out to cross the mountains on his way home! He had three silver cups, two fine guns, and a silver coffee-pot; the pot would be useful when he set up housekeeping. But all this was of minor importance; he carried, or rather was carried homewards across the mountains by something much weightier. The weather was raw, dark, and inclined to rain, and the clouds descended like a mourning veil upon the mountain heights, shrouding their glittering peaks. From the woods below came the sound of the axe, and down the mountain slope rolled the trunks of trees that looked from the heights like thin sticks, but which were nevertheless as stout as ship's masts. The Liitschine murmured monotonously, the wind whistled, and the clouds sailed along. Suddenly Rudy found a young maiden walking at his side; he had not noticed her till she was quite close to him. She was also about to ascend the mountain. The maiden's eyes had a peculiar power that compelled one to look into them; they were so strange, so clear, so deep and unfathomable.

"Have you a sweetheart?" asked Rudy; all his thoughts ran on love.

"I have none, answered the maiden, with a laugh, but she did not seem to be speaking the truth. "Don't let us go a long way round," she said. "We must keep more to the left; it is a shorter way."

"Oh, yes!" said Rudy, "and fall into a crevasse. You don't know the way better than that, and want to be the guide?

"I know the way well enough!" said the maiden, "and I have my thoughts collected. Yours are no doubt down in the valley. Up here one should think of the Ice Maiden; men say she bears their race no goodwill."

"I do not fear her," said Rudy, "she had to give me up when I was still a child, and I shall not give myself up to her now that I am older."

The darkness increased, the rain came down, snow fell, and the lightning was quite blinding.

"Give me your hand," said the maiden, "I will help you to mount," and he felt the touch of her icy fingers.

"You help me!" exclaimed Rudy, "I do not want a woman's help in climbing yet." And he strode on more quickly away from her.

The snow-flakes covered him as with a veil, the wind whistled, and behind him he heard the maiden laughing and singing; it sounded quite strangely.

"It must be a specter in the service of the Ice Maiden," thought Rudy, who had heard such things talked about when, still a boy, he had passed the night up here in his journey over the mountains.

The snow no longer fell so thickly, and the cloud lay beneath him; looking back, no one was to be seen, but he heard laughing and singing, and the sounds did not seem to proceed from a human throat.

When Rudy at last reached the topmost plateau, from which the path leads down into the Rhone valley, he saw two bright stars shining in the clear blue heavens in the direction of Chamouny; and he thought of Babette, of himself, and of his good fortune, and his heart glowed at the thought.

The Visit to the Mill

"What grand things you have brought home!" said his old foster-mother, and her strange eagle eyes sparkled as she wriggled and twisted her skinny neck more strangely and quickly than ever.

"You are a lucky fellow, Rudy! I must kiss you, my sweet boy."

And Rudy allowed her to kiss him, but it was written in his face that he forced himself to put up with these little home afflictions.

"How handsome you are, Rudy!" said the old woman.

"Don't talk such nonsense!" said Rudy, with a laugh, but he was pleased all the same.

"I must say it again," said the old woman; "you are a lucky fellow."

"Well, you may be right," said he, thinking of Babette. Never had he felt such a longing to get down into the deep valley.

"They must have come home!" he said to himself; "it is already two days over the time when they had intended to be back. I must go to Bex."

So Rudy walked over to Bex and found them at home in the mill. He was received very kindly, and they had brought him greetings from the family in Interlaken. Babette did not say much; she had become very silent, but her eyes spoke and that was quite sufficient for Rudy.

At other times the miller had always led the conversation, and was accustomed to hear people laugh at his jokes and sayings—for was he not the wealthy miller? But now he seemed to prefer listening to Rudy's adventures, as the latter told of the difficulties and dangers that the chamois-hunter has to endure on the lofty mountain peaks—how he has to creep along the flimsy ledges of snow which are only cemented as it were by wind and weather to the edge of the cliff, and across the frail bridge that the snowdrift has thrown over the deep ravines.

The eyes of the brave Rudy sparkled as he spoke of the life of a hunter, of the cunning of the chamois and of their bold leaps, of the powerful "Föhn" and the rolling avalanches. He noticed that at every fresh description the miller became more and more interested, and that he was especially moved by what he heard of the vulture and the royal eagle.

Not far off, in the Canton Valais, there was an eagle's nest, very skillfully built under a high projecting ledge of rock. In that nest was a young eagle, but it was impossible to get at it. An Englishman had a few days before offered Rudy a whole handful of gold if he brought him the young eagle alive. "But everything has its limits," said Rudy; "the eagle is not to be had, it would be madness to attempt it."

The wine flowed freely and the conversation too, but the evening seemed much too short for Rudy, although it was past midnight when he left the miller's after this his first visit.

The lights in the windows of the miller's house still shone for a short time through the green branches; out of the open skylight in the roof came the parlor cat, while along the water-pipe came the kitchen cat to meet her.

"Is there any news at the mill?" asked the parlor cat. "Here in the house there is a secret engagement. Father knows nothing of it yet. Rudy and Babette have been treading on each other's paws under the table all the evening; they trod on me twice, but I didn't mew, for that would have attracted attention."

"I should have mewed though," said the kitchen cat.

"What suits the kitchen would not suit the parlor," said the parlor cat. "But I am curious to know what the miller will say when he hears of the engagement."

Yes, what the miller would say—that Rudy would also have liked to know, but it was impossible for him to wait long to hear it. When a few days later the omnibus rattled over the Rhone bridge between the cantons of Valais and Vaud, Rudy was sitting in it in as good spirits as ever, indulging in pleasant thoughts of the favorable answer he expected to receive that evening.

And when evening came, and the omnibus was driving back along the same road, Rudy was again sitting inside, whilst the parlor cat was running about in the mill with the news.

"Have you heard it, you in the kitchen? The miller knows all now. It has come to a fine end. Rudy came here towards the evening; and there was a great deal of whispering and secret talk between him and Babette, as they stood in the passage before the miller's room. I was lying at their feet, but they had neither eyes nor thoughts for me. 'I will go to your father at once,' said Rudy, 'that is the most honorable way.' 'Shall I go with you?' asked Babette; 'it will give you courage.' 'I have courage enough,' said Rudy; 'but if you are there, he must be friendly, whether he will or not.' Upon that they went in, Rudy treading heavily on my tail. He's very clumsy; I mewed; but neither he nor Babette had ears to hear. They opened the door and entered together. I was in first and sprang upon the back of a chair, for I didn't know how Rudy would open the ball. However, the miller opened it with a mighty kick, and the other was out of the house and up the mountain to the chamois in a jiffy. Master Rudy will have to stick to those now, and give up aiming at our Babette."

"But do tell me what they said," said the kitchen cat.

"What they said? Why, everything that people say when they go a-wooing: 'I love her, and she loves me. And if there is milk enough in the can for one, there is enough for two.' 'But she is too far above you,' said the miller, 'she sits on heaps of grit—gold grit, as you know. You will never reach her.' 'There is nothing too high for a man to reach if he only has the will,' answered Rudy, for he is a bold fellow. 'But you yourself said a little while ago that you couldn't reach the young eagle; well, Babette is still higher than that nest.' 'I'll take them both,' said Rudy. 'I'll give you Babette if you bring me the young eagle alive,' said the miller, laughing till the tears stood in his eyes. 'But now I thank you for your visit, Rudy; come again tomorrow when there's no one at home. Good-bye, Rudy!' And Babette said good-bye too, but as mournfully as a little kitten that cannot see its mother yet. 'A man's word is his bond,' said Rudy. 'Don't cry, Babette; I shall bring the young eagle.' 'You'll break your neck, I hope,' said the miller, 'and we shall then be spared your company here." That's what I call a mighty kick. And now Rudy is gone and Babette sits and weeps, but the miller sings German songs that he learnt on his last journey. I'm not going to pull a long face about the matter—that will not do any good."

"Still there's a chance left for all that," said the kitchen cat.

The Eagle's Nest

From the mountain path a voice trolled out some joyous and vigorous notes, giving proofs of good humor and undaunted courage. It was Rudy going to see his friend Vesinand.

"You must help me. I must take the young eagle out of the nest at the top of the cliff; we will take Nagli with us."

"Will you not have a try to reach the moon first? It would be just as easy," said Vesinand. "You seem to be in good spirits."

"Of course I am. I am thinking of marrying. But to be serious, I will tell you how matters stand."

And soon both Vesinand and Nagli knew Rudy's intentions.

"You are a bold fellow," they said. "It can't be done; you'll break your neck."

"I shall not fall as long as I don't think of it," said Rudy.

They set out about midnight, carrying with them poles, ladders, and ropes. The road lay through forest and underwood, over rolling stones, leading ever higher and higher in the dark night. Water foamed beneath them and trickled down from above, while damp clouds hung in the air. At last the hunters reached the edge of the precipice, where it was even darker, for the rocky walls almost met, and the sky could only be seen through the narrow crevice at the top; close beside them yawned the abyss with the foaming waters beneath. The three sat down on the stones to await the dawn, for when the parent eagle flew out they would have to shoot the old bird before they could think of obtaining possession of the young one. Rudy crouched down, as motionless as if he had been part of the stone on which he was sitting, holding his gun cocked ready to fire, and his gaze fixed steadily upon the highest point of the cliff, where the eagle's nest was hidden beneath the overhanging rock. The three hunters had a long time to wait. But now they heard a loud rustling high above them, and a great hovering object darkened the air. Two guns took aim as the black body of the eagle flew out of the nest. A shot was fired; for a moment only the wide-spreading wings moved, then the bird slowly sank, crushing the branches and bushes in its way. For a moment it seemed as if it would completely fill the chasm, and drag the hunters down in its fall by its bulk and its great outstretched pinions; but at last it lay in the abyss beneath.

Now the hunters moved themselves. Three of the longest ladders were bound together; it was thought that they would reach far enough. They were fixed on the ground as close to the edge of the precipice as safety would permit, but they did not reach far enough; and higher up, where the nest was protected by the projecting ledge, the cliff was as smooth as a wall. After consulting together, they determined to bind two ladders together, and by letting them down into the chasm from above, make them communicate with the three set up below. With great difficulty they dragged the two ladders up, binding them fast with ropes to the top; they were then let out over the projecting ledge, and hung swaying there over the abyss. Rudy was already seated on the lowest rung. It was a bitterly cold morning, and clouds of mist were rising up out of the dark ravine. Rudy sat there like a fly upon a piece of swinging straw which a bird, while making its nest, had dropped upon the edge of some tall factory chimney; but the fly can fly away if the straw gives way, whilst Rudy could only break his neck. The wind whistled round him, and beneath him in the abyss foamed the waters of the thawing glacier, the palace of the Ice Maiden.

He now made the ladder swing to and fro, like the spider swings its body when it wants to seize anything in its long wavy threads; and when Rudy for the fourth time touched the top of the ladders set up from below he had grasped it, bound them securely together with skillful hands—but they swayed and rattled as if they hung on worn-out hinges.

The five long ladders, which seemed to reach up to the nest, and which stood up perpendicularly against the cliff, looked like a waving reed; and now the most dangerous part of the work was to be accomplished. There was climbing to be done as only a cat can climb, but that was just what Rudy understood, for he had learnt it from the cat; he did not even know the Spirit of Giddiness was in the air behind him, trying to grasp him with its polypus-like arms.

When he at length stood upon the topmost rung of the ladder he saw that it did not reach high enough to enable him to look into the nest, and that he could only get up to it by using his hands.

He first tried the strength of the stout interwoven branches that formed the nethermost part of the nest; and having secured a firm hold on one of the strongest, he swung himself up from the ladder, and hanging on to the branch soon had his head and shoulders in the nest. He was met by a suffocating stench of carrion, for in the nest were sheep, chamois, and birds, all in a state of decomposition. The Spirit of Giddiness, who had little power over him, blew the poisonous vapors into his face, in order to make him dizzy and faint, whilst down in the black yawning gulf the Ice Maiden herself, with her long pale green hair, sat by the rushing waters staring at him with eyes as deadly as two gun-barrels.

"Now I'll have you," she was thinking.

In a corner of the nest he saw the eaglet, a great strong bird, but still unfledged. Rudy kept his gaze rivetted upon it, and holding on with all his might with one hand, he with the other threw a noose over the young eagle. It was caught—alive, its legs fixed in the tightly drawn cord.

Rudy slung the noose with the bird across his shoulder, so that the creature hung a good way beneath him whilst he held on to a rope flung out to help him, until his toes touched the topmost rung of the ladder.

"Hold tight! Don't think it possible to fall and you will not do so!" It was the old lesson; and Rudy acting on it, held tight, clambered down, and being convinced that he could not fall, of course did not.

Then arose loud and joyous hurrahs, as Rudy landed on the firm rock with his young eagle.

What News the Parlor Cat Had to Tell

"Here is what you asked for!" said Rudy, as he came into the miller's house at Bex, and placing a large basket on the floor, took off the cloth that covered it. Two yellow eyes set in black rings glared forth, flashing fire, and so wild that they seemed to wish to burn and penetrate everything they beheld; the short strong beak was opened to bite, and the neck was red and covered with young feathers.

"The young eagle," cried the miller. Babette shrieked and sprang back, but could not take her eyes either from Rudy or from the eagle.

"You are not easily frightened!" said the miller.

"And you are a man of your word," said Rudy. "We both have our characteristics."

"But how is it that you did not break your neck?" asked the miller.

"Because I held tight," replied Rudy. "And that I do still. Now I shall hold Babette tight."

"First see that you get her," said the miller, laughing; and Babette knew that was a good sign.

"We must get him out of the basket—it is terrible the way he glares. But how did you manage to get him?" Rudy had to describe the capture, and the miller opened his eyes wider and wider.

"With your courage and your good fortune you can support three wives!" said the miller.

"I thank you!" cried Rudy.

"It is true, you have not got Babette yet!" said the miller, slapping the young Alpine hunter good-humoredly on the shoulder.

"Do you know the latest news in the mill?" said the parlor cat to the kitchen cat. "Rudy has brought us the young eagle and takes Babette in exchange. They kissed each other, and the old man saw it. That's as good as an engagement. The old man was quite good-natured about it; he drew back his claws, took his afternoon nap, and left the two to sit and chatter. They have so much to talk about that they will not have finished by Christmas."

And they had not finished by Christmas either. The wind whisked away the yellow leaves, and the snow whirled through the valley as well as on the high mountains. The Ice Maiden sat in her stately castle, which increases in size in winter; the cliffs stood there covered with frost, and icicles, as thick as trees and as heavy as elephants, hung down, where in summer the water veil of the mountain streams flutters in the breeze; fantastic garlands of crystal ice hung glittering upon the snow-powdered pine trees. The Ice Maiden rode upon the howling wind away over the deepest valleys. The snow-blanket reached right down as far as Bex, and the Ice Maiden, coming down there, beheld Rudy sitting at the miller's; he sat indoors that winter much more than was his wont, for he was generally near Babette. The wedding was to take place the following summer; his ears often tingled, for friends spoke a good deal about it. In the mill all was sunshine, and there bloomed the loveliest Alpine rose, the merry, laughing Babette, beautiful as the coming spring— the spring which makes all the birds sing of summer-time and marriage.

"How those two are always sitting stuck together there," said the parlor cat. "I am tired of their mewing!"

The Ice Maiden

Spring had unfolded her fresh green garlands of walnut and chestnut-trees, and beautifully did they rear their stately heads along the banks of the Rhone from the bridge at St. Moritz as far as the Lake of Geneva. The river rushes along with wild speed from its source under the green glacier—the ice-palace, where the Ice Maiden dwells, whence she has herself borne up by the keen wind to the highest snow-field to bask in the warm sunshine on the snow-covered pools. Here she sat gazing fixedly down into the deep valleys where the people were busily moving about like ants on a sunlit stone.

"Beings of mental power, as the children of the sun call you," said the Ice Maiden, "you are only vermin. One rolling snowball—and you, your houses and cities, are crushed and wiped out." She raised her proud head higher and looked far and wide with her death-dealing eyes. From the valley beneath arose a rolling sound: rocks were being blasted—the work of men. Roads and tunnels for railways were being laid down.

"They are playing at being moles," she said; "they are digging passages under the earth: hence this noise, like the reports of a gun. When I move my castles, the noise is greater than the roar of thunder."

Out of the valley ascended a wreath of smoke moving forwards like a fluttering veil. It formed the waving plumes of the engine, which was dragging along the newly opened line the train that looked like a winding serpent with carriages for its joints. It shot past swift as an arrow.

"They pretend to be the masters down there, these mental powers," said the Ice Maiden. "But the powers of mighty Nature are still the ruling ones."

She laughed and sang, making the valley tremble.

"An avalanche is falling," cried the people.

But the children of the sun sang still louder of the ruling power of human thought which places a yoke upon the ocean, levels mountains and fills up valleys, and is lord over the powers of Nature.

Just at that moment a party of travelers came across the snow-field where the Ice Maiden sat; they had bound themselves fast to each other by ropes, so that they formed one large body as it were upon the slippery surface of the ice, at the edge of the deep abyss.

"Vermin!" said the Ice Maiden. "You lords of the powers of Nature!" and she turned her gaze from the party and looked scornfully down into the deep valley where the train was rushing along.

"There they sit, these thoughts! But they are in the power of Nature's forces. I can see them, one and all. One sits proudly alone, like a king, while the others are all heaped up together. Here again half of them are asleep, and when the steam-dragon stops, they get out and go their ways. The thoughts go out into the world!" And she laughed.

"There goes another avalanche!" said the people down in the valley.

"It will not reach us," said two who sat together on the back of the dragon—two souls but one mind—as they say. They were Rudy and Babette, and the miller was there too.

"Like baggage," he said; "I am there as a necessary encumbrance."

"There sit the two," said the Ice Maiden. "Many chamois have I crushed, millions of Alpine roses have I snapped and broken, and not even spared the roots. I will destroy them—these thoughts, these powers of mind."

And again she laughed.

"There goes another avalanche," said those down in the valley.

The Godmother

At Montreux, one of the nearest towns, which with Clarens, Vevey, and Crin encircle the north-east part of the Lake of Geneva, resided Babette's god-mother, the grand English lady, with her daughters and a young gentleman, a relation of theirs. They had only lately arrived, but the miller had already visited them, announced Babette's engagement, and told them about Rudy and the young eagle and the visit to Interlaken—in short, the whole story. It had pleased them very much, and made them feel very kindly towards Rudy, Babette, and the miller too; they also insisted upon all three coming over to Montreux, and that is why they had come. Babette was to see her godmother, and her godmother was to see Babette.

At the little town of Villeneuve, at one end of the Lake of Geneva lay the steamer that made the journey to Vevey, below Montreux, in half an hour. These shores have often been celebrated in song; here, under the walnut-trees, by the deep blue lake, sat Byron, and wrote his melodious verses of the prisoner in the dark rocky castle of Chillon. Here, where Clarens with its weeping willows is reflected in the water, wandered Rousseau, dream-ing of Heloise. The Rhone flows along at the foot of the high snow-capped mountains of Savoy, and here, not far from its mouth, lies a little island in the lake, so small that, seen from the shore, it looks like a ship upon the water. The island is a rock which about a hundred years ago a lady caused to be dammed up, and covered with earth; she also planted three acacia-trees which now overshadow the whole island. Babette was enchanted with this spot, which appeared to her the loveliest in the whole voyage; she would very much have liked to land there, it was so beautiful. But the steamer went on and did not stop till it reached Vevey. The small party walked slowly up from here between the white sun-lit walls that enclose the vineyards around the little mountaintown of Montreux, where the fig-trees overshadow the peasant's houses, and where laurels and cypresses grow in the gardens. Halfway up the mountain stood the hotel in which Babette's godmother resided.

The reception was very cordial. The godmother was a pleasant woman with a round, smiling countenance; as a child she must certainly have resembled one of Raphael's cherubs. Even at her age her head was still that of an angel, richly crowned with silver locks. Her daughters were fine, elegant girls, tall and slender. The young cousin whom they had brought with them was clad in white from head to foot; he had golden hair and golden whiskers, so large that they might have been divided among three gentlemen; he immediately paid Babette the greatest attention.

Richly bound books, music and drawings lay strewn about on the large table. The doors leading to the balcony stood open, affording a lovely view of the great lake, which lay so clear and still that the mountains of Savoy, with their towns, woods and snowy peaks were reflected in it.

Rudy, who was at other times so lively and gay, did not in the least feel himself at home; he moved about as if he were walking on peas over a slippery floor. The time seemed as long and tedious to him as if he were on a treadmill. And then they had to go out for a walk. That was just as slow and tedious; Rudy could have taken two steps forward and one backwards to keep pace with the others. They walked down to Chillon, the gloomy old castle on the rocky island, merely to see the instruments of torture, the dungeons in which people were buried alive, the rusty chains hanging from the walls of rock, the stone benches for those condemned to death, the trap doors through which the unfortunate creatures were hurled down and impaled upon iron spikes amidst the surge. They called looking at all this pleasure. It was a place of execution, made famous by Byron's lines. But Rudy could not forget its original use. He leaned out of one of the great stone windows and looked down into the deep blue water and across to the little island with the three acacias, wishing himself there away from the whole chattering party. Babette however was unusually lively; she had amused herself famously, she said, and thought the cousin perfection itself.

"Yes, a perfect fop!" said Rudy; it was the first time that Rudy had said anything that did not please Babette. The Englishman had given her a little book as a souvenir of Chillon; it was Byron's poem "The Prisoner of Chillon" translated into French so that she could read it.

"It may be a good book," said Rudy, "but I don't like the finely combed fellow who gave it you."

"He looked just like a flour-sack without any flour," said the miller, laughing at his own wit.

Rudy laughed too, and said that that was just what he was like.

The Cousin

When a few days later Rudy went to pay a visit to the mill, he found the young Englishman there. Babette was just placing a dish of boiled trout before him, which she had doubtless herself garnished with parsley to make it look nice and appetizing. But Rudy thought all this quite unnecessary. What did the Englishman want there? What was his business there? To be treated and waited upon by Babette? Rudy was jealous, and that made Babette happy. It pleased her to study every corner of his heart—both the strong and the weak spots. Love was to her as yet only a game, and she played with Rudy's whole heart.

It must, however, be said that in him was centered all her happiness and all her life; he was her one thought, and her ideal of all that was good and noble in the world. Still, the darker his looks grew, the more her eyes laughed; she would even have kissed the fair Englishman with the golden whiskers if by doing so she could have enraged Rudy and sent him rushing away, for that would have proved how much he loved her. This was certainly not right in Babette, but then she was only nineteen years old. She did not reflect much on her conduct, and still less did she consider that it might be interpreted as flighty by the young Englishman, and as not at all becoming for the modest betrothed daughter of the miller.

Where the high road from Bex passes under the snow-clad rocky heights, which in the language of the country are called "Diablerets," stood the mill, not far from a rushing mountain stream, which lashed itself into a gray foam like soapsuds. It was not this stream, however, that turned the mill-wheel, but a smaller one, which came tumbling down the rocks on the other side of the river, and which, gaining a greater impetus and power by being dammed up with stones, ran out, through a wooden trough like a wide gutter, over the large stream. The trough was always so full of water that it overflowed and offered a wet slippery path to any one who took it into his head to get to the mill by this shorter road. The young Englishman, however, thought he would try it. Dressed in white like a miller's boy, he was climbing up the path one evening, guided by the light that streamed from Babette's bedroom window. But as he had never learned to climb, he nearly went head first into the stream, escaping with wet arms and bespattered trousers. All dripping and covered with slime, he arrived beneath Babette's window, and, clambering up the old lime-tree, he began to mimic the owl, that being the only bird he could imitate. Babette, hearing him, looked out through the thin curtains; but when she saw the man in white, and guessed who it was, her little heart beat with terror and also with anger. She quickly put out the light, and, after having assured herself that the window had been securely fastened, she left him to hoot and to screech as much as he liked.

What a terrible thing it would be if Rudy were now at the mill! But Rudy was not at the mill; no—what was worse still—he was standing right under the lime-tree. Loud angry words were spoken; there might be blows—perhaps even murder!

Babette, in great terror, opened her window, and calling Rudy's name, begged him to go away, adding that she could not allow him to stay there.

"You cannot allow me to stay here!" he cried. "Then this is an appointment. You are expecting some good friend whom you prefer to me. Shame on you, Babette!"

"You are unbearable," cried Babette. "I hate you!" she added, in tears. "Go—go!"

"This I have not deserved," said he, as he strode away, his cheeks and his heart burning like fire.

Babette threw herself on the bed weeping.

"I love you so dearly, Rudy! How can you think so ill of me?"

She worked herself into quite a passion, and that was a good thing for her; otherwise she would have been very grieved. As it was, she could fall asleep and enjoy the refreshing slumber that virtue brings.

Evil Powers

Rudy left Bex and took his way homewards, ascending the mountain path, with its fresh cool air, where amidst the snow the Ice Maiden reigns. The trees, with their thick foliage, were far beneath him, and looked like potato-tops; the pines and the bushes became smaller up there; the Alpine roses grew next to the snow, which lay in solitary patches, like linen put out to bleach. A blue gentian that grew in his path he crushed with the butt-end of his gun.

Higher up two chamois showed themselves; Rudy's eyes sparkled, and his thoughts took a new turn. But as he was not near enough for a sure aim, he mounted higher up, where only thick stubble grew from between the boulders; seeing the chamois calmly crossing the snow-field, he pressed on. Thick mists gathered round him, and suddenly he found himself on the brink of a steep precipice. The rain began to pour down in torrents.

He felt a burning thirst; his head was hot, while his limbs were shivering. He seized his hunting-flask, but it was empty; he had not thought of filling it when he rushed up the mountains. He had never been ill before, but now he had a feeling as if he were so; he was tired, and felt an inclination to lie down, a desire to sleep, but the rain was streaming down all around him. He tried to rouse himself, but every object danced and trembled strangely before his eyes.

Suddenly he perceived what he had never seen here before—a newly built low hut that leaned against the rock, and in the doorway stood a young girl. It almost seemed to him as if it were Annette, the schoolmaster's daughter, whom he had once kissed in the dance; but though it was not Annette, still he had seen the girl somewhere before, perhaps near Grindelwald the evening he was returning from the shooting-match at Interlaken.

"How did you come here?" he asked.

"This is my home. I am minding my flocks."

"Your flocks? Where do they graze? Here there is only snow and rocks."

"You know much about what is here!" said the girl, laughing. "Here behind us, a little way down, is a fine piece of pasture. That is where my goats go. I take great care of them. I never lose one; what is mine, remains mine."

"You're pretty sharp," said Rudy.

"So are you," replied the girl.

"If you have any milk in the house, give me some to drink; I am dreadfully thirsty."

"I have something better than the milk," said the girl, "and you shall have it. There were some travelers here yesterday with a guide and they left half a bottle of wine behind them, such as you have never tasted. They will not come back for it, and as I shall not drink it, you can have it."

And the girl brought the wine, poured it into a wooden goblet, and handed it to Rudy.

"That's excellent," he said. "I never tasted wine so warming and so fiery."

His eyes sparkled: he was filled with fresh life, and with a glow as if every care and vexation had vanished; the strongest feelings of a man's nature welled up within him.

"But surely you are Annette," he cried. "Give me a kiss."

"If you give me the pretty ring you have on your finger."

"My engagement ring?"

"Yes, that's it," said the girl, and re-filling the goblet with wine she held it to his lips, and he drank. The pleasure of life coursed through his veins; he felt as though the whole world belonged to him—then why torment himself? Everything was created for our enjoyment and our happiness. The stream of life is the stream of pleasure; to be carried, to be torn along by it, is happiness. He looked at the young girl. She was Annette, and yet not Annette; still less was she the phantom, the ghost, as he had called it, that he had met near Grindelwald. The girl up here on the mountain was fresh as the driven snow, blooming as an Alpine rose, and swift as a kid; but still formed from Adam's rib, like himself. He flung his arms around the beautiful creature and looked into her eyes, so strangely clear. A moment only did he gaze, but in that moment who shall express or describe it in words? Was it the life of the spirit, or the spirit of death that took possession of him? Was he carried on high, or was he sinking into the deep deadly crevasse, deeper, ever deeper?

He saw the walls of ice looking like blue-green glass; fathomless chasms yawned around him, and the water dripped down with a sound like the chime of bells—clear as a pearl, and lit up by bluish flames.

The Ice Maiden kissed him—a kiss that sent an icy shudder through his whole frame; a cry of pain escaped him and, tearing himself away, he staggered and all became dark to his eyes; but he opened them again. The evil powers had played their game.

Gone was the Alpine maiden, gone the sheltering hut; the water trickled down the naked rocks, and the snow lay all around. Rudy was shivering with cold, soaked through to the skin, and his ring—the engagement ring that Babette had given him—had disappeared. His gun lay in the snow beside him; taking it up he tried to discharge it, but it missed fire. Damp clouds filled the chasm like masses of snow, and up above sat the Spirit of Giddiness watching her powerless prey; while from the depths came a sound as if a mass of rock were falling, crushing and carrying away everything that obstructed its course.

At the miller's Babette sat and wept. Rudy had not been there for six days—he who was in the wrong, he who ought to ask her pardon, and whom she loved with all her heart.

In the Mill

"What a life these people do lead!" said the parlor cat to the kitchen cat. "Babette and Rudy have fallen out again. She sits and cries, and I suppose he thinks no more about her."

"I don't like that," said the kitchen cat.

"Neither do I," said the parlor cat, "but I shall not take it to heart. Babette can become engaged to the red-whiskered fellow. But he has not been here either since the time he wanted to get on the roof."

Evil powers carry on their game around us and in us. Rudy had found that out and thought a great deal about it. What was it that had gone on about and within him on the mountain? Was it a ghost that he had seen, or only the result of a feverish dream? He had never had fever, or any other illness, before. But while judging Babette he had examined the workings of his own heart, and there he had found traces of the wild course of the fierce storm that had raged there. Could he confess all to Babette, every thought that in the hour of temptation might have led to deeds? He had lost her ring, and by that very loss she had won him back. Would she be able to confess to him? It seemed as if his heart would burst when he thought of her; how many recollections rose within him! He saw her as if she were standing before him in the flesh, a laughing, saucy child. Many a loving word that she had uttered out of the fullness of her love came like a ray of sunshine to his heart, and soon it was filled with nothing but sunshine at the thought of Babette. Yes, she would undoubtedly be able to confess to him, and she should, too.

He went to the mill. There was a confession; it began with a kiss, and ended with Rudy remaining the sinner. It was all his fault in having doubted Babette's fidelity—it was abominable of him. Such mistrust, such violence, could only lead them both into unhappiness. That, indeed, they could! And therefore

Babette read him a little sermon, which amused her greatly and which she delivered with a pretty little air. On one point she admitted that Rudy was right: her godmother's nephew was a fop. She would burn the book that he had given her, so that she should not possess the least thing that could remind her of him.

"Now it's all over," said the parlor cat. "Rudy has come back, and they are friends again, which they say is the greatest happiness of all."

"I heard the rats say last night," said the kitchen cat, "that the greatest happiness consists in eating tallow candles and having plenty of rancid bacon. Whom is one to believe—the rats, or the lovers?"

"Neither," said the parlor cat, "that is the safest."

The greatest happiness for Rudy and Babette, the happy day, as they called it, their wedding-day, was drawing near.

But the wedding was not to take place in the church at Bex, nor at the mill; Babette's godmother wished the marriage to be solemnized in the pretty little church at Montreux, and the festivities to be held at her house. The miller was very anxious that her wish should be acceded to; he alone knew what she had determined to do for the newly married couple. They were to receive a wedding present from her which was well worth some such concession to her will.

The day was fixed. They were to travel as far as Villeneuve on the previous evening to be in time to take the boat across to Montreux early the next morning, so that the godmother's daughters might dress the bride.

"I suppose there will be a wedding feast in this house too," said the parlor cat; "if not, I wouldn't give a mew for the whole thing."

"Of course there'll be a feast here," said the kitchen cat. "Ducks have been killed, pigeons plucked, and a whole roebuck is hanging on the wall. My mouth waters when I think of it. They start to-morrow!"

Yes, to-morrow! That evening Rudy and Babette for the last time sat together as an engaged couple in the miller's house. Outside the glow was on the Alps, the evening bells rang out and the daughter of the sun sang: "Let what is best, happen!"

Night Visions

The sun had gone down, and the clouds lay low in the Rhone valley between the mountain-peaks. The wind blew from the south across the high Alps It was the wind from Africa—a hurricane that scattered the clouds; and when it had passed, all was still for a moment. The rent clouds hung in fantastic forms between the wooded hills and over the rapid Rhone river. They hung in shapes like the sea-monsters of old, like the eagle hovering in the air, like the jumping frogs in the marsh; they lay low upon the rushing stream, and sailed down upon it, though floating in the air. The stream carried an up-rooted fir-tree down with it, making eddying circles all around it; the Spirits of Giddiness were there, more than one, circling on the foaming waters. The moon lit up the snow-clad mountain peaks, the dark woods, and the strange white clouds—those forms of night that are the spirits of Nature's powers. The mountain-dwellers saw them through the window-panes, sailing past in troops before the Ice Maiden as she came out of her glacier-castle, sitting on the frail bark formed by the uprooted fir; the glacier-water carried her down the stream to the open sea.

"The wedding-guests are coming," was whistled in the air and sung upon the waters.

There were visions without and visions within.

Babette was dreaming a strange dream.

She dreamt that she had been married to Rudy for many years. He was gone out chamois-hunting, but she was sitting at home, and the young Englishman with the golden whiskers was with her. His eyes were so eloquent, and his words possessed such power, that when he held out his hand to her, she was obliged to follow him. They strode away from the house by a path that led ever downwards. Babette felt as though a weight lay upon her heart, which continually grew heavier; she was sinning against Rudy and against God. Suddenly she found herself deserted, her clothes torn by thorns, and her hair turned gray; looking upwards in her grief, she saw Rudy standing on a cliff. She stretched her arms out towards him, but did not venture to call or beg him to come; besides, that would have been useless, for she soon discovered that it was not Rudy, but only his coat and hat which he had hung upon his alpenstock as the hunters do to deceive the chamois. In her boundless grief Babette exclaimed: "Oh! would that I had died on my wedding-day, the happiest day of my life! My God! that would have been a mercy and a blessing. That would have been the best that could have happened for Rudy and me. No one knows the future!" Then, in godless despair, she hurled herself into the deep ravine. A sound like the breaking of a harpstring and one plaintive note was heard, and then Babette awoke.

The dream was past and effaced; but she knew that she had dreamt something terrible about the young Englishman whom she had not seen nor thought of for several months. She wondered whether he was at Montreux, and whether she should see him at the wedding. A slight shadow passed over her pretty face, and her eyebrows contracted. But soon a smile played around her lips and her eyes sparkled with joy, for the sun was shining gloriously, and to-morrow she and Rudy were to be married.

Rudy was already in the parlor when she entered it, and soon they were off to Villeneuve. Both were exceedingly happy, and so was the miller; he laughed and proved himself in the best of humors. He was a kind father and an honest soul.

"Now we are the masters of the house," said the parlor cat.

Conclusion

Evening had not yet fallen when the three joyous companions reached Villeneuve and sat down to dinner. This over, the miller sat in an armchair, smoked his pipe and had a little nap. The young bridal pair walked through the town arm in arm, and along the high road, at the foot of the wooded rocks by the side of the deep blue lake. The gloomy castle of Chillon, with its gray walls and ponderous towers, was reflected in the clear waters; the little island with the acacias was still nearer, and looked like a bouquet lying on the lake.

"How charming it must be there!" said Babette. She again felt her former desire come over her to cross to the island; this wish could now be gratified, for on the shore lay a boat, and the rope by which it was moored could easily be loosened. Seeing no one whom they could ask for permission, they took the boat without more ado, Rudy knowing how to row very well. The oars moved through the pliant water like the fins of a fish—that water which is so yielding and yet so strong, which has a back for carrying and jaws for swallowing, which though mild and smiling when at peace can inspire such terror in its destroying moods. A white streak of foam followed in the wake of the boat, which in a few minutes took them both over to the island, where they landed. There was only just room enough for two to dance.

Rudy swung Babette round two or three times, and then they sat down, hand in hand, on the little bench under the drooping acacias, looking into each other's eyes, while all around was bathed in the splendor of the setting sun. The pine-woods on the mountains assumed a purplish red tint like that of the blooming heather, and where the rocks were no longer covered with trees, they glowed as if the hills were transparent. The clouds in the sky were brilliant with a crimson glow, and the whole lake was like a fresh blooming rose-leaf. Gradually the shadows crept up the snow-clad mountains of Savoy and lent them a dark-blue hue till only the topmost peak glowed like red lava. They thus represented a moment in the history of the creation of the mountains, when these masses had just arisen in full glow out of the bowels of the earth and had not yet cooled down. Rudy and Babette thought they had never beheld such an Alpine glow before. The snow-clad "Dent du Midi" shone like the disk of the full moon when it rises above the horizon.

"What beauty! what happiness!" both exclaimed.

"Earth can bestow no more on me," said Rudy. "An evening such as this is a whole life. How often have I felt my happiness, as I feel it now, and thought that if all were to come to a sudden end, what a happy life I should have lived, and how beautiful this world would have been for me. But the day passed, and a new one, more beautiful even than the other, dawned for me. How infinitely good God is, Babette."

"I am truly happy," said she.

"Earth can bestow no more on me," exclaimed Rudy. And the evening bells rang out from the hills of Savoy and the mountains of Switzerland, while in the west the dark-blue Jura stood out in golden splendor.

"God grant you all that is brightest and best!" said Babette.

"He will," said Rudy. "To-morrow I shall have it. Tomorrow you will be entirely mine. My own sweet wife!"

"The boat!" cried Babette suddenly.

The boat which was to carry them back had become unfastened and was floating away from the island.

"I'll bring it back," said Rudy; and taking off his coat and boots, he plunged into the lake and swam with vigorous strokes after the boat.

Cold and deep was the clear blue ice-water from the mountain glacier. Rudy looked down into it; he took only a single glance, yet he thought he saw a golden ring rolling, shining, and sparkling in the depths. He remembered his engagement ring, and the ring became larger, extending itself into a shining circle within which appeared the clear glacier; deep chasms yawned around it, and the water dropped tinkling like the sound of bells, and gleaming with pale blue flames. In a second he saw what it takes us many words to describe.

Young hunters and young girls, men and women who had once fallen into the crevasses of the glaciers stood, there alive with smiles upon their lips, and far beneath the church bells of buried towns were ringing. The congregation knelt under the vaulted roof; the organ-pipes were formed of icicles and the mountain torrent furnished the music. The Ice Maiden sat on the clear transparent ground, and raising herself up towards Rudy kissed his feet. There passed through his limbs an icy death-like chill, an electric shock—ice and fire: for it is impossible to distinguish one from the other in a brief touch.

"Mine, mine!" sounded around him and within him.

"I kissed you when you were a child, kissed you on your mouth. Now I kiss you on your toes and heels, and you are entirely mine."

And he disappeared in the clear blue waters.

All was still; the church bells ceased ringing, their last notes dying away with the glow on the red clouds above.

"You are mine," resounded in the depths; "you are mine," re-echoed from on high—from the infinite.

How glorious to pass from love to love, from earth to Heaven!

A sound like the breaking of a harp-string, and a plaintive note were heard—the icy kiss of death had conquered what is mortal. The prelude had ended so that the real drama of life might begin; discord had resolved itself into harmony.

Do you call this a sad story?

Poor Babette! For her it was unspeakable anguish.

The boat floated farther and farther away. No one on the shore knew that the bridal pair had crossed over to the little island. The clouds began to gather, and evening came on. Alone, despairing and wailing, she stood there. A storm burst over her; the vivid lightning lit up the Jura mountains and the heights of Switzerland and Savoy; from all sides followed flash upon flash, while the peals of thunder came one upon the other, each lasting several minutes. One moment the lightning would light up the sky, so that every single vine stem could be seen as though it were broad day, and the next everything would again be plunged into darkness. The flashes formed bands, circles, and zigzags of light, darting into the lake on all sides, while the roar of the thunder increased by its own echo. On land the boats were drawn up on the beach, and every living thing had sought a shelter. And now the rain poured down in torrents.

"Where can Rudy and Babette be in this terrible storm?" said the miller.

Babette sat with folded hands, her head in her lap, dumb with grief; she wept, she wailed no more.

"In the deep water," she said to herself. "He is deep down, as under a glacier."

Then came into her mind what Rudy had told her of his mother's death, and of his escape when brought up almost dead out of the crevasse. "The Ice Maiden has him again."

There came a flash of lightning as dazzling as the sun's rays on the white snow. Babette sprang up; the lake rose at that moment like a shining glacier, and there stood the Ice Maiden, majestic, and encircled by a pale blue light, while at her feet lay Rudy's corpse. "Mine," she said, and again all was darkness and rolling water.

"How horrible!" wailed Babette. "Why was he to die just as the day of our happiness dawned? Oh, God! enlighten my understanding, shed light into my heart. I do not understand Thy ways, nor the inscrutable decrees of Thy omnipotence and wisdom."

And God enlightened her heart. A thought, a merciful ray of understanding shot through her, reminding her of her vivid dream of the past night; and she remembered the words and the wish she had uttered concerning what might be best for Rudy and herself.

"Woe is me! Was that the germ of sin in my heart? Was my dream a glimpse of our future lives, one of which had to be thus violently taken to effect my salvation? Miserable wretch that I am!"

She sat there wailing in the dark night. Through the deep stillness she still seemed to hear Rudy's words, the last he had spoken here: "Earth can bestow no more on me!" They had been uttered in the fulness of joy, they re-echoed in the midst of deep sorrow.

Years have passed since then. The lake and its shores still smile, and the vines yield luscious grapes. Steamboats with waving flags shoot past; pleasure-boats with swelling sails fly swiftly over the water like white butterflies. The railway past Chillon is opened, leading far into the Rhone valley. At every station strangers get out, and, holding their red-bound guide-books in their hands, read what sights they have to see. They visit Chillon, they see out in the lake the little island with the three acacias, and they read in their guide-book of the bridal pair who one evening in the year 1856 sailed over to it. They read how the bridegroom met his death, and how it was only on the following morning that the despairing cries of the bride were heard from the shore.

But the guide-book does not speak of Babette's quiet life with her father, not at the mill—for strangers live there now—but in the fine house near the railway-station. Many an evening she sits at her window and looks out over the chestnut trees to the snow-clad mountains which Rudy once climbed. She sees the evening Alpine glow as the children of the sun settle down upon the lofty peaks, repeating the song of the traveler whose cloak the whirlwind tore away—taking the covering, but not the man.

There is a rosy tint on the mountain snow, and a rosy gleam in every heart in which dwells the thought: "God's will is best!" But the truth of it is not always revealed to us, as it was revealed to Babette in her dream.

The Boy Who Found Fear at Last

(FROM *THE OLIVE FAIRY BOOK*)

Once upon a time there lived a woman who had one son whom she loved dearly. The little cottage in which they dwelt was built on the outskirts of a forest, and as they had no neighbors, the place was very lonely, and the boy was kept at home by his mother to bear her company.

They were sitting together on a winter's evening, when a storm suddenly sprang up, and the wind blew the door open. The woman started and shivered, and glanced over her shoulder as if she half expected to see some horrible thing behind her. "Go and shut the door," she said hastily to her son, "I feel frightened."

"Frightened?" repeated the boy. "What does it feel like to be frightened?"

"Well—just frightened," answered the mother. "A fear of something, you hardly know what, takes hold of you."

"It must be very odd to feel like that," replied the boy. "I will go through the world and seek fear till I find it." And the next morning, before his mother was out of bed, he had left the forest behind him.

After walking for some hours he reached a mountain, which he began to climb. Near the top, in a wild and rocky spot, he came upon a band of fierce robbers, sitting round a fire. The boy, who was cold and tired, was delighted to see the bright flames, so he went up to them and said, "Good greeting to you, sirs," and wriggled himself in between the men, till his feet almost touched the burning logs.

The robbers stopped drinking and eyed him curiously, and at last the captain spoke.

"No caravan of armed men would dare to come here, even the very birds shun our camp, and who are you to venture in so boldly?"

"Oh, I have left my mother's house in search of fear. Perhaps you can show it to me?"

"Fear is wherever we are," answered the captain.

"But *where*?" asked the boy, looking round. "I see nothing."

"Take this pot and some flour and butter and sugar over to the churchyard which lies down there, and bake us a cake for supper," replied the robber. And the boy, who was by this time quite warm, jumped up cheerfully, and slinging the pot over his arm, ran down the hill.

When he got to the churchyard he collected some sticks and made a fire; then he filled the pot with water from a little stream close by, and mixing the flour and butter and sugar together, he set the cake on to cook. It was not long before it grew crisp and brown, and then the boy lifted it from the pot and placed it on a stone, while he put out the fire. At that moment a hand was stretched from a grave, and a voice said:

"Is that cake for me?"

"Do you think I am going to give to the dead the food of the living?" replied the boy, with a laugh. And giving the hand a tap with his spoon, and picking up the cake, he went up the mountain side, whistling merrily.

"Well, have you found fear?" asked the robbers when he held out the cake to the captain.

"No; was it there?" answered the boy. "I saw nothing but a hand which came from a grave, and belonged to someone who wanted my cake, but I just rapped the fingers with my spoon, and said it was not for him, and then the hand vanished. Oh, how nice the fire is!" And he flung himself on his knees before it, and so did not notice the glances of surprise cast by the robbers at each other.

"There is another chance for you," said one at length. "On the other side of the mountain lies a deep pool; go to that, and perhaps you may meet fear on the way."

"I hope so, indeed," answered the boy. And he set out at once.

He soon beheld the waters of the pool gleaming in the moonlight, and as he drew near he saw a tall swing standing just over it, and in the swing a child was seated, weeping bitterly.

"That is a strange place for a swing," thought the boy; "but I wonder what he is crying about." And he was hurrying on towards the child, when a maiden ran up and spoke to him.

"I want to lift my little brother from the swing," cried she, "but it is so high above me, that I cannot reach. If you will get closer to the edge of the pool, and let me mount on your shoulder, I think I can reach him."

"Willingly," replied the boy, and in an instant the girl had climbed to his shoulders. But instead of lifting the child from the swing, as she could easily have done, she pressed her feet so firmly on either side of the youth's neck, that he felt that in another minute he would be choked, or else fall into the water beneath him. So gathering up all his strength, he gave a mighty heave, and threw the girl backwards. As she touched the ground a bracelet fell from her arm, and this the youth picked up.

"I may as well keep it as a remembrance of all the queer things that have happened to me since I left home," he said to himself, and turning to look for the child, he saw that both it and the swing had vanished, and that the first streaks of dawn were in the sky.

With the bracelet on his arm, the youth started for a little town which was situated in the plain on the further side of the mountain, and as, hungry and thirsty, he entered its principal street, an ogre stopped him. "Where did you get that bracelet?" asked the ogre. "It belongs to me."

"No, it is mine," replied the boy.

"It is not. Give it to me at once, or it will be the worse for you!" cried the ogre.

"Let us go before a judge, and tell him our stories," said the boy. "If he decides in your favor, you shall have it; if in mine, I will keep it!"

To this the ogre agreed, and the two went together to the great hall, in which the kadi was administering justice. He listened very carefully to what each had to say, and then pronounced his verdict. Neither of the two claimants had proved his right to the bracelet, therefore it must remain in the possession of the judge till its fellow was brought before him.

When they heard this, the ogre and the boy looked at each other, and their eyes said: "Where are we to go to find the other one?" But as they knew there was no use in disputing the decision, they bowed low and left the hall of audience.

Wandering he knew not whither, the youth found himself on the sea-shore. At a little distance was a ship which had struck on a hidden rock, and was rapidly sinking, while on deck the crew were gathered, with faces white as death, shrieking and wringing their hands.

"Have you met with fear?" shouted the boy. And the answer came above the noise of the waves.

"Oh, help! help! We are drowning!"

Then the boy flung off his clothes, and swam to the ship, where many hands were held out to draw him on board.

"The ship is tossed hither and thither, and will soon be sucked down," cried the crew again. "Death is very near, and we are frightened!"

"Give me a rope," said the boy in reply, and he took it, and made it safe round his body at one end, and to the mast at the other, and sprang into the sea. Down he went, down, down, down, till at last his feet touched the bottom, and he stood up and looked about him. There, sure enough, a sea-maiden with a wicked face was tugging hard at a chain which she had fastened to the ship with a grappling iron, and was dragging it bit by bit beneath the waves. Seizing her arms in both his hands, he forced her to drop the chain, and the ship above remaining steady, the sailors were able gently to float her off the rock. Then taking a rusty knife from a heap of seaweed at his feet, he cut the rope round his waist and fastened the sea-maiden firmly to a stone, so that she could do no more mischief, and bidding her farewell, he swam back to the beach, where his clothes were still lying.

The youth dressed himself quickly and walked on till he came to a beautiful shady garden filled with flowers, and with a clear little stream running through. The day was hot, and he was tired, so he entered the gate, and seated himself under a clump of bushes covered with sweet-smelling red blossoms, and it was not long before he fell asleep. Suddenly a rush of wings and a cool breeze awakened him, and raising his head cautiously, he saw three doves

plunging into the stream. They splashed joyfully about, and shook themselves, and then dived to the bottom of a deep pool. When they appeared
again they were no longer three doves, but three beautiful damsels, bearing
between them a table made of mother of pearl. On this they placed drinking
cups fashioned from pink and green shells, and one of the maidens filled a
cup from a crystal goblet, and was raising it to her mouth, when her sister
stopped her.

"To whose health do you drink?" asked she.

"To the youth who prepared the cake, and rapped my hand with the
spoon when I stretched it out of the earth," answered the maiden, "and was
never afraid as other men were! But to whose health do you drink?"

"To the youth on whose shoulders I climbed at the edge of the pool, and
who threw me off with such a jerk, that I lay unconscious on the ground for
hours," replied the second. "But you, my sister," added she, turning to the
third girl, "to whom do you drink?"

"Down in the sea I took hold of a ship and shook it and pulled it till it
would soon have been lost," said she. And as she spoke she looked quite different from what she had done with the chain in her hands, seeking to work
mischief. "But a youth came, and freed the ship and bound me to a rock. To
his health I drink," and they all three lifted their cups and drank silently.

As they put their cups down, the youth appeared before them.

"Here am I, the youth whose health you have drunk; and now give me the
bracelet that matches a jewelled band which of a surety fell from the arm of
one of you. An ogre tried to take it from me, but I would not let him have it,
and he dragged me before the kadi, who kept my bracelet till I could show
him its fellow. And I have been wandering hither and thither in search of it,
and that is how I have found myself in such strange places."

"Come with us, then," said the maidens, and they led him down a passage into a hall, out of which opened many chambers, each one of greater
splendor than the last. From a shelf heaped up with gold and jewels the eldest
sister took a bracelet, which in every way was exactly like the one which was
in the judge's keeping, and fastened it to the youth's arm.

"Go at once and show this to the kadi," said she, "and he will give you the
fellow to it."

"I shall never forget you," answered the youth, "but it may be long before
we meet again, for I shall never rest till I have found fear." Then he went his

way, and won the bracelet from the kadi. After this, he again set forth in his quest of fear.

On and on walked the youth, but fear never crossed his path, and one day he entered a large town, where all the streets and squares were so full of people, he could hardly pass between them.

"Why are all these crowds gathered together?" he asked of a man who stood next him.

"The ruler of this country is dead," was the reply, "and as he had no children, it is needful to choose a successor. Therefore each morning one of the sacred pigeons is let loose from the tower yonder, and on whomsoever the bird shall perch, that man is our king. In a few minutes the pigeon will fly. Wait and see what happens."

Every eye was fixed on the tall tower which stood in the center of the chief square, and the moment that the sun was seen to stand straight over it, a door was opened and a beautiful pigeon, gleaming with pink and gray, blue and green, came rushing through the air. Onward it flew, onward, onward, till at length it rested on the head of the boy. Then a great shout arose:

"The king! the king!" but as he listened to the cries, a vision, swifter than lightning, flashed across his brain. He saw himself seated on a throne, spending his life trying, and never succeeding, to make poor people rich; miserable people happy; bad people good; never doing anything he wished to do, not able even to marry the girl that he loved.

"No! no!" he shrieked, hiding his face in his hands; but the crowds who heard him thought he was overcome by the grandeur that awaited him, and paid no heed.

"Well, to make quite sure, let fly more pigeons," said they, but each pigeon followed where the first had led, and the cries arose louder than ever:

"The king! the king!" And as the young man heard, a cold shiver, that he knew not the meaning of, ran through him.

"This is fear whom you have so long sought," whispered a voice, which seemed to reach his ears alone. And the youth bowed his head as the vision once more flashed before his eyes, and he accepted his doom, and made ready to pass his life with fear beside him.

A Christmas Tree

CHARLES DICKENS

I have been looking on, this evening, at a merry company of children assembled round that pretty German toy, a Christmas Tree. The tree was planted in the middle of a great round table, and towered high above their heads. It was brilliantly lighted by a multitude of little tapers; and everywhere sparkled and glittered with bright objects. There were rosy-cheeked dolls, hiding behind the green leaves; and there were real watches (with movable hands, at least, and an endless capacity of being wound up) dangling from innumerable twigs; there were French-polished tables, chairs, bedsteads, wardrobes, eight-day clocks, and various other articles of domestic furniture (wonderfully made, in tin, at Wolverhampton), perched among the boughs, as if in preparation for some fairy housekeeping; there were jolly, broad-faced little men, much more agreeable in appearance than many real men—and no wonder, for their heads took off, and showed them to be full of sugar-plums; there were fiddles and drums; there were tambourines, books, workboxes, paint-boxes, sweetmeat-boxes, peep-show boxes, and all kinds of boxes; there were trinkets for the elder girls, far brighter than any grown-up gold and jewels; there were baskets and pincushions in all devices; there were guns, swords, and banners; there were witches standing in enchanted rings of pasteboard, to tell fortunes; there were teetotums, humming-tops, needle-cases, pen-wipers, smelling-bottles, conversation-cards, bouquet-holders; real fruit, made artificially dazzling with gold leaf; imitation apples, pears, and walnuts, crammed with surprises; in short, as a pretty child, before me, delightedly whispered to another pretty child, her bosom friend, "There was everything, and more." This motley collection of odd objects, clustering on the tree like magic fruit, and flashing back the bright looks directed towards it from every side—some of the diamond-eyes admiring it were hardly on a level with the table, and a few were languishing in timid wonder on the bosoms of pretty mothers, aunts, and nurses—made a lively realization of the fancies of childhood; and set me thinking how all the trees that grow and all the things that come into existence on the earth, have their wild adornments at that well-remembered time.

Being now at home again, and alone, the only person in the house awake, my thoughts are drawn back, by a fascination which I do not care to resist, to my own childhood. I begin to consider, what do we all remember best upon the branches of the Christmas Tree of our own young Christmas days, by which we climbed to real life.

Straight, in the middle of the room, cramped in the freedom of its growth by no encircling walls or soon-reached ceiling, a shadowy tree arises; and, looking up into the dreamy brightness of its top—for I observe in this tree the singular property that it appears to grow downward towards the earth— I look into my youngest Christmas recollections!

All toys at first, I find. Up yonder, among the green holly and red berries, is the Tumbler with his hands in his pockets, who wouldn't lie down, but whenever he was put upon the floor, persisted in rolling his fat body about, until he rolled himself still, and brought those lobster eyes of his to bear upon me—when I affected to laugh very much, but in my heart of hearts was extremely doubtful of him. Close beside him is that infernal snuff-box, out of which there sprang a demoniacal Counselor in a black gown, with an obnoxious head of hair, and a red cloth mouth, wide open, who was not to be endured on any terms, but could not be put away either; for he used suddenly, in a highly magnified state, to fly out of Mammoth Snuff-boxes in dreams, when least expected. Nor is the frog with cobbler's wax on his tail, far off; for there was no knowing where he wouldn't jump; and when he flew over the candle, and came upon one's hand with that spotted back—red on a green ground—he was horrible. The cardboard lady in a blue-silk skirt, who was stood up against the candlestick to dance, and whom I see on the same branch, was milder, and was beautiful; but I can't say as much for the larger cardboard man, who used to be hung against the wall and pulled by a string; there was a sinister expression in that nose of his; and when he got his legs round his neck (which he very often did), he was ghastly, and not a creature to be alone with.

When did that dreadful Mask first look at me? Who put it on, and why was I so frightened that the sight of it is an era in my life? It is not a hideous visage in itself; it is even meant to be droll; why then were its stolid features so intolerable? Surely not because it hid the wearer's face. An apron would have done as much; and though I should have preferred even the apron away, it would not have been absolutely insupportable, like the mask. Was it the immovability of the mask? The doll's face was immovable, but I was not afraid of her. Perhaps that fixed and set change coming over a real face, infused into my quickened heart some remote suggestion and dread of the universal change that is to come on every face, and make it still? Nothing reconciled me to it. No drummers, from whom proceeded a melancholy chirping on the turning of a handle; no regiment of soldiers, with a mute band, taken out of a box, and fitted, one by one, upon a stiff and lazy little set of lazy-tongs; no old woman, made of wires and a brown-paper composition, cutting up a pie for two small children; could give me a permanent comfort, for a long time. Nor was it any satisfaction to be shown the Mask, and see that it was made of paper, or to have it locked up and be assured that no one wore it. The mere recollection of that fixed face, the mere knowledge of its existence anywhere, was sufficient to awake me in the night all perspiration and horror, with, "O I know it's coming! O the mask!"

I never wondered what the dear old donkey with the panniers—there he is! was made of, then! His hide was real to the touch, I recollect. And the great black horse with the round red spots all over him—the horse that I could even get upon—I never wondered what had brought him to that strange condition, or thought that such a horse was not commonly seen at Newmarket. The four horses of no color, next to him, that went into the wag-gon of cheeses, and could be taken out and stabled under the piano, appear to have bits of fur-tippet for their tails, and other bits for their manes, and to stand on pegs instead of legs, but it was not so when they were brought home for a Christmas present. They were all right, then; neither was their harness unceremoniously nailed into their chests, as appears to be the case now. The tinkling works of the music-cart, I *did* find out, to be made of quill tooth-picks and wire; and I always thought that little tumbler in his shirt sleeves, perpetually swarming up one side of a wooden frame, and coming down, head foremost, on the other, rather a weak-minded person—though good-natured; but the Jacob's Ladder, next him, made of little squares of red wood, that went flapping and clattering over one another, each developing a different picture, and the whole enlivened by small bells, was a mighty mar-vel and a great delight.

Ah! The Doll's house!—of which I was not proprietor, but where I visited. I don't admire the Houses of Parliament half so much as that stone-fronted mansion with real glass windows, and door-steps, and a real balcony—greener than I ever see now, except at watering places; and even they afford but a poor imitation. And though it did open all at once, the entire house-front (which was a blow, I admit, as cancelling the fiction of a staircase), it was but to shut it up again, and I could believe. Even open, there were three distinct rooms in it: a sitting-room and bed-room, elegantly furnished, and best of all, a kitchen, with uncommonly soft fire-irons, a plentiful assortment of diminutive utensils—oh, the warming-pan!—and a tin man-cook in profile, who was always going to fry two fish. What Barmecide justice have I done to the noble feasts wherein the set of wooden platters figured, each with its own peculiar delicacy, as a ham or turkey, glued tight on to it, and garnished with something green, which I recollect as moss! Could all the Temperance Societies of these later days, united, give me such a tea-drinking as I have had through the means of yonder little set of blue crockery, which really would hold liquid (it ran out of the small wooden cask, I recollect, and tasted of matches), and which made tea, nectar. And if the two legs of the ineffectual little sugar-tongs did tumble over one another, and want purpose, like Punch's hands, what does it matter? And if I did once shriek out, as a poisoned child, and strike the fashionable company with consternation, by reason of having drunk a little teaspoon, inadvertently dissolved in too hot tea, I was never the worse for it, except by a powder!

Upon the next branches of the tree, lower down, hard by the green roller and miniature gardening-tools, how thick the books begin to hang. Thin books, in themselves, at first, but many of them, and with deliciously smooth covers of bright red or green. What fat black letters to begin with! "A was an archer, and shot at a frog." Of course he was. He was an apple-pie also, and there he is! He was a good many things in his time, was A, and so were most of his friends, except X, who had so little versatility, that I never knew him to get beyond Xerxes or Xantippe—like Y, who was always confined to a Yacht or a Yew Tree; and Z condemned for ever to be a Zebra or a Zany. But, now, the very tree itself changes, and becomes a bean-stalk—the marvelous bean-stalk up which Jack climbed to the Giant's house! And now, those dreadfully interesting, double-headed giants, with their clubs over their shoulders, begin to stride along the boughs in a perfect throng, dragging knights and ladies home for dinner by the hair of their heads. And Jack—how noble, with his sword of sharpness, and his shoes of swiftness! Again those old meditations come upon me as I gaze up at him; and I debate within myself whether there was more than one Jack (which I am loth to believe possible), or only one genuine original admirable Jack, who achieved all the recorded exploits.

Good for Christmas-time is the ruddy color of the cloak, in which—the tree making a forest of itself for her to trip through, with her basket—Little Red Riding-Hood comes to me one Christmas Eve to give me information of the cruelty and treachery of that dissembling Wolf who ate her grand-mother, without making any impression on his appetite, and then ate her, after making that ferocious joke about his teeth. She was my first love. I felt that if I could have married Little Red Riding-Hood, I should have known perfect bliss. But, it was not to be; and there was nothing for it but to look out the Wolf in the Noah's Ark there, and put him late in the procession on the table, as a monster who was to be degraded. O the wonderful Noah's Ark! It was not found seaworthy when put in a washing-tub, and the ani-mals were crammed in at the roof, and needed to have their legs well shaken down before they could be got in, even there—and then, ten to one but they began to tumble out at the door, which was but imperfectly fastened with a wire latch—but what was *that* against it! Consider the noble fly, a size or two smaller than the elephant: the lady-bird, the butterfly—all triumphs of art! Consider the goose, whose feet were so small, and whose balance was so indifferent, that he usually tumbled forward, and knocked down all the ani-mal creation. Consider Noah and his family, like idiotic tobacco-stoppers; and how the leopard stuck to warm little fingers; and how the tails of the larger animals used gradually to resolve themselves into frayed bits of string!

Hush! Again a forest, and somebody up in a tree—not Robin Hood, not Valentine, not the Yellow Dwarf (I have passed him and all Mother Bunch's wonders, without mention), but an Eastern King with a glittering scimitar and turban. By Allah! two Eastern Kings, for I see another, looking over his shoulder! Down upon the grass, at the tree's foot, lies the full length of a coal-black Giant, stretched asleep, with his head in a lady's lap; and near them is a glass box, fastened with four locks of shining steel, in which he keeps the lady prisoner when he is awake. I see the four keys at his girdle now. The lady makes signs to the two kings in the tree, who softly descend. It is the setting-in of the bright Arabian Nights.

Oh, now all common things become uncommon and enchanted to me. All lamps are wonderful; all rings are talismans. Common flower-pots are full of treasure, with a little earth scattered on the top; trees are for Ali Baba to hide in; beef-steaks are to throw down into the Valley of Diamonds, that the precious stones may stick to them, and be carried by the eagles to their nests, whence the traders, with loud cries, will scare them. Tarts are made, according to the recipe of the Vizier's son of Bussorah, who turned pastry-cook after he was set down in his drawers at the gate of Damascus; cobblers are all Mustaphas, and in the habit of sewing up people cut into four pieces, to whom they are taken blindfold.

Any iron ring let into stone is the entrance to a cave which only waits for the magician, and the little fire, and the necromancy, that will make the earth shake. All the dates imported come from the same tree as that unlucky date, with whose shell the merchant knocked out the eye of the genie's invisible son. All olives are of the stock of that fresh fruit, concerning which the Commander of the Faithful overheard the boy conduct the fictitious trial of the fraudulent olive merchant; all apples are akin to the apple purchased (with two others) from the Sultan's gardener for three sequins, and which the tall black slave stole from the child. All dogs are associated with the dog, really a transformed man, who jumped upon the baker's counter, and put his paw on the piece of bad money. All rice recalls the rice which the awful lady, who was a ghoul, could only peck by grains, because of her nightly feasts in the burial-place. My very rocking horse,—there he is, with his nostrils turned completely inside-out, indicative of Blood!—should have a peg in his neck, by virtue thereof to fly away with me, as the wooden horse did with the Prince of Persia, in the sight of all his father's Court.

Yes, on every object that I recognize among those upper branches of my Christmas Tree, I see this fairy light! When I wake in bed, at daybreak, on the cold, dark, winter mornings, the white snow dimly beheld, outside, through the frost on the window-pane, I hear Dinarzade. "Sister, sister, if you are yet awake, I pray you finish the history of the Young King of the Black Islands." Scheherazade replies, "If my lord the Sultan will suffer me to live another day, sister, I will not only finish that, but tell you a more wonderful story yet." Then, the gracious Sultan goes out, giving no orders for the execution, and we all three breathe again.

At this height of my tree I begin to see, cowering among the leaves— it may be born of turkey, or of pudding, or mince pie, or of these many fancies, jumbled with Robinson Crusoe on his desert island, Philip Quarll among the monkeys, Sandford and Merton with Mr. Barlow, Mother Bunch, and the Mask—or it may be the result of indigestion, assisted by imagination and over-doctoring—a prodigious nightmare. It is so exceedingly indistinct, that I don't know why it's frightful—but I know it is. I can only make out that it is an immense array of shapeless things, which appear to be planted on a vast exaggeration of the lazy-tongs that used to bear the toy soldiers, and to be slowly coming close to my eyes, and receding to an immeasurable distance. When it comes closest, it is worse. In connection with it I descry remembrances of winter nights incredibly long; of being sent early to bed, as a punishment for some small offense, and waking in two hours, with a sensation of having been asleep two nights; of the laden hopelessness of morning ever dawning; and the oppression of a weight of remorse.

And now, I see a wonderful row of little lights rise smoothly out of the ground, before a vast green curtain. Now, a bell rings—a magic bell, which still sounds in my ears unlike all other bells—and music plays, amidst a buzz of voices, and a fragrant smell of orange-peel and oil. Anon, the magic bell commands the music to cease, and the great green curtain rolls itself up majestically, and The Play begins! The devoted dog of Montargis avenges the death of his master, foully murdered in the Forest of Bondy; and a humorous Peasant with a red nose and a very little hat, whom I take from this hour forth to my bosom as a friend (I think he was a Waiter or an Hostler at a village Inn, but many years have passed since he and I have met), remarks that the sassigassity of that dog is indeed surprising; and evermore this jocular conceit will live in my remembrance fresh and unfading, overtopping all possible jokes, unto the end of time. Or now, I learn with bitter tears how poor Jane Shore, dressed all in white, and with her brown hair hanging down, went starving through the streets; or how George Barnwell killed the worthiest uncle that ever man had, and was afterwards so sorry for it that he ought to have been let off. Comes swift to comfort me, the Pantomime— stupendous Phenomenon!—when clowns are shot from loaded mortars into the great chandelier, bright constellation that it is; when Harlequins, covered all over with scales of pure gold, twist and sparkle, like amazing fish; when Pantaloon (whom I deem it no irreverence to compare in my own mind to my grandfather) puts red-hot pokers in his pocket, and cries "Here's somebody coming!" or taxes the Clown with petty larceny, by saying, "Now, I sawed you do it!" when Everything is capable, with the greatest ease, of being changed into Anything; and "Nothing is, but thinking makes it so."

Now, too, I perceive my first experience of the dreary sensation—often to return in after-life—of being unable, next day, to get back to the dull, settled world; of wanting to live for ever in the bright atmosphere I have quitted; of doting on the little Fairy, with the wand like a celestial Barber's Pole, and pining for a Fairy immortality along with her. Ah, she comes back, in many shapes, as my eye wanders down the branches of my Christmas Tree, and goes as often, and has never yet stayed by me!

Out of this delight springs the toy-theater,—there it is, with its familiar proscenium, and ladies in feathers, in the boxes!—and all its attendant occupation with paste and glue, and gum, and water colors, in the getting-up of The Miller and his Men, and Elizabeth, or the Exile of Siberia. In spite of a few besetting accidents and failures (particularly an unreasonable disposition in the respectable Kelmar, and some others, to become faint in the legs, and double up, at exciting points of the drama), a teeming world of fancies so suggestive and all-embracing, that, far below it on my Christmas Tree, I see dark, dirty, real Theaters in the day-time, adorned with these associations as with the freshest garlands of the rarest flowers, and charming me yet.

But hark! The Waits are playing, and they break my childish sleep! What images do I associate with the Christmas music as I see them set forth on the Christmas Tree? Known before all the others, keeping far apart from all the others, they gather round my little bed. An angel, speaking to a group of shepherds in a field; some travelers, with eyes uplifted, following a star; a baby in a manger; a child in a spacious temple, talking with grave men; a solemn figure, with a mild and beautiful face, raising a dead girl by the hand; again, near a city gate, calling back the son of a widow, on his bier, to life; a crowd of people looking through the opened roof of a chamber where he sits, and letting down a sick person on a bed, with ropes; the same, in a tempest, walking on the water to a ship; again, on a sea-shore, teaching a great multitude; again, with a child upon his knee, and other children round; again, restoring sight to the blind, speech to the dumb, hearing to the deaf, health to the sick, strength to the lame, knowledge to the ignorant; again, dying upon a Cross, watched by armed soldiers, a thick darkness coming on, the earth beginning to shake, and only one voice heard, "Forgive them, for they know not what they do."

Still, on the lower and maturer branches of the Tree, Christmas associations cluster thick. School-books shut up; Ovid and Virgil silenced; the Rule of Three, with its cool impertinent inquiries, long disposed of; Terence and Plautus acted no more, in an arena of huddled desks and forms, all chipped, and notched, and inked; cricket-bats, stumps, and balls, left higher up, with the smell of trodden grass and the softened noise of shouts in the evening air; the tree is still fresh, still gay. If I no more come home at Christmas-time, there will be boys and girls (thank Heaven!) while the World lasts; and they do! Yonder they dance and play upon the branches of my Tree, God bless them, merrily, and my heart dances and plays too!

And I *do* come home at Christmas. We all do, or we all should. We all come home, or ought to come home, for a short holiday—the longer, the better—from the great boarding-school, where we are for ever working at our arithmetical slates, to take, and give a rest. As to going a visiting, where can we not go, if we will; where have we not been, when we would; starting our fancy from our Christmas Tree!

Away into the winter prospect. There are many such upon the tree! On, by low-lying, misty grounds, through fens and fogs, up long hills, winding dark as caverns between thick plantations, almost shutting out the sparkling stars; so, out on broad heights, until we stop at last, with sudden silence, at an avenue. The gate-bell has a deep, half-awful sound in the frosty air; the gate swings open on its hinges; and, as we drive up to a great house, the glancing lights grow larger in the windows, and the opposing rows of trees seem to fall solemnly back on either side, to give us place. At intervals, all day, a frightened hare has shot across this whitened turf; or the distant clatter of a herd of deer trampling the hard frost, has, for the minute, crushed the silence too. Their watchful eyes beneath the fern may be shining now, if we could see them, like the icy dewdrops on the leaves; but they are still, and all is still. And so, the lights growing larger, and the trees falling back before us, and closing up again behind us, as if to forbid retreat, we come to the house.

There is probably a smell of roasted chestnuts and other good comfortable things all the time, for we are telling Winter Stories—Ghost Stories, or more shame for us—round the Christmas fire; and we have never stirred, except to draw a little nearer to it. But, no matter for that. We came to the house, and it is an old house, full of great chimneys where wood is burnt on ancient dogs upon the hearth, and grim portraits (some of them with grim legends, too) lower distrustfully from the oaken panels of the walls. We are a middle-aged nobleman, and we make a generous supper with our host and hostess and their guests—it being Christmas-time, and the old house full of company—and then we go to bed. Our room is a very old room. It is hung with tapestry. We don't like the portrait of a cavalier in green, over the fireplace. There are great black beams in the ceiling, and there is a great black bedstead, supported at the foot by two great black figures, who seem to have come off a couple of tombs in the old baronial church in the park, for our particular accommodation. But, we are not a superstitious noble-man, and we don't mind. Well! we dismiss our servant, lock the door, and sit before the fire in our dressing-gown, musing about a great many things. At length we go to bed. Well! we can't sleep. We toss and tumble, and can't sleep. The embers on the hearth burn fitfully and make the room look ghostly. We can't help peeping out over the counterpane, at the two black figures and the cavalier—that wicked-looking cavalier—in green. In the flickering light they seem to advance and retire: which, though we are not by any means a superstitious nobleman, is not agreeable. Well! we get nervous—more and more nervous. We say "This is very foolish, but we can't stand this; we'll pretend to be ill, and knock up somebody." Well! we are just going to do it, when the locked door opens, and there comes in a young woman, deadly pale, and with long fair hair, who glides to the fire, and sits down in the chair we have left there, wringing her hands. Then, we notice that her clothes are wet. Our tongue cleaves to the roof of our mouth, and we can't speak; but, we observe her accurately. Her clothes are wet; her long hair is dabbled with moist mud; she is dressed in the fashion of two hundred years ago; and she has at her girdle a bunch of rusty keys. Well! there she sits, and we can't even faint, we are in such a state about it. Presently she gets up, and tries all the locks in the room with the rusty keys, which won't fit one of them; then, she fixes her eyes on the portrait of the cavalier in green, and says, in a low, terrible voice, "The stags know it!" After that, she wrings her hands again, passes the bedside, and goes out at the door. We hurry on our dressing-gown, seize our pistols (we always travel with pistols), and are following, when we find the door locked. We turn the key, look out into the dark gallery; no one there. We wander away, and try to find our servant. Can't be done. We pace the gallery till daybreak; then return to our deserted room, fall asleep, and are awakened by our servant (nothing ever haunts *him*) and the shining sun. Well! we make a wretched breakfast, and all the company say we look queer. After breakfast, we go over the house with our host, and then we take him to the portrait of the cavalier in green, and then it all comes out. He was false to a young housekeeper once attached to that family, and famous for her beauty, who drowned herself in a pond, and whose body was discovered, after a long time, because the stags refused to drink of the water. Since which, it has been whispered that she traverses the house at midnight (but goes especially to that room where the cavalier in green was wont to sleep), trying the old locks with the rusty keys. Well! we tell our host of what we have seen, and a shade comes over his features, and he begs it may be hushed up; and so it is. But, it's all true; and we said so, before we died (we are dead now) to many responsible people.

There is no end to the old houses, with resounding galleries, and dismal state-bedchambers, and haunted wings shut up for many years, through which we may ramble, with an agreeable creeping up our back, and encounter any number of ghosts, but (it is worthy of remark perhaps) reducible to a very few general types and classes; for, ghosts have little originality, and "walk" in a beaten track. Thus, it comes to pass, that a certain room in a certain old hall, where a certain bad lord, baronet, knight, or gentleman, shot himself, has certain planks in the floor from which the blood *will* *not* be taken out. You may scrape and scrape, as the present owner has done, or plane and plane, as his father did, or scrub and scrub, as his grandfather did, or burn and burn with strong acids, as his great-grandfather did, but, there the blood will still be—no redder and no paler—no more and no less—always just the same. Thus, in such another house there is a haunted door, that never will keep open; or another door that never will keep shut; or a haunted sound of a spinning-wheel, or a hammer, or a footstep, or a cry, or a sigh, or a horse's tramp, or the rattling of a chain. Or else, there is a turret-clock, which, at the midnight hour, strikes thirteen when the head of the family is going to die; or a shadowy, immovable black carriage which at such a time is always seen by somebody, waiting near the great gates in the stable-yard. Or thus, it came to pass how Lady Mary went to pay a visit at a large wild house in the Scottish Highlands, and, being fatigued with her long journey, retired to bed early, and innocently said, next morning, at the breakfast-table, "How odd, to have so late a party last night, in this remote place, and not to tell me of it, before I went to bed!" Then, every one asked Lady Mary what she meant? Then, Lady Mary replied, "Why, all night long, the carriages were driving round and round the terrace, underneath my window!" Then, the owner of the house turned pale, and so did his Lady, and Charles Macdoodle of Macdoodle signed to Lady Mary to say no more, and every one was silent. After breakfast, Charles Macdoodle told Lady Mary that it was a tradition in the family that those rumbling carriages on the terrace betokened death. And so it proved, for, two months afterwards, the Lady of the mansion died. And Lady Mary, who was a Maid of Honor at Court, often told this story to the old Queen Charlotte; by this token that the old King always said, "Eh, eh? What, what? Ghosts, ghosts? No such thing, no such thing!" And never left off saying so, until he went to bed.

Or, a friend of somebody's whom most of us know, when he was a young man at college, had a particular friend, with whom he made the compact that, if it were possible for the Spirit to return to this earth after its separation from the body, he of the twain who first died, should reappear to the other. In course of time, this compact was forgotten by our friend; the two young men having progressed in life, and taken diverging paths that were wide asunder. But, one night, many years afterwards, our friend being in the North of England, and staying for the night in an inn, on the Yorkshire Moors, happened to look out of bed; and there, in the moonlight, leaning on a bureau near the window, steadfastly regarding him, saw his old college friend! The appearance being solemnly addressed, replied, in a kind of whisper, but very audibly, "Do not come near me. I am dead. I am here to redeem my promise. I come from another world, but may not disclose its secrets!" Then, the whole form becoming paler, melted, as it were, into the moonlight, and faded away.

Or, there was the daughter of the first occupier of the picturesque Elizabethan house, so famous in our neighborhood. You have heard about her? No! Why, *She* went out one summer evening at twilight, when she was a beautiful girl, just seventeen years of age, to gather flowers in the garden; and presently came running, terrified, into the hall to her father, saying, "Oh, dear father, I have met myself!" He took her in his arms, and told her it was fancy, but she said, "Oh no! I met myself in the broad walk, and I was pale and gathering withered flowers, and I turned my head, and held them up!" And, that night, she died; and a picture of her story was begun, though never finished, and they say it is somewhere in the house to this day, with its face to the wall.

Or, the uncle of my brother's wife was riding home on horseback, one mellow evening at sunset, when, in a green lane close to his own house, he saw a man standing before him, in the very center of a narrow way. "Why does that man in the cloak stand there!" he thought. "Does he want me to ride over him?" But the figure never moved. He felt a strange sensation at seeing it so still, but slackened his trot and rode forward. When he was so close to it, as almost to touch it with his stirrup, his horse shied, and the figure glided up the bank, in a curious, unearthly manner—backward, and without seeming to use its feet—and was gone. The uncle of my brother's wife, exclaiming, "Good Heaven! It's my cousin Harry, from Bombay!" put spurs to his horse, which was suddenly in a profuse sweat, and, wondering at such strange behavior, dashed round to the front of his house. There, he saw the same figure, just passing in at the long French window of the drawing-room, opening on the ground. He threw his bridle to a servant, and hastened in after it. His sister was sitting there, alone. "Alice, where's my cousin Harry?" "Your cousin Harry, John?" "Yes. From Bombay. I met him in the lane just now, and saw him enter here, this instant." Not a creature had been seen by any one; and in that hour and minute, as it afterwards appeared, this cousin died in India.

Or, it was a certain sensible old maiden lady, who died at ninety-nine, and retained her faculties to the last, who really did see the Orphan Boy; a story which has often been incorrectly told, but, of which the real truth is this—because it is, in fact, a story belonging to our family—and she was a connection of our family. When she was about forty years of age, and still an uncommonly fine woman (her lover died young, which was the reason why she never married, though she had many offers), she went to stay at a place in Kent, which her brother, an Indian-Merchant, had newly bought. There was a story that this place had once been held in trust by the guardian of a young boy; who was himself the next heir, and who killed the young boy by harsh and cruel treatment. She knew nothing of that. It has been said that there was a Cage in her bedroom in which the guardian used to put the boy. There was no such thing. There was only a closet. She went to bed, made no alarm whatever in the night, and in the morning said composedly to her maid when she came in, "Who is the pretty forlorn-looking child who has been peeping out of that closet all night?" The maid replied by giving a loud scream, and instantly decamping. She was surprised; but she was a woman of remarkable strength of mind, and she dressed herself and went down-stairs, and closeted herself with her brother. "Now, Walter," she said, "I have been disturbed all night by a pretty, forlorn-looking boy, who has been constantly peeping out of that closet in my room, which I can't open. This is some trick."

"I am afraid not, Charlotte," said he, "for it is the legend of the house. It is the Orphan Boy. What did he do?" "He opened the door softly," said she, "and peeped out. Sometimes, he came a step or two into the room. Then, I called to him, to encourage him, and he shrunk, and shuddered, and crept in again, and shut the door." "The closet has no communication, Charlotte," said her brother, "with any other part of the house, and it's nailed up." This was undeniably true, and it took two carpenters a whole forenoon to get it open, for examination. Then, she was satisfied that she had seen the Orphan Boy. But, the wild and terrible part of the story is, that he was also seen by three of her brother's sons, in succession, who all died young. On the occasion of each child being taken ill, he came home in a heat, twelve hours before, and said, Oh, Mamma, he had been playing under a particular oak-tree, in a certain meadow, with a strange boy—a pretty, forlorn-looking boy, who was very timid, and made signs! From fatal experience, the parents came to know that this was the Orphan Boy, and that the course of that child whom he chose for his little playmate was surely run.

Legion is the name of the German castles, where we sit up alone to wait for the Specter—where we are shown into a room, made comparatively cheerful for our reception—where we glance round at the shadows, thrown on the blank walls by the crackling fire—where we feel very lonely when the village innkeeper and his pretty daughter have retired, after laying down a fresh store of wood upon the hearth, and setting forth on the small table such supper-cheer as a cold roast capon, bread, grapes, and a flask of old Rhine wine—where the reverberating doors close on their retreat, one after another, like so many peals of sullen thunder—and where, about the small hours of the night, we come into the knowledge of divers supernatural mysteries. Legion is the name of the haunted German students, in whose society we draw yet nearer to the fire, while the schoolboy in the corner opens his eyes wide and round, and flies off the footstool he has chosen for his seat, when the door accidentally blows open. Vast is the crop of such fruit, shining on our Christmas Tree; in blossom, almost at the very top; ripening all down the boughs!

Among the later toys and fancies hanging there—as idle often and less pure—be the images once associated with the sweet old Waits, the softened music in the night, ever unalterable! Encircled by the social thoughts of Christmastime, still let the benignant figure of my childhood stand unchanged! In every cheerful image and suggestion that the season brings, may the bright star that rested above the poor roof, be the star of all the Christian World! A moment's pause, O vanishing tree, of which the lower boughs are dark to me as yet, and let me look once more! I know there are blank spaces on thy branches, where eyes that I have loved have shone and smiled; from which they are departed. But, far above, I see the raiser of the dead girl, and the Widow's Son; and God is good! If Age be hiding for me in the unseen portion of thy downward growth, O may I, with a gray head, turn a child's heart to that figure yet, and a child's trustfulness and confidence!

Now, the tree is decorated with bright merriment, and song, and dance, and cheerfulness. And they are welcome. Innocent and welcome be they ever held, beneath the branches of the Christmas Tree, which cast no gloomy shadow! But, as it sinks into the ground, I hear a whisper going through the leaves. "This, in commemoration of the law of love and kindness, mercy and compassion. This, in remembrance of Me!"

The Language of Beasts

(FROM *THE CRIMSON FAIRY BOOK*)

Once upon a time a man had a shepherd who served him many years faithfully and honestly. One day, whilst herding his flock, this shepherd heard a hissing sound, coming out of the forest near by, which he could not account for. So he went into the wood in the direction of the noise to try to discover the cause. When he approached the place he found that the dry grass and leaves were on fire, and on a tree, surrounded by flames, a snake was coiled, hissing with terror.

The shepherd stood wondering how the poor snake could escape, for the wind was blowing the flames that way, and soon that tree would be burning like the rest. Suddenly the snake cried: "O shepherd! for the love of heaven save me from this fire!"

Then the shepherd stretched his staff out over the flames and the snake wound itself round the staff and up to his hand, and from his hand it crept up his arm, and twined itself about his neck. The shepherd trembled with fright, expecting every instant to be stung to death, and said: "What an unlucky man I am! Did I rescue you only to be destroyed myself?" But the snake answered: "Have no fear; only carry me home to my father who is the King of the Snakes." The shepherd, however, was much too frightened to listen, and said that he could not go away and leave his flock alone; but the snake said: "You need not be afraid to leave your flock, no evil shall befall them; but make all the haste you can."

So he set off through the wood carrying the snake, and after a time he came to a great gateway, made entirely of snakes intertwined one with another. The shepherd stood still with surprise, but the snake round his neck whistled, and immediately all the arch unwound itself.

"When we are come to my father's house," said his own snake to him, "he will reward you with anything you like to ask—silver, gold, jewels, or whatever on this earth is most precious; but take none of all these things, ask rather to understand the language of beasts. He will refuse it to you a long time, but in the end he will grant it to you."

Soon after that they arrived at the house of the King of the Snakes, who burst into tears of joy at the sight of his daughter, as he had given her up for dead. "Where have you been all this time?" he asked, directly he could speak, and she told him that she had been caught in a forest fire, and had been rescued from the flames by the shepherd. The King of the Snakes, then turning to the shepherd, said to him: "What reward will you choose for saving my child?"

"Make me to know the language of beasts," answered the shepherd, "that is all I desire."

The king replied: "Such knowledge would be of no benefit to you, for if I granted it to you and you told any one of it, you would immediately die; ask me rather for whatever else you would most like to possess, and it shall be yours."

But the shepherd answered him: "Sir, if you wish to reward me for saving your daughter, grant me, I pray you, to know the language of beasts. I desire nothing else"; and he turned as if to depart.

Then the king called him back, saying: "If nothing else will satisfy you, open your mouth." The man obeyed, and the king spat into it, and said: "Now spit into my mouth." The shepherd did as he was told, then the King of the Snakes spat again into the shepherd's mouth. When they had spat into each other's mouths three times, the king said:

"Now you know the language of beasts, go in peace; but, if you value your life, beware lest you tell any one of it, else you will immediately die."

So the shepherd set out for home, and on his way through the wood he heard and understood all that was said by the birds, and by every living creature. When he got back to his sheep he found the flock grazing peacefully, and as he was very tired he laid himself down by them to rest a little. Hardly had he done so when two ravens flew down and perched on a tree near by, and began to talk to each other in their own language: "If that shepherd only knew that there is a vault full of gold and silver beneath where that lamb is lying, what would he not do?" When the shepherd heard these words he went straight to his master and told him, and the master at once took a waggon, and broke open the door of the vault, and they carried off the treasure. But instead of keeping it for himself, the master, who was an honorable man, gave it all up to the shepherd, saying: "Take it, it is yours. The gods have given it to you." So the shepherd took the treasure and built himself a house. He married a wife, and they lived in great peace and happiness, and he was acknowledged to be the richest man, not only of his native village, but of all the country-side. He had flocks of sheep, and cattle, and horses without end, as well as beautiful clothes and jewels.

One day, just before Christmas, he said to his wife: "Prepare everything for a great feast, to-morrow we will take things with us to the farm that the shepherds there may make merry." The wife obeyed, and all was prepared as he desired. Next day they both went to the farm, and in the evening the master said to the shepherds: "Now come, all of you, eat, drink, and make merry. I will watch the flocks myself to-night in your stead." Then he went out to spend the night with the flocks.

When midnight struck the wolves howled and the dogs barked, and the wolves spoke in their own tongue, saying:

"Shall we come in and work havoc, and you too shall eat flesh?" And the dogs answered in their tongue: "Come in, and for once we shall have enough to eat."

Now amongst the dogs there was one so old that he had only two teeth left in his head, and he spoke to the wolves, saying: "So long as I have my two teeth still in my head, I will let no harm be done to my master."

All this the master heard and understood, and as soon as morning dawned he ordered all the dogs to be killed excepting the old dog. The farm servants wondered at this order, and exclaimed: "But surely, sir, that would be a pity?"

The master answered: "Do as I bid you"; and made ready to return home with his wife, and they mounted their horses, her steed being a mare. As they went on their way, it happened that the husband rode on ahead, while the wife was a little way behind. The husband's horse, seeing this, neighed, and said to the mare: "Come along, make haste; why are you so slow?" And the mare answered: "It is very easy for you, you carry only your master, who is a thin man, but I carry my mistress, who is so fat that she weights as much as three." When the husband heard that he looked back and laughed, which the wife perceiving, she urged on the mare till she caught up with her husband, and asked him why he laughed. "For nothing at all," he answered; "just because it came into my head." She would not be satisfied with this answer, and urged him more and more to tell her why he had laughed. But he controlled himself and said: "Let me be, wife; what ails you? I do not know myself why I laughed." But the more he put her off, the more she tormented him to tell her the cause of his laughter. At length he said to her: "Know, then, that if I tell it you I shall immediately and surely die." But even this did not quiet her; she only besought him the more to tell her.

Meanwhile they had reached home, and before getting down from his horse the man called for a coffin to be brought; and when it was there he placed it in front of the house, and said to his wife:

"See, I will lay myself down in this coffin, and will then tell you why I laughed, for as soon as I have told you I shall surely die." So he lay down in the coffin, and while he took a last look around him, his old dog came out from the farm and sat down by him, and whined. When the master saw this, he called to his wife: "Bring a piece of bread to give to the dog." The wife brought some bread and threw it to the dog, but he would not look at it. Then the farm cock came and pecked at the bread; but the dog said to it: "Wretched glutton, you can eat like that when you see that your master is dying?" The cock answered: "Let him die, if he is so stupid. I have a hundred wives, which I call together when I find a grain of corn, and as soon as they are there I swallow it myself; should one of them dare to be angry, I would give her a lesson with my beak. He has only one wife, and he cannot keep her in order."

As soon as the man understood this, he got up out of the coffin, seized a stick, and called his wife into the room, saying: "Come, and I will tell you what you so much want to know"; and then he began to beat her with the stick, saying with each blow: "It is that, wife, it is that!" And in this way he taught her never again to ask why he had laughed.

At the Mole's Court

(TRADITIONAL SWEDISH TALE)

Autumn had gone and winter begun. The wind came icy cold from the north, and every leaf on the trees, every blade on the bushes was blown away. The grass lay beaten down on the ground, and the rain lashed it with its great, heavy drops. No ray of sunlight pierced the thick, dark clouds, which chased each other so wildly over the sky.

The birds that had their dwelling-places on the mountains or in the forests had long ago flown to warmer lands, because they felt that winter was approaching.

Only one little lark remained hopping among the rye stubble on the fields. She would gladly have flown with the others, but she was not able, for she had injured her wing on a brier-bush, so she could not fly with the rest. Now she sat there so dishevelled and sick, and shook herself again and again to get rid of the rain. But soon it got just as wet again, and that smarted so in the little wing.

Then the rain grew colder, and soon the drops were white. It was snow that came and the flakes fell faster and faster. Terrified, the lark hopped through the fence, and in between the bushes of the hedge, and sprang further and further, as fast as her tiny feet could move.

By and by she saw a large mound in front of her, with a dark opening on the side of it, and she hopped in there. It was very dark there, so the lark could not see anything at first, but when her eyes became used to the dim light, she found that the hole was the entrance to a long tunnel going inwards. She was now so weak and tired, she stuck her head under the well wing and went to sleep.

When she woke up and tried to look out, no opening was to be found. The snow had fallen deep outside, and a great drift lay over the mound. The lark was shut into the passage!

Dejected, she sat and thought over the situation.

"Perhaps there is a way out on the other side," said she, and began to go forward on the dark path.

After she had walked awhile, the roof grew higher, and she was inside a great cave. There was creeping and crawling on all sides, and the lark, who was now accustomed to the darkness, which was broken only by the glow-worm's pale light, saw that she was in the company of slugs, dew-worms, and such creatures. But farther away, on the other side of the cave, sat the mole and his mate, ruling over the whole, because it was to his court the lark had come.

"Here stands a beggar," said a big slug, poking the lark with his long, sticky horn. "What shall we do with him?" The slug was chief court marshal, and his duty was to preserve order down there.

"We have enough of such," said the mole, lowering his eyebrows. "Come here, I want to talk to you."

The poor lark hopped forward and placed herself before him.

"What is your name and where do you come from?" asked the mole.

"My name is Lark, and I am from the hedge up there."

"Well, I can easily believe that you are one of that pack that travels and tramps over our heads when we walk in the corridors. What are you good for?"

But the lark did not understand what she was to answer.

"She does not understand Your Majesty's language," said the dew-worm. "She is evidently not accustomed to speak with such distinguished folks. Can you dig caves in the ground?"

"No," replied the lark.

"Can you gather ants' eggs, grains of rye, and such things?"

"No, I can only sing," said the lark, looking anxiously around.

"A ballad singer, a musician, a good-for-nothing!" said the mole, scratch-ing his head. And then the whole court did the same.

"What shall we do with her?" inquired the slug.

"Well, she deserves to be put to death and buried in silence," said the mole, "when she can not do her part towards providing the food. But as my

454

former court fool, the lame, tailless field-mouse, is dead, she can have the position. I need some one who can entertain me with merry tricks."

"Did you ever hear of such luck! Twist yourself forward as I do and bow!" said the dew-worm.

But the lark did not know of what her luck consisted, and so did not move.

"Do you not hear that you are allowed to remain here?" said the slug sharply. "You are to have food and house-room in return for singing and entertaining His Majesty's high court. Do you not know enough to say 'thank you,' for it?"

What was the poor little lark to do? She bent her head to the mole, and then wiped away her tears with her wing.

"Sing now," said the court marshal, "and rejoice that the royal family and we will listen to you."

"It is so hard to sing when one is not happy! I cannot," replied the lark.

But the mole was angry now. "Cannot! what kind of nonsense is that? If I give you food and shelter, is it not your duty to sing when I wish? So now, let us hear."

The lark began to think of how the sun shone so clear in summer, and how dark it was here. And so she sang about the sunlight and the blue sky, but that did not suit the company present at all.

"What kind of nonsense and stupidity is that?" asked the mole. "I will not hear such talk about sun and light, for there is no such thing. That is only an old legend that we have outgrown."

The mole and his court had never seen the sun, and so they would not believe that the sunlight existed.

"But I assure you"—began the lark.

"Silence!" said the dew-worm. "You shall not stand here and contradict those who are greater than you. Do you not know that I have been up there hundreds of times, and yet I never saw sun or sky?"

That was true enough, because the dew-worm has no eyes, as you know.

"You must know," said the queen, "that it is forbidden on penalty of death, to tell such untruths here, and if you prize your neck, you will keep quiet about such things."

"Just hear! what kindness and grace!" said the slug. "Thank the gracious queen, who forgives your wicked falsehoods, and now sing. Sing how fine it is here, how much food we have, how kind the noble company is, how the dew-worm creeps; yes, you can sing about me, too, and it will not be too much."

"Yes, sing about them," said the king, "provided you value your life."

It was a difficult thing for the lark to sing about the mole digging caves, the dew-worm crawling, the slug swinging his horn and so on.

"Indeed!" said the mole.

"Indeed!" said the whole court after him.

"Let her take a place among the other servants," said the queen, and so the lark had to eat in the kitchen.

It was an eternity, the lark thought, that she sang songs; she could not know how many days and nights there were, for here the days and nights were alike.

Her longing after the sun and light grew active and strong, but she was not allowed to speak of them without death resulting.

But one time her longing grew too strong; she began to sing about the slug's great horn which she had praised a thousand times before, when all at once she changed—she could not help it—and began to sing of the sun and the light and the soft west wind and the fragrant flowers.

Then there was such a bustle that one who was not there could not imagine it.

"Down with her! She scorns us in our wisdom; sings of what is above, and that towards the end of the nineteenth century," shrieked the moles, slugs, dew-worms and all the other creeping things that burrow in the ground, and they rushed upon the lark.

But she escaped—her wing was healed—and came into the passage through which she had entered the mole's court. She hurried forward, faster and faster.

When she came way out, she saw a ray of light. Her eyes, which were now used to the darkness, were blinded at first, but she soon became accustomed to day again—the beloved day, that grew ever clearer and clearer. Finally she saw a ray of sunlight, then many and many more.

The ice was melted, the snow gone; it was spring, and glowing sunshine.

The lark rose on outstretched wings, with exulting song over the green meadows and blue lakes. But the company which followed the little songstress stopped when it began to be daylight.

"It is too disagreeable here," said the mole, and turned back.

"Yes, she deserved her fate," said the slug. "To think of her having everything so fine, and still to run away, just of conceit!"

"Yes," said the dew-worm, "to try to make us believe that there are such things as sun and sky! One could have laughed at it, if it had not been so annoying."

"And think of coming with such prating in the enlightened nineteenth century," said the mole. "Ha, ha, ha! but she received her deserts for it!"

The whole company laughed at the lark, who wanted to make folks believe such stupidity as that sky and sun existed. They still laugh when they think of it, though it angers them at the same time.

The Bird of Popular Song

Hans Christian Andersen

It is winter-time. The earth wears a snowy garment, and looks like marble hewn out of the rock; the air is bright and clear; the wind is sharp as a well-tempered sword, and the trees stand like branches of white coral or blooming almond twigs, and here it is keen as on the lofty Alps.

The night is splendid in the gleam of the Northern Lights, and in the glitter of innumerable twinkling stars.

The storms come; the clouds arise and shake out their swan's-down; the snow-flakes fly; they cover road and house, open fields and closed-in streets. But we sit in the warm room, by the hot stove, and talk about the old times. And we listen to this story:

By the open sea was a grave-mound; and on it sat at midnight the spirit of the buried hero, who had been a king. The golden circlet gleamed on his brow, his hair fluttered in the wind, and he was clad in steel and iron. He bent his head mournfully, and sighed in deep sorrow, as an unquiet spirit might sigh.

And a ship came sailing by. Presently the sailors lowered the anchor and landed. Among them was a singer, and he approached the royal spirit, and said,

"Why mournest thou, and wherefore dost thou suffer thus?"

And the dead man answered,

"No one has sung the deeds of my life; they are dead and forgotten: song doth not carry them forth over the lands, nor into the hearts of men; therefore I have no rest and no peace."

And he spoke of his works, and of his warlike deeds, which his contemporaries had known, but which had not been sung, because there was no singer among his companions.

Then the old bard struck the strings of his harp, and sang of the youthful courage of the hero, of the strength of the man, and of the greatness of his good deeds. Then the face of the dead one gleamed like the margin of the cloud in the moonlight. Gladly and of good courage, the form arose in splendor and in majesty, and vanished like the glancing of the Northern Lights. Nought was to be seen but the green turfy mound, with the stones on which no Runic record has been graven; but at the last sound of the harp there soared over the hill, as though he had fluttered from the harp, a little bird, a charming singing-bird, with ringing voice of the thrush, with the moving voice pathos of the human heart, with a voice that told of home, like the voice that is heard by the bird of passage. The singing-bird soared away, over mountain and valley, over field and wood—he was the Bird of Popular Song, who never dies.

We hear his song—we hear it now in the room on a winter's evening while the "white bees" are swarming without, and the storm takes firm hold. The bird sings not alone the requiem of heroes; he sings also sweet gentle songs of love, so many and so warm, of Northern fidelity and truth. He has stories in words and in tones; he has proverbs and snatches of proverbs; songs which, like Runes laid under a dead man's tongue, force him to speak; and thus Popular Song tells of the land of his birth.

In the old heathen days, in the times of the Vikings, its nest was in the harp of the bard.

In the days of knightly castles, when the strong fist held the scales of justice, when only might was right, and a peasant and a dog were of equal importance, where did the Bird of Song find shelter and protection? Neither violence nor stupidity gave him a thought.

But in the gabled window of the knightly castle, the lady of the castle sat with the parchment roll before her, and wrote down the old recollections in song and legend, while near her stood the old woman from the wood, and the traveling peddler who went wandering through the country. As these told their tales, there fluttered around them, with twittering and song, the Bird of Popular Song, who never dies so long as the earth has a hillock upon which his foot may rest.

And now he looks in upon us and sings. Without are the night and the snow-storm. He lays the Runes beneath our tongues, and we know the land of our home. Heaven speaks to us in our native tongue, in the voice of the Bird of Popular Song. The old remembrances awake, the faded colors glow with a fresh luster, and story and song pour us a blessed draught which lifts up our minds and our thoughts, so that the evening becomes as a Christmas festival.

The snow-flakes chase each other, the ice cracks, the storm rules without, for he has the might, he is lord—but not the LORD OF ALL.

It is winter time. The wind is sharp as a two-edged sword, the snow-flakes chase each other; it seems as though it had been snowing for days and weeks, and the snow lies like a great mountain over the whole town, like a heavy dream of the winter night. Everything on the earth is hidden away, only the golden cross of the church, the symbol of faith, arises over the snow grave, and gleams in the blue air and in the bright sunshine.

And over the buried town fly the birds of heaven, the small and the great; they twitter and they sing as best they may, each bird with his beak.

First comes the band of sparrows: they pipe at every trifle in the streets and lanes, in the nests and the houses; they have stories to tell about the front buildings and the back buildings.

"We know the buried town," they say; "everything living in it is piep! piep! piep!"

The black ravens and crows flew on over the white snow.

"Grub, grub!" they cried. "There's something to be got down there; something to swallow, and that's most important. That's the opinion of most of them down there, and the opinion is goo—goo—good!"

The wild swans come flying on whirring pinions, and sing of the noble and the great, that will still sprout in the hearts of men, down in the town which is resting beneath its snowy veil.

No death is there—life reigns yonder; we hear it on the notes that swell onward like the tones of the church organ, which seize us like sounds from the elf-hill, like the songs of Ossian, like the rushing swoop of the War-maidens' wings. What harmony! That harmony speaks to our hearts, and lifts up our souls! It is the Bird of Popular Song whom we hear.

And at this moment the warm breath of heaven blows down from the sky. There are gaps in the snowy mountains, the sun shines into the clefts; spring is coming, the birds are returning, and new races are coming with the same home sounds in their hearts.

Hear the story of the year: "The night of the snow-storm, the heavy dream of the winter night, all shall be dissolved, all shall rise again in the beauteous notes of the Bird of Popular Song, who never dies!"

"Thou Wert Right, Little Dove"

(TRADITIONAL SWEDISH TALE)

It was cold, and stormy besides. The north wind rushed through the streets, wild and angry, and heaped the snow high here and there. People who had business out hurried home, and those who had warm garments wrapped them around themselves as carefully as possible, while the poor ran to keep themselves warm.

"It is terrible weather to-night," said one fur-cloaked man to another. It was no news he told, but people are apt to talk that way, so as to have something to say.

"Yes, indeed, it is,' replied the other. "But look! the vagabonds are out, too." He pointed at an old woman, who reeled out from an ale-house, which was now locked behind her.

"Pack yourself home, you scum," said he to the woman.

At this she uttered some such words as that kind of people know well, and stumbled onward again.

"Hie, look out, old whiskey witch!" It was two street urchins who ran past; they jostled the woman so she fell headlong in a drift. She got up, threw out an oath, and went on.

"Let us punish her," said the snowflakes, and crept in among the rags in her garments.

"Yes, let us lash her," said the north wind, and drove her from the curbstone to the rows of houses, and from the houses to the curbstone again.

"No, spare her, spare her!" said a little dove, which sat curled up under the eaves. "Perhaps there is some good still left in her."

"No, there is not," answered the wind. The snowflakes agreed to this, and the dogs that looked out through the gates barked loudly.

Farther and farther wandered the woman. The high houses disappeared, the streets became more and more empty and deserted, and only one or two cottages could be seen.

"Oh! I am so cold, I am so cold," sobbed a child's voice. It was a little girl about six years old, who was wailing in distress.

The drunken woman stopped. Her hazy brain lighted up, and she took the child's hands in hers. "Poor little thing," said she, and stood firmly on her feet again. "Poor little thing!"

She carried the small hands, blue with cold, to her mouth, breathed on them until they became warm again, and rubbed the girl's cheeks till the blood returned to them.

"Hurry home, little one." She drew the worn shawl from her shoulders and wrapped it around the child. "Now run!"

And away hurried the child. But the woman remained standing there looking after her till she disappeared around a corner.

The intoxication wore away more and more. The aged one looked up towards heaven; the clouds parted, and a gleaming star shone down from on high.

"My God," whispered she very softly, and sank down on the cold drift; she kept her eyes fixed on the clear star, around which the sky grew brighter and brighter. A smile lay on the cold lips —such a one as had not rested there for many a year—but the aged one saw nothing more.

The north wind blew so soft and low, and laid the snowflakes for a covering over the woman—a covering so white and spotless that no queen rests beneath one more pure. In the morning the people found a woman frozen to death in the street.

"Any one might know that Whiskey Witch would come to such an end," they said. "She seems to look so happy," said an old woman; "I never saw her look so contented when alive."

The little dove looked down from the roof on the simple funeral procession.

"Thou wert right, little dove," whispered the wind and snowflakes.

461

The Fox and the Lapp

(FROM *THE BROWN FAIRY BOOK*)

Once upon a time a fox lay peeping out of his hole, watching the road that ran by at a little distance, and hoping to see something that might amuse him, for he was feeling very dull and rather cross. For a long while he watched in vain; everything seemed asleep, and not even a bird stirred overhead. The fox grew crosser than ever, and he was just turning away in disgust from his place when he heard the sound of feet coming over the snow. He crouched eagerly down at the edge of the road and said to himself: "I wonder what would happen if I were to pretend to be dead! This is a man driving a reindeer sledge, I know the tinkling of the harness. And at any rate I shall have an adventure, and that is always something!"

So he stretched himself out by the side of the road, carefully choosing a spot where the driver could not help seeing him, yet where the reindeer would not tread on him; and all fell out just as he had expected. The sledge-driver pulled up sharply, as his eyes lighted on the beautiful animal lying stiffly beside him, and jumping out he threw the fox into the bottom of the sledge, where the goods he was carrying were bound tightly together by ropes. The fox did not move a muscle though his bones were sore from the fall, and the driver got back to his seat again and drove on merrily.

But before they had gone very far, the fox, who was near the edge, contrived to slip over, and when the Laplander saw him stretched out on the snow he pulled up his reindeer and put the fox into one of the other sledges that was fastened behind, for it was market-day at the nearest town, and the man had much to sell.

They drove on a little further, when some noise in the forest made the man turn his head, just in time to see the fox fall with a heavy thump on to the frozen snow. "That beast is bewitched!" he said to himself, and then he threw the fox into the last sledge of all, which had a cargo of fishes. This was exactly what the cunning creature wanted, and he wriggled gently to the front and bit the cord which tied the sledge to the one before it so that it remained standing in the middle of the road.

Now there were so many sledges that the Lapp did not notice for a long while that one was missing; indeed, he would have entered the town without knowing if snow had not suddenly begun to fall. Then he got down to secure more firmly the cloths that kept his goods dry, and going to the end of the long row, discovered that the sledge containing the fish and the fox was missing. He quickly unharnessed one of his reindeer and rode back along the way he had come, to find the sledge standing safe in the middle of the road; but as the fox had bitten off the cord close to the noose there was no means of moving it away.

The fox meanwhile was enjoying himself mightily. As soon as he had loosened the sledge, he had taken his favorite fish from among the piles neatly arranged for sale, and had trotted off to the forest with it in his mouth. By-and-by he met a bear, who stopped and said: "Where did you find that fish, Mr. Fox?"

"Oh, not far off," answered he; "I just stuck my tail in the stream close by the place where the elves dwell, and the fish hung on to it of itself."

"Dear me," snarled the bear, who was hungry and not in a good temper, "if the fish hung on to your tail, I suppose he will hang on to mine."

"Yes, certainly, grandfather," replied the fox, "if you have patience to suffer what I suffered."

"Of course I can," replied the bear, "what nonsense you talk! Show me the way."

So the fox led him to the bank of a stream, which, being in a warm place, had only lightly frozen in places, and was at this moment glittering in the spring sunshine.

"The elves bathe here," he said, "and if you put in your tail the fish will catch hold of it. But it is no use being in a hurry, or you will spoil everything."

Then he trotted off, but only went out of sight of the bear, who stood still on the bank with his tail deep in the water. Soon the sun set and it grew very cold and the ice formed rapidly, and the bear's tail was fixed as tight as if a vice had held it; and when the fox saw that everything had happened just as he had planned it, he called out loudly:

"Be quick, good people, and come with your bows and spears. A bear has been fishing in your brook!"

And in a moment the whole place was full of little creatures each one with a tiny bow and a spear hardly big enough for a baby; but both arrows and spears could sting, as the bear knew very well, and in his fright he gave such a tug to his tail that it broke short off, and he rolled away into the forest as fast as his legs could carry him. At this sight the fox held his sides for laughing, and then scampered away in another direction. By-and-by he came to a fir tree, and crept into a hole under the root. After that he did something very strange.

Taking one of his hind feet between his two front paws, he said softly:

"What would you do, my foot, if someone was to betray me?"

"I would run so quickly that he should not catch you."

"What would you do, mine ear, if someone was to betray me?"

"I would listen so hard that I should hear all his plans."

"What would you do, my nose, if someone was to betray me?"

"I would smell so sharply that I should know from afar that he was coming."

"What would you do, my tail, if someone was to betray me?"

"I would steer you so straight a course that you would soon be beyond his reach. Let us be off; I feel as if danger was near."

But the fox was comfortable where he was, and did not hurry himself to take his tail's advice. And before very long he found he was too late, for the bear had come round by another path, and guessing where his enemy was began to scratch at the roots of the tree. The fox made himself as small as he could, but a scrap of his tail peeped out, and the bear seized it and held it tight. Then the fox dug his claws into the ground, but he was not strong enough to pull against the bear, and slowly he was dragged forth and his body flung over the bear's neck. In this manner they set out down the road, the fox's tail being always in the bear's mouth.

After they had gone some way, they passed a tree-stump, on which a bright colored woodpecker was tapping.

"Ah! those were better times when I used to paint all the birds such gay colors," sighed the fox.

"What are you saying, old fellow?" asked the bear.

"I? Oh, I was saying nothing," answered the fox drearily. "Just carry me to your cave and eat me up as quick as you can."

The bear was silent, and thought of his supper; and the two continued their journey till they reached another tree with a woodpecker tapping on it.

"Ah! those were better times when I used to paint all the birds such gay colors," said the fox again to himself.

"Couldn't you paint me too?" asked the bear suddenly.

But the fox shook his head; for he was always acting, even if no one was there to see him do it.

"You bear pain so badly," he replied, in a thoughtful voice, "and you are impatient besides, and could never put up with all that is necessary. Why, you would first have to dig a pit, and then twist ropes of willow, and drive in posts and fill the hole with pitch, and, last of all, set it on fire. Oh, no; you would never be able to do all that."

"It does not matter a straw how hard the work is," answered the bear eagerly, "I will do it every bit." And as he spoke he began tearing up the earth so fast that soon a deep pit was ready, deep enough to hold him.

"That is all right," said the fox at last, "I see I was mistaken in you. Now sit here, and I will bind you." So the bear sat down on the edge of the pit, and the fox sprang on his back, which he crossed with the willow ropes, and then set fire to the pitch. It burnt up in an instant, and caught the bands of willow and the bear's rough hair; but he did not stir, for he thought that the fox was rubbing the bright colors into his skin, and that he would soon be as beautiful as a whole meadow of flowers. But when the fire grew hotter still he moved uneasily from one foot to the other, saying, imploringly: "It is getting rather warm, old man." But all the answer he got was: "I thought you would never be able to suffer pain like those little birds."

The bear did not like being told that he was not as brave as a bird, so he set his teeth and resolved to endure anything sooner than speak again; but by this time the last willow band had burned through, and with a push the fox sent his victim tumbling into the grass, and ran off to hide himself in the forest. After a while he stole cautiously and found, as he expected, nothing left but a few charred bones. These he picked up and put in a bag, which he slung over his back.

By-and-by he met a Lapp driving his team of reindeer along the road, and as he drew near, the fox rattled the bones gaily.

"That sounds like silver or gold," thought the man to himself. And he said politely to the fox:

"Good-day, friend! What have you got in your bag that makes such a strange sound?"

"All the wealth my father left me," answered the fox. "Do you feel inclined to bargain?"

"Well, I don't mind," replied the Lapp, who was a prudent man, and did not wish the fox to think him too eager; "but show me first what money you have got."

"Ah, but I can't do that," answered the fox, "my bag is sealed up. But if you will give me those three reindeer, you shall take it as it is, with all its contents."

The Lapp did not quite like it, but the fox spoke with such an air that his doubts melted away. He nodded, and stretched out his hand; the fox put the bag into it, and unharnassed the reindeer he had chosen.

"Oh, I forgot!" he exclaimed, turning round, as he was about to drive them in the opposite direction, "you must be sure not to open the bag until you have gone at least five miles, right on the other side of those hills out there. If you do, you will find that all the gold and silver has changed into a parcel of charred bones." Then he whipped up his reindeer, and was soon out of sight.

For some time the Lapp was satisfied with hearing the bones rattle, and thinking to himself what a good bargain he had made, and of all the things he would buy with the money. But, after a bit, this amusement ceased to content him, and besides, what was the use of planning when you did not know for certain how rich you were? Perhaps there might be a great deal of silver and only a little gold in the bag; or a great deal of gold, and only a little silver. Who could tell? He would not, of course, take the money out to count it, for that might bring him bad luck. But there could be no harm in just one peep! So he slowly broke the seal, and untied the strings, and, behold, a heap of burnt bones lay before him! In a minute he knew he had been tricked, and flinging the bag to the ground in a rage, he ran after the fox as fast as his snow-shoes would carry him.

Now the fox had guessed exactly what would happen, and was on the look out. Directly he saw the little speck coming towards him, he wished that the man's snow-shoes might break, and that very instant the Lapp's shoes snapped in two. The Lapp did now know that this was the fox's work, but he had to stop and fetch one of his other reindeer, which he mounted, and set off again in pursuit of his enemy. The fox soon heard him coming, and this time he wished that the reindeer might fall and break its leg. And so it did; and the man felt it was a hopeless chase, and that he was no match for the fox.

So the fox drove on in peace till he reached the cave where all his stores were kept, and then he began to wonder whom he could get to help him kill his reindeer, for though he could steal reindeer he was too small to kill them. "After all, it will be quite easy," thought he, and he bade a squirrel, who was watching him on a tree close by, take a message to all the robber beasts of the forest, and in less than half an hour a great crashing of branches was heard, and bears, wolves, snakes, mice, frogs, and other creatures came pressing up to the cave.

When they heard why they had been summoned, they declared themselves ready each one to do his part. The bear took his crossbow from his neck and shot the reindeer in the chin; and, from that day to this, every reindeer has a mark in that same spot, which is always known as the bear's arrow. The wolf shot him in the thigh, and the sign of his arrow still remains; and so with the mouse and the viper and all the rest, even the frog; and at the last the reindeer all died. And the fox did nothing, but looked on.

"I really must go down to the brook and wash myself," said he (though he was perfectly clean), and he went under the bank and hid himself behind a stone. From there he set up the most frightful shrieks, so that the animals fled away in all directions. Only the mouse and the ermine remained where they were, for they thought that they were much too small to be noticed.

The fox continued his shrieks till he felt sure that the animals must have got to a safe distance; then he crawled out of his hiding-place and went to the bodies of the reindeer, which he now had all to himself. He gathered a bundle of sticks for a fire, and was just preparing to cook a steak, when his enemy, the Lapp, came up, panting with haste and excitement.

"What are you doing there?" cried he; "why did you palm off those bones on me? And why, when you had got the reindeer, did you kill them?"

"Dear brother," answered the fox with a sob, "do not blame me for this misfortune. It is my comrades who have slain them in spite of my prayers."

The man made no reply, for the white fur of the ermine, who was crouching with the mouse behind some stones, had just caught his eye. He hastily seized the iron hook which hung over the fire and flung it at the little creature; but the ermine was too quick for him, and the hook only touched the top of its tail, and that has remained black to this day. As for the mouse, the Lapp threw a half-burnt stick after him, and though it was not enough to hurt him, his beautiful white skin was smeared all over with it, and all the washing in the world would not make him clean again. And the man would have been wiser if he had let the ermine and the mouse alone, for when he turned round again he found he was alone.

Directly the fox noticed that his enemy's attention had wandered from himself he watched his chance, and stole softly away till he had reached a clump of thick bushes, when he ran as fast as he could, till he reached a river, where a man was mending his boat.

"Oh, I wish, I wish, I had a boat to mend too!" he cried, sitting up on his hind-legs and looking into the man's face.

"Stop your silly chatter!" answered the man crossly, "or I will give you a bath in the river."

"Oh, I wish, I do wish, I had a boat to mend," cried the fox again, as if he had not heard. And the man grew angry and seized him by the tail, and threw him far out in the stream close to the edge of an island; which was just what the fox wanted. He easily scrambled up, and sitting on the top, he called: "Hasten, hasten, O fishes, and carry me to the other side!" And the fishes left the stones where they had been sleeping, and the pools where they had been feeding, and hurried to see who could get to the island first.

"I have won," shouted the pike. "Jump on my back, dear fox, and you will find yourself in a trice on the opposite shore."

"No, thank you," answered the fox, "your back is much too weak for me. I should break it."

"Try mine," said the eel, who had wriggled to the front.

"No, thank you," replied the fox again, "I should slip over your head and be drowned."

"You won't slip on *my* back," said the perch, coming forward.

"No; but you are really *too* rough," returned the fox.

"Well, you can have no fault to find with *me*," put in the trout.

"Good gracious! are *you* here?" exclaimed the fox. "But I'm afraid to trust myself to you either."

At this moment a fine salmon swam slowly up.

"Ah, yes, you are the person I want," said the fox; "but come near, so that I may get on your back, without wetting my feet."

So the salmon swam close under the island, and when he was touching it the fox seized him in his claws and drew him out of the water, and put him on a spit, while he kindled a fire to cook him by. When everything was ready, and the water in the pot was getting hot, he popped him in, and waited till he thought the salmon was nearly boiled. But as he stooped down the water gave a sudden fizzle, and splashed into the fox's eyes, blinding him. He started backwards with a cry of pain, and sat still for some minutes, rocking himself to and fro. When he was a little better he rose and walked down a road till he met a grouse, who stopped and asked what was the matter.

"Have you a pair of eyes anywhere about you?" asked the fox politely.

"No, I am afraid I haven't," answered the grouse, and passed on.

A little while after the fox heard the buzzing of an early bee, whom a gleam of sun had tempted out.

"Do you happen to have an extra pair of eyes anywhere?" asked the fox.

"I am sorry to say I have only those I am using," replied the bee. And the fox went on till he nearly fell over an asp who was gliding across the road.

"I should be so glad if you would tell me where I could get a pair of eyes," said the fox. "I suppose you don't happen to have any you could lend me?"

"Well, if you only want them for a short time, perhaps I could manage," answered the asp; "but I can't do without them for long."

"Oh, it is only for a very short time that I need them," said the fox; "I have a pair of my own just behind that hill, and when I find them I will bring yours back to you. Perhaps you will keep these till them." So he took the eyes out of his own head and popped them into the head of the asp, and put the asp's eyes in their place. As he was running off he cried over his shoulder: "As long as the world lasts the asps' eyes will go down in the heads of foxes from generation to generation."

And so it has been; and if you look at the eyes of an asp you will see that they are all burnt; and though thousands and thousands of years have gone by since the fox was going about playing tricks upon everybody he met, the asp still bears the traces of the day when the sly creature cooked the salmon.

Joel's Talk with Santa Claus

Eugene Field

One Christmas Eve Joel Baker was in a most unhappy mood. He was lonesome and miserable; the chimes making merry Christmas music outside disturbed rather than soothed him, the jingle of the sleigh-bells fretted him, and the shrill whistling of the wind around the corners of the house and up and down the chimney seemed to grate harshly on his ears.

"Humph," said Joel, wearily, "Christmas is nothin' to me; there was a time when it meant a great deal, but that was long ago—fifty years is a long stretch to look back over. There is nothin' in Christmas now, nothin' for me at least; it is so long since Santa Claus remembered me that I venture to say he has forgotten that there ever was such a person as Joel Baker in all the world. It used to be different; Santa Claus used to think a great deal of me when I was a boy. Ah! Christmas nowadays ain't what it was in the good old time—no, not what it used to be."

As Joel was absorbed in his distressing thoughts he became aware very suddenly that somebody was entering or trying to enter the room. First came a draft of cold air, then a scraping, grating sound, then a strange shuffling, and then,—yes, then, all at once, Joel saw a pair of fat legs and a still fatter body dangle down the chimney, followed presently by a long white beard, above which appeared a jolly red nose and two bright twinkling eyes, while over the head and forehead was drawn a fur cap, white with snowflakes.

"Ha, ha," chuckled the fat, jolly stranger, emerging from the chimney and standing well to one side of the hearthstone; "ha, ha, they don't have the big, wide chimneys they used to build, but they can't keep Santa Claus out—no, they can't keep Santa Claus out! Ha, ha, ha. Though the chimney were no bigger than a gas pipe, Santa Claus would slide down it!"

It didn't require a second glance to assure Joel that the new-comer was indeed Santa Claus. Joel knew the good old saint—oh, yes—and he had seen him once before, and, although that was when Joel was a little boy, he had never forgotten how Santa Claus looked.

Nor had Santa Claus forgotten Joel, although Joel thought he had; for now Santa Claus looked kindly at Joel and smiled and said: "Merry Christmas to you, Joel!"

"Thank you, old Santa Claus," replied Joel, "but I don't believe it's going to be a very merry Christmas. It's been so long since I've had a merry Christmas that I don't believe I'd know how to act if I had one.

"Let's see," said Santa Claus, "it must be going on fifty years since I saw you last—yes, you were eight years old the last time I slipped down the chimney of the old homestead and filled your stocking. Do you remember it?"

"I remember it well," answered Joel. "I had made up my mind to lie awake and see Santa Claus; I had heard tell of you, but I'd never seen you, and Brother Otis and I concluded we'd lie awake and watch for you to come."

Santa Claus shook his head reproachfully.

"That was very wrong," said he, "for I'm so scarey that if I'd known you boys were awake I'd never have come down the chimney at all, and then you'd have had no presents."

"But Otis couldn't keep awake," explained Joel. "We talked about everythin' we could think of, till father called out to us that if we didn't stop talking he'd have to send one of us up into the attic to sleep with the hired man. So in less than five minutes Otis was sound asleep and no pinching could wake him up. But I was bound to see Santa Claus and I don't believe anything would've put me to sleep. I heard the big clock in the sitting-room strike eleven, and I had begun wonderin' if you never were going to come, when all of a sudden I heard the tinkle of the bells around your reindeers' necks. Then I heard the reindeers prancin' on the roof and the sound of your sleigh-runners cuttin' through the crust and slippin' over the shingles. I was kind o' scared and I covered my head up with the sheet and quilts—only I left a little hole so I could peek out and see what was goin' on. As soon as I saw you I got over bein' scared—for you were jolly and smilin' like, and you chuckled as you went around to each stockin' and filled it up."

"Yes, I can remember the night, "said Santa Claus. "I brought you a sled, didn't I?"

"Yes, and you brought Otis one, too," replied Joel. "Mine was red and had 'Yankee Doodle' painted in black letters on the side; Otis' was black and had 'Snow Queen' in gilt letters."

"I remember those sleds distinctly," said Santa Claus, "for I made them specially for you boys."

"You set the sleds up against the wall," continued Joel, "and then you filled the stockin's."

"There were six of 'em, as I recollect?" said Santa Claus.

"Let me see," queried Joel. "There was mine, and Otis', and Elvira's, and Thankful's, and Susan Prickett's—Susan was our help, you know. No, there were only five, and, as I remember, they were the biggest we could beg or borrer of Aunt Dorcas, who weighed nigh unto two hundred pounds. Otis and I didn't like Susan Prickett, and we were hopin' you'd put a cold potato in her stockin'."

"But Susan was a good girl," remonstrated Santa Claus. "You know I put cold potatoes only in the stockin's of boys and girls who are bad and don't believe in Santa Claus."

"At any rate," said Joel, "you filled all the stockin's with candy and pop-corn and nuts and raisins, and I can remember you said you were afraid you'd run out of pop-corn balls before you got around. Then you left each of us a book. Elvira got the best one, which was 'The Garland of Frien'ship,'and had poems in it about the bleeding of hearts, and so forth. Father wasn't expectin' anything, but you left him a new pair of mittens, and mother got a new fur boa to wear to meetin'."

"Of course," said Santa Claus, "I never forgot father and mother."

"Well, it was as much as I could do to lay still," continued Joel, "for I'd been longin' for a sled, an' the sight of that red sled with 'Yankee Doodle' painted on it jest made me wild. But, somehow or other, I began to get powerful sleepy all at once, and I couldn't keep my eyes open. The next thing I knew Otis was nudgin' me in the ribs. 'Git up, Joel,' says he; 'it's Chris'mas an' Santa Claus has been here.' 'Merry Chris'mas! Merry Chris'mas!' we cried as we tumbled out o' bed. Then Elvira an' Thankful came in, not more 'n half dressed, and Susan came in, too, an' we just made Rome howl with 'Merry Chris'mas! Merry Chris'mas!' to each other. 'Ef you children don't make less noise in there,' cried father, 'I'll hev to send you all back to bed.' The idea of askin' boys an' girls to keep quiet on Chris'mas mornin' when they've got new sleds an' 'Garlands of Frien'ship'!"

Santa Claus chuckled; his rosy cheeks fairly beamed joy.

"Otis an' I didn't want any breakfast," said Joel. "We made up our minds that a stockin'ful of candy and pop-corn and raisins would stay us for a while. I do believe there wasn't buckwheat cakes enough in the township to keep us indoors that mornin'; buckwheat cakes don't size up much 'longside of a red sled with 'Yankee Doodle' painted onto it and a black sled named 'Snow Queen.' We didn't care how cold it was—so much the better for slidin' down hill! All the boys had new sleds—Lafe Dawson, Bill Holbrook, Gum Adams, Rube Playford, Leander Merrick, Ezra Purple—all on 'em had new sleds excep' Martin Peavey, and he said he calculated Santa Claus had skipped him this year 'cause his father had broke his leg haulin' logs from the Pelham woods and had been kep' indoors six weeks. But Martin had his ol' sled, and he didn't hev to ask any odds of any of us, neither."

"I brought Martin a sled the *next* Christmas," said Santa Claus.

"Like as not—but did you ever slide down hill, Santa Claus? I don't mean such hills as they hev out here in this new country, but one of them old-fashioned New England hills that was made 'specially for boys to slide down, full of bumpers an' thank-ye-marms, and about ten times longer comin' up than it is goin' down! The wind blew in our faces and almos' took our breath away. 'Merry Chris'mas to ye, little boys!' it seemed to say, and it untied our mufflers an' whirled the snow in our faces, just as if it was a boy, too, an' wanted to play with us. An ol' crow came flappin' over us from the corn field beyond the meadow. He said: 'Caw, caw,' when he saw my new sled—I s'pose he'd never seen a red one before. Otis had a hard time with his sled—the black one—an' he wondered why it wouldn't go as fast as mine would. 'Hev you scraped the paint off'n the runners?' asked Wralsey Goodnow. 'Course I hev,' said Otis; 'broke my own knife an' Lute Ingraham's a-doin' it, but it don't seem to make no dif'rence—the darned ol' thing won't go!' Then, what did Simon Buzzell say but that, like's not, it was because Otis's sled's name was 'Snow Queen.' 'Never did see a girl sled that was worth a cent, anyway,' sez Simon. Well, now, that jest about broke Otis up in business. 'It ain't a girl sled,' sez he, 'and its name ain't "Snow Queen"! I'm a-goin' to call it' "Dan'l Webster," or "Oliver Optic," or "Sheriff Robbins," or after some other big man!' An' the boys plagued him so much about that pesky girl sled that he scratched off the name, an', as I remember, it *did* go better after that!

"About the only thing," continued Joel, "that marred the harmony of the occasion, as the editor of the 'Hampshire County Phoenix' used to say, was the ashes that Deacon Morris Frisbie sprinkled out in front of his house. He said he wasn't going to have folks breakin' their necks jest on account of a lot of frivolous boys that was goin' to the gallows as fas' as they could! Oh, how we hated him! and we'd have snowballed him, too. if we hadn't been afraid of the constable that lived next door. But the ashes didn't bother us much, and every time we slid side-saddle we'd give the ashes a kick, and that sort of scattered 'em."

The bare thought of this made Santa Claus laugh.

"Goin' on about nine o'clock," said Joel, "the girls come along—Sister Elvira an' Thankful, Prudence Tucker, Belle Yocum, Sophrone Holbrook, Sis Hubbard, an' Marthy Sawyer. Marthy's brother Increase wanted her to ride on *his* sled, but Marthy allowed that a red sled was her choice every time. 'I don't see how I'm goin' to hold on,' said Marthy. 'Seems as if I would hev my hands full keepin' my things from blowin' away.' 'Don't worry about yourself, Marthy,' sez I, 'for if you 'll look after your things, I kind o' calc'late I'll manage not to lose you on the way.' Dear Marthy—seems as if I could see you now, with your tangled hair a-blowin' in the wind, your eyes all bright and sparklin', an' your cheeks as red as apples. Seems, too, as if I could hear you laughin' an' callin', jist as you did as I toiled up the old New England hill that Chris'mas mornin'—a callin': 'Joel, Joel, Joel—ain't ye ever comin', Joel?' But the hill is long and steep, Marthy, an' Joel ain't the boy he used to be; he's old, an' gray, an' feeble, but there's love an' faith in his heart, an' they kind o' keep him totterin' tow'rds the voice he hears a-callin': 'Joel, Joel, Joel!'"

"I know—I see it all," murmured Santa Claus, very softly.

"Oh, that was so long ago," sighed Joel; "so very long ago! And I've had no Chris'mas since—only once, when our little one—Marthy's an' mine—you remember him, Santa Claus?"

"Yes," said Santa Claus, "a toddling little boy with blue eyes—"

"Like his mother," interrupted Joel; "an' he was like her, too—so gentle an' lovin', only we called him Joel, for that was my father's name and it kind o' run in the fam'ly. He wa'n't more 'n three years old when you came with your Chris'mas presents for him, Santa Claus. We had told him about you, and he used to go to the chimney every night and make a little prayer about what he wanted you to bring him. And you brought 'em, too—a stick-horse, an' a picture-book, an' some blocks, an' a drum—they 're on the shelf in the closet there, and his little Chris'mas stockin' with 'em—I've saved 'em all, an' I've taken 'em down an' held 'em in my hands, oh, so many times!"

"But when I came again," said Santa Claus—

"His little bed was empty, an' I was alone. It killed his mother—Marthy was so tenderhearted; she kind o' drooped an' pined after that. So now they've been asleep side by side in the buryin'-ground these thirty years.

"That's why I'm so sad-like whenever Chris'mas comes," said Joel, after a pause. "The thinkin' of long ago makes me bitter almost. It's so different now from what it used to be."

"No, Joel, oh, no," said Santa Claus. "'Tis the same world, and human nature is the same and always will be. But Christmas is for the little folks, and you, who are old and grizzled now, must know it and love it only through the gladness it brings the little ones."

"True," groaned Joel; "but how may I know and feel this gladness when I have no little stocking hanging in my chimney corner—no child to please me with his prattle? See, I am alone."

"No, you're not alone, Joel," said Santa Claus. "There are children in this great city who would love and bless you for your goodness if you but touched their hearts. Make them happy, Joel; send by me this night some gift to the little boy in the old house yonder—he is poor and sick; a simple toy will fill his Christmas with gladness."

"His little sister, too—take her some present," said Joel; "make them happy for me, Santa Claus—you are right—make them happy for me."

How sweetly Joel slept! When he awoke, the sunlight streamed in through the window and seemed to bid him a merry Christmas. How contented and happy Joel felt! It must have been the talk with Santa Claus that did it all; he had never known a sweeter sense of peace. A little girl came out of the house over the way. She had a new doll in her arms, and she sang a merry little song and she laughed with joy as she skipped along the street. Ay, and at the window sat the little sick boy, and the toy Santa Claus left him seemed to have brought him strength and health, for his eyes sparkled and his cheeks glowed, and it was plain to see his heart was full of happiness.

And, oh! how the chimes did ring out, and how joyfully they sang their Christmas carol that morning! They sang of Bethlehem and the manger and the Babe; they sang of love and charity, till all the Christmas air seemed full of angel voices.

Carol of the Christmas morn—
Carol of the Christ-child born—
  Carol to the list'ning sky
Till it echoes back again
"Glory be to God on high,
Peace on earth, good will tow'rd men!"

So all this music—the carol of the chimes, the sound of children's voices, the smile of the poor little boy over the way—all this sweet music crept into Joel's heart that Christmas morning; yes, and with these sweet, holy influences came others so subtile and divine that, in its silent communion with them, Joel's heart cried out amen and amen to the glory of the Christmas time.

The Bishop of Börglum and His Kinsmen

HANS CHRISTIAN ANDERSEN

Now we are up in Jutland, quite beyond the "wild moor." We hear what is called the "Western wow-wow"—the roar of the North Sea as it breaks against the western coast of Jutland—and we are quite near to it, but before us rises a great mound of sand—a mountain we have long seen, and towards which we are wending our way, driving slowly along through the deep sand. On this mountain of sand is a lofty old building—the convent of Börglum. In one of its wings (the larger one) there is still a church. And at this we arrive in the late evening hour; but the weather is clear in the bright June night around us, and the eye can range far, far over field and moor to the Bay of Aalborg, over heath and meadow, and far across the sea.

Now we are there, and roll past between barns and other farm buildings; and at the left of the gate we turn aside to the old Castle Farm, where the lime trees stand in lines along the walls, and, sheltered from the wind and weather, grow so luxuriantly that their twigs and leaves almost conceal the windows.

We mount the winding staircase of stone, and march through the long passages under the heavy roof-beams. The wind moans very strangely here, both within and without. It is hardly known how, but the people say—yes, people say a great many things when they are frightened or want to frighten others—they say that the old dead canons glide silently past us into the church, where mass is sung. They can be heard in the rushing of the storm, and their singing brings up strange thoughts in the hearers—thoughts of the old times into which we are carried back.

On the coast a ship is stranded; and the bishop's warriors are there, and spare not those whom the sea has spared. The sea washes away the blood that has flowed from the cloven skulls. The stranded goods belong to the bishop, and there is a store of goods here. The sea casts up casks and barrels filled with costly wine for the convent cellar, and in the convent is already good store of beer and mead. There is plenty in the kitchen—dead game and poultry, hams and sausages; and fat fish swim in the ponds without.

The Bishop of Börglum is a mighty lord. He has great possessions, but still he longs for more—everything must bow before the mighty Olaf Glob. His rich cousin at Thyland is dead. "Kinsman is worst to kinsman": his widow will find this saying true. Her husband has possessed all Thyland, with the exception of the Church property. Her son was not at home. In his boyhood he had already been sent abroad to learn foreign customs, as it was his wish to do. For years there had been no news of him. Perhaps he had long been laid in the grave, and would never come back to his home, to rule where his mother then ruled.

"What has a woman to do with rule?" said the bishop.

He summoned the widow before a law court; but what did he gain thereby? The widow had never been disobedient to the law, and was strong in her just rights.

Bishop Olaf of Börglum, what dost thou purpose? What writest thou on yonder smooth parchment, sealing it with thy seal, and entrusting it to the horsemen and servants, who ride away—far away—to the city of the Pope?

It is the time of falling leaves and of stranded ships, and soon icy winter will come.

Twice had icy winter returned before the bishop welcomed the horsemen and servants back to their home. They came from Rome with a papal decree—a ban, or bull, against the widow who had dared to offend the pious bishop. "Cursed be she and all that belongs to her. Let her be expelled from the congregation and the Church. Let no man stretch forth a helping hand to her, and let friends and relations avoid her as a plague and a pestilence!"

"What will not bend must break," said the Bishop of Börglum.

And all forsake the widow; but she holds fast to her God. He is her helper and defender.

One servant only—an old maid—remained faithful to her; and, with the old servant, the widow herself followed the plough; and the crop grew, although the land had been cursed by the Pope and by the bishop.

"Thou child of perdition, I will yet carry out my purpose!" cried the Bishop of Börglum. "Now will I lay the hand of the Pope upon thee, to summon thee before the tribunal that shall condemn thee!"

Then did the widow yoke the two last oxen that remained to her to a wagon, and mounted up on the wagon, with her old servant, and traveled away across the heath out of the Danish land. As a stranger she came into a foreign country, where a strange tongue was spoken and where new customs prevailed. Farther and farther she journeyed, to where green hills rise into mountains, and the vine clothes their sides. Strange merchants drive by her, and they look anxiously after their wagons laden with merchandise. They fear an attack from the armed followers of the robber-knights. The two poor women, in their humble vehicle drawn by two black oxen, travel fearlessly through the dangerous sunken road and through the darksome forest. And now they were in France. And there met them a stalwart knight, with a train of twelve armed followers. He paused, gazed at the strange vehicle, and questioned the women as to the goal of their journey and the place whence they came. Then one of them mentioned Thyland in Denmark, and spoke of her sorrows—of her woes—which were soon to cease, for so Divine Providence had willed it. For the stranger knight is the widow's son! He seized her hand, he embraced her, and the mother wept. For years she had not been able to weep, but had only bitten her lips till the blood started.

* * *

It is the time of falling leaves and of stranded ships.

The sea rolled wine-casks to the shore for the bishop's cellar. In the kitchen the deer roasted on the spit before the fire. At Börglum it was warm and cheerful in the heated rooms, while cold winter raged without, when a piece of news was brought to the bishop: "Jens Glob, of Thyland, has come back, and his mother with him." Jens Glob laid a complaint against the bishop, and summoned him before the temporal and the spiritual court.

"That will avail him little," said the bishop. "Best leave off thy efforts, knight Jens."

Again it is the time of falling leaves, of stranded ships—icy winter comes again, and the "white bees" are swarming, and sting the traveler's face till they melt.

"Keen weather to-day!" say the people, as they step in.

Jens Glob stands by the fire, so deeply wrapped in thought that he singes the skirt of his long garment.

"Thou Börglum bishop," he exclaims, "I shall subdue thee after all! Under the shield of the Pope, the law cannot reach thee; but Jens Glob shall reach thee!"

Then he writes a letter to his brother-in-law, Olaf Hase, in Sallingland, and prays that knight to meet him on Christmas Eve, at matins, in the church at Widberg. The bishop himself is to say the mass, and consequently will journey from Börglum to Thyland; and this is known to Jens Glob.

Moorland and meadow are covered with ice and snow. The marsh will bear horse and rider, the bishop with his priests and armed men. They ride the shortest way, through the brittle reeds, where the wind moans sadly.

Blow thy brazen trumpet, thou trumpeter clad in fox-skin! it sounds merrily in the clear air. So they ride on over heath and moorland—over what is the garden of Fata Morgana in the hot summer, towards the church of Widberg.

The wind is blowing his trumpet too—blowing it harder and harder. He blows up a storm—a terrible storm—that increases more and more. Towards the church they ride, as fast as they may through the storm. The church stands firm, but the storm careers on over field and moorland, over land and sea.

Börglum's bishop reaches the church; but Olaf Hase will scarce do so, hard as he may ride. He journeys with his warriors on the farther side of the bay, to help Jens Glob, now that the bishop is to be summoned before the judgment seat of the Highest.

The church is the judgment hall; the altar is the council table. The lights burn clear in the heavy brass candelabra. The storm reads out the accusation and the sentence, resounding in the air over moor and heath, and over the rolling waters. No ferry-boat can sail over the bay in such weather as this.

Olaf Hase makes halt at Ottesund. There he dismisses his warriors, presents them with their horses and harness, and gives them leave to ride home and greet his wife. He intends to risk his life alone in the roaring waters; but they are to bear witness for him that it is not his fault if Jens Glob stands without reinforcement in the church at Widberg. The faithful warriors will not leave him, but follow him out into the deep waters. Ten of them are carried away; but Olaf Hase and two of the youngest men reach the farther side. They have still four miles to ride.

It is past midnight. It is Christmas. The wind has abated. The church is lighted up; the gleaming radiance shines through the window-panes, and pours out over meadow and heath. The mass has long been finished, silence reigns in the church, and the wax is heard dropping from the candles to the stone pavement. And now Olaf Hase arrives.

In the forecourt Jens Glob greets him kindly, and says,

"I have just made an agreement with the bishop."

"Sayest thou so?" replied Olaf Hase. "Then neither thou nor the bishop shall quit this church alive."

And the sword leaps from the scabbard, and Olaf Hase deals a blow that makes the panel of the church door, which Jens Glob hastily closes between them, fly in fragments.

"Hold, brother! First hear what the agreement was that I made. I have slain the bishop and his warriors and priests. They will have no word more to say in the matter, nor will I speak again of all the wrong that my mother has endured."

The long wicks of the altar lights glimmer red; but there is a redder gleam upon the pavement, where the bishop lies with cloven skull, and his dead warriors around him in the quiet of the holy Christmas night.

And four days afterwards the bells toll for a funeral in the convent of Börglum. The murdered bishop and the slain warriors and priests are displayed under a black canopy, surrounded by candelabra decked with crape. There lies the dead man, in the black cloak wrought with silver; the crosier in the powerless hand that was once so mighty. The incense rises in clouds, and the monks chant the funeral hymn. It sounds like a wail—it sounds like a sentence of wrath and condemnation that must be heard far over the land, carried by the wind—sung by the wind—the wail that sometimes is silent, but never dies; for ever again it rises in song, singing even into our own time this legend of the Bishop of Börglum and his hard nephew. It is heard in the dark night by the frightened husbandman, driving by in the heavy sandy road past the convent of Börglum. It is heard by the sleepless listener in the thickly-walled rooms at Börglum. And not only to the ear of superstition is the sighing and the tread of hurrying feet audible in the long echoing passages leading to the convent door that has long been locked. The door still seems to open, and the lights seem to flame in the brazen candlesticks; the fragrance of incense arises; the church gleams in its ancient splendor; and the monks sing and say the mass over the slain bishop, who lies there in the black silver-embroidered mantle, with the crosier in his powerless hand; and on his pale proud forehead gleams the red wound like fire, and there burn the worldly mind and the wicked thoughts. . . .

Sink down into his grave—into oblivion—ye terrible shapes of the times of old!

Hark to the raging of the angry wind, sounding above the rolling sea! Outside a storm approaches, calling aloud for human lives. The sea has not put on a new mind with the new time. This night it is a horrible pit to devour up lives, and to-morrow, perhaps, it may be a glassy mirror—even as in the old time that we have buried. Sleep sweetly, if thou canst sleep!

Now it is morning.

The new time flings sunshine into the room. The wind still keeps up mightily. A wreck is announced—as in the old time.

During the night, down yonder by Lökken, the little fishing village with the red-tiled roofs—we can see it up here from the window—a ship has come ashore. It has struck, and is fast embedded in the sand; but the rocket apparatus has thrown a rope on board, and formed a bridge from the wreck to the mainland; and all on board are saved, and reach the land, and are wrapped in warm blankets; and to-day they are invited to the farm at the convent of Börglum. In comfortable rooms they encounter hospitality and friendly faces. They are addressed in the language of their country, and the piano sounds for them with melodies of their native land; and before these have died away, the chord has been struck, the wire of thought that reaches to the land of the sufferers announces that they are rescued. Then their anxieties are dispelled; and in the evening they join in the dance, at the feast given in the great hall at Börglum. Waltzes and other dances will be danced, and songs will be sung of Denmark and of "The Gallant Soldier" of the present day.

Blessed be thou, new time! Speak thou of summer and of purer gales! Send thy sunbeams gleaming into our hearts and thoughts! On thy glowing canvas let them be painted—the dark legends of the rough hard times that are past!

The Strange Guests

(TRADITIONAL NATIVE AMERICAN TALE)

Many years ago there lived, near the borders of Lake Superior, a noted hunter, who had a wife and one child. His lodge stood in a remote part of the forest, several days' journey from that of any other person. He spent his days in hunting, and his evenings in relating to his wife the incidents that had befallen him in the chase. As game was very abundant, he seldom failed to bring home in the evening an ample store of meat to last them until the succeeding evening; and while they were seated by the fire in his lodge partaking the fruits of his day's labour, he entertained his wife with conversation, or by occasionally relating those tales, or enforcing those precepts, which every good Indian esteems necessary for the instruction of his wife and children. Thus, far removed from all sources of disquiet, surrounded by all they deemed necessary to their comfort, and happy in one another's society, their lives passed away in cheerful solitude and sweet contentment.

The breast of the hunter had never felt the compunctions of remorse, for he was a just man in all his dealings. He had never violated the laws of his tribe by encroaching upon the hunting-grounds of his neighbors, by taking that which did not belong to him, or by any act calculated to displease the village chiefs or offend the Great Spirit. His chief ambition was to support his family with a sufficiency of food and skins by his own unaided exertions, and to share their happiness around his cheerful fire at night. The white man had not yet taught them that blankets and clothes were necessary to their comfort, or that guns could be used in the killing of game.

The life of the Chippewa hunter peacefully glided away.

One evening during the winter season, it chanced that he remained out later than usual, and his wife sat lonely in the lodge, and began to be agitated with fears lest some accident had befallen him. Darkness had already fallen. She listened attentively to hear the sound of coming footsteps; but nothing could be heard but the wind mournfully whistling around the sides of the lodge. Time passed away while she remained in this state of suspense, every moment augmenting her fears and adding to her disappointment.

Suddenly she heard the sound of approaching footsteps upon the frozen surface of the snow. Not doubting that it was her husband, she quickly unfastened the loop which held, by an inner fastening, the skin door of the lodge, and throwing it open she saw two strange women standing before it. Courtesy left the hunter's wife no time for deliberation. She invited the strangers to enter and warm themselves, thinking, from the distance to the nearest neighbors, they must have walked a considerable way. When they were entered she invited them to remain. They seemed to be total strangers to that part of the country, and the more closely she observed them the more curious the hunter's wife became respecting her guests.

No efforts could induce them to come near the fire. They took their seats in a remote part of the lodge, and drew their garments about them in such a manner as to almost completely hide their faces. They seemed shy and reserved, and when a glimpse could be had of their faces they appeared pale, even of a deathly hue. Their eyes were bright but sunken: their cheek-bones were prominent, and their persons slender and emaciated.

Seeing that her guests avoided conversation as well as observation, the woman forbore to question them, and sat in silence until her husband entered. He had been led further than usual in the pursuit of game, but had

483

returned with the carcass of a large and fat deer. The moment he entered the lodge, the mysterious women exclaimed—

"Behold! what a fine and fat animal!" and they immediately ran and pulled off pieces of the whitest fat, which they ate with avidity.

Such conduct appeared very strange to the hunter, but supposing the strangers had been a long time without food, he made no remark; and his wife, taking example from her husband, likewise restrained herself.

On the following evening the same scene was repeated. The hunter brought home the best portions of the game he had killed, and while he was laying it down before his wife, according to custom, the two strange women came quickly up, tore off large pieces of fat, and ate them with greediness. Such behavior might well have aroused the hunter's displeasure; but the deference due to strange guests induced him to pass it over in silence.

Observing the parts to which the strangers were most partial, the hunter resolved the next day to anticipate their wants by cutting off and tying up a portion of the fat for each. This he did: and having placed the two portions of fat upon the top of his burden, as soon as he entered the lodge he gave to each stranger the part that was hers. Still the guests appeared to be dissatisfied, and took more from the carcass lying before the wife.

Except for this remarkable behavior, the conduct of the guests was unexceptionable, although marked by some peculiarities. They were quiet, modest, and discreet. They maintained a cautious silence during the day, neither uttering a word nor moving from the lodge. At night they would get up, and, taking those implements which were then used in breaking and preparing wood, repair to the forest. Here they would busy themselves in seeking dry branches and pieces of trees blown down by the wind. When a sufficient quantity had been gathered to last until the succeeding night they carried it home upon their shoulders. Then carefully putting everything in its place within the lodge, they resumed their seats and their studied silence. They were always careful to return from their labors before the dawn of day, and were never known to stay out beyond that hour. In this manner they repaid, in some measure, the kindness of the hunter, and relieved his wife from one of her most laborious duties.

Thus nearly the whole year passed away, every day leading to some new development of character which served to endear the parties to each other. The visitors began to assume a more hale and healthy aspect; their faces daily lost something of that deathly hue which had at first marked them, and they visibly improved in strength, and threw off some of that cold reserve and forbidding austerity which had kept the hunter so long in ignorance of their true character.

One evening the hunter returned very late after having spent the day in toilsome exertion, and having laid the produce of his hunt at his wife's feet, the silent women seized it and began to tear off the fat in such an unceremonious manner that the wife could no longer control her feelings of disgust, and said to herself—

"This is really too bad. How can I bear it any longer!"

She did not, however, put her thought into words, but an immediate change was observed in the two visitors. They became unusually reserved, and showed evident signs of being uneasy in their situation. The good hunter immediately perceived this change, and, fearful that they had taken offense, as soon as they had retired demanded of his wife whether any harsh expression had escaped her lips during the day. She replied that she had uttered nothing to give the least offense. The hunter tried to compose himself to sleep, but he felt restive and uneasy, for he could hear the sighs and lamentations of the two strangers. Every moment added to his conviction that his guests had taken some deep offense; and, as he could not banish this idea from his mind, he arose, and, going to the strangers, thus addressed them—

"Tell me, ye women, what is it that causes you pain of mind, and makes you utter these unceasing sighs? Has my wife given you any cause of offense during the day while I was absent in the chase? My fears persuade me that, in some unguarded moment, she has forgotten what is due to the rights of hospitality, and used expressions ill-befitting the mysterious character you sustain. Tell me, ye strangers from a strange country, ye women who appear not to be of this world, what it is that causes you pain of mind, and makes you utter these unceasing sighs."

They replied that no unkind expression had ever been used towards them during their residence in the lodge, that they had received all the affectionate attention they could reasonably expect.

"It is not for ourselves," they continued, "it is not for ourselves that we weep. We are weeping for the fate of mankind; we are weeping for the fate of mortals whom Death awaits at every stage of their existence. Proud mortals, whom disease attacks in youth and in age. Vain men, whom hunger pinches, cold benumbs, and poverty emaciates. Weak beings, who are born in tears, who are nurtured in tears, and whose whole course is marked upon the thirsty sands of life in a broad line of tears. It is for these we weep.

"You have spoken truly, brother; we are not of this world. We are spirits from the land of the dead, sent upon the earth to try the sincerity of the living. It is not for the dead but for the living that we mourn. It was by no means necessary that your wife should express her thoughts to us. We knew them as soon as they were formed. We saw that for once displeasure had arisen in her heart. It is enough. Our mission is ended. We came but to try you, and we knew before we came that you were a kind husband, an affectionate father, and a good friend. Still, you have the weaknesses of a mortal, and your wife is wanting in our eyes; but it is not alone for you we weep, it is for the fate of mankind.

"Often, very often, has the widower exclaimed, 'O Death, how cruel, how relentless thou art to take away my beloved friend in the spring of her youth, in the pride of her strength, and in the bloom of her beauty! If thou wilt permit her once more to return to my abode, my gratitude shall never cease; I will raise up my voice continually to thank the Master of Life for so excellent a boon. I will devote my time to study how I can best promote her happiness while she is permitted to remain; and our lives shall roll away like a pleasant stream through a flowing valley!' Thus also has the father prayed for his son, the mother for her daughter, the wife for her husband, the sister for her brother, the lover for his mistress, the friend for his bosom companion, until the sounds of mourning and the cries of the living have pierced the very recesses of the dead.

"The Great Spirit has at length consented to make a trial of the sincerity of these prayers by sending us upon the earth. He has done this to see how we should be received,—coming as strangers, no one knowing from where. Three moons were allotted to us to make the trial, and if, during that time, no impatience had been evinced, no angry passions excited at the place where we took up our abode, all those in the land of spirits, whom their relatives had desired to return, would have been restored. More than two moons have already passed, and as soon as the leaves began to bud our mission would have been successfully terminated. It is now too late. Our trial is finished, and we are called to the pleasant fields whence we came.

"Brother, it is proper that one man should die to make room for another. Otherwise, the world would be filled to overflowing. It is just that the goods gathered by one should be left to be divided among others; for in the land of spirits there is no want, there is neither sorrow nor hunger, pain nor death. Pleasant fields, filled with game spread before the eye, with birds of beautiful form. Every stream has good fish in it, and every hill is crowned with groves of fruit-trees, sweet and pleasant to the taste. It is not here, brother, but there that men begin truly to live. It is not for those who rejoice in those pleasant groves but for you that are left behind that we weep.

"Brother, take our thanks for your hospitable treatment. Regret not our departure. Fear not evil. Thy luck shall still be good in the chase, and there shall ever be a bright sky over thy lodge. Mourn not for us, for no corn will spring up from tears."

The spirits ceased, but the hunter had no power over his voice to reply. As they had proceeded in their address he saw a light gradually beaming from their faces, and a blue vapor filled the lodge with an unnatural light. As soon as they ceased, darkness gradually closed around. The hunter listened, but the sobs of the spirits had ceased. He heard the door of his tent open and shut, but he never saw more of his mysterious visitors.

The success promised him was his. He became a celebrated hunter, and never wanted for anything necessary to his ease. He became the father of many boys, all of whom grew up to manhood, and health, peace, and long life were the rewards of his hospitality.

The Cat on the Dovrefell

PETER CHRISTEN ASBJØRNSEN

Once on a time there was a man up in Finnmark who had caught a great white bear, which he was going to take to the King of Denmark. Now, it so fell out, that he came to the Dovrefell just about Christmas Eve, and there he turned into a cottage where a man lived, whose name was Halvor, and asked the man if he could get house-room there, for his bear and himself.

"Heaven never help me, if what I say isn't true!" said the man; "but we can't give any one house-room just now, for every Christmas Eve such a pack of Trolls come down upon us, that we are forced to flit, and haven't so much as a house over our own heads, to say nothing of lending one to any one else."

"Oh!" said the man, "if that's all, you can very well lend me your house; my bear can lie under the stove yonder, and I can sleep in the side-room."

Well, he begged so hard, that at last he got leave to stay there; so the people of the house flitted out, and before they went, everything was got ready for the Trolls; the tables were laid, and there were rice porridge, and fish boiled in lye, and sausages, and all else that was good, just as for any other grand feast.

So, when everything was ready, down came the Trolls. Some were great and some were small; some had long tails and some had no tails at all; some, too, had long, long noses; and they ate and drank, and tasted everything. Just, then, one of the little Trolls caught sight of the white bear, who lay under the stove; so he took a piece of sausage and stuck it on a fork, and went and poked it up against the bear's nose, screaming out:

"Pussy, will you have some sausage?"

Then the white bear rose up and growled, and hunted the whole pack of them out of doors, both great and small.

Next year Halvor was out in the wood, on the afternoon of Christmas Eve, cutting wood before the holidays, for he thought the Trolls would come again; but just as he was hard at work, he heard a voice in the wood calling out:

"Halvor, Halvor!"

"Well," said Halvor, "here I am."

"Have you got your big cat with you still?"

"Yes, that I have," said Halvor; "she's lying at home under the stove, and what's more, she has now got seven kittens, far bigger and fiercer than she is herself."

"Oh, then, we'll never come to see you again," bawled out the Troll away in the wood, and he kept his word; for since that time the Trolls have never eaten their Christmas brose with Halvor on the Dovrefell.

The Elfin Hill

Hans Christian Andersen

S ome large lizards were nimbly running about in the clefts of an old tree;
they understood one another very well, for they all spoke the lizard
language.

"I wonder what is rumbling and rattling in yon old elfin hill," said the
first lizard. "I have been unable to shut an eye for the last two nights, so great
was the noise; it was just as bad as toothache, for that also prevents me from
sleeping."

"I am sure there is something on," said another lizard; "they had the top
of the hill propped up on four red pillars until the cock crowed this morning;
it must be well aired; the elfin girls have also learnt new dances. Surely, there
is something on."

"Yes," said a third lizard, "I have seen an earthworm of my acquaintance, just when it came out of the hill where it had been groping about in
the ground day and night. It has heard a good deal; the unfortunate animal
cannot see, but knows well enough how to wriggle about and listen. They
expect visitors in the elfin hill, and very distinguished ones too; but whom
the earthworm was unwilling or unable to tell me. All the will-o'-the wisps
are ordered to take part in a torchlight procession, as it is called; the silver
and gold, of which there is plenty in the hill, is polished and placed out in
the moonlight."

"Who may these visitors be?" asked all the lizards. "What are they doing?
Listen, how it hums and rumbles!" No sooner had they said this than the
elfin hill opened and an old elfin girl, hollow at the back,[1] came tripping out;
she was the housekeeper of the old elfin king, and being distantly connected
with the family, she wore an amber heart on her forehead. Her feet moved

---

1. Elfin girls are, according to the popular superstition, to be looked at only from one side,
as they are supposed to be hollow, like a mask.

so nimbly—trip, trip. Good gracious! how she could trip—she went straight down to the sea to the night-raven.[1]

"I have to invite you to the elfin hill for to-night," she said; "but you would do us a great favor if you would undertake the invitations. You ought to do something, as you do not entertain yourself. We expect some very distinguished friends, sorcerers, who can tell us something; that is why the old king of the elves wishes to show off."

"Who is to be invited?" asked the night-raven.

"All the world may attend the grand ball, even human beings, if they can talk in their sleep or know anything of the like which is according to our ways. But for the feast the company has to be strictly select: we only wish to have tiptop society. I have had an argument with the king, for in my opinion not even ghosts ought to be admitted. The merman and his daughters have to be invited first of all. Perhaps they may not like to come to the dry land, but we shall provide them with wet stones to sit on, or with something still better; and under these circumstances I think they will not refuse this time. All the old demons of the first class, with tails such as the goblins, we must invite, of course; further, I think, we must not forget the grave-pig,[2] the death-horse, nor the church dwarf; they belong, it is true, to the clergy, who are not of our class, but that is only their vocation; they are our near relatives, and frequently call upon us."

"Croak," said the night-raven, and flew off at once to invite the people.

The elfin girls were already dancing on the hill, they were wrapped in shawls made of mist and moonshine, which look very pretty to people who like things of this kind. The large hall in the center of the elfin hill was beautifully adorned; the floor had been washed with moonshine, while the walls had been polished with a salve prepared by witches, so that they shone like tulip-leaves in the light. In the kitchen they were very busy; frogs were

---

1. When in former days a ghost appeared the priest banished it into the earth; on the spot where this had happened they drove a stake into the ground. At midnight there was suddenly a cry heard: "Let me go." The stake was then removed, and the banished ghost escaped in the shape of a raven with a hole in his left wing. This ghostly bird was called the night-raven.

2. In Denmark, superstitious people believe that under every church a living horse or pig is buried. It is supposed that the ghost of the horse limps on three legs every night to some house where somebody is going to die.

roasting on the spit, dishes of snail-skins with children's fingers and salads of mushroom-seed, hemlock and mouse noses were preparing; there was beer of the marshwoman's make, sparkling wine of saltpeter from the grave vaults: all was very substantial food; the dessert consisted of rusty nails and glass from church windows. The old king of the elves had his golden crown polished with crushed slate-pencil; it was the same as used by the first form, and indeed it is difficult for an elf king to obtain such slate-pencils. In the bedroom, curtains were hung up and fastened with snail-slime. There was a running, rumbling and jostling everywhere.

"Now let us perfume the place by burning horse-hair and pig's bristles, and then, I think, I have done all I can," said the old elfin girl.

"Father, dear," said the youngest daughter, "may I now know who our distinguished guests will be?"

"Well, I suppose I may tell you now," he said. "Two of my daughters must be prepared for marriage; for two will certainly be married. The old goblin of Norway, who lives in the old Dovre-mountains and possesses many strong castles built on the cliffs and a gold mine, which is much better than people think, will come down with his two sons, who are both looking out for a wife. The old goblin is as genuine and honest an old chap as Norway ever brought forth; he is merry and straightforward too. I have known him a very long time, we used to drink together to our good friendship; he was last here to fetch his wife, she is dead now; she was a daughter of the king of the chalk-hills near Moen. He took his wife on tick, as people say. Oh, how I am longing for the dear old goblin again! They say his sons are somewhat naughty and forward, but people may do them wrong by supposing that, and I think they will be all right when they grow older. Let me see that you can teach them good manners."

"When are they coming?" asked one of the daughters.

"That depends on wind and weather," replied the king of the elves. "They travel economically. They will come when they have the chance to go by ship. I wished them to come through Sweden, but that was not to the old man's liking. He does not advance with time, and I do not like that at all."

Just then two will-o'-the-wisps came leaping in, the one much quicker than the other, and therefore one arrived first.

"They are coming, they are coming," they cried.

"Give me my crown, and let me stand in the moonshine," said the elf king.

The daughters raised their shawls and bowed to the ground. There stood the old goblin from Dovre; he wore a crown of hardened ice and polished fir-cones; he was wrapt in a bear-skin and had large warm boots on; his sons, on the contrary, had nothing round their necks and no braces on their trousers, for they were strong men.

"Is that a hill?" asked the youngest of the boys, pointing to the elfin hill. "We should call it a hole, in Norway."

"Boys," said the old man, "you ought to know better, a hole goes in, a hill stands out; have you no eyes in your heads?"

The only thing that struck them, they said, was that they were able to understand the language without any difficulty.

"Don't be so foolish," said the old goblin; "people might think you are still unfledged."

Then they all went into the elfin hill, where, the distinguished visitors had assembled, and so quickly, that it seemed as if the wind had blown them together. But every one was nicely and well accommodated. The sea folks sat at dinner in big water-tubs; they said they felt quite at home. All showed very good breeding except the two young goblins of the north, who put their legs on the table, for they imagined that they might take such liberties.

"Take your feet off the table," said the old goblin; and they obeyed, though reluctantly. They tickled their fair neighbors at table with fir-cones which they brought in their pockets; they took their boots off, in order to be at ease, and gave them to the ladies to hold. But their father, the old Dovre goblin, was quite different; he talked so well about the stately Norwegian rocks, and of the waterfalls which rushed down with a noise like thunder and the sound of an organ, forming white foam; he told of the salmon which leap against the rushing water when the Reck begins to play on the golden harp; he spoke of the fine moonlight winter nights, when the sledge-bells are ringing and the young men skate with burning torches in their hands over the ice, which is so clear and transparent that they frighten the fishes under their feet. He could talk so well that those who listened to him saw all in reality; it was just as if the sawmills were going, and as if servants and maids were singing and dancing; suddenly the old goblin gave the old elfin girl a kiss, and it was a real kiss, and yet they were almost strangers to each other.

After this the elfin girls had to perform their dances, first in the ordinary way, and then with stamping of their feet, and it looked very well; afterwards came the artistic and solo dance. Good gracious! how they threw their legs up; nobody knew where they began or where they ended, nor which were the legs and which the arms; all were flying about like sawdust, and they turned so quickly round that the death-horse and the grave-pig became unwell and had to leave the room.

"Hallo!" cried the old goblin, "that is a strange way of working about with the legs! But what do they know besides dancing, stretching the legs, and producing a whirlwind?"

"That you shall soon see," said the elf king, and called the youngest of his daughters. She was as nimble and bright as moonshine; she was indeed the finest-looking of all the sisters. She took a white chip of wood into her mouth, and disappeared instantly; that was her accomplishment. But the old goblin said he should not like his wife to possess such a power, and was sure his sons would be of the same opinion. The second could walk by her own side as if she had a shadow, while everybody knows that goblins never have a shadow. The third was quite different in her accomplishments; she had been apprenticed to the marsh-woman in the brewery, and knew well how to lard elder-tree logs with glow-worms.

"She will make a good housekeeper," said the old goblin, drinking her health with his eyes, as he did not wish to take anything more.

Now came the fourth, with a large harp to play upon; no sooner had she struck the first chord than all lifted up the left leg—for the goblins are left-legged—and when she touched the strings again every one had to do what she wished.

"That is a dangerous person," said the old goblin; and his two sons went out of the hill, for now they had seen quite enough. "What does your next daughter know?" asked the old goblin.

"I have learnt to admire all that is Norwegian, and I shall never marry unless I can go to Norway."

But the smallest of the sisters whispered into the old man's ear: "That is only because she has heard in a Norwegian song that when the world is destroyed through water the Norwegian cliffs will remain standing like monuments; therefore she wishes to go there, because she is so much afraid of being drowned."

"Ho, ho!" said the old goblin; "is that really what she meant? But tell me, what can the seventh and last do?"

493

"The sixth comes before the seventh," said the elf king, for he could count; but the sixth was rather timid.

"I can only tell people the truth," she said at last. "Nobody cares for me, and I am sufficiently occupied in making my shroud."

Now came the seventh and last; what could she do? Why, she could tell fairy tales, and as many as ever she wished.

"Here are my five fingers," said the old goblin; "tell me one for each of them."

And she took him by the wrist, and he laughed so much that he was nearly choked; when she came to the ring-finger, which had a golden ring upon it, as if it was aware that a betrothal should take place, the old goblin said, "Hold fast what you have; this hand is yours; I shall marry you myself."

Then the elfin girl said that the tales of the ring-finger and that of Peter Playman had yet to be told.

"Those we shall hear in the winter," said the old goblin, "and also those of the birch-tree, of the ghosts' presents, and of the creaking frost. You shall relate all your stories, for nobody up there can tell stories well; and then we shall sit in the rooms of stone where the pine logs are burning, and we shall drink mead out of the drinking-horns of the old Norwegian kings—Reck has made me a present of a couple of them—and when we are sitting there the mermaid will come to see us; she will sing to you all the songs of the shepherd-girls in the mountains. We shall enjoy it very much. The salmon will leap up in the waterfalls against the stone walls, but they cannot come in. Indeed, life is very pleasant in dear old Norway. But where are my boys?"

Where had they gone to? They were running about in the fields and blowing out the will-o'-the-wisps who had so kindly come to march in the torchlight procession.

"What have you been doing?" asked the old goblin. "I have taken a new mother for you; now you can each choose one of the aunts."

But the boys declared that they preferred to make speeches and drink; they had no wish to marry. And they began to make speeches, drank to other people's health, and emptied their glasses to the dregs. Afterwards they took off their coats and placed themselves on the tables to sleep, for they did not stand on ceremonies. But the old goblin danced with his young sweetheart about the room, and exchanged boots with her, for that is more fashionable than exchanging rings.

"The cock is crowing," cried the old elfin girl that did the housekeeping; "now we must close the shutters, lest the sun burn us."

Then the hill was closed up. But outside, the lizards were running about in the cleft tree, and one said to the other: "I like the old Norwegian goblin very much."

"I prefer the boys," said the earthworm; but the unfortunate animal could not see.

The Nightingale and the Rose

OSCAR WILDE

"She said that she would dance with me if I brought her red roses," cried the young Student; "but in all my garden there is no red rose."

From her nest in the holm-oak tree the Nightingale heard him, and she looked out through the leaves, and wondered.

"No red rose in all my garden!" he cried, and his beautiful eyes filled with tears. "Ah, on what little things does happiness depend! I have read all that the wise men have written, and all the secrets of philosophy are mine, yet for want of a red rose is my life made wretched."

"Here at last is a true lover," said the Nightingale. "Night after night have I sung of him, though I knew him not: night after night have I told his story to the stars, and now I see him. His hair is dark as the hyacinth-blossom, and his lips are red as the rose of his desire; but passion has made his face like pale ivory, and sorrow has set her seal upon his brow."

"The Prince gives a ball to-morrow night," murmured the young Student, "and my love will be of the company. If I bring her a red rose she will dance with me till dawn. If I bring her a red rose, I shall hold her in my arms, and she will lean her head upon my shoulder, and her hand will be clasped in mine. But there is no red rose in my garden, so I shall sit lonely, and she will pass me by. She will have no heed of me, and my heart will break."

"Here indeed is the true lover," said the Nightingale. "What I sing of, he suffers: what is joy to me, to him is pain. Surely Love is a wonderful thing.

495

It is more precious than emeralds, and dearer than fine opals. Pearls and pomegranates cannot buy it, nor is it set forth in the market-place. It may not be purchased of the merchants, nor can it be weighed out in the balance for gold."

"The musicians will sit in their gallery," said the young Student, "and play upon their stringed instruments, and my love will dance to the sound of the harp and the violin. She will dance so lightly that her feet will not touch the floor, and the courtiers in their gay dresses will throng round her. But with me she will not dance, for I have no red rose to give her"; and he flung himself down on the grass, and buried his face in his hands, and wept.

"Why is he weeping?" asked a little Green Lizard, as he ran past him with his tail in the air.

"Why, indeed?" said a Butterfly, who was fluttering about after a sunbeam.

"Why, indeed?" whispered a Daisy to his neighbor, in a soft, low voice.

"He is weeping for a red rose," said the Nightingale.

"For a red rose!" they cried; "how very ridiculous!" and the little Lizard, who was something of a cynic, laughed outright.

But the Nightingale understood the secret of the Student's sorrow, and she sat silent in the oak-tree, and thought about the mystery of Love.

Suddenly she spread her brown wings for flight, and soared into the air. She passed through the grove like a shadow, and like a shadow she sailed across the garden.

In the center of the grass-plot was standing a beautiful Rose-tree, and when she saw it, she flew over to it, and lit upon a spray.

"Give me a red rose," she cried, "and I will sing you my sweetest song."

But the Tree shook its head.

"My roses are white," it answered; "as white as the foam of the sea, and whiter than the snow upon the mountain. But go to my brother who grows round the old sun-dial, and perhaps he will give you what you want."

So the Nightingale flew over to the Rose-tree that was growing round the old sun-dial.

"Give me a red rose," she cried, "and I will sing you my sweetest song."

But the Tree shook its head.

"My roses are yellow," it answered; "as yellow as the hair of the mer-maiden who sits upon an amber throne, and yellower than the daffodil that blooms in the meadow before the mower comes with his scythe. But go to my brother who grows beneath the Student's window, and perhaps he will give you what you want."

So the Nightingale flew over to the Rose tree that was growing beneath the Student's window.

"Give me a red rose," she cried, "and I will sing you my sweetest song."

But the Tree shook its head.

"My roses are red," it answered, "as red as the feet of the dove, and redder than the great fans of coral that wave and wave in the ocean-cavern. But the winter has chilled my veins, and the frost has nipped my buds, and the storm has broken my branches, and I shall have no roses at all this year."

"One red rose is all I want," cried the Nightingale, "only one red rose! Is there no way by which I can get it?"

"There is a way," answered the Tree; "but it is so terrible that I dare not tell it to you."

"Tell it to me," said the Nightingale, "I am not afraid."

"If you want a red rose," said the Tree, "you must build it out of music by moonlight, and stain it with your own heart's-blood. You must sing to me with your breast against a thorn. All night long you must sing to me, and the thorn must pierce your heart, and your life-blood must flow into my veins, and become mine."

"Death is a great price to pay for a red rose," cried the Nightingale, "and Life is very dear to all. It is pleasant to sit in the green wood, and to watch the Sun in his chariot of gold, and the Moon in her chariot of pearl. Sweet is the scent of the hawthorn, and sweet are the bluebells that hide in the valley, and the heather that blows on the hill. Yet Love is better than Life, and what is the heart of a bird compared to the heart of a man?"

So she spread her brown wings for flight, and soared into the air. She swept over the garden like a shadow, and like a shadow she sailed through the grove.

The young Student was still lying on the grass, where she had left him, and the tears were not yet dry in his beautiful eyes.

"Be happy," cried the Nightingale, "be happy; you shall have your red rose. I will build it out of music by moonlight, and stain it with my own heart's-blood. All that I ask of you in return is that you will be a true lover, for Love is wiser than Philosophy, though she is wise, and mightier than Power, though he is mighty. Flame-colored are his wings, and colored like flame is his body. His lips are sweet as honey, and his breath is like frankincense."

The Student looked up from the grass, and listened, but he could not understand what the Nightingale was saying to him, for he only knew the things that are written down in books.

But the Oak-tree understood, and felt sad, for he was very fond of the little Nightingale who had built her nest in his branches.

"Sing me one last song," he whispered; "I shall feel very lonely when you are gone."

So the Nightingale sang to the Oak-tree, and her voice was like water bubbling from a silver jar.

When she had finished her song the Student got up, and pulled a note-book and a lead-pencil out of his pocket.

"She has form," he said to himself, as he walked away through the grove—"that cannot be denied to her; but has she got feeling? I am afraid not. In fact, she is like most artists; she is all style, without any sincerity. She would not sacrifice herself for others. She thinks merely of music, and everybody knows that the arts are selfish. Still, it must be admitted that she has some beautiful notes in her voice. What a pity it is that they do not mean anything, or do any practical good." And he went into his room, and lay down on his little pallet-bed, and began to think of his love; and, after a time, he fell asleep.

And when the Moon shone in the heavens the Nightingale flew to the Rose-tree, and set her breast against the thorn. All night long she sang with her breast against the thorn, and the cold crystal Moon leaned down and listened. All night long she sang, and the thorn went deeper and deeper into her breast, and her life-blood ebbed away from her.

She sang first of the birth of love in the heart of a boy and a girl. And on the topmost spray of the Rose-tree there blossomed a marvelous rose, petal following petal, as song followed song. Pale was it, at first, as the mist that hangs over the river—pale as the feet of the morning, and silver as the wings of the dawn. As the shadow of a rose in a mirror of silver, as the shadow of a rose in a water-pool, so was the rose that blossomed on the topmost spray of the Tree.

But the Tree cried to the Nightingale to press closer against the thorn. "Press closer, little Nightingale," cried the Tree, "or the Day will come before the rose is finished."

So the Nightingale pressed closer against the thorn, and louder and louder grew her song, for she sang of the birth of passion in the soul of a man and a maid.

And a delicate flush of pink came into the leaves of the rose, like the flush in the face of the bridegroom when he kisses the lips of the bride. But the thorn had not yet reached her heart, so the rose's heart remained white, for only a Nightingale's heart's-blood can crimson the heart of a rose.

And the Tree cried to the Nightingale to press closer against the thorn. "Press closer, little Nightingale," cried the Tree, "or the Day will come before the rose is finished."

So the Nightingale pressed closer against the thorn, and the thorn touched her heart, and a fierce pang of pain shot through her. Bitter, bitter was the pain, and wilder and wilder grew her song, for she sang of the Love that is perfected by Death, of the Love that dies not in the tomb.

And the marvelous rose became crimson, like the rose of the eastern sky. Crimson was the girdle of petals, and crimson as a ruby was the heart.

But the Nightingale's voice grew fainter, and her little wings began to beat, and a film came over her eyes. Fainter and fainter grew her song, and she felt something choking her in her throat.

Then she gave one last burst of music. The white Moon heard it, and she forgot the dawn, and lingered on in the sky. The red rose heard it, and it trembled all over with ecstasy, and opened its petals to the cold morning air. Echo bore it to her purple cavern in the hills, and woke the sleeping shepherds from their dreams. It floated through the reeds of the river, and they carried its message to the sea.

"Look, look!" cried the Tree, "the rose is finished now"; but the Nightingale made no answer, for she was lying dead in the long grass, with the thorn in her heart.

And at noon the Student opened his window and looked out.

"Why, what a wonderful piece of luck!" he cried; "here is a red rose! I have never seen any rose like it in all my life. It is so beautiful that I am sure it has a long Latin name"; and he leaned down and plucked it.

Then he put on his hat, and ran up to the Professor's house with the rose in his hand.

The daughter of the Professor was sitting in the doorway winding blue silk on a reel, and her little dog was lying at her feet.

"You said that you would dance with me if I brought you a red rose," cried the Student. "Here is the reddest rose in all the world. You will wear it to-night next your heart, and as we dance together it will tell you how I love you."

But the girl frowned.

"I am afraid it will not go with my dress," she answered; "and, besides, the Chamberlain's nephew has sent me some real jewels, and everybody knows that jewels cost far more than flowers."

"Well, upon my word, you are very ungrateful," said the Student angrily; and he threw the rose into the street, where it fell into the gutter, and a cart-wheel went over it.

"Ungrateful!" said the girl. "I tell you what, you are very rude; and, after all, who are you? Only a Student. Why, I don't believe you have even got silver buckles to your shoes as the Chamberlain's nephew has"; and she got up from her chair and went into the house.

"What a silly thing Love is," said the Student as he walked away. "It is not half as useful as Logic, for it does not prove anything, and it is always telling one of things that are not going to happen, and making one believe things that are not true. In fact, it is quite unpractical, and, as in this age to be practical is everything, I shall go back to Philosophy and study Metaphysics."

So he returned to his room and pulled out a great dusty book, and began to read.

The Snow-Maiden

(Traditional Russian Tale)

Many years ago, in a distant Russian village, there lived a peasant, by name Akem, with his wife Masha; they lived in a small wooden hut, where they spent their days in love and harmony; but children had they none. This was a very sore point with both of them, they used to sit by the window or at the door of their little hut looking at their neighbors' children playing about, and wished that they had some of their own; but finding that it was no use wishing, they at last became sad in their old age.

One cold winter's day, when the snow lay thick upon the uneven country roads, and the little village boys were running about throwing snowballs to keep themselves warm, and making snow-men and women, old Akem and Masha sat by their window looking at them in silence. Suddenly Akem looked up at his wife, and said, laughing,—

"Masha, what do you say to coming out into the road and making ourselves a snow-man or woman, like those little boys yonder?"

Masha laughed, too, it seemed such a queer thing to do at their time of life!

"Yes, if you like," she replied; "let us go, it may cheer us up a bit; but I don't see why we should make a snow-man or woman, let us rather make a child out of snow, as Providence does not seem to wish us to have a real one!"

"I do believe you are getting quite clever in your old age, Masha! Come along, then, and let us set to work."

Off went the old couple, laughing at themselves all the while, and sure enough they commenced making a snow-child! They made the legs, arms, hands, feet, and a snowball for the head.

"What, in the name of wonder, are you up to?" exclaimed a passer-by, stopping suddenly in front of the two old people.

"A snow-child!" laughed Masha, as she began to explain everything to the stranger.

"May the Saints help you!" said he, as he went his way.

When they had got the legs, arms, hands, feet, and head fixed up together, Akem began making the nose, two holes for the eyes, and was just drawing a small line for the mouth, when he suddenly, much to his surprise, felt warm breath come out of it. He took his hand away quickly, and on looking up at the two holes made for the eyes, beheld two real, beautiful blue eyes; the lips became full and rosy, and as for the nose, it was the dearest little nose ever seen.

"Good heavens! what does this mean? is it a temptation of the Evil One?" cried Akem, crossing himself several times, while the snow-child threw her arms round his neck, and kissed him as though she were alive.

"O Akem! Akem!" cried Masha, trembling with joy, "Providence has at last taken pity on us, and sent us this child to cheer us in our old age."

She was about to throw her arms around the snow-child and embrace it, when, to the astonishment of both the old man and woman, the snow fell off, and left in Masha's arms a beautiful little girl.

"Oh, my little Snow-Maiden! my little darling!" cried the happy Masha, as she led the lovely child into their hut. Meanwhile, Akem could not get over his wonder. He rubbed his head, and felt sorely puzzled; he did not know whether he was asleep or awake, but felt almost sure that something had gone wrong with him somewhere.

But to return to the Snow-Maiden (as Masha was pleased to call her). She grew very rapidly—not only daily but hourly—into a tall, beautiful, and graceful girl; the peasants were delighted with her—Akem had come to the conclusion that it was all right—their hut was now always in constant mirth. The village girls and boys were frequent visitors to it; they played, read, and sang with the Snow-Maiden, who understood it all thoroughly, and did her best to amuse all around her. She talked, laughed, and was altogether so cheerful and good-natured, that everybody loved her dearly, and tried to please her in every possible way,—at the same time a better and more obedient daughter never was. She had the most lovely white skin, just like snow; her eyes were like forget-me-nots, her lips and cheeks like roses; in fact, she was the very picture of health and beauty; with her lovely golden hair hanging down her back, she looked just like a girl of seventeen, though she was only a few days old.

"Akem," said Masha, one day to her husband, "how good Providence has been to us; how Snow-Maiden has brightened us, in these few days, and how wicked we were to grumble as we did."

"Yes, Masha," returned Akem, "we ought to thank Providence for all that He has done for us, and thank Him that we have mirth instead of gloom, in our little home."

Winter passed, the heavens rejoiced, the spring sun came out, the swallows began to fly about, and the grass and trees became green once more.

The lovely Russian peasant-girls gathered themselves together, and met their young cavaliers under the trees in the forest, where they danced and sang their pretty Russian songs. But the Snow-Maiden was dull.

"What is the matter with you, my darling?" asked Masha; "are you ill? You are always so bright and cheerful as a rule, and now you are so dull all at once. Has any bad man thrown a spell over you?"

502

"No, mother mine; nothing is the matter with me, darling," the Snow-Maiden replied, but still she continued to be dull, and by degrees she lost her beautiful color, and began to droop sadly, greatly to the alarm of those around her.

The last snow had now vanished, the gardens began to bloom, the rivers and lakes rippled, the birds sang merrily; in fact all the wide world seemed happy; yet our little Snow-Maiden drooped and looked sad. She sat with her hands folded in the coolest part of the hut. She loved the cold winter, it was her best friend, but this horrid heat she hated. She was glad when it rained a little, there was no broiling sun then. She did not mind the winter sun, but the summer sun was her enemy; and quite natural, too, poor thing, when she was born in the winter in the snow! At last the great summer feast arrived, the village youths and maidens came to the Snow-Maiden and asked her to join them in a romp through the woods, and begged Masha to let her go with them. At first Masha refused, but the girls begged so hard that at last, on thinking it over, she consented, for she thought it might cheer Snow-Maiden up.

"But," said she, "take care of her, for she is the apple of my eye, and if anything happens to her, I don't know what I shall do!"

"All right! all right! we shall take care of her, she is just as dear to us!" cried the young people, as they took Snow-Maiden and ran off with her into the forest, where the girls wove themselves wreaths, while the young men gathered sticks, which they piled up high; and at sunset they set fire to them, and then they arranged themselves all in a row one after another, boys and girls, and prepared to jump over the burning heap. Our Snow-Maiden was the last in the row.

"Mind," said the girls to her, "don't stay behind but jump after us."

One! two! three! and away they went, jumping over the flames in great delight. Suddenly they heard a piercing scream, and on looking round discovered that Snow-Maiden was missing.

"Ah," cried they, laughing, "she is up to one of her tricks again, and has most likely gone and hidden herself somewhere. Come, let us go and search for her."

They all ran off in pairs in different directions, but nowhere could they find their missing companion. Their happy young faces soon turned very grave, and their joy gave place to sorrow and alarm. They met at last in the road outside the forest, and began asking each other what they had best do.

"Perhaps she has run home," said one.

This seemed a happy thought; so they ran to the hut, but no Snow-Maiden was there. They looked for her all through the next day and night, and on the third, and fourth. They sought her in the village, hut after hut, and in the forest, tree after tree, bush after bush; but all in vain, nowhere could they find her. As for poor Akem and Masha, it is needless to say, that their grief was too great for words, no one could comfort them. Day after day, night after night, did poor Masha wander into the forest, calling like the cuckoo,—

"Oh, my little Snow-Maiden! Oh, my little darling."

But there was no answer to her call, not one word from that sweet voice did Masha get in reply. Snow-Maiden was not to be found, that was certain, but how had she vanished, and whither had she gone? Had the wild beasts of the forest eaten her up? or had the robber-bird carried her off to the blue sea? No, it was not the wild beasts, nor was it the robber-bird, but—as our little friend was jumping over the flames after her companions she evaporated into a thin cloud, and flew to the heights of the heavens.

The Old Bachelor's Nightcap

HANS CHRISTIAN ANDERSEN

In Copenhagen there is a street with a strange name—"Hysken Sträde." Where did this name come from, and what is its meaning? It is said to be German, but that is unjust to the Germans, as then it would have to be called "Hauschen"—not "Hysken." "Hauschen" means little house, and a few little houses stood here once long ago. They were very little more substantial than the wooden booths we see now in the market-places at fair-time. They were, perhaps, a little larger and had windows; but the panes consisted of horn or bladder, as glass was then too expensive to be used by every one.

But then, the time we are speaking of was long ago—so long ago that our grandfathers and great-grandfathers would speak of these days as "olden times"—it was in fact several centuries back.

The rich merchants in Bremen and Lubeck carried on trade with Copenhagen; they did not reside in the town themselves, but sent their clerks, who lived in the wooden booths in Hauschen Street, and sold beer and spices. The German beer was good, and there were many kinds of it; for instance, Bremen, Prussinger, and Sono beer, and even Brunswick mumm; and quantities of spices were sold—saffron, aniseed, ginger, and especially pepper. Yes, pepper was the chief article, and so it happened the German clerks got the nickname of "pepper gentry," and there was a condition made with them when they left Bremen and Lubeck that they would not marry in Copenhagen. Many of them became very old, and had to take care of themselves, look after their own comforts, and light their own fires when they had any; and some of them became very solitary old boys with eccentric ideas and habits. From this, all unmarried men who have passed a certain age are called in Denmark "pepper gentry," and this must be remembered by all who wish to understand this tale.

The "pepper gentleman" becomes a butt for ridicule, and is continually told that he ought to put on his nightcap, draw it over his eyes and go to sleep. The boys sing,

> Take your nightcap, go to rest,
> Poor old bachelor so good;
> Your warm bed you'll find the best
> When you've finished chopping wood.

So they sing of the "pepper gentlemen," and make game of the poor bachelor and his nightcap, and turn them into ridicule, because they know very little of either. That sort of nightcap no one would wish to have! And why not? We shall hear.

In olden times Small House Street was not paved, and foot passengers stumbled out of one hole into another, as in a neglected byway, and it was also very narrow. The booths leaned side by side, and were so close together that often in the summer time a sail was stretched from one booth to its opposite neighbor, and at this time the smell of pepper, saffron, and ginger became doubly powerful. One seldom saw young men behind the counters: the clerks were generally old boys, but they did not look as we should be apt to picture them, with wigs, nightcaps, and velvet knee-breeches, and with coat and waistcoat buttoned up to the chin. No, our grandfathers' great-grandfathers may have looked like that in their portraits, but the "pepper gentlemen" had no money to spare and did not have their portraits painted, although it would indeed be interesting now to have a picture of one of them as he stood behind the counter or went to church on holy days. His hat was high crowned and broad brimmed, and sometimes one of the younger clerks would have a feather in his. The woolen shirt was concealed by a broad linen collar; the close jacket buttoned up to the chin, and a cloak hung loosely over it; the trousers were tucked into broad-toed shoes, for the clerks did not wear stockings. In their belt they usually had a table-knife and spoon; also a larger knife for the defense of the owner, and it was often very necessary.

Anthony, one of the oldest clerks, was dressed in this way on holidays and festivals, with the exception that instead of the high-crowned hat, he wore a low bonnet, and under it a knitted cap, a regular nightcap, and to which he had grown so accustomed that it was always on his head, and he had two, nightcaps I mean, not heads.

The old man would have made a good artist's model, for he was as thin as a lath, had many crows-feet round his eyes and mouth, long bony fingers, and bushy gray eyebrows. Over his left eye grew quite a tuft of hair, which was not beautiful, although it gave him a striking appearance. People knew that he came from Bremen, but this was not his native place, although his master lived there; his own home was in Thuringia, the town of Eisenach, near the Wartburg. Old Anthony did not speak of this often, but he thought of it a great deal. The old clerks of Small House Street very seldom met one another; each remained in his own booth, which was closed early in the evening, and then it looked very dark and melancholy out in the street; a faint glimmer of light forced its way through the little horn-pane on the roof, and the old clerk sat inside the booth, usually on his bed, his German hymn-book in his hand, singing an evening hymn in a low voice. Sometimes he went about in the booth until late at night, busy about all kinds of things.

Indeed it was not a very pleasant life; to be in a strange country is a hard lot; nobody takes any notice of you unless you happen to come in their way.

The place often looked very deserted and gloomy when it was dark outside with rain or snow falling. There were no lamps in the street, except one solitary light hanging before a picture of the Virgin which was fastened against the wall. One could distinctly hear the splash of waves against the breakwater at the castle wharf.

Evenings like this are long and dreary, unless people can find something to do; there are not always things to be packed or unpacked, nor can scales be polished nor paper bags be made continually. Failing these, one must invent some other employment, and Anthony did so; he mended his clothes and put pieces on his boots. When he at last went to bed he used from habit to keep his nightcap on; he drew it down a little farther over his face, but he soon pushed it up again to see if the light had been properly put out. He would touch it, press the wick together, and then lie down on the other side and pull his nightcap down again. But very often a doubt would arise in his mind as to whether every coal in the little firepan below had been properly put out—a little spark might remain burning, and might set fire to something and cause damage. Therefore he got up, crept down the ladder—it could hardly be called a staircase—and when he came to the firepan, not a spark was to be seen, so he might just as well go to bed again. Then sometimes when he got half-way back he would wonder if the shutters were securely fastened; then his thin legs would carry him downstairs again. When at last he crept into bed, he would be so cold that his teeth chattered; cold seems to be doubly severe when it knows it cannot stay much longer. He drew up the bed-covering and drew the nightcap lower over his face, and tried to think of something other than trade and the labors of the day.

But this was not always agreeable, for old memories would come sometimes and raise the curtain of the past, bringing such painful thoughts that they pierce the heart and fill the eyes with tears—and that often happened to Anthony; scalding tears like large pearls would fall from his eyes to the quilt or the floor, and it would sound as if one of his heart-strings had broken. Sometimes they seemed to rise up again in a flame, illuminating a picture of life which never faded from his heart. Then he dried his eyes with his nightcap; the tear and the picture were indeed crushed, but the source of the tears remained and would well up again in his heart. The pictures did not come before him in the order in which they had occurred; often the most painful would come together; then at another time the happiest would come, but these always had the deepest shadows on them.

Every one admits that the beechwoods of Denmark are very beautiful, but the woods of Thuringia were far more beautiful in Anthony's eyes. The old oaks around the old baronial castle, where the creeping plants hung down over the rocks, seemed grander and more venerable to him, and the apple blossoms were sweeter there than in the Danish land.

He remembered all this very clearly; a glittering tear rolled over his cheek, and in this tear he could distinctly see two children at play—a boy and a girl. The boy had rosy cheeks, curly, golden hair, and clear blue eyes; he was the son of the merchant Anthony—it was he himself. The little girl had brown eyes and black hair, and had a bright intelligent expression. She was the burgomaster's daughter Molly. The two children were playing with an apple; they shook it, and heard the pips rattling inside. Then they cut it in two, and each of them took half; they even divided the pips and ate them all but one, which the little girl suggested they should put in the ground. "Then you shall see what will come out," she said. "It will be something you do not at all expect. A whole apple-tree will come out, but not at once."

She put the pip in a flower-pot, and they were both very busy and excited about it. The boy made a hole in the earth with his finger; the little girl dropped the pip into it, and they both covered it over with earth.

"Now you must not take it out to-morrow to see if it has taken root," said Molly. "That does not do at all. I did it with my flowers, but only twice; I wanted to see if they were growing—I did not know any better then—and they all died."

Anthony took the flower-pot away with him, and all through the winter he looked at it every morning, but nothing was to be seen except the black earth. At last, however, the spring came, the sun shone warmly again, and two little green leaves came up out of the pot.

"They represent Molly and myself," said the boy. "That's beautiful, that's wonderfully beautiful."

Soon a third leaf came. Whom did that represent? And another came, and yet another. Day after day and week after week it grew larger, until at last it began to look like a real tree.

All this was mirrored in a single tear which was wiped away, and disappeared; but it might come again from its source in old Anthony's heart.

There is a chain of stony mountains in the neighborhood of Eisenach. One of them has a rounded outline, and rises above the rest; it is quite bare and without tree, bush, or grass. It is called the Venus Mount, and in it dwells Venus, one of the old heathen deities. She is also called Lady Holle, and every child in the neighborhood of Eisenach has heard of her. It was she who enticed Tannhauser, the noble knight and minstrel, from the circle of the singers of the Wartburg into her mountain. Little Molly and Anthony often stood near this mountain, and one day Molly said, "Knock and say, Lady Holle, open the door—Tannhauser is here!"

But Anthony was not courageous enough. However, Molly did it, but she only said the words "Lady Holle, Lady Holle," aloud and distinctly; the rest she muttered so indistinctly that Anthony felt sure she really said nothing, yet she was as bold and saucy as possible; as saucy as she was sometimes when she came round him with other little girls in the garden, and they all tried to kiss him, because he did not like it and endeavored to send them away. Molly was the only one who took no notice of his resistance.

"*I* may kiss him!" she would say proudly; and Anthony put up with it and thought no more of it—it was only her vanity.

How charming Molly was, and what a dreadful tease! They said that Lady Holle was beautiful too, but that her beauty was tempting like that of an evil spirit. Saint Elizabeth possessed the greatest beauty and grace; she was the patron saint of the country, the pious princess of Thuringia, whose good deeds have been immortalized in so many lands by means of stories and legends. Her picture hung in the chapel surrounded by silver lamps, but it was not at all like Molly.

The apple-tree which the two children had planted grew year by year, and became larger and larger—so large that it had to be put out in the garden at last, in the fresh air where the dew fell and the sun shone. There it became so strong that it was able to stand the cold of the winter, and it seemed as if, when the severity of the winter was over, it put forth flowers in the spring for joy. It had two apples upon it in the autumn—one for Molly and one for Anthony. It could not very well do less.

So the tree grew very rapidly, and Molly grew with the tree. She looked as fresh as an apple-blossom; but Anthony was not to behold this flower for long. All things change; Molly's father left his old home, and Molly went far away with him. In our time the railways have made this a journey of a few hours only, but then it took a day and a night to go as far eastward from Eisenach to the city which is still called Weimar, at the farthest border of Thuringia. Molly and Anthony wept; but their tears united and had the sweet rosy hue of joy, for Molly told him that she loved him, loved him more than all the splendors of Weimar.

One, two, three years went by, and during this time he only received two letters: one came by the carrier, and a traveler brought the other. The way was long, difficult and circuitous, and passed through many towns and villages.

Molly and Anthony had often heard the story of Tristram and Isold, and the boy had applied it to himself and Molly, though the name Tristram was said to mean "born in tribulation," and that did not apply to Anthony, nor would he ever think, like Tristram, "She has forgotten me." But, indeed, Isold did not forget her faithful knight, and when they were both laid to rest in the earth, one on each side of the church, the lime-trees grew from their graves over the church roof and there mingled their blossoms and leaves together.

Anthony thought this a beautiful story, but sad—he was not afraid of anything sad happening to him or Molly—and he whistled a song composed by Walter of the Vogelweide, the old minnesinger:

Under the lindens on the heath.
One part of it he liked best of all:
Through the wood and in the vale
Sweetly trills the nightingale.

This song was often upon his lips, and he sang and whistled it on the moonlight night when he rode along the deep hollow way, on the road to Weimar, to visit Molly. He wished to arrive unexpectedly, and he did so. He was welcomed with full goblets of wine, and introduced to many pleasant people; a pretty room and a good bed were provided for him. Yet his reception was not what he had imagined and hoped it would be; he could not understand himself, or the others, but we may understand why it was so. One may go into a house and associate with the family without becoming one of them; one may talk together as people do in a stage-coach with a fellow-traveler, each inconveniencing the other, and wishing that either his good neighbor or himself were away. It was something of this kind that Anthony felt.

"I am a straightforward girl," said Molly, "and I will myself tell you how things stand. Much has changed since we were children together—both inwardly and outwardly. Habit and will cannot control our hearts. Anthony, now that I shall soon be far away from here, I should not like to make an enemy of you: I shall always think of you kindly, but I have never felt for you what I now feel for another man. You must reconcile yourself to this. Farewell, Anthony."

And Anthony bade her "good-bye" without a tear, but he felt he was no longer Molly's friend. Hot and cold iron both take the skin from our lips, and we have the same sensation when we kiss it; so his hatred sprang to life in a kiss just as his love had done.

Within twenty-four hours Anthony was back to Eisenach, but the horse he had ridden was ruined.

"What does it matter?" he said. "My life is ruined also—I will destroy everything that can remind me of her, or of Lady Holle—or Venus, the heathen woman! I will break down the apple-tree, and tear it up by the roots, so that it will never blossom or bear fruit again!'"

But the apple-tree was not broken down—he himself broke down, and was confined to his bed by a fever. But what raised him up again? A medicine that he was forced to take was given him—the bitterest medicine, which both body and spirit alike shrink from. Anthony's father was no longer a rich merchant. Hard days of trial came—misfortune came rolling into the house like the waves of the sea. Suffering and anxiety took away the father's strength, and Anthony had something else to think of beside nursing his love-sorrows and his anger against Molly. He had to take his father's place: to give orders, to help, to act with energy, and at last to go out into the world to earn his own living. He went to Bremen, and there learnt what poverty and hardships meant; these sometimes make the heart callous, but at other times soften it too much.

How different the world and the people in it were to what he had imagined them to be in his boyhood! What were the minnesinger's songs to him now? An echo of something that had vanished long ago. Yes, so he thought at times: but once more the songs would sound in his soul, and his heart would become gentle again.

"God's will be done!" he would say then. "It is a good thing that I was not permitted to keep Molly's love—that she did not remain true to me. What misery might it not have brought about now fortune has turned away from me! She left me before she knew of this disaster, or what the future held in store for me. That is the mercy of Providence. Everything has happened for the best; she was not to blame—and yet I have been so hard and bitter towards her!"

Years rolled on—Anthony's father died, and strangers lived in the old house, but Anthony was destined to see it once more. His rich employer sent him journeys on business, and his way led through Eisenach, his native town.

The old Wartburg stood unaltered, with "the monk and the nun" hewn out of stone. The old oaks made it look the same as in his childish days, and the Venus Mount stood gray and bare over the valley. He would have cried gladly:

"Lady Holle, Lady Holle, unlock the mountain; I will enter and remain in my native earth!"

But that was a sinful desire, and he crossed himself to drive it away. A little bird among the bushes sang sweetly, and the old minne-song was recalled to his memory:

> Through the wood and in the vale
> Sweetly trills the nightingale.

Here, in the town of his childhood, which he saw again through tears, much came back into his remembrance—his father's house stood just as it had done in the old times, but the garden was altered. A path leading across the fields led through part of the old ground, and the apple-tree that he had not broken down stood there still, but it was outside the garden, on the further side of the path. But the sun threw his rays on the apple tree as in former days, the dew fell gently upon it as it did then, and its branches were filled with such a load of fruit that they bent down towards the ground.

"How it thrives," he said; "the tree may well do so!"

One of its branches, however, was broken; mischievous hands had torn it down, as the tree stood near the high road.

"People break its blossoms off without an expression of thanks, they steal its fruit, and break its branches; one could say of the tree as it has been said of some people, it was not sung at its cradle that this should happen to it. Its story began so pleasantly, and to what has it come now? Forsaken and forgotten, a garden tree near a ditch in the field close by the high road. There it stands without protection, ransacked, and broken! It is not yet dead, but in time its blossoms will become fewer, and there will be no fruit at all—and then its story will be ended."

Thus thought Anthony while he stood under the tree, thus he thought during many a long night in the solitary chamber of the wooden house in the distant land—in Small House Street, Copenhagen, whither his rich master, the Bremen merchant, had sent him, on condition that he should never marry.

"Marry! Ha, ha," he laughed bitterly to himself.

Winter had come early, it was freezing hard. Outside a snowstorm was raging; every one who could remained at home. Thus it happened that the people who lived opposite Anthony did not notice that his door had not been unlocked for two days, nor had he shown himself, for who would go out in such weather if he could help it? These were gray, gloomy days, and in the house, the windows of which were not made of glass, there was only alternately twilight and dark night. Old Anthony had not left his bed for these two days; he had not the strength to get up, already for a long time he had felt the effects of the weather in his limbs; forsaken by all, the bachelor lay there and could not help himself, he could hardly reach the water-jug which he had put by his bedside, and he had taken all to the last drop. It was not fever, nor illness, but old age that had laid him up. Where he lay it was as dark as if it were perpetual night. A little spider, which, however, he could not see, spun its web over him, busily and contentedly, as if it were weaving a band of crape, which should wave over him when the old man closed his eyes.

Time was hanging heavily and painfully with him; he had no tears to shed, and he felt no pain. No thought of Molly entered his mind; he felt as if the world and its noise had no longer anything to do with him, as if he were lying outside the world, and nobody thought of him. For a moment he felt hungry or thirsty—yes, he felt both—but no one came to look after him. He thought of all who had suffered from want of food sometimes; of Saint Elizabeth when she wandered on earth, the saint of his native place, and of his childhood, the noble duchess of Thuringia, the kind-hearted lady who used to visit the humblest cottages administering food and comfort to its poor inmates. The thought of her pious deeds was as light to his soul. He remembered how she came to say words of consolation, dressing the wounds of the afflicted and feeding the hungry, although her severe husband had often scolded her for it. He remembered the legend about her, in which she is said to have carried a basket full of food and wine, and her husband who watched her, came and asked her angrily what she was carrying, and she answered, with fear and trembling, "Roses which I have picked in the garden"; how he had then torn the white cloth from the basket, and how a miracle had been performed for the good woman, as bread and wine, and everything in the basket, had been transformed into roses! Thus the memory of the saint filled Anthony's calm mind; she stood as if real, before his dim sight in his simple dwelling in the Danish land. He uncovered his head and looked into her mild eyes, and everything around him was bright and rosy—indeed the roses seemed to breathe forth fragrance—and a sweet strange smell of apples reached him; he saw an apple tree in full bloom spreading its branches above him—it was the tree which he and Molly had planted together.

And the tree dropped its fragrant petals upon him, and cooled his hot brow; the petals fell upon his parched lips, and were like strengthening wine and bread; they also fell upon his breast, and he became calm and felt inclined to sleep.

"Now I shall sleep," he whispered to himself; "sleep will do me good. To-morrow I shall get up again and be strong and well. Wonderful, wonderful! The apple tree planted in love I see now in magnificence!" And he slept.

The day after this—it was the third day that his booth remained locked—the snowstorm raged no longer; then a neighbor from the opposite house came to the booth where Anthony dwelled as he had not yet shown himself. He lay there stretched on his bed—dead—clutching his old cap tightly in both hands. They did not put it on when he was in his coffin; he had a clean white one on then.

Where now were the tears he had shed? What had become of the pearls? They remained in the nightcap—and the real ones do not come out in the wash—they were preserved in the nightcap, and in time forgotten; but the old thoughts and the old dreams, they still remained in the bachelor's night-cap. Don't wish for such a cap, it would make your forehead burn, your pulse beat quicker, and produce dreams which appear like reality.

The man who first wore the cap afterwards felt all this, though it was fifty years later, and he was the burgomaster himself who was tolerably wealthy, and had a wife and eleven children. He was immediately seized with dreams of unfortunate love, of bankruptcy and times of hardship.

"Good heavens! how the nightcap burns!" he cried, tearing it from his head; a pearl rolled out and then another, and another, and they sparkled and made a rattling sound.

"I must be suffering from gout," said the burgomaster; "something glitters before my eyes!"

They were tears, shed fifty years before by old Anthony of Eisenach.

Every one who put the nightcap on his head afterwards, had visions and dreams that excited him a great deal. His own life-history was changed into that of Anthony and became a story—in fact many stories. But some one else must tell these; we have told the first one, and our parting word to you is—Don't wish for "the old bachelor's nightcap."

The Old Secretary's Christmas Eve

(TRADITIONAL SWEDISH TALE)

Both large and small all through the city knew the old secretary, which was not surprising, because he always wore the same dress, and expression, too. The thin, smoothly combed gray hair was always covered by the same tall gray hat; the bushy eyebrows, the sharp eyes and the firmly closed mouth were forever unchanged. As long as any one could remember the secretary, he had worn the round blue cape with the many wide collars, the checked cotton umbrella, and the gray knee-breeches. The large galoshes went by the name of "boats" among the boys of the city; "klapp! klapp!" they sounded on the rough stones of the street. The old secretary looked so comical, many thought, but no one dared to say so, because the young folks were afraid of the man who went on his way silent and alone.

No one knew where the secretary had come from, or what his childhood had been. He wrote for people now, and helped them with their accounts, and that is the reason he was called secretary; because a person must be called something.

He did not earn much, to be sure, but he did not need much, either, where he lived in his attic room, to which no one came without an errand there. The secretary had no need to invite strangers there, it is true, for he never went out except to his work—the lonely old man.

Christmas Eve had come, and just here the story begins. In the forenoon, people hurried back and forth on the streets; the shops were crowded, and Christmas presents were bought, wrapped up and sealed.

In the market place stood many Christmas spruces, both large and small, so the purchasers could choose according to their own liking and taste; and the beautiful green trees found ready sale.

In the afternoon it grew more quiet, and when evening came it was very silent out-of-doors, but in the windows light after light appeared both in the stately rooms of the rich, and the lowly hut of the poor man, because

515

Christmas is such a blessed time that people share with each other, so that no one shall entirely miss Christmas joys.

The old secretary wandered alone through the streets towards his lonely, silent home, as he had done for many, many years. Now and then the sound of happy voices reached his ears, shadows danced gaily out on the curtains, and travelers, one and all, hastened past him with quickened steps.

"Ah, yes! this is Christmas Eve," said he to himself, but silently, so that no one heard it.

"Christmas Eve!"—he stopped an instant as if something special passed through his mind—"Christmas Eve!"

He had now come as far as the great market place. A little boy still stood there with a small spruce-tree. He would so gladly have sold it, but now it looked hopeless to him.

The old secretary stopped before the little tree.

"What do you ask for the spruce?" he said shyly, as if he appeared stupid in asking such a question. The boy named the price; it was only twenty-five *öre*.

"Here you have it, little one," said the old secretary, and handed the boy a *krona*. "I will take the spruce with me." He moved his head a little, and that was for a nod, and walked away, while the boy, his face red with delight, ran home.

"I wonder if I had better dress the Christmas-tree for Pettersson's girl!" said the secretary to himself, just as quietly as before. He decided to do so.

He then went into several shops, and bought trinkets such as one hangs on a Christmas-tree, to the great wonderment of the clerks in the stores and the purchasers who were in them. "What has happened to the old secretary? He had a spruce in his hand," said they.

But the secretary neither heard nor thought about what the people might say. With his hands and pockets full he came home, and then began to trim up the Christmas-tree. It went slowly, for it was many, many years since he had done so, but at last it was ready with candles and everything.

"I will light the candles before I call the girl in"; and the old man lighted one after another of the small wax candles, and it became then more brilliant than it had ever been in the little room before. The old man sat down and gazed at the little tree. He clasped his hands.

"Oh! how beautiful," he exclaimed out loud, so that anybody could have heard it, if there had been any one there.

His eyebrows moved rapidly; in the corner of each eye there gleamed a tear, then many followed and fell like a soft, warm May rain, on the aged, wrinkled cheeks.

Whether it was because he saw the tree through tears or for what reason, he beheld such wonderful pictures! The room became large, the spruce grew, and a host of curly-headed children moved around it, in gleeful dance. Father and mother, yes, his own father and mother joined the ring and, yes, there was his own self, not as an old secretary, no, as a gay, blue-eyed boy with rosy cheeks, and the other children were his brothers and sisters! Faster fell the tears, but they did not burn, as when one usually weeps, but they fell softly, like dew on a summer night, on the parched plains. The old secretary hardly dared to breathe, because he was afraid the vision would vanish.

Now, the picture changes. The little ones stand beside father and mother with clasped hands.

"O, hear!" whispered the secretary. "Dear God, hear! it is surely the old Christmas psalm."

The tones rose, so distinct and clear, the delicate childish voices sounded so fresh in the evening stillness!

The secretary sang with them—

A Virgin bears a child today—

and so on through the beautiful psalm. The voice is weak and trembling, but he does not hear it, he hears the voices of father and mother, brothers and sisters, he hears his own childish tones; he is no longer in his dreary little chamber; he is in his childhood's home again, among the dear ones, whom he never thought to see again in this life.

In the outer room stood Madam Pettersson, the one who let him his room, and prepared his food for him. She never had heard him sing before; it was so strange!

"Hush, Lina!" says she to the girl, who stood right by the door, listening. "We must not go in before he is done! What do you suppose he can have there?"

—he never from us parteth!

now sang the secretary; that is the last verse of the psalm, and so it was ended.

Madam Pettersson opened the door. "Oh, see!" exclaimed she, clapping her hands, "the secretary has trimmed a Christmas-tree for himself!"

But the secretary did not answer. He sat leaning back in his chair, with his hands clasped and a beautiful smile on his lips. Madam Pettersson had never seen him look so cheerful.

"Secretary—oh! what! I believe he is dead!" She moved his hands, his head, but he sat the same as before.

Yes, he was dead, as she said, but he had never looked so happy, as Madam Pettersson could remember.

Ripple, the Water-Spirit

Louisa May Alcott

Down in the deep blue sea lived Ripple, a happy little Water-Spirit; all day long she danced beneath the coral arches, made garlands of bright ocean flowers, or floated on the great waves that sparkled in the sunlight; but the pastime that she loved best was lying in the many-colored shells upon the shore, listening to the low, murmuring music the waves had taught them long ago; and here for hours the little Spirit lay watching the sea and sky, while singing gayly to herself.

But when tempests rose, she hastened down below the stormy billows, to where all was calm and still, and with her sister Spirits waited till it should be fair again, listening sadly, meanwhile, to the cries of those whom the wild waves wrecked and cast into the angry sea, and who soon came floating down, pale and cold, to the Spirits' pleasant home; then they wept pitying tears above the lifeless forms, and laid them in quiet graves, where flowers bloomed, and jewels sparkled in the sand.

This was Ripple's only grief, and she often thought of those who sorrowed for the friends they loved, who now slept far down in the dim and silent coral caves, and gladly would she have saved the lives of those who lay around her; but the great ocean was far mightier than all the tender-hearted Spirits dwelling in its bosom. Thus she could only weep for them, and lay them down to sleep where no cruel waves could harm them more.

One day, when a fearful storm raged far and wide, and the Spirits saw great billows rolling like heavy clouds above their heads, and heard the wild winds sounding far away, down through the foaming waves a little child came floating to their home; its eyes were closed as if in sleep, the long hair fell like sea-weed round its pale, cold face, and the little hands still clasped the shells they had been gathering on the beach, when the great waves swept it into the troubled sea.

With tender tears the Spirits laid the little form to rest upon its bed of flowers, and, singing mournful songs, as if to make its sleep more calm and deep, watched long and lovingly above it, till the storm had died away, and all was still again.

While Ripple sang above the little child, through the distant roar of winds and waves she heard a wild, sorrowing voice, that seemed to call for help. Long she listened, thinking it was but the echo of their own plaintive song, but high above the music still sounded the sad, wailing cry. Then, stealing silently away, she glided up through foam and spray, till, through the parting clouds, the sunlight shone upon her from the tranquil sky; and, guided by the mournful sound, she floated on, till, close before her on the beach, she saw a woman stretching forth her arms, and with a sad, imploring voice praying the restless sea to give her back the little child it had so cruelly borne away. But the waves dashed foaming up among the bare rocks at her feet, mingling their cold spray with her tears, and gave no answer to her prayer.

When Ripple saw the mother's grief, she longed to comfort her; so, bending tenderly beside her, where she knelt upon the shore, the little Spirit told her how her child lay softly sleeping, far down in a lovely place, where sorrowing tears were shed, and gentle hands laid garlands over him. But all in vain she whispered kindly words; the weeping mother only cried,—

"Dear Spirit, can you use no charm or spell to make the waves bring back my child, as full of life and strength as when they swept him from my side? O give me back my little child, or let me lie beside him in the bosom of the cruel sea."

"Most gladly will I help you if I can, though I have little power to use; then grieve no more, for I will search both earth and sea, to find some friend who can bring back all you have lost. Watch daily on the shore, and if I do not come again, then you will know my search has been in vain. Farewell, poor mother, you shall see your little child again, if Fairy power can win him back." And with these cheering words Ripple sprang into the sea; while, smiling through her tears, the woman watched the gentle Spirit, till her bright crown vanished in the waves.

When Ripple reached her home, she hastened to the palace of the Queen, and told her of the little child, the sorrowing mother, and the promise she had made.

"Good little Ripple," said the Queen, when she had told her all, "your promise never can be kept; there is no power below the sea to work this charm, and you can never reach the Fire-Spirits' home, to win from them a flame to warm the little body into life. I pity the poor mother, and would most gladly help her; but alas! I am a Spirit like yourself, and cannot serve you as I long to do."

"Ah, dear Queen! if you had seen her sorrow, you too would seek to keep the promise I have made. I cannot let her watch for *me* in vain, till I have done my best: then tell me where the Fire-Spirits dwell, and I will ask of them the flame that shall give life to the little child and such great happiness to the sad, lonely mother: tell me the path, and let me go."

"It is far, far away, high up above the sun, where no Spirit ever dared to venture yet," replied the Queen. "I cannot show the path, for it is through the air. Dear Ripple, do not go, for you can never reach that distant place: some harm most surely will befall; and then how shall we live, without our dearest, gentlest Spirit? Stay here with us in your own pleasant home, and think no more of this, for I can never let you go."

But Ripple would not break the promise she had made, and besought so earnestly, and with such pleading words, that the Queen at last with sorrow gave consent, and Ripple joyfully prepared to go. She, with her sister Spirits, built up a tomb of delicate, bright-colored shells, wherein the child might lie, till she should come to wake him into life; then, praying them to watch most faithfully above it, she said farewell, and floated bravely forth, on her long, unknown journey, far away.

"I will search the broad earth till I find a path up to the sun, or some kind friend who will carry me; for, alas! I have no wings, and cannot glide through the blue air as through the sea," said Ripple to herself, as she went dancing over the waves, which bore her swiftly onward towards a distant shore.

Long she journeyed through the pathless ocean, with no friends to cheer her, save the white sea-birds who went sweeping by, and only stayed to dip their wide wings at her side, and then flew silently away. Sometimes great ships sailed by, and then with longing eyes did the little Spirit gaze up at the faces that looked down upon the sea; for often they were kind and pleasant ones, and she gladly would have called to them and asked them to be friends. But they would never understand the strange, sweet language that she spoke, or even see the lovely face that smiled at them above the waves; her blue, transparent garments were but water to their eyes, and the pearl chains in her hair but foam and sparkling spray; so, hoping that the sea would be most gentle with them, silently she floated on her way, and left them far behind.

At length green hills were seen, and the waves gladly bore the little Spirit on, till, rippling gently over soft white sand, they left her on the pleasant shore.

"Ah, what a lovely place it is!" said Ripple, as she passed through sunny valleys, where flowers began to bloom, and young leaves rustled on the trees.

"Why are you all so gay, dear birds?" she asked, as their cheerful voices sounded far and near; "is there a festival over the earth, that all is so beautiful and bright?"

"Do you not know that Spring is coming? The warm winds whispered it days ago, and we are learning the sweetest songs, to welcome her when she shall come," sang the lark, soaring away as the music gushed from his little throat.

"And shall I see her, Violet, as she journeys over the earth?" asked Ripple again.

"Yes, you will meet her soon, for the sunlight told me she was near; tell her we long to see her again, and are waiting to welcome her back," said the blue flower, dancing for joy on her stem, as she nodded and smiled on the Spirit.

"I will ask Spring where the Fire-Spirits dwell; she travels over the earth each year, and surely can show me the way," thought Ripple, as she went journeying on.

Soon she saw Spring come smiling over the earth; sunbeams and breezes floated before, and then, with her white garments covered with flowers, with wreaths in her hair, and dewdrops and seeds falling fast from her hands, the beautiful season came singing by.

"Dear Spring, will you listen, and help a poor little Spirit, who seeks far and wide for the Fire-Spirits' home?" cried Ripple; and then told why she was there, and begged her to tell what she sought.

"The Fire-Spirits' home is far, far away, and I cannot guide you there; but Summer is coming behind me," said Spring, "and she may know better than I. But I will give you a breeze to help you on your way; it will never tire nor fail, but bear you easily over land and sea. Farewell, little Spirit! I would gladly do more, but voices are calling me far and wide, and I cannot stay."

"Many thanks, kind Spring!" cried Ripple, as she floated away on the breeze; "give a kindly word to the mother who waits on the shore, and tell her I have not forgotten my vow, but hope soon to see her again."

Then Spring flew on with her sunshine and flowers, and Ripple went swiftly over hill and vale, till she came to the land where Summer was dwelling. Here the sun shone warmly down on the early fruit, the winds blew freshly over fields of fragrant hay, and rustled with a pleasant sound among the green leaves in the forests; heavy dews fell softly down at night, and long, bright days brought strength and beauty to the blossoming earth.

"Now I must seek for Summer," said Ripple, as she sailed slowly through the sunny sky.

"I am here, what would you with me, little Spirit?" said a musical voice in her ear; and, floating by her side, she saw a graceful form, with green robes fluttering in the air, whose pleasant face looked kindly on her, from beneath a crown of golden sunbeams that cast a warm, bright glow on all beneath.

Then Ripple told her tale, and asked where she should go; but Summer answered, —

"I can tell no more than my young sister Spring where you may find the Spirits that you seek; but I too, like her, will give a gift to aid you. Take this sunbeam from my crown; it will cheer and brighten the most gloomy path through which you pass. Farewell! I shall carry tidings of you to the watcher by the sea, if in my journey round the world I find her there."

And Summer, giving her the sunbeam, passed away over the distant hills, leaving all green and bright behind her.

So Ripple journeyed on again, till the earth below her shone with yellow harvests waving in the sun, and the air was filled with cheerful voices, as the reapers sang among the fields or in the pleasant vineyards, where purple fruit hung gleaming through the leaves; while the sky above was cloudless, and the changing forest-trees shone like a many-colored garland, over hill and plain; and here, along the ripening corn-fields, with bright wreaths of crimson leaves and golden wheat-ears in her hair and on her purple mantle, stately Autumn passed, with a happy smile on her calm face, as she went scattering generous gifts from her full arms.

But when the wandering Spirit came to her, and asked for what she sought, this season, like the others, could not tell her where to go; so, giving her a yellow leaf, Autumn said, as she passed on,—

"Ask Winter, little Ripple, when you come to his cold home; he knows the Fire-Spirits well, for when he comes they fly to the earth, to warm and comfort those dwelling there; and perhaps he can tell you where they are. So take this gift of mine, and when you meet his chilly winds, fold it about you, and sit warm beneath its shelter, till you come to sunlight again. I will carry comfort to the patient woman, as my sisters have already done, and tell her you are faithful still."

Then on went the never-tiring Breeze, over forest, hill, and field, till the sky grew dark, and bleak winds whistled by. Then Ripple, folded in the soft, warm leaf, looked sadly down on the earth, that seemed to lie so desolate and still beneath its shroud of snow, and thought how bitter cold the leaves and flowers must be; for the little Water-Spirit did not know that Winter spread a soft white covering above their beds, that they might safely sleep below till Spring should waken them again. So she went sorrowfully on, till Winter, riding on the strong North-Wind, came rushing by, with a sparkling ice-crown in his streaming hair, while from beneath his crimson cloak, where glittering frost-work shone like silver threads, he scattered snow-flakes far and wide.

"What do you seek with me, fair little Spirit, that you come so bravely here amid my ice and snow? Do not fear me; I am warm at heart, though rude and cold without," said Winter, looking kindly on her, while a bright smile shone like sunlight on his pleasant face, as it glowed and glistened in the frosty air.

When Ripple told him why she had come, he pointed upward, where the sunlight dimly shone through the heavy clouds, saying,—

"Far off there, beside the sun, is the Fire-Spirits' home; and the only path is up, through cloud and mist. It is a long, strange path, for a lonely little

Spirit to be going; the Fairies are wild, willful things, and in their play may harm and trouble you. Come back with me, and do not go this dangerous journey to the sky. I'll gladly bear you home again, if you will come."

But Ripple said, "I cannot turn back now, when I am nearly there. The Spirits surely will not harm me, when I tell them why I am come; and if I win the flame, I shall be the happiest Spirit in the sea, for my promise will be kept, and the poor mother happy once again. So farewell, Winter! Speak to her gently, and tell her to hope still, for I shall surely come."

"Adieu, little Ripple! May good angels watch above you! Journey bravely on, and take this snow-flake that will never melt, as my gift," Winter cried, as the North-Wind bore him on, leaving a cloud of falling snow behind.

"Now, dear Breeze," said Ripple, "fly straight upward through the air, until we reach the place we have so long been seeking; Sunbeam shall go before to light the way, Yellow-leaf shall shelter me from heat and rain, while Snow-flake shall lie here beside me till it comes of use. So farewell to the pleasant earth, until we come again. And now away, up to the sun!"

When Ripple first began her airy journey, all was dark and dreary; heavy clouds lay piled like hills around her, and a cold mist filled the air; but the Sunbeam, like a star, lit up the way, the leaf lay warmly round her, and the tireless wind went swiftly on. Higher and higher they floated up, still darker and darker grew the air, closer the damp mist gathered, while the black clouds rolled and tossed, like great waves, to and fro.

"Ah!" sighed the weary little Spirit, "shall I never see the light again, or feel the warm winds on my cheek? It is a dreary way indeed, and but for the Seasons' gifts I should have perished long ago; but the heavy clouds must pass away at last, and all be fair again. So hasten on, good Breeze, and bring me quickly to my journey's end."

Soon the cold vapors vanished from her path, and sunshine shone upon her pleasantly; so she went gayly on, till she came up among the stars, where many new, strange sights were to be seen. With wondering eyes she looked upon the bright worlds that once seemed dim and distant, when she gazed upon them from the sea; but now they moved around her, some shining with a softly radiant light, some circled with bright, many-colored rings, while others burned with a red, angry glare. Ripple would have gladly stayed to watch them longer, for she fancied low, sweet voices called her, and lovely faces seemed to look upon her as she passed; but higher up still, nearer to the sun, she saw a far-off light, that glittered like a brilliant crimson star, and seemed to cast a rosy glow along the sky.

"The Fire-Spirits surely must be there, and I must stay no longer here," said Ripple. So steadily she floated on, till straight before her lay a broad, bright path, that led up to a golden arch, beyond which she could see shapes flitting to and fro. As she drew near, brighter glowed the sky, hotter and hotter grew the air, till Ripple's leaf-cloak shrivelled up, and could no longer shield her from the heat; then she unfolded the white snow-flake, and, gladly wrapping the soft, cool mantle round her, entered through the shining arch.

Through the red mist that floated all around her, she could see high walls of changing light, where orange, blue, and violet flames went flickering to and fro, making graceful figures as they danced and glowed; and underneath these rainbow arches, little Spirits glided, far and near, wearing crowns of fire, beneath which flashed their wild, bright eyes; and as they spoke, sparks dropped quickly from their lips, and Ripple saw with wonder, through their garments of transparent light, that in each Fairy's breast there burned a steady flame, that never wavered or went out.

As thus she stood, the Spirits gathered round her, and their hot breath would have scorched her, but she drew the snow-cloak closer round her, saying,—

"Take me to your Queen, that I may tell her why I am here, and ask for what I seek."

So, through long halls of many-colored fire, they led her to a Spirit fairer than the rest, whose crown of flames waved to and fro like golden plumes, while, underneath her violet robe, the light within her breast glowed bright and strong.

"This is our Queen," the Spirits said, bending low before her, as she turned her gleaming eyes upon the stranger they had brought.

Then Ripple told how she had wandered round the world in search of them, how the Seasons had most kindly helped her on, by giving Sunbeam, Breeze, Leaf, and Flake; and how, through many dangers, she had come at last to ask of them the magic flame that could give life to the little child again.

When she had told her tale, the spirits whispered earnestly among themselves, while sparks fell thick and fast with every word; at length the Fire-Queen said aloud,—

"We cannot give the flame you ask, for each of us must take a part of it from our own breasts; and this we will not do, for the brighter our bosom-fire bums, the lovelier we are. So do not ask us for this thing; but any other gift we will most gladly give, for we feel kindly towards you, and will serve you if we may."

But Ripple asked no other boon, and, weeping sadly, begged them not to send her back without the gift she had come so far to gain.

"O dear, warm-hearted Spirits! give me each a little light from your own breasts, and surely they will glow the brighter for this kindly deed; and I will thankfully repay it if I can." As thus she spoke, the Queen, who had spied out a chain of jewels Ripple wore upon her neck, replied,—

"If you will give me those bright, sparkling stones, I will bestow on you a part of my own flame; for we have no such lovely things to wear about our necks, and I desire much to have them. Will you give it me for what I offer, little Spirit?"

Joyfully Ripple gave her the chain; but, as soon as it touched her hand, the jewels melted like snow, and fell in bright drops to the ground; at this the Queen's eyes' flashed, and the Spirits gathered angrily about poor Ripple, who looked sadly at the broken chain, and thought in vain what she could give, to win the thing she longed so earnestly for.

"I have many fairer gems than these, in my home below the sea; and I will bring all I can gather far and wide, if you will grant my prayer, and give me what I seek," she said, turning gently to the fiery Spirits, who were hovering fiercely round her.

"You must bring us each a jewel that will never vanish from our hands as these have done," they said, "and we will each give of our fire; and when the child is brought to life, you must bring hither all the jewels you can gather from the depths of the sea, that we may try them here among the flames; but if they melt away like these, then we shall keep you prisoner, till you give us back the light we lend. If you consent to this, then take our gift, and journey home again; but fail not to return, or we shall seek you out."

And Ripple said she would consent, though she knew not if the jewels could be found; still, thinking of the promise she had made, she forgot all else, and told the Spirits what they asked most surely should be done. So each one gave a little of the fire from their breasts, and placed the flame in a crystal vase, through which it shone and glittered like a star.

Then, bidding her remember all she had promised them, they led her to the golden arch, and said farewell.

So, down along the shining path, through mist and cloud, she traveled back; till, far below, she saw the broad blue sea she left so long ago.

Gladly she plunged into the clear, cool waves, and floated back to her pleasant home; where the Spirits gathered joyfully about her, listening with tears and smiles, as she told all her many wanderings, and showed the crystal vase that she had brought.

"Now come," said they, "and finish the good work you have so bravely carried on." So to the quiet tomb they went, where, like a marble image, cold and still, the little child was lying. Then Ripple placed the flame upon his breast, and watched it gleam and sparkle there, while light came slowly back into the once dim eyes, a rosy glow shone over the pale face, and breath stole through the parted lips; still brighter and warmer burned the magic fire, until the child awoke from his long sleep, and looked in smiling wonder at the faces bending over him.

Then Ripple sang for joy, and, with her sister Spirits, robed the child in graceful garments, woven of bright sea-weed, while in his shining hair they wreathed long garlands of their fairest flowers, and on his little arms hung chains of brilliant shells.

"Now come with us, dear child," said Ripple; "we will bear you safely up into the sunlight and the pleasant air; for this is not your home, and yonder, on the shore, there waits a loving friend for you."

So up they went, through foam and spray, till on the beach, where the fresh winds played among her falling hair, and the waves broke sparkling at her feet, the lonely mother still stood, gazing wistfully across the sea. Suddenly, upon a great blue billow that came rolling in, she saw the Water-Spirits smiling on her; and high aloft, in their white gleaming arms, her child stretched forth his hands to welcome her; while the little voice she so longed to hear again cried gayly,—

"See, dear mother, I am come; and look what lovely things the gentle Spirits gave, that I might seem more beautiful to you."

Then gently the great wave broke, and rolled back to the sea, leaving Ripple on the shore, and the child clasped in his mother's arms.

"O faithful little Spirit! I would gladly give some precious gift to show my gratitude for this kind deed; but I have nothing save this chain of little pearls: they are the tears I shed, and the sea has changed them thus, that I might offer them to you," the happy mother said, when her first joy was passed, and Ripple turned to go.

"Yes, I will gladly wear your gift, and look upon it as my fairest ornament," the Water-Spirit said; and with the pearls upon her breast, she left the
shore, where the child was playing gayly to and fro, and the mother's glad
smile shone upon her, till she sang beneath the waves.

And now another task was to be done; her promise to the Fire-Spirits
must be kept. So far and wide she searched among the caverns of the sea, and
gathered all the brightest jewels shining there; and then upon her faithful
Breeze once more went journeying through the sky.

The Spirits gladly welcomed her, and led her to the Queen, before whom
she poured out the sparkling gems she had gathered with such toil and care;
but when the Spirits tried to form them into crowns, they trickled from
their hands like colored drops of dew, and Ripple saw with fear and sorrow how they melted one by one away, till none of all the many she had
brought remained. Then the Fire-Spirits looked upon her angrily, and when
she begged them to be merciful, and let her try once more, saying, —

"Do not keep me prisoner here. I cannot breathe the flames that give
you life, and but for this snow-mantle I too should melt away, and vanish
like the jewels in your hands. O dear Spirits, give me some other task, but
let me go from this warm place, where all is strange and fearful to a Spirit
of the sea."

They would not listen; and drew nearer, saying, while bright sparks showered from their lips, "We will not let you go, for you have promised to be ours
if the gems you brought proved worthless; so fling away this cold white cloak,
and bathe with us in the fire fountains, and help us bring back to our bosom
flames the light we gave you for the child."

Then Ripple sank down on the burning floor, and felt that her life was
nearly done; for she well knew the hot air of the fire-palace would be death to
her. The Spirits gathered round, and began to lift her mantle off; but underneath they saw the pearl chain, shining with a clear, soft light, that only
glowed more brightly when they laid their hands upon it.

"O give us this!" cried they; "it is far lovelier than all the rest, and does
not melt away like them; and see how brilliantly it glitters in our hands. If we
may but have this, all will be well, and you are once more free."

And Ripple, safe again beneath her snow-flake, gladly gave the chain to
them; and told them how the pearls they now placed proudly on their breasts
were formed of tears, which but for them might still be flowing. Then the

Spirits smiled most kindly on her, and would have put their arms about her, and have kissed her cheek, but she drew back, telling them that every touch of theirs was like a wound to her.

"Then, if we may not tell our pleasure so, we will show it in a different way, and give you a pleasant journey home. Come out with us," the Spirits said, "and see the bright path we have made for you." So they led her to the lofty gate, and here, from sky to earth, a lovely rainbow arched its radiant colors in the sun.

"This is indeed a pleasant road," said Ripple. "Thank you, friendly Spirits, for your care; and now farewell. I would gladly stay yet longer, but we cannot dwell together, and I am longing sadly for my own cool home. Now Sunbeam, Breeze, Leaf, and Flake, fly back to the Seasons whence you came, and tell them that, thanks to their kind gifts, Ripple's work at last is done."

Then down along the shining pathway spread before her, the happy little Spirit glided to the sea.

The Snowdrop, or Summer-Geck

Hans Christian Andersen

It was winter-time; the air was cold, the wind sharp; but indoors it was snug and warm. Indoors lay the flower; it lay in its bulb under the earth and the snow.

One day rain fell; the drops trickled through the snow-coverlet, down into the ground, touched the flower-bulb, and told about the bright world up above; soon a sunbeam, fine and pointed, pierced its way through the snow, down to the bulb, and tapped on it.

"Come in!" said the flower.

"I can't," said the sunbeam, "I am not strong enough to open the door; I shall be strong when summer comes."

"When will it be summer?" asked the flower, and repeated it every time a new sunbeam pierced down to it. But it was a long time till summer: the snow still lay on the ground, and every night ice formed on the water.

"How long it is in coming! How long it is!" said the flower; "I feel a prickling and tingling, I must stretch myself, I must stir myself, I must open up, I must get out and nod good morning to the summer; that will be a happy time!"

And the flower stretched itself and strained itself inside against the thin shell, which the water outside had softened, which the snow and the earth had warmed, and the sunbeam had tapped upon; it shot out under the snow, with its whitey-green bud on its green stalk, with narrow, thick leaves, which seemed trying to shelter it. The snow was cold, but permeated with light and easy to push through; and here the sunbeams came with greater strength than before.

"Welcome! welcome!" sang every sunbeam, and the flower raised itself above the snow, out into the world of light. The sunbeams patted and kissed it, so that it opened itself completely, white as snow, and adorned with green stripes. It bowed its head in gladness and humility.

"Beautiful flower," sang the sunbeams, "how fresh and pure thou art! Thou art the first; thou art the only one! Thou art our darling! Thou ringest in summer, lovely summer, over town and field! All the snow shall melt! the cold winds shall be chased away! we shall rule! Everything will become green! And then thou wilt have company, lilacs, and laburnum, and last of all the roses; but thou art the first, so fine and pure!"

It was a great delight. It seemed as if the air was music, as if the beams of light penetrated into its leaves and stalk. There it stood, so fine and fragile, and yet so strong, in its young beauty; it stood there in its white kirtle with green ribbons, and praised the summer. But it was far from summer-time, clouds hid the sun, and sharp winds blew upon the flowers.

"Thou art come a little too early," said Wind and Weather; "we still have power, and that thou shalt feel and submit to. Thou shouldst have kept indoors, not run out to make a show. It is not time yet!"

It was biting cold! The days which came, brought not a single sunbeam; it was weather to freeze to pieces in, for such a little delicate flower. But there was more strength in it than it knew of; it was strong in joy and faith in the summer, which must come, which was foretold to it by its own deep longing, and confirmed by the warm sunshine; and so it stood with confident hope, in its white dress, in the white snow, bowing its head, when the snow-flakes fell heavy and thick, whilst the icy winds swept over it.

"Thou wilt be broken!" said they, "wither and freeze: what didst thou seek out here! Why wert thou lured abroad! the sunbeam has fooled thee! Now canst thou enjoy thyself, thou summer-geck?"

"Summer-geck!" echoed in the cold morning hours.

"Summer-geck!" shouted some children who came down into the garden, "there stands one so pretty, so beautiful, the first, the only one!"

And these words did the flower so much good; they were words like warm sunbeams. The flower did not even notice in its gladness that it was being plucked: it lay in a child's hand, was kissed by a child's lips, was brought into a warm room, gazed at by kind eyes, and put in water, so strengthening, so enlivening. The flower believed that it was come right into summer, all at once.

The daughter of the house, a pretty little girl, was just confirmed; she had a dear friend, and he was also just confirmed. "He shall be my summer-geck," said she; so she took the fragile little flower, laid it in a piece of scented paper, on which were written verses, verses about the flower. Yes, it was all in the verses, and it was made up as a letter; the flower was laid inside, and it was all dark about it, as dark as when it lay in the bulb. The flower went on a journey, lay in the post-bag, was pressed and squeezed, and that was not pleasant, but it came to an end at last.

The journey was over, the letter was opened and read by the dear friend; he was so delighted he kissed the flower, and laid it, with the verses around it, in a drawer, in which were many delightful letters, but all without a flower; this was the first, the only one, as the sunbeams had called it, and that was very pleasant to think about. It got a long time to think about it, it thought whilst the summer passed, and the long winter passed, and it was summer once more; then it was brought out again. But this time the young man was not at all delighted; he gripped the paper hard and threw away the verses, so that the flower fell on the floor; it had become flat and withered, but it should not have been thrown on the floor for all that; still it was better lying there than on the fire, where the letter and verses were blazing. What had happened? What so often happens. The flower had fooled him; it was a jest, the maiden had fooled him, and that was no jest; she had chosen another sweetheart in mid-summer. In the morning, the sun shone in on the little flattened summer-geck, which looked as if it were painted on the floor. The girl who was sweeping took it up and put it in one of the books on the table;

she thought it had fallen out, when she was clearing up and putting things in order. And so the flower lay again amongst verses, printed verses, and they are grander than written ones; at least more is spent upon them.

Years passed away, and the book stood on the shelf. At length it was taken down, opened and read; it was a good book,—songs and poems by the Danish poet, Ambrosius Stub, who is well worth knowing. And the man who read the book, turned the page. "Here is a flower!" said he, "a summer-geck! not without some meaning does it lie here. Poor Ambrosius Stub! he was also a summer-geck, a befooled poet! he was too early in his time; and so he got sleet and sharp winds, and went his rounds amongst the gentlemen of Fyen, like the flower in the flower-glass, the flower in the verses. A summer-geck, a winter-fool, all jest and foolery, and yet the first, the only, the youthfully fresh Danish poet. Yes, lie as a mark in the book, little summer-geck! Thou art laid there with some meaning."

And so the summer-geck was laid in the book again, and felt itself both honored and delighted with the knowledge that it was a mark in the lovely song-book, and that the one who had first sung and written about it, had also been a summer-geck, had been befooled in the winter. Of course the flower understood this in its own way, just as we understand anything in our own way.

This is the story of the summer-geck.

Prince Ring

(FROM *THE YELLOW FAIRY BOOK*)

Once upon a time there was a King and his Queen in their kingdom. They had one daughter, who was called Ingiborg, and one son, whose name was Ring. He was less fond of adventures than men of rank usually were in those days, and was not famous for strength or feats of arms. When he was twelve years old, one fine winter day he rode into the forest along with his men to enjoy himself. They went on a long way, until they caught sight of a hind with a gold ring on its horns. The Prince was eager to catch it, if possible, so they gave chase and rode on without stopping until all the horses began to founder beneath them. At last the Prince's horse gave way too, and then there came over them a darkness so black that they could no longer see the hind. By this time they were far away from any house, and thought it was high time to be making their way home again, but they found they had got lost now. At first they all kept together, but soon each began to think that he knew the right way best; so they separated, and all went in different directions.

The Prince, too, had got lost like the rest, and wandered on for a time until he came to a little clearing in the forest not far from the sea, where he saw a woman sitting on a chair and a big barrel standing beside her. The Prince went up to her and saluted her politely, and she received him very graciously. He looked down into the barrel then, and saw lying at the bottom an unusually beautiful gold ring, which pleased him so much that he could not take his eyes off it. The woman saw this, and said that he might have it if he would take the trouble to get it; for which the Prince thanked her, and said it was at least worth trying. So he leaned over into the barrel, which did not seem very deep, and thought he would easily reach the ring; but the more he stretched down after it the deeper grew the barrel. As he was thus bending down into it the woman suddenly rose up and pushed him in head first, saying that now he could take up his quarters there. Then she fixed the top on the barrel and threw it out into the sea.

The Prince thought himself in a bad plight now, as he felt the barrel floating out from the land and tossing about on the waves.

How many days he spent thus he could not tell, but at last he felt that the barrel was knocking against rocks, at which he was a little cheered, thinking it was probably land and not merely a reef in the sea. Being something of a swimmer, he at last made up his mind to kick the bottom out of the barrel, and having done so he was able to get on shore, for the rocks by the sea were smooth and level; but overhead there were high cliffs. It seemed difficult to get up these, but he went along the foot of them for a little, till at last he tried to climb up, which at last he did.

Having got to the top, he looked round about him and saw that he was on an island, which was covered with forest, with apples growing, and altogether pleasant as far as the land was concerned. After he had been there several days, he one day heard a great noise in the forest, which made him terribly afraid, so that he ran to hide himself among the trees. Then he saw a Giant approaching, dragging a sledge loaded with wood, and making straight for him, so that he could see nothing for it but to lie down just where he was. When the Giant came across him, he stood still and looked at the Prince for a little; then he took him up in his arms and carried him home to his house, and was exceedingly kind to him. He gave him to his wife, saying he had found this child in the wood, and she could have it to help her in the house. The old woman was greatly pleased, and began to fondle the Prince with the utmost delight. He stayed there with them, and was very willing and obedient to them in everything, while they grew kinder to him every day.

One day the Giant took him round and showed him all his rooms except the parlor; this made the Prince curious to have a look into it, thinking there must be some very rare treasure there. So one day, when the Giant had gone into the forest, he tried to get into the parlor, and managed to get the door open half-way. Then he saw that some living creature moved inside and ran along the floor towards him and said something, which made him so frightened that he sprang back from the door and shut it again. As soon as the fright began to pass off he tried it again, for he thought it would be interesting to hear what it said; but things went just as before with him. He then got angry with himself, and, summoning up all his courage, tried it a third time, and opened the door of the room and stood firm. Then he saw that it was a big Dog, which spoke to him and said:

"Choose me, Prince Ring."

The Prince went away rather afraid, thinking with himself that it was no great treasure after all; but all the same what it had said to him stuck in his mind.

It is not said how long the Prince stayed with the Giant, but one day the latter came to him and said he would now take him over to the mainland out of the island, for he himself had no long time to live. He also thanked him for his good service, and told him to choose some-one of his possessions, for he would get whatever he wanted. Ring thanked him heartily, and said there was no need to pay him for his services, they were so little worth; but if he did wish to give him anything he would choose what was in the parlor. The Giant was taken by surprise, and said:

"There, you chose my old woman's right hand; but I must not break my word."

Upon this he went to get the Dog, which came running with signs of great delight; but the Prince was so much afraid of it that it was all he could do to keep from showing his alarm.

After this the Giant accompanied him down to the sea, where he saw a stone boat which was just big enough to hold the two of them and the Dog. On reaching the mainland the Giant took a friendly farewell of Ring, and told him he might take possession of all that was in the island after he and his wife died, which would happen within two weeks from that time. The Prince thanked him for this and for all his other kindnesses, and the Giant returned home, while Ring went up some distance from the sea; but he did not know what land he had come to, and was afraid to speak to the Dog. After he had walked on in silence for a time the Dog spoke to him and said:

"You don't seem to have much curiosity, seeing you never ask my name."

The Prince then forced himself to ask, "What is your name?"

"You had best call me Snati-Snati," said the Dog. "Now we are coming to a King's seat, and you must ask the King to keep us all winter, and to give you a little room for both of us."

The Prince now began to be less afraid of the Dog. They came to the King and asked him to keep them all the winter, to which he agreed. When the King's men saw the Dog they began to laugh at it, and make as if they would tease it; but when the Prince saw this he advised them not to do it, or they might have the worst of it. They replied that they didn't care a bit what he thought.

After Ring had been with the King for some days the latter began to think there was a great deal in him, and esteemed him more than the others. The King, however, had a counselor called Red, who became very jealous when he saw how much the King esteemed Ring; and one day he talked to him, and said he could not understand why he had so good an opinion of this stranger, who had not yet shown himself superior to other men in anything. The King replied that it was only a short time since he had come there. Red then asked him to send them both to cut down wood next morning, and see which of them could do most work. Snati-Snati heard this and told it to Ring, advising him to ask the King for two axes, so that he might have one in reserve if the first one got broken. Next morning the King asked Ring and Red to go and cut down trees for him, and both agreed. Ring got the two axes, and each went his own way; but when the Prince had got out into the wood Snati took one of the axes and began to hew along with him. In the evening the King came to look over their day's work, as Red had proposed, and found that Ring's wood-heap was more than twice as big.

"I suspected," said the King, "that Ring was not quite useless; never have I seen such a day's work."

Ring was now in far greater esteem with the King than before, and Red was all the more discontented. One day he came to the King and said, "If Ring is such a mighty man, I think you might ask him to kill the wild oxen in the wood here, and flay them the same day, and bring you the horns and the hides in the evening."

"Don't you think that a desperate errand?" said the King, "seeing they are so dangerous, and no one has ever yet ventured to go against them?"

Red answered that he had only one life to lose, and it would be interesting to see how brave he was; besides, the King would have good reason to ennoble him if he overcame them. The King at last allowed himself, though rather unwillingly, to be won over by Red's persistency, and one day asked Ring to go and kill the oxen that were in the wood for him, and bring their horns and hides to him in the evening. Not knowing how dangerous the oxen were, Ring was quite ready, and went off at once, to the great delight of Red, who was now sure of his death.

As soon as Ring came in sight of the oxen they came bellowing to meet him; one of them was tremendously big, the other rather less. Ring grew terribly afraid.

"How do you like them?" asked Snati.

"Not well at all," said the Prince.

"We can do nothing else," said Snati, "than attack them, if it is to go well; you will go against the little one, and I shall take the other."

With this Snati leapt at the big one, and was not long in bringing him down. Meanwhile the Prince went against the other with fear and trembling, and by the time Snati came to help him the ox had nearly got him under, but Snati was not slow in helping his master to kill it.

Each of them then began to flay their own ox, but Ring was only half through by the time Snati had finished his. In the evening, after they had finished this task, the Prince thought himself unfit to carry all the horns and both the hides, so Snati told him to lay them all on his back until they got to the Palace gate. The Prince agreed, and laid everything on the Dog except the skin of the smaller ox, which he staggered along with himself. At the Palace gate he left everything lying, went before the King, and asked him to come that length with him, and there handed over to him the hides and horns of the oxen. The King was greatly surprised at his valor, and said he knew no one like him, and thanked him heartily for what he had done.

After this the King set Ring next to himself, and all esteemed him highly, and held him to be a great hero; nor could Red any longer say anything against him, though he grew still more determined to destroy him. One day a good idea came into his head. He came to the King and said he had something to say to him.

"What is that?" said the King.

Red said that he had just remembered the gold cloak, gold chess-board, and bright gold piece that the King had lost about a year before.

"Don't remind me of them!" said the King.

Red, however, went on to say that, since Ring was such a mighty man that he could do everything, it had occurred to him to advise the King to ask him to search for these treasures, and come back with them before Christmas; in return the King should promise him his daughter.

The King replied that he thought it altogether unbecoming to propose such a thing to Ring, seeing that he could not tell him where the things were; but Red pretended not to hear the King's excuses, and went on talking about it until the King gave in to him. One day, a month or so before Christmas, the King spoke to Ring, saying that he wished to ask a great favor of him.

"What is that?" said Ring.

"It is this," said the King: "that you find for me my gold cloak, my gold chess-board, and my bright gold piece, that were stolen from me about a year ago. If you can bring them to me before Christmas I will give you my daughter in marriage."

"Where am I to look for them, then?" said Ring.

"That you must find out for yourself," said the King: "I don't know."

Ring now left the King, and was very silent, for he saw he was in a great difficulty: but, on the other hand, he thought it was excellent to have such a chance of winning the King's daughter. Snati noticed that his master was at a loss, and said to him that he should not disregard what the King had asked him to do; but he would have to act upon his advice, otherwise he would get into great difficulties. The Prince assented to this, and began to prepare for the journey.

After he had taken leave of the King, and was setting out on the search, Snati said to him, "Now you must first of all go about the neighborhood, and gather as much salt as ever you can." The Prince did so, and gathered so much salt that he could hardly carry it; but Snati said, "Throw it on my back," which he accordingly did, and the Dog then ran on before the Prince, until they came to the foot of a steep cliff.

"We must go up here," said Snati.

"I don't think that will be child's play," said the Prince.

"Hold fast by my tail," said Snati; and in this way he pulled Ring up on the lowest shelf of the rock. The Prince began to get giddy, but up went Snati on to the second shelf. Ring was nearly swooning by this time, but Snati made a third effort and reached the top of the cliff, where the Prince fell down in a faint. After a little, however, he recovered again, and they went a short distance along a level plain, until they came to a cave. This was on Christmas Eve. They went up above the cave, and found a window in it, through which they looked, and saw four trolls lying asleep beside the fire, over which a large porridge-pot was hanging.

"Now you must empty all the salt into the porridge-pot," said Snati.

Ring did so, and soon the trolls wakened up. The old hag, who was the most frightful of them all, went first to taste the porridge.

"How comes this?" she said; "the porridge is salt! I got the milk by witch-craft yesterday out of four kingdoms, and now it is salt!"

All the others then came to taste the porridge, and thought it nice, but after they had finished it the old hag grew so thirsty that she could stand it no longer, and asked her daughter to go out and bring her some water from the river that ran near by.

"I won't go," said she, "unless you lend me your bright gold piece."

"Though I should die you shan't have that," said the hag.

"Die, then," said the girl.

"Well, then, take it, you brat," said the old hag, "and be off with you, and make haste with the water."

The girl took the gold and ran out with it, and it was so bright that it shone all over the plain. As soon as she came to the river she lay down to take a drink of the water, but meanwhile the two of them had got down off the roof and thrust her, head first, into the river.

The old hag began now to long for the water, and said that the girl would be running about with the gold piece all over the plain, so she asked her son to go and get her a drop of water.

"I won't go," said he, "unless I get the gold cloak."

"Though I should die you shan't have that," said the hag.

"Die, then," said the son.

"Well, then, take it," said the old hag, "and be off with you, but you must make haste with the water."

He put on the cloak, and when he came outside it shone so bright that he could see to go with it. On reaching the river he went to take a drink like his sister, but at that moment Ring and Snati sprang upon him, took the cloak from him, and threw him into the river.

The old hag could stand the thirst no longer, and asked her husband to go for a drink for her; the brats, she said, were of course running about and playing themselves, just as she had expected they would, little wretches that they were.

"I won't go," said the old troll, "unless you lend me the gold chess-board."

"Though I should die you shan't have that," said the hag.

"I think you may just as well do that," said he, "since you won't grant me such a little favor."

"Take it, then, you utter disgrace!" said the old hag, "since you are just like these two brats."

The old troll now went out with the gold chess-board, and down to the river, and was about to take a drink, when Ring and Snati came upon him, took the chess-board from him, and threw him into the river. Before they had got back again, however, and up on top of the cave, they saw the poor old fellow's ghost come marching up from the river. Snati immediately sprang upon him, and Ring assisted in the attack, and after a hard struggle they mastered him a second time. When they got back again to the window they saw that the old hag was moving towards the door.

"Now we must go in at once," said Snati, "and try to master her there, for if she once gets out we shall have no chance with her. She is the worst witch that ever lived, and no iron can cut her. One of us must pour boiling porridge out of the pot on her, and the other punch her with red-hot iron."

In they went then, and no sooner did the hag see them than she said, "So you have come, Prince Ring; you must have seen to my husband and children."

Snati saw that she was about to attack them, and sprang at her with a red-hot iron from the fire, while Ring kept pouring boiling porridge on her without stopping, and in this way they at last got her killed. Then they burned the old troll and her to ashes, and explored the cave, where they found plenty of gold and treasures. The most valuable of these they carried with them as far as the cliff, and left them there. Then they hastened home to the King with his three treasures, where they arrived late on Christmas night, and Ring handed them over to him.

The King was beside himself with joy, and was astonished at how clever a man Ring was in all kinds of feats, so that he esteemed him still more highly than before, and betrothed his daughter to him; and the feast for this was to last all through Christmastide. Ring thanked the King courteously for this and all his other kindnesses, and as soon as he had finished eating and drinking in the hall went off to sleep in his own room. Snati, however, asked permission to sleep in the Prince's bed for that night, while the Prince should sleep where the Dog usually lay. Ring said he was welcome to do so, and that he deserved more from him than that came to. So Snati went up into the Prince's bed, but after a time he came back, and told Ring he could go there himself now, but to take care not to meddle with anything that was in the bed.

Now the story comes back to Red, who came into the hall and showed the King his right arm wanting the hand, and said that now he could see what kind of a man his intended son-in-law was, for he had done this to him without any cause whatever. The King became very angry, and said he would soon find out the truth about it, and if Ring had cut off his hand without good cause he should be hanged; but if it was otherwise, then Red should die. So the King sent for Ring and asked him for what reason he had done this. Snati, however, had just told Ring what had happened during the night, and in reply he asked the King to go with him and he would show him some-thing. The King went with him to his sleeping-room, and saw lying on the bed a man's hand holding a sword.

"This hand," said Ring, "came over the partition during the night, and was about to run me through in my bed, if I had not defended myself."

The King answered that in that case he could not blame him for protect-ing his own life, and that Red was well worthy of death. So Red was hanged, and Ring married the King's daughter.

The first night that they went to bed together Snati asked Ring to allow him to lie at their feet, and this Ring allowed him to do. During the night he heard a howling and outcry beside them, struck a light in a hurry and saw an ugly dog's skin lying near him, and a beautiful Prince in the bed. Ring instantly took the skin and burned it, and then shook the Prince, who was lying unconscious, until he woke up. The bridegroom then asked his name; he replied that he was called Ring, and was a King's son. In his youth he had lost his mother, and in her place his father had married a witch, who had laid a spell on him that he should turn into a dog, and never be released from the spell unless a Prince of the same name as himself allowed him to sleep at his feet the first night after his marriage. He added further, "As soon as she knew that you were my namesake she tried to get you destroyed, so that you might not free me from the spell. She was the hind that you and your companions chased; she was the woman that you found in the clearing with the barrel, and the old hag that we just now killed in the cave."

After the feasting was over the two namesakes, along with other men, went to the cliff and brought all the treasure home to the Palace. Then they went to the island and removed all that was valuable from it. Ring gave to his name-sake, whom he had freed from the spell, his sister Ingiborg and his father's kingdom to look after, but he himself stayed with his father-in-law the King, and had half the kingdom while he lived and the whole of it after his death.

An Old-Fashioned Christmas Eve

Peter Christen Asbjørnsen

The wind was whistling through the old lime and maple trees opposite my windows, the snow was sweeping down the street, and the sky was black as a December sky can possibly be here in Christiania. I was in just as black a mood. It was Christmas Eve, the first I was to spend away from the cozy fireside of my home. I had lately received my officer's commission, and had hoped that I should have gladdened my aged parents with my presence during the holidays, and had also hoped that I should be able to show myself in all my glory and splendor to the ladies of our parish. But a fever had brought me to the hospital, which I had left only a week before, and now I found myself in the much-extolled state of convalescence. I had written home for a horse and sledge and my father's fur coat, but my letter could scarcely reach our valley before the day after Christmas, and the horse could not be in town before New Year's Eve.

My comrades had all left town, and I knew no family with whom I could make myself at home during the holidays. The two old maids I lodged with were certainly very kind and friendly people, and they had taken great care of me in the commencement of my illness, but the peculiar ways and habits of these ladies were too much of the old school to prove attractive to the fancies of youth. Their thoughts dwelt mostly on the past, and when they, as often might occur, related to me some stories of the town, its people and its customs, these stories reminded me, not only by their contents, but also by the simple unaffected way in which they were rendered, of a past age.

The antiquated appearance of these ladies was also in the strictest harmony with the house in which they lived. It was one of those old houses in Custom-house Street, with deep windows, long dark passages and staircases, gloomy rooms and garrets, where one could not help thinking of ghosts and brownies; in short, just such a house, and perhaps it was the very one, which Mauritz Hansen has described in his story, *The Old Dame with the Hood*. Their circle of acquaintances was very limited; besides a married sister and her children, no other visitors came there but a couple of tiresome old ladies. The only relief to this kind of life was a pretty niece and some merry little cousins of hers, who always made me tell them fairy tales and stories.

I tried to divert myself in my loneliness and melancholy mood by looking out at all the people who passed up and down the street in the snow and wind with blue noses and half-shut eyes. It amused me to see the bustle and the life in the apothecary's shop across the street. The door was scarcely shut for a moment. Servants and peasants streamed in and out, and commenced to study the labels and directions when they came out in the street. Some appeared to be able to make them out, but sometimes a lengthy study and a dubious shake of the head showed that the solution was too difficult. It was growing dusk, I could not distinguish the countenances any longer, but gazed across at the old building. The apothecary's house, "The Swan," as it is still called, stood there with its dark, reddish-brown walls, its pointed gables and towers, with weathercocks and latticed windows, as a monument of the architecture of the time of King Christian the Fourth. The Swan looked then as now a most respectable and sedate bird, with its gold ring around the neck, its spur-boots and its wings stretched out as if ready to fly. I was about to plunge myself into reflection on imprisoned birds, when I was disturbed by noise and laughter proceeding from some children in the adjoining room, and by a gentle, old-maidenish knock at my door.

On my requesting the visitor to come in, the elder of my landladies, Miss Mette, entered the room with a courtesy in the good old style; she inquired after my health, and invited me without further ceremony to come and make myself at home with them for the evening. "It isn't good for you, dear lieutenant, to sit thus alone here in the dark," she added; "will you not come in to us now at once? Old Mother Skau and my brother's little girls have come; they will perhaps amuse you a little. You are so fond of the dear children."

I accepted the friendly invitation. As I entered the room, the fire from the large square stove, where the logs were burning lustily, threw a red, flickering light through the wide-open door over the room, which was very deep, and furnished in the old style with high-backed Russia leather chairs, and one of those settees which were intended for farthingales and straight up-and-down positions. The walls were adorned with oil paintings, portraits of stiff ladies with powdered coiffures, of bewigged Oldenborgians and other redoubtable persons in mail and armor or red coats.

"You must really excuse us, lieutenant, for not having lighted the candles yet," said Miss Cicely, the younger sister, who was generally called "Cilly," and who came towards me and dropped a courtesy, exactly like her sister's; "but the children do so like to tumble about here before the fire in the dusk of the evening, and Madam Skau does also enjoy a quiet little chat in the chimney corner."

"Oh, chat me here and chat me there, there is nothing you like yourself better than a little bit of gossip in the dusk of the evening, Cilly, and then we are to get the blame of it," answered the old asthmatic lady whom they called Mother Skau.

"Eh, good evening, sir," she said to me, as she drew herself up to make the best of her own inflated bulky appearance, "come and sit down here and tell me how it fares with you; but, by my troth, you are nothing but skin and bones!"

I had to tell her all about my illness, and in return I had to endure a very long and circumstantial account of her rheumatism and her asthmatical ailments, which fortunately was interrupted by the noisy arrival of the children from the kitchen, where they had paid a visit to old Stine, a fixture in the house.

"Oh, auntie, do you know what Stine says?" cried a little brown-eyed beauty; "she says I shall go with her into the hayloft to-night and give the brownie his Christmas porridge. But I won't go, I am afraid of the brownies!"

"Never mind, my dear, Stine says it only to get rid of you; she dare not go into the hayloft herself, the foolish old thing, in the dark, for she knows well enough she was frightened once by the brownies herself," said Miss Mette; "but are you not going to say good evening to the lieutenant, children?"

"Oh, is that you, lieutenant?—I did not know you! How pale you are! It is such a long time since I saw you," shouted the children all at once as they flocked round me. "Now you must tell us something awful jolly! It is such a long time since you told us anything. Oh, tell us about Buttercup, dear Mr. Lieutenant, do tell us about Buttercup and Goldentooth!"

I had to tell them about Buttercup and the dog Goldentooth, but they would not let me off till I gave them a couple of stories into the bargain about the brownies at Vager and at Bure, who stole hay from each other and who met at last with a load of hay on their backs, and how they fought till they vanished in a cloud of hay-dust. I had also to tell the story of the brownie at Hesselberg, who teased the housedog till the farmer came out and threw him over the barn bridge. The children clapped their hands in great joy and laughed heartily.

"It served him right, the naughty brownie," they shouted, and asked for another story.

"No, no, children! you bother the lieutenant too much," said Miss Cicely, "Aunt Mette will tell you a story now."

"Yes, do auntie, do! "was the general cry.

"I don't know exactly what I shall tell you," said Aunt Mette, "but since we have commenced telling about the brownies, I think I will tell you something about them too. You remember of course old Kari Gausdal, who came here and baked bread and who always had so many tales to tell you."

"Oh, yes, yes !" shouted the children.

"Well, old Kari told me, that she was in service at the orphan asylum some years ago, and at that time it was still more dreary and lonely in that part of the town than it is now. That asylum is a dark and dismal place, I can tell you. Well, when Kari came there she was cook, and a very smart and clever girl she was. She had one day to get up very early in the morning to brew, when the other servants said to her: 'You had better mind you don't get up too early, and you mustn't put any fire under the copper before two o'clock.' 'Why?' she asked. 'Don't you know there is a brownie here; and you ought to know that these people don't like to be disturbed so early,' they said, 'and before two o'clock you mustn't light the fire by any means.' 'Is that all?' said Kari; she was anything but chicken-hearted. 'I have nothing to do with that brownie of yours, but if he comes in my way, why, by my faith, I will send him head over heels through the door.' The others warned her, but she did not care a bit, and next morning, just as the clock struck one, she got up and lighted the fire under the copper in the brew-house. But the fire went out every moment. Somebody appeared to be throwing the logs about on the hearth, but she could not see who it was. She gathered the logs together one time after the other, but it was of no use and the chimney would not draw either. She got tired of this at last, took a burning log and ran round the room with it, swinging it high and low while she shouted: 'Be gone, be gone whence you came! If you think you can frighten me, you are mistaken.' 'Curse you!' somebody hissed in one of the darkest corners, 'I have had seven souls in this house; I thought I should have got eight in all!' But from that time nobody saw or heard the brownie in the asylum, said Kari Gausdal."

"I am getting so frightened," said one of the children; "no, you must tell us some more stories, lieutenant; I never feel afraid when you tell us anything, because you tell us such jolly tales." Another proposed that I should tell them about the brownie who danced the Halling dance with the lassie. That was a tale I didn't care much about, as there was some sing-ing in it. But they would on no account let me off, and I was going to clear my throat and prepare my exceedingly inharmonious voice to sing the Halling dance, which belongs to the story, when the pretty niece whom I have already referred to entered the room, to the great joy of the children and to my rescue.

"Well, my dear children, I will tell you the story, if you can get Cousin Lizzie to sing the Halling for you," said I, as she sat down, "and then you'll dance to it yourselves, won't you?"

Cousin Lizzie was besieged by the children, and had to promise to do the singing, so I commenced my story:—

"There was once upon a time—I almost think it was in Hallingdal—a lassie who was sent up into the hay-loft with the cream porridge for the brownie—I cannot recollect if it was on a Thursday or on a Christmas Eve, but I think it was a Christmas Eve. Well, she thought it was a great pity to give the brownie such a dainty dish, so she eat the porridge herself, and the melted butter in the bargain, and went up into the hay-loft with plain oatmeal porridge and sour milk, in a pig's trough instead. 'There, that's good enough for you, Master Brownie,' she said. But no sooner had she spoken the words, than the brownie stood right before her, seized her round the waist, and danced about with her, which he kept up till she lay gasping for breath, and when the people came up into the hay-loft in the morning, she was more dead than alive. But as long as they danced, the brownie sang (and here Cousin Lizzie undertook his part, and sang to the tune of the Halling:—

> And you have eaten the porridge for the brownie,
> And you shall dance with the little brownie!
> And have you eaten the porridge for the brownie?
> Then you shall dance with the little brownie!

I assisted in keeping time by stamping on the floor with my feet, while the children romped about the room in uproarious joy.

"I think you are turning the house upside down, children!" said old Mother Skau; "if you'll be quiet, I'll give you a story."

The children were soon quiet, and Mother Skau commenced as follows:—

"You hear a great deal about brownies and fairies and such like beings, but I don't believe there is much in it. I have neither seen one nor the other,—of course I have not been so very much about in my lifetime, but I believe it is all nonsense. But old Stine out in the kitchen there, she says she has seen the brownie. About the time when I was confirmed, she was in service with my parents. She came to us from a captain's, who had given up the sea. It was a very quiet place. They never went anywhere, and nobody came to see them. The captain only took a walk as far as the quay every day. They always went to bed early. People said there was a brownie in the house. Well, it so happened that Stine and the cook were sitting in their room one evening, mending and darning their things; it was near bedtime, for the watchman had already sung out 'Ten o'clock,' but somehow the darning and the sewing went on very slowly indeed; every moment 'Jack Nap' came and played his tricks upon them! At one moment Stine was nodding and nodding, and then came the cook's turn—they could not keep their eyes open; they had been early up that morning to wash clothes. But just as they were sitting thus, they heard a terrible crash down stairs in the kitchen and Stine shouted: 'Lor' bless and preserve us! it must be the brownie.' She was so frightened she dared scarcely move a foot, but at last the cook plucked up courage and went down into the kitchen, closely followed by Stine. When they opened the kitchen door, they found all the crockery on the floor, but none of it broken, while the brownie was standing on the big kitchen table with his red cap on and hurling the one dish after the other on to the floor and laughing in great glee. The cook had heard that the brownies could sometimes be tricked into moving to another house, when anybody would tell them of a very quiet place, and as she long had been wishing for an opportunity to play a trick upon this brownie, she took courage and spoke to him—her voice was a little shaky at the time— that he ought to remove to the tinman's over the way, where it was so very quiet and pleasant, because they always went to bed at nine o'clock every evening; which was true enough, as the cook told Stine later, but then the master and all his apprentices and journeymen were up every morning at three o'clock, and hammered away and made a terrible noise all day. Since that day they never saw the brownie any more at the captain's. He seemed to feel quite at home at the tinman's, although they were hammering and tapping away there all day, but people said that the gudewife put a dish of porridge up in the garret for him every Thursday evening; and it's no wonder that they got on well and became rich when they had a brownie in the house. Stine believed he brought things to them. Whether it was the brownie or not who really helped them, I cannot say," said Mother Skau, in conclusion, and got a fit of coughing and choking after the exertion of telling this, for her, unusually long story.

When she had taken a pinch of snuff she felt better, and became quite cheerful again, and began:—

"My mother, who, by the by, was a truthful woman, told a story, which happened here in the town one Christmas Eve. I know it is true, for an untrue word never passed her lips."

"Let us hear it, Madam Skau," said I.

"Yes, tell, tell, Mother Skau," cried the children.

She coughed a little, took another pinch of snuff, and proceeded:—

"When my mother still was in her teens, she used sometimes to visit a widow whom she knew, and whose name was,—dear me, what was her name?—Madam,—yes, Madame Evensen, of course. She was a woman who had seen the best part of her life, but whether she lived up in Mill Street, or down in the corner by Little Church Hill, I cannot say for certain. Well, one Christmas Eve, just like to-night, she thought she would go to the morning service on the Christmas Day, for she was a great churchgoer, and so she left out some coffee with the girl before she went to bed, that she might get a cup next morning—she was sure a cup of warm coffee would do her a great deal of good at that early hour! When she woke the moon was shining into the room, but when she got up to look at the clock she found it had stopped and that the fingers pointed to half-past eleven. She had no idea what time it could be, so she went to the window and looked across to the church. The light was streaming out through all the windows. She must have overslept herself! She called the girl and told her to get the coffee ready, while she dressed herself. So she took her hymn-book and started for church. The street was very quiet; she did not meet a single person on her way to church. When she came inside, she sat down in her customary seat in one of the pews, but when she looked around her she thought that the people were so pale and so strange, exactly as if they were all dead. She did not know any of them, but there were several she seemed to recollect having seen before, but when and where she had seen them she could not call to mind. When the minister came into the pulpit, she saw that he was not one of the ministers in the town, but a tall pale man, whose face however she thought she could recollect. He preached very nicely indeed, and there was not the usual noisy coughing and hawking, which you always hear at the morning services on a Christmas Day; it was so quiet, you could have heard a needle drop on the floor,—in fact, it was so quiet she began to feel quite uneasy and uncomfortable. "When the singing commenced again, a female, who sat next to her, leant towards her and whispered in her ear: 'Throw the cloak loosely around you and go, because if you wait here till the service is over they will make short work of you! It is the dead who are keeping service.'"

"Oh, Mother Skau, I feel so frightened. I feel so frightened," whimpered one of the children, and climbed up on a chair.

"Hush, hush, child," said Mother Skau; "she got away from them safe enough; only listen!—When the widow heard the voice of the person next to her, she turned round to look at her—but what a start she got! She recognized her, it was her neighbor, who died many years ago; and when she looked around the church, she remembered well that she had seen both the minister and several of the congregation before, and that they had died long ago. This sent quite a cold shiver through her, she became that frightened. She threw the cloak loosely round her, as the female next to her had said, and went out of the pew; but she thought they all turned round and stretched out their hands after her. Her legs shook under her, till she thought she would sink down on the church floor. When she came out on the steps, she felt that they had got hold of her cloak; she let it go and left it in their clutches, while she hurried home as quickly as she could. When she came to the door the clock struck one, and by the time she got inside she was nearly half dead—she was that frightened. In the morning, when the people went to church, they found the cloak lying on the steps but it was torn into a thousand pieces. My mother had often seen the cloak before, and I think she saw one of the pieces also; but that doesn't matter—it was a short, pink, woolen cloak with fur lining and borders, such as was still in use in my childhood! They are very rarely seen nowadays, but there are some old ladies in the town and down at the 'home' whom I see with such cloaks in church at Christmas time."

The children, who had expressed considerable fear and uneasiness during the latter part of the story, declared they would not hear any more such terrible stories. They had crept up into the sofa and on the chairs, but still they thought they felt somebody plucking at them from underneath the table. Suddenly the lights were brought in, and we discovered then to our great amusement that the children had put their legs on to the table. The lights, the Christmas cake, the jellies, the tarts, and the wine soon chased away the horrible ghost story and all fear from their minds, revived everybody's spirits, and brought the conversation on to their neighbors and the topics of the day. Finally our thoughts took a flight towards something more substantial on the appearance of the Christmas porridge and the roast ribs of pork. We broke up early and parted with the best wishes for a Merry Christmas. I passed however a very uneasy night. I do not know whether it was the stories, the substantial supper, my weak condition, or all these combined,

549

which was the cause of it; I tossed myself hither and thither in my bed and got mixed up with brownies, fairies, and ghosts the whole night. Finally I sailed through the air towards the church, while some merry sledge bells were ringing in my ears. The church was lighted up, and when I came inside I saw it was our own church up in the valley. There were nobody there but peasants in their red caps, soldiers in full uniform, country lasses with their white head-dresses and red cheeks. The minister was in the pulpit; it was my grandfather, who died when I was a little boy. But just as he was in the middle of the sermon, he made a somersault—he was known as one of the smartest men in the parish—right into the middle of the church; the surplice flew one way and the collar another. "There lies the parson, and here am I," he said, with one of his well known airs, "and now let us have a spring-dance!" In an instant the whole congregation was in the midst of a wild dance; a big tall peasant came towards me and took me by the shoulder and said: "You'll have to join us, my lad!"

At this moment I awoke and felt some one pulling at my shoulder. I could scarcely believe my eyes when I saw the same peasant whom I had seen in my dream leaning over me. There he was with the red cap down over his ears, a big fur coat over his arm, and a pair of big eyes looking fixedly at me.

"You must be dreaming," he said, "the perspiration is standing in big drops on your forehead, and you were sleeping as heavily as a bear in his lair! God's peace and a merry Christmas to you, I say, and greetings to you from your father and all yours up in the valley. Here's a letter from your father, and the horse is waiting for you out in the yard."

"But, good heavens, is that you, Thor?" I shouted in great joy. It was indeed my father's man, a splendid specimen of a Norwegian peasant. "How in the world have you come here already?"

"Ah, that I can soon tell you," answered Thor. "I came with your favorite, the bay mare. I had to take your father down to Næs, and then he says to me, 'Thor,' says he, 'it isn't very far to town from here. Just take the bay mare and run down and see how the lieutenant is, and if he is well and can come with you, you must bring him back along with you,' says he."

When we left the town, it was daylight. The roads were in splendid condition. The bay mare stretched out her old smart legs and we arrived at length in sight of the dear old house. Thor jumped off the sledge to undo the gate, and as we merrily drove up to the door we were met by the boisterous welcome of old Rover, who in his frantic joy at hearing my voice almost broke his chain in trying to rush at me.

Such a Christmas as I spent that year I cannot recollect before or since.

The Thistle's Experiences

HANS CHRISTIAN ANDERSEN

Beside the lordly manor-house lay a lovely, well-kept garden with rare trees and flowers; the guests of the house expressed their admiration of it; the people of the district, from town and country, came on Sundays and holidays and begged permission to see the garden, even whole schools came to visit it.

Outside the garden, close to the palings beside the field-path, stood a huge thistle; it was very big and spread from the root in several branches, so that it might be called a thistle-bush. No one looked at it except the old ass which drew the milk-cart. It stretched out its neck to the thistle, and said, "You are lovely! I could eat you!" but the halter was not long enough for the ass to get near enough to eat it.

There was a great deal of company at the manor-house—some very noble people from the capital, young pretty girls, and amongst them a young lady who came from a distance; she came from Scotland, was of high birth, rich in lands and gold, a bride worth winning, more than one young gentleman said, and their mothers said the same thing.

The young people amused themselves on the lawn and played croquet; they walked about amongst the flowers, and each of the young girls picked a flower and put it in the button-hole of one of the young gentlemen. But the young Scottish lady looked round for a long time, rejecting one after the other; none of the flowers seemed to please her; then she looked over the paling, outside stood the great thistle-bush with its strong, purple flowers; she saw it, she smiled and begged the son of the house to pick one of them for her.

"It is the flower of Scotland!" said she, "it blooms in the scutcheon of the country, give it to me!"

And he brought her the most beautiful of the thistles, and pricked his fingers, as if it were the most prickly rosebush that it grew on.

She fastened the thistle-flower in the button-hole of the young man, and he felt himself highly honored. Each of the other young men would willingly have given his own beautiful flower to have worn the one given by the Scottish girl's fair hand. And if the son of the house felt himself honored, what did not the thistle-bush feel?" It seemed as if the dew and the sunshine were going through it.

"I am something more than I thought!" it said to itself. "I really belong inside the paling and not outside! One is strangely placed in the world! but now I have one of mine over the paling, and even in a button-hole!"

Every bud which came forth and unfolded was told of this event, and not many days went past before the thistle-bush heard, not from people, nor from the twittering of the birds, but from the air itself, which preserves and carries sound, from the most retired walks of the garden and the rooms of the house, where the doors and windows stood open, that the young gentleman who got the thistle-flower from the fair Scottish girl's hand, had now got her hand and heart as well. They were a handsome pair—it was a good match.

"I have brought that about!" thought the thistle-bush, and thought of the flower it had given for a button-hole. Each flower that opened heard of this occurrence.

"I shall certainly be planted in the garden!" thought the thistle; "perhaps put in a pot which pinches: that is the greatest honor of all!"

And the thistle thought of this so strongly that it said with full conviction, "I shall be put in a pot!"

It promised every little thistle-flower which opened that it also should be put in a pot, perhaps in a button-hole—the highest honor that was to be attained; but none of them was put in a pot, to say nothing of a button-hole; they drank in the air and the light, licked the sunshine by day and the dew by night, bloomed, were visited by bees and hornets which searched for the dowry, the honey in the flowers, and they took the honey and left the flower standing. "The thieving pack!" said the thistle, "if I could only stab them! But I cannot!"

The flowers hung their heads and faded, but new ones came again.

"You come in good time!" said the thistle, "every minute I expect to get across the fence."

A few innocent daisies and narrow-leaved plantains stood and listened with deep admiration, and believed everything that was said.

The old ass of the milk-cart looked along from the wayside to the thistle-bush, but the halter was too short to reach it.

And the thistle thought so long of the Scottish thistle to whose family it thought it belonged, that at last it believed it came from Scotland and that its parents had been put into the national scutcheon. It was a great thought, but great thistles can have great thoughts!

"One is often of such a noble family, that one dare not know it!" said the nettle, which grew close by; it also had an idea that it might turn into nettle-cloth if it were properly handled. And the summer passed and the autumn passed; the leaves fell off the trees, the flowers got strong colors and less scent. The gardener's apprentice sang in the garden, across the fence:

Up the hill and down the hill,
That is all the story still.

The young fir-trees in the wood began to long for Christmas, but it was a long time to Christmas.

"Here I stand still!" said the thistle. "It seems as if no one thought about me, and yet *I* have made the match; they were betrothed, and they held their wedding eight days ago. I won't take a step, for I cannot."

Some more weeks went past; the thistle stood with its last single flower, big and full, it had shot up close by the root. The wind blew cold over it, the colors went, the splendor vanished, the calyx of the flower, big as that of an artichoke bloom, looked like a silver sunflower. Then the young couple, now man and wife, came into the garden; they went along by the paling, and the young wife looked across it.

"There stands the big thistle yet!" said she; "now it has no more flowers!"

"Yes, there is the ghost of the last one!" said he, and pointed to the silvery remains of the flower, itself a flower.

"It is lovely!" said she, "such a one must be carved round about the frame of our picture!"

And the young man had to climb the paling again to break off the calyx of the thistle. It pricked him in the fingers,—he had called it a "ghost." And it came into the garden, into the house, and into the drawing-room; there stood a picture—"the young couple." In the bridegroom's button-hole was painted a thistle. They talked about this and about the thistle-flower they brought, the last thistle-flower now gleaming like silver, a copy of which was to be carved on the frame.

And the breeze carried what was said, away, far away.

"What one can experience!" said the thistle-bush. 'My firstborn was put in a button-hole, my last in a frame! Where shall *I* go?'"

And the ass stood by the road-side and looked long at the thistle.

"Come to me, my kitchen-love! I cannot come to you, the halter is not long enough!"

But the thistle did not answer; it became more and more thoughtful; it thought, and it thought, right up to Christmas-time, and then the thought came into flower: "If one's children have got inside, a mother can be content to stand outside the fence!"

"That is an honorable thought!" said the sunbeam. "You shall also get a good place!"

"In a pot or in a frame ?'" asked the thistle.

"In a story!" said the sunbeam. And here it is!

The Witch-Dancer's Doom
(TRADITIONAL BRETON TALE)

I

Long, long ago, in the days of good King Arthur, Count Morriss dwelt in the old château of La Roche Morice, near Landerneau, in Brittany. With him lived his beautiful niece, Katel. Although charming in face and figure, this maiden had a somewhat uncanny reputation. For it was said—and with reason—that she was a witch.

The Count had often urged Katel to marry, but in vain. The lady had no mind to lose her freedom. Dancing was the one passion of her life. "When," said she, "I can find a knight who shall be able to dance continuously with me for twelve hours, with no break, to him I promise to give my hand!"

This scornful challenge was proclaimed by heralds in every neighboring town and hamlet. In response came many wooers to attempt the impossible task. Those whom Katel favored she made her partners at the rustic fêtes and open-air dances which were then in vogue. In the soft-swarded meadows, by sunlight or starlight, the dancers would meet, and, to the dreamy music of the pipes, eager couples would whirl until the hills around began to blush in the light of the early dawn. The wildest, giddiest, yet most graceful of the throng was Katel, who danced madly on until one by one her partners sank fainting upon the ground, and death released them from the heartless sorceress who had lured them into her toils.

Thus perished many suitors, until the cruel maiden became an object of general hatred and horror. When her doings came to the ears of the Count, he sternly forbade her to attend any more of the dances. In order to enforce her obedience, he shut her up in a tower, where, said he, she was to remain until she should choose a husband from among such suitors as still persisted in offering her marriage.

Now, Katel had a wizened little page, no bigger than a leveret, and as black as a raven's wing. This creature she summoned to her one morning before dawn, and, with her finger at her lips, she said to him: "Be swift and silent! My uncle still slumbers. Get thee gone by the ladder, and hie thee to the castle of Salaün, who is waiting for a message from her he loves. The guards will allow thee to pass; take horse, ride like the wind, and tell Salaün that Katel calls him to deliver her from this tower before the day dawns."

The infatuated young knight obeyed the summons immediately. In an hour's time he was assisting the lady to mount his horse, after having got her in safety down the rope-ladder. As, from the window of the donjon, the dwarf watched them ride away, he chuckled to himself:

"Ha! ha! And so they are off to the great ball held to-day in the Martyrs' Meadow! Ah, my dear Salaün! before another sun shall rise your death-knell will be tolled!"

II

When Katel and her gallant cavalier arrived at the Martyrs' Meadow, they excited general surprise and admiration. Some, however, shook their heads forebodingly, as they heard that Salaün, now Katel's affianced lover, was to be her partner, for they knew that the brave young knight must needs fall a victim to her spell.

The ball began. Some of the most skillful pipers in the land had been engaged for the occasion, and they played gavottes, rondes, courantes, and many other dances, without intermission. But Katel waited until night came and the torches were lit. Then she took Salaün's hand and they began to dance together.

"Round again! Once more! Ha! ha!" laughed the witch-maiden, as they spun along. "What! are you tired already? Do you give in so soon as this?"

"Never—while I am with you!" was the fervent reply. The fatal spell had begun to work.

Thus on they whirled, yet more swiftly than before, so that the other dancers stood aside to watch them. After a time, however, Katel observed that her partner was gradually becoming weaker, and that he would soon be unable to keep pace with her.

"Courage!" exclaimed she, in a bantering tone. "We cannot stop yet; it wants but a very short time to midnight, and then I shall be yours!"

Salaün, although almost exhausted, strained every nerve and muscle in a frantic, final effort to continue the dance. Round the field they flew, at lightning speed; but it was for the last time. The knight's knees shook—his breath came more quickly—then with difficulty he gasped out the words:

"Oh, Katel! have mercy! I can do no more! Katel, my love, have I not won you yet?"

But as he sank lifeless upon the grass Katel turned coldly away. His fate was nothing to her. At that moment the clock in a neighboring tower struck twelve. All the lights flickered and expired; darkness reigned supreme. And through the darkness, shrilling high above every other sound, rang the mocking laugh of the impish dwarf.

III

"What!" exclaimed Katel derisively, glancing angrily at the worn-out pipers, who had at last paused in their wild music, "exhausted already by such slight exertions? I wish the Evil One would send me some musicians and dancers worthy of me! Of what use are these miserable, puny creatures?"

As she uttered the words, stamping her foot in her fury, a weird, red light gleamed in the sky; there was a terrible peal of thunder, and a strange stir in the trees. Then suddenly, in the center of the field, appeared two phantom forms, at the sight of whom the panic-stricken by-standers would fain have fled. To their horror, however, they found flight impossible; they were rooted to the spot!

One of the phantoms was attired in a red garment, covered with a black cloak. Beneath his arm he held a large double pipe, coiled around which were five hissing, writhing serpents. The other stranger, who was exceedingly tall, was dressed in a tightly fitting black suit, and heavy, red mantle, while upon his head waved an imposing tuft of vultures' plumes.

The ghostly piper began at once to play an unearthly dance-tune, so wild and maddening that it made all the hearers tremble. His tall, grim companion seized Katel by the waist, and the couple whirled round to the mad measure, which grew ever faster and more furious. In an instant the torches were relit. A few others joined in the dance; not for long, however. Katel and her phantom were soon the only dancers. Shriller still shrieked the pipes, faster yet grew the music, more and more swiftly spun the feet. Ere long the witch-maiden felt that her strength was deserting her; the torches swam before her eyes, and, in the last extremity of terror, she struggled to release herself from the iron grip which held her so relentlessly.

"What! so soon tired?" cried the specter, jeering at her. "Do you give in so soon as this? Come! round once more! Ha! ha!"

Thus was Katel treated as she had treated others. She had no breath left wherewith to answer; her last hour had come. She made one more wild, despairing bound, then fell to the ground in the throes of death. At the same moment, the phantoms vanished. There was a vivid lightning-blaze, a terrific crash of thunder; then fell black darkness hiding everything. A tempestuous wind arose, and rain fell in torrents.

When the storm had cleared, and the morning sun shone out, those who found courage to visit the spot beheld the forms of Katel and her lover Salaün lying dead upon the shrivelled turf.

Ever since that time, the spot has been shunned by all, and still, by their firesides on the winter nights, the peasants tell the tale of Katel, the witch-dancer, and her fearful fate.

What Christmas Is as We Grow Older

CHARLES DICKENS

Time was, with most of us, when Christmas Day encircling all our limited world like a magic ring, left nothing out for us to miss or seek; bound together all our home enjoyments, affections, and hopes; grouped everything and every one around the Christmas fire; and made the little picture shining in our bright young eyes, complete.

Time came, perhaps, all so soon, when our thoughts overleaped that narrow boundary; when there was some one (very dear, we thought then, very beautiful, and absolutely perfect) wanting to the fulness of our happiness; when we were wanting too (or we thought so, which did just as well) at the Christmas hearth by which that some one sat; and when we intertwined with every wreath and garland of our life that some one's name.

That was the time for the bright visionary Christmases which have long arisen from us to show faintly, after summer rain, in the palest edges of the rainbow! That was the time for the beatified enjoyment of the things that were to be, and never were, and yet the things that were so real in our resolute hope that it would be hard to say, now, what realities achieved since, have been stronger!

What! Did that Christmas never really come when we and the priceless pearl who was our young choice were received, after the happiest of totally impossible marriages, by the two united families previously at daggers-drawn on our account? When brothers and sisters-in-law who had always been rather cool to us before our relationship was effected, perfectly doted on us, and when fathers and mothers overwhelmed us with unlimited incomes? Was that Christmas dinner never really eaten, after which we arose, and generously and eloquently rendered honor to our late rival, present in the company, then and there exchanging friendship and forgiveness, and founding an attachment, not to be surpassed in Greek or Roman story, which subsisted until death? Has that same rival long ceased to care for that same priceless pearl, and married for money, and become usurious? Above all, do we really know, now, that we should probably have been miserable if we had won and worn the pearl, and that we are better without her?

That Christmas when we had recently achieved so much fame; when we had been carried in triumph somewhere, for doing something great and good; when we had won an honored and ennobled name, and arrived and were received at home in a shower of tears of joy; is it possible that *that* Christmas has not come yet?

And is our life here, at the best, so constituted that, pausing as we advance at such a noticeable mile-stone in the track as this great birthday, we look back on the things that never were, as naturally and full as gravely as on the things that have been and are gone, or have been and still are? If it be so, and so it seems to be, must we come to the conclusion that life is little better than a dream, and little worth the loves and strivings that we crowd into it?

No! Far be such miscalled philosophy from us, dear Reader, on Christmas Day! Nearer and closer to our hearts be the Christmas spirit, which is the spirit of active usefulness, perseverance, cheerful discharge of duty, kindness and forbearance! It is in the last virtues especially, that we are, or should be, strengthened by the unaccomplished visions of our youth; for, who shall say that they are not our teachers to deal gently even with the impalpable nothings of the earth!

Therefore, as we grow older, let us be more thankful that the circle of our Christmas associations and of the lessons that they bring, expands ! Let us welcome every one of them, and summon them to take their places by the Christmas hearth.

Welcome, old aspirations, glittering creatures of an ardent fancy, to your shelter underneath the holly! We know you, and have not outlived you yet. Welcome, old projects and old loves, however fleeting, to your nooks among the steadier lights that burn around us. Welcome, all that was ever real to our hearts; and for the earnestness that made you real, thanks to Heaven! Do we build no Christmas castles in the clouds now? Let our thoughts, fluttering like butterflies among these flowers of children, bear witness! Before this boy, there stretches out a Future, brighter than we ever looked on in our old romantic time, but bright with honor and with truth. Around this little head on which the sunny curls lie heaped, the graces sport, as prettily, as airily,

559

as when there was no scythe within the reach of Time to shear away the curls of our first-love. Upon another girl's face near it—placider but smiling bright—a quiet and contented little face, we see Home fairly written. Shining from the word, as rays shine from a star, we see how, when our graves are old, other hopes than ours are young, other hearts than ours are moved; how other ways are smoothed; how other happiness blooms, ripens, and decays— no, not decays, for other homes and other bands of children, not yet in being nor for ages yet to be, arise, and bloom and ripen to the end of all!

Welcome, everything! Welcome, alike what has been, and what never was, and what we hope may be, to your shelter underneath the holly, to your places round the Christmas fire, where what is sits open-hearted! In yonder shadow, do we see obtruding furtively upon the blaze, an enemy's face? By Christmas Day we do forgive him! If the injury he has done us may admit of such com- panionship, let him come here and take his place. If otherwise, unhappily, let him go hence, assured that we will never injure nor accuse him.

On this day we shut out Nothing!

"Pause," says a low voice. "Nothing? Think!"

"On Christmas Day, we will shut out from our fireside, Nothing."

"Not the shadow of a vast City where the withered leaves are lying deep?" the voice replies. "Not the shadow that darkens the whole globe? Not the shadow of the City of the Dead?"

Not even that. Of all days in the year, we will turn our faces towards that City upon Christmas Day, and from its silent hosts bring those we loved, among us. City of the Dead, in the blessed name wherein we are gathered together at this time, and in the Presence that is here among us according to the promise, we will receive, and not dismiss, thy people who are dear to us!

Yes. We can look upon these children angels that alight, so solemnly, so beautifully among the living children by the fire, and can bear to think how they departed from us. Entertaining angels unawares, as the Patriarchs did, the playful children are unconscious of their guests; but we can see them— can see a radiant arm around one favorite neck, as if there were a tempting of that child away. Among the celestial figures there is one, a poor mis-shapen boy on earth, of a glorious beauty now, of whom his dying mother said it grieved her much to leave him here, alone, for so many years as it was likely would elapse before he came to her—being such a little child. But he went quickly, and was laid upon her breast, and in her hand she leads him.

There was a gallant boy, who fell, far away, upon a burning sand beneath a burning sun, and said, "Tell them at home, with my last love, how much I could have wished to kiss them once, but that I died contented and had done my duty!" Or there was another, over whom they read the words, "Therefore we commit his body to the deep," and so consigned him to the lonely ocean and sailed on. Or there was another, who lay down to his rest in the dark shadow of great forests, and, on earth, awoke no more. O shall they not, from sand and sea and forest, be brought home at such a time!

There was a dear girl—almost a woman—never to be one —who made a mourning Christmas in a house of joy, and went her trackless way to the silent City. Do we recollect her, worn out, faintly whispering what could not be heard, and falling into that last sleep for weariness? O look upon her now! O look upon her beauty, her serenity, her changeless youth, her happiness! The daughter of Jairus was recalled to life, to die; but she, more blest, has heard the same voice, saying unto her, "Arise for ever!"

We had a friend who was our friend from early days, with whom we often pictured the changes that were to come upon our lives, and merrily imagined how we would speak, and walk, and think, and talk, when we came to be old. His destined habitation in the City of the Dead received him in his prime. Shall he be shut out from our Christmas remembrance? Would his love have so excluded us? Lost friend, lost child, lost parent, sister, brother, husband, wife, we will not so discard you! You shall hold your cherished places in our Christmas hearts, and by our Christmas fires; and in the season of immortal hope, and on the birthday of immortal mercy, we will shut out Nothing!

The winter sun goes down over town and village; on the sea it makes a rosy path, as if the Sacred tread were fresh upon the water. A few more moments, and it sinks, and night comes on, and lights begin to sparkle in the prospect. On the hill-side beyond the shapelessly-diffused town, and in the quiet keeping of the trees that gird the village-steeple, remembrances are cut in stone, planted in common flowers, growing in grass, entwined with lowly brambles around many a mound of earth. In town and village, there are doors and windows closed against the weather, there are flaming logs heaped high, there are joyful faces, there is healthy music of voices. Be all ungentleness and harm excluded from the temples of the Household Gods, but be those remembrances admitted with tender encouragement!

561

They are of the time and all its and peaceful reassurances; and of the history that re-united even upon earth the living and the dead; and of the broad beneficence and goodness that too many men have tried to tear to narrow shreds.

How Sampo Lappelil Saw the Mountain King

(TRADITIONAL SWEDISH TALE)

Far away in Lapland, at a place called Aïmïo, near the River Jana, there lived, in a little hut, a Laplander and his wife, with their small son, Sampo.

Sampo Lappelill was now between seven and eight years of age. He had black hair, brown eyes, a snub nose, and a wide mouth, which last is considered a mark of beauty in curious Lapland. Sampo was a strong child for his age; he delighted to dance down the hills in his little snow-shoes, and to drive his own reindeer in his own little sledge. The snow whirled about him as he passed through the deep drifts, until nothing of him could be seen except the tuft of his black forelock.

"I shall never feel comfortable while he is from home!" said the mother. "He may meet Hisü's reindeer with the golden antlers."

Sampo overheard these words, and wondered what reindeer it could be that had golden antlers. "It must be a splendid animal!" said he; "how much I should like to drive to Rastekaïs with it!" Rastekaïs is a high, dreary mountain, and can be seen from Aïmïo, from which it is five or six miles distant.

"You audacious boy!" exclaimed the mother; "how dare you talk so? Rastekaïs is the home of the trolls, and Hisü dwells there also."

"Who is Hisü?" inquired Sampo.

"What ears that boy has!" thought the Lapp-wife. "But I ought not to have spoken of such things in his presence; the best thing I can do now is to frighten him well." Then she said aloud: "Take care, Lappelill, that you never go near Rastekaïs, for there lives Hisü, the Mountain King, who can eat a whole reindeer at one mouthful, and who swallows little boys like flies."

Upon hearing these words, Sampo could not help thinking what good fun it would be to have a peep at such a wonderful being—from a safe distance, of course!

Three or four weeks had elapsed since Christmas, and darkness brooded still over Lapland. There was no morning, noon, or evening; it was always night. Sampo was feeling dull. It was so long since he had seen the sun that he had nearly forgotten what it was like. Yet he did not desire the return of summer, for the only thing he remembered about that season was that it was a time when the gnats stung very severely. His one wish was that it might soon become light enough for him to use his snow-shoes.

One day, at noon (although it was dark), Sampo's father said: "Come here! I have something to show you."

Sampo came out of the hut. His father pointed towards the south.

"Do you know what that is?" asked he.

"A southern light," replied the boy.

"No," said his father, "it is the herald of the sun. To-morrow, maybe, or the day after that, we shall see the sun himself. Look, Sampo, how weirdly the red light glows on the top of Rastekaïs!"

Sampo perceived that the snow upon the gloomy summit, which had been so long shrouded in darkness, was colored red. Again the idea flashed into his mind what a grand sight the terrible Mountain King would be— from a distance. The boy brooded on this for the remainder of the day, and throughout half the night, when he should have been asleep.

He thought, and thought, until at length he crept silently out of the reindeer skins which formed his bed, and then through the door-hole. The cold was intense. Far above him the stars were shining, the snow scrunched beneath his feet. Sampo Lappelill was a brave boy, who did not fear the cold. He was, moreover, well wrapped up in fur. He stood gazing at the stars, considering what to do next.

Then he heard a suggestive sound. His little reindeer pawed the ground with its feet. "Why should I not take a drive?" thought Sampo, and proceeded straightway to put his thought into action. He harnessed the reindeer to the sledge, and drove forth into the wilderness of snow.

"I will drive only a little way towards Rastekaïs," said Sampo to himself, and off he went, crossing the frozen River Jana to the opposite shore, which—although the child was unaware of this fact—belonged to the kingdom of Norway.

As Sampo drove, he sang a bright little song. The wolves were running round his sledge like gray dogs, but he did not mind them. He knew well that no wolf could keep pace with his dear, swift little reindeer. Up hill and down dale he drove on, with the wind whistling in his ears. The moon seemed to be racing with him, and the rocks to be running backwards. It was thoroughly delightful!

Alas! at a sudden turning upon the downward slope of a hill the sledge overturned, and Sampo was pitched into a snow-drift. The reindeer did not observe this, and, in the belief that its master was still sitting behind it, it ran on. Sampo could not cry "Stop!" for his mouth was stuffed with snow.

He lay there in the darkness, in the midst of the vast snowy wilderness, in which was no human habitation for miles around.

At first, he naturally felt somewhat bewildered. He scrambled unhurt out of the big snow-drift. Then, by the wan moonlight, he saw that he was surrounded on all sides by snow-drifts and huge mountains. One mountain towered above the others, and this he knew must be Rastekaïs, the home of the fierce Mountain King, who swallowed little boys like flies!

Sampo Lappelill was frightened now, and heartily wished himself safe at home. But how was he to get there?

There sat the poor child, alone in the darkness, amongst the desolate, snow-covered rocks, with the big, black shadow of Rastekaïs frowning down upon him. As he wept his tears froze immediately, and rolled down over his jacket in little round lumps like peas; so Sampo thought that he had better leave off crying, and run about in order to keep himself warm.

"Rather than freeze to death here," he said to himself, "I would go straight to the Mountain King. If he has a mind to swallow me, he must do so, I suppose; but I shall advise him to eat instead some of the wolves in this neighborhood. They are much fatter than I, and their fur would not be so difficult to swallow."

Sampo began to ascend the mountain. Before he had gone far, he heard the trotting of some creature behind him, and a moment after a large wolf overtook him. Although inwardly trembling, Sampo would not betray his fear. He shouted:

"Keep out of my way! I am the bearer of a message to the King, and you hinder me at your peril!"

"Dear me!" said the wolf (on Rastekaïs all the animals can speak). "And, pray, what little shrimp are you, wriggling through the snow?"

"My name is Sampo Lappelill," replied the boy. "Who are you?"

"I," answered the wolf, "am first gentleman-usher to the Mountain King. I have just been all over the kingdom to call together his subjects for the great sun festival. As you are going my way, you may, if you please, get upon my back, and so ride up the mountain."

Sampo instantly accepted the invitation. He climbed upon the shaggy back of the wolf, and they went off at a gallop.

"What do you mean by the sun festival?" inquired Sampo.

"Don't you know *that*?" said the wolf. "We celebrate the sun's feast the day he first appears on the horizon after the long night of winter. All trolls, goblins, and animals in the north then assemble on Rastekaïs, and on that day they are not permitted to hurt each other. Lucky it was for you, my boy, that you came here to-day. On any other day, I should have devoured you long ago."

"Is the King bound by the same law?" asked Sampo anxiously.

"Of course he is," answered the wolf. "From one hour before sunrise until one hour after sunset he will not dare to harm you. If, however, you are on the mountain when the time expires, you will be in great danger. For the King will then seize whoever comes first, and a thousand bears and a hundred thousand wolves will also be ready to rush upon you. There will soon be an end of Sampo Lappelill!"

"But perhaps, sir," said Sampo timidly, "you would be so kind as to help me back again before the danger begins?"

The wolf laughed. "Don't count on any such thing, my dear Sampo; on the contrary, I mean to seize you first myself. You are such a very nice, plump little boy! I see that you have been fattened on reindeer milk and cheese. You will be splendid for breakfast to-morrow morning!"

Sampo began to think that his best course might be to jump off the wolf's back at once. But it was too late. They had now arrived at the top of Rastekaïs. Many curious and marvelous things were there to be seen. There sat the terrible Mountain King on his throne of cloudy rocks, gazing out over the snow-fields. He wore on his head a cap of white snow-clouds; his eyes were like a full moon; his nose resembled a mountain-ridge. His mouth was an abyss;

his beard was like tufts of immense icicles; his arms were as thick and strong as fir trees; his coat was like an enormous snow-mountain. Sampo Lappelill had a good view of the King and his subjects, for a bow of dazzling northern lights shone in the sky and illuminated the scene.

All around the King stood millions of goblins, trolls, and brownies; tiny, gray creatures, who had come from remotest parts of the world to worship the sun. This they did from fear, not from love; for trolls and goblins hate the sun, and always hope that he will never return when they see him disappear at the end of summer.

Farther off stood all the animals of Lapland, thousands and thousands of them of all sizes; from the bear, the wolf, and the glutton, to the little mountain-rat, and the brisk, tiny reindeer-flea. No gnats appeared, however; *they* had all been frozen.

Sampo was greatly astonished at what he saw. Unobserved, he slipped from the wolf's back, and hid behind a ponderous stone, to watch the proceedings.

The Mountain King shook his head, and the snow whirled about him. The northern lights shone around his head like a crown of glory, sending long, red streamers across the deep blue sky; they whizzed and sparkled, expanded and drew together, fading sometimes, then again darting out like lightning over the snow-clad mountains. This performance amused the King. He clapped with his icy hands until the sound echoed like thunder, causing the trolls to scream with joy, and the animals to howl with fear. At this the King was still more delighted, and he shouted across the desert:

"This is to my mind! Eternal darkness! Eternal night! May they never end!"

"May they never end!" repeated all the trolls at the top of their voices. Then arose a dispute amongst the animals. All the beasts of prey agreed with the trolls, but the reindeer and other gentle creatures felt that they should like to have summer back again, although they disliked the gnats that would certainly return with it. One creature alone was ready to welcome summer quite unreservedly. This was the reindeer-flea. She piped out as loudly as she could:

"If you please, your Majesty, have we not come here to worship the sun, and to watch for his coming?"

"Nonsense!" growled a polar bear. "Our meeting here springs from a stupid old custom. The sooner it ends the better! In my opinion, the sun has set for ever; he is dead!"

At these words the animals shuddered, but the trolls and goblins were much pleased with them, and reiterated them gaily, shaking with laughter to such an extent that their tiny caps fell off their heads. Then the King roared, in a voice of thunder:

"Yea! Dead is the sun! Now must the whole world worship me, the King of Eternal Night and Eternal Winter!"

Sampo, sitting behind the stone, was so greatly enraged by this speech that he came forth from his hiding-place, exclaiming:

"That, O King, is a lie as big as yourself! The sun is not dead, for only yesterday I saw his forerunner. He will be here very shortly, bringing sweet summer with him, and thawing the icicles in your funny, frozen beard!"

The King's brow grew black as a thunder-cloud. Forgetful of the law, he lifted his tremendous arm to strike Sampo; but at that moment the northern light faded. A red streak shot suddenly across the sky, shining with such brilliancy into the King's face that it entirely dazzled him. His arm fell useless at his side. Then the golden sun rose in slow stateliness on the horizon, and that flood of glorious light caused even those who had rejoiced in his supposed death to welcome his re-appearance.

But the goblins were considerably astonished. From under their red caps they stared at the sun with their little gray eyes, and grew so excited that they stood on their heads in the snow. The beard of the Mountain King began to melt and drip, until it was flowing down his jacket like a running stream.

By-and-by, Sampo heard a reindeer say to her little one:

"Come, my child, we must be going, or we shall be eaten by the wolves."

"Such will be *my* fate also if I linger longer," thought Sampo. So he sprang upon the back of a beautiful reindeer with golden antlers, which started off with him at once, darting down the rocks with lightning speed.

"What is that rustling sound that I hear behind us?" asked the boy presently.

"It is made by the thousand bears; they are pursuing us in order to eat us up," replied the reindeer. "You need not fear, however, for I am the King's own enchanted reindeer, and no bear has ever been able as yet to nibble my heels!"

They went on in silence for a time, then Sampo put another question.

"What," asked he, "is that strange panting I hear behind us?"

"That," returned the reindeer, "is made by the hundred thousand wolves; they are at full gallop behind us, and wish to tear us in pieces. But fear nothing from them! No wolf has ever beaten me in a race yet!"

Again Sampo spoke:

"Is it not thundering over there amongst the rocky mountains?"

"No," answered the now trembling reindeer; "that noise is made by the King, who is chasing us. Now, indeed, all hope has fled, for no one can escape *him*!"

"Can we do nothing?" asked Sampo.

"There is no safety to be found here," said the reindeer, "but there is just one chance for us. We must try to reach the priest's house over yonder by Lake Enare. Once there, we shall be safe, for the King has no power over Christians."

"Oh, make haste! make haste! dear reindeer!" cried Sampo, "and you shall feed on golden oats, and out of a silver manger."

On sped the reindeer. As they entered the priest's house, the Mountain King crossed the courtyard, and knocked at the door with such violence that it is a wonder he did not knock the house down.

"Who is there?" called the priest from within.

"It is I!" answered a thundering voice; "it is the mighty Mountain King! Open the door! You have there a child, whom I claim as my prey."

"Wait a moment!" cried the priest. "Permit me to robe myself, in order that I may give your Majesty a worthier reception."

"All right!" roared the King; "but be quick about it, or I may break down your walls!" A moment later he raised his enormous foot for a kick, yelling: "Are you not ready yet?"

Then the priest opened the door, and said solemnly, "Begone, King of Night and Winter! Sampo Lappelill is under my protection, and he shall never be yours!"

Upon this, the King flew into such a violent passion that he exploded in a great storm of snow and wind. The flakes fell and fell, until the snow reached the roof of the priest's house, so that every one inside it expected to be buried alive. But as soon as the sun rose, the snow began to melt, and all was well. The Mountain King had completely vanished, and no one knows exactly what became of him, although some think that he is still reigning on Rastekaïs.

Sampo thanked the priest heartily for his kindness, and begged, as an additional favor, the loan of a sledge. To this sledge the boy harnessed the golden-antlered reindeer, and drove home to his parents, who were exceedingly glad to see him.

How Sampo became a great man, who fed his reindeer with golden oats out of a silver manger, is too lengthy a story to tell now.

Ole the Tower-Keeper

HANS CHRISTIAN ANDERSEN

In the world it's always going up and down—and now I can't go up any higher!" So said Ole the tower-keeper. "Most people have to try both the ups and the downs; and, rightly considered, we all get to be watchmen at last, and look down upon life from a height."

Such was the speech of Ole, my friend, the old tower-keeper, an amusing talkative old fellow, who seemed to speak out everything that came into his head, and who for all that had many a serious thought deep in his heart. Yes, he was the child of respectable people, and there were even some who said that he was the son of a privy councilor, or that he might have been; he had studied too, and had been assistant teacher and deputy clerk; but of what service was all that to him? In those days he lived in the dean's house, and was to have everything in the house, to be at free quarters, as the saying is; but he was still, so to speak, a fine young gentleman. He wanted to have his boots cleaned with patent blacking, and the dean would only give ordinary grease; and upon that point they split—one spoke of stinginess, the other of vanity, and the blacking became the black cause of enmity between them, and at last they parted.

But what he demanded from the dean he also demanded from the world—namely, patent blacking—and he got nothing but grease. Accordingly he at last drew back from all men, and became a hermit; but the church tower is the only place in a great city where hermitage, office, and bread can be found together. So he betook himself up thither, and smoked his pipe on his solitary rounds. He looked upward and downward, and had his own thoughts, and told in his way of what he saw and did not see, of what he read in books and in himself. I often lent him books, good books; and you may know a man by the company he keeps. He loved neither the English governess-novels, nor the French ones, which he called a mixture of empty wind and raisin-stalks: he wanted biographies and descriptions of the wonders of the world. I visited him at least once a year, generally directly after New Year's Day, and then he always spoke of this and that which the change of the year had put into his head.

I will tell the story of two of these visits, and will give his own words if I can do so.

First Visit

Among the books which I had lately lent Ole, was one about cobble-stones, which had greatly rejoiced and occupied him.

"Yes, they are rare old fellows, those cobble-stones!" he said; "and to think that we should pass them without noticing them! I have often done that myself in the fields and on the beach, where they lie in great numbers. And over the street pavement, those fragments of the oldest remains of antiquity, one walks without ever thinking about them. I have done the very thing myself. But now I look respectfully at every paving-stone. Many thanks for the book! It has filled me with thought, has pushed old thoughts and habits aside, and has made me long to read more on the subject. The romance of the earth is, after all, the most wonderful of all romances. It's a pity one can't read the first volumes of it, because they're written in a language that we don't understand. One must read in the different strata, in the pebble-stones, for each separate period. And it is only in the sixth volume that the human personages first appear, Adam and Eve; that is a little too late for some readers, they would like to have them at once, but it is all the same to me. Yes, it is a romance, a very wonderful romance, and we all have our place in it. We grope and ferret about, and yet remain where we are, but the ball keeps turning, without emptying the ocean over us; the crust we walk upon holds together, and does not let us through. And then it's a story that has been acting for millions of years, with constant progress. My best thanks for the book about the cobble-stones. Those are fellows indeed! they could tell us something worth hearing, if they only know how to talk. It's really a pleasure, now and then to become a mere nothing, especially when a man is as highly placed as I am. And then to think that we all, even with patent lacquer, are nothing more than insects of a moment on that anthill the earth, though we may be insects with stars and garters, places and offices! One feels quite a novice beside these venerable million-year-old cobble-stones. On last New Year's Eve I was reading the book, and had lost myself in it so completely, that I forgot my usual New Year's diversion, namely, the wild hunt to Amager. Ah, you don't know what that is!

"The journey of the witches on broomsticks is well enough known—that journey is taken on St. John's Eve, to the Brocken; but we have a wild journey also, which is national and modern, and that is the journey to Amager on the eve of the New Year. All indifferent poets and poetesses, musicians, newspaper writers, and artistic notabilities, I mean those who are no good, ride in the New Year's Eve through the air to Amager. They sit astride on their painting brushes or quill pens, for steel pens won't bear them, they're too stiff. As I told you, I see it every New Year's Eve, and could mention most of them by name, but I should not like to draw their enmity upon myself, for they don't like people to talk about their ride to Amager on quill pens. I've a kind of niece, who is a fishwife, and who, as she tells me, supplies three respectable newspapers with the terms of abuse they use, and she has herself been there as an invited guest; but she was carried out thither, for she does not own a quill pen, nor can she ride. She has told me all about it. Half of what she says is not true, but the half is quite enough. When she was out there, the festivities began with a song: each of the guests had written his own song, and each one sang his own song, for he thought that the best, and it was all one, all the same melody. Then those came marching up, in little bands, who are only busy with their mouths. There were ringing bells that sang alternately; and then came the little drummers that beat their tattoo in the family circle; and acquaintance was made with those who write without putting their names, which here means as much as using grease instead of patent blacking; and then there was the hangman with his boy, and the boy was the smartest, otherwise he would not be noticed; then too there was the good street-sweeper with his cart, who turns over the dust-bin, and calls it 'good, very good, remarkably good.' And in the midst of the pleasure there shot up out of the great dirt-heap a stem, a tree, an immense flower, a great mushroom, a perfect roof, which formed a sort of storehouse for the worthy company, for in it hung everything they had given to the world during the Old Year. Out of the tree poured sparks like flames of fire; these were the ideas and thoughts, borrowed from others, which they had used, and which now got free and rushed away like so many fireworks. They played at 'the fuse burns,' and the young poets played at 'heartburns,' and the witlings played off their jests, and the jests rolled away with a thundering sound, as if empty pots were being shattered against doors. 'It was very amusing!' my niece said; in fact, she said many things that were very malicious but very amusing, but I won't mention them, for a man must be good-natured and not a carping critic. But you will easily perceive that when a man once knows the rights of the festival out there, as I know them, it's quite natural that on the New Year's Eve one should look out to see the wild chase go by. "If in the New Year I miss certain persons who used to be there, I am sure to notice others who are new arrivals; but this year I omitted taking my look at the guests. I bowled away on the cobble-stones, rolled back through millions of years, and saw the stones break loose high up in the North, saw them drifting about on icebergs, long before Noah's ark was constructed, saw them sink down to the bottom of the sea, and reappear again on a sand-bank, the one that stuck up out of the water and said, 'This shall be Zealand!' I saw them become the dwelling-place of birds that are unknown to us, and then became the seat of wild chiefs of whom we know nothing, until with their axes they cut their Runic signs into a few of these stones, which then came into the calendar of time. But as for me, I had quite gone out of it, and had become a nothing. Then three or four beautiful falling stars came down, which cleared the air, and gave my thoughts another direction. You know what a falling star is, do you not? The learned men are not at all clear about it. I have my own ideas about shooting stars, and my idea is this: How often are silent thanksgivings offered up for one who has done a good and noble action! the thanks are often speechless, but they are not lost for all that. I think these thanks are caught up, and the sunbeams bring the silent, hidden thankfulness over the head of the benefactor; and if it be a whole people that has been expressing its gratitude through a long lapse of time, the thankfulness appears as a nose-gay of flowers, and falls in the form of a shooting star over the good man's grave. I am always very much pleased when I see a shooting star, especially in the New Year's Eve, and then find out for whom the gift of gratitude was intended. Lately a gleaming star fell in the southwest, as a tribute of thanks-giving to many, many! 'For whom was that star intended?' thought I. It fell, no doubt, on the hill by the Bay of Flensborg, where the Danebrog waves over the graves of Schleppegrell, Laessoe, and their comrades. One star also fell in the midst of the land, fell upon Soro, a flower on the grave of Holberg, the thanks of the year from a great many—thanks for his charming plays!

"It is a great and pleasant thought to know that a shooting star falls upon our graves: on mine certainly none will fall—no sunbeam brings thanks to me, for here there is nothing worthy of thanks. I shall not get the patent lac-quer," said Ole; "for my fate on earth is only grease, after all."

Second Visit

It was New Year's Day, and I went up the tower. Ole spoke of the toasts that were drunk at the passing of the Old Year into the New. And he told me a story about the glasses, and this story had a very deep meaning. It was this:

"When on the New Year's Eve the clock strikes twelve, the people at the table rise up, with full glasses in their hands, and drink success to the New Year. They begin the year with the glass in their hands; that is a good beginning for topers. They begin the New Year by going to bed, and that's a good beginning for drones. Sleep is sure to play a great part in the course of the year, and the glass likewise. Do you know what dwells in the glass?" asked Ole. "There dwell in the glass, health, pleasure, and the wildest delight; and misfortune and the bitterest woe dwell there also. Now suppose we count the glasses—of course I count the different degrees in the glasses for different people.

"You see, the *first glass*, that's the glass of health, and in that the herb of health is found growing; put it up on the beam in the ceiling, and at the end of the year you may be sitting in the arbor of health.

"If you take the *second glass*—from this a little bird soars upwards, twittering in guileless cheerfulness, so that a man may listen to his song and perhaps join in, 'Fair is life! no downcast looks! Take courage and march onward!'

"Out of the *third glass* rises a little winged urchin, who cannot certainly be called an angel-child, for there is goblin blood in his veins, and he has the spirit of a goblin; not wishing to hurt or harm you, indeed, but very ready to play off tricks upon you. He'll sit at your ear and whisper merry thoughts to you; he'll creep into your heart and warm you, so that you grow very merry and become a wit, so far as the wits of the others can judge.

"In the *fourth glass* is neither herb, bird, nor urchin: in that glass is the pause drawn by reason, and one may never go beyond that sign.

"Take the *fifth glass*, and you will weep at yourself, you will feel such a deep emotion; or it will affect you in a different way. Out of the glass there will spring with a bang Prince Carnival, impertinent and extravagantly merry: he'll draw you away with him, you'll forget your dignity, if you have any, and you'll forget more than you should or ought to forget. All is dance, song, and sound; the masks will carry you away with them, and the daughters of vanity, clad in silk and satin, will come with loose hair and alluring charms;—tear yourself away if you can!

573

"The *sixth, glass*! Yes, in that glass sits a demon, in the form of a little, well-dressed, attractive and very fascinating man, who thoroughly understands you, agrees with you in everything, and becomes quite a second self to you. He has a lantern with him, to give you light as he accompanies you home. There is an old legend about a saint who was allowed to choose one of the seven deadly sins, and who accordingly chose drunkenness, which appeared to him the least, but which led him to commit all the other six. The man's blood is mingled with that of the demon—it is the sixth glass, and with that the germ of all evil shoots up within us; and each one grows up with a strength like that of the grains of mustard seed, and shoots up into a tree, and spreads over the whole world; and most people have no choice but to go into the oven, to be recast in a new form.

"That's the history of the glasses," said the tower-keeper Ole, "and it can be told with lacquer or only with grease; but I give it you with both!"

That was my second visit to Ole, and if you want to hear about more of them, then the visits must be—continued.

Jack Frost

(TRADITIONAL RUSSIAN TALE)

Once upon a time there lived an old Russian peasant with his wife and three daughters—Martha, Pasha, and Masha. Now the eldest, Martha, happened to be a step-daughter, therefore she was, of course, greatly disliked by her step-mother. Early in the morning, till late at night, the step-mother would do nothing but chide the unfortunate Martha, and give her more work than was good for her. She had to go out and get the wood to heat the stoves, wash the floors, feed the cocks and hens, milk the cows, and do a number of other things. Yet the step-mother was not satisfied, and would keep on telling her that she was a lazy, good-for-nothing girl, and that she never by any chance put the hut in proper order, nor put the potatoes in the right dish, and various other little domestic trifles, which do not belong to our story. Martha was, so to speak, always in hot water; still, she wisely held her tongue, trying hard all the time to please her step-mother, who, unfortunately, was the sort of woman that nothing would please. As for the other two girls, they naturally took after their mother, and snubbed Martha right and left, so that the poor girl was scolded by all, except her father, who loved her dearly.

Years went by, and these young girls grew into beautiful young women, and were beginning to think of getting married. The father, though anxious to find them all good partners, was sorely afraid to part with Martha, who had become a wonderfully beautiful girl; the step-mother, on the other hand, was anxious to get rid of her. She was not particular in what way; but she knew that Martha was the chief attraction in the house, and that while she was there, the other two girls were not likely to stand any chance. Many a young man had already asked for her hand, but Martha was in no hurry, as she cared for none of them very much; so she refused them all; but no one had yet proposed to the other two girls. The step-mother began thinking what she had better do to get Martha out of the way. At last she thought of something that seemed to her a very good idea.

"Martha must really make up her mind to marry some one," said she one night to her husband.

"But she does not care for any one; besides, what should we do if she did? who would feed the animals and look after the hut, if Martha were to marry?"

"Stuff! you surely don't want her to stop at home altogether, and die an old maid?"

"Certainly not; yet who is to look after everything, and cheer us in our old age. I am sure neither Pasha nor Masha would care about that."

"Of course not; they will soon be snatched up. In fact, they would have been married now, only the dear, good girls thought that Martha being the eldest ought to marry first."

The old man hesitated.

"Well, yes, wife," he said at last. "My Martha ought certainly to marry, but the question is to *whom*; she cares for no one."

The woman laughed to herself.

"*I* know of a suitable husband," she said.

"Indeed, and who is he?" asked her husband astonished.

"Why, Jack Frost. He is rich, he is handsome, what more could she want? Look at all the fir and pine-trees, look at the ice and the snow,—they all belong to him, every one of them. I hear that he is looking about for a wife, and if he takes a fancy to Martha, which he is sure to do, no one could help it,—how rich she would be!"

The old peasant opened his eyes and mouth very wide, and stood staring at his wife in great surprise. However, thinking that she knew best, he at last asked her,—

"But where is this Jack Frost you speak of to be found?"

"In the forest, of course, you silly!"

"Yes, but that's rather a large order."

"Well, look here! Early to-morrow morning you must harness the horses to the sledge, take a large empty box, and drive into the forest with Martha—drive on until you come to a very dark pine thicket. In front of you, you will see an ice-hill, upon which stands a large fir-tree; put the box under this tree, and leave Martha with it; but don't tell her the reason for anything about it; only just say that you will come back and fetch her in a few minutes; and that she must wait patiently till your return—and all is sure to turn out well, just as I wish it."

"But she will die of the cold."

"No, not she; Jack Frost will look after her."

But the woman's idea was that Martha should sit on that box until she died of the bitter cold which surrounded the ice-hill, near which Jack Frost resided.

Next morning the old man did as his wife had ordered him; he harnessed his horses, and drove off with his daughter to the ice-hill, where he left her to sit on the box under the big fir-tree, telling her that he would come back soon and fetch her away.

Poor Martha sat there for a long time, trembling with the cold. Not knowing why she had to stop there; but only that her father had told her to wait for him and not to move, she meant to obey him come what might. She felt dreadfully miserable, as she saw that the day was drawing to a close, and yet her father did not come. Had he forgotten his promise? or had something happened to him? She tried to cry, but no tears came. Suddenly she heard a slight noise close to her ear: it was Jack Frost jumping from tree to tree. When he saw her he came nearer to where she sat.

"Are you warm, pretty maiden? are you warm?" he asked, in a cold, clear voice, from the top of the fir-tree.

"I hardly know," she said with a shudder, as she tried to look up, but had not the strength to do so.

Jack Frost jumped from branch to branch, coming nearer to her. Suddenly he sprang from the tree and stood by her side, his ice-cold fingers touching her shoulders. He was a handsome-looking old man, with a long white beard, and curly white locks hanging down his back; he had a kind-looking old face, with a good-natured smile on it.

"Are you warm, pretty maiden?" he asked again, stooping down to look into her face.

"Yes," she replied, "I am burning."

Martha was really freezing, but the cold was so great that she thought she was broiling.

Jack Frost felt very sorry for the poor girl, and coming closer to her, covered her up with what seemed to her fur cloaks and rugs, but she knew no more until she found herself at home again, surrounded by her father, step-mother, and sisters; she was clad in a beautiful silk dress, with a lovely fur mantle, and the box which was taken to the forest empty was now full of beautiful presents. It was really funny to see how cross the step-mother became on seeing Martha actually back again with such a number of rich presents and things round her; she tried, however, to keep her rage down, as well as she could. She never thought for a moment that her step-daughter's trip to the forest would have ended in this way. Nevertheless, she took the old man aside, and said proudly,—

"Was I not right in making you take Martha to the forest? See how rich she has become; Jack Frost has evidently taken a great fancy to her. I always said he would, and if you had not been in such a hurry to go and fetch her back he would have married her by this time, and she wouid have been richer still; but it is no good talking about it now."

Her thoughts were very different from her speech.

"No, my dear," she thought to herself; "I am not going to be beaten by *you*."

A few days later the woman ordered her unfortunate husband to harness his horses and take her own two daughters, Pasha and Masha, into the wood to try their luck, and see what Jack Frost would give *them*. Away went the old man, with Pasha and Masha, to the pine forest, and told them to sit on the box under the fir-tree, just as Martha had done. He then left them and went home.

At first the girls enjoyed it very much, and talked and laughed together.

"It does seem such a queer idea," said Pasha, "to send us *here* to find a lot of dresses and things, just as though we could not buy everything we want in the village, or wait till we go to Moscow."

"We should have to wait long in that case, Pasha, as we are not likely to go there in a hurry."

"Mamma said that we should see some very handsome young men here, if we waited long enough. I wonder whether that is true?"

"I don't know! All I know is that it's getting frightfully cold"; and Masha shivered as she drew her warm furs round her.

But Pasha did not mind the cold; she did not feel it half as much as her sister, for she was blessed with the gift of the gab, and chatted away right merrily, laughing and talking about every possible thing.

"What did you say, Pasha?" Masha would ask almost every minute. "I am so cold I can hardly hear what you are talking about. I wonder whether those young men really will come."

"Have patience, my dear; men always keep one waiting; they can't be punctual to save their lives."

"I don't believe they *will* come, say what you like; but supposing only one man comes, which of us do you think he will choose—you or me?"

"*Maybe* he will take *you*," snarled Pasha.

"No, he will *most* likely choose *you*, my dear!" retorted Masha.

With that they began to sneer at each other, till they heard Jack Frost jumping from tree to tree, shaking them as though they were so many bells. Now it so happened that the girls did not know that it was Jack Frost who had given Martha all those presents, and that it was for him they were waiting.

"There, Masha!" cried Pasha, "I hear something. I believe the young men are coming at last in their troikas; don't you hear the bells?"

Jack Frost came near them.

"Are you warm, pretty maidens?" he asked; "are you warm, my dears?"

"*Warm*, you old stupid!" cried Pasha, looking up at him; "warm, indeed! oh, yes, of course we are; it's a wonder we are not dead with the heat."

"What are you waiting for?" he asked.

"What business is that of yours?"

Jack Frost smiled.

"We are waiting for our lovers," said Masha, who thought her sister had been rather rude. "But I suppose they have lost their way in this horrid, dark forest."

"Queer place to wait for lovers," Jack Frost said. "I hardly think they would be such asses as to come here. Are you still warm, pretty maidens?"

"Get away with you, you old stupid, do! Can't you see that we are nearly frozen to death," cried Pasha angrily.

Still Jack Frost kept on coming closer and closer to them, and at last he leaped from the fir-tree, touched them with his ice-cold hands, which froze them to death, for Jack Frost had somehow taken a dislike to the girls, and thus Pasha and Masha departed this world of sorrow.

In the morning the woman sent her husband to go and fetch them home again, with all the treasures that she thought they would be sure to have. Away went the old man to the pine forest, where, to his horror, he found the dead bodies of his two daughters lying on the ice-hill. He took them up, kissed their pale, cold faces, put them in his sledge, and drove home to his wife, who came out smiling to meet him; but alas for those smiles! they died away, as Pasha and Masha had done.

"Where are my children?" she cried out.

The old man, after uncovering the rugs, displayed the bodies of the two unfortunate girls lying dead in the cart. Angry words did not remain long unuttered by the mother's lips.

"What have you done to them, you wicked, wicked man? My poor little darlings, they were the delight of my life. My Pasha, my Masha, what shall I do without them? my darling little doves. What did you do to them, you horrid old wretch? Tell me this instant."

"Leave off talking that nonsense, this is no time for scolding. You told me to take the girls to the forest; you thought of nothing but riches all the time, and this is what you get for it. You can't find fault with me, I did what you told me to do, and these are the thanks I get."

The woman after a little more scolding and howling came to herself again, and actually forgave her husband, who had done nothing. After that they lived happily for many a long year, not forgetting, however, to bury Pasha and Masha. As for Martha, she soon married a rich and handsome young man, and lived happily ever after, as people always do in Fairy Tales.

The Enchanted Watch

(From *The Green Fairy Book*)

Once upon a time there lived a rich man who had three sons. When they grew up, he sent the eldest to travel and see the world, and three years passed before his family saw him again. Then he returned, magnificently dressed, and his father was so delighted with his behavior, that he gave a great feast in his honor, to which all the relations and friends were invited.

When the rejoicings were ended, the second son begged leave of his father to go in his turn to travel and mix with the world. The father was enchanted at the request, and gave him plenty of money for his expenses, saying, "If you behave as well as your brother, I will do honor to you as I did to him." The young man promised to do his best, and his conduct during three years was all that it should be. Then he went home, and his father was so pleased with him that his feast of welcome was even more splendid than the one before.

The third brother, whose name was Jenik, or Johnnie, was considered the most foolish of the three. He never did anything at home except sit over the stove and dirty himself with the ashes; but he also begged his father's leave to travel for three years. "Go if you like, you idiot; but what good will it do you?"

The youth paid no heed to his father's observations as long as he obtained permission to go. The father saw him depart with joy, glad to get rid of him, and gave him a handsome sum of money for his needs.

Once, as he was making one of his journeys, Jenik chanced to cross a meadow where some shepherds were just about to kill a dog. He entreated them to spare it, and to give it to him instead which they willingly did, and he went on his way, followed by the dog. A little further on he came upon a cat, which someone was going to put to death. He implored its life, and the cat followed him. Finally, in another place, he saved a serpent, which was also handed over to him and now they made a party of four—the dog behind Jenik, the cat behind the dog, and the serpent behind the cat.

Then the serpent said to Jenik, "Go wherever you see me go," for in the autumn, when all the serpents hide themselves in their holes, this serpent was going in search of his king, who was king of all the snakes.

Then he added: "My king will scold me for my long absence, everyone else is housed for the winter, and I am very late. I shall have to tell him what danger I have been in, and how, without your help, I should certainly have lost my life. The king will ask what you would like in return, and be sure you beg for the watch which hangs on the wall. It has all sorts of wonderful properties, you only need to rub it to get whatever you like."

No sooner said than done. Jenik became the master of the watch, and the moment he got out he wished to put its virtues to the proof. He was hungry, and thought it would be delightful to eat in the meadow a loaf of new bread and a steak of good beef washed down by a flask of wine, so he scratched the watch, and in an instant it was all before him. Imagine his joy!

Evening soon came, and Jenik rubbed his watch, and thought it would be very pleasant to have a room with a comfortable bed and a good supper. In an instant they were all before him. After supper he went to bed and slept till morning, as every honest man ought to do. Then he set forth for his father's house, his mind dwelling on the feast that would be awaiting him. But as he returned in the same old clothes in which he went away, his father flew into a great rage, and refused to do anything for him. Jenik went to his old place near the stove, and dirtied himself in the ashes without anybody minding.

The third day, feeling rather dull, he thought it would be nice to see a three-story house filled with beautiful furniture, and with vessels of silver and gold. So he rubbed the watch, and there it all was. Jenik went to look for his father, and said to him: "You offered me no feast of welcome, but permit me to give one to you, and come and let me show you my plate."

The father was much astonished, and longed to know where his son had got all this wealth. Jenik did not reply, but begged him to invite all their relations and friends to a grand banquet.

So the father invited all the world, and everyone was amazed to see such splendid things, so much plate, and so many fine dishes on the table. After the first course Jenik prayed his father to invite the King, and his daughter the Princess. He rubbed his watch and wished for a carriage ornamented with gold and silver, and drawn by six horses, with harness glittering with precious stones. The father did not dare to sit in this gorgeous coach, but went to the palace on foot. The King and his daughter were immensely surprised with the beauty of the carriage, and mounted the steps at once to go to Jenik's banquet. Then Jenik rubbed his watch afresh, and wished that for six miles the way to the house should be paved with marble. Who ever felt so astonished as the King? Never had he traveled over such a gorgeous road.

When Jenik heard the wheels of the carriage, he rubbed his watch and wished for a still more beautiful house, four stories high, and hung with gold, silver, and damask; filled with wonderful tables, covered with dishes such as no king had ever eaten before. The King, the Queen, and the Princess were speechless with surprise. Never had they seen such a splendid palace, nor such a high feast! At dessert the King asked Jenik's father to give him the young man for a son-in-law. No sooner said than done! The marriage took place at once, and the King returned to his own palace, and left Jenik with his wife in the enchanted house.

Now Jenik was not a very clever man, and at the end of a very short time he began to bore his wife. She inquired how he managed to build palaces and to get so many precious things. He told her all about the watch, and she never rested till she had stolen the precious talisman. One night she took the watch, rubbed it, and wished for a carriage drawn by four horses; and in this carriage she at once set out for her father's palace. There she called to her own attendants, bade them follow her into the carriage, and drove straight to the sea-side. Then she rubbed her watch, and wished that the sea might be crossed by a bridge, and that a magnificent palace might arise in the middle of the sea. No sooner said than done. The Princess entered the house, rubbed her watch, and in an instant the bridge was gone.

Left alone, Jenik felt very miserable. His father, mother, and brothers, and, indeed, everybody else, all laughed at him. Nothing remained to him but the cat and dog whose lives he had once saved. He took them with him and went far away, for he could no longer live with his family. He reached at last a great desert, and saw some crows flying towards a mountain. One of them was a long way behind, and when he arrived his brothers inquired what had made him so late. "Winter is here," they said, "and it is time to fly to other countries." He told them that he had seen in the middle of the sea the most wonderful house that ever was built.

On hearing this, Jenik at once concluded that this must be the hiding-place of his wife. So he proceeded directly to the shore with his dog and his cat. When he arrived on the beach, he said to the dog: "You are an excellent swimmer, and you, little one, are very light; jump on the dog's back and he will take you to the palace. Once there, he will hide himself near the door, and you must steal secretly in and try to get hold of my watch."

No sooner said than done. The two animals crossed the sea; the dog hid near the house, and the cat stole into the chamber. The Princess recognized him, and guessed why he had come; and she took the watch down to the cellar and locked it in a box. But the cat wriggled its way into the cellar, and the moment the Princess turned her back, he scratched and scratched till he had made a hole in the box. Then he took the watch between his teeth, and waited quietly till the Princess came back. Scarcely had she opened the door when the cat was outside, and the watch into the bargain.

The cat was no sooner beyond the gates than she said to the dog:

"We are going to cross the sea; be very careful not to speak to me."

The dog laid this to heart and said nothing; but when they approached the shore he could not help asking, "Have you got the watch?"

The cat did not answer—he was afraid that he might let the talisman fall. When they touched the shore the dog repeated his question.

"Yes," said the cat.

And the watch fell into the sea. Then our two friends began each to accuse the other, and both looked sorrowfully at the place where their treasure had fallen in. Suddenly a fish appeared near the edge of the sea. The cat seized it, and thought it would make them a good supper.

"I have nine little children," cried the fish. "Spare the father of a family!"

"Granted," replied the cat; "but on condition that you find our watch."

The fish executed his commission, and they brought the treasure back to their master. Jenik rubbed the watch and wished that the palace, with the Princess and all its inhabitants, should be swallowed up in the sea. No sooner said than done. Jenik returned to his parents, and he and his watch, his cat and his dog, lived together happily to the end of their days.

Poultry Meg's Family

HANS CHRISTIAN ANDERSEN

Poultry Meg was the only human occupant in the handsome new house which was built for the fowls and ducks on the estate. It stood where the old baronial mansion had stood, with its tower, crow-step gable, moat, and drawbridge. Close by was a wilderness of trees and bushes; the garden had been here and had stretched down to a big lake, which was now a bog. Rooks, crows, and jackdaws flew screaming and cawing over the old trees, a perfect swarm of birds. They did not seem to decrease, but rather to increase, although one shot amongst them. One could hear them inside the poultry-house, where Poultry Meg sat with the ducklings running about over her wooden shoes. She knew every fowl, and every duck, from the time it crept out of the egg; she was proud of her fowls and ducks, and proud of the splendid house which had been built for them.

Her own little room was clean and neat, that was the wish of the lady to whom the poultry-house belonged; she often came there with distinguished guests and showed them the "barracks of the hens and ducks," as she called it.

Here was both a wardrobe and an easy-chair, and even a chest of drawers, and on it was a brightly polished brass plate on which was engraved the word "Grubbe," which was the name of the old, noble family who had lived here in the mansion. The brass plate was found when they were digging here, and the parish clerk had said that it had no other value except as an old relic. The clerk knew all about the place and the old time, for he had knowledge from books; there were so many manuscripts in his table-drawer. He had great knowledge of the old times; but the oldest of the crows knew more perhaps, and screamed about it in his own language, but it was crow-language, which the clerk did not understand, clever as he might be. The bog could steam after a warm summer day so that it seemed as if a lake lay behind the old trees, where the crows, rooks, and jackdaws flew; so it had appeared when the Knight Grubbe had lived here, and the old manor-house stood with its thick, red walls. The dog's chain used to reach quite past the gateway in those days; through the tower, one went into a stone-paved passage which led to the rooms; the windows were narrow and the panes small, even in the great hall, where the dancing took place, but in the time of the last Grubbe there was no dancing as far back as one could remember, and yet there lay there an old kettledrum which had served as part of the music. Here stood a curious carved cupboard, in which rare flower bulbs were kept, for Lady Grubbe was fond of gardening, and cultivated trees and plants; her husband preferred riding out to shoot wolves and wild boars, and his little daughter Marie always went with him. When she was only five years old, she sat proudly on her horse, and looked round bravely with her big black eyes. It was her delight to hit out with her whip amongst the hounds; her father would have preferred to see her hit out amongst the peasant boys who came to look at the company.

The peasant in the clay house close to the manor had a son called Sören, the same age as the little noble lady. He knew how to climb, and had always to go up and get the bird's nests for her. The birds screamed as loud as they could scream, and one of the biggest of them cut him over the eye, so that the blood poured out. It was thought at first that the eye had been destroyed; but it was very little damaged after all. Marie Grubbe called him her Sören—that was a great favor, and it was a good thing for his father, poor John; he had committed a fault one day, and was to be punished by riding the wooden horse. It stood in the yard, with four poles for legs, and a single narrow plank for a back; on this John had to ride astride, and have some heavy bricks fastened to his legs, so that he might not sit too comfortably; he made horrible grimaces, and Sören wept and implored little Marie to interfere; immediately she ordered that Sören's father should be taken down, and when they did not obey her she stamped on the stone pavement, and pulled her father's coat sleeve till it was torn. She would have her way, and she got it, and Sören's father was taken down.

The Lady Grubbe, who now came up, stroked her little daughter's hair, and looked at her affectionately; Marie did not understand why. She would go to the hounds, and not with her mother, who went into the garden, down to the lake, where the white and yellow water-lilies bloomed, and the bulrushes nodded amongst the reeds. She looked at all this luxuriance and freshness. "How pleasant!" said she. There stood in the garden a rare tree which she herself had planted; it was called a "copper-beech," a kind of blackamoor amongst the other trees, so dark brown were the leaves; it must have strong sunshine, otherwise in continual shade it would become green like the other trees and so lose its distinctive character. In the high chestnut-trees were many birds' nests, as well as in the bushes and the grassy meadows. It seemed as if the birds knew that they were protected here, for here no one dared to fire a gun.

The little Marie came here with Sören; he could climb, as we know, and he fetched both eggs and young downy birds. The birds flew about in terror and anguish, little ones and big ones! Peewits from the field, rooks, crows, and jackdaws from the high trees, screamed and shrieked; it was a shriek exactly the same as their descendants shriek in our own day.

"What are you doing, children?" cried the gentle lady. "This is ungodly work!"

Sören stood ashamed, and even the high-born little girl looked a little abashed, but then she said, shortly and sulkily, "My father lets me do it!"

"Afar! afar!" screamed the great blackbirds, and flew off, but they came again next day, for their home was here.

But the quiet, gentle lady did not stay long at home here; our Lord called her to Himself, with Him she was more at home than in the mansion, and the church bells tolled solemnly when her body was carried to the church. Poor men's eyes were wet, for she had been good to them. When she was gone, no one cared for her plants, and the garden ran to waste.

Sir Grubbe was a hard man, they said, but his daughter, although she was so young, could manage him; he had to laugh, and she got her way. She was now twelve years old, and strongly built; she looked through and through people, with her big black eyes, rode her horse like a man, and shot her gun like a practiced hunter.

One day there came great visitors to the neighborhood, the very greatest, the young king and his half-brother and comrade Lord Ulrik Frederick Gyldenlöwe; they wanted to hunt the wild boar there, and would stay some days at Sir Grubbe's castle.

Gyldenlöwe sat next Marie at table; he took her round the neck and gave her a kiss, as if they had been relations, but she gave him a slap on the mouth and said that she could not bear him. At that there was great laughter, as if it was an amusing thing.

And it may have been amusing too, for five years after, when Marie had completed her seventeenth year, a messenger came with a letter; Lord Gyldenlöwe we proposed for the hand of the noble lady; that was something!

"He is the grandest and most gallant gentleman in the kingdom!" said Sir Grubbe. "That is not to be despised."

"I don't care much about him!" said Marie Grubbe, but she did not reject the grandest man in the country, who sat by the king's side.

Silver plate, woolen and linen went with a ship to Copenhagen; she traveled overland in ten days. The outfit had contrary winds, or no wind at all; four months passed before it arrived, and when it did come Lady Gyldenlöwe had departed.

"I would rather lie on coarse sacking, than in his silken bed!" said she; "I'd rather walk on my bare feet than drive with him in a carriage!"

Late one evening in November, two women came riding into the town of Aarhus; it was Lady Gyldenlöwe and her maid: they came from Veile, where they had arrived from Copenhagen by ship. They rode up to Sir Grubbe's stone mansion. He was not delighted with the visit. She got hard words, but she got a bedroom as well; got nice food for breakfast, but not nice words, for the evil in her father was roused against her, and she was not accustomed to that. She was not of a gentle temper, and as one is spoken to, so one answers. She certainly did answer, and spoke with bitterness and hate about her husband, with whom she would not live; she was too honorable for that.

So a year went past, but it did not pass pleasantly. There were evil words between father and daughter, and that there should never be. Evil words have evil fruit. What could be the end of this?

"We two cannot remain under the same roof," said the father one day. "Go away from here to our old manor-house, but rather bite your tongue out than set lies going!"

So these two separated; she went with her maid to the old manor-house, where she had been born and brought up, and where the gentle pious lady, her mother, lay in the church vault; an old cowherd lived in the house, and that was the whole establishment. Cobwebs hung in the rooms, dark and heavy with dust; in the garden everything was growing wild. Hops and other climbing plants twisted a net between the trees and bushes; and hemlock and nettles grew larger and stronger. The copper beech was overgrown by the others and now stood in shade, its leaves were now as green as the other common trees, and its glory had departed. Rooks, crows, and daws flew in thick swarms over the high chestnut-trees, and there was a cawing and screaming, as if they had some important news to tell each other: now she is here again, the little one who had caused their eggs and their young ones to be stolen from them. The thief himself, who had fetched them, now climbed on a leafless tree, sat on the high mast, and got good blows from the rope's end if he did not behave himself.

The clerk told all this in our own time; he had collected it and put it together from books and manuscripts; it lay with many more manuscripts in the table-drawer.

"Up and down is the way of the world!" said he, "it is strange to hear!" And we shall hear how it went with Marie Grubbe, but we will not forget Poultry Meg, who sits in her grand hen-house in our time; Marie Grubbe sat there in her time, but not with the same spirit as old Poultry Meg.

The winter passed, spring and summer passed, and then again came the stormy autumn-time, with the cold, wet sea-fogs. It was a lonely life, a wearisome life there in the old manor-house. So Marie Grubbe took her gun and went out on the moors, and shot hares and foxes, and whatever birds she came across. Out there she met oftener than once noble Sir Palle Dyre from Nörrebæk, who was also wandering about with his gun and his dogs. He was big and strong, and boasted about it when they talked together. He could have dared to measure himself with the late Mr. Brockenhus of Egeskov, of whose strength there were still stories. Palle Dyre had, following his example, caused an iron chain with a hunting-horn to be hung at his gate, and when he rode home he caught the chain, and lifted himself with the horse from the ground, and blew the horn.

"Come yourself and see it, Dame Marie!" said he, "there is fresh air blowing at Nörrebæk!"

When she went to his house is not recorded, but on the candlesticks in Nörrebæk Church one can read that they were given by Palle Dyre and Marie Grubbe of Nörrebæk Castle.

Bodily strength had Palle Dyre: he drank like a sponge; he was like a tub that could never be filled; he snored like a whole pig-sty, and he looked red and bloated.

"He is piggish and rude!" said Dame Palle Dyre, Grubbe's daughter. Soon she was tired of the life, but that did not make it any better. One day the table was laid, and the food was getting cold; Palle Dyre was fox-hunting and the lady was not to be found. Palle Dyre came home at midnight, Dame Dyre came neither at midnight nor in the morning, she had turned her back on Nörrebæk had ridden away without greeting or farewell.

It was gray wet weather; the wind blew cold, and a flock of black screaming birds flew over her, they were not so homeless as she.

First she went south, quite up to Germany; a couple of gold rings with precious stones were turned into money; then she went east, and then turned again to the west; she had no goal before her eyes, and was angry with every one, even with the good God Himself, so wretched was her mind; soon her whole body became wretched too, and she could scarcely put one foot before another. The peewit flew up from its tussock when she fell over it: the bird screamed as it always does, "You thief! You thief!" She had never stolen her neighbor's goods, but birds' eggs and young birds she had had brought to her when she was a little girl; she thought of that now.

From where she lay she could see the sand-hills by the shore; fishermen lived there, but she could not get so far, she was so ill. The great white sea-mews came flying above her and screamed as the rooks and crows screamed over the garden at home. The birds flew very near her, and at last she imagined that they were coal-black, but then it became night before her eyes. When she again opened her eyes she was being carried; a big, strong fellow had taken her in his arms. She looked straight into his bearded face; he had a scar over his eye, so that the eyebrow appeared to be divided in two. He carried her, miserable as she was, to the ship, where he got a rating from the captain for it.

The day following, the ship sailed; Marie Grubbe was not put ashore, so she went with it. But she came back again, no doubt? Yes, but when and where?

The clerk could also tell about this, and it was not a story which he himself had put together. He had the whole strange story from a trustworthy old book; we ourselves can take it out and read it.

The Danish historian, Ludwig Holberg, who has written so many useful books and the amusing comedies from which we can get to know his time and people, tells in his letters of Marie Grubbe, where and how he met her; it is well worth hearing about, but we will not forget Poultry Meg, who sits so glad and comfortable in her grand hen-house.

The ship sailed away with Marie Grubbe; it was there we left off.

Years and years went past.

The plague was raging in Copenhagen; it was in the year 1711. The Queen of Denmark went away to her German home, the king quitted the capital, every one who could, hastened away. The students, even if they had board and lodging free, left the city. One of them, the last who still remained at the so-called Borch's College, close by Regensen, also went away. It was two o'clock in the morning; he came with his knapsack, which was filled more with books and manuscripts than with clothes. A damp, clammy mist hung over the town; not a creature was to be seen in the whole street; round about on the doors and gates crosses were marked to show that the plague was inside, or that the people were dead. No one was to be seen either in the broader, winding Butcher's Row, as the street was called which led from the Round Tower to the King's Castle. A big ammunition wagon rumbled past; the driver swung his whip and the horses went off at a gallop, the wagon was full of dead bodies. The young student held his hand before his face, and smelt at some strong spirits which he had on a sponge in a brass box.

From a tavern in one of the streets came the sound of singing and unpleasant laughter, from people who drank the night through, to forget that the plague stood before the door and would have them to accompany him in the wagon with the other corpses. The student turned his steps towards the castle bridge, where one or two small ships lay; one of them was weighing anchor to get away from the plague-stricken city.

"If God spares our lives and we get wind for it, we are going to Grönsund in Falster," said the skipper, and asked the name of the student who wished to go with him.

"Ludwig Holberg," said the student, and the name sounded like any other name; now the sound is one of the proudest names in Denmark; at that time he was only a young, unknown student.

The ship glided past the castle. It was not yet clear morning when they came out into the open water. A light breeze came along, and the sails swelled, the young student set himself with his face to the wind, and fell asleep, and that was not quite the wisest thing to do. Already on the third morning the ship lay off Falster.

"Do you know any one in this place, with whom I could live cheaply?" Holberg asked the captain.

"I believe that you would do well to go to the ferrywoman in Borrehouse," said he. "If you want to be very polite, her name is Mother Sören Sörensen Möller! yet it may happen that she will fly into a rage if you are too polite to her! Her husband is in custody for a crime; she herself manages the ferry-boat, she has fists of her own!"

The student took his knapsack and went to the ferry-house. The door was not locked, he lifted the latch, and went into a room with a brick-laid floor, where a bench with a big leather coverlet was the chief article of furniture. A white hen with chickens was fastened to the bench, and had upset the water-dish, and the water had run across the floor. No one was here, or in the next room, only a cradle with a child in it. The ferry-boat came back with only one person in it, whether man or woman was not easy to say. The person was wrapped in a great cloak, and wore a fur cap like a hood on the head. The boat lay to.

It was a woman who got out and came into the room. She looked very imposing when she straightened her back; two proud eyes sat under the black eyebrows. It was Mother Sören, the ferry-woman; rooks, crows, and daws would scream out another name which we know better.

She looked morose, and did not seem to care to talk, but so much was said and settled, that the student arranged for board and lodging for an indefinite time, whilst things were so bad in Copenhagen. One or other honest citizen from the neighboring town came regularly out to the ferry-house. Frank the cutler and Sivert the excise-man came there; they drank a glass of ale and talked with the student. He was a clever young man, who knew his "Practica," as they called it; he read Greek and Latin, and was well up in learned subjects.

"The less one knows, the less one is burdened with it," said Mother Sören.

"You have to work hard!" said Holberg, one day when she soaked her clothes in the sharp lye, and herself chopped the tree-roots for firewood.

"That's my affair!" said she.

"Have you always from childhood been obliged to work and toil?"

"You can see that in my hands!" said she, and showed him two small but strong, hard hands with bitten nails. "You have learning and can read."

At Christmas it began to snow heavily. The cold came on, the wind blew sharply, as if it had vitriol to wash people's faces with. Mother Sören did not let that disturb her. She drew her cloak around her, and pulled her hood down over her head. It was dark in the house, early in the afternoon. She laid wood and turf on the fire, and set herself down to darn her stockings, there was no one else to do it. Towards evening she talked more to the student than was her custom. She spoke about her husband.

"He has by accident killed a skipper of Dragör, and for that he must work three years in irons. He is only a common sailor, and so the law must take its course."

"The law applies also to people of higher position," said Holberg.

"Do you think so?" said Mother Sören, and looked into the fire, but then she began again, "Have you heard of Kai Lykke, who caused one of his churches to be pulled down, and when the priest thundered from the pulpit about it, he caused the priest to be laid in irons, appointed a court, and adjudged him to have forfeited his head, which was accordingly struck off; that was not an accident, and yet Kai Lykke went free that time!"

"He was in the right according to the times!" said Holberg, "now we are past that!"

"You can try to make fools believe that,' said Mother Sören as she rose and went into the room where the child lay, eased it and laid it down again, and then arranged the student's bed; he had the leather covering, for he felt the cold more than she did, and yet he had been born in Norway.

On New Year's morning it was a real bright sunshiny day; the frost had been and still was so strong that the drifted snow lay frozen hard, so that one could walk upon it. The bells in the town rang for church, and the student Holberg took his woolen cloak about him and would go to the town.

Over the ferry-house the crows and rooks were flying with loud cries, one could scarcely hear the church bells for their noise. Mother Sören stood outside, filling a brass kettle with snow, which she was going to put on the fire to get drinking-water. She looked up to the swarm of birds, and had her own thoughts about it.

The student Holberg went to church; on the way there and back he passed Sivert the tax-collector's house, by the town gate; there he was invited in for a glass of warm ale with syrup and ginger. The conversation turned on Mother Sören, but the tax-collector did not know much about her—indeed, few people did. She did not belong to Falster, he said; she had possessed a little property at one time; her husband was a common sailor with a violent temper, who had murdered a skipper of Dragör. "He beats his wife, and yet she takes his part."

"I could not stand such treatment!" said the tax-collector's wife. "I am also come of better people; my father was stocking-weaver to the Court!"

"Consequently you have married a Government official," said Holberg, and made a bow to her and the tax-collector.

It was Twelfth Night, the evening of the festival of the Three Kings. Mother Sören lighted for Holberg a three-king candle—that is to say, a tallow-candle with three branches, which she herself had dipped.

"A candle for each man!" said Holberg.

"Each man?" said the woman, and looked sharply at him.

"Each of the wise men from the east!" said Holberg.

"That way!" said she, and was silent for a long time. But on the evening of the Three Kings he learned more about her than he did before.

"You have an affectionate mind to your husband," said Holberg, "and yet people say that he treats you badly."

"That is no one's business but mine!" she answered. "The blows could have done me good as a child; now I get them for my sin's sake! I know what good he has done me," and she rose up. "When I lay ill on the open heath, and no one cared to come in contact with me, except perhaps the crows and the rooks to peck at me, he carried me in his arms and got hard words for the catch he brought on board. I am not used to be ill, and so I recovered. Every one has his own way, Sören has his, and one should not judge a horse by the halter! With him I have lived more comfortably than with the one they called the most gallant and noble of all the king's subjects. I have been married to the Stadtholder Gyldenlöwe, the half-brother of the king; later on I took Palle Dyre! Right or wrong, each has his own way, and I have mine. That was a long story, but now you know it!" And she went out of the room.

It was Marie Grubbe! so strange had been the rolling ball of her fortune. She did not live to see many more anniversaries of the festival of the Three Kings; Holberg has recorded that she died in 1716, but he has not recorded, for he did not know it, that when Mother Sören, as she was called, lay a corpse in the ferry-house, a number of big blackbirds flew over the place. They did not scream, as if they knew that silence belonged to a burial. As soon as she was laid in the earth the birds disappeared, but the same evening over at the old manor in Jutland an enormous number of crows and rooks were seen; they all screamed as loud as they could, as if they had something to announce, perhaps about him who as a little boy took their eggs and young ones, the farmer's son who had to wear a garter of iron, and the noble lady who ended her life as a ferrywoman at Grönsund.

"Brave! brave!" they screamed.

And the whole family screamed "Brave! brave!" when the old manor-house was pulled down. "They still cry, and there is no more to cry about!" said the clerk, when he told the story. "The family is extinct, the house pulled down, and where it stood, now stands the grand hen-house with the gilded weathercock and with old Poultry Meg. She is so delighted with her charming dwelling; if she had not come here, she would have been in the workhouse."

The pigeons cooed over her, the turkeys gobbled round about her, and the ducks quacked.

"No one knew her!" they said. "She has no relations. It is an act of grace that she is here. She has neither a drake father nor a hen mother, and no descendants!"

Still she had relations, although she did not know it, nor the clerk either, however much manuscript he had in the table-drawer, but one of the old crows knew about it, and told about it. From its mother and grandmother it had heard about Poultry Meg's mother and her grandmother, whom we also know from the time she was a child and rode over the bridge looking about her proudly, as if the whole world and its birds' nests belonged to her; we saw her out on the heath by the sand-dunes, and last of all in the ferry-house. The grandchild, the last of the race, had come home again where the old house had stood, where the wild birds screamed, but she sat among the tame birds, known by them and known along with them. Poultry Meg had no more to wish for, she was glad to die, and old enough to die.

"Grave! grave!" screamed the crows.

And Poultry Meg got a good grave, which no one knew except the old crow, if he is not dead also.

And now we know the story of the old manor, the old race, and the whole of Poultry Meg's family.

The Star-Child

Oscar Wilde

Once upon a time two poor Woodcutters were making their way home through a great pine-forest. It was winter, and a night of bitter cold. The snow lay thick upon the ground, and upon the branches of the trees: the frost kept snapping the little twigs on either side of them, as they passed: and when they came to the Mountain-Torrent she was hanging motionless in air, for the Ice-King had kissed her.

So cold was it that even the animals and the birds did not know what to make of it.

"Ugh!" snarled the Wolf, as he limped through the brushwood with his tail between his legs, "this is perfectly monstrous weather. Why doesn't the Government look to it?"

"Weet! weet! weet!" twittered the green Linnets, "the old Earth is dead, and they have laid her out in her white shroud."

"The Earth is going to be married, and this is her bridal dress," whispered the Turtle-doves to each other. Their little pink feet were quite frost-bitten, but they felt that it was their duty to take a romantic view of the situation.

"Nonsense!" growled the Wolf. "I tell you that it is all the fault of the Government, and if you don't believe me I shall eat you." The Wolf had a thoroughly practical mind, and was never at a loss for a good argument.

"Well, for my own part," said the Woodpecker, who was a born philosopher, "I don't care an atomic theory for explanations. If a thing is so, it is so, and at present it is terribly cold."

Terribly cold it certainly was. The little Squirrels, who lived inside the tall fir-tree, kept rubbing each other's noses to keep themselves warm, and the Rabbits curled themselves up in their holes, and did not venture even to look out of doors. The only people who seemed to enjoy it were the great horned Owls. There feathers were quite stiff with rime, but they did not mind, and they rolled their large yellow eyes, and called out to each other across the forest, "Tu-whit! Tu-whoo! Tu-whit! Tu-whoo! what delightful weather we are having!"

On and on went the two Woodcutters, blowing lustily upon their fingers, and stamping with their huge iron-shod boots upon the caked snow. Once they sank into a deep drift, and came out as white as millers are when the stones are grinding; and once they slipped on the hard smooth ice where the marsh-water was frozen, and their faggots fell out of their bundles, and they had to pick them up and bind them together again; and once they thought that they had lost their way, and a great terror seized on them, for they knew that the Snow is cruel to those who sleep in her arms. But they put their trust in the good Saint Martin, who watches over all travelers, and retraced their steps, and went warily, and at last they reached the outskirts of the forest, and saw, far down in the valley beneath them, the lights of the village in which they dwelt.

So overjoyed were they at their deliverance that they laughed aloud, and the Earth seemed to them like a flower of silver, and the Moon like a flower of gold.

Yet, after that they had laughed they became sad, for they remembered their poverty, and one of them said to the other, "Why did we make merry, seeing that life is for the rich, and not for such as we are? Better that we had died of cold in the forest, or that some wild beast had fallen upon us and slain us."

"Truly," answered his companion, "much is given to some, and little is given to others. Injustice has parcelled out the world, nor is there equal division of aught save of sorrow."

But as they were bewailing their misery to each other this strange thing happened. There fell from heaven a very bright and beautiful star. It slipped down the side of the sky, passing by the other stars in its course, and, as they watched it wondering, it seemed to them to sink behind a clump of willow-trees that stood hard by a little sheepfold no more than a stone's throw away.

"Why! there is a crock of gold for whoever finds it," they cried, and they set to and ran, so eager were they for the gold.

And one of them ran faster than his mate, and outstripped him, and forced his way through the willows, and came out on the other side, and lo! there was indeed a thing of gold lying on the white snow. So he hastened towards it, and stooping down placed his hands upon it, and it was a cloak of golden tissue, curiously wrought with stars, and wrapped in many folds. And he cried out to his comrade that he had found the treasure that had fallen from the sky, and when his comrade had come up, they sat them down in the snow, and loosened the folds of the cloak that they might divide the pieces of gold. But, alas! no gold was in it, nor silver, nor, indeed, treasure of any kind, but only a little child who was asleep.

And one of them said to the other, "This is a bitter ending to our hope, nor have we any good fortune, for what doth a child profit to a man? Let us leave it here, and go our way, seeing that we are poor men, and have children of our own whose bread we may not give to another."

But his companion answered him: "Nay, but it were an evil thing to leave the child to perish here in the snow, and though I am as poor as thou art, and have many mouths to feed, and but little in the pot, yet will I bring it home with me, and my wife shall have care of it."

So very tenderly he took up the child, and wrapped the cloak around it to shield it from the harsh cold, and made his way down the hill to the village, his comrade marveling much at his foolishness and softness of heart.

And when they came to the village, his comrade said to him, "Thou hast the child, therefore give me the cloak, for it is meet that we should share."

But he answered him: "Nay, for the cloak is neither mine nor thine, but the child's only," and he bade him Godspeed, and went to his own house and knocked.

And when his wife opened the door and saw that her husband had returned safe to her, she put her arms round his neck and kissed him, and took from his back the bundle of faggots, and brushed the snow off his boots, and bade him come in.

But he said to her, "I have found something in the forest, and I have brought it to thee to have care of it," and he stirred not from the threshold.

"What is it?" she cried. "Show it to me, for the house is bare, and we have need of many things." And he drew the cloak back, and showed her the sleeping child.

"Alack, goodman!" she murmured," have we not children enough of our own, that thou must needst bring a changeling to sit by the hearth? And who knows if it will not bring us bad fortune? And how shall we tend it?" And she was wroth against him.

"Nay, but it is a Star-Child," he answered; and he told her the strange manner of the finding of it.

But she would not be appeased, but mocked at him, and spoke angrily, and cried: "Our children lack bread, and shall we feed the child of another? Who is there who carest for us? And who giveth us food?"

"Nay, but God careth for the sparrows even, and feedeth them," he answered.

"Do not the sparrows die of hunger in the winter?" she asked. "And is it not winter now?" And the man answered nothing, but stirred not from the threshold.

And a bitter wind from the forest came in through the open door, and made her tremble, and she shivered, and said to him: "Wilt thou not close the door? There cometh a bitter wind into the house, and I am cold."

"Into a house where a heart is hard cometh there not always a bitter wind?" he asked. And the woman answered him nothing, but crept closer to the fire.

And after a time she turned round and looked at him, and her eyes were full of tears. And he came in swiftly, and placed the child in her arms, and she kissed it, and laid it in a little bed where the youngest of their own children was lying. And on the morrow the Woodcutter took the curious cloak of gold and placed it in a great chest, and a chain of amber that was round the child's neck his wife took and set it in the chest also.

So the Star-Child was brought up with the children of the Woodcutter, and sat at the same board with them, and was their playmate. And every year he became more beautiful to look at, so that all those who dwelt in the village were filled with wonder, for, while they were swarthy and black-haired, he was white and delicate as sawn ivory, and his curls were like the rings of the daffodil. His lips, also, were like the petals of a red flower, and his eyes were like violets by a river of pure water, and his body like the narcissus of a field where the mower comes not.

Yet did his beauty work him evil. For he grew proud, and cruel, and selfish. The children of the Woodcutter, and the other children of the village, he despised, saying that they were of mean parentage, while he was noble, being sprung from a Star, and he made himself master over them, and called them his servants. No pity had he for the poor, or for those who were blind or maimed or in any way afflicted, but would cast stones at them and drive them forth on to the highway, and bid them beg their bread elsewhere, so that none save the outlaws came twice to that village to ask for alms. Indeed, he was as one enamoured of beauty, and would mock at the weakly and ill-favored, and make jest of them; and himself he loved, and in summer, when the winds were still, he would lie by the well in the priest's orchard and look down at the marvel of his own face, and laugh for the pleasure he had in his fairness.

Often did the Woodcutter and his wife chide him, and say: "We did not deal with thee as thou dealest with those who are left desolate, and have none to succour them. Wherefore art thou so cruel to all who need pity?"

Often did the old priest send for him, and seek to teach him the love of living things, saying to him: "The fly is thy brother. Do it no harm. The wild birds that roam through the forest have their freedom. Snare them not for thy pleasure. God made the blind-worm and the mole, and each has its place. Who art thou to bring pain into God's world? Even the cattle of the field praise Him."

But the Star-Child heeded not their words, but would frown and flout, and go back to his companions, and lead them. And his companions followed him, for he was fair, and fleet of foot, and could dance, and pipe, and make music. And wherever the Star-Child led them they followed, and whatever the Star-Child bade them do, that did they. And when he pierced with a sharp reed the dim eyes of the mole, they laughed, and when he cast stones at the leper they laughed also. And in all things he ruled them, and they became hard of heart, even as he was.

Now there passed one day through the village a poor beggar-woman. Her garments were torn and ragged, and her feet were bleeding from the rough road on which she had traveled, and she was in very evil plight. And being weary she sat her down under a chestnut-tree to rest.

But when the Star-Child saw her, he said to his companions, "See! There sitteth a foul beggar-woman under that fair and green-leaved tree. Come, let us drive her hence, for she is ugly and ill-favored."

So he came near and threw stones at her, and mocked her, and she looked at him with terror in her eyes, nor did she move her gaze from him. And when the Woodcutter, who was cleaving logs in a haggard hard by, saw what the Star-Child was doing, he ran up and rebuked him, and said to him: "Surely thou art hard at heart and knowest not mercy, for what evil has this poor woman done to thee that thou should'st treat her in this wise?"

And the Star-Child grew red with anger, and stamped his foot upon the ground, and said, "Who art thou to question me what I do? I am no son of thine to do thy bidding."

"Thou speakest truly," answered the Woodcutter, "yet did I show thee pity when I found thee in the forest."

And when the woman heard these words she gave a loud cry, and fell into a swoon. And the Woodcutter carried her to his own house, and his wife had care of her, and when she rose up from the swoon into which she had fallen, they set meat and drink before her, and bade her have comfort.

But she would neither eat nor drink, but said to the Woodcutter, "Didst thou not say that the child was found in the forest? And was it not ten years from this day?"

And the Woodcutter answered, "Yea, it was in the forest that I found him, and it is ten years from this day."

"And what signs didst thou find with him?" she cried. "Bare he not upon his neck a chain of amber? Was not round him a cloak of gold tissue broidered with stars?"

"Truly," answered the Woodcutter, "It was even as thou sayest." And he took the cloak and the amber chain from the chest where they lay, and showed them to her.

And when she saw them she wept for joy, and said, "He is my little son whom I lost in the forest. I pray thee send for him quickly, for in search of him have I wandered over the whole world."

So the Woodcutter and his wife went out and called to the Star-Child, and said to him, "Go into the house, and there shalt thou find thy mother, who is waiting for thee."

So he ran in, filled with wonder and great gladness. But when he saw her who was waiting there, he laughed scornfully and said, "Why, where is my mother? For I see none here but this vile beggar-woman."

And the woman answered him, "I am thy mother."

"Thou art mad to say so," cried the Star-Child angrily. "I am no son of thine, for thou art a beggar, and ugly, and in rags. Therefore get thee hence, and let me see thy foul face no more."

"Nay, but thou art indeed my little son, whom I bare in the forest," she cried, and she fell on her knees, and held out her arms to him. "The robbers stole thee from me, and left thee to die," she murmured, "but I recognized thee when I saw thee, and the signs also have I recognized, the cloak of golden tissue and the amber-chain. Therefore I pray thee come with me, for over the whole world have I wandered in search of thee. Come with me, my son, for I have need of thy love."

But the Star-Child stirred not from his place, but shut the doors of his heart against her, nor was there any sound heard save the sound of the woman weeping for pain.

And at last he spoke to her, and his voice was hard and bitter. "If in very truth thou art my mother," he said, "it had been better hadst thou stayed away, and not come here to bring me to shame, seeing that I thought I was the child of some Star, and not a beggar's child, as thou tellest me that I am. Therefore get thee hence, and let me see thee no more."

"Alas! my son," she cried, "wilt thou not kiss me before I go? For I have suffered much to find thee."

"Nay," said the Star-Child, "but thou art too foul to look at, and rather would I kiss the adder or the toad than thee."

So the woman rose up, and went away into the forest weeping bitterly, and when the Star-Child saw that she had gone, he was glad, and ran back to his playmates that he might play with them.

But when they beheld him coming, they mocked him and said, "Why thou art as foul as the toad, and as loathsome as the adder. Get thee hence, for we will not suffer thee to play with us," and they drave him out of the garden.

And the Star-Child frowned and said to himself, "What is this that they say to me? I will go to the well of water and look into it, and it shall tell me of my beauty."

So he went to the well of water and looked into it, and lo! his face was as the face of a toad, and his body was scaled like an adder. And he flung himself down on the grass and wept, and said to himself, "Surely this has come upon me by reason of my sin. For I have denied my mother, and driven her away, and been proud, and cruel to her. Wherefore I will go and seek her through the whole world, nor will I rest till I have found her."

And there came to him the little daughter of the Woodcutter, and she put her hand upon his shoulder and said, "What doth it matter if thou hast lost thy comeliness? Stay with us, and I will not mock at thee."

And he said to her, "Nay, but I have been cruel to my mother, and as a punishment has this evil been sent to me. Wherefore I must go hence, and wander through the world till I find her, and she give me her forgiveness."

So he ran away into the forest and called out to his mother to come to him, but there was no answer. All day long he called to her, and when the sun set he lay down to sleep on a bed of leaves, and the birds and the animals fled from him, for they remembered his cruelty, and he was alone save for the toad that watched him, and the slow adder that crawled past.

And in the morning he rose up, and plucked some bitter berries from the trees and ate them, and took his way through the great wood, weeping sorely. And of everything that he met he made enquiry if perchance they had seen his mother.

He said to the Mole, "Thou canst go beneath the earth. Tell me, is my mother there?"

And the Mole answered, "Thou hast blinded mine eyes. How should I know?"

He said to the Linnet, "Thou canst fly over the tops of the tall trees, and canst see the whole world. Tell me, canst thou see my mother?"

And the Linnet answered, "Thou hast clipt my wings for thy pleasure. How should I fly?"

And to the little Squirrel who lived in the fir-tree, and was lonely, he said, "Where is my mother?"

And the Squirrel answered, "Thou hast slain mine. Dost thou seek to slay thine also?"

And the Star-Child wept and bowed his head, and prayed forgiveness of God's things, and went on through the forest, seeking for the beggar-woman. And on the third day he came to the other side of the forest and went down into the plain.

And when he passed through the villages the children mocked him, and threw stones at him, and the carlots would not suffer him even to sleep in the byres lest he might bring mildew on the stored corn, so foul was he to look at, and their hired men drave him away, and there was none who had pity on him. Nor could he hear anywhere of the beggar-woman who was his mother, though for the space of three years he wandered over the world, and often seemed to see her on the road in front of him, and would call to her, and run after her till the sharp flints made his feet to bleed. But overtake her he could not, and those who dwelt by the way did ever deny that they had seen her, or any like to her, and they made sport of his sorrow.

For the space of three years he wandered over the world, and in the world there was neither love nor loving-kindness nor charity for him, but it was even such a world as he had made for himself in the days of his great pride.

And one evening he came to the gate of a strong-walled city that stood by a river, and, weary and footsore though he was, he made to enter in. But the soldiers who stood on guard dropped their halberts across the entrance, and said roughly to him, "What is thy business in the city?"

"I am seeking for my mother," he answered, "and I pray ye to suffer me to pass, for it may be that she is in this city."

But they mocked at him, and one of them wagged a black beard, and set down his shield and cried, "Of a truth, thy mother will not be merry when she sees thee, for thou art more ill-favored than the toad of the marsh, or the adder that crawls in the fen. Get thee gone. Get thee gone. Thy mother dwells not in this city."

And another, who held a yellow banner in his hand, said to him, "Who is thy mother, and wherefore art thou seeking for her?"

And he answered, "My mother is a beggar even as I am, and I have treated her evilly, and I pray ye to suffer me to pass that she may give me her forgiveness, if it be that she tarrieth in the city." But they would not, and pricked him with their spears.

And, as he turned away weeping, one whose armor was inlaid with gilt flowers, and on whose helmet couched a lion that had wings, came up and made enquiry of the soldiers who it was who had sought entrance. And they said to him, "It is a beggar and the child of a beggar, and we have driven him away."

"Nay," he cried, laughing, "but we will sell the foul thing for a slave, and his price shall be the price of a bowl of sweet wine."

And an old and evil-visaged man who was passing by called out, and said, "I will buy him for that price," and, when he had paid the price, he took the Star-Child by the hand and led him into the city.

And after that they had gone through many streets they came to a little door that was set in a wall that was covered with a pomegranate tree. And the old man touched the door with a ring of graved jasper and it opened, and they went down five steps of brass into a garden filled with black poppies and green jars of burnt clay. And the old man took then from his turban a scarf of figured silk, and bound with it the eyes of the Star-Child, and drave him in front of him. And when the scarf was taken off his eyes, the Star-Child found himself in a dungeon, that was lit by a lantern of horn.

And the old man set before him some mouldy bread on a trencher and said, "Eat," and some brackish water in a cup and said, "Drink," and when he had eaten and drunk, the old man went out, locking the door behind him and fastening it with an iron chain.

And on the morrow the old man, who was indeed the subtlest of the magicians of Libya and had learned his art from one who dwelt in the tombs of the Nile, came into him and frowned at him, and said, "In a wood that is nigh to the gate of this city of Giaours there are three pieces of gold. One is of white gold, and another is of yellow gold, and the gold of the third one is red. To-day thou shalt bring me the piece of white gold, and if thou bringest it not back, I will beat thee with a hundred stripes. Get thee away quickly, and at sunset I will be waiting for thee at the door of the garden. See that thou bringest the white gold, or it shall go ill with thee, for thou art my slave, and I have bought thee for the price of a bowl of sweet wine." And he bound the eyes of the Star-Child with the scarf of figured silk, and led him through the house, and through the garden of poppies, and up the five steps of brass. And having opened the little door with his ring he set him in the street.

And the Star-Child went out of the gate of the city, and came to the wood of which the Magician had spoken to him.

Now this wood was very fair to look at from without, and seemed full of singing birds and of sweet-scented flowers, and the Star-Child entered it gladly. Yet did its beauty profit him little, for wherever he went harsh briars and thorns shot up from the ground and encompassed him, and evil nettles stung him, and the thistle pierced him with her daggers, so that he was in sore distress. Nor could he anywhere find the piece of white gold of which the Magician had spoken, though he sought for it from morn to noon, and from noon to sunset. And at sunset he set his face towards home, weeping bitterly, for he knew what fate was in store for him.

But when he had reached the outskirts of the wood, he heard from a thicket a cry as of someone in pain. And forgetting his own sorrow he ran back to the place, and saw there a little Hare caught in a trap that some hunter had set for it.

And the Star-Child had pity on it, and released it, and said to it, "I am myself but a slave, yet may I give thee thy freedom."

And the Hare answered him, and said: "Surely thou hast given me freedom, and what shall I give thee in return?"

And the Star-Child said to it, "I am seeking for a piece of white gold, nor can I anywhere find it, and if I bring it not to my master he will beat me."

"Come thou with me," said the Hare, "and I will lead thee to it, for I know where it is hidden, and for what purpose."

So the Star-Child went with the Hare, and lo! in the cleft of a great oak-tree he saw the piece of white gold that he was seeking. And he was filled with joy, and seized it, and said to the Hare, "The service that I did to thee thou hast rendered back again many times over, and the kindness that I showed thee thou hast repaid a hundred fold."

"Nay," answered the Hare, "but as thou dealt with me, so I did deal with thee," and it ran away swiftly, and the Star-Child went towards the city.

Now at the gate of the city there was seated one who was a leper. Over his face hung a cowl of gray linen, and through the eyelets his eyes gleamed like red coals. And when he saw the Star-Child coming, he struck upon a wooden bowl, and clattered his bell, and called out to him and said, "Give me a piece of money, or I must die of hunger. For they have thrust me out of the city, and there is no one who has pity on me."

"Alas!" cried the Star-Child, "I have but one piece of money in my wallet, and if I bring it not to my master he will beat me, for I am his slave."

But the leper entreated him, and prayed of him, till the Star-Child had pity, and gave him the piece of white gold.

And when he came to the Magician's house, the Magician opened to him, and brought him in, and said to him, "Hast thou the piece of white gold?" And the Star-Child answered, "I have it not." So the Magician fell upon him, and beat him, and set before him an empty trencher, and said, "Eat," and an empty cup, and said, "Drink," and flung him again into the dungeon.

And on the morrow the Magician came to him, and said, "If to-day thou bringest me not the piece of yellow gold, I will surely keep thee as my slave, and give thee three hundred stripes."

So the Star-Child went to the wood, and all day long he searched for the piece of yellow gold, but nowhere could he find it. And at sunset he set him down and began to weep, and as he was weeping there came to him the little Hare that he had rescued from the trap.

And the Hare said to him, "Why art thou weeping? And what dost thou seek in the wood?"

And the Star-Child answered, "I am seeking for a piece of yellow gold that is hidden here, and if I find it not my master will beat me, and keep me as a slave."

"Follow me," cried the Hare, and it ran through the wood till it came to a pool of water. And at the bottom of the pool the piece of yellow gold was lying.

"How shall I thank thee?" said the Star-Child, "for lo! this is the second time that you have succoured me."

"Nay, but thou hadst pity on me first," said the Hare, and it ran away swiftly.

And the Star-Child took the piece of yellow gold, and put it in his wallet, and hurried to the city. But the leper saw him coming, and ran to meet him, and knelt down and cried, "Give me a piece of money or I shall die of hunger."

And the Star-Child said to him, "I have in my wallet but one piece of yellow gold, and if I bring it not to my master he will beat me and keep me as his slave."

But the leper entreated him sore, so that the Star-Child had pity on him, and gave him the piece of yellow gold.

And when he came to the Magician's house, the Magician opened to him, and brought him in, and said to him, "Hast thou the piece of yellow gold?" And the Star-Child said to him, "I have it not." So the Magician fell upon him, and beat him, and loaded him with chains, and cast him again into the dungeon.

And on the morrow the Magician came to him, and said, "If to-day thou bringest me the piece of red gold I will set thee free, but if thou bringest it not I will surely slay thee."

So the Star-Child went to the wood, and all day long he searched for the piece of red gold, but nowhere could he find it. And at evening he sat him down, and wept, and as he was weeping there came to him the little Hare.

And the Hare said to him, "The piece of red gold that thou seekest is in the cavern that is behind thee. Therefore weep no more but be glad."

"How shall I reward thee," cried the Star-Child, "for lo! this is the third time thou hast succoured me."

"Nay, but thou hadst pity on me first," said the Hare, and it ran away swiftly.

And the Star-Child entered the cavern, and in its farthest corner he found the piece of red gold. So he put it in his wallet, and hurried to the city. And the leper seeing him coming stood in the center of the road, and cried out, and said to him, "Give me the piece of red money, or I must die," and the Star-Child had pity on him again, and gave him the piece of red gold, saying, "Thy need is greater than mine." Yet was his heart heavy, for he knew what evil fate awaited him.

But lo! as he passed through the gate of the city, the guards bowed down and made obeisance to him, saying, "How beautiful is our lord!" and a crowd of citizens followed him, and cried out, "Surely there is none so beautiful in the whole world!" so that the Star-Child wept, and said to himself, "They are mocking me, and making light of my misery." And so large was the concourse of the people, that he lost the threads of his way, and found himself at last in a great square, in which there was a palace of a King.

And the gate of the palace opened, and the priests and the high officers of the city ran forth to meet him, and they abased themselves before him, and said, "Thou art our lord for whom we have been waiting, and the son of our King."

And the Star-Child answered them and said, "I am no king's son, but the child of a poor beggar-woman. And how say ye that I am beautiful, for I know that I am evil to look at?"

Then he, whose armor was inlaid with gilt flowers, and on whose helmet couched a lion that had wings, held up a shield, and cried, "How saith my lord that he is not beautiful?"

And the Star-Child looked, and lo 1 his face was even as it had been, and his comeliness had come back to him, and he saw that in his eyes which he had not seen there before.

And the priests and the high officers knelt down and said to him, "It was prophesied of old that on this day should come he who was to rule over us.

Therefore, let our lord take this crown and this scepter, and be in his justice and mercy our King over us."

But he said to them, "I am not worthy, for I have denied the mother who bare me, nor may I rest till I have found her, and known her forgiveness. Therefore, let me go, for I must wander again over the world, and may not tarry here, though ye bring me the crown and the scepter." And as he spake he turned his face from them towards the street that led to the gate of the city, and lo! amongst the crowd that pressed round the soldiers, he saw the beggar-woman who was his mother, and at her side stood the leper, who had sat by the road.

And a cry of joy broke from his lips, and he ran over, and kneeling down he kissed the wounds on his mother's feet, and wet them with his tears. He bowed his head in the dust, and sobbing, as one whose heart might break, he said to her: "Mother, I denied thee in the hour of my pride. Accept me in the hour of my humility. Mother, I gave thee hatred. Do thou give me love. Mother, I rejected thee. Receive thy child now." But the beggar-woman answered him not a word.

And he reached out his hands, and clasped the white feet of the leper, and said to him: "Thrice did I give thee of my mercy. Bid my mother speak to me once." But the leper answered him not a word.

And he sobbed again, and said: "Mother, my suffering is greater than I can bear. Give me thy forgiveness, and let me go back to the forest." And the beggar-woman put her hand on his head, and said to him, "Rise," and the leper put his hand on his head, and said to him "Rise," also.

And he rose up from his feet, and looked at them, and lo! they were a King and a Queen.

And the Queen said to him, "This is thy father whom thou hast succoured."

And the King said, "This is thy mother, whose feet thou hast washed with thy tears."

And they fell on his neck and kissed him, and brought him into the palace, and clothed him in fair raiment, and set the crown upon his head, and the scepter in his hand, and over the city that stood by the river he ruled, and was its lord. Much justice and mercy did he show to all, and the evil Magician he banished, and to the Woodcutter and his wife he sent many fair gifts, and to their children he gave high honor. Nor would he suffer any to be cruel to bird or beast, but taught love and loving-kindness and charity, and to the poor he gave bread, and to the naked he gave raiment, and there was peace and plenty in the land.

Yet ruled he not long, so great had been his suffering, and so bitter the fire of his testing, for after the space of three years he died. And he who came after him ruled evilly.

The Peasant Wife Who Was So Discontented

(TRADITIONAL SWEDISH TALE)

There was once a peasant, who had a wife; and she was so discontented with everything they had that she complained all the time and grew very cross. When she went out into the farmyard and looked at their cows, she thought they were miserable creatures compared to other cows. When she sat with her husband to eat, she thought the food and the plates were wretched, that the kitchen was too small and the fields not large enough. She wanted everything as good as the richest in the parish, you may believe.

One Christmas Eve, there came walking into the kitchen, a woman who looked very peculiar. It was no other than the old witch who had her abode in the high hill over beyond the pasture.

The old peasant woman was standing beside the stove, cooking Christmas porridge and muttering as usual, of course. But the witch, who was one of the good-natured sort, spoke to the peasant couple and said:

"As long as Lisa here"—that was the old peasant woman, you must know—"is not satisfied with the way things are, you may wish for three things and you shall have them. But think well for eight days before you wish for the first, so you may wish wisely." With this the witch disappeared.

Lisa was beside herself with delight, you may know, and pondered all Christmas Eve and Christmas day over what she should wish for herself. But at night, when she put the potatoes on the supper table, she thought the sausages were not good enough for her, so she said:

609

"If only a body had a fine, great sausage!" and immediately a great sausage appeared on the platter before her. But this made the old man angry to see her so dissatisfied, so he said:

"I wish the sausage were hanging on your nose, I do!" At once the sausage was hanging on Lisa's nose, and the old man was not strong enough to pull it off.

Now, for the first time they remembered, that they had already made two wishes, and so had only one left. But what good would it do the old woman to be ever so rich, if she had to go around with a sausage hanging on her nose all her days?

So the old man was obliged to wish the sausage off again, and then they were just as rich as they were to start with, as any one can guess.

Removing-Day

Hans Christian Andersen

You remember Ole the watchman in the tower! I have told of two visits to him, now I shall tell about a third one, but that is not the last.

It is usually at New Year time that I go up to him; now on the contrary it was on removing-day, for then it is not very pleasant down in the streets of the town; they are so heaped-up with sweepings and rubbish of all kinds, not to speak of cast-out bed-straw, which one must wade through. I came by just now, and saw that in this great collection of rubbish several children were playing; they played at going to bed; it was so inviting for this game, they thought; they snuggled down in the straw, and pulled an old ragged piece of wallpaper over them for a coverlet. "It was so lovely!" they said; it was too much for me, and so I had to run off up to Ole.

"It is removing-day!" said he, "The streets and lanes serve as an ash-box, an enormous ash-box. A cart-load is enough for me. I can get something out of that, and I did get something shortly after Christmas. I came down into the street, which was raw, wet, dirty, and enough to give one a cold. The dust-man stopped with his cart, which was full, a kind of sample of the streets of

Copenhagen on a removing-day. In the back of the cart was a fir-tree, still quite green and with gold-tinsel on the branches; it had been used for a Christmas-tree and was now thrown out into the street, and the dustman had stuck it up at the back of the heap. It was pleasant to look at, or something to weep over; yes, one can say either, according to how one thinks about it, and I thought about it, and so did one and another of the things which lay in the cart, or they might have thought, which is about one and the same thing. A lady's torn glove lay there; what did it think about? Shall I tell you? It lay and pointed with the little finger at the fir-tree. 'That tree concerns me,' it thought; 'I have also been at a party where there were chandeliers! my real life was one ball-night; a hand-clasp, and I split! there my recollection stops; I have nothing more to live for!' That is what the glove thought, or could have thought. 'How silly the fir-tree is!' said the potsherd. Broken crockery thinks everything foolish. 'If one is on the dust-cart,' they said, 'one should not put on airs and wear tinsel! I know that I have been of use in this world, of more use than a green branch like that.' That was also an opinion such as many people may have; but the fir-tree looked well, it was a little poetry on the pile of rubbish, and there is plenty of that about in the streets on removing-day! The way got heavy and troublesome for me down there, and I became eager to come away, up into the tower again, and to stay up here: here I sit and look down with good humor.

"The good people down there play at changing houses! they drag and toil with their belongings; and the brownie sits in the tub and removes with them. House rubbish, family troubles, sorrows and afflictions remove from the old to the new dwelling, and so what do they and we get out of the whole? Yes, it is already written down long ago in the good, old verse in the news-paper: 'Think of Death's great removing-day!' It is a serious thought, but I suppose it is not unpleasant for you to hear about it. Death is, and remains, the most trustworthy official, in spite of his many small occupations. Have you never thought over this?

"Death is the omnibus conductor, he is the passport-writer, he puts his name to our character book, and he is the director of the great savings bank of life. Can you understand it? All the deeds of our earthly life, great and small, we put in the savings bank, and when Death comes with his removing-day omnibus, and we must go into it and drive to the land of eternity, then at the boundary he gives us our character-book as a passport. For pocket-money on the journey he takes out of the savings bank one or other of the deeds we have done, the one that most shows our worth. That may be delightful, but it may also be terrible.

"No one has escaped yet from the omnibus drive. They certainly tell about one who was not allowed to go with it—the shoemaker of Jerusalem, he had to run behind; if he had got leave to come into the omnibus, then he would have escaped being a subject for the poets. Peep just once with your thoughts into the great omnibus of the removing-day! It is a mixed company! The king and the beggar sit side by side, the genius and the idiot; they must set off, without goods or gold, only with their character-book and the savings bank pocket-money; but which of one's deeds will be brought forward and sent with one? Perhaps a very little one, as small as a pea, but the pea can send out a blossoming plant.

"The poor outcast, who sat on the low stool in the corner, and got blows and hard words, will perhaps get his worn-out stool with him as a token and a help. The stool becomes a sedan-chair to carry him into the land of eternity; it raises itself there to a throne, shining like gold, and flowering like an arbor.

"One, who in this life always went about and tippled pleasure's spicy drink to forget other mischief he had done, gets his wooden keg with him and must drink from it on the omnibus journey; and the drink is pure and clear, so that the thoughts are cleared; all good and noble feelings are awakened, he sees and feels what he did not care to see before, or could not see, and so he has his punishment in himself, 'the gnawing worm, which dies not for ages and ages.' If there was written on the glass 'Oblivion,' there is written on the keg 'Remembrance.'

"If I read a good book, an historical writing, I must always think of the person I read about as coming into Death's omnibus at last; I must think about which of his deeds Death took out of the savings bank for him, what pocket-money he took into the land of eternity.

"There was once a French king, I have forgotten his name; the names of good things are forgotten sometimes, even by me, but they are sure to come back again. It was a king who in time of famine became his people's benefactor, and the people raised a monument of snow to him, with this inscription: 'Quicker than this melts, you helped!' I can imagine, that Death gave him, in allusion to this monument, a single snow-flake which never melt, and that it flew like a white snow-bird over his royal head into the land of immortality.

"There was also Louis XI; yes, I remember his name, one always remembers bad things well. A trait of him comes often into my mind; I wish that one could say the story was untrue. He ordered his constable to be beheaded; he could do that, whether it was just or unjust; but the constable's innocent children, the one eight years old, the other seven, he ordered to be stationed at the place of execution and to be sprinkled with their father's blood; then to be taken to the Bastille and put in an iron cage, where they did not even get a blanket to cover them; and King Louis sent the executioners to them every week and had a tooth pulled from each of them, so that they should not have too good a time; and the eldest said: 'My mother would die of sorrow, if she knew that my little brother suffered so much; pull out two of my teeth, and let him go free!' The tears came to the executioner's eyes at that, but the King's will was stronger than the tears, and every week two children's teeth were brought to the king on a silver salver; he had demanded them, and he got them. These two teeth, I imagine, Death took out of life's savings bank for King Louis XI, and gave him them to take with him on his journey into the great land of immortality; they fly, like two flames of fire, before him; they shine, they burn, they pinch him, these innocent children's teeth.

"Yes, it is a serious journey, the omnibus drive on the great removing-day; and when will it come?

"That is the serious thing about it, that any day, any hour, any minute, one may expect the omnibus. Which of our deeds will Death take out of the savings bank and give to us? Let us think about it; that removing-day is not to be found in the Almanac."

Manabozho the Wolf

(TRADITIONAL NATIVE AMERICAN TALE)

Manabozho set out to travel. He wished to out-do all others, and see new countries, but after walking over America, and encountering many adventures, he became satisfied as well as fatigued. He had heard of great feats in hunting, and felt a desire to try his power in that way.

One evening, as he was walking along the shores of a great lake, weary and hungry, he encountered a great magician in the form of an old wolf, with six young ones, coming towards him. The wolf, as soon as he saw him, told his whelps to keep out of the way of Manabozho.

"For I know," said he, "that it is he we see yonder."

The young wolves were in the act of running off, when Manabozho cried out—

"My grandchildren, where are you going? Stop, and I will go with you."

He appeared rejoiced to see the old wolf, and asked him whither he was journeying. Being told that they were looking out for a place where they could find the most game, and best pass the winter, he said he should like to go with them, and addressed the old wolf in these words—

"Brother, I have a passion for the chase. Are you willing to change me into a wolf?"

The old wolf was agreeable, and Manabozho's transformation was effected.

He was fond of novelty. He found himself a wolf corresponding in size with the others, but he was not quite satisfied with the change, crying out—

"Oh! make me a little larger."

They did so.

"A little larger still," he cried.

They said—

"Let us humor him," and granted his request

"Well," said he, "that will do." Then looking at his tail—

"Oh!" cried he, "make my tail a little longer and more bushy."

They made it so, and shortly after they all started off in company, dashing up a ravine. After getting into the woods some distance, they fell in with the tracks of moose. The young wolves went after them, Manabozho and the old wolf following at their leisure.

"Well," said the wolf, "who do you think is the fastest of my sons? Can you tell by the jumps they take."

"Why," replied he, "that one that takes such long jumps; he is the fastest, to be sure."

"Ha, ha! You are mistaken," said the old wolf. "He makes a good start, but he will be the first to tire out. This one who appears to be behind will be the first to kill the game."

Soon after they came to the place where the young ones had killed the game. One of them had dropped his bundle there.

"Take that, Manabozho," said the old wolf.

"Esa," he replied, "what will I do with a dirty dog-skin?"

The wolf took it up; it was a beautiful robe.

"Oh! I will carry it now," said Manabozho.

"Oh no," replied the wolf, who at the moment exerted his magic power. "It is a robe of pearls."

From that moment he lost no opportunity of displaying his superiority, both in the hunter's and magician's art, over his conceited companion.

Coming to a place where the moose had lain down, they saw that the young wolves had made a fresh start after their prey.

"Why," said the wolf, "this moose is poor. I know by the tracks, for I can always tell whether they are fat or not."

They next came to n place where one of the wolves had tried to bite the moose, and, failing, had broken one of his teeth on a tree.

"Manabozho," said the wolf, "one of your grandchildren has shot at the game. Take his arrow. There it is."

"No," replied he, "what will I do with a dirty tooth?"

The old wolf took it up, and, behold! it was a beautiful silver arrow.

When they overtook the young ones, they found they had killed a very fat moose. Manabozho was very hungry, but, such is the power of enchantment, he saw nothing but bones, picked quite clean. He thought to himself—

"Just as I expected. Dirty, greedy fellows!"

However, he sat down without saying a word, and the old wolf said to one of the young ones—

"Give some meat to your grandfather."

The wolf, coming near to Manabozho, opened his mouth wide as if he had eaten too much, whereupon Manabozho jumped up, saying—

"You filthy dog, you have eaten so much that you are ill. Get away to some other place."

The old wolf, hearing these words, came to Manabozho, and, behold! before him was a heap of fresh ruddy meat with the fat lying all ready prepared. Then Manabozho put on a smiling face.

"Amazement!" cried he, "how fine the meat is!"

"Yes," replied the wolf; "it is always so with us. We know our work, and always get the best. It is not a long tail that makes a hunter."

Manabozho bit his lip.

They then commenced fixing their winter quarters, while the young ones went out in search of game, of which they soon brought in a large supply. One day, during the absence of the young wolves, the old one amused himself by cracking the large bones of a moose.

"Manabozho," said he, "cover your head with the robe, and do not look at me while I am at these bones, for a piece may fly in your eye."

Manabozho covered his head, but, looking through a rent in the robe, he saw all the other was about. At that moment a piece of bone flew off and hit him in the eye. He cried out—

"Tyau! Why do you strike me, you old dog!"

The wolf said—

"You must have been looking at me."

"No, no," replied Manabozho; "why should I want to look at you?"

"Manabozho," said the wolf, "you must have been looking, or you would not have got hurt."

"No, no," said Manabozho; and he thought to himself, "I will repay the saucy wolf for this."

Next day, taking up a bone to obtain the marrow, he said to the old wolf—

"Cover your head, and don't look at me, for I fear a piece may fly in your eye."

The wolf did so. Then Manabozho took the leg-bone of the moose, and, looking first to see if the old wolf was well covered, he hit him a blow with all his might. The wolf jumped up, and cried out—

"Why do yon strike me so?"

"Strike you!" exclaimed Manabozho. "I did not strike you!"

"You did," said the wolf.

"How can you say I did, when you did not see me. Were you looking?" said Manabozho.

He was an expert hunter when he undertook the work in earnest, and one day he went out and killed a fat moose. He was very hungry, and sat down to eat, but fell into great doubts as to the proper point in the carcass to begin at.

"Well," said he, "I don't know where to commence. At the head? No. People would laugh, and say, 'He ate him backward!'"

Then he went to the side.

"No," said he, "they will say I ate him sideways."

He then went to the hind-quarter.

"No," said he, "they will say I ate him forward."

At last, however, seeing that he must begin the attack somewhere, he commenced upon the hindquarter. He had just got a delicate piece in his mouth when the tree just by began to make a creaking noise, rubbing one large branch against another. This annoyed him.

"Why!" he exclaimed, "I cannot eat when I hear such a noise. Stop, stop!" cried he to the tree.

He was again going on with his meal when the noise was repeated.

"I cannot eat with such a noise," said he; and, leaving the meal, although he was very hungry, he went to put a stop to the noise. He climbed the tree, and having found the branches which caused the disturbance, tried to push them apart, when they suddenly caught him between them, so that he was held fast. While he was in this position a pack of wolves came near.

"Go that way," cried Manabozho, anxious to send them away from the neighborhood of his meat.

"Go that way; what would you come to get here?"

The wolves talked among themselves, and said "Manabozho wants to get us out of the way. He must have something good here."

"I begin to know him and all his tricks," said an old wolf. "Let us see if there is anything."

They accordingly began to search, and very soon finding the moose made away with the whole carcass. Manabozho looked on wistfully, and saw them eat till they were satisfied, when they left him nothing but bare bones. Soon after a blast of wind opened the branches and set him free. He went home, thinking to himself—

"See the effect of meddling with frivolous things when certain good is in one's possession!"

Snowflake

(Traditional German Tale)

Snowflake was a poor enchanted princess flying about the world, and seeking love. She was a beautiful child, snow-white and pretty of complexion, with eyes of heavenly blue and fair curls, and her father was a powerful king in India. When she was six years old her mother died and she got a wicked stepmother. The latter brought two daughters to the king, but they were as ugly as crows, and Snowflake looked all the lovelier by their side. This vexed the queen, who was an evil witch, and she pondered how she might ruin the pretty child who was now twelve years of age. But she had to be careful before the king, who loved Snowflake more than his own life. She might have killed the child with poison or steel, yet it seemed too risky; it might be betrayed, and she thought it safer to mar her by sorcery. One day as she bathed her and put her a clean dress on, she anointed her with some salve, moved round her very quickly, kissed and embraced her, and suddenly turned into a black fox, who licked the frightened child all over with her quick tongue, and murmured the following words:

> Snowflake, Snowflake, fly away,
> Fly through the wide world away;
> Cold to-day, to-morrow warm,
> Never rest in lover's arm;
> But who with unchanging faith
> Five years follows thee apace.

And instantly the pretty princess was turned to a snowflake; the old witch opened the window and snowflake was wafted out into the air. This happened on a cold winter's day, and the wicked stepmother called mockingly after her: "Now you may fly and shiver until eternity! It is more likely that I should become young as you, than that you will find a man who will be faithful to you for five years even in his innermost thoughts."

And the sweet little snowflake flew about in the cold wind with other snowflakes, and was cold and shivered as they, and made a plaintive noise like them. But she knew why she grieved, for she had retained her sweet warm soul, although she was outwardly so miserably changed, and even in this guise she had to fly about the wide and barren world to look for love. And the saddest things that used to happen to her were, when she chanced to alight on a pretty face, or cling to a warm breast or a hot little hand, and was shaken off unkindly or blown off, as if she brought only an unpleasant sensation of cold like other snowflakes. Thus whenever she had hoped that she might rest a little in somebody's love, she had to fly off again all through the long dreary winter, and she lay on the cold breast of frozen mountains and stones and the icy lakes, and wept and sighed for love, which she found nowhere. And as the weather grew warmer and the first little flowers raised their tiny heads and the first birds sang again, she was not allowed to remain in the beautiful air, but had to go into darkness, for old winter caught her with the other snowflakes and locked them all up in the depths and caverns of the old mountains, to lie there until he should return to the earth.

There Snowflake lay through beautiful spring and warm summer and autumn, and spent her time in longing and sadness—in longing, for all her memories had been retained; in sadness, for she doubted that she should ever meet with love. Then she whispered many melancholy sounds and uttered many sorrowful songs, which only the silent rock walls heard, and which were like an echo of her own fate. And at last winter returned and opened his gates and drove the light-winged snowflakes out into the world. And she flew among the others, but again in search of love; and light winds came and carried her along over continents and oceans. Thus she alighted in her travels on the top of cold Caucasus, and sighed and groaned pitifully in the bitter feeling of abandonment among her cold and loveless mates. And as she was here sick to death with yearning, she heard from below her in a deep ravine such painful sighs and groans, that they might have moved a stone, and instantly she flew to the spot whence the voice proceeded. There she saw underneath a leafless tree, through whose branches the winter wind howled and whistled, a youth of stately bearing and beautiful face. His coat of mail, helmet and shield lay about on the snow, his noble horse stood aside and tried to paw up the snow for some grass, his spurs lay broken by his side, his coat was torn, and in his right hand he flourished a shining sword. His hair hung unkempt about his face, and his eyes looked troubled, like some one staring into vacancy, and miserable wails fell from his lips.

In silent anguish Snowflake fell down at his feet and thought: "Alas! if the man is as sorrowful as I am, and unhappy through longing for love, he may crush me here in his despair, so that I lose life and consciousness! Such death would be sweet to me." But thus ran his wail:

"Welcome, ye places of sorrow! ye barren rocks and bare trees, you rough and dark ravine, and ye winds which rush along with the snowdrift; ye are my funeral procession, the dirge I like. Gone is my strength in which I defied the world; faded is the beauty which women and maidens have praised; my poor sick soul, starved and bled to death, here thou shalt find the rest and peace which the cold earth could not give thee. O cold earth, soon thou wilt no longer be cold, but a quiet, cool bed to the senseless dead. Come, my faithful sword, true friend and protector in many a battle and adventure! render me thy last service; pierce this heart which is already so much cut up, this poor heart to whom were given all goods and treasures, save the highest treasure, love. Oh, if this ugly thorn could love, I would embrace it, press it to my breast; aye, into my breast that it should bleed from its many thorns, and yet I would shout with exultation; yes, this cold snow I would pick up if its cold would warm to love, would fill my hands with it and carry it away as my most precious possession, and heaven and earth should hear my exulting cry, 'I am being loved! I am happy!' Even an otter or a toad I would embrace and call it my darling love, if it would love me. But no! no! never, never. Come then, my sword! come on, death! thou deliverer from all pain, and make an end to this miserable farce." And he prepared to pierce his heart.

And like lightning a thought flew through the tender soul of Snowflake. She raised herself and settled on the hand that was going to heave its last stroke. He felt a warm sensation as of something burning. And he looked into his hand and saw a snowflake lying there in its beautiful fragile form. And Snowflake, who was herself looking for a loving soul, grew warmer and burnt his hand. The man dropped his sword in wonder and looked at her, as if he understood the tender child which lay on his hand no heavier than a breath of air, and with delight he exclaimed, "What, is it she? Gracious Heaven! now I will live! And were it for eternity, I shall not find time too long!" Hearing these words, Snowflake melted with delight and became a

620

glittering drop which lay clear in his hand, like the heavenly blue eye of an angel, and seemed to implore his love.

And the man saw the sparkling drop, which glowed warm in his hand, and ran towards a tree that had still a few green leaves, picked off the freshest leaf and poured the drop into it and hid it carefully in his bosom. Then he put on his armor, swung himself on his horse, and rode at a flying pace to the nearest town.

Now I have to tell you who this man was, whence he came, and what had happened to him.

He was a noble prince, the son of the king of Arabia, the country where gold grows, and myrrh and other precious herbs. He had been born under the most miraculous circumstances, and with such incomparable beauty, that the king his father and the wise men of the land paid great attention to him from his earliest childhood; for they thought that his life would also be full of unusual events. They cast the lot, they inquired from the stars about him, they toyed with riddles and soothsayers; but the lot would not fall, the stars would not speak, the soothsayers could not explain; they all remained in the dark about his future. But they did not remain in the dark about his disposition. The prince showed from infancy an unusual tenderness and softness of heart. In his big black eyes lay so much sorrow and yearning that the old king was frightened, and would say to his wise men and counselors: "The boy will have to be brought up severely, and must always be among crowds of men, else he might become a dreamer or star-gazer, who make the worst kings; or love, the most pernicious and dangerous of all passions, might drive him altogether from the path of virtue." All the actions and movements of the prince were as gentle and tender as his little heart, and his voice sounded softly and lovely, like a summer's breeze when it plays among the spring flowers. Therefore he was named Prince Bisbiglio, which means lisping sounds.

When Prince Bisbiglio was four years of age, his father did not put him under the care of a wise man in the desert, as is the custom with Oriental kings, who fancy that in the noise of the capital and the glamor and luxury of court-life a man could hardly be brought up to, and exercised in, austere virtue; but he sent him to an old tried warrior, who, with an ever-ready armed troop, was always on the watch guarding the frontiers. There he was to be brought up a warrior, see nothing but horses and arms, hear only the clang of arms, trumpets, and clarions; know no other bed but the hard soldier's camp-bed, and no other field and pasture but the hard-trodden wrestling-places and drilling-places whereon men and horses did not allow the grass to grow.

He was to learn no arts, for the king feared arts might make him soft and disgust him with hard work, which is the best art for him who is to rule as a man over other men. In this camp the prince lived for ten years, and became a perfect warrior, practiced in all arms, a master in the managing of horses and throwing of spears; besides, he was slim and warrior-like in appearance, and strong for his age. In his fifteenth year his father bade him return to court, and rejoiced at the sight of the handsome youth and his wise bringing-up. But what availed him the latter? Whatever nature has sown in a man must shoot forth sooner or later; it is indelible like life, and can only be exterminated with life. Prince Bisbiglio had for ten years seen nothing but rough and iron men, masters of war and lances, bow and sword; he had gazed into no stars, listened not to nightingales, nor turned in merry dance. And yet there were so many stars and nightingales and dances in his soul that they would not be suppressed by all the iron noise and exercise. No; they became all the more alive in him the more they were repressed into the innermost recesses of his mind.

Bisbiglio was a child of longing and love, and amidst the hard and rude warriors his heart had unconsciously yearned for love, he had absorbed it out of every sign and glance, out of every song and story, however differently they sounded, even out of every word spoken carelessly before him; his own heart had early opened him this heaven with its stars and nightingales. Thus powerful is inborn impulse.

Bisbiglio was in the flower of his age, the time when imagination is liveliest; he longed to get out into the beautiful wide world, to explore its beauty and splendor, and he went to the king, his father, and begged to be allowed to go out as other princes do, that he might make a name through princely and knightly adventures. The king was pleased to allow it, for, thought he, he is a firm youth, grown up among iron and steel; the cooing love-doves and the flattering sirens of tenderness will not tempt him from the path of heroic deeds. But Bisbiglio's purpose differed from that of his father; he wanted no adventures but those of love, desired to ride out after love and to search for it in the wide world, until he should find that love, the highest and rarest possession which had always been in his thoughts. For in the camp on Euphrates he had often heard the tale of the Persian prince Sospirio, who had wandered over the world for twenty years in search of love, and who at last found it in the shape of a snow-white briar-rose, flowering secretly and lonely in the midst of the African desert. This was the high mysterious star towards which Bisbiglio gazed early in life, this was the sweet nightingale which sang to him even among the neighing of war-horses and the clashing of spear and shield; he had dreamt night and day of marvelous adventures, of combats with giants and dragons, of transformations and enchantments—not as knightly and royal occupations and games, no—all for love, and again for love. So he had gone out into the world, and now for four years, with pain and longing, he had been looking for love and had not found it.

Of adventures he had had enough, of combats he had had plenty, of beautiful women and maidens, princesses and queens, Amazons and sirens, of marvelous flowers and birds he had seen abundance; some he had liked and been fond of, but alas! he had not found love—the heavenly, glowing, feeling, living, singing, exulting love. He had attracted all that was beautiful and lovely, as a magnet attracts the iron; he had also been tenderly loved, but alas! after a few days, aye, sometimes after a few minutes, he had felt something was lacking, and had to ride on to find the true love he was in search of. This had again occurred a month ago. In Damascus he had seen the king's daughter, beautiful as a rose, slender as a lily, lovely as a violet in the hidden valley, and she had grown very fond of him, as he of her. And yet the unfortunate prince was compelled to ride onward, feeling hers was not the love he was searching for; and now he despaired of ever finding it, and had ridden up to the wild snow-covered mountains, to the highest top of Mount Caucasus, and there sweet Snowflake had preserved his life.

When the prince came into the town, he stopped at the house of a jeweller, bought a tiny phial cut out of pure diamond, poured his sparkling drop, his snowflake, into it, sealed it up and hid it in his bosom, saying: "Thou wilt surely become a princess some day like the briar-rose in the desert, and even if thou never become one, I shall be the happiest of men as long as I feel thy flame."

For you must know, he had wrought a little bag that' lay close to his heart, into which he put his phial, and he felt in his heart a gentle pricking, which he would not have missed for the world. So he rode on merrily through the wood. He had a foreboding that the drop would be transformed and could not remain thus; he also knew that he must not ride home before the fate was fulfilled. And Snowflake was as a tiny drop in the diamond phial, and was overjoyed, for she felt herself beloved; yet she often trembled at the thought— five years! how long, five years! Will he stand the test? It is sweet to rest on his heart, but how much sweeter would it be to embrace him and press him to my heart! And she trembled with delight at the prospect, and at the same time with fear that she might lose him.

For three years Prince Bisbiglio rode through the world with her, and they passed to him like three days. Then came the time of severe tests which he had to undergo before her fate could be fulfilled. And this was the first of them:

He rode past a house burning in bright flame. Then he doubted in himself: if she, who is my love, were human, instead of being a liquid drop, and I lay in the flame, would she jump into it and save me? And hardly had he conceived the wicked thought, when he felt the phial with irresistible strength tear his shirt and coat and burst his iron armor. And quick as lightning it threw itself into the fire; he saw the phial bursting, and the pure drop wept and sighed in the fiery trouble and soon only looked like a duller flame than the others. Then an unspeakable anguish seized his soul, he vaulted from his horse and into the fire, seized the small flame and hid it in his hand. And it burned a deep wound into his hand, and then resolved itself again into a drop. But he hurried to the nearest town and purchased another diamond phial in which he confined it and laid it in its old place. His hair had got scorched in the fire, his cheeks burnt, and the wound in his hand was very deep. And he suffered great pain and lay ill for three weeks before he recovered. Then he grieved at his want of faith, but Snowflake was full of joy that he had so faithfully jumped into the fire for her, yet she wept inwardly to see him suffer so much pain. And he was well aware of it, for he fancied often he heard a groaning in the phial, although in reality he heard nothing.

Then came the second trial:

He rode over a high bridge which crosses a rapid stream, called Tigris. From there he saw the nest of a halcyon (or kingfisher) floating on the stream, and the female sat on the nest, feeding her young. And deeply moved by this sight, he said: "Oh, what love! Are men ever so faithful? Truly, if the current swallowed this little brood, the mother would dive after them and save them or die herself." And Snowflake felt his heart's thought, and in her anguish of soul she burst again through coat and armor and the phial dashed against a stone, and the drop poured itself into the stream and hissed as if one pours hot water into cold, and away it was carried by the rapid current. Quick as lightning the prince dashed into the stream and struggled with current and whirlpool, dived up and down and wrestled with death and life and filled his hands again and again with water, until he had found the gently hissing drop, which he now felt as a burning coal in his hand. Then he swam to the bank and sank down exhausted, but the little drop again burnt a wound in his hand. When he recovered his senses, he felt bruised all over from the rocks he had knocked against and the burn in his hand smarted, but his soul exulted in delight. And Snowflake was also exulting at this proof of his valiant faithfulness. In the nearest town he got another phial, confined his drop in it, laid it on his heart, and rode on.

Now came the third and last trial:

One morning as the prince was riding through a thick and high mountain-forest, he perceived a gigantic rider who rode on a white charger and was so tall that his head towered above the tops of the oaks and beeches. He carried a lance which wavered like a ship's mast in the air, and lowered it when he saw the prince. This giant carried an ugly wrinkled old woman behind him on a pillion, who clung to him with her bony arms. He carried her along against his wishes, in consequence of a vow he had taken, but meant to rid himself of her by bestowing her on the first comer. Thus, when he saw Bisbiglio, he called with a voice to make all the hill-tops and ravines echo as if a hundred thunderstorms had let off all the heavenly guns, "Stop, my boy; I have here something for you. You are young and can do with a sweetheart, which is rather an inconvenience to a man of my years. Take this lady on your horse and swear to me that you will give her knightly treatment and fight anybody you meet who will not acknowledge her to be the handsomest princess whom the sun has ever shone upon. On this condition I will let you pass scot free, otherwise your mother will soon have to bury a dead son."

"As long as a warm drop of blood is in my body that will never happen," cried Bisbiglio, burning with rage. "Beware, you braggart! for I will fight you!" With these words he jumped off his horse and let it run away; for he well perceived that he could not attack the giant and his colossal steed on horseback, but that skill and suppleness would have to be his arms against the latter's superior strength.

And the giant, who felt ashamed to be less brave than the youth, jumped also from his horse. They threw their lances away and took to their swords.

And now took place a finer and rarer combat than was ever seen in the lists. The ground trembled when the giant moved a foot, and it seemed as if the rocks must break under his blows. Lightly as on the wings of the wind the prince moved about, and skillfully evaded each stroke and blow, owing to the slow heaviness of the giant. Thus they had fought a long time, and the giant's blood oozed out of many a wound, but they were not deep wounds. The prince was still unhurt, and played nimbly with his light weapon about the monster. When the giant saw his own blood flow, he grew furious in his soul, and called out, "Enough of this; or, rather, too much! No longer shall the mouse play with the lion!" And he lifted his arm to strike a terrible blow with which he meant to cut the prince in two like a turnip. Yet his sword slipped off the helmet, but caught on the shield and coat of mail, and the prince felt the point of the iron touch his heart. In this extremity he gathered his last strength and drove his sword to its entire length into the giant's breast, so that the big warrior fell down swearing and groaning.

You may imagine Snowflake's anxiety during this terrible contest, and how she shivered and trembled in her phial when the giant rattled with his weapons and when she heard his blows whistling through the air. But when she saw the red blood stream down over the prince's armor, she could no longer contain herself in her prison; she burst her phial and mingled with the purple stream of blood on the ground. And, oh, marvel and miracle! the moment she was surrounded by the prince's blood, there stood the most beautiful maiden. Snowflake had returned to human shape and figure.

The prince was so exhausted from the fight and loss of blood that he swooned away. Snowflake threw herself down beside him with a thousand tears, opened his coat of mail, and dried the blood in his wound with her beautiful long curls; she wept over him as over a dead man. But as she wept and wailed, he opened his eyes and breathed again, and saw his sweet darling, for whose sake he had traveled so many years over the world. And at the sight of her, new strength seemed to rush through his veins; he felt regenerated, and no longer noticed his wound nor how the blood streamed down, but only saw the lovely Snowflake, and embraced her and kissed her. But she cut up some of her dress and laid it on his wound, and the blood was stanched. The wound was deep, but not deadly, which it might easily have been if slightly deeper, for the giant had hit him near the heart.

But the monster lay there dead, never to rise again. They looked at his huge lance and his heavy armor, which no ordinary mortal could have lifted, and there they let him lie; the ugly old woman, on whose account the terrible fight arose, they allowed to go in peace whither she liked. As a memorial of this fight with the giant, the prince only took the big white horse on which the monster rode, and his sword, but as they lifted the sword from the ground and looked at it they saw a new wonder: the point had melted like iron when a smith lays it into a hot fire to soften it. When Snowflake saw that, her eyes sparkled with delight, and tears streamed down her cheeks, and she pressed the prince to her heart with great warmth and said: "O you most faithful soul, with unconquerable love, your heart is so hot with love that it has melted the giant's iron! Do I now own this warm heart of which I dreamt in bitter sorrow during my enchantment? Now I see that everything is fulfilled which my stepmother, the evil witch, murmured when she made me fly out of the window." And she related to the prince the history of her transformation, and how she had miserably flown about for two winters as a snowflake, until in his hand she melted to a drop of water.

The day of the combat with the giant happened just to be the last day of the fifth year since Snowflake met with the despairing Bisbiglio in the barren ravine of the Caucasus. And as both saw that their fate was fulfilled, and as they were longing to crown their true and incomparable love by a wedding, they rode no further after adventures—for the last five years had been the very prettiest adventure—but they took the straightest road to the castle in which lived the old king of Araby, Bisbiglio's father. And they arrived there safely, and the prince duly told his father everything that had happened to him. And the old gentleman saw now that the wisdom he fancied he had shown in the education of his son was not very successful, but he did not grumble at his adventures, as he brought such a beautiful daughter into his house; for Snowflake was so handsome and lovely that she pleased not only him and all men, but also the angels in heaven. And when he had given sufficient scope to his delight, and the wedding had been celebrated, Bisbiglio and his Snowflake traveled to the old king in India. And Snowflake related to him all her story: how the stepmother had changed herself into a fox, and sung, "Snowflake, Snowflake, fly away!" and how she had become a snowflake and been let out of the window, and had lived seven sad years under the enchantment. And the king grew furious and had the old witch punished by death; and he disowned her ugly daughters, and sent them up into the hills of India, and had them married to low-born men. But Snowflake became Queen of India after his death, and thus India and Araby were joined in one empire. But never in the world did one see a more tender and faithful couple than the faithful Bisbiglio and his sweet Snowflake; so that their love and faith is to this day told of in fable and song through all the Orient. They also had the prettiest and loveliest children, who had hearts to enjoy the gracefulness and beauty of heaven and earth and who were equal to their parents in kindness and goodness.

The Springtide of Love

PLEYDELL NORTH

The mists of the early twilight were falling, and Elsa, the little girl who lived at the woodman's cottage, was still far from home. She had wandered out in the spring sunshine in search of the bluebells and wild anemones with which the wood abounded, for the child loved the company of the birds and flowers better than the rough play of the boys who were called her brothers.

The woodman and his wife said she was strange and dreamy, full of curious fancies which they found it hard to understand; but, then, they were not Elsa's real parents, which might account for their difficulty. They were kind to her, however, in their fashion, and Elsa always tried to remember to obey them; but sometimes she forgot. She had forgotten to-day—for although the good wife had told her to remain near the cottage, the eagerness of her search for the flowers she loved had led her farther into the wood than she had ever been before.

The sunlight disappeared, and the darkness seemed to come quite suddenly under the thick branches of the trees; the birds had chanted their last evening song and gone to their nests—only a solitary thrush sang loudly just overhead; Elsa thought it was warning her to hurry homewards. She turned quickly, taking as she thought the direction of the cottage; but as she was barely seven years old, and felt a little frightened, it is not surprising that she only plunged deeper into the wood.

Now she found herself in the midst of a great silence; the beautiful tracery of young green leaves through which she had hitherto caught glimpses of the sky had disappeared, and over her head stretched only bare brown branches, between which she saw the shining stars, clear as on a frosty winter's night. The stars looked friendly, and she was glad to see them, but it was growing dreadfully cold. The plucked flowers withered and fell from her poor little numbed hands, and she shivered in her thin cotton frock.

Ah! what would she not have given for a sight of the open door and the fire in the woodman's cottage, and a basin of warm bread and milk, even though it was given with a scolding from the woodman's wife! She struggled on, with her poor little tired feet, for it seemed to her that the wood was growing thinner—perhaps there might be a house hereabouts.

But, oh! how terribly cold. Now there was frost upon the ground at her feet, frost upon dead leaves and blades of grass, frost upon the bare tree branches. The moon had risen, and she could see that all the world around her was white and chill and dead. Surely she had wandered back into the cruel bitter winter, frost-bound and hard.

It was strange that she had strength to go on, but she looked up at the stars, and thought that they were guiding her. At length she came to the border of the wood, and there stretched before her a wide, open space, with only a few trees scattered here and there, and through an opening of the trees the cold moon shone down upon a white, silent house.

The house looked as dead and winter-bound as everything else; but still it was a house, and Elsa said to herself that surely some one must live in it. So she thanked the friendly stars for leading her aright, and with what remaining strength she had, dragged her poor little numbed feet up the broad path or road between the trees. At the end of the road an iron gate hung open upon its hinges, and Elsa found herself in what once had been a garden. Now the lawns and flower-beds were all alike one blinding sheet of ice and frozen snow.

But, oh, joy! there was the great white house, and from one window shone a light, surely the light of a fire. All the rest was dark. Up a flight of stone steps the child dragged her weary feet, across a terrace that had surely once been gay with flowers, until she stood before a huge door, brown and black, except where the frost gleamed, closed and barred with iron bars. The great knocker hung high above her reach; but with her poor little hands she beat against the woodwork. Surely, if some one did not let her in soon, she must fall down there and sleep and die upon the step. But at the sound of her faint knocking there came from within the deep baying of a hound, and Elsa was terrified anew, but could not run away; then in a few moments a heavy bar seemed to be withdrawn and the great door opened slowly.

A tall man stood within—a man in the dress of a hunter, pale-faced in the moonlight, but strong and powerful, and wearing a long, dark beard that reached almost to his waist. His was a figure to fill any child with fear, but Elsa saw only the scene behind him. A great blazing wood fire upon an open hearth, with rugs in front of it upon which were stretched two large hounds; a third, shaking himself slowly, had followed his master to the door. Elsa stretched out her little hands to the blazing warmth, with the cry of a perishing child.

"Take me in—oh! take me in!" she pleaded. "Please let me come in!"

She ran forward. Then with a strange hoarse sound, that she did not understand, the man stooped and lifted her in his arms, and carried her forward and laid her gently down upon the rugs in the grateful warmth, and the hounds sniffed round her and seemed well pleased, and ready to welcome her—and—for a little while she remembered no more.

When Elsa came to herself (she thought she must have been asleep, but the waking was a little strange and difficult) she found that she was propped up among soft cushions still upon the rugs; the dogs now lay at a respectful distance, each with his forepaws stretched out and his nose held between them, while with gleaming eyes he watched with keenest interest all that going was on.

The rough-looking man with the long, dark beard and the pale face knelt beside her, holding a basin of warm, steaming broth. Then Elsa sat up and tried to drink, but she was so weak with fatigue and cold that her new friend was obliged to feed her with a spoon, which he did rather awkwardly. After she had swallowed the broth, the warm blood flowed once more freely through her veins, and she sank into a deep, sweet sleep, her little head falling serenely against the stranger's breast and her hair spreading out in golden waves over the arm that held her.

When Elsa once more opened her eyes, the cold gray light of morning fell through the uncurtained windows into the hall. She found herself lying on a couch covered with rugs of warm fur, at the side of the hearth, where logs of pine wood, newly kindled, leapt and blazed, filling the air with sweet, pungent odors.

For a while she was bewildered, wondering how she came to be there, instead of in her little room at the woodman's cottage. Then she saw her friend of the night before kneeling in front of the fire, evidently preparing food, while the dogs, grouped around, sat on their haunches with ears erect, keen and observant, watching his movements. Then Elsa remembered; and she clapped her hands with a merry laugh, the laugh of a happy, waking child. The man kneeling by the fire started at the sound, and then turned his grave face towards her with a wistful expression strange to see.

"I want to get up," said Elsa promptly. "If you please, I can wash and dress myself; I've been taught how."

"Wait a few minutes, little lady, then you shall have all you want."

The voice sounded strangely, and the man seemed listening to its tones as though surprised to hear himself speak. But the rough, halting accents seemed less out of keeping with the old house than Elsa's laugh. The dogs came and licked her hands, and she played with them until the man rose from his place before the fire, and lifting her up bade her come with him.

He led her to a small room off the hall, which was indeed curious in its arrangements. A toilet-table stood there with most costly fittings; brushes with silver and ivory handles were lying upon the faded silk; a little pair of satin shoes had been thrown carelessly upon the floor; a cloak of crimson satin was flung over a chair. All these things looked as though a hand had cast them aside but yesterday—yet all were faded and soiled, and the dust lay thick as though that yesterday had been many years ago.

And among these relics of an unknown past the child made her simple toilet. She had never seen such magnificence, or felt, she thought, so sad. But when she returned to the hall ten minutes later, the sadness was forgotten.

She looked a quaint little figure, indeed, clad in a silken wrapper provided by her host, which trailed far behind on the ground, greatly to her delight; her little feet were cased in dainty slippers which, small as they were, yet were many sizes too large. In spite of misfits, however, she contrived to walk with a stately grandeur quite amazing to behold, until the dogs jumped and fawned upon her, when she forgot her finery in a game of play and lost her slippers in the rug.

On the table, a breakfast was rudely spread: cold meats for the master of the house, who fed his dogs from his own plate, while for Elsa was provided a bowl of goat's milk and some crisp cakes, which she thought delicious.

When the meal was over, Elsa pleaded to be allowed to do for her new friend the household duties she had been taught to fulfil by the woodman's wife; and soon, with the wrapper deftly pinned about her waist, and the silken sleeves tucked up from bare and dimpled arms, she stood before a bowl of steaming water, washing plates and dishes. Only the table was rather high, and she was forced to stand upon a stool.

From that day a strange new life began for little Elsa.

The rough-looking man who had given her shelter seemed to be living quite alone with his dogs. Every morning he went out with them and his gun, apparently to hunt and shoot in the forest, for he usually returned laden with game, which served to keep the larder stocked.

Of other kinds of provisions there seemed to be a plentiful supply on the premises; the granaries were well stocked with corn, which the master ground himself, while some goats tethered in the outhouses gave a sufficient quantity of milk for the daily needs of the little household.

Of Elsa's return to the woodman's cottage there seemed to be no question. She was terrified at the thought of being again lost in the wood, and pleaded hard to remain with her new friend, who, on his side, was equally loth to part with her.

Soon, having learned many useful ways from the woodman's wife, she became a clever little housekeeper, and could make a good stew, while Ulric, as the master of the house bade her call him, was out with his dogs in the forest, though now only two of the hounds accompanied him in his expeditions; one was always left as Elsa's companion and guardian. Then, too, she could milk and feed the goats, and keep the house-place clean and tidy. But all the day was not given to such work as this.

When Ulric had returned, and they had dined together, he would bring the great carved wooden chair with the huge back up to the fire, and Elsa would fetch a stool to his side and busy herself with needle and thread, while he told her strange stories; or sometimes he would fetch a ponderous volume from a library the house contained and read, either to himself or aloud to her, such things as she could understand.

Now, if you wonder where Elsa found the needle and thread which I have mentioned, I must tell you that Ulric had given her a little work-basket neatly fitted, but the silk lining of which was much faded, and some of the needles were rusty. There was in it also a golden thimble, which Elsa found a little too large.

And as for the clothes she worked at, one day he brought her a quantity of beautiful garments, some of silk and satin, and some of fine cloth, and in these, having nothing of her own but her one poor little cotton frock, the child managed to dress herself, till she looked like a quaint little fairy princess. Her stitches were awkward and badly done at first, but as time went on, instinct helped her small knowledge, and she grew handy with her needle.

When she was cooking and feeding the goats, she wore a woollen petticoat and an apron, a costume more suited to the occasion.

In the evenings Ulric taught her many things: to read and to write, and even to speak in strange languages, so that her education was by no means neglected. He let her wander over the great mansion where she would, and showed her many of the rooms himself. All bore signs of having been used quite recently, and yet a long time ago. Dust was thick everywhere, and soon Elsa grew to understand that the dust must remain and accumulate; no hand was to be allowed to touch anything in that strange, silent house beyond the hall and the little room which Ulric had arranged for her sleeping apartment. One part of the mansion, however, she never penetrated. At the end of a long passage hung a heavy velvet curtain, and behind this was a door, always securely locked. Only Ulric passed beyond it, at stated times, and when he returned from these visits he was more than usually sad for many hours.

The weeks slipped into months, and Elsa dwelt on in this strange home. Every day at first she looked eagerly for the breaking of the frost—for the promise of the sunshine and flowers she had left behind her in the wood. But the spring never came. The bitter cold and the frost continued, and in time the child's heart must have frozen too, but for the strong, warm love which had sprung up within it for Ulric.

Old and thoughtful she grew, beyond her years, but never unhappy. Ulric needed her, was glad of her presence; she could minister to his wants and brighten his sad life.

So Ulric's love grew more to her than the flowers and sunshine of the outer world; to think of leaving him now would break her heart, but she wondered often over the mystery that shadowed his life and hers. And the months grew to years, and Elsa was twelve years old.

Then one evening Ulric came in from one of his visits to the closed chamber, more sad and thoughtful even than usual, and taking Elsa's hand in his, bade her sit beside him for a little while and put aside her work. She came obediently, looking anxiously into his face.

"Little Elsa," he said, "I have counted the time, and it is now five years since you came to me. You told me then you were seven years old, now you are therefore twelve, and will soon be growing into a maiden. The time has come—"

Instinctively the child clasped his hand closer.

"Not to part us, father?" (for so she had learned to call him.)

"That, my child, must rest with you."

"Then it is soon settled," said Elsa, trying to laugh, "for I will never leave you."

Something like the light of hope shone in the man's clouded eyes—eyes in which Elsa had never seen a smile, although his lips had smiled at her often.

"Listen," he said; "before you speak rash words, I must tell you all. Then you shall decide.

"It is a little more than eleven years since the curse fell upon me. I was a hard man then, Elsa—hard and cruel and strong—it was my boast that I never forgave a debt, or pardoned an enemy.

"I had married a young and beautiful wife, and her I loved passionately, but in my own hard and selfish fashion. Often I refused to heed even her gentle pleadings for the suffering, the sinful, and the poor. And we had one child—a girl—then only a few months old.

"It was a New Year's Eve that I decided upon giving a great entertainment to all the country round. I did it for my own glorification. Among the rich I was disliked, but tolerated on account of my position; by the poor far and wide I was feared and hated.

"Every one invited came to my ball. My wife looked exquisitely lovely, more lovely I thought than on our bridal day—everything ministered to my pride and satisfaction.

"We had mustered here, here in this hall, to drink the health of the dying year and welcome the incoming of the new, when above the sounds of laughter and good cheer was heard from without a pitiful, feeble wail—the wail of a child in pain. That feeble cry rang then above every other sound—it rings in my heart still.

"Before I could interfere, my wife, with her own hands, had flung wide the great barred door, and I saw a sight which I alone could explain.

"Upon the step was huddled a woman, with a child in her arms. A man, gaunt and hunger-stricken, towered behind her in the darkness; two other children clung to her, shivering and weeping. We were in the midst of the cruel, bitter winter; the earth was frost-bound, hard and cold, even as now. That day I had given orders that these people, poor and starving as they were, should be turned from their home. The man I had suspected of being a poacher, and he was doing no work—a good-for-nothing—but she, my wife, had pleaded for them that I would wait, at least, until the summer. Now she bent down to that poor creature on the step, who was striving to nurse and warm her babe in her chill arms, and whispered something—I guessed it was a promise of shelter.

"In my fierce pride and anger I laid my hand upon her arm, and with a strong grip drew her back—then without a word I closed the door and barred it. But within there was no more laughter. A voice rose upon the still night air—the sound of a bitter curse—a curse that should rest upon me and mine, the chill of winter and of death, of pitiless desolation and remorse, until human love should win me back to human pity and God's forgiveness.

"One by one, with cold good-nights, my guests departed. My wife stole away to her own apartments without a word; upon her arm I saw the mark of my cruel hand.

"In the morning the curse had fallen. The woman I had turned away had been found at my gates, dead, her child still clasped to her breast.

"The servants fled and left me alone, taking with them our child; my wife—that night—she, too—died—to me."

The man's head drooped upon his hands. For a moment there was silence in the hall.

Elsa stood—her child's heart grieved at the terrible story, her whole nature sorrowing, pitiful, shocked.

Presently Ulric recovered himself and continued: "Now, Elsa, you know all. My child, if you will return to the world and leave me to work out my fate, you shall not go penniless. I have wealth. For your sake I will venture once more among the haunts of men and see you placed in a safe home, then—I will try to forget. It is right that you should shrink."

"Father, dear father, I love you—you are sorry—I will not leave you—do not send me away."

A look almost of rapture changed the worn and tear-stained face of the man who had owned his sin—and the child's arms closed once more around his neck, and her golden head nestled to his breast. A few minutes later he led her to the closed chamber. Together they passed beyond it, and Elsa found herself standing in a richly furnished room.

Near a window was a couch covered with dark velvet, and upon the couch a figure lay stretched as if in quiet, death-like sleep, or carved in marble. The figure was that of a young and very fair woman. Her dress of white satin had yellowed with time; her hands were clasped upon her breast as though in prayer; her golden hair lay unbound upon the pillow.

"It is fitting now," said Ulric, "that you should come here."

Softly Elsa advanced. She stood beside the couch, gazing down upon the still, white face, so sweet in its settled grief, but which in this long silence seemed to have lost its first youth. Elsa bent lower, lower. What new instinct filled her warm, young heart, and made her speak?

"Mother, awake!" she said. "Mother!" and kissed the cold, quiet lips.

Was it a ray of sunlight that stole through the open window and trembled upon the mouth, curving it into a smile? Slowly the dark eyes opened and rested with a look of ineffable love upon Elsa's face.

And so the curse and the shadows of eternal winter passed away from the house of Ulric, and his young bride came back from her long slumber. In due time the garden, too, awoke to the touch of spring, and the flowers bloomed, and the birds mated once more and sang in budding trees, and the sun shone. And Elsa's love bound closely together the hearts of her father and mother; for perhaps you have been clever enough to find out that the woodman's wife was the nurse who had carried away with her in her flight Ulric's little daughter on the night of the New Year's ball.

The Forest Trees

(TRADITIONAL SWEDISH TALE)

Summer was over. The mists began to exhale from the marshes, and the autumn wind swept over field and forest. The birds sought shelter among the branches or flew to warmer climes, for they knew that a cold and severe time was coming.

Out in the forest sat a little bird on a branch; he could not fly away, because his wings were wounded. He beseeched the birch: "Dear birch, let me hide myself among your green leaves, because the autumn wind blows so cold, so cold!"

But the birch answered: "That you cannot do, because you might injure my buds, and ruin my fine attire; away with you!"

So the little creature, shivering with cold, hopped to the strong oak and begged:

"Dear oak, let me hide among your green branches and leaves, because I shiver so much, so much!"

But the oak answered: "Away with you! You might steal some of my acorns, and soil my spotless garments. You cannot stay with me!"

Then the poor bird hopped to the willow beside the brook and said: "Kind willow, let me creep in among your leaves or I shall die of cold."

But the willow answered: "I do not know you, and besides, I am afraid for my garments. What would the other trees think if they should see me conversing with one so poor and wretched looking as you?"

Thus the little bird went to all the leafy trees in the forest and begged for shelter, but none would protect him, and he came near dying with cold. At last he came to the place where the spruce, pine and juniper stood, but he could not speak then, for he was nearly frozen.

When the spruce caught sight of the poor little thing it said: "Come here to me, you poor little bird, and you shall warm yourself! Come under my branches, they are soft and warm!"

The pine said: "I have not such thick branches as my sister, the spruce, but I shall stand here and defy the north wind, so that he cannot harm you, poor little bird! "

And the pine stretched out its tall limbs and helped the spruce to protect the forlorn little one.

The juniper said: "I am small and humble, but when you are hungry, come to me, because I have good, soft berries, and you shall have them so freely, so freely! "

And thus the wounded bird received food and shelter from the warm-hearted trees.

But night came on with frost and storm, and in the morning the leaf trees' green attire lay on the ground, ruined, and the autumn wind shook their naked branches; but the evergreen trees that had shown kindness and given shelter to the poor defenseless little bird, stood there just as green and beautiful as ever. For no winter cold could rob them of their magnificent robes.

The History of a Nutcracker

ALEXANDRE DUMAS

Preface

There was a juvenile party at the house of my friend Lord M—; and I had helped to add to the number and noise of the company by taking my little daughter.

It is true that in half an hour, during which I joined in four or five games of blind-man's buff, hot cockles, and hunt the slipper—in spite of the noise which was made by a couple of dozen delightful little rogues from eight to ten years old, and who seemed to try which would talk the loudest—I slipt out of the drawing-room, and sought a certain snug parlor which I knew, and where I hoped to enjoy a little peace for an hour or so.

I had effected my retreat with as much skill as success, escaping not only without being perceived by the juvenile guests, which was not very difficult, considering how intent they were upon their games, but also unnoticed by their parents, which was not so easy a matter. I had reached the wished-for parlor, when I observed, on entering it, that it was for the moment converted into a supper-room, the side boards being heaped up with confectionary and other refreshments. Now as these appearances seemed to promise that I should not be disturbed until supper-time, I threw myself into a comfortable arm-chair, quite delighted with the idea that I was about to enjoy an hour's peace after the dreadful noise which had deafened me in the drawing-room.

I don't know exactly how it was, but at the end of about ten minutes I fell fast asleep.

I cannot say how long I had thus lost all knowledge of what was passing around, when I was suddenly aroused by loud peals of laughter. I opened my eyes in terror, and saw nothing but the beautifully-painted ceiling over my head. Then I tried to get up; but the attempt was useless, for I was fastened to my chair as firmly as Gulliver was on the shore of Lilliput.

I immediately understood in what a scrape I had got myself: I had been surprised in the enemy's country, and was a prisoner of war.

The best thing for me to do in such a case was to put a good face upon the matter, and treat for my liberty.

My first proposal was to take my conquerors the very next morning to Farrance's, and treat them to anything they liked; but, unhappily, the moment was not well chosen for such an offer: I was addressing myself to an audience already well stuffed with tarts, and whose hands were filled with patties.

My proposal was therefore refused in plain terms.

I then offered to take the entire party to Vauxhall next evening, and amuse them with the exhibition of fire-works.

The proposal was well-received by the little boys; but the little girls would not listen to it, because they were dreadfully afraid of fire-works: they could not endure the noise of the crackers, and the smell of the gunpowder annoyed them.

I was about to make a third offer, when I heard a sweet little musical voice whispering in the ears of a companion certain words which made me tremble: "Ask papa, who writes novels, to tell us some pretty story."

I was on the point of protesting against this; but my voice was drowned by cries of "Oh! yes, a story—we will have a story!"

"But, my dear children," I said, as loud as I could, "you ask me the most difficult thing in the world. A story indeed! Ask me to recite one of Gay's fables, or *My Name is Norval,* if you will; and I may consent. But a story!"

"We don't want anything out of the *Speaker,*" cried the children altogether: "we want a story!"

"My dear little friends, if—"

"There is no *if* in the cause: we will have a story!"

"But, my dear little friends, I say again—"

"There is no *but*: we will have a story!"

"Yes: we will have a story! we will have a story!" now echoed on all sides, and in a manner which was too positive to object to any longer.

"Well," I said with a sign: "if you must, you must."

"Ah! that's capital," cried my little tormentors.

"But I must tell you one thing," said I: "the story I am about to relate is not my own."

"Never mind that, so long as it amuses us."

I must confess that I was a little vexed to think that my audience set so light a value upon my own writings.

"Whose tale is it, then, sir!" asked a pretty voice, belonging, no doubt, to some little being more curious than the others.

"It is by Hoffmann, miss. Have you ever heard of Hoffmann?"

"No, sir; I never heard of him."

"And what is the name of your story, sir?" asked a young gentleman, who, being the son of the nobleman that gave the party, felt a right to question me.

"*The History of a Nutcracker,*" was my answer. Does the title please you, my dear Henry?"

"Hem! I don't think the title promises anything particularly fine. But, never mind; go on! If it does not please us, we will stop you, and you must begin another; and so on, I can tell you, until you really do fix upon a good one."

"One moment!" I exclaimed. "I will not accept those conditions. If you were grown-up persons, well and good!"

"Nevertheless, those are our conditions: if not, a prisoner you must remain with us for ever."

"My dear Henry, you are a charming boy—well brought up—and I shall be much surprised if you do not some day become Prime Minister of England. Let me go free, and I will do all you ask."

"On your word of honor?"

"On my word of honor."

At the same moment I felt the thousand threads that held me suddenly become loose: each of the little tormentors had set to work to untie a knot; and in half a minute I was at liberty.

Now as every one must keep his word, even when it is pledged to children, I desired my audience to sit round me; and when the children had all placed themselves in a manner so comfortable that I fancied they would soon fall off to sleep in their chairs, I began my story in the following manner.

Godfather Drosselmayer

Once upon a time there lived at Nuremberg, in Germany, a judge of great respectability, and who was called Judge Silberhaus, which means "silver-house."

This judge had a son and daughter. The son was nine years old, and was named Fritz: the daughter, who was seven and a half, was called Mary.

They were two beautiful children; but so different in disposition and features, that no one would have believed them to be brother and sister.

Fritz was a fine stout boy with ruddy cheeks and roguish looks. He was very impatient, and stamped on the floor whenever he was contradicted; for he thought that everything in the world had been made for his amusement, or to suit his fancy. In this humor he would remain until the judge, annoyed by his cries and screams, or by his stamping, came out of his study, and, raising his fore-finger, said with a frown, "Master Fritz!"

These two words were quite sufficient to make Master Fritz wish that the earth would open and swallow him up.

As for his mother, it was no matter how much or how often she raised her fore-finger; for Fritz did not mind her at all.

His sister Mary was, on the contrary, a delicate and pale child, with long hair curling naturally, and flowing over her little white shoulders like a flood of golden light upon a vase of alabaster. She was sweet, amiable, bashful, and kind to all who were in sorrow, even to her dolls: she was very obedient to her mamma, and never contradicted her governess, Miss Trudchen; so that Mary was beloved by every one.

Now, the 24th of December, 17—, had arrived. You all know, my dear young friends, that the 24th of December is called Christmas Eve, being the day before the one on which the Redeemer Jesus was born.

But I must now explain something to you. You have all heard, perhaps, that every country has its peculiar customs; and the best read amongst you are aware that Nuremberg, in Germany, is a town famous for its toys, puppets, and playthings, of which it exports great quantities to other countries. You will admit, therefore, that the little boys and girls of Nuremberg ought to be the happiest children in the world, unless, indeed, they are like the inhabitants of Ostend, who seem only to delight in their oysters for the purpose of sending them to foreign markets. Germany, being quite a different country from England, has altogether other customs. In England, New Year's Day is the grand day for making presents, so that many parents would be very glad if the year always commenced with the 2nd of January.

But in Germany the great day for presents is the 24th of December, the one preceding Christmas Day. Moreover, in Germany, children's presents are given in a peculiar way. A large shrub is placed upon a table in the drawing-room; and to all its branches are hung the toys to be distributed among the children. Such play-things as are too heavy to hang to the shrub, are placed on the table; and the children are then told that it is their guardian angel who sends them all those pretty toys. This is a very innocent deception, after all; and perhaps it can scarcely be called a deception, because all the good things of this world are sent to us by heaven.

I need scarcely tell you that among those children of Nuremberg who received most presents were the son and daughter of Judge Silberhaus; for besides their father and mother, who doted on them, they also had a god-father who loved them dearly, and whose name was Drosselmayer.

I must describe in a few words the portrait of this illustrious person, who occupied in the town of Nuremberg a position almost as high as that of Judge Silberhaus himself.

Godfather Drosselmayer, who was a great physician and doctor of medicine, was by no means a very good-looking person. He was a tall thin man, about six feet high, but who stooped very much, so that, in spite of the length of his legs, he could almost pick up his handkerchief, if it fell, without stooping any lower. His face was wrinkled as a golden rennet that has withered and fallen from the tree. Being blind of the right eye, he wore a black patch; and, being entirely bald, he wore a shining and frizzled wig, which he had made himself with spun glass, such as you may have seen the glass-blowers spin at the Adelaide Gallery or Polytechnic Institution. He was, however, compelled, for fear of damaging this ingenious contrivance, to carry his hat under his arm. His remaining eye was sparkling and bright, and seemed not only to perform its own duty, but that of its absent companion, so rapidly did it glance round any room which Godfather Drosselmayer was desirous to scrutinize in all points, or fix upon any person whose secret thoughts he wished to read.

Now, Godfather Drosselmayer, who was a learned doctor, did not follow the example of those physicians who allow their patients to die, but occupied his time in giving life to dead things: I mean that, by studying the formation of men and animals, he had gained so deep a knowledge of the manner in which they are made, that he was able to manufacture men who could walk, bow to each other, and go through their exercises with a musket. He also made ladies who danced, and played upon the harpsichord, the harp, and the viol; dogs that ran, carried, and barked; birds that flew, hopped, and sang; and fish that swam, and ate crumbs of bread. He had even succeeded in making puppets and images of Punch utter a few words—not many, it is true, but such as "papa," "mamma," &c. The tones were certainly harsh, and always the same in sound; because you can very well understand that all this was done merely by means of machinery concealed inside the toys; and no machinery can ever perform the same wonders as the beings which God has created.

Nevertheless, in spit of all difficulties, Godfather Drosselmayer did not despair of being some day able to make real men, real women, real dogs, real birds, and real fish. It is scarcely necessary to add that his two godchildren, to whom he had promised the first proofs of his success in this line, awaited the happy moment with great impatience.

Godfather Drosselmayer, having reached this state of perfection in mechanical science, was a most useful man to his friends. Thus, for instance, if a time-piece at the house of Judge Silberhaus got out of order, in spite of the attentions of the usual clock-makers—if the hands suddenly stopped—if the tick-tick seemed to go badly—or if the wheels inside would not move— Godfather Drosselmayer was immediately sent for; and he hastened to the house as quick as he could, for he was a man devoted to the art of mechanics. He was no sooner shown the poor clock, than he instantly opened it, took out the works, and placed them between his knees. Then, with his eye glittering like a carbuncle, and his wig laid upon the floor, he drew from his pocket a number of little tools which he had made himself, and the proper use of which he alone knew. Choosing the most pointed one, he plunged it into the very midst of the works, to the great alarm of little Mary, who could not believe that the poor clock did not suffer from the operation. But in a short time when the old gentleman had touched the works in various parts, and placed them again in their case, or on their stand, or between the four pillars of the time-piece, as the case might be, the clock soon began to revive, to tick as loud as ever, and to strike with its shrill clear voice at the proper time; a circumstance that gave new life, as it were, to the room itself, which without it seemed a melancholy place.

Moreover, in compliance with the wishes of little Mary, who was grieved to see the kitchen dog turning the spit, Godfather Drosselmayer made a wooden dog, which by means of mechanism connected inside, turned the spit without annoyance to itself. Turk, who had done this duty for three years, until he had become quite shaky all over, was now able to lie down in peace in front of the kitchen fire, and amuse himself by watching the movements of his successor.

Thus, after the judge, after the judge's wife, after Fritz, and after Mary, the dog Turk was certainly the next inmate of the house who had most reason to love and respect Godfather Drosselmayer. Turk was indeed grateful, and showed his joy, whenever Drosselmayer drew near the house, by leaping up against the front door and wagging his tail, even before the old gentleman had knocked.

On the evening of the 24th of December, just as the twilight was approaching, Fritz and Mary, who had not been allowed to enter the drawing-room all day, were huddled together in a corner of the dining-parlor. Miss Trudchen, the governess, was knitting near the window, to which she had moved her chair, in order to catch the last rays of day-light. The children were seized with a kind of vague fear, because candles had not been brought into the room, according to custom; so they were talking in a low tone to each other, just as children talk when they are afraid.

"Fritz," said Mary, "I am sure papa and mamma are busy in preparing the Christmas tree; for ever since the morning I have heard a great deal going on in the drawing-room, which we were forbidden to enter."

"And I know," said Fritz, "by the way Turk barked ten minutes ago, that Godfather Drosselmayer has arrived."

"Oh! I wonder what our dear kind godfather has brought us!" exclaimed Mary, clapping her little hands. "I am sure it will be a beautiful garden, planted with trees, and with a beautiful river running between the banks, covered with flowers. And on the river, too, there will be some silver swans with collars of gold, and a little girl will bring them sweet-cake, which they will eat out of her apron."

"In the first place, Miss," said Fritz, in that authoritative tone which was natural to him, and which his parents considered to be one of his greatest faults, "you must know that swans do not eat sweet-cake."

"I thought they did," answered Mary; "but as you are a year and a half older than I, you must know best."

Fritz tossed his head up with an air of importance.

"And, for my part," he continued, "I feel certain that if Godfather Drosselmayer brings anything at all, it will be a castle with soldiers to watch it, and enemies to attack it. We shall then have some famous battles."

"I do not like battles," said Mary. "If he does bring a castle, as you think he will, it must be for you: I shall, however, take care of the wounded."

"Whatever it is that he brings," returned Fritz, "you know very well that it is neither for you nor for me; because the toys which Godfather Drosselmayer gives us are always taken away again immediately afterwards, under pretense that they really are works of great art. Then, you know, they are always put into that great cupboard with the glass doors, and on the top shelves, which papa himself can only reach when he stands upon a chair. So, after all, I much prefer the toys which papa and mamma give us, and which we are allowed to play with until we break them into a thousand pieces."

"And so do I," answered Mary; "only we must not say so to godfather."

"And why not?"

"Because he would feel annoyed to think that we do not like his toys as much as those which papa and mamma give us. He gives them to us, thinking to please us; and it would be wrong to tell him the contrary."

"Oh! nonsense," cried Fritz.

"Miss Mary is quite right, Master Fritz," said Dame Trudchen, who was generally very silent, and only spoke on important occasions.

"Come," said Mary hastily, in order to prevent Fritz from giving an impudent answer to the poor governess; "let us guess what our parents intend to give us. For my part I told mamma—but upon condition that she would not scold—that Miss Rose, my doll, grows more and more awkward, in spite of the lessons which I am constantly giving her; and that she does nothing but fall upon her nose, which never fails to leave most disagreeable marks upon her face; so that I can no longer take her into decent society, because her face does not at all correspond with her frocks.

"And I," said Fritz, "did not hesitate to assure papa that a nice little horse would look admirably well in my stables; I also took the opportunity to inform him that no army can possibly exist without cavalry, and that I want a squadron of hussars to complete the division which I command."

These words made Miss Trudchen conclude that the moment was favorable for her to speak a second time.

"Master Fritz and Miss Mary," said she, "you know very well that it is your guardian angel who sends and blesses all those fine toys which are given to you. Do not therefore say beforehand what you want; because the angel knows much better than you what will please you."

"Oh!" cried Fritz; "and yet last year he sent me foot soldiers, although, as I have just said, I should have been better satisfied with a squadron of hussars."

"For my part I have only to thank my good angel," said Mary; "for did I but ask for a doll last year, and I not only had the doll, but also a beautiful white dove with red feet and beak."

In the meantime the night had altogether drawn in, and the children, who by degrees spoke lower and lower, and grew closer and closer together, fancied that they heard the wings of their guardian angels fluttering near them, and a sweet music in the distance, like that of an organ accompanying the Hymn of the Nativity, beneath the gloomy arches of a cathedral. Presently a sudden light shone upon the wall for a moment, and Fritz and Mary believed that it was their guardian angel, who, after depositing in the toys in the drawing-room, flew away in the midst of a golden luster to visit other children who were expecting him with the same impatience as themselves.

Immediately afterward a bell rang—the door was thrown violently open—and so strong a light burst into the apartment that the children were dazzled, and uttered cries of surprise and alarm.

The judge and his wife then appeared at the door, and took the hands of their children, saying, "Come, little dears, and see what the guardian angels have sent you."

The children hastened to the drawing-room; and Miss Trudchen, having placed her work upon a chair, followed them.

The Christmas Tree

My dear children, you all know the beautiful toy-stalls in the Soho Bazaar, the Pantheon, and the Lowther Arcade; and your parents have often taken you there, to permit you to choose whatever you liked best. Then you have stopped short, with longing eyes and open mouth; and you have experienced a pleasure which you will never again know in your lives—no, not even when you become men and acquire titles or fortunes. Well, the same joy was felt by Fritz and Mary when they entered the drawing-room and saw the great tree growing as it were from the middle of the table, and covered with blossoms made of sugar, and sugar-plums instead of fruit—the whole glittering by the light of a hundred Christmas candles concealed amidst the leaves. At the beautiful sight Fritz leapt for joy, and danced about in a manner which showed how well he had attended to the lessons of his dancing-master. On her side, Mary could not restrain two large tears of joy which, like liquid pearls, rolled down her countenance, that was open and smiling as a rose in June. But the children's joy knew no bounds when they came to examine all the pretty things which covered the table. There was a beautiful doll, twice as large as Miss Rose; and there was also a charming silk frock, hung on a stand in such a manner that Mary could walk around it. Fritz was also well pleased; for he found upon the table a squadron of hussars, with red jackets and gold lace, and mounted on white horses; while on the carpet, near the table, stood the famous horse which he also much longed to see in his stables. In a moment did this modern Alexander leap upon the back of that brilliant Bucephalus, which was already saddled and bridled; and, having ridden two or three times around the table, he got off again, declaring that though the animal was very spirited and restive, he should soon be able to tame him in such a manner that ere a month passed the horse would be quiet as a lamb.

But at the moment when Fritz set his foot upon the ground, and when Mary was baptizing her new doll by the name of Clara, the bell rang a second time; and the children turned towards that corner of the room when the sound came.

They then beheld something which had hitherto escaped their attention, so intent had they been upon the beautiful Christmas tree. In fact, the corner of the room of which I have just spoken, was concealed, or cut off as it were, by a large Chinese screen, behind which there was a certain noise accompanied by a certain sweet music, which proved that something unusual was going on in that quarter. The children then recollected that they had not yet seen the doctor; and they both exclaimed at the same moment, "Oh! Godpapa Drosselmayer!"

At these words—and as if it had only waited for that exclamation to put itself in motion—the screen opened inwards, and showed not only Godfather Drosselmayer, but something more!

In the midst of a green meadow, decorated with flowers, stood a magnificent country-seat, with numerous windows, all made of real glass, in front, and two gilt towers on the wings. At the same moment the jingling of bells was heard from within—the doors and windows opened—and the rooms inside were discovered lighted up by wax-tapers half an inch high. In those rooms were several little gentlemen and ladies, all walking about: the gentlemen splendidly dressed in laced coats, and silk waistcoats and breeches, each with a sword by his side, and a hat under his arm; the ladies gorgeously attired in brocades, their hair dressed in the style of the eighteenth century, and each one holding a fan in her hand, wherewith they all fanned themselves as if overcome by the heat. In the central drawing-room, which actually seemed to be on fire, so splendid was the luster of the crystal chandelier, filled with wax candles, a number of children were dancing to the jingling music; the boys all in round jackets, and the girls all in short frocks. At the same time a gentleman, clad in a furred cloak, appeared at the window of an adjoining chamber, made signs, and then disappeared again; while Godfather Drosselmayer himself, with his drab frock-coat, the patch on his eye, and the glass wig—so like the original, although only three inches high, that the puppet might be taken for the doctor, as if seen at a great distance— went out and in the front door of the mansion with the air of a gentleman, inviting those who were walking outside to enter his abode.

The first moment was one of surprise and delight for the two children; but, having watched the building for a few minutes with his elbows resting on the table, Fritz rose and exclaimed, "But, Godpapa Drosselmayer, why do you keep going out and coming in by the same door? You must be tired of going backwards and forwards like that. Come, enter by that door there, and come out by this one here."

And Fritz pointed with his finger to the doors of the two towers.

"No, that cannot be done," answered Godfather Drosselmayer.

"Well, then," said Fritz, "do me the pleasure of going up those stairs, and taking the place of that gentleman at the window: then tell him to go down to the door."

"It is impossible, my dear Frtiz," again said the doctor.

"At all events the children have danced enough: let them go and walk, while the gentlemen and ladies who are now walking, dance in their turn."

"But you are not reasonable, you little rogue," cried the godpapa, who began to grow angry: "the mechanism must move in a certain way."

"Then let me go into the house," said Fritz.

"Now you are silly, my dear boy," observed the judge: "you see that it is impossible for you to enter the house, since the vanes on the top of the towers scarcely come up to your shoulders."

Fritz yielded to this reasoning and held his tongue; but in a few moments, seeing that the ladies and gentlemen kept on walking, that the children would not leave off dancing, that the gentleman with the furred cloak appeared and disappeared at regular intervals, and that Godfather Drosselmayer did not leave the door, he again broke his silence.

"My dear godpapa," said he, "if all these little figures can do nothing more than what they are doing over and over again, you may take them away to-morrow, for I do not care about them; and I like my horse much better, because it runs when I choose—and my hussars, because they maneuver at my command, and wheel to the right or left, or march forward or backward, and are not shut up in any house like your poor little people who can only move over and over in the same way.

With these words he turned his back upon Godfather Drosselmayer and the house, hastened to the table, and drew up his hussars in battle array.

As for Mary, she had slipped away very gently, because the motions of the little figures in the house seemed to her to be very tiresome: but as she was a charming child, she said nothing, for fear of wounding the feelings of Godpapa Drosselmayer. Indeed, the moment Fritz turned his back, the doctor said to the judge and his wife, in a tone of vexation, "This master-piece is not fit for children; and I will put my house back again into the box, and take it away."

But the judge's wife approach him, and, in order to atone for her son's rudeness, begged Godfather Drosselmayer to explain to her all the secrets of the beautiful house, and praise the ingenuity of the mechanism to such an extent, that she not only made the doctor forget his vexation, but put him into such a good humor, that he drew from the pockets of his drab coat a number of little men and women with horn complexions, white eyes, and gilt hands and feet. Besides the beauty of their appearance, these little men and women set forth a delicious perfume, because they were made of cinnamon.

At this moment Miss Trudchen called Mary, and offered to help her to put on the pretty little silk frock which she had so much admired on first entering the drawing-room; but Mary, in spite of her usual politeness, did not answer the governess, so much was she occupied with a new personage whom she had discovered amongst the toys, and to whom, my dear children, I must briefly direct your attention, since he is actually the hero of my tale, in which Miss Trudchen, Mary, Fritz, the judge, the judge's lady, and even Godfather Drosselmayer, are only secondary characters.

The Little Man with the Wooden Cloak

I told you that Mary did not reply to the invitation of Miss Trudchen, because she had just discovered a new toy which she had not before perceived.

Indeed, by dint of making his hussars march and counter-march about the table, Fritz had brought to light a charming little gentleman, who, leaning in a melancholy mood against the trunk of the Christmas tree, awaited, in silence and polite reserve, the moment when his turn to be inspected should arrive. We must pause to notice the appearance of this little man, to whom I gave the epithet "charming" somewhat hastily; for, in addition to his body being too long and large for the miserable little thin legs which supported it, his head was of a size so enormous that it was quite at variance with the proportions indicated not only by nature, but also by those drawing-masters who know much better than even Nature herself.

But if there were any fault in his person, that defect was atoned for by the excellence of his toilette, which denoted at once a man of education and taste. He wore a braided frock coat of violet-colored velvet, all frogged and covered with buttons; trousers of the same material; and the most charming little Wellington boots ever seen on the feet of a student or an officer. But these were two circumstances which seemed strange in respect to a man who preserved such elegant taste: the one was an ugly narrow cloak made of wood, and which hung down like a pig's tail from the nape of his neck to the middle of his back; and the other was a wretched cap, such as peasants sometimes wear in Switzerland, upon his head. But Mary, when she perceived those two objects which seemed so unsuitable to the rest of the costume, remembered that Godfather Drosselmayer himself wore above his drab coat a little collar of no better appearance than the wooden cloak belonging to the little gentleman in the military frock; and that the doctor often covered his own bald head with an ugly—an absolutely frightful cap, unlike all other ugly caps in the world—although this circumstance did not prevent the doctor from being an excellent godpapa. She even thought to herself that were Godpapa Drosselmayer to imitate altogether the dress of the little gentleman with the wooden cloak, he could not possibly become so genteel and interesting as the puppet.

You can very well believe that these reflections on the part of Mary were not made without a close inspection of the little man, whom she liked from the very first moment that she saw him. Then, the more she looked at him, the more she was struck by the sweetness and amiability which were expressed by his countenance. His clear green eyes, which were certainly rather goggle, beamed with serenity and kindness. The frizzled beard of white cotton, extending beneath his chin, seemed to become him amazingly, because it set off the charming smile of his mouth, which was rather wide perhaps; but then, the lips were as red as vermilion!

Thus was it that, after examining the little man for upwards of ten minutes, without daring to touch it, Mary exclaimed, "Oh! dear papa, whose is that funny figure leaning against the Christmas tree?"

"It belongs to no one in particular," answered the judge; "but to both of you together."

"How do you mean, dear papa? I do not understand you."

"This little man," continued the judge, "will help you both; for it is he who in future will crack all your nuts for you; and he belongs as much to Fritz as to you, and as much to you as Fritz."

Thus speaking, the judge took up the little man very carefully, and raising his wood cloak, made him open his mouth by a very simple motion, and display two rows of sharp white teeth. Mary then placed a nut in the little man's mouth; and crack—crack—the shell was broken into a dozen pieces, and the kernel fell whole and sound into Mary's hand. The little girl then learnt that the dandified gentleman belonged to that ancient and respectable race of Nutcrackers whose origin is as ancient as that of the town of Nuremberg, and that he continued to exercise the honorable calling of his forefathers. Mary, delighted to have made this discovery, leapt for joy; where-upon the Judge said, "Well, my dear little Mary, since the Nutcracker pleases you so much, although it belongs equally to Fritz and yourself, it is to you that I especially trust it. I place it in your care."

With these words the judge handed the little fellow to Mary, who took the puppet in her arms, and began to practice it in its vocation, choosing, however—so good was her heart—the smallest nuts, that it might not be compelled to open its mouth too wide, because by so doing its face assumed a most ridiculous expression. Then Miss Trudchen drew near to behold the little puppet in her turn; and for her also did it perform its duty in the most unassuming and obliging manner in the world, although she was but a dependant

While he was employed in training his horse and parading his Hussars, Master Fritz heard the crack—crack so often repeated, that he felt sure something new was going on. He accordingly looked up and turned his large inquiring eyes upon the group composed of the judge, Mary, and Miss Trudchen; and when he observed the little man with the wooden cloak in his sister's arms, he leapt from his horse, and, without waiting to put the animal in its stable, hastened towards Mary. Then what a joyous shout of laughter burst from his lips as he espied the funny appearance of the little man open-ing his large mouth. Fritz also demanded his share of the nuts which the puppet cracked; and this was of course granted. Next he wanted to hold the little man while he cracked the nuts; and this wish was also gratified. Only, in spite of the remonstrances of his sister; Fritz chose the largest and hardest nuts to cram into his mouth; so that at the fifth of sixth c-r-r-ack! and out fell three of the poor little fellow's teeth. At the same time his chin fell and became tremulous like that of an old man.

"Oh! my poor Nutcracker!" ejaculated Mary, snatching the little man from the hands of Fritz.

"What a stupid fellow he is!" cried the boy: "he pretends to be a Nutcracker, and his jaws are as brittle as glass. He is a false Nutcracker, and he does not understand his duty. Give him to me, Mary; I will make him go on cracking my nuts, even if he loses all his teeth in doing so, and his chin is dislocated entirely. But how you seem to feel for the lazy fellow!"

"No—no—no!" cried Mary, clasping the little man in her arms: "no—you shall not have my Nutcracker! See how he looks at me, as much as to tell me that his poor jaw is hurt. Fie, Fritz! you are very ill-natured—you beat your horses; and the other day you shot one of your soldiers."

"I beat my horses when they are restive," said Fritz, with an air of importance; "and as for the soldier whom I shot the other day, he was a wretched scoundrel that I never have been able to do anything with for the last year, and who deserted one fine morning with his arms and baggage—a crime that is punishable by death in all countries. Besides, all these things are matters of discipline which do no regard women. I do not prevent you from boxing your doll's ears; so don't try to hinder me from whipping my horses or shooting my soldiers. But I want the Nutcracker."

"Papa—papa!—help—help!" cried Mary, wrapping the little man in her pocket-handkerchief: "help! Fritz is going to take the Nutcracker from me!"

At Mary's cries, not only the judge drew near the children; but his wife and Godfather Drosselmayer also ran towards them. The two children told their stories in their own way—Mary wishing to keep the Nutcracker, and Fritz anxious to have it again. But to the astonishment of Mary, Godfather Drosselmayer, with a smile that seemed perfectly frightful to the poor little girl, decided in favor of Fritz. Happily for the poor Nutcracker, the judge and his wife took little Mary's part.

"My dear Fritz," said the judge, "I trusted the Nutcracker to the care of your sister; and as far as my knowledge of surgery goes, I see that the poor creature is unwell and requires attention. I therefore give him over solely to the care of Mary, until he is quite well; and no one must say a word against my decision. And you, Fritz, who stand up so firmly in behalf of military discipline, when did you ever hear of making a wounded soldier return to his duty? The wounded always go to the hospital until they are cured; and if they be disabled by their wounds, they are entitled to pensions."

Fritz was about to reply; but the judge raised his forefinger to a level with his right eye, and said, "Master Fritz!"

You have already seen what influence those two words had upon the little boy: thus, ashamed at having drawn upon himself the reprimand conveyed in those words, he slipped quietly off, without giving any answer, to the table where his hussars were posted: then, having placed the sentinels in their stations, he marched off the rest to their quarters for the night.

In the meantime Mary picked up the three little teeth which had fallen from the Nutcracker's mouth, and kept the Nutcracker himself well wrapped up in the pocket-handkerchief; she had also bound up his chin with a pretty white ribbon which she cut from the frock. On his side, the little man, who was at first very pale and much frightened, seemed quite contented in the care of his protectress, and gradually acquired confidence, when he felt himself gently rocked in her arms. Then Mary perceived that Godfather Drosselmayer watched with mocking smiles the care which she bestowed upon the little man with the wooden cloak; and it struck her that the single eye of the doctor had acquired an expression of spite and malignity which she had never before seen. She therefore tried to get away from him; but Godfather Drosselmayer burst out laughing, saying, "Well, my dear god-daughter, I am really astonished that a pretty girl like you can be so devoted to an ugly little urchin like that.

Mary turned round; and much as she loved her godfather, even the com-pliment which he paid her did not make amends for the unjust attack he made upon the person of her Nutcracker. She even felt—contrary to her usual disposition—very angry; and that vague comparison which she had before formed between the little man with the wooden cloak and her godfa-ther, returned to her memory.

"Godpapa Drosselmayer," she said, "you are unkind towards my little Nutcracker, whom you call an ugly urchin. Who knows whether you would even look so well as he, even if you had his pretty little military coat, his pretty little breeches, and his pretty little boots!"

At these words Mary's parents burst out laughing; and the doctor's nose grew prodigiously longer.

Why did the doctor's nose grow so much longer? Mary, surprised by the effect of her remark, could not guess the reason.

But there are never any effects without causes, that reason no doubt belonged to some strange and unknown cause, which we must explain.

Wonderful Events

I do not know, my dear little friends, whether you remember that I spoke of a certain large cupboard, with glass windows, in which the children's toys were locked up. This cupboard was on the right side of the door of the judge's own room. Mary was still a baby in the cradle, and Fritz had only just began to walk, when the judge had that cupboard made by a very skillful carpenter, who put such brilliant glass in the frames, that the toys appeared a thousand times finer when ranged on the shelves than when they were held in the hand. Upon the top shelf of all, which neither Fritz nor Mary could reach, the beautiful pieces of workmanship of Godfather Drosselmayer were placed. Immediately beneath was the shelf containing the picture-books; and the two lower shelves were given to Fritz and Mary, who filled them in the way they liked best. It seemed, however, to have been tacitly agreed upon between the two children, that Fritz should hold possession of the higher shelf of the two, for the marshalling of his troops, and that Mary should keep the lower shelf for her dolls and their households. This arrangement was entered into on the eve of Christmas Day. Fritz placed his soldiers upon his own shelf; and Mary, having thrust Miss Rose into a corner, gave the bed-room, formed by the lowest shelf, to Miss Clara, with whom she invited herself to pass the evening and enjoy a supper of sugar plums. Miss Clara, on casting her eyes around, saw that everything was in proper order; her table well spread with sugar plums and conserved fruits, and her nice white bed with its white counterpane, all so neat and comfortable. She therefore felt very well satisfied with her new apartment.

While all these arrangements were being made, the evening wore away: midnight was approaching—Godfather Drosselmayer had been gone a long time—and yet the children could not be persuaded to quit the cupboard.

Contrary to custom, it was Fritz that yielded first to the persuasion of his parents, who told him that it was time to go to bed.

"Well," said he, "after all the exercise which my poor hussars have had to-day, they must be fatigued; and as those excellent soldiers all know their duty towards me—and as, so long as I remain here, they will not close their eyes—I must retire."

With these words—and having given them the watch-word, to prevent them from being surprised by a patrol of the enemy—Fritz went off to bed.

But this was not the case with Mary; and as her mamma, who was about to follow her husband to their bed-chamber, desired her to tear herself away from the dearly- beloved cupboard, little Mary said, "Only one moment, dear mamma—a single moment: do let me finish all I have to do here. There are a hundred or more important things to put to rights; and the moment I have settled them, I promise to go to bed."

Mary requested this favor in so touching and plaintive a tone,—she was, moreover, so glad an obedient a child—that her mother did not hesitate to grant her request. Nevertheless, as Miss Trudchen had already gone up stairs to get Mary's bed ready, the judge's wife, thinking that her daughter might forget to put out the candles, performed that duty herself, leaving only a light in the lamp hanging from the ceiling.

"Do not be long before you go to your room, dear little Mary," said the judge's wife; for if you remain up too long, you will not be able to rise at your usual hour to-morrow morning."

With these words the lady quitted the room and closed the door behind her.

The moment Mary found herself alone, she bethought herself, above all things, of her poor little Nutcracker; for she contrived to keep it in her arms, wrapped up in her pocket handkerchief. She placed him upon the table very gently, unrolled her handkerchief, and examined his chin. The Nutcracker still seemed to suffer much pain, and appeared very cross.

"Ah! my dear little fellow," she said in a low tone, "do not be angry, I pray, because my brother Fritz hurt you so much. He had no evil intention, rest well assured; only his manners have become rough, and his heart is a little hardened by his soldier's life. Otherwise he is a very good boy, I can assure you; and I know that when you are better acquainted with him, you will forgive him. Besides, to atone for the injury which he has done you, I will take care of you; which I will do so attentively that in a few days you will be quite well. As for putting in the teeth again and fastening your chin properly, that is the business of Godpapa Drosselmayer, who perfectly understands those kinds of things."

Mary could say no more; for the moment she pronounced the name of her Godfather Drosselmayer, the Nutcracker, to whom this discourse was addressed, made so dreadful a grimace, and his eyes suddenly flashed so brightly, that the little girl stopped short in affright, and stepped a pace back. But as the Nutcracker immediately afterwards resumed its amiable expression and its melancholy smile, she fancied that she must have been the sport of an illusion, and that the flame of the lamp, agitated by a current of air, had thus disfigured the little man. She even laughed at herself, saying, "I am indeed very foolish to think that this wooden puppet could make faces to me. Come, let me draw near the poor fellow, and take that care of him which he requires."

Having thus mused within herself, Mary took the puppet once more in her arms, drew near the cupboard, knocked at the glass door, which Fritz had closed, and said to the new doll, "I beg of you, Miss Clara, to give up your bed to my poor Nutcracker, who is unwell, and to shift for yourself on the sofa to-night. Remember that you are in excellent health yourself, as your round and rosy cheeks sufficiently prove. Moreover, a night is soon passed; the sofa is very comfortable, and there will not be many dolls in Nuremberg as well lodged as yourself."

Miss Clara, as you may well suppose, did not utter a word; but it struck Mary that she seemed very sulky and discontented; but Mary, whose conscience told her that she had treated Miss Clara in the most considerate manner, used no farther ceremony with her, but, drawing the bed towards her, placed the Nutcracker in it, covering him with the clothes up to the very chin: she then thought that she knew nothing as yet of the real disposition of Miss Clara, whom she had only seen for a few hours; but that as Miss Clara had appeared to be in a very bad humor at losing her bed, some evil might happen to the poor invalid if he were left with so insolent a person. She therefore placed the bed, with the Nutcracker in it, upon the second shelf, close by the ridge where Fritz's cavalry were quartered: then, having laid Miss Clara upon the sofa, she closed the cupboard, and was about to rejoin Miss Trudchen in the bed-chamber, when all around the room the poor girl heard a variety of low scratching sounds coming from behind the chairs, the store, and the cupboard. The large clock which hung against the wall, and which was surmounted by a large gilt owl, instead of a cuckoo, as is usual with old German clocks, began that usual whirring sound which gives warning of striking; and yet it did not strike. Mary glanced towards it, and saw that the immense gilt owl had drooped its wings in such a way that they covered the entire clock, and that the bird thrust forward as far as it could its hideous cat-like head, with the round eyes and the crooked beak. Then the whirring sound of the clock became louder and louder, and gradually changed into the resemblance of a human voice, until it appeared as if these words issued from the beak of the owl: "Clocks, clocks, clocks! whir, whir, whir! in a low tone! The king of the mice has a sharp ear! Sing him his old song! Strike, strike, strike, clocks all: sound his last hour—for his fate is right at hand!"

And then, dong—dong—dong—the clock struck twelve in a hollow and gloomy tone.

Mary was very much frightened. She began to shudder from head to foot; and she was about to run away from the room, when she beheld

Godfather Drosselmayer seated upon the clock instead of the owl, the two skirts of his coat having taken the place of the drooping wings of the bird. At that spectacle, Mary remained nailed as it were to the spot with astonishment; and she began to cry, saying, "What are you doing up there, Godpapa Drosselmayer? Come down here, and don't frighten me like that, naughty Godpapa Drosselmayer."

But at these words there began a sharp whistling and furious kind of tittering all around: then in a few moments Mary heard thousands of little feet treading behind the walls; and next she saw thousands of little lights through the joints in the wainscot. When I say little lights, I am wrong—I mean thousands of little eyes. Mary full well perceived that there was an entire population of mice about to enter the room. And, in fact, in the course of five minutes, thousands and thousands of mice made their appearance by the creases of the door and the joints of the floor, and began to gallop hither and thither, until at length they ranged themselves in order of battle, as Fritz was wont to draw upon his wood soldiers. All this seemed very amusing to Mary; and as she did not feel towards mice that absurd alarm which so many foolish children experience, she thought she should divert herself with the sight, when there suddenly rang through the room a whistling so sharp, so terrible, and so long, that a cold shudder passed over her.

At the same time, a plank was raised up by some power underneath, and the king of the mice, with seven heads all wearing gold crowns, appeared at her very feet, in the midst of the mortar and plaster that was broken up; and each of his seven mouths began to whistle and scream horribly, while body to which those seven heads belonged forced its way through the opening. The entire army advanced towards the king, speaking with their little mouths three times in chorus. Then the various regiments marched across the room, directing their course towards the cupboard, and surrounding Mary on all sides, so that she began to beat a retreat. I have already told you that Mary was not a timid child; but when she saw herself surrounded by crowds of mice, commanded by that monster with seven heads, fear seized upon her, and her heart began to beat so violently, that it seemed as if it would burst from her chest. Her blood appeared to freeze in her veins, her breath failed her; and, half fainting, she retreated with trembling steps. At length—pir-r-r-r! and the pieces of the panes in the cupboard, broken by her elbow which knocked against it, fell upon the floor. She felt at the moment an acute pain in the left arm; but at the same time her heart grew lighter, for she no longer heard that squeaking which had so much frightened her. Indeed, everything had again become quiet around her; the mice had disappeared; and she thought that, terrified by the noises of the glass which was broken, they had sought refuge in their holes.

But almost immediately afterwards a strange noise commenced in the cupboard; and numerous little sharp voices exclaimed, "To arms! to arms! to arms!" At the same time the music of Godfather Drosselmayer's country-house, which had been placed upon the top shelf of the cupboard, began to play; and on all sides she heard the words, "Quick! rise to arms! to arms!"

Mary turned round. The cupboard was lighted up in a wondrous manner, and all was bustle within. All the harlequins, the clowns, the punches, and the other puppets scampered about; while the dolls set to work to make lint and prepare bandages for the wounded. At length the Nutcracker himself threw off all the clothes, and jumped off the bed, crying, "Foolish troop of mice! return to your holes, or you must encounter me!"

But at that menace a loud whistling echoed through the room; and Mary perceived that the mice had not returned to their holes; but that, frightened by the noise of the broken glass, they had sought refuge beneath the chairs and tables, whence they were now beginning to issue again.

On his side, Nutcracker, far from being terrified by the whistling, seemed to gather fresh courage.

"Despicable king of the mice," he exclaimed; "it is thou, then! Thou acceptest the death which I have so long offered you? Come on, and let this night decide between us. And you, my good friends—my companions—my brethren, if it be indeed true that we are united in bonds of affection, support me in this perilous contest! On! on!—let those who love me follow!"

Never did a proclamation produce such an effect. Two harlequins, a clown, two punches, and three other puppets, cried out in a loud tone, "Yes, my lord, we are yours in life and death! We will conquer under your command, or die with you!"

At these words, which proved that there was an echo to his speech in the heart of his friends, Nutcracker felt himself so excited, that he drew his sword, and without calculating the dreadful height on which he stood, leapt from the second shelf. Mary, upon perceiving that dangerous leap, gave a piercing cry; for Nutcracker seemed on the point of being dashed to pieces; when Miss Clara, who was on the lower shelf, darted from the sofa and received him in her arms.

"Ah! my dear little Clara," said Mary, clasping her hands together with emotion: "how have I mistaken your disposition!"

But Miss Clara, thinking only of the present events, said to the Nutcracker, "What! my lord—wounded and suffering as you are, you are plunging head-long into new dangers! Content yourself with commanding the army, and let the others fight. Your courage is known; and you can do no good by giving fresh proof of it!"

And as she spoke, Clara endeavored to restrain the gallant Nutcracker by holding him tight in her arms; but he began to struggle and kick in such a manner that Miss Clara was obliged to let him glide down. He slipped from her arms, and fell on his knees at her feet in a most graceful manner, saying, "Princess, believe me, that although at a certain period you were unjust towards me, I shall always remember you, even in the midst of battle!"

Miss Clara stooped as low down as possible, and, taking him by his little arm, compelled him to rise: then taking off her waist-band all glittering with spangles, she made a scarf of it, and sought to pass it over the shoulder of the young hero; but he, stepping back a few paces, and bowing at the same time in acknowledgment of so great a favor, untied the little white ribbon with which Mary had bound up his chin, and tied it round his waist, after pressing it to his lips. Then, light as a bird, he leapt from the shelf on the floor, brandishing his saber all the time. Immediately did the squeakings and creakings of the mice begin over again; and the king of the mice, as if to reply to the challenge of the Nutcracker, issued from beneath the great table in the middle of the room, followed by the main body of his army. At the same time, the wings, on the right and left, began to appear from beneath the arm-chair, under which they had taken refuge.

The Battle

"Trumpets, sound the charge! drums, beat the alarm!" exclaimed the valiant Nutcracker.

And at the same moment the trumpets of Fritz's hussars began to sound, while the drums of his infantry began to beat, and the rumbling of canon was also heard. At the same time a band of musicians was formed with fat

Figaros with their guitars, Swiss peasants with their horns, and Negroes with their triangles. And all these persons, though not called upon by the Nutcracker, did not the less begin to descend from shelf to shelf, playing the beautiful march of the "British Grenadiers." The music no doubt excited the most peaceably-inclined puppets; for, at the same moment, a kind of militia, commanded by the beadle of the parish, was formed, consisting of harlequins, punches, clowns, and pantaloons. Arming themselves with anything that fell in their way, they were soon ready for battle. All was bustle, even to a man-cook, who, quitting his fire, came down with his spit, on which was a half-roasted turkey, and went and took his place in the ranks. The Nutcracker placed himself at the head of this valiant battalion, which, to the shame of the regular troops, was ready first.

I must tell you everything, or else you might think that I am inclined to be too favorable to that glorious militia; and therefore I must say that if the infantry and cavalry of Master Fritz were not ready so soon as the others, it was because they were all shut up in four boxes. The poor prisoners might therefore well hear the trumpet and drum which called them to battle: they were shut up, and could not get out. Mary heard them stirring in their boxes, like cray-fish in a basket; but, in spite of their efforts, they could not free themselves. At length the grenadiers, less tightly fastened in than the others, succeeded in raising the lid of their box, and then helped to liberate the light infantry. In another instant, these were free; and, well knowing how useful cavalry is in a battle, they hastened to release the hussars, who began to canter gaily about, and range themselves four deep upon the flanks.

But if the regular troops were thus somewhat behind-hand, in consequence of the excellent discipline in which Fritz maintained them, they speedily repairs the lost time: for infantry, cavalry, and artillery began to descend with the fury of an avalanche, amidst the plaudits of Miss Rose and Miss Clara, who clapped their hands as they passed, and encouraged them with their voices, as the ladies from whom they were descended most likely were wont to do in the days of ancient chivalry.

Meantime the king of the mice perceived that he had to encounter an entire army. In fact, the Nutcracker was in the center of his gallant band of militia; on the left was the regiment of hussars, waiting only the moment to charge; on the right was stationed a formidable battalion of infantry; while, upon a footstool which commanded the entire scene of battle, was a park of ten cannon. In addition to these forces, a powerful reserve, composed of gingerbread men, and warriors made of sugar of different colors, had remained in the cupboard, and already began to bustle about. The king of the mice had, however, gone too far to retreat; and he gave the signal by a squeak, which was repeated by all the forces under his command.

At the same moment the battery on the footstool replied with a volley of shot amongst the masses of mice.

The regiment of hussars rushed onward to the charge, so that on one side the dust raised by their horses feet, and on the other the smoke of the cannon, concealed their plain of battle from the eyes of Mary.

But in the midst of the roar of cannon, the shouts of the combatants, and the groans of the dying, she heard the voice of the Nutcracker ever rising above the din.

"Serjeant Harlequin," he cried, "take twenty men, and fall upon the flank of the enemy. Lieutenant Punch, form into a square. Captain Puppet, fire in platoons. Colonel of Hussars, charge in masses, and not four deep, as you are doing. Bravo, good leaden soldiers—bravo! If all my troops behave as well as you, the day is ours!"

But, by these encouraging words even, Mary was at no loss to perceive that the battle was deadly, and that the victory remained doubtful. The mice, thrown back by the hussars—decimated by the fire of platoons—and shattered by the park of artillery, returned again and again to the charge, biting and tearing all who came in their way. It was like the combats in the days of chivalry—a furious struggle foot to foot and hand to hand, each one bent upon attack or defense, without waiting to think of his neighbor. Nutcracker vainly endeavored to direct the evolutions in a disciplined manner, and forms his troops into dense columns. The hussars, assailed by numerous corps of mice, were scattered, and failed to rally round their colonel; a vast battalion of enemy had cut them off from the main body of their army, and had actually advanced up to the militia, which performed prodigies of valor. The beadle of the parish used his battle-axe most gallantly; the man-cook ran whole ranks of mice through with his spit; the leaden soldiers remained firm as a wall; but Harlequin and his twenty men had been driven back, and were forced to retreat under cover of the battery; and Lieutenant Punch's square had been broken up. The remains of his troops fled and threw the militia into disorder; and Captain Puppet, doubtless for want of cartridges, had ceased to fire, and was in full retreat. In consequence of this backward movement through the line, the park of cannon was exposed. The king of the mice, perceiving that the success of the fight depend upon the capture of that battery, ordered his bravest troops to attack it. The footstool was accordingly stormed in a moment, and the artillerymen were cut to pieces by the side of their cannon. One of them set fire to his powder-wagon, and met an heroic death with twenty of his comrades. But all this display was useless against numbers; and in a short time a volley of shot, fired upon them from their own cannon, and which swept the forces commanded by the Nutcracker, convinced him that the battery of the footstool had fallen into the hands of the enemy.

From that moment the battle was lost, and the Nutcracker now thought only of beating an honorable retreat: but, in order to give breathing time to his troops, he summoned the reserve to his aid.

Thereupon, the gingerbread men and the corps of sugar warriors descended from the cupboard and took part in the battle. They were certainly fresh, but very inexperienced, troops: the gingerbread men especially were very awkward, and, hitting right and left, did as much injury to friends as to enemies. The sugar warriors stood firm; but they were of such different natures—emperors, knights, Tyrolese peasants, gardeners, cupids, monkeys, lions, and crocodiles—that they could not combine their movements, and were strong only as a mass. Their arrival, however, produced some good; for scarcely had the mice tasted the gingerbread men and the sugar warriors, when they left the leaden soldiers, whom they found very hard to bite, and turned also from the punches, harlequins, beadles, and cooks, who were only stuffed with brann, to fall upon the unfortunate reserve, which in a moment was surrounded by thousands of mice, and, after an heroic defense, devoured arms and baggage.

Nutcracker attempted to profit by that moment to rally his army; but the terrible spectacle of the destruction of the reserve had struck terror to the bravest hearts. Captain puppet was as pale as death; Harlequin's clothes were in rags; a mouse had penetrated into Punch's hump, and, like the youthful Spartan's fox, began to devour his entrails; and not only was the colonel of the hussars a prisoner with a large portion of his troops, but the mice had even formed a squadron of cavalry, by means of horses thus taken.

The unfortunate Nutcracker had no chance of victory left: he could not even retreat with honor; and therefore he determined to die.

He placed himself at the head of a small body of men, resolved like himself to sell their lives dearly.

In the meantime terror reigned among the dolls: Miss Clara and Miss Rose wrung their hands, and gave vent to loud cries.

"Alas!" exclaimed Miss Clara; "must I die in the flower of my youth— I, the daughter of a king, and born to such brilliant destinies?"

"Alas!" said Miss Rose; "am I doomed to fall into the hands of the enemy, and be devoured by the filthy mice?"

The other dolls ran about in tears; their cries mingling with those of Miss Clara and Miss Rose. Meanwhile matters went worse and worse with Nutcracker: he was abandoned by the few friends who had remained faithful to him. The remains of the squadron of hussars took refuge in the cupboard; the leaden soldiers had all fallen into the power of the enemy; the cannoneers had long previously been dispersed; and the militia was cut to pieces, like the three hundred Spartans of Leonidas, without yielding a step. Nutcracker had planted himself against the lower part of the cupboard, which he vainly sought to climb up: he could not do so without the aid of Miss Rose or Miss Clara; and they had found nothing better to do than to faint. Nutcracker made a last effort, collected all his courage, and cried in an agony of despair, "A horse! a horse! my kingdom for a horse!" But, as in the case of Richard III, his voice remained without even an echo—or rather betrayed him to the enemy. Two of the rifle-brigade of the mice seized upon his wooden cloak; and at the same time the king of the mice cried with his seven mouths, "On your heads, take him alive! Remember that I have my mother to avenge! This punishment must serve as an example to all future Nutcrackers!"

And, with these words, the king rushed upon the prisoner.

But Mary could no longer support that horrible spectacle.

"Oh! my poor Nutcracker!" she exclaimed: "I love you with all my heart, and cannot see you die thus!"

At the same moment, by a natural impulse and without precisely knowing what she was doing, Mary took off one of her shoes, and threw it with all her force in the midst of the combatants. Her aim was so good that the shoe hit the king of the mice, and made him roll over in the dust. A moment afterwards, king and army—conquerors and conquered—all alike disappeared, as if by enchantment. Mary felt a more severe pain than before in her arm. She endeavored to reach an arm-chair to sit down; but her strength failed her—and she fainted!

The Illness

When Mary awoke from her deep sleep, she found herself lying in her little bed, and the sun penetrated radiant and brilliant through the windows. By her side was seated a gentleman whom she shortly perceived to be a surgeon named Vandelstern, and who said in a low voice, the moment she opened her eyes, "She is awake."

Then the judge's wife advanced towards the bed, and gazed upon her daughter for a long time with an anxious air.

"Ah! my dear mamma," exclaimed little Mary, upon seeing her mother; "are all those horrible mice gone? and is my poor Nutcracker saved?"

"For the love of heaven, my dear Mary, do not repeat all that nonsense," said the lady. "What have mice, I should like to know, to do with the Nutcracker? But you, naughty girl, have frightened us all sadly. And it is always so when children are obstinate and will not obey their parents. You played with your toys very late last night: you most likely fell asleep; and it is probable that a little mouse frightened you. At all events, in your alarm, you thrust your elbow through one of the panes of the cupboard, and cut your arm in such a manner that Mr. Vandlestern, who has just extracted the fragments of glass, declares that you ran a risk of cutting an artery and dying through loss of blood. Heaven be thanked that I awoke—I know not at what o'clock—and that, recollecting how I had left you in the room, I went down to look after you. Poor child! you were stretched upon the floor, near the cupboard; and all round you were strewed the dolls, the puppets, the punches, the leaden soldiers, pieces of the gingerbread men, and Fritz's hussars—all scattered about pell-mell—while in your arms you held the Nutcracker. But how was it that you had taken off one of your shoes, and that it was at some distance from you?"

"Ah! my dear mother," said Mary, shuddering as she thought of what had taken place; "all that you saw was caused by the great battle that took place between the puppets and the mice: but the reason of my terror was that I saw the victorious mice about to seize upon the poor Nutcracker, who commanded the puppets;—and it was then that I threw my shoe at the king of the mice. After that, I know not what happened."

The surgeon made a sign to the judge's lady, who said in a soft tone to Mary, "Do not think any more of all that, my dear child. All the mice are gone, and the little Nutcracker is safe and comfortable in the glass cupboard."

The judge then entered the room, and conversed for a long time with the surgeon; but of all that they said Mary could only catch these words—"It is delirium."

Mary saw immediately that her story was not believed, but that it was looked upon as fable; and she did not say any more upon the subject, but allowed those around her to have their own way. For she was anxious to get up as soon as possible and pay a visit to the poor Nutcracker. She, however, knew she had escaped safe and sound from the battle; and that was all she cared about for the present.

Nevertheless Mary was very restless. She could not play, on account of her wounded arm; and when she tried to read or look over her picture-books, everything swam so before her eyes that she was obliged to give up the task. The time hung very heavily upon her hands; and she looked forward with impatience to the evening, because her momma would come and sit by her, and tell her pleasant stories.

One evening, the judge's wife had just ended the pretty tale of "Prince Facardin," when the door opened, and Godfather Drosselmayer thrust in his head, saying, "I must see with my own eyes how the little invalid gets on."

But when Mary perceived Godfather Drosselmayer with his glass wig, his black patch, and his drab frock coat, the remembrance of the night when the Nutcracker lost the famous battle against the mice, returned so forcibly to her mind, that she could not prevent herself from crying out, "O Godpapa Drosselmayer, you were really very ugly! I saw you quite plainly, when you were astride upon the clock, and when you covered it with your wings to prevent it from striking, because it would have frightened away the mice. I heard you call the king with the seven heads. Why did you not come to the aid of my poor Nutcracker, naughty Godpapa Drosselmayer; for, by not coming, you were the cause of my hurting myself and having to keep to my bed."

The judge's wife listened to all this with a kind of stupor; for she thought that the poor little girl was relapsing into delirium. She therefore said, in a low tone of alarm, "What are you talking about, Mary? are you taking leave of your senses?"

"Oh! no," answered Mary; "and Godpapa Drosselmayer knows that I am telling the truth."

But the godfather, without saying a word, made horrible faces, like a man who was sitting upon thorns; then all of a sudden he began to chaunt these lines in a gloomy sing-song tone:—

> Old Clock-bell, beat
>   Low, dull, and hoarse:—
> Advance, retreat,
>   Thou gallant force!

> The bell's lone sound proclaims around
>   The hour of deep mid-night;
> And the piercing note from the screech-owl's throat
>   Puts the king himself to flight

> Old clock-bell, beat
>   Low, dull, and hoarse:—
> Advance, retreat,
>   Thou gallant force!"

Mary contemplated Godfather Drosselmayer with increasing terror; for he now seemed to her more hideously ugly than usual. She would indeed have been dreadfully afraid of him, if her mother had not been present, and if Fritz had not at that moment entered the room with a loud shout of laughter.

"Do you know, Godpapa Drosselmayer," said Fritz, "that you are uncommonly amusing to-day: you seem to move about just like my punch that stands behind the store; and, as for the song, it is not common sense."

"My dear doctor," she said, "your song is indeed very strange, and appears to me to be only calculated to make little Mary worse."

"Nonsense!" cried Godfather Drosselmayer: "do you not recognize the old chant which I am in the habit of humming when I mend your clocks?"

At the same time he seated himself near Mary's bed, and said to her in a rapid tone, "do not be angry with me, my dear child, because I did not tear out the fourteen eyes of the king of the mice with my own hands; but I knew what I was about—and now, as I am anxious to make it up with you, I will tell you a story."

"What story?" asked Mary.

"*The History of the Crackatook Nut and Princess Pirlipata.* Do you know it?"

"No, my dear godpapa," replied Mary, whom the offer of a story reconciled to the doctor that moment. "Go on."

"My dear doctor," said the judge's wife, "I hope that your story will not be so melancholy as your song?"

"Oh, no, my dear lady," returned Godfather Drosselmayer. "On the contrary, it is very amusing."

"Tell it to us, then!" cried both the children.

Godfather Drosselmayer accordingly began in the following manner.

The History of the Crackatook Nut and Princess Pirlipata

How Princess Pirlipata was born, and how the event produced the greatest joy to her parents

There was lately, in the neighborhood of Nuremberg, a little kingdom, which was not Prussia, nor Poland, nor Bavaria, nor the Palatinate, and which was governed by a king.

This king's wife, who was consequently a queen, became the mother of a little girl, who was therefore a princess by birth, and received the sweet name of Pirlipata.

The king was instantly informed of the event, and he hastened out of breath to see the pretty infant in her cradle. The joy which he felt in being the father of so charming a child, carried him to such an extreme that, quite forgetting himself, he uttered loud cries of joy, and began to dance around the room, crying, "Oh! who has ever seen anything so beautiful as my Pirlapatetta?"

Then, as the king had been followed into the room by his ministers, his generals, the great officers of state, the chief judges, the councilors, and the puisine judges, they all began dancing around the room as the king, singing:

> Great monarch, we ne'er
> In this world did see
> A child so fair
> As the one that there
> Has been given to thee!
> Oh! ne'er, and Oh! ne'er,
> Was there child so fair!

And, indeed—although I may surprise you by saying so—there was not a word of flattery in all this; for, since the creation of the world, a sweeter child than Princess Pirlipata never has been seen. Her little face appeared to be made of the softest silken tissue, like the white rosy tints of the lily combined. Here eyes were of the purest and brightest blue; and nothing was more charming than to behold the golden thread of her hair, flowing in delicate curls over shoulders as white as alabaster. Moreover, Pirlipata, when born, was already provided with two complete rows of the most pearly teeth, with which—two hours after her birth—she bit the finger of the lord chancellor so hard, when being near sighted, he stooped down to look close at her, that, although she belonged to the sect of stoic philosophers, he cried out according to some, "Oh! the dickens!" whereas others affirm, to the honor of philosophy, that he only said, "Oh! Oh!" However, up to the present day opinions are divided upon this important subject, neither party being willing to yield to the other. Indeed, the only point on which the *Dickensonians* and the *Ohists* are agreed is, that the princess really did bite the finger of the lord high chancellor. The country thereby learnt that there was as much spirit as beauty belonging to the charming Pirlipata.

Everyone was therefore happy in a kingdom so blest by heaven, save the queen herself, who was anxious and uneasy, no person knew why. But what chiefly struck people with surprise, was the care with which the timid mother had the cradle of the infant watched. In fact, besides having all the doors guarded by sentinels, and in addition to the two regular nurses, the queen had six other nurses to sit round the cradle, and who were relieved by a half-a-dozen others at night. But what caused the greatest interest, and which no one could understand, was that each of these six nurses was compelled to hold a cat upon her knees, and to tickle it all night so as to prevent it from sleeping, and keep it purring.

I am certain, my dear children, that you are as curious as the inhabitants of that little kingdom without a name, to know why these extra nurses were forced to hold cats upon their knees, and to tickle them in such a way that they should never cease purring; but, as you would vainly endeavor to find out the secret of that enigma, I shall explain it to you, in order to save you the headache which would not fail to be the result of your guess-work.

It happened one day that half-a-dozen great kings took it into their heads to pay a visit to the future father of Princess Pirlipata, for at that time the princess was not born. They were accompanied by the royal princes, the hereditary grand dukes, and the heirs apparent, all most agreeable personages. This arrival was the signal for the king whom they visited, and who was a most hospitable monarch, to make a large drain upon his treasury, and give tournaments, feasts, and dramatic representations. But this was not all. He having learnt from the intendant of the royal kitchen, that the astronomer royal of the court was favorable for killing pigs, and the conjunction of the stars foretold that the year would be propitious for sausage-making, the king commanded a tremendous slaughter of pigs to take place in the court-yard. Then, ordering his carriage, he went in person to call upon all the kings and princes staying in his capital, and invite them to dine with him; for he was resolved to surprise them by the splendid banquet which he intended to give them. On his return to the palace, he retired to the queen's apartment, and going to her, said in a coaxing tone, with which he was always accustomed to make her do anything he wished, "My most particular and very dear love, you have not forgotten—have you—how dotingly fond I am of black puddings? You surely have not forgotten that?"

The queen understood by the first word what the king wanted of her. In fact she knew by his cunning address, that she must now proceed, as she had done many times before, to the very useful occupation of making, with her own royal hands, the greatest possible quantity of sausages, polonies, and black puddings. She therefore smiled at that proposal of her husband; for although filling with dignity the high situation of queen, she was less proud of the compliments paid her upon the manner in which she bore the scepter and the crown, than of those bestowed on her skill in making a black pudding, or any other dish. She therefore contented herself by curtseying gracefully to her husband, saying that she was quite ready to make him the puddings which he required.

The grand treasurer accordingly received orders to carry the immense enameled cauldron and the large silver saucepans to the royal kitchens, so that the queen might make the black puddings, the polonies, and the sausages. An enormous fire was made with sandal-wood; the queen put on her apron of white damask, and in a short time delicious odors steamed from the cauldron. Those sweet perfumes spread through the passages, penetrated into all the rooms, and reached the throne room where the king was holding a privy council. The king was very fond of good eating, and the smell made a profound impression upon him. Nevertheless, as he was a wise prince, and was famed for his habits of self-command, he resisted for a long time the feeling which attracted him towards the kitchens; but at last, in spite of the command which he exercised over himself, he was compelled to yield to the inclination that now ruled him.

"My lords and gentlemen," he accordingly said, rising from his throne, "with your permission I will retire for a few moments; pray wait for me." Then this great king hastened through the passages and corridors to the kitchen, embraced his wife tenderly, stirred the contents of the cauldron with his golden scepter, and tasted them with the tip of his tongue. Having thus calmed his mind, he returned to the council, and resumed, though somewhat abstractedly, the subject of discussion.

He had left the kitchen just at the important moment when the fat, cut up in small pieces, was about to be broiled upon the silver gridirons. The queen, encouraged by his praises, now commenced that important operation; and the first drops of grease had just dripped upon the live coals, when a squeaking voice was heard to chant the following lines:

> Dear sister, pray give to the queen of the Mice,
> A piece of that fat which is grilling so nice;
> To me a good dinner is something so rare,
> That I hope of the fat you will give me a share.

The queen immediately recognized the voice that thus spoke; it was the voice of Dame Mousey.

Dame Mousey had lived for many years in the palace. She declared herself to be a relation of the royal family, and was Queen of the kingdom of Mice. She therefore maintained a numerous court beneath the kitchen hearth-stone.

The queen was a kind and good-natured woman; and although she would not publicly recognize Dame Mousey as a sister and a sovereign, she nevertheless showed her in private a thousand flattering attentions. Her husband, more particular than herself, had often reproached her for thus lowering herself. But on the present occasion she could not find it in her heart to refuse the request of her little friend; and she accordingly said, "Come, Dame Mousey, without fear, and taste my pork-fat as much as you like. I give you full leave to do so."

Same Mousey accordingly leapt upon the hearth, quite gay and happy, and took with her little paws the pieces of fat which the queen gave her.

But, behold! the murmurs of joy which escaped the mouth of Dame Mousey, and the delicious smell of the morsels of fat on the gridiron, reached her seven sons, then her relations, and next her friends, all of whom were terribly addicted to gourmandizing, and who now fell upon the fat with such fury, that the queen was obliged, hospitable as she was, to remind them that if they continued at that rate only five minutes more, there would not be enough fat left for the black puddings. But, in spite of the justice of this remonstrance, the seven sons of Dame Mousey took no heed of them; and setting a bad example to their relations and friends, rushed upon their aunt's fat, which would have entirely disappeared, had not the cries of the queen brought the man-cook and scullery boys, all armed with brushes and brooms, to drive the mice back again under the hearth-stone. But the victory, although complete, came somewhat too late; for there scarcely remained a quarter enough fat necessary for the polonies, the sausages, and the black puddings. The remnant, however, was scientifically divided by the royal mathematician, who was sent for in all possible haste, between the large cauldron containing the materials for the puddings, and the two saucepans in which the sausages and polonies were cooking.

Half an hour after this event, the cannon fired, the clarions and trumpets sounded, and then came the potentates, the royal princes, the hereditary dukes, and the heirs apparent to the thrones, all dressed in their most splendid clothes, and some riding on gallant chargers. The king received them on the threshold of the palace, in the most courteous manner possible; then, having conducted them to the banqueting room, he took his seat at the head of the table in his quality of sovereignhood, and having the crown upon his head and the scepter in his hand. The guests all placed themselves at table according to their rank, as crowned kings, royal princes, hereditary dukes, or heirs apparent.

The board was covered with dainties, and everything went well during the soup and the first course. But when the polonies were placed on the table, the king seemed to be agitated; when the sausages were serve up, he grew very pale; and when the black puddings were brought in, he raised his eyes to heaven, sighs escaped his breast, and a terrible greed seemed to rend his soul. At length he fell back in his chair, and covered his face with his hands, sobbing and moaning in so lamentable a manner, that all the guests rose from their seats and surrounded him with great anxiety. At length the crisis seemed very serious; the court physician could not feel the beating of the pulse of the unfortunate monarch, who was thus overwhelmed with the weight of the most profound, the most frightful, and the most unheard of calamity. At length, upon the most violent remedies, such as burnt feathers, volatile salts, and cold keys thrust down the back, had been employed, the king seemed to return to himself. He opened his eyes, and said in a scarcely audible tone, "*not enough fat!*"

At these words, the queen grew pale in her turn, she threw herself at his feet, crying in a voice interrupted by sobs, "Oh! my unfortunate, unhappy, and royal husband, What grief have I not caused you, by refusing to listen to the advice which you have so often given me! But you behold the guilty one at your feet, and you can punish her as severely as you think fit."

"What is the matter?" demanded the king, "and what has happened that I know not of?"

"Alas! alas!" answered the queen, to whom her husband had never spoken in so cross a tone; "Alas! Dame Mousey, her seven sons, her nephews, her cousins, and her friends, devoured the fat."

But the queen could not say any more; her strength failed her, she fell back and fainted.

Then the king rose in a great rage, and cried in a terrible voice, "Let her ladyship the royal housekeeper explain what all this means! Come, speak!"

Then the royal housekeeper related all that she knew; namely, that being alarmed by the queen's cries, she ran and beheld the majesty beset by the entire family of Dame Mousey, and that, having summoned the cooks and scullery boys, the plunderers were compelled to retreat.

The king, perceiving that this was a case of high treason, resumed all his dignity and calmness, and commanded the privy council to meet that minute, the matter being of the utmost importance. The council assembled, the business was explained, and it was decided by a majority of voices, "That Dame Mousey, being accused of having eaten the fat destined for the sausages, the polonies, and the black puddings of the king, should be tried for the same offense; and that if the said Dame Mousey was found guilty, she and all her race should be banished from the kingdom, and all her good or possessions, namely, lands, castles, palaces, and royal residencies should be confiscated."

Then the king observed to his councilors that while the trial lasted, Dame Mousey and her family would have sufficient time to devour all the fat in the royal kitchens, which would expose him to the same privation as that which he had just endured in the presence of six crowned heads, without reckoning royal princes, hereditary dukes, and heirs apparent. He therefore demanded a discretionary power in respect to Dame Mousey and her family.

The privy council divided, for the form of the thing, but the discretionary power was voted, as you may well suppose, by a large majority.

Then the king sent one of his best carriages, preceded by a courier that greater speed might be used, to a very skillful mechanic who lived at Nuremberg, and whose name was Christian Elias Drosselmayer. This mechanic was requested to proceed that moment to the palace upon urgent business. Christian Elias Drosselmayer immediately obeyed, for he felt convinced that the king required him to make some work of art. Stepping into the vehicle, he traveled day and night, until he arrived in the king's presence. Indeed, such was his haste, that he had not waited to change the drab-colored coat which he usually wore. But instead of being angry at that breach of etiquette, the king was much pleased with his haste; for if the famous mechanic had committed a fault, it was in his anxiety to obey the king's commands.

The king took Christian Elias Drosselmayer into his private chamber, and explained to him the position of affairs; namely, that it was decided upon to make a striking example of the race of mice throughout the kingdom; that attracted by the fame of his skill, the king had fixed upon him to put the decree of justice into execution; and that the said king's only fear was lest the mechanic, skillful though he were, should perceive insurmountable difficulties in the way of appeasing the royal anger.

But Christian Elias Drosselmayer reassured the king, promising that in eight days there should not be a single mouse left in the kingdom.

In a word, that very same day he set to work to make several ingenious little oblong boxes, inside which he placed a morsel of fat at the end of a piece of wire. By seizing upon the fat, the plunderer, whoever he might be, caused the door to shut down behind him, and thus became a prisoner. In less than a week, a hundred of these boxes were made, and placed, not only beneath the hearthstone, but in all the garrets, lofts, and cellars of the palace. Dame Mousey was far too cunning and sagacious not to discover at the first glance the stratagem of Master Drosselmayer. She therefore assembled her seven sons, their nephews, and their cousins, to warn them of the snare that was laid for them. But, after having appeared to listen to her, and the veneration which her years commanded, they withdrew, laughing at her terrors; then, attracted by the smell of the fried pork-fat, they resolved, in spite of the representations made to them, to profit by the charity that came they knew not whence.

At the expiration of twenty-four hours, the seven sons of Dame Mousey, eighteen of her nephews, fifty of her cousins, and two hundred and thirty-five of her other connections, without reckoning thousands of her subjects, were caught in the mouse-traps and ignominiously executed.

Then did Dame Mousey, with the remnant of her court and the rest of her subjects, resolve upon abandoning a place covered with the blood of her massacred relatives and friends. The tidings of that resolution became known and reached the ears of the king. His majesty expressed his satisfaction, and the poets of the court composed sonnets upon his victory, while the courtiers compared him to Sesostris, Alexander, and Cæsar.

The queen was alone anxious and uneasy; she knew Dame Mousey well, and suspected that she would not leave unavenged the death of her relations and friends. And, in fact, at the very moment when the queen, by way of atoning for her previous fault, was preparing with her own hands a liver soup for the king, who doted upon that dish, Dame Mousey suddenly appeared and chanted the following lines:

Thine husband, void of pity and of fear,
Hath slain my cousins, sons, and nephews dear;
   But list, O Queen! to the decrees of fate:
The child which heaven will shortly give to thee,
And which the object of thy love will be,
   Shall bear the rage of my vindictive hate.
Thine husband owneth castles, cannons, towers,
A council's wisdom, and an army's powers,
   Mechanics, ministers, mouse-traps, and snares:
None of all these, alas! to me belong;
But heaven hath given me teeth, sharp, firm, and strong,
   That I may rend in pieces royal heirs.

Having sung these words she disappeared, and no one saw her afterwards. But the queen, who expected a little baby, was so overcome by the prophecy, that she upset the liver soup into the fire.

Thus, for the second time, was Dame Mousey the cause of depriving the king of one of his favorite dishes, whereat he fell into a dreadful rage. He, however, rejoiced more than ever at the step he had taken to ride his country of the mice.

It is scarcely necessary to say that Christian Edward Drosselmayer was sent away well rewarded, and returned in triumph to Nuremberg.

How, in spite of the precautions taken by the queen, Dame Mousey accomplishes her threat in regard to Princess Pirlipata

And now, my dear children, you know as well as I do, wherefore the queen had Princess Pirlipata watched with such wonderful care. She feared the vengeance of Dame Mousey; for, according to what Dame Mousey had said, there could be nothing less in store for the heiress of this little kingdom without a name, than the loss of her life, or at all events her beauty; which last affliction is considered by some people worse for one of her sex. What redoubled the fears of the queen was, that the machines invented by Master Drosselmayer were totally useless against the experience of Dame Mousey. The astronomer of the court, who was also grand prophet and grand astrologer, was fearful lest his office should be suppressed unless he gave his opinion at this important juncture: he accordingly declared that he read in the stars the great fact that the illustrious family of the cat Murr was alone capable of defending the cradle against the approach of Dame Mousey. It was for this reason that each of his six nurses was forced to hold a cat constantly upon her knees. Those cats might be considered as under-officers attached to the court; and the nurses sought to lighten the cares of the duty performed by the cats, by gently rubbing them with their fair hands.

You know, my dear children, that there are certain times when a person watches even while actually dozing; and so it was that, one evening, in spite of all the efforts which the six nurses made to the contrary, as they sate round the cradle of the princess with the cats upon their knees, they felt sleep rapidly gaining upon them. Now, as each nurse kept her own ideas to herself, and was afraid of revealing them to their companions, hoping all the time that their drowsiness would not be perceived by others, the result was, that, one after another, they closed their eyes—their hands stopped from stroking the cats—and the cats themselves, being no longer rubbed and scratched, profited by circumstance to take a nap.

I cannot say how long this strange slumber had lasted, when, towards midnight, one of the nurses awoke with a start. All the others were in a state of profound lethargy: not a sound—not even their very breathing, was heard: the silence of death reigned around, broken only by the slight creak of the worm biting the wood. But how frightened was the nurse when she beheld a large and horrible mouse standing up near her on its hind legs, and, having plunged its head into the cradle, seemed very busy in biting the face of the princess! She rose with a cry of alarm; and at that exclamation, all the other nurses jumped up. But Dame Mousey—for she indeed it was—sprang towards one corner of the room. The cats leapt after her: alas! it was too late—Dame Mousey had disappeared by a crevice in the floor. At the same moment Princess Pirlipata, who was awoke by all that din, began to cry. Those sounds made the nurses leap with joy. "Thank God!" they said; "since Princess Pirlipata cries she is not dead!" They then all ran towards the cradle—but their despair was great indeed when they saw what had happened to that delicate and charming creature!

In fact, instead of that face of softly blended white and red—that little head, with its golden hair—those mild blue eyes, azure as the sky itself—instead of all these charms the nurses beheld an enormous and mis-shapen head upon a deformed and ugly body. Her two sweet eyes had lost their heavenly hue, and became goggle, fixed, and haggard. Her little mouth had grown from ear to ear; and her chin was covered with a beard like grizzly cotton. All this would have suited old Punch; but seemed very horrible for a young princess.

At that moment the queen entered. The twelve nurses threw themselves with their faces against the ground; while the six cats walked about to discover if there were not some open window by which they might escape upon the tiles. At the sight of her child the despair of the poor mother was something frightful to behold; and she was carried off in a fainting fit into the royal chamber. But it was chiefly the unhappy father whose sorrow was the most desperate and painful to witness. The courtiers were compelled to put padlocks upon the windows, for fear he should throw himself out; and they were also forced to line the walls with mattresses, lest he should dash out his brains against them. His sword was of course taken away from him; and neither knife nor fork, nor any sharp or pointed instruments were left in his way. This was the more easily effected; inasmuch as he ate nothing for the two or three following days, crying without ceasing, "Oh! miserable king that I am! Oh! cruel destiny that thou art!"

Perhaps, instead of accusing destiny, the king should have remembered that, as is generally the case with mankind, he was the author of his own misfortunes; for had he known how to content himself with black pudding containing a little less fat than usual, and had he abandoned his ideas of vengeance, and left dame Mousey and her family in peace beneath the hearth-stone, the affliction which he deplored would not have happened. But we must confess that the ideas of the royal father of Princess Pirlipata did not tend at all in that direction.

On the contrary—believing, as all great men do, that they must necessarily attribute their misfortunes to others—he threw all the blame upon the skillful mechanic Christian Elias Drosselmayer. Well convinced, moreover, that if he invited him back to court to be hung or beheaded, he would not accept the invitation, he desired him to come in order to receive a new order of knighthood which had just been created for men of letters, artists, and mechanics. Master Drosselmayer was not exempt from human pride: he thought that a star would look well upon the breast of his drab surtout coat; and accordingly set off for the king's court. But his joy was soon changed into fear; for on the frontiers of the kingdom, guards awaited him. They seized upon him, and conducted him from station to station, until they reached the capital.

The king, who was afraid of being won over to mercy, would not see Master Drosselmayer when the latter arrived at the palace; but he ordered him to be immediately conducted to the cradle of Pirlipata, with the assurance that if the princess were not restored by that day month to her former state of beauty, he would have the mechanic's head cut off.

Master Drosselmayer did not pretend to be bolder than his fellow-men, and had always hoped to die a natural death. He was therefore much frightened at this threat. Nevertheless, trusting a a great deal to his knowledge, which his own modesty had never prevented him being aware of to its full extent, he acquired courage. Then he set to work to discover whether the evil would yield to any remedy, or whether it were really incurable, as he had from the first believed it to be.

With this object in view, he skillfully took off the head of the Princess, and next all her limbs. He likewise dissected the hands and feet, in order to examine, with more accuracy, not only the joints and the muscles, but also the internal formation. But, alas! the more he worked into the frame of Pirlipata, the more firmly did he become convinced that as the princess grew, the uglier she would become. He therefore joined Pirlipata together again; and then, seating himself by the side of her cradle, which he was not to quit until she had resumed her former beauty, he gave way to his melancholy thoughts.

The fourth week had already commenced, and Wednesday made its appearance, when, according to custom, the king came in to see if any change had taken place in the exterior of the princess. But when he saw that it was just the same, he shook his scepter at the mechanic, crying, "Christian Elias Drosselmayer, take care of yourself! you have only three days left to restore me my daughter just as she was wont to be; and if you remain obstinate in refusing to cure her, on Monday next you shall be beheaded."

Master Drosselmayer, who could not cure the princess, not through any obstinacy on his part, but through actual ignorance how to do it, began to weep bitterly, surveying, with tearful eyes, Princess Pirlipata, who was cracking nuts as comfortably as if she were the most beautiful child upon the earth. Then as he beheld that melting spectacle, the mechanic was struck for the first time by that particular taste for nuts which the princess had shown since her birth; and he remembered also the singular fact that she was born with teeth. In fact, immediately after her change from beauty to ugliness she had begun to cry bitterly, until she found a nut near her: she had then cracked it, eaten the kernel, and turned around to sleep quietly. From that moment the nurses had taken good care to fill their pockets with nuts, and give her one or more whenever she made a face.

"Oh! instinct of nature! Eternal and mysterious sympathy of all created beings!" cried Christian Elias Drosselmayer, "thou showest me the door which leads to the discovery of thy secrets! I will knock at it, and it will open!"

At these words, which surprised the king, the mechanic turned towards his majesty and requested the favor of being conducted into the presence of the astronomer of the court. The king consented, but on condition that it should be with a guard. Master Drosselmayer would perhaps have been better pleased to take that little walk all alone; but, as under the circumstances he could not help himself, he was obliged to submit to what he could not prevent, and processed through the streets of the capital escorted like a felon.

On reaching the house of the astrologer, Master Drosselmayer threw himself into his arms; and they embraced each other amidst torrents of tears, for they were acquaintances of long standing, and were much attached to each other. They then retired to a private room, and examined a great number of books which treated upon likings and dislikings, and a host of other matters not a whit less profound. At length night came; and the astrologer ascending to his tower, and aided by Master Drosselmayer, who was himself very skillful in such matters, discovered, in spite of the difficulty of the heavenly circles which crossed each other in all directions, that in order to break the spell which rendered Princess Pirlipata hideous, and to restore her former beauty, she must eat the kernel of the Crackatook nut, the shell of which was so hard that the wheel of a forty-eight pounder might pass over it without breaking it. Moreover, it was necessary that this nut should be cracked in the presence of the princess, and by a young man who had never been shaved, and who had always worn boots. Lastly, it was requisite that he should present the nut to the princess, with his eyes closed, and in the same way step seven paces backward without stumbling. Such was the answer of the stars.

Drosselmayer and the astronomer had worked without ceasing for four days and four nights, to clear up this mysterious affair. It was on the Sunday evening—the king had finished his dinner, and was just beginning on the dessert—when the mechanic, who was to be beheaded the next day, entered the royal dining room, full of joy, and announced that he had discovered the means of restoring Princess Pirlipata to her beauty. At these news, the king caught him in his arms, with the most touching kindness, and asked him what those means were.

The mechanic thereupon explained to the king the result of his consultation with the astrologer.

"I knew perfectly well, Master Drosselmayer," said the king, "that all your delay was only through obstinacy. It is, however, settled at last; and after dinner we will set to work. Take care, then, dearest mechanic, to have the young man who has never been shaved, and who wears boots, in readiness in ten minutes, together with the nut Crackatook. Let him, moreover, abstain from drinking wine for the next hour, for fear he should stumble while walking backwards like a crab; but when once it is all over, tell him that he is welcome to my whole cellar, and may get as tipsy as he chooses."

But, to the great astonishment of the king, Master Drosselmayer seemed quite frightened at these words; and, as he held his tongue, the king insisted upon knowing why he remained silent and motionless instead of hastening to execute the orders of his sovereign.

"Sire," replied the mechanician, throwing himself on his knees before the king, "it is perfectly true that we have found the means of curing Princess Pirlipata, and that those means consist of her eating a Crackatook nut when it shall have been cracked by a young man who has never been shaved, and who has always worn boots; but we have not as yet either the young man or the nut—we know not where to find them, and in all probability we shall have the greatest difficulty in discovering both the nut and the Nutcracker."

At these words, the king brandished his scepter above the head of the mechanician, crying, "Then hasten to the scaffold!"

But the queen, on her side, hastened to kneel by the side of Master Drosselmayer, and begged her august husband to remember that by cutting off the head of the mechanician he would be losing even that ray of hope which remained to them during his lifetime; that the chances were that he who had discovered the horoscope would also find the nut and the Nutcracker; that they ought to believe more firmly in the present prediction of the astronomer, inasmuch as nothing which he had hitherto prophesied had ever come to pass, but that it was evident his presages must be fulfilled some day or another; inasmuch as the king had named him his grand prophet; and that, as the princess was not yet of an age to marry (she being now only three months old), and would not even be marriageable until she was fifteen, there was consequently a period of fourteen years and nine months during which Master Drosselmayer and the astrologer might search after the Crackatook nut and the young man who was to break it. The queen therefore suggested that a reprieve might be awarded to Christian Elias Drosselmayer, at the expiration of which he should return to surrender himself into the king's power, whether he had found the means of curing the princess, or not; and either to be generously rewarded, or put to death without mercy.

The king, who was a very just man, and who on that day especially had dined splendidly upon his two favorite dishes—namely, liver soup and black puddings—lent a favorable ear to the prayer of his wise and courageous queen. He therefore decided that the astrologer and the mechanician should that moment set out in search of the nut and the Nutcracker; for which purpose he granted fourteen years and nine months, with the condition that they should return, at the expiration of that reprieve, to place themselves in his power, so that, if they were empty-handed, he might deal with them according to his own royal pleasure.

If, on the contrary, they should make their re-appearance with the Crackatook nut which was to restore the princess to all her former beauty, the astrologer would be rewarded with a yearly pension of six hundred pounds and a telescope of honor; and the mechanician would receive a sword set with diamonds, the Order of the Golden Spider (the grand order of the state), and new frock-coat.

As for the young man who was to crack the nut, the king had no doubt of being able to find one suitable for the purpose, by means of advertisements constantly inserted in the national and foreign newspapers.

Touched by this declaration on the part of the king, which relieved them from half the difficulty of their task, Christian Elias Drosselmayer pledged his honor that he would either find the Crackatook-nut, or return, like another Regulus, to place himself in the hands of the king.

That same evening the astrologer and the mechanician departed from the capital of the kingdom to commence their researches.

How the mechanician and the astrologer wander over the four quarters of the world, and discover a fifth, without finding the Crackatook nut

It was now fourteen years and five months since the astrologer and the mechanician first set out on their wanderings through all parts, without discovering a vestige of what they sought. They had first of all traveled through Europe; then they visited America, next Africa, and afterwards Asia: they even discovered a fifth part of the world, which learned men have since called New Holland, because it was discovered by two Germans! But throughout that long series of travels, although they had seen many nuts of different shapes and sizes, they never fell in with the Crackatook nut. They had, however, in alas! a vain hope, passed several years at the court of the King of Dates and at that of the Prince of Almonds: they had uselessly consulted the celebrated Academy of Grau Monkeys and the famous Naturalist Society of Squirrels; until at length they arrived, sinking with fatigue, upon the borders of the great forest which touches the feet of the Himalayan Mountains. And now they dolefully said to each other that they had only a hundred and twenty-two days to find what they sought, after a useless search of fourteen years and five months.

If I were to tell you, my dear children, the strange adventures which happened to the two travelers during that long wandering, I should occupy you every evening for an entire month, and should then weary you in the long run. I will therefore only tell you that Christian Elias Drosselmayer, who was the most eager in search after the nut,—since his head depended upon finding it,—gave himself up to greater dangers than his companion, and lost all his hair by a stroke of the sun received in the tropics. He also lost his right eye by an arrow which a Caribbean Chief aimed at him. Moreover, his drab frock-coat, which was not new when he left Germany, had literally fallen into rags and tatters. His situation was therefore most deplorable; and yet, so much do men cling to life, that, damaged as he was by the various accidents which had befallen him, he beheld with increasing terror the approach of the moment when he must return to place himself in the power of the king.

Nevertheless, the mechanician was a man of honor: he would not break a promise so sacred as that which he had made. He accordingly resolved, whatever might happen, to set out the very next morning on his return to Germany. And indeed there was no time to lose; four-teen years and five months had passed away, and the two travelers had only a hundred and twenty-two days, as we have already said, to reach the capital of Princess Pirlipata's father.

Christian Elias Drosselmayer accordingly made known his noble intention to his friend the astrologer; and both decided that they would set out on their return the next morning.

And, true to this intention, the travelers resumed their jour-ney at daybreak, taking the direction of Bagdad. From Bagdad they proceeded to Alexandria, where they embarked for Venice. From Venice they passed through the Tyrol; and from the Tyrol they entered into the kingdom of Pirlipata's father, both sincerely hoping that he was either dead or in his dotage.

But, alas! it was no such thing! Upon reaching the capital, the unfortunate mechanician learnt that the worthy monarch not only had not lost his intellectual faculties, but was also in better health than ever. There was consequently no chance for him—unless Princess Pirlipata had become cured of her ugliness without any remedy at all, which was not possible; or, that the king's heart had softened, which was not probable—of escaping the dreadful fate which threatened him.

He did not however present himself the less boldly at the gate of the palace, for he was sustained by the idea that he was doing an heroic action; and he accordingly desired to speak to the king.

The king, who was of easy access, and who gave an audience to whomsoever he had business with, ordered the grand master of the ceremonies to bring the strangers into his presence.

The grand master of the ceremonies then stated that the strangers were of a most villainous appearance, and could not possibly be worse dressed. But the king answered that it was wrong to judge the heart by the countenance, and the gown did not make the parson.

Thereupon, the grand master of the ceremonies, having perceived the correctness of these observations, bowed respectfully and proceeded to fetch the mechanician and the astrologer.

The king was the same as ever, and they immediately recognized him; but the travelers were so changed, especially poor Elias Drosselmayer, that they were obliged to declare who they were.

Upon seeing the two travelers return of their own accord, the king gave a sign of joy, for he felt convinced that they would not have come back if they had not found the Crackatook nut. But he was speedily undeceived; and the mechanician, throwing himself at his feet, confessed that, in spite of the most earnest and constant search, his friend and himself had returned empty-handed.

The king, as we have said, although of a passionate disposition, was an excellent man at bottom; he was touched by the punctuality with which Christian Elias Drosselmayer had kept his word; and he changed the sentence of death, long before pronounced against him, into imprisonment for life. As for the astrologer, he contented himself by banishing that great sage.

But as three days were still remaining of the period of fourteen years and nine months' delay, granted by the king, Master Drosselmayer, who was deeply attached to his country, implored the king's permission to profit by those three days to visit Nuremberg once more.

This request seemed so just to the king, that he granted it without any restriction.

Master Drosselmayer, having only three days left, resolved to profit by that time as much as possible; and, having fortunately found that two places in the mail were not taken, he secured them that moment.

Now, as the astrologer was himself condemned to banishment, and as it was all the same to him which way he went, he took his departure with the mechanician.

Next morning, at about ten o'clock, they were at Nuremberg. As Master Drosselmayer had only one relation in the world, namely his brother, Christopher Zacharais Drosselmayer, who kept one of the principal toy-shops in Nuremberg, it was at his house that he alighted.

Christopher Zacharias Drosselmayer was overjoyed to see his poor brother Christian Elias, whom he had believed to be dead. In the first instance he would not admit that the man with the bald head and the black patch upon the eye was in reality his brother; but the mechanician showed him his famous drab surtout coat, which, all tattered as it was, had retained in certain parts some traces of its original color; and in support of that first proof he mentioned so many family secrets, unknown to all save Zacharias and himself, that the toy-merchant was compelled to yield to the evidence brought forward.

He then inquired of him what had kept him so long absent from his native city, and in what country he had left his hair, his eye, and the missing pieces of his coat.

Christian Elias Drosselmayer had no motive to keep secret from his brother the events which had occurred. He began by introducing his companion in misfortune; and, this formal usage having been performed, he related his adventures from A to Z, ending them by saying that he had only a few hours to stay with his brother, because, not having found the Crackatook nut, he was on the point of being shut up in a dungeon forever.

While Christian Elias was telling his story, Christopher Zacharias had more than once twiddled his finger and thumb, turned round upon one leg, and made a certain knowing noise with his tongue. Under any other circumstances, the mechanician would have demanded of him what those signs meant; but he was so full of thought, that he saw nothing; and it was only when his brother exclaimed, "Hem! Hem!" twice, and "Oh! oh! oh!" three times, that he asked the reason of those expressions.

"The reason is," said Christopher Zacharias, "that it would be strange indeed if—but, no—and yet—"

"What do you mean?" cried the mechanician.

"If—" continued the toy merchant.

"If what?" again said Master Drosselmayer.

But instead of giving any answer, Christopher Zacharias, who, during those short questions and answers, had no doubt collected his thoughts, threw his wig up into the air, and began to caper about, crying, "Brother, you are saved! You shall not go to prison; for either I am much mistaken, or I myself am in possession of the Crackatook nut."

And, without giving any further explanation to his astonished brother, Christopher Zacharaias rushed out of the room, but returned in a moment with a box containing a large gilt filbert, which he presented to the mechanician.

The mechanician, who dared not believe in such good luck, took the nut with hesitation, and turned it round in all directions so as to examine it with the attention which it deserved. He then declared that he was of the same opinion as his brother, and that he should be much astonished if that filbert were not indeed the Crackatook nut. Thus saying, he handed it to the astrologer, and asked his opinion.

The astrologer examined it with as much attention as Master Drosselmayer had done; but shaking his head, he replied, "I should also be of the same opinion as yourself and brother, if the nut were not gilt; but I have not seen anything in the stars showing that the nut we are in search of ought to be so ornamented. Besides, how came your brother by the Crackatook nut?"

"I will explain the whole thing to you," said Christopher, "and tell you how the nut fell into my hands, and how it came to have gilding which prevents you from recognizing it, and which indeed is not its own naturally."

Then—having made them sit down, for he very wisely thought that after traveling for fourteen years and nine months they must be tired—he began as follows:—

"The very day on which the king sent for you under pretense of giving you an Order of Knighthood, a stranger arrived at Nuremberg, carrying with him a bag of nuts which he had to sell. But the nut merchants of this town, being anxious to keep the monopoly them-selves, quarreled with him just opposite my shop. The stranger, with a view to defend himself more easily, placed his bag of nuts upon the ground, and the fight continued, to the great delight of the little boys and the ticket-porters; when a wagon, heavily laden, passed over the bag of nuts. Upon seeing this accident, which they attributed to the justice of heaven, the merchants considered that they were sufficiently avenged, and left the stranger alone. He picked up his bag, and all his nuts were found to be cracked, save ONE—one only—which he handed to me with a strange kind of smile requesting me to buy it for a new zwanziger of the year 1720, and declaring that the day would come when I should not repent the bargain, dear as it might seem. I felt in my pocket, and was much surprised to find a zwanziger of the kind mentioned by this man. The coincidence seemed so strange, that I gave him my zwanziger; he handed me the nut, and took his departure.

"I placed the nut in my window for sale; and although I only asked two kreutzers more than the money I had given for it, it remained in the window for seven or eight years without finding a purchaser. I then had it gilt to increase its value; but for that purpose I uselessly spent two zwanzigers more; for the nut has been here ever since the day I bought it."

At that moment the astrologer, in whose hands the nut had remained, uttered a cry of joy. While Master Drosselmayer was listening to his brother's story, the astrologer had delicately scraped off some of the gilding of the nut; and on the shell he had found the word "Crackatook" engraven in Chinese characters.

All doubts were now cleared up; and the three individuals danced for joy, the real Crackatook nut being actually in their possession.

How, after having found the Crackatook nut, the mechanician and the astrologer find the young man who is to crack it

Christian Elias Drosselmayer was in such a hurry to announce the good news to the king, that he was anxious to return by the mail that very moment; but Christian Zacharias begged him to stay at least until his son should come in. The mechanician yielded the more easily to this request, because he had not seen his nephew for fifteen years, and because, on recalling the idea of the past, he remembered that at the time when he quitted Nuremberg, he had left the said nephew a fine fat romping fellow of only three and a half, but of whom he (the uncle) was dotingly fond.

While he was thinking of these things, a handsome young man of between eighteen and nineteen entered the shop of Christopher Zacharias, whom he saluted by the name of "Father." Then Christopher Zacharaias, having embraced him, presented him to Christian Elias, saying to the young man, "And now embrace your uncle."

The young man hesitated; for Uncle Drosselmayer, with his frock-coat in rags, his bald head, and the plaster upon his eye, did not seem a very inviting person. But his father observed the hesitation, and as he was fearful that Christian Elias's feelings would be wounded, he pushed his son forward, and thrust him into the arms of the mechanician.

In the meantime the astrologer had kept his eyes fixed upon the young man with a steady attention which seemed so singular that the youth felt ill at his ease in being so stared at, and left the room.

The astrologer then put several questions to Christopher Zacharias concerning his son; and the father answered them with all the enthusiasm of a fond parent.

Young Drosselmayer was, as his appearance indicated, between seventeen and eighteen. From his earliest years he had been so funny and yet so tractable, that his mother had taken a delight in dressing him like some of the puppets which her husband sold: namely, sometimes as a student, sometimes as a postilion, sometimes as a Hungarian, but always in a garb that required boots; because, as he possessed the prettiest little foot in the world, but had a rather small calf, the boots showed off the little foot, and concealed the fault of the calf.

"And so," said the astrologer to Christopher Zacharias, "your son has always worn boots?"

Christian Elias now stared in his turn.

"My son has never worn anything but boots," replied the toy-man. "At the age of ten," he continued, "I sent him to the university of Tubingen, where he remained till he was eighteen, without contracting any of the bad habits of his companions, such as drinking, swearing, and fighting. The only weakness of which I believe him to be guilty, is that he allows the four or five wretched hairs which he has upon his chin to grow, without permitting a barber to touch his countenance.

"And thus," said the astrologer, "your son has never been shaved?"

Christian Elias stared more and more.

"Never," answered Christopher Zacharias.

"And during the holidays," continued the astrologer, "how did he pass his time?"

"Why," replied the father, "he used to remain in the shop, in his becoming student's dress; and, through pure good-nature, he cracked nuts for all the young ladies who came to the shop to buy toys and who, on that account, called him *Nutcracker*."

"Nutcracker!" cried the mechanician.

"Nutcracker!" repeated the astrologer in his turn.

And then they looked at each other while Christopher Zacharias looked at them both.

"My dear sir," said the astrologer to the toy-man, "in my opinion your fortune is as good as made."

The toy-man, who had not heard this prophecy without a feeling of pleasure, required an explanation, which the astrologer, however, put off until the next morning.

When the mechanician and the astrologer were shown to their apartment, and were alone together, the astrologer embraced his friend, crying, "It is he! We have him!"

"Do you think so?" demanded Christian Elias, in the tone of a man who had his doubts, but who only wished to be convinced.

"Can there be any uncertainty?" exclaimed the astrologer: "he has all the necessary qualifications!"

"Let us sum them up."

"He has never warn anything but boots."

"True!"

"He has never been shaved."

"True, again!"

"And through good-nature, he has stood in his father's shop to crack nuts for young persons, who never called him by any other name than *Nutcracker.*"

"All this is quite true."

"My dear friend," added the astrologer, "one stroke of good luck never comes alone. But if you still doubt, let us go and consult the stars."

They accordingly ascended to the roof of the house; and, having drawn the young man's horoscope, discovered that he was intended for great things.

This prophecy, which confirmed all the astrologer's hopes, forced the mechanician to adopt his opinion.

"And now," said the astrologer, in a triumphant tone, "there are only two things which we must not neglect."

"What are they?" demanded Christian Elias.

The first, is that you must fit to the nape of your nephew's neck a large piece of wood, which must be so well connected to the lower jaw that it will increase its power by the fact of pressure."

"Nothing is more easy," answered Christian Elias; "it is the A, B, C of mechanics."

"The second thing," continued the astrologer, "is, that on arriving at the residence of the king, we must carefully conceal the fact that we have brought with us the young man who is destined to crack the Crackatook nut. For my opinion is that the more teeth there are broken, and the more jaws there are dislocated in trying to break the Crackatook nut, the more eager the king will be to offer a great reward to him who shall succeed where so many have failed."

"My dear friend," answered the mechanician, "you are a man of sound sense. Let us go to bed."

And, with these words, having quitted the top of the house, they descended to their bed-room, where, having drawn their cotton night-caps over their ears, they slept more comfortably than they had done for fourteen years and nine months past.

On the following morning, at an early hour, the two friends went down to the apartment of Christopher Zacharias, and told him all the fine plans they had formed the evening before. Now, as the toyman was not wanting in ambition, and as, in his paternal fondness, he fancied that his son must certainly possess the strongest jaws in all Germany, he gladly assented to the arrangement, which was to take from his shop not only the nut but also the *Nutcracker.*

The young man himself was more difficult to persuade. The wooden counter-balance which it was proposed to fix to the back of his neck, insteady of the pretty little tie which kept his hair in such neat folds, particularly vexed him. But his father, his uncle, and the astrologer made him such splendid promises, that he consented. Christian Elias Drosselmayer, therefore, went to work that moment; the wooden balance was soon made; and it was strongly fixed to the nape of the young man now so full of hope. Let me also state, to satisfy your curiosity, that the contrivance worked so well that on the very first the skillful mechanician received brilliant proofs of his success, for the young man was enabled to crack the hardest apricot-stones, and the most obstinate peach-stones.

These trials having been made, the astrologer, the mechanician, and young Drosselmayer set out immediately for the king's dwellings. Christopher Zacharias was anxious to go with them; but, as he was forced to take care of his shop, that excellent father resigned himself to necessity, and remained behind at Nuremberg.

End of the History of Princess Pirlipata

The mechanician, on reaching the capital, took good care to leave young Drosselmayer at the inn where they put up. They then proceeded to the palace to announce that having vainly sought the Crackatook nut all over the world, they had at length found it at Nuremberg. But of him who was to crack it, they said not a word, according to the arrangement made between them.

The joy at the palace was very great. The king sent directly for the privy councilor who had the care of the public mind, and who acted as censor in respect to the newspapers; and this great man, by the king's command, drew up an article to be inserted in the Royal Gazette, and which all other newspapers were ordered to copy, to the effect that *"all persons who fancied that they had teeth good enough to break the*

Crackatook nut, were to present themselves at the palace, and if they succeeded, would be liberally rewarded for their trouble."

This circumstance was well-suited to show how rich the kingdom was in strong jaws. The candidates were so numerous, that the king was forced to form a jury, the foreman of whom was the crown dentist; and their duty was to examine all the competitors, to see if they had all their thirty-two teeth perfect, and whether any were decayed.

Three thousand five hundred candidates were admitted to this first trial, which lasted a week, and which produced only an immense number of broken teeth and jaws out of place.

It was therefore necessary to make a second appeal; and all the national and foreign newspapers were crammed with advertisements to that purpose. The king offered the post of Perpetual President of the Academy, and the Order of the Golden Spider to whomsoever should succeed in cracking the Crackatook nut. There was no necessity to have a degree of Doctor of Philosophy, or Master of Arts, to be competent to stand as a candidate.

This second trial produced five thousand candidates. All the learned societies of Europe sent deputies to this important assembly. Several members of the English Royal Society were present; and a great number of critics belonging to the leading London newspapers and literary journals; but they were not able to stand as candidates, because their teeth had all been broken long before in their frequent attempts to tear to pieces the works of their brother authors. This second trial, which lasted a fortnight, was, alas! as fruitless as the first. The deputies of the learned societies disputed amongst themselves, for the honor of the association to which they respectively belonged, as to who should break the nut; but they only left their best teeth behind them.

As for the nut itself, its shell did not even bear the marks of the attempts that had been made to crack it.

The king was in despair. He resolved, however, to strike one grand blow; and, as he had no male descendant, he declared, by means of a third article in the *Royal Gazette*, the national newspapers, and the foreign journals, that the hand of Princess Pirlipata and the inheritance of the throne should be given to him who might crack the Crackatook nut. There was one condition to this announcement;

namely, that this time the candidates must be from sixteen to twenty-four years of age. The promise of such a reward excited all Germany. Competitors poured in from all parts of Europe; and they would even have come from Asia, Africa, and America, and that fifth quarter of the world which had been discovered by Christian Elias Drosselmayer and his friend the astrologer, if there had been sufficient time.

On this occasion the mechanician and the astrologer thought that the moment was now come to produce young Drosselmayer; for it was impossible for the king to offer a higher reward than that just announced. Only, certain of success as they were, and although this time a host of princes and royal and imperial jaws had presented themselves, the mechanician and the astronologer did not appear with their young friend at the register-office until just as it was about to close; so that the name NATHANIEL DROSSELMAYER was number the 11,375th, and stood last.

It was on this occasion as on the preceding ones. The 11,374 rivals of young Drosselmayer were foiled; and on the nineteenth day of the trial, at twenty-five minutes to twelve o'clock, and just as the princess accomplished her fifteenth year, the name of Nathaniel Drosselmayer was called.

The young man presented himself, accompanied by his two guardians, the mechanician and the astrologer. It was the first time that these two illustrious persons had seen the princess since they had beheld her in the cradle; and since that period great changes had taken place with her. But I must inform you, with due candor, that those changes were not to her advantage. When a child, she was shockingly ugly: she was now frightfully so.

Her form had lost, with its growth, none of its important features. It is therefore difficult to understand how those skinny legs, those flat hips, and that distorted body, could have supported such a monstrous head. And that head had the same grizzled hair—the same green eyes—the same enormous mouth—and the same cotton beard on the chin, as we have already described; only all these features were just fifteen years older.

Upon perceiving that monster of ugliness, poor Nathaniel shuddered and inquired of the mechanician and the astrologer if they were quite sure that the kernel of the Crackatook nut would restore the princess to her beauty: because, if she were to remain in that state, he was quite willing to make the trial in a matter where all the others had failed; but he should leave the honor of the marriage and the profit of the heirship of the throne to any one who might be inclined to accept them. It is hardly necessary to state that both the mechanician and the astrologer reassured their young friend, promising that the nut, once broke, and the kernel, once eaten, Pirlipata would become that very moment the most beautiful princess on the face of the earth.

But if the sight of Princess Pirlipata had struck poor Nathaniel with dismay, I must tell you, in honor of the young man, that *his* presence had produced a very different effect upon the sensitive heart of the heiress of the crown; and she could not prevent herself from exclaiming, when she saw him, "Oh! how glad I should be if he were to break the nut!"

Thereupon the chief governess of the princess replied, "I think I have often observed to your highness, that it is not customary for a young and beautiful princess like yourself to express her opinion aloud relative to such matters.

Nathaniel was indeed calculated to turn the heads of all the princesses in the world. He wore a little military frock-coat, of a violet color, all braided, and with golden buttons, and which his uncle had made for this solemn occasion. His breeches were of the same stuff; and his boots were so well blacked, and sat in such admirable manner, that they seemed as if they were painted. The only thing which somewhat spoilt his appearance was the ugly piece of wood fitted to the nape of his neck; but Uncle Drosselmayer had so contrived that it seemed like a little bag attached to his wig, and might at a stretch have passed as an eccentricity of the toilet, or else as a new fashion which Nathaniel's tailor was trying to push into vogue at the court.

Thus it was, that when this charming young man entered the great hall, what the princess had the imprudence to say aloud, the other ladies present said to themselves; and there was not a person, not even excepting the king and the queen, who did not desire at the bottom of his heart that Nathaniel might prove triumphant in the adventure which he had undertaken.

On his side, young Drosselmayer approached with a confidence which encouraged the hopes that were placed in him. Having reached the steps leading to the throne, he bowed to the king and queen, then to Princess Pirlipata, and then to the spectators; after which he received the Crackatook nut from the grand master of the ceremonies, took it delicately between his fore-finger and thumb, placed it in his mouth, and gave violent pull at the wooden balance hanging behind him.

Crack! crack!—and the shell was broken in several pieces.

He then skillfully detached the kernel from the fibers hanging to it, and presented it to the princess, bowing gracefully but respectfully at the same time; after which he closed his eyes, and began to walk backwards. At the same moment the princess swallowed the kernel; and, O! wonder! her horrible ugliness disappeared, and she became a young lady of angelic beauty. Her face seemed to have borrowed the hues of the rose and the lily: her eyes were of sparkling azure; and thick tresses, resembling masses of golden thread, flowed over her alabaster shoulders.

The trumpets and the cymbals sounded enough to make one deaf; and the shouts of the people responded to the noise of the instruments. The king, the ministers, the councilors of state, and the judges began to dance, as they had done at the birth of Pirlipata; and eau-de-cologne was obliged to be thrown in the face of the queen, who had fainted for joy.

The great tumult proved very annoying to young Nathaniel Drosselmayer, who, as you must remember, had yet to step seven paces backwards. He, however, behaved with a coolness which gave the highest hopes relative to the period when he should be called upon to reign in his turn; and he was just stretching out his leg to take the seventh step, when the queen of the mice suddenly appeared through a crevice in the floor. With horrible squeaks she ran between his legs; so that just at that very moment when the future Prince Royal placed his foot upon the ground, his heel came so fully on the body of the mouse that he stumbled in such a manner as to nearly fall.

O sorrow! At the same instant the handsome young man became as ugly as the princess was before him; his shrunken form could hardly support his enormous head; his eyes became green, haggard, and goggle; his mouth split from ear to ear; and his delicate little sprouting beard changed into a white and soft substance, which was afterward found to be cotton.

But the cause of this event was punished at the same moment that she produced it. Dame Mousey was weltering in her own blood upon the floor. Her wickedness did not therefore go without its punishment. In fact, young Drosselmayer had trampled so hard upon her with his heel, that she was crushed beyond all hope of recovery. But, while still writhing on the floor, Dame Mousey squeaked forth the following words, with all the strength of her agonizing voice:

> Crackatook! Crackatook! fatal nut that thou art,
> Through thee has Death reached me, at length, with his dart!
> Heigho! heigho!
> But the Queen of the Mice has thousands to back her,
> And my son will yet punish that wretched Nutcracker,
> I know! I know!
>
> Sweet life, adieu!
> Too soon snatch'd away!
> And thou heaven of blue,
> And thou world so gay,
> Adieu! adieu!"

The verses of Dame Mousey might have been better; but one cannot be very correct, as you will all agree, when breathing the last sigh!

And when that last sigh was rendered, a great officer of the court took up Dame Mousey by the tail, and carried her away for the purpose of interring her remains in the hole where so many of her family had been buried fifteen years and some months beforehand.

As, in the middle of all this, no one had troubled themselves about Nathaniel Drosselmayer except the mechanician and the astrologer, the princess, who was unaware of the accident which had happened, ordered the young hero to be brought into her presence; for, in spite of the lesson read to her by the governess, she was in haste to thank him. But scarcely had she perceived the unfortunate Nathaniel, than she hid her face in her hands; and, forgetting the service which he had rendered her, cried, "Turn out the horrible Nutcracker! turn him out! turn him out!"

The grand marshal of the palace accordingly took poor Nathaniel by the shoulders and pushed him down stairs. The king, who was very angry at having a Nutcracker proposed to him as his son-in-law, attacked the astrologer and the mechanician; and, instead of the income of six hundred pounds a year and the telescope of honor which he had promised the first—instead, also, of the sword set with diamonds, the Order of the Golden Spider, and the drab frock-coat, which he ought to have given the latter—he banished them both from his kingdom, granting them only twenty-four hours to cross the frontiers.

Obedience was necessary. The mechanician, the astrologer, and young Drosselmayer (now become a Nutcracker), left the capital and quitted the country. But when night came, the two learned men consulted the stars once more, and read in them that, all deformed though he were, Nathaniel would not the less become a prince and king, unless indeed he chose to remain a private individual, which was left to his own choice. This was to happen when his deformity should disappear; and that deformity would disappear when he should have commanded an army in battle—when he should have killed the seven-headed king of the mice, who was born after Dame Mousey's seven first sons had been put to death,—and, lastly, when a beautiful lady should fall in love with him.

But while awaiting these brilliant destinies, Nathaniel Drosselmayer, who had left the paternal shop as the only son and heir, now returned to it in the form of a Nutcracker!

I need scarcely tell you that his father did not recognize him; and that, when Christopher Zacharias inquired of the mechanician and his friend the astrologer, what had become of his dearly-beloved son, those two illustrious persons replied, with the seriousness of learned men, that the king and the queen would not allow the savior of the princess to leave them, and that young Nathaniel remained at court covered with honor and glory. As for the unfortunate Nutcracker, who felt how deeply painful was his situation, he uttered not a word, but resolved to await patiently the change which must some day or another take place in him. Nevertheless, I must candidly admit, that in spite of the good nature of his disposition, he was desperately vexed with Uncle Drosselmayer, who, coming at a moment he was so little expected, and having enticed him away by so many fine promises, was the sole and only cause of the frightful misfortune that had occurred to him.

Such, my dear children, is the History of the Crackatook Nut, not just as Godfather Drosselmayer told it to little Mary and Fritz; and you can now understand why people often say, when speaking of anything difficult to do, "That is a hard nut to crack."

The Uncle and the Nephew

If any one of my young friends now around me has ever cut himself with glass, which he has most likely done in the days of his disobedience, he must know by experience that it is a particularly disagreeable kind of cut, because it is so long in healing. Mary was, therefore, forced to stay a whole week in bed; for she always felt giddy whenever she tried to get up. But at last she got well altogether, and was able to skip about the room as she was wont to do.

You would not do my little heroine the injustice to suppose that her first visit was to any other place than the glass cupboard, which now seemed quite charming to look at. A new pane had been put in; and all the windows had been so well cleaned by Miss Trudchen, that all the trees, houses, dolls, and other toys of the Christmas Eve seemed quite new, gay, and polished. But in the midst of all the treasures of her little kingdom, and before all other things, Mary perceived her Nutcracker smiling upon her from the second shelf where he was placed, and with his teeth all in as good order as ever they were. While thus joyfully examining her favorite, an idea which had more than once presented itself to the mind of Mary touched her to the quick. She was persuaded that all Godfather Drosselmayer had told her was not a mere fable, but the true history of the disagreement between the Nutcracker on one side, and the late queen of the mice and her son, the reigning king, on the other side. She, therefore, knew that the Nutcracker could be neither more nor less than Nathaniel Drosselmayer, of Nuremberg, the amiable but enchanted nephew of her godfather; for that the skillful mechanician who had figured at the court of Pirlipata's father, was Doctor Drosselmayer, she had never doubted from the moment when he introduced his drab frock-coat into his tale. This belief was strengthened when she found him losing first his hair by a sun-stroke, and then his eye by an arrow, events which had rendered necessary the invention of the ugly black patch, and of the ingenious glass wig, of which I have already spoken.

"But why did not your uncle help you, poor Nutcracker?" said Mary, as she stood at the glass cupboard, gazing up at her favorite; for she remembered that on the success of the battle depended the disenchantment of the poor little man and his elevation to the rank of king of the kingdom of toys. Then she thought that all the dolls, puppets, and little men must be well prepared to receive him as their king; for did they not obey the Nutcracker as soldiers obey a general? That indifference on the part of Godfather Drosselmayer was so much the more annoying to little Mary, because she was certain that those dolls and puppets to which, in her imagination, she gave life and motion, really did live and move.

Nevertheless, there was now no appearance of either life or motion in the cupboard, where everything was still and quiet. But Mary, rather than give up her sincere belief, thought that all this was occasioned by the sorcery of the late queen of the mice and her son; and so firm was she in this belief, that, while she gazed up at the Nutcracker, she continued to say aloud what she had only begun to say to herself.

"And yet," she resumed, "although you are unable to move, and are prevented by enchantment from saying a single word to me, I am very sure, my dear Mr. Drosselmayer, that you understand me perfectly, and that you are well aware of my good intentions with regard to you. Reckon, then upon my support when you require it; and in the meantime, do not vex yourself. I will go straight to your uncle, and beg him to assist you; and if he only loves you a little, he is so clever that I am sure he can help you."

In spite of the eloquence of this speech, the Nutcracker did not move an inch; but it seemed to Mary that a sigh came from behind the glass, the panes of which began to sound very low, but wonderfully soft and pleasing; while it appeared to Mary that a sweet voice, like a small silver bell, said, "Dear little Mary, thou art my guardian angel! I will be thine, and Mary shall be mine!" And at these words, so mysteriously heard, Mary felt a singular sensation of happiness, in spite of the shudder which passed through her entire frame.

Twilight had now arrived; and the judge returned home, accompanied by Doctor Drosselmayer. In a few moments Miss Trudchen got tea ready, and all the family were gathered round the table, talking gaily. As for Mary, she had been to fetch her little arm-chair, and had seated herself in silence at the feet of Godfather Drosselmayer. Taking advantage of a moment when no one was speaking, she raised her large blue eyes towards the doctor, and, looking earnestly at him, said, "I now know, dear godpapa, that my Nutcracker is your nephew, young Drosselmayer, of Nuremberg. He has become a prince, and also a king of the kingdom of toys, as your friend the astrologer prophesied. But you know that he is at open war with the king of the mice. Come, dear godpapa, tell me why you did not help him when you were sitting astride upon the clock? and why do you now desert him?"

And, with these words, Mary again related, amidst the laughter of her father, her mother, and Miss Trudchen, the events of that famous battle which she had seen. Fritz and Godfather Drosselmayer alone did not enjoy the whole scene.

"Where," said the godfather, "does that little girl get all those foolish ideas which enter her head?"

"She has a very lively imagination," replied Mary's mother; "and, after all, these are only dreams and visions occasioned by fever."

"And I can prove *that*," shouted Fritz; "for she says that my red hussars took to flight, which cannot possibly be true—unless indeed they are abominable cowards, in which case they would not get the better of me, for I would flog them all soundly."

Then, with a singular smile, Godfather Drosselmayer took Mary upon his knees, and said with more kindness than before, "My dear child, you do not know what course you are pursuing in espousing so warmly the cause of your Nutcracker. You will have to suffer much if you persist in taking the part of one who is in disgrace; for the king of the mice, who considers him to be the murderer of his mother, will persecute him in all ways. But, in any case, remember that it is not I—but you alone—who can save him. Be firm and faithful—and all will go well."

Neither Mary nor anyone else understood the words of Godfather Drosselmayer: on the contrary, those words seemed so strange to the judge, that he took the doctor's hand, felt his pulse for some moments in silence, and then said, "My dear friend, you are very feverish, and I should advise you to go home to bed."

The Duel

During the night, which followed the scene just related, and while the moon, shining in all its splendor, cast its bright rays through the openings in the curtains, Mary, who now slept with her mother, was awakened by a noise that seemed to come from the corner of the room, and was mingled with sharp screeches and squeakings.

"Alas!" cried Mary, who remembered to have heard the same noise on the occasion of the famous battle; "alas! the mice are coming again! Mamma, mamma, mamma!"

But her voice was stifled in her throat, in spite of all her efforts: she endeavored to get up to run out of the room, but seemed to be nailed to her bed, unable to move her limbs. At length, turning her affrighted eyes towards the corner of the room, when the noise came, she beheld the king of the mice scraping for himself a way through the wall, and thrusting in first one of his heads, then another, then a third, and so on until the whole seven, each with a crown, made their appearance. Having entered the room, he walked several times round it like a victor who takes possession of his conquest: he then leapt with one bound upon a table that was standing near the bed. Gazing upon her with his fourteen eyes, all as bright as carbuncles, and with a gnashing of his teeth and a horrible squeaking noise, he said, "Fe, fa fum! You must give me all your sugar-plums and your sweet cakes, little girl, and if not, I will eat up your friend the Nutcracker."

Then, having uttered this threat, he fled from the room by the same hole as he had entered by.

Mary was so frightened by this terrible apparition, that she awoke in the morning very pale and broken-hearted, the more so that she dared not mention what had taken place during the night, for fear of being laughed at. Twenty times was she on the point of telling all, either to her mother or to Fritz; but she stopped, still thinking that neither the one nor the other would believe her. It was, however, pretty clear that she must sacrifice her sugar-plums and her sweet cakes to the safety of the poor Nutcracker. She accordingly placed them all on the ledge of the cupboard that very evening.

Next morning, the judge's wife said, "I really do not know whence come all the mice that have suddenly invaded the house; but those naughty creatures have actually eaten up all my poor little Mary's sugar-plums."

703

The lady was not quite right; the sugar-plums and cakes were only *spoilt*, not *eaten up*; for the gluttonous king of the mice, not finding the sweet cakes as good as he expected, messed them about so that the were forced to be thrown away.

But as it was not sugar-plums that Mary liked best, she did not feel much regret at the sacrifice which the king of the mice had extorted from her; and, thinking that he would be content with the first contribution with which he had taxed her, she was much pleased at the idea of having saved Nutcracker upon such good terms.

Unfortunately her satisfaction was not of long duration; for the following night she was again awoke by hearing squeaking and whining close by her ears.

Alas! it was the king of the mice again, his eyes shining more horribly than on the preceding night; and, in a voice interrupted by frequent whines and squeaks, he said, "You must give me your little sugar dolls and figures made of biscuit, little girl; if not, I will eat up your friend the Nutcracker."

Thereupon the king of the mice went skipping away, and disappeared by the hole in the wall.

Next morning, Mary, now deeply afflicted, went straight to the glass cupboard, and threw a mournful look upon her figures of sugar and biscuit; and her grief was very natural, for never were such nice-looking sweet things seen before.

"Alas!" she said, as she turned towards the Nutcracker, "what would I not do for you, my dear Mr. Drosselmayer? But you must admit all the same that what I am required to do is very hard."

At these words the Nutcracker assumed so piteous an air, that Mary, who fancied that she was for ever beholding the jaws of the king of the mice opening to devour him, resolved to make this second sacrifice to save the unfortunate young man. That very evening, therefore, she placed her sugar figures and her biscuits upon the ledge of the cupboard, where the night before she had put her sugar-plums and sweet cakes. Kissing them, however, one after another, as a token of farewell, she yielded up her shepherds and shepherdesses, and her sheep, concealing behind the flock at the same time a little sugar baby with fat round cheeks, and which she loved above all the other things.

"Now really this is too bad!" cried the judge's wife next morning: "it is very clear that these odious mice have taken up their dwelling in the glass cupboard; for all poor Mary's sugar figures are eaten up."

At these words large tears started from Mary's eyes; but she dried them up almost directly, and even smiled sweetly as she thought to herself, "What matter my shepherds, shepherdesses, and sheep, since the Nutcracker is saved!"

"Mamma," cried Fritz, who was present at the time, "I must remind you that our baker has an excellent gray cat, which we might send for, and which would soon put an end to all this by snapping up the mice one after another, and even Dame Mousey herself afterwards, as well as her son the king."

"Yes," replied the judge's wife; "but that same cat would jump upon the table and shelves, and break my glasses and cups to pieces."

"Oh! there is no fear of *that*!" cried Fritz. "The baker's cat is too polite to do any such thing; and I wish I could walk along the pipes and the roofs of houses as skillfully as he can."

"No cats here, if you please!" cried the judge's wife, who could not bear those domestic animals.

"But, after all," said the judge, who overheard what was going on, "some good may follow from the remarks of Fritz: if you will not have a cat, get a mouse-trap."

"Capital!" cried Fritz: "that idea is very happy, since Godpapa Drosselmayer invented mouse-traps."

Every one now laughed; and as, after a strict search, no such thing as a mouse-trap was found in the house, the servants went to Godfather Drosselmayer, who sent back a famous one, which was baited with a bit of bacon, and placed in the spot where the mice had made such havock.

Mary went to bed with the hope that morning would find the king of the mice a prisoner in the box, to which his gluttony was almost certain to lead him. But at about eleven o'clock, and while she was in her first sleep, she was awoke by something cold and velvety that leapt about her arms and face; and, at the same moment, the whining and squeaking which she knew so well, rang in her ears. The horrible king of the mice was there—seated on her pillow, with his eyes shooting red flames and his seven mouths wide open, as if he were about to eat poor Mary up.

"I laugh at the trap—I laugh at the trap," said the king of the mice: "I shall not go into the little house, and the bacon will not tempt me. I shall not be taken: I laugh at the trap! But you must give me your picture-books and your little silk frock; if not, I will eat up your friend the Nutcracker."

You can very well understand that after such a demand as this, Mary awoke in the morning with her heart full of sorrow and her eyes full of tears. Her mother, moreover, told her nothing new when she said that the trap had remained empty, and that the king of the mice had suspected the snare. Then, as the judge's wife left the room to see after the breakfast, Mary entered her papa's room, and going up to the cupboard, said, "Alas, my dear good Mr. Drosselmayer, where will all this end? When I have given my picture-books to the king of the mice to tear, and my pretty little silk frock, which my guardian angel sent me, to rend into pieces, he will not be content, but will every day be asking me for more. And when I have nothing else left to give him, he will perhaps eat me up in your place. Alas! what can a poor little girl like me do for you, dear good Mr. Drosselmayer? what can I do?"

While Mary was weeping and lamenting in this manner, she observed that the Nutcracker had a drop of blood upon his neck. From the day when she had discovered that her favorite was the son of the toyman and the nephew of the Doctor, she had left off carrying him in her arms, and had neither kissed nor caressed him. Indeed, so great was her timidity in this respect, that she had not even dared to touch him with the tip of her finger. But at this moment, seeing that he was hurt, and fearing lest his wound might be dangerous, she took him gently out of the cupboard, and began to wipe away with her handkerchief the drop of blood which was upon his neck. But how great washer astonishment, when she suddenly felt the Nutcracker moving about in her hands! She replaced him quickly upon the shelf: his lips quivered from ear to ear, which made his mouth seem larger still; and, by dint of trying to speak, he concluded by uttering the following words:— "Ah, dear Miss Silberhaus—excellent friend—what do I not owe you? and how much gratitude have I to express to you? Do not sacrifice for me your picture-books and your silk frock; but get me a sword—a good sword—and I will take care of the rest!"

The Nutcracker would have said more; but his words became unintelligible—his voice sank altogether—and his eyes, for a moment animated by an expression of the softest melancholy, grew motionless and vacant. Mary felt no alarm: on the contrary, she leapt for joy, for she was very happy at the idea of being able to save the Nutcracker, without being compelled to give up her picture-books or her silk frock. One thing alone vexed her—and that was where could she find the good sword that the little man required? Mary resolved to explain her difficulty to Fritz, who, in spite of his blustering manners, she knew to be a good-natured boy. She accordingly took him up close to the glass cupboard, told him all that had happened between the Nutcracker and the king of the mice, and ended by explaining the nature of the service she required of him. The only thing which made a great impression upon Fritz was the idea that his hussars had really acted in a cowardly manner in the thickest of the battle: he therefore asked Mary if the accusations were really true; and as he knew that she never told a story, he believed her words. Then, rushing up to the cupboard, he made a speech to his soldiers, who seemed quite ashamed of themselves. But this was not all: in order to punish the whole regiment in the person of its officers, he degraded them one after the other, and expressly ordered the band not to play the *Hussar's March* during parade.

Then, turning to Mary, he said, "As for the Nutcracker, who seems to me to be a brave little fellow, I think I can manage his business; for, as I put a veteran major of horse-guards upon half pay yesterday, he having finished his time in the service, I should think he cannot want his sword any longer. It is an excellent blade, I can assure you!"

It now remained to find the major. A search was commenced, and he was found living on his half-pay in a little tavern which stood in a dark corner of the third shelf in the cupboard. As Fritz had imagined, he offered no objection to give up his sword, which had become useless to him, and which was that instant fastened to the Nutcracker's neck.

The fear which Mary now felt prevented her from sleeping all the next night; and she was so wide awake that she heard the clock strike twelve in the room where the cupboard was. Scarcely had the hum of the last stroke ceased, when strange noises came from the direction of the cupboard; and then there was a great clashing of swords, as if two enemies were fighting in mortal combat. Suddenly one of the duelists gave a squeak!

"The king of the mice!" cried Mary, full of joy and terror at the same time.

There was then a dead silence; but presently some one knocked gently—very gently—at the door; and a pretty little voice said, "Dearest Miss Silberhaus, I have glorious news for you: open the door, I beseech you!"

Mary recognized the voice of young Drosselmayer. She hastily put on her little frock, and opened the door. The Nutcracker was there, holding the blood-stained sword in his right hand and a candle in his left. The moment he saw Mary he knelt down, and said, "It is you alone, O dearest lady! who have nerved me up with the chivalrous courage which I have just shown, and who gave me strength to fight that insolent wretch who dared to threaten you. The vile king of the mice is bathed in his blood. Will you, O lady! deign to accept the trophies of the victory—trophies that are offered by the hand of a knight who is devoted to you until death?"

With these words the Nutcracker drew from his left arm the seven gold crowns of the king of the mice, which he had placed there as if they were bracelets, and which he now offered to Mary, who received them with joy.

The Nutcracker, encouraged by this amiability on her part, then rose and spoke thus:—"Oh! dear Miss Silberhaus, now that I have conquered my enemy, what beautiful things can I show you, if you would have the conde-scension to go with me only a few paces hence! Oh! do not refuse me—do not refuse me, dear lady—I implore you!"

Mary did not hesitate a moment to follow the Nutcracker, knowing how great were her claims upon his gratitude, and being quite certain that he had no evil intention towards her.

"I will follow you," she said, "my dear Mr. Drosselmayer; but you must not take me very far, nor keep me long away, because I have not yet slept a wink."

"I will choose the shortest, although the most difficult, path," said the Nutcracker; and, thus speaking, he led the way, Mary following him.

The Kingdom of Toys

They both reached, in a short time, a large old cupboard standing in a passage near the door, and which was used as a clothes'-press. There the Nutcracker stopped; and Mary observed, to her great astonishment, that the folding-doors of the cupboard, which were nearly always kept shut, were now wide open, so that she could see plainly her father's traveling-cloak lined with fox-skin, which was hanging over the other clothes. The Nutcracker climbed very skill-fully along the border of the cloak; and, clinging to the braiding, he reached the large cape, which, fastened by a piece of lace, fell over the back of the cloak. From beneath this cape the Nutcracker drew down a pretty little ladder of cedar-wood, which he placed in such a manner that the foot touched the bot-tom of the cupboard, and the top was lost in the sleeve of the cloak.

"Now, dear young lady," said the Nutcracker, "have the goodness to give me your hand and ascend with me."

Mary complied; and scarcely had she glanced up the sleeve, when a brilliant light burst upon her view, and she suddenly found herself transported into the midst of a fragrant meadow, which glittered as if it were strewed with precious stones.

"Oh! how charming!" cried Mary, dazzled by the sight, "where are we?"

"We are in the Field of Sugar-candy, Miss; but we will not remain here, unless you wish to do so. Let us pass through this door."

Then Mary observed a beautiful gate through which they left the field. The gate seemed to be made of white marble, red marble, and blue marble; but when Mary drew near it she saw that it was made of preserves, candied orange-peel, burnt almonds, and sugared raisins. This was the reason, as she learnt from the Nutcracker, why that gate was called the Gate of Burnt Almonds.

The gate opened into a long gallery, the roof of which was supported by pillars of barley-sugar. In the gallery there were five monkeys, all dressed in red, and playing music, which, if it were not the most melodious in the world, was at least the most original. Mary made so much haste to see more, that she did not even perceive that she was walking upon a pavement of pistachio-nuts and macaroons, which she took for marble. At length she reached the end of the gallery, and scarcely was she in the open air, when she found herself surrounded by the most delicious perfumes, which came from a charming little forest that opened before her. This forest, which would have been dark were it not for the quantity of lamps that it contained, was lighted up in so brilliant a manner that it was easy to distinguish the golden and silver fruits, which were suspended to branches ornamented with white ribands and nosegays, resembling marriage favors.

"Oh! my dear Mr. Drosselmayer," cried Mary, "what is the name of this charming place, I beseech you?"

"We are now in the Forest of Christmas, Miss," answered the Nutcracker; "and it is here that people come to fetch the trees to which the presents sent by the guardian angels are fastened."

"Oh!" continued Mary, "may I not remain here one moment? Everything is so nice here and smells so sweet!"

The Nutcracker clapped his hands together; and several shepherds and shepherdesses, hunters and huntresses, came out of the forest, all so delicate and white that they seemed made of refined sugar. They carried on their shoulders an arm-chair, made of chocolate, incrusted with angelica, in which they placed a cushion of jujube, inviting Mary most politely to sit down. Scarcely had she done so when, as at operas, the shepherds and shepherd-esses, the hunters and huntresses, took their places and began to dance a charming ballet to an accompaniment of horns and bugles, which the hunt-ers blew with such good will that their faces became flushed just as if they were made of conserve of roses. Then, the dance being finished, they all dis-appeared in a grove.

"Pardon me, dear Miss Silberhaus," said the Nutcracker, holding out his hand towards Mary,—"pardon me for having exhibited to you so poor a bal-let; but those simpletons can do nothing better than repeat, over and over again, the same step. As for the hunters, they blew their bugles as if they were afraid of them; and I can promise you that I shall not let it pass so quietly. But let us leave those creatures for the present, and continue our walk, if you please."

"I really found it all very delightful," said Mary, accepting the invitation of the Nutcracker; "and it seems to me, my dear Mr. Drosselmayer, that you are harsh towards the little dancers."

The Nutcracker made a face, as much as to say, "We shall see; but your plea in their favor shall be considered." They then continued their journey, and reached a river which seemed to send forth all the sweet scents that per-fumed the air.

"This," said the Nutcracker, without even waiting to be questioned by Mary, "is the River of Orange Juice. It is one of the smallest in the kingdom; for, save in respect to its, sweet odor, it cannot be compared to the River of Lemonade, which falls into the southern sea, or the Sea of Punch. The Lake of Sweet Whey is also finer: it joins the northern sea, which is called the Sea of Milk of Almonds."

At a short distance was a little village, in which the houses, the church, and the parsonage were all brown; the roofs however were gilt, and the walls were resplendent with incrustations of red, blue, and white sugar-plums.

"This is the Village of Sweet Cake," said the Nutcracker; "it is a pretty little place, as you perceive, and is situated on the Streamlet of Honey. The inhabitants are very agreeable to look upon; but they are always in a bad humor, because they are constantly troubled with the tooth-ache. But, my dear Miss Silberhaus," continued the Nutcracker, "do not let us stop at all the villages and little towns of the kingdom. To the capital! to the capital!"

The Nutcracker advanced, still holding Mary's hand, but walking more confidently than he hitherto had done; for Mary, who was full of curiosity, kept by his side, light as a bird. At length, after the expiration of some minutes, the odor of roses was spread through the air, and everything around them now seemed to be of a rose-tint. Mary remarked that this was the perfume and the reflection of a River of Essence of Roses, which flowed along, its waves rippling melodiously. Upon the sweet-scented waters, silver swans, with collars of gold round their necks, swam gently along, warbling the most delicate songs, so that this harmony, with which they were apparently much pleased, made the diamond fishes leap up around them.

"Ah! cried Mary," this is the pretty river which Godpapa Drosselmayer made me at Christmas; and I am the girl who played with the swans!"

The Journey

The Nutcracker tapped his hands together once more; and, at the moment, the River of Essence of Roses began to rise visibly; and from its swelling waves came forth a chariot made of shells, and covered with precious stones that glittered in the sun. It was drawn by golden dolphins; and four charming little Moors, with caps made of scales of gold-fish and clothes of humming-birds' feathers, leapt upon the bank. They first carried Mary, and then the Nutcracker, very gently down to the chariot, which instantly began to advance upon the stream.

You must confess that it was a ravishing spectacle, and one which might even be compared to the voyage of Cleopatra upon the Cydnus, which you read of in Roman History, to behold little Mary in the chariot of shells, surrounded by perfume, and floating on the waves of essence of roses. The golden dolphins that drew the chariot, tossed up their heads, and threw into the air the glittering jets of of rosy crystal, which fell in variegated showers of all the colors of the rainbow. Moreover, that pleasure might penetrate every sense, a soft music began to echo round; and sweet silvery voices were heard singing in the following manner:

Who art thou, thus floating where essence of rose
In a stream of sweet perfume deliciously flows?
    Art thou the Fairies Queen?
Say, dear little fishes that gleam in the tide;
Or answer, ye cygnets that gracefully glide
    Upon that flood serene!

And all this time the little Moors, who stood behind the seat on the chariot of shells, shook two parasols, hung with bells, in such a manner that those sounds formed an accompaniment to the vocal melody. And Mary, beneath the shade of the parasols, leant over the waters, each wave of which as it passed reflected her smiling countenance.

In this manner she traversed the Riddle of Essence of Roses and reached the bank on the opposite side. Then, when they were within an oar's length of the shore, the little Moors leapt, some into the water, others on the bank, the whole forming a chain so as to convey Mary and the Nutcracker ashore upon a carpet made of angelica, all covered with mint-drops.

The Nutcracker now conducted Mary through a little grove, which was perhaps prettier than the Christmas Forest, so brilliantly did each tree shine, and so sweetly did they all smell with their own peculiar essence. But what was most remarkable was the quantity of fruits hanging to the branches, those fruits being not only of singular color and transparency—some yellow as the topaz, others red like the ruby—but also of a wondrous perfume.

"We are now in the Wood of Preserved Fruits," said the Nutcracker, "and beyond that boundary is the capital."

And, as Mary thrust aside the last branches, she was stupefied at beholding the extent, the magnificence, and the novel appearance of the city which rose before her upon a mound of flowers. Not only did the walls and steeples glitter with the most splendid colors, but, in respect to the shape of the buildings, it was impossible to see any so beautiful upon the earth. The fortifications and the gates were built of candied fruits, which shone in the sun with their own gay colors, all rendered more brilliant still by the crystallized sugar that covered them. At the principal gate, which was the one by which they entered, silver soldiers presented arms to them, and a little man, clad in a dressing-gown of gold brocade, threw himself into the Nutcracker's arms, crying "Oh! dear prince, have you come at length? Welcome—welcome to the City of Candied Fruits!"

Mary was somewhat astonished at the great title given to the Nutcracker; but she was soon drawn from her surprise by the noise of an immense quantity of voices all chattering at the same time; so that she asked the Nutcracker if there were some disturbance or some festival in the Kingdom of Toys?

"There is nothing of all that, dear Miss Silberhaus," answered the Nutcracker; "but the City of Candied Fruits is so happy a place, and all its people are so joyful, that they are constantly talking and laughing. And this is always the same as you see it now. But come with me; let us proceed, I implore of you."

Mary, urged by her own curiosity and by the polite invitation of the Nutcracker, hastened her steps, and soon found herself in a large market-place, which had seen the most magnificent aspects that could possibly be seen. All the houses around were of sugar, open with fretwork, and having balcony over balcony; and in the middle of the market-place was an enormous cake, from the inside of which flowed four fountains, namely, lemonade, orangeade, sweet milk, and gooseberry syrup. The basins around were filled with whipped syllabub, so delicious in appearance, that several well-dressed persons publicly ate of it by means of spoons. But the most agreeable and amusing part of the whole scene, was the crowd of little people who walked about, arm-in-arm, by the thousands and tens of thousands, all laughing, singing, and chattering at the tops of their voices, so that Mary could now account for the joyous din which she had heard. Besides the inhabitants of the capital, there were men of all countries—Armenians, Jews, Greeks, Tyrolese, officers, soldiers, clergymen, monks, shepherds, punches, and all kinds of funny people, such as one meets with in the world.

Presently the tumult redoubled at the entrance of a street looking upon the great square; and the people stood aside to allow the cavalcade to pass. It was the Great Mogul, who was carried upon a palanquin, attended by ninety-three lords of his kingdom and seven hundred slaves: but, at the same time, it happened that from the opposite street the Grand Sultan appeared on horseback, followed by three hundred janissaries. The two sovereigns had always been rivals, and therefore enemies; and this feeling made it impossible for their attendants to meet each other without quarreling. It was even much worse, as you may well suppose, when those two powerful monarchs found themselves face to face: in the first place there was a great confusion, from the midst of which the citizens sought to save themselves; but cries of fury and despair were soon heard, for a gardener, in the act of running away, had knocked off the head of a Brahmin, greatly respected by his own class; and the Grand Sultan's horse had knocked down a frightened punch, who endeavored to creep between the animal's legs to get away from the riot. The din was increasing, when the gentleman in the gold brocade dressing-gown, who had saluted the Nutcracker by the title of "Prince" at the gate of the city, leapt to the top of the huge cake with a single bound; and having run a silvery sweet-toned bell three times, cried out three times, "Confectioner! confectioner! confectioner!"

That instant did the tumult subside and the combatants separate. The Grand Sultan was brushed, for he was covered with dust; the Brahmin's head was fixed on, with the injunction that he must not sneeze for three days, for fear it should fall off again; and order was restored. The pleasant sports began again, and everyone hastened to quench his thirst with the lemonade, the orangeade, the sweet milk, or the gooseberry syrup, and to regale himself with the whip-syllabub.

"My dear Mr. Drosselmayer," said Mary, "what is the cause of the influence exercised upon those little folks by the word confectioner repeated thrice?"

"I must tell you, Miss," said the Nutcracker, "that the people of the City of Candied Fruits believe, by experience, in the transmigration of souls, and are in the power of a superior principle, called confectioner, which principle can bestow on each individual what form he likes by merely baking, for a shorter or longer period, as the case may be. Now, as everyone believes his own existing shape to be the best, he does not like to change it. Hence the magic influence of the word confectioner upon the head of the City of Candied Fruits, when pronounced by the chief magistrate. It is sufficient, as you perceive, to appease all that tumult; everyone in an instant, forgets earthly things, broken ribs, and bumps upon the head; and, restored to himself, says, "*What is man? and what may he not become?*"

While they were thus talking, they reached the entrance of the palace, which shed around a rosy luster, and was surmounted by a hundred light and elegant towers. The walls were strewed with nosegays, of violets, narcissi, tulips, and jasmine, which set of with their various hues the rose-colored ground from which they stood forth. The great dome in the center was covered with thousands of gold and silver stars.

"O, heavens!" exclaimed Mary, "what is that wonderful building?"

"The Palace of Sweet Cake," answered the Nutcracker; "and it is one of the most famous monuments in the capital of the Kingdom of Toys."

Nevertheless, lost in wonder as she was, Mary could not help observing that the roof of one of the great towers was totally wanting and that the little gingerbread men, mounted on a scaffold of cinnamon, were occupied in repairing it. She was about to question the Nutcracker relative to this accident, when he said, "Alas! It is only a disgrace, if not with absolute ruin. The giant Glutton ate up the top of that tower; and he was already on the point of biting the dome, when the people hastened to give him as a tribute the quarter of the city called Almond and Honey-cake District, together with a large portion of the Forest of Angelica, in consideration of which he agreed to take himself off without making any worse ravages than those which you see."

At that moment a soft an delicious music was heard. The gates of the palace opened themselves, and twelve little pages came forth, carrying in their hands branches of aromatic herbs, lighted like torches. Their heads were made of pearl, six of them had bodies made of rubies, and the six others of emeralds, wherewith they trotted joyously along upon two little feet of gold, sculptured with all the taste and care of Benvenuto Cellini.

They were followed by four ladies, about the same size as Miss Clara, Mary's new doll; but all so splendidly dressed and so richly adorned, that Mary was not at a loss to perceive in them the royal princesses of the City of Preserved Fruits. They all four, upon perceiving the Nutcracker, hastened to embrace him with the utmost tenderness, exclaiming at the same time, and as it were with one voice, "Oh! prince—dear prince! Dear—dear brother!"

The Nutcracker seemed much moved; he wiped away the tears which flowed from his eyes, and, taking Mary by the hand, said, in a feeling tone, to the four princesses, "My dear sisters, this is Miss Silberhaus whom I now introduce to you. She is the daughter of Chief-Justice Silberhaus, of Nuremberg, a gentleman of the highest respectability. It is this young lady who saved my life; for, if at the moment when I lost a battle she had not thrown her shoe at the king of the mice—and, again, if she had not afterward lent me the sword of a major whom her brother had placed on the half-pay list—I should even now be sleeping in my tomb, or what is worse, be devoured by the king of the mice. "Ah! My dear Miss Silberhaus," cried the Nutcracker, with an enthusiasm which he could not control, "Pirlipata, although the daughter of a king, was not worthy to unloose the latchet of your pretty little shoes."

"Oh! No—no; certainly not!" repeated the four princesses in chorus; and, throwing their arms round Mary's neck, they cried, "Oh! Noble liberatrix of our dear and much-loved prince and brother! Oh! Excellent Miss Silberhaus!"

And, with these exclamations, which their heart-felt joy cut short, the four princesses conducted the Nutcracker and Mary into the palace, made them sit down upon beautiful little sofas of cedar-wood, covered with golden flowers, and then insisted upon preparing a banquet with their own hands. With this object, they hastened to fetch a number of little vases and bowls made of the finest Japanese porcelain, and silver knives, forks, spoons, and other articles of the table. They then brought in the finest fruits and most delicious sugar-plums that Mary had ever seen, and began to bustle about so nimbly that Mary was at no loss to perceive how well they understood everything connected with cooking. Now, as Mary herself was well acquainted with such matters, she wished inwardly to take a share in all that was going on; and, as if she understood Mary's wishes, the most beautiful of the Nutcracker's four sisters, handed her a little golden mortar, saying, "Dear liberatrix of my brother, pound me some sugar-candy, if you please."

Mary hastened to do as she was asked; and while she was pounding the sugar-candy in the mortar, when a delicious music came forth, the Nutcracker began to relate all his adventures: but, strange as it was, it seemed to Mary during that recital, as if the words of young Drosselmayer and the noise of the pestle came gradually more and more indistinct to her ears. In a short time she seemed to be surrounded by a light vapor turned into a silvery mist, which spread more and more densely around her, so that it presently concealed the Nutcracker and the princesses from her sight. Strange songs, which reminded her of those she had heard on the River of Essence of Roses, met her ears, commingled with the increasing murmur of waters; and then Mary thought that the waves flowed beneath her, raising her up in their swell. She felt as if she were rising high up—higher—and higher; when, suddenly, down she fell from a precipice that she could not measure.

Conclusion

One does not fall several thousand feet without awaking. Thus it was that Mary awoke; and, on awaking, she found herself in her little bed. It was broad daylight, and her mother, who was standing by her, said, "Is it possible to be so lazy as you are? Come, get up, and dress yourself, dear little Mary, for breakfast is waiting."

"Oh! my dear mamma," said Mary, opening her eyes wide with astonishment, "whither did young Mr. Drosselmayer take me last night? And what splendid things did he show me?"

Then Mary related all that I have just told you; and when she had done her mother said, "You have had a very long and charming dream, dear little Mary; but now that you are awake, you must forget it all, and come and have your breakfast."

But Mary, while she dressed herself, persisted in maintaining the she had really seen all she spoke of. Her mother accordingly went to the cupboard and took out the Nutcracker, who, according to custom, was upon the third shelf. Bringing it to her daughter, she said, "How can you suppose, silly child, that this puppet, which is made of wood and cloth, can be alive, or move, or think?"

"But, my dear mamma," said Mary, perpetually, I am well aware that the Nutcracker is none other than young Mr. Drosselmayer, the nephew of godpapa."

At that moment Mary heard a loud shout of laughter behind her.

It was the judge, Fritz, and Miss Trudchen, who made themselves merry at her expense.

"Ah!" cried Mary, "how can you laugh at me, dear papa, and at my poor Nutcracker? He spoke very respectfully of you, nevertheless, when we went to the Palace of Sweet Cake, and he introduced me to his sisters."

The shouts of laughter redoubled to such an extent that Mary began to see the necessity of giving some proof of the truth of what she said, for fear of being treated as a simpleton. She therefore went into the adjoining room and brought back a little box in which she had carefully placed the seven crowns of the king of the mice.

"Here, mamma," she said, "are the seven crowns of the king of the mice, which the Nutcracker gave me last night as a proof of his victory."

The judge's wife, full of surprise, took the seven little crowns, which were made of an unknown but very brilliant metal, and were carved with a delicacy of which human hands were incapable. The judge himself could not take his eyes off them, and considered them to be so precious, that, in spite of the prayers of Fritz, he would not let him touch one of them.

The judge and his wife then pressed Mary to tell them whence came those little crowns; but she could only persist in what she had said already: and when her father, annoyed at what he heard and at what he considered obstinacy on her part, called her a little "story-teller," she burst into tears, exclaiming, "Alas! unfortunate child that I am! What would you have me tell you?"

At that moment the door opened, and the doctor made his appearance.

"What is the matter?" he said, "and what have they done to my little god-daughter that she cries and sobs like this? What is it? what is it all?"

The judge acquainted Dr. Drosselmayer with all that had occurred; and, when the story was ended, he showed him the seven crowns. But scarcely had the doctor seen them, when he burst out laughing, and said, "Well, really this is too good! These are the seven crowns that I used to wear to my watch-chain some years ago, and which I gave to my god-daughter on the occasion of her second birthday. Do you not remember, my dear friend?"

But the judge and his wife could not recollect anything about the present stated to have been given. Nevertheless, believing what the godfather said, their countenances became more calm. Mary, upon seeing this, ran up to Doctor Drosselmayer, saying, "But you know all, godpapa! confess that the Nutcracker is your nephew, and that it was he who gave me the seven crowns."

But Godfather Drosselmayer did not at all seem to like these words; and his face became so gloomy, that the judge called little Mary to him, and taking her upon his knees, said "Listen to me, my dear child, for I wish to speak to you very seriously. Do me the pleasure, once for all, to put an end to these silly ideas; because, if you should again assert that this ugly and deformed Nutcracker is the nephew of our friend the doctor, I give you due warning that I will throw, not only the Nutcracker, but all the other toys, Miss Clara amongst them, out of the window."

Poor Mary was therefore unable to speak any more of all the fine things with which her imagination was filled but you can well understand that when a person has once traveled in such a fine place as the Kingdom of Toys, and seen such a delicious town as the City of Preserved Fruits, were it only for an hour, it is not easy to forget such sights.

Mary therefore endeavored to speak of her brother of the whole business; but she had lost all of his confidence since the moment when she had said that his hussars had taken to flight. Convinced, therefore, that Mary was a story-teller, as her father had said so, he restored his officers to the rank from which he had reduced them, and allowed the band to play as usual the Hussar's March—a step which did not prevent Mary from entertaining her own opinion relative to their courage.

Mary dared not therefore speak further of her adventures. Nevertheless, the remembrance of the Kingdom of Toys followed her without ceasing; and when she thought of all that, she looked upon it as it she were still in the Christmas Forest, or on the River of Essence of Roses, or in the City of Preserved Fruits;—so that, instead of playing with her toys as she had been wont to do, she remained silent and pensive, occupied only with her own thoughts, while every one called her "the little dreamer."

But one day, when the doctor, with his wig laid upon the ground, his tongue thrust into one corner of his mouth, and the sleeves of his yellow coat turned up, was mending a clock by the aid of a long pointed instrument, it happened that Mary, who was seated near the glass cupboard contemplating the Nutcracker, and buried in her own thoughts, suddenly said, quite forgetful that both the doctor and her mamma were close by, "Ah! my dear Mr. Drosselmayer, if you were not a little man made of wood, as my papa declares, and if you really were alive, I would not do as Princess Pirlipata did, and desert you because, in serving me, you had ceased to be a handsome young man; for I love you sincerely!"

But scarcely had she uttered these words, when there was such a noise in the room, that Mary fell off her chair in a fainting fit.

When she came to herself, she found that she was in the arms of her mother, who said, "How is it possible that a great girl like you, I ask, can be so foolish as to fall off your chair—and just at the moment, too, when young Mr. Drosselmayer, who has finished his travels, arrives at Nuremberg? Come, wipe your eyes, and be a good girl."

Indeed, as Mary wiped her eyes, the door opened and Godpapa Drosselmayer, with his glass wig upon his head, his hat under his arm, and his drab frock-coat upon his back, entered the room. He wore a smiling

719

countenance, and held by the hand a young man, who, although very little, was handsome. This young man wore a superb frock-coat of red velvet embroidered with gold, white silk stockings, and shoes brilliantly polished. He had a charming nosegay on the bosom of his shirt, and was very dandified with his curls and hair-powder; moreover, long tresses, neatly braided, hung behind his back. The little sword that he wore by his side was brilliant with precious stones; and the hat which he carried under his arm was of the finest silk.

The amiable manners of this young man showed who he was directly; for scarcely had he entered the room, when he placed at Mary's feet a quantity of magnificent toys and nice confectionary—chiefly sweet cake and sugar-plum, the finest she had ever tasted, save in the Kingdom of Toys. As for Fritz, the doctor's nephew seemed to have guessed his martial taste, for he brought him a sword with a blade of the finest Damascus steel. At table, when the dessert was placed upon it, the amiable youth cracked nuts for all the company: the hardest could not resist his teeth for a moment. He placed them in his mouth with his right hand; with the left he pulled his hair behind; and, crack! the shell was broken.

Mary had become very red when she first saw that pretty little gentleman; but she blushed deeper still, when, after the dessert, he invited her to go with him into the room where the glass cupboard was.

"Yes, go my dear children, and amuse yourselves together," said Godpapa Drosselmayer: "I do not want that room any more to-day, since all the clocks of my friend the judge now go well."

The two young people proceeded to the room; but scarcely was young Drosselmayer alone with Mary, when he fell upon one knee, and spoke thus:

"My dear Miss Silberhaus, you see at your feet the happy Nathaniel Drosselmayer, whose life you saved on this very spot. You also said that you would not have repulsed me, as Princess Pirlipata did, if, in serving *you*, I had become hideous. Now, as the spell which the queen of the mice threw upon me was destined to lose all its power on that day when, in spite of my ugly face, I should be beloved by a young and beautiful girl, I at that moment ceased to be a vile Nutcracker and resumed my proper shape, which is not disagreeable, as you may see. Therefore, my dear young lady, if you still possess the same sentiments in respect to myself, do me the favor to bestow your much-loved hand upon me, share my throne and my crown, and reign with me over the Kingdom of Toys, of which I ere now become the king."

Then Mary raised young Drosselmayer gently, and said "You are an amiable and a good king, sir; and as you have moreover a charming kingdom, adorned with magnificent palaces, and possessing a very happy people, I receive you as my future husband, provided my parents give their consent."

Thereupon, as the door of the room had opened very gently without the two young folks having heard it, so occupied were they with their own sentiments, the judge, his wife, and Godpapa Drosselmayer came forward, crying "Bravo!" with all their might; which made Mary as red as a cherry. But the young man was not abashed; and, advancing towards the judge and his wife, he bowed gracefully to them, paid them a handsome compliment, and ended by soliciting the hand of Mary in marriage. The request was immediately granted.

That same day Mary was engaged to Nathaniel Drosselmayer, on condition that the marriage should not take place for a year.

At the expiration of the year, the bridegroom came to fetch the bride in a little carriage of mother of pearl incrusted with gold and silver, and drawn by ponies of the size of sheep, but which were of countless worth, because there were none like them in the world. The young king took his bride to the Palace of Sweet cake, where they were married by the chaplain. Twenty-two thousand little people, all covered with pearls, diamonds, and brilliant stones, danced at the bridal.

Even at the present day, Mary is still queen of that beautiful country, where may be seen brilliant forests of Christmas; rivers of orangeade, sweet milk, and essence of roses; transparent palaces of sugar whiter than snow and cleaner than ice;—in a word, all kinds of wonderful and extraordinary things may there be seen by those who have eyes sharp enough to discover them.

SELECT BIBLIOGRAPHY

Alcott, Louisa May. *Flower Fables*. Boston: George W. Briggs & Co., 1855.

Andersen, Hans Christian (William Alexander Craigie and Jessie K. Craigie, trans.) *Fairy Tales and Other Stories*. London: Oxford University Press, 1914.

Arndt, Ernst Moritz (Anna Dabis, trans.) *Fairy Tales from the Isle of Rügen*. London: David Nutt, 1896.

Asbjørnsen, Peter Christen and Moe, Jørgen (G. W. Dasent, trans.) *East o' the Sun and West o' the Moon*. Philadelphia: David McKay, 1921.

Asbjørnsen, Peter Christen (H. L. Bræksted, trans.) *Fairy Tales from the Far North*. London: David Nutt, 1897.

Asbjørnsen, Peter Christen (H. L. Bræksted, trans.) *Folk and Fairy Tales*. New York: A. C. Armstrong & Son, 1883.

Baring Gould, S. *A Book of Fairy Tales*. London: Methuen and Company, 1894.

Bay, J. Christian. *Danish Fairy and Folk Tales*. New York: Harper & Brothers, 1899.

Caballero, Fernan. *The Bird of Truth and Other Fairy Tales*. London: W. Swan Sonnenschein & Co., 1882.

Craik, Dinah Maria. *The Fairy Book: The Best Popular Fairy Stories Selected and Rendered Anew*. London: Macmillan and Co., 1868.

Dickens, Charles. *Christmas Stories from* Household Words *and* All the Year Round. New York: Charles Scribner's Sons, 1905.

—— *The Pickwick Papers*. London: The Amalgamated Press, 1905.

Field, Eugene. *The Writings in Prose and Verse of Eugene Field: The Holy Cross and Other Tales*. New York: Charles Scribner's Sons, 1896.

Hodgetts, Edith M. S. *Tales and Legends from the Land of the Tzar*. London: Griffith Farran & Co., Limited, 1891.

Hunt, Margaret (ed.) *Grimm's Household Tales*. London: George Bell and Sons, 1884.

Jacobs, Joseph (ed.) *More English Fairy Tales*. London: David Nutt, 1894.

Jones, W. Henry and Kropf, Lewis L. (eds.) *The Folk-Tales of the Magyars*. London: Elliot Stock, 1889.

Lang, Andrew. *The Blue Fairy Book*. London: Longmans, Green, and Co., 1889.

—— *The Brown Fairy Book*. London: Longmans, Green, and Co., 1904.

—— *The Crimson Fairy Book*. London: Longmans, Green, and Co., 1903.

—— *The Green Fairy Book*. London: Longmans, Green, and Co., 1893.

—— *The Lilac Fairy Book*. London: Longmans, Green, and Co., 1910.

—— *The Olive Fairy Book*. London: Longmans, Green, and Co., 1907.

—— *The Orange Fairy Book*. London: Longmans, Green, and Co., 1906.

—— *The Red Fairy Book*. London: Longmans, Green, and Co., 1890.

—— *The Violet Fairy Book*. London: Longmans, Green, and Co., 1901.

—— *The Yellow Fairy Book*. London: Longmans, Green, and Co., 1904.

Morris, Harrison S. (ed.) *In the Yule-Log Glow: Christmas Stories from 'Round the World*. Philadelphia: J. B. Lippincott Company, 1892.

Ralston, W. R. S. *Russian Folk-Tales*. New York: R. Worthington, 1880.

Rydingsvärd, Anna Von (Albert Segerstedt, trans.) *My Lady Legend and Other Folk Tales from the North*. Boston: D. Lothrop Company, 1891.

Wilde, Oscar. *The Happy Prince and Other Tales*. London: David Nutt, 1889.

—— *A House of Pomegranates*. London: James R. Oscgood McIlvaine and Co., 1891.

Wratislaw, A. H. *Sixty Folk-Tales from Exclusively Slavonic Sources*. London: Elliot Stock, 1849.